Praise for
John Gwynne and
The Bloodsworn Trilogy

"A satisfying and riveting read. The well-realized characters move against the backdrop of a world stunning in its immensity. It's everything I've come to expect from a John Gwynne book."

—Robin Hobb

"A masterfully crafted, brutally compelling Norse-inspired epic."

—Anthony Ryan, author of *The Pariah*

"The world is wonderfully rendered with attention paid to what makes the Norse sagas entertaining....The many layers provide a lavish feast for any reader. A great companion to Neil Gaiman's *Norse Mythology.*"

—*Booklist* (starred review)

"There is not a dull chapter in this fantasy epic. As tension mounts with each passing page, Gwynne delivers exhilarating fights and gruesome battles with such vivid prose the choreography jumps off the page."

—*Vulture* (Best of the Year)

"Gwynne, a Viking reenactor, puts in the work, with fine historical details...that make the story come to life....Fans of the era will be delighted with the accuracy. This is a duly exciting start to the series."

—*Publishers Weekly*

"Visceral, heartbreaking, and unputdownable."

—Jay Kristoff

"*The Shadow of the Gods* is truly an epic in every fashion....[Gwynne] should be in the conversation with the best the genre has to offer today."

—Daniel Greene

"A masterclass in storytelling....Epic, gritty fantasy with an uncompromising amount of heart."

—*FanFiAddict*

"*The Shadow of the Gods* is absolutely stunning, one hell of an epic series opener and a spectacular dose of Viking-flavoured fantasy."

—*Tattooed Book Geek*

THE
HUNGER
OF THE
GODS

By John Gwynne

THE FAITHFUL AND THE FALLEN

Malice
Valor
Ruin
Wrath

OF BLOOD AND BONE

A Time of Dread
A Time of Blood
A Time of Courage

THE BLOODSWORN TRILOGY

The Shadow of the Gods
The Hunger of the Gods

THE HUNGER OF THE GODS

BOOK TWO OF
THE BLOODSWORN TRILOGY

JOHN GWYNNE

orbitbooks.net

Copyright © 2022 by John Gwynne
Excerpt from *The Justice of Kings* copyright © 2022 by Richard Swan

Cover design by Bekki Guyatt
Cover illustration by Marcus Whinney
Map by Tim Paul
Author photograph by Caroline Gwynne

Orbit
Hachette Book Group
1290 Avenue of the Americas
New York, NY 10104
orbitbooks.net

First Edition: April 2022
Simultaneously published in Great Britain by Orbit

Orbit is an imprint of Hachette Book Group.
The Orbit name and logo are trademarks of Little, Brown Book Group Limited.

The publisher is not responsible for websites (or their content) that are not owned by the publisher.

The Hachette Speakers Bureau provides a wide range of authors for speaking events. To find out more, go to www.hachettespeakersbureau.com or call (866) 376-6591.

Library of Congress Control Number: 2021949500

ISBNs: 9780316539920 (trade paperback), 9780316539937 (ebook)

Printed in the United States of America

LSC-C

Printing 1, 2022

For my darling Harriett,
surely there can be no more tears left in all the world,
for we have wept them all over you.

Pronunciation Guide

ð: sounds like "th" in "they"; Guðvarr is pronounced "Guthvarr"

j: sound like "y" in "yellow"; Brynja is pronounced "Brynya"

ø: sounds like "ir" in "bird"; Røkia is pronounced "Rirkia"

CAST OF CHARACTERS

The Battle-Grim

Agnar Broksson – chief of the Battle-Grim, slain in an act of betrayal by Biórr on the ash-plain of Oskutreð

Elvar Fire-Fist – daughter of Jarl Störr. She has sworn the blood oath to find Bjarn, son of Uspa the Seiðr-witch, to rescue him from Ilska the Cruel and her Raven-Feeders, in return for Uspa guiding the Battle-Grim to fabled Oskutreð, the heart of where the gods fought and died

Grend – companion and guardian of Elvar. Has also sworn the blood oath to find Bjarn

Huld – youngest of the Battle-Grim after Elvar. She grew up on the hard streets of Svelgarth

Sighvat the Fat – second to Agnar, a fierce warrior, though more interested in food than making decisions. Swore the blood oath to rescue Bjarn from Ilska's Raven-Feeders

Sólín Spittle – one of the longest-serving of the Battle-Grim, she lost some teeth during a fight with a swarm of tennúr

Urt the Unwashed – warrior of the Battle-Grim, bynamed because of his aversion to cleanliness

Orv the Sneak – the only archer in the Battle-Grim, a scout and hunter. Bynamed because of his stealth

Uspa – a Seiðr-witch. Captured by the Battle-Grim on Iskalt

Island (along with her husband, Berak, and child, Bjarn) where she was destroying the Galdrabok, the *Graskinna*. She swears a pact with Agnar and Elvar, where she will lead the Battle-Grim to Oskutreð if they swear to do all they can to rescue her son, Bjarn, from the clutches of Ilska the Cruel. The blood oath seals their pact

The Bloodsworn

Æsa – a member of the Bloodsworn with a worrying disregard for pain or life. The blood of Fjalla the mountain goat is in her vein

Edel – chief scout and huntswoman of the Bloodsworn. The blood of Hundur the hound is in her veins. Old, shrewd, guarded. Two hounds are her companions

Einar Half-Troll – big as a tree, strongest of the Bloodsworn. A lover of food and well-told tales. Also a *Berserkir*

Glornir Shield-Breaker – chief of the Bloodsworn. A *Berserkir*, with the bear-god's blood in his veins. Husband of Vol and older brother of Thorkel

Gunnar Prow – so-named on account of his nose, which fills most of his face and is curved like a prow-beast on a *drakkar*. The blood of Gröfu the badger is in his veins

Halja Flat-Nose – the blood of Orna the eagle-god is in her veins. Sister of Vali Horse-Breath, who was slain by a troll during the battle at Rota's chamber

Revna Hare-Legs – named Hare-Legs because of her speed in battle, she has the blood of Státa the stoat in her veins

Ingmar Ice – a *Berserkir*

Jökul Hammer-Hand – blacksmith and warrior. Has the blood of Gröfu the badger in his veins

Røkia – *Úlfhéðnar*, the blood of Ulfrir the wolf in her veins. Given the task of training Varg in weapons craft

Svik Tangle-Hair – the blood of Refur the fox is in his veins. Chief skáld/storyteller of the Bloodsworn. He has a particular fondness for cheese

Varg No-Sense – once a thrall of Kolskegg, a wealthy farmer and landowner. Killed Kolskegg when he was betrayed by him, and fled, searching for the killers of his sister, Frøya. Joined the Bloodsworn to gain access to their Seiðr-witch, Vol, in order for her to perform an akáll, a magical invocation that will allow Varg to see the last moments of his sister's life, and so reveal how she died. Since joining the Bloodsworn he has discovered that he is Tainted, an *Úlfhéðnar* with the blood of Ulfrir in his veins

Vol – a Seiðr-witch, wife of Glornir

The Raven-Feeders and their companions

Lik-Rifa – dragon-god, caged for hundreds of years in a chamber among the roots of Oskutreð, the Ash Tree. She has now been freed by a magical ceremony performed by her Tainted offspring, the dragon-born

Rotta – the rat-god. Imprisoned and tortured by Ulfrir and Orna for his part in the slaying of their daughter

Biórr – Tainted, with the blood of Rotta the rat in his veins. He infiltrated the Battle-Grim, slew Agnar Battle-Grim and led Ilska to Oskutreð, so instrumental in the release of Lik-Rifa from her chamber beneath Oskutreð. He is now back with the Raven-Feeders

Brák Trolls-Bane – Tainted, with the blood of Státa the Stoat god in his veins, one of Drekr's crew, a huntsman and trapper

Drekr – Tainted, a dragon-born, brother of Ilska and Myrk. Abducted Breca and slew Thorkel

Ilmur – Tainted, the hound-god Hundur is in his blood. Once a thrall of the Battle-Grim, freed by Biórr and now a member of the Raven-Feeders

Ilska the Cruel – chief of the Raven-Feeders, a dragon-born with Lik-Rifa's blood in her veins. Older sister of Drekr and Myrk

Kalv – Tainted, with the blood of Svin the boar in his veins. Son of Red Fain and brother of Storolf Wartooth

Kráka – Seiðr-witch, once a thrall of the Battle-Grim, but freed by Biórr and now part of the Raven-Feeders

Myrk Sharp-Claw – Tainted, dragon-born with Lik-Rifa's blood in her veins. Younger sister of Ilska and Drekr

Red Fain – Tainted, with Svin the boar's blood in his veins. Father of Kalv and Storolf Wartooth

Storolf Wartooth – Tainted, with the blood of Svin the boar in his veins, son of Red Fain and brother of Kalv. Named Wartooth because he left some teeth in an enemy's shield when he bit into it and tore it from his opponent's grip

Oleif Gap-Tooth – Tainted, the blood of Hraeg the vulture in his veins. One of Drekr's crew, and now part of the Raven-Feeders

Bjarn Beraksson – Tainted, son of Uspa and Berak. Abducted by Ilska and the Raven-Feeders

Breca Thorkelsson – Tainted, son of Orka and Thorkel. Abducted by Drekr

Harek Asgrimsson – Tainted, son of Asgrim and Idrun, who were slain by Drekr and his crew

Others

Orka Skullsplitter – husband of Thorkel and mother of Breca. Once chief of the Bloodsworn and known as Skullsplitter. Thorkel has been slain and her son abducted, and she has followed his trail north, leading her to the Grimholt, where she was captured by *drengrs* and Skalk the Galdurman. She escaped in a bloody battle

Lif Virksson – a fisherman of Fellur village. Son of Virk, and brother of Mord. Orka rescued him from execution, and he travelled north with her. His brother Mord was slain while in chains by Guðvarr the *drengr*

Sæunn – a Tainted thrall with the blood of Hundur the hound in her veins

Gudleif Arnesson – has built a steading with his family north of the Boneback Mountains

Queen Helka – ruler of Darl and the surrounding regions. An ambitious, ruthless woman with a view to ruling all of Vigrið. She has one son, Hakon, and one daughter, Estrid

Prince Hakon Helkasson – son and eldest child of Queen Helka

Princess Estrid Helkasdottir – daughter of Queen Helka

Frek the Úlfhéðnar – Tainted, with the blood of Ulfrir the wolf-god in his veins. Thralled to Queen Helka and one of her honour-guard

Skalk the Galdurman – Galdurman of Darl, in the service of Queen Helka. Sent by Helka with the Bloodsworn to discover what is happening on the northern borders of her realm. He steals Orna's talon and abducts Vol the Seiðr-witch

Sturla – Skalk's Galdur-apprentice

Guðvarr – a *drengr* of Fellur village and nephew to Jarl Störr. He is tasked with leading the band sent after Orka, Lif and Mord

Vilja – a whore of Darl, resident of *The Dead Drengr*

Jarl Sigrún – Jarl of Fellur village and the surrounding district. Embroiled in the political expansion of Queen Helka. Her lover slain and her face scarred by Orka, she sends her nephew Guðvarr after Orka

Yrsa – a *drengr* of Darl in the service of Skalk the Galdurman

Arild – a *drengr* of Fellur village

Skapti – a *drengr*, captain of the Grimholt. In the employ of Prince Hakon and involved in the plans of Drekr and his movement of abducted children

Hrolf – a *drengr* of the Grimholt

Jarl Glunn Iron-Grip – a petty jarl allied to Queen Helka

Jarl Svard the Scratcher – a petty jarl allied to Queen Helka

Jarl Logur of Liga – ruler of the port town of Liga. Friend to the Bloodsworn

Jarl Orlyg of Svelgarth – ruler of the town of Svelgarth and the surrounding region. Old and grizzled, a veteran of war, an enemy of Queen Helka

Prince Jaromir of Iskidan – a prince of Iskidan, one of the many sons of Kirill the Magnificent, lord of Iskidan

Ilia – a *druzhina* of Iskidan

Taras the Bull – a bruised man, Tainted with the blood of Naut the bull in his veins. Thralled into the service of Prince Jaromir of Iskidan

Iva – a Seiðr-witch and Prince Jaromir's thrall

Jarl Störr – lord of Snakavik and most of the western districts of Vigrið. Father of Thorun, Elvar and Broðir. Famed for his *Berserkir-guard*

Silrið – Jarl Störr's Galdurwoman

Thorun Störrsson – eldest child of Jarl Störr

Broðir Störrsson – youngest child of Jarl Störr

Berak Bjornasson – Tainted, a *Berserkir* with the blood of Berser the bear-god in his veins. Husband of Uspa the Seiðr-witch and father of Bjarn. Captured by Agnar and the Battle-Grim and sold as a thrall to Jarl Störr, to become one of the famed *Berserkir-guard*

Gytha – a *drengr* and champion of Jarl Störr

Syr – a *drengr* of Jarl Störr, guard of Snakavik's gate

Hjalmar Peacemaker – leader of the Fell-Hearted mercenary warband

Hrung – a giant's head, magically animated by the power of dying Snaka

Njal Olafsson – jarl of a small fishing village on the banks of the River Drammur

Terna – a thrall of Njal Olafsson, originally a thrall from Kolskegg's farm

Brimil – a slaver based in Darl

Rog – bartender of *The Dead Drengr*

Frøya – sister of Varg

Leif Kolskeggson – son of Kolskegg, he hunted Varg for his father's murder, but upon catching Varg, Glornir and the Bloodsworn took Varg into their care and saved him from Leif's vengeance

Sterkur death-in-the-eye – a warrior and chief of a mercenary band for hire, the Red-Hands

Creatures

Grok – a giant raven
Kló – a giant raven
Spert – a spertus, vaesen, and bound to Orka and her household
Vesli – a tennúr, wounded and found by Breca, she swears an oath
to Breca and Spert

Norse Titles, Terms and Items

Akáll – an invocation, a magic ceremony to reveal the last moments of the dead

Althing – meeting, an assembly of free people

Berserkir – person descended from Berser the bear-god. Capable of great strength and savagery

blóð svarið – a magical blood oath

Brynja – a coat of ring mail

Byrding – coastal boat

Drakkar – a longship

Drengr – an oathsworn warrior, trained to a high level

Druzhina – elite horse-mounted warrior

Galdrabok – book of magic

Galdurman – magician, specifically rune-magic.

Graskinna – grey-skin, a book of magic scribed on flayed skin

Guðfalla – the gods-fall

Guðljós – god-lights

Hangerock – a type of dress

Hird – warriors belonging to a lord's household

Heya – agreed

Holmganga – a duel recognised by law, a way of settling disputes

Jarl – lord or earl

Knarr – a merchant/trade ship

Maður-boy – a human child

Niðing – nothing, nobody, an insult, meaning without honour

Nålbinding – to bind or weave. An early form of knitting used to make clothing

Raudskinna – red-skin, a book of magic, made from the flayed skin of a dead god

Seax – single-edged knife, often with a broken back, of varying sizes. A multi-purpose tool, from cooking/shaving to combat

Seiðr – a type of magical power, inherited from Snaka, the father of the gods

Seiðr-witch – a woman who wields magical power

Skáld – a poet, teller of tales, often employed by a jarl or chief to sing of their heroic deeds

Skál – good health

Snekke – a smaller version of a longship

Tafl – a game of strategy played upon a board with carved figures

Thrall – a slave

Úlfhéðnar – person descended from Ulfrir the wolf-god

Vaesen – creatures created by Lik-Rifa the dragon-god

Weregild – a blood-debt

Winnigas – cloth covering for the legs, from ankle to just below the knee

Whale-road – the open sea

WHAT HAS GONE BEFORE

Orka: Orka lives a solitary life in the hills with her husband Thorkel, and their ten-year-old son, Breca. They have built a home for themselves in the wild, and trade in furs and skins with a nearby village when they need supplies.

During a hunting trip they discover a homestead burned out, two people murdered and the murdered couple's son gone.

Orka reports this to the local village, to Guðvarr, a *drengr* (warrior) and nephew of the local jarl, or lord, Jarl Sigrún.

Breca, Orka's son, finds a wounded tennúr (a magical creature with a liking for teeth) in the woods and brings it home.

Orka, Thorkel and Breca attend an Althing, or meeting, as all residents of the district are summoned by Jarl Sigrún, the local lord. At this meeting they hear that Jarl Sigrún has sworn an oath of allegiance to Queen Helka, a powerful woman with ambitions to rule all Vigrið. A *holmganga* duel is also fought between Virk, a local fisherman, and Guðvarr. Virk wins the duel but breaks the *holmganga* rules and so is slain by Jarl Sigrún's Tainted warrior-thrall.

Upon returning home Orka and Thorkel decide that it is time for them to move on and build a new home elsewhere. Orka goes to consult the Froa-spirit (the powerful spirit and guardian of the Ash Tree) for guidance but finds the Froa-spirit dead, slain with fire and axes. Upon returning to her steading she finds her home in flames, her husband, Thorkel, slain, and her son, Breca, gone. She tracks the abductors, catches up with some of them and kills them, questions one and discovers that the man who took her son is called Drekr.

She returns home, buries her husband and swears an oath, both of vengeance and to recover her abducted son. She arms herself and slips into Fellur village at night, finding Virk's two sons, Mord and Lif, tied to a post to await punishment for their attack on Guðvarr (in a failed attempt at vengeance for their dead father). Orka sets them free, then breaks into Jarl Sigrún's hall, wounds the jarl and interrogates her warrior-thrall, a woman named Vafri with the blood of Ulfrir the wolf-god in her veins. Vafri tells Orka that she should be looking for a man named Drekr, and that he can be found in the fortress town of Darl. A fight ensues and Orka escapes, fleeing Fellur village by boat with Mord and Lif.

They head for Darl, Mord and Lif agreeing to row Orka in return for training in weapons craft. When they reach Darl Orka leaves the two brothers, advising them to bide their time before they return to Fellur to seek their vengeance against Guðvarr.

Orka searches for Drekr, eventually finding him in a secret meeting with Prince Hakon, the son of Queen Helka. They fight, but the fight is split up by the arrival of town guards. Lif and Mord appear and pull Orka to safety.

Orka discovers that Drekr has left Darl and is headed to the Grimholt, a tower that guards a pass through the Boneback Mountains, and at the same time Guðvarr appears, hunting Orka, Mord and Lif for their crimes in Fellur village. They leave Darl, chasing after Drekr, with Guðvarr in pursuit.

Orka, Mord and Lif reach the Grimholt, and during an altercation with some frost-spiders and two giant ravens, they are captured by Skalk the Galdurman and warriors from the Grimholt. They are taken to the tower and put to the question, where it is revealed that Drekr has some kind of business arrangement with Prince Hakon.

Guðvarr arrives with his *drengrs*, bursts into the tower and kills Mord, who is in chains. During this Orka hears the cry of a child and suspects it is her son, Breca. The hope, fear and rage combine to release the wolf in her blood, because Orka is Tainted, an *Úlfhéðnar*, with the blood of Ulfrir the wolf-god in her veins. She proceeds to break free and go on a killing spree. At first the guardians of the Grimholt fight back, but they cannot stand against her savage fury and so they break and run.

Varg: Varg is on the run. He is a thrall who has recently killed his owner, a wealthy farmer, and fled. Varg's sister has been killed and he is seeking either a Galdurman or a Seiðr-witch (two forms of magic-users) to perform an akáll for him, which is a magical invocation revealing the last few moments of the dead. Varg wishes this done for his sister so that he can discover who or what killed her.

Varg reaches the trading port of Liga, where he discovers that the famed mercenary warriors, the Bloodsworn, are in town and have a Seiðr-witch among their ranks. But she only uses her magic for the Bloodsworn, so Varg enters a tournament where he fights one of the Bloodsworn to earn the right to join them. He is beaten unconscious and left on the banks of a fjord. When he wakes, he tends to his wounds and builds a fire, only to be set upon by Leif Kolskeggson and his crew, son of the farm owner whom Varg killed. Varg is captured, but then rescued by the Bloodsworn.

They take Varg in as one of their own, but on an "apprenticeship" agreement, so Varg has to learn weapons craft and prove his loyalty and trustworthiness to the Bloodsworn before Vol their Seiðr-witch will perform the akáll he seeks.

As the Bloodsworn leave Liga they are attacked by Prince Jaromir of Iskidan and his mounted *druzhina*, who wish for one of the Bloodsworn, a man named Sulich, to be handed over to them for crimes he is alleged to have committed in the far-off country of Iskidan. Glornir, chief of the Bloodsworn, refuses to hand Sulich over, and so a short and bloody battle follows, broken up by the arrival of Liga's guards and three longships carrying Queen Helka and her retinue into port.

Queen Helka hires the Bloodsworn for a job. People on her north-western border have been going missing and turning up dead. She wants the Bloodsworn to find out who or what is doing this and kill them. She sends her Galdurman, Skalk, and his two *drengr* guards with the Bloodsworn.

Once in the Boneback Mountains the Bloodsworn discover an old mine that is being excavated by a collection of warriors and vaesen – skraeling and a troll – who have enslaved the local populace and forced them to work in the excavation. As the Bloodsworn investigate a battle ensues, where a dragon-born (a strain of the Tainted descended from the dragon-god, Lik-Rifa, long thought to be extinct, if they had ever existed at all) emerges from the mine with a bone of the dead god Orna in his fist. In a bloody battle Varg kills the dragon-born but is seriously injured himself.

When Varg awakes he is told that the Bloodsworn have found evidence to suggest that the mine is in fact the chambers of Rotta, the rat-god, who was chained here and sentenced to a life of pain and torture by his brother and sister. Copied fragments of a Galdurbok (magic book) called the *Raudskinna* are found.

Vol comes to tend Varg's wounds, and while she is there Skalk and his two *drengr* guards enter the room. They club Vol unconscious, kill Varg's friend, Torvik and steal the bone fragment of the god Orna, along with other items of worth that have been discovered.

Skalk gives Varg the choice to go with him, offering to perform the ákáll that Varg so desperately wants, but instead Varg hurls himself at the *drengr* who killed his friend, and in a frenzied blood rush he rips the man's throat out with his teeth. Skalk strikes Varg unconscious.

Upon regaining consciousness, Varg discovers that Skalk has escaped with Orna's talon, a chest full of relics and Vol as his prisoner. He is told by Svik and Røkia of the Bloodsworn that he is Tainted, that he has the wolf-god Ulfrir in his veins. Not only this, he is told that all the Bloodsworn are Tainted, and that they recruited him because they discovered his bloodline. This comes as a bit of a shock to Varg, but soon he comes to terms with it and joins the Bloodsworn as they set out in chase of Skalk, vowing to avenge Torvik and get Vol back.

They follow Skalk's trail, which takes them to the Grimholt. Here they find a scene of death and savagery, Orka sitting upon the steps of the Grimholt. She is blood-drenched with her dead enemies piled at her feet. Children are gathered around her.

Glornir, the chief of the Bloodsworn, dismounts, because he

knows Orka. She was known as the Skullsplitter, most famed warrior of Vigrið, and the once-chief of the Bloodsworn. Thorkel, Orka's husband, was Glornir's brother. Orka is grief-stricken because she has not found her son, Breca.

Glornir and Orka embrace.

Elvar: Elvar is a young warrior, a member of the famed mercenary warband the Battle-Grim, and she is out to make her name, her battle-fame.

The Battle-Grim land their longship at Iskalt, a volcanic island off the north-west coast of Vigrið. They are hunting a man named Berak, who is believed to be of Tainted blood, a *Berserkir* with the blood of Berser the bear-god in his veins. Their chase leads them through a battle in a village and up into the mountains, where they eventually catch up with Berak as he is locked in combat with a bull troll. Elvar sees a woman and child, the woman throwing some kind of book into a pool of molten lava.

Agnar, chief of the Battle-Grim, orders his warriors to kill the bull troll before it harms or kills Berak, and a brief, bloody fight ensues, where Elvar lands the killing blow against the troll. Berak is then captured, subdued and chained, his wife and child also captured. His wife, Uspa, is revealed to be a Seiðr-witch.

The Battle-Grim leave Iskalt Island with their prisoners and travel to Snakavik, a fortress built within the skull of the dead serpent-god, Snaka. Jarl Störr rules here, and he is famed for having an honour-guard of enslaved *Berserkir* warriors.

He is also Elvar's father, although there is little love between them. Elvar left her family and life of privilege to escape her father's plans for her, and to make a name of her own.

Jarl Störr purchases the *Berserkir* Berak from Agnar. While the Battle-Grim are still in Snakavik they are ambushed and Bjarn, the son of Berak, is abducted by Ilska the Cruel, who is the chief of a mercenary band called the Raven-Feeders. Uspa the Seiðr-witch then makes a deal with Agnar; if he will swear a magical blood oath to get her son back, she will lead them to the fabled battle-ground of Oskutreð, where the war between the gods was fought and riches beyond imagination are said to be found.

Elvar swears the blood oath, along with Grend, her faithful companion, and a few others. The Battle-Grim set out for Oskutreð, along the way encountering a swarm of tennúr, a magical bridge and a forest full of long-dead gods. During the journey Elvar takes Biórr, a young warrior of the Battle-Grim, as her lover.

Upon reaching Oskutreð they find an ash-covered plain full of the scattered bones of dead gods, and the blasted stump of a great tree. A Froa-spirit named Vörn confronts them, forbidding them access to the tree, but allows them to scavenge the treasure from the plain. Before the Battle-Grim can do this Ilska the Cruel and her Raven-Feeders arrive. Agnar and Ilska's champion, a giant of a man named Skrið, fight a *holmganga* duel to decide who has access to Oskutreð. Agnar wins, but is then slain traitorously by his own warrior, Biórr, who we discover is Tainted and is part of Ilska's crew. It was Biórr who arranged the abduction of Bjarn, and enabled Ilska and her Raven-Feeders to follow the Battle-Grim north to Oskutreð.

A shield wall battle ensues between the Battle-Grim and the Raven-Feeders, though at the same time Ilska leads a number of warriors who are all revealed to be dragon-born against the Froa-spirit and Uspa. Once they are defeated, a large number of chained children are unloaded from wagons and led onto the shattered stump of the Ash Tree. Here Ilska conducts a spell, using blood magic and a Galdurbok, and breaks the magical bonds that keep Lik-Rifa the dragon-god caged inside a chamber deep within the bowels of the great tree. Lik-Rifa explodes into the light of day and fights a brief and bloody battle with her gaolers, three winged sisters, children of the gods Ulfrir and Orna. One of the winged women is thrown unconscious to the ground, and the other two are slain.

Lik-Rifa meets Ilska and the dragon-born who set her free, and she flies away, leading them south.

Elvar is wounded during the battle against the Raven-Feeders and watches in shock, horror and awe as the dragon flies into the distance.

Eagles should show their claws, though dying.
The Saga of Olaf Haraldsson

CHAPTER ONE

ORKA

Orka stood in a tempest of fire and smoke. Flickering flame and clouds of ash were a storm-lash all about her. Death's-reek hovered thick in the air, clawing into her throat. The crackle and hiss of fire drowned all else out as the world burned. A shadow overhead and a turbulence in the air, like the beating of great wings. Then a child's scream ripped through the storm, her son Breca calling for her and she twisted and turned, searching, desperately seeking in stumbling footfalls, but the world was all acrid clouds of billowing smoke and grasping, flayed fingers of bright-searing flame. She tripped over something, a figure lying prone upon the ground at her feet, blood oozing, dead eyes staring. Thorkel, her husband, her friend. Her love. His glazed, empty eyes held her gaze and his lips moved, a death-rasped, snake-slithering hiss of breath issuing from his husked corpse.

"*They took him.*"

She jerked awake with a gasp, eyes snapping wide, and saw a shadow looming over her in the wolf-grey light. Without thought she was moving, one hand shooting out to grip the shadow's throat, her other hand ripping a seax from its scabbard on her weapons belt, which was rolled and clutched close like a pillow.

A choked gurgle.

"It's . . . me," a voice squeaked. "Lif."

Orka froze, the seax's sharp tip a finger's width from Lif's eye.

She fought the urge to kill, the silent storm that had been lurking dormant in her veins now whipped to sudden life. A tremor rippled through her and she shoved Lif away, sat up, sheathed the seax.

She tasted blood in her mouth, licked her teeth, crusted and clotted, spat and rose to her feet with a groan. Her body ached, muscles and joints protesting, the weight of her mail *brynja* heavy on her shoulders and she glowered at Lif.

"What?" she growled.

They were standing in the burned-out remains of the Grimholt's hall, Queen Helka's fortress that guarded a pass through the Boneback Mountains. Members of the Bloodsworn lay about them, wrapped in cloaks, snoring and twitching. One man groaned, face shuddering in some dark dream. A hearth fire had burned itself out, grey ash in this grey world. It was *sólstöður*, the long day, when night was banished from the sky for thirty days, but judging by the pewter haze that leaked through the roof of the torn hall it was somewhere around dawn. Orka stretched, bones clicking.

"Wanted to talk to you," Lif said. His face was pale, blue-tinged lips looking black in the half-light, the remnants of frost-spider venom still lingering in his veins. He held something in his arms.

Orka stooped and swept up a long-axe from the floor. Earlier, she had taken it from a warrior, carved him open with it, and then turned that hooked blade on a score of others. Its blade was clean, now, as were her two seaxes and a hand-axe hanging from her belt. The rest of her was thick with clotted blood, but she had tended her weapons before sleep had taken her. She rested the long-axe across her shoulder, a shiver running through her at the familiar weight. She loved it and hated it at the same time.

"Talk, then," she said striding away, towards the hall's entrance and out into the day. She bit back the harsh words that formed on her tongue, not wanting to talk to anyone. The sound of Breca's voice from her dream still lingered in her thought-cage, echoing like some Seiðr-magic spell. All she wanted was to find her son. She thought she had found him yesterday, thought she had heard him calling for her, and the joy of it had lit a fire in her veins. She had carved a bloody path to get to him. But it had not been Breca, though she had found other Tainted children, bound like thralls, all stolen by Drekr for the dead gods knew what.

But not my Breca. His absence had hit her like a sword-blow, piercing deep, almost breaking her. Grief had flowed from her like blood from a sword thrust. But today the wound was seared and stitched closed again, her heart cold and hard. She would go on. She would find him, and did not want the distraction of anything else. Of any*one* else. But there was grief carved into Lif's face and dripping from his lips like poison from a wound. He had watched his brother Mord die, shackled to a wall and gut-stabbed by that *niðing*, Guðvarr. A bad death, and so Orka pressed her teeth together and did not snarl at him to leave her be when the slap and scrape of his footfalls followed her.

A cold breeze tugged at her blonde-braided hair as she marched down wide steps splattered with congealed blood. The bodies were gone, now, piled in a fresh-dug trench in the courtyard. Despite the mountain-cold, the flies were already buzzing, a cloud hovering over the heaped corpses. The courtyard was ringed by a cluster of outbuildings that tumbled down to a river, a track curling down a slope towards walls and a barred gate. Near the gate a hearth fire crackled, a pot hanging over it and Orka saw Glornir, chief of the Bloodsworn, standing and talking with a handful of his warriors. Einar Half-Troll was there, a shadowed boulder of a man, stirring whatever was in the pot and talking to Jökul the smith. He had a bandage wrapped around his thinning hair, and his snarl of a beard had more grey in it than she remembered. She put a hand to her belt and the bronze buckle and fixings, remembered him forging them for her. She saw other figures lurking in the shadows of buildings, another by the gates of the Grimholt. One of them looked at her, a man, wolf-lean, his hair short for a warrior of the Bloodsworn. His mail coat glimmered and he held a spear in his fist, shield slung across his back and a helm buckled at his belt. She returned his gaze with her own flat-eyed stare and he looked away.

Orka reached the river, flowing cold and fierce from the Boneback Mountains, the sound beneath her feet changing as she walked out a few strides on to a wooden pier. There had been two *snekkes* moored here yesterday, shallow-hulled and sleek-straked, like a *drakkar*, but smaller, only a dozen oars on each. They were both gone now, frayed ropes dangling in the water testifying to the haste and desperation of those fleeing her vengeance as they leaped from the pier to the boats, cutting at the ropes, rather than taking the time to untie them from mooring posts. Peering over the pier's edge, she searched the ice-blue, white spume frothing around boulders that rose from the riverbed like slime-covered broken teeth. Deep in the clear water, nestled among the boulders she saw the tip of a chitinous, segmented tail. Spert, sleeping still after yesterday's fight. His tail twitched and thrashed as if he were dreaming, stirring a cloud of silt. Close by on the riverbank, Orka spied the shape of Vesli the tennúr laying curled asleep, one thin, membranous wing cast over her hairless body like a cloak. She held a small spear clutched in one pale fist.

Breca's spear.

Orka placed her long-axe and weapons belt on the wooden boards of the pier, then leaned over, heaving her *brynja* up and slithering out of it like a serpent shedding its scaled skin, tugged her boots and nålbinding socks off and then her breeches, finally pulled both her woollen and linen undertunics off in one movement, and stood there, huffing clouds of cold breath as her skin goose-bumped. Then she bent her legs and leaped into the river.

A shock like a hammer blow, snatching her breath away as she splashed into the river and sank beneath the surface, felt the current tugging at her but she kicked her legs and carved through the water like a salmon, swimming out into deeper waters, almost to the bottom, then turned, her feet and toes sinking into mud. She paused there a moment, looking around. Sound muted, light filtering around her in fractured beams from above, a many-hued flickering like the glow of the *guðljós* in the northern skies. Here everything seemed to slow, the noise of the world, the anger and terror that raged through her, all stilled for a moment, frozen and languid in this mountain's heart-water. Her chest began to burn, aching for a breath, pressure building in her head, and still she waited, grateful for this respite from the world above. Finally, when her burning lungs could not take any more, she pushed hard against the riverbed, shooting towards the light and breaking the surface in a spray of water. Lif was standing on the pier beside her weapons and discarded clothes, holding something in his arms. With sharp, deft strokes she swam to the riverbank and stood, still half submerged. Reached down and took a stone from the riverbed, sat on the flat side of a rock and began scrubbing it across her skin, scrapping away what blood and filth the river's current had not managed to scour from her.

Eventually she waded from the river, water falling away like glittering streams of ice. Lif held out a woollen cloak for her, which she took and dried herself with. She looked at her pile of clothes on the pier, all stiff and coated in blood and sweat.

"Here," Lif said, holding out the bundle he had been carrying in his hands. "I found it over there, think it was a store-room for the garrison here." He held clean breeches, linen under-tunic and a thick wool over-tunic. "They're the biggest I could find; I think they'll fit you."

"My thanks," Orka said, taking the clothes and tugging on the breeches, thick wool, then a plain linen under-tunic and finally a blue-grey woollen over-tunic. She rolled her shoulders, stretching the linen and wool, which clung to her damp skin. Then she fetched her nålbinding socks and boots from the pier, tugged them on and hefted her *brynja*, realised it needed cleaning before she put it back on. Buckling her weapons belt around her waist, she slung the coat of mail over her shoulder then squatted and lifted the long-axe, leaning on it like a staff.

"You wanted to talk?" she said, fixing Lif with her gaze.

He sucked in a breath, mouth open, the words sticking in his throat.

"Three things," he muttered, then closed his mouth again, shuffled his feet.

Orka looked at the sky, then back at Lif.

"The day will not wait for you," she said. "Nor will I."

"You are Tainted, the blood of a dead god in your veins, a remnant of their power in you," Lif blurted, the words spilling from his mouth in a rush.

"Aye," Orka nodded. She pushed her tongue into a gap in her teeth and worked free a sliver of something stuck there, spat out a glob of meat, not wanting to think about where it had come from. More than her long-axe had been used to carve her way through the warriors of the Grimholt yesterday. "I am Tainted," she said. A shiver rippled through her at hearing the words out loud. Such a closely guarded secret that her life had depended upon. She looked hard into Lif's face, waiting for the disgust and revulsion, for the fear and hatred that usually accompanied such a revelation. But what she saw in his eyes was . . . hurt.

"You never told me. Us," Lif said. "All that time together, fighting together. We saved your life in Darl, pulled you out from under Drekr's axe . . ."

Orka sighed, wiped her palm over her face.

"It is not something I am used to saying out loud," Orka said. "It is the kind of thing that could put a thrall-collar around my neck, or see me swinging in a cage. It has been a secret long-guarded."

But Lif trusted me, followed me, and I have kept this secret from him.

"I should have told you and Mord," she shrugged. "You are right, you both deserved that."

Lif nodded. "We did," he said. "In the tower, you said that this Drekr is stealing *Tainted* children." He paused again, chewing over his words. "I did not know that, but of course it makes sense, now. So Breca is Tainted, too?"

"Aye. Breca is Tainted, has my wolf-blood flowing in his veins."

Lif nodded, clearly thinking it all through.

"The second thing?" Orka asked.

Lif looked back up at Orka.

"That man yesterday, the bald grey-beard."

"Glornir, chief of the Bloodsworn," Orka said.

"He called you *Skullsplitter*."

Orka looked away, then slowly nodded.

"*You* are the Skullsplitter? You said the Skullsplitter was dead?"

"Skullsplitter died the day I walked away from the Bloodsworn," Orka said. Fractured images burst into life in her thought-cage. She did not want to talk about it, had never spoken of those times, even with Thorkel. They had walked away from that life, locked the memories in a cage, buried all physical reminders in a chest in the earth of their steading. Lif looked at her, grief and awe carved into his face like runes in an oath stone, and she felt the sting of her shame, and the whisper of her old life, like a ghost-fech in her ear. She sucked in a deep breath.

"Breca was in my belly, then, and I wanted no more of the Bloodsworn's life. Death and blood, never ending. Thorkel felt the same, so we left." She shrugged. "A harder decision than saying it makes it sound, and a longer one, but that is the short of it. That is what we did. During a ship battle we leaped into the sea and swam for shore. The Bloodsworn thought we had fallen in battle. Many did that day, never to be found, their bones lying in those murky depths still, no doubt."

"When I saw you yesterday, saw what you did . . ." Lif said. "You were like . . . someone else."

Orka blew out a long breath. "I have locked the Skullsplitter away all these years. Breca's scream, what I *thought* was Breca's scream, it burst the bars of her cage. And then this came to my hands . . ." she looked at the long-axe in her fist and shrugged. "Skullsplitter is back now, and she will help me find my Breca."

A silence grew. Vesli the tennúr whimpered in her sleep, twisting on the ground.

"The third thing?" Orka said.

Lif looked back over his shoulder at the remains of the hall and tower, frowned hard. "Will you help me bring Mord down and raise a cairn over him? I tried, but he is chained to the wall, still."

Orka looked up at the tower, or what was left of it. Most of the roof gone and two walls burned away, blackened beams twisted like desiccated fingers.

"I will," she said.

Together they strode back across the courtyard, up the stairs and into the hall. Bodies were stirring, warriors rising from their cloaks. Orka walked past them all to the rear of the hall, where a doorway led to rising stairs. Timber creaked as she began to climb, ash thick on the floor and walls, Orka's feet stirring small clouds as the stair-well groaned and shifted beneath her weight. Then she was in a corridor, one wall fallen away so that she could look out across the Grimholt's courtyard to the river. A room stood before her, the door charred to nothing and she walked carefully in.

Bodies littered the ground, limbs severed, all blackened, twisted husks.

The floor creaked as Lif joined her and they both stood, staring at the dead. Mord lay against the far wall, a charred corpse. One arm was raised, manacled to the wall, the rest of his body slumped and curled around the sword-wound in his belly.

Orka stepped on a twisted, charred staff and it crumbled beneath her weight. She strode forwards carefully, raised her long-axe and swung it, sparks exploding, as she chopped into the iron chain pinned to the wall. A crack and screech of metal as the chain broke and Mord's arm dropped to the ground. Orka took off her cloak, lay it next to Mord's corpse and then rolled him into it, Lif helping her.

Patches of charred flesh fell away under their fingertips as they moved him and Lif turned away, vomiting on to the blackened floorboards. Orka rolled the cloak around Mord, tied it tight, then lifted his body, which felt weightless to her now, and gently laid him across her shoulder.

"Let me help," Lif said, spitting a mouthful of bile and wiping tears from his eyes.

"I have him," Orka said.

Footsteps on the stairwell, the framework protesting, and a figure appeared in the doorway. A man of medium build, braided red hair tied back at the nape, a silver ring holding his oiled, rope-knotted beard in place. He wore a gleaming *brynja* with sword and seax hanging at his belt, rings of silver thick on his arms. His breeches were pale blue wool with dark *winnigas* wraps from knee to ankle.

"Skullsplitter," the man said, dipping his head.

"Svik," Orka nodded, pausing for a moment and the two warriors regarded each other.

"You look like shite," Svik said.

"And you look as if you are fresh-scrubbed for the Yule-Blot," Orka answered.

"It's important to look your best," he said with a shrug. "Who knows what each day will bring. What lucky lady may find herself in my presence."

"Still an arseling, then," Orka said with a snort.

Svik laughed, small white teeth glistening through his beard, but the laughter did not reach his eyes. They stared at Orka, and slowly his expression changed, the humour flickering to something else. Something tragic, a fleeting image of grief and heartbreak.

"You left us. You swore your oath, and still just left us," he breathed.

Orka stared at him, the words in her head not finding their way to her tongue.

Svik blinked, looked away. "Glornir asks for you," he said.

Orka just grunted and walked on, Svik stepping aside to let her through the doorway. Lif swept up Orka's long-axe and followed her, Svik falling in behind them. The three of them strode down the stairwell and out into the courtyard. More fires had been started, pots bubbling, and Orka smelled porridge and honey. Warriors of the Bloodsworn milled around the courtyard and grounds of the Grimholt; a few stood on the palisaded walls to north and south.

Glornir was waiting for her, his beard more grey than black, now. He was regarding her with his dour eyes, his long-axe resting easily in one large fist. The echo of his brother lurked in his eyes, in the lines and crags of his face, making Orka wince at the memory of her dead husband. Others stood around Glornir that Orka recognised. Einar Half-Troll, blotting out the sun, and Jökul Hammer-Hand, the smith. Edel with her braided silver hair, ruined eye and wolfhounds, and Røkia, lean and whip-hard. There were others that Orka did not know, most of them younger. A dark-skinned man with head shaved clean, apart from one long black braid, no beard but long, leather-tied moustaches. A curved sabre hung at his hip and he wore the baggy breeches of Iskidan. A gold-haired woman with a nose that had been smashed almost flat on her face, and the man Orka had seen watching her earlier, his hair short and beard little more than tufts of stubble among these braided warriors. He wore good kit, though, his *brynja* dark-oiled and gleaming, a seax and hand-axe hanging at his waist alongside a fine spectacled helm buckled to his belt. A silver ring coiled around one arm.

Orka strode to Glornir, stopping and gently laying Mord's wrapped corpse at her feet. Lif stopped at her shoulder and handed her the long-axe, and Svik walked back to stand with Glornir and the other Bloodsworn.

"Much to talk on, Orka," Glornir said. "When we found you, you were *Úlfhéðnar* and in your grief, yesterday, the wolf loose in your blood."

She just nodded, knew the truth of that. She remembered broken moments, of blood, the screams of the dying, finding a shed full of bairns. How she had thrown her head back and howled when she realised Breca was not among them. And Glornir's arrival with the Bloodsworn at his back as she had sat on the steps, gore-drenched and drowning in misery. She remembered him holding her.

Looking at him now, though, she saw a misery of his own in his eyes, in the set of his muscled back and shoulders.

"What is it?" Orka asked him.

"Vol," Glornir said, his lips twitching into a snarl. "She has been taken. By a *niðing* Galdurman."

"Skalk," Orka said, putting a hand to her head, a blood-crusted lump where he had clumped her with his staff. "He was here," she spat. "With a *drengr* warrior and a prisoner, slung across a horse's back."

"That is them," Glornir said, more growl than words. Orka could see the *Berserkir* in Glornir shivering and pulsing in his blood. "I have searched for their bodies, for any sign of them."

Orka closed her eyes, thinking, sifting through the fractured images of yesterday's slaughter. "They fled. On a *snekke* moored at the river." She nodded towards the pier, Glornir and the others following her gaze.

Vesli the tennúr shifted in her sleep beside the riverbank, twitching and crying out. She let out a high, piercing shriek and Orka strode over to the vaesen. Vesli's eyes snapped open and she sat up, whimpering.

"The corpse-ripper is free," Vesli squeaked, cowering, her small eyes searching the skies above them. Some of the Bloodsworn lifted their gaze and looked, too.

"A dream," Orka said, resting a big hand on Vesli's shoulder, even as she recalled her own dream, of fire and ash and beating wings.

"No," Vesli said, "Lik-Rifa has been freed from her cage beneath the ground."

Orka frowned, and voices among the Bloodsworn muttered.

"I also dreamed of a dragon last night," a voice among the Bloodsworn said.

"Just bad dreams," Glornir said, though even his brow was knotted in a scowling thundercloud.

A bubbling from the river and Spert's head burst through the surface of the water, the vaesen bobbing on the current. He looked at them all with his bulbous black eyes in his grey, candle-melted face.

"Vesli speak true," Spert rasped, "Lik-Rifa is free." He licked his lips with a thick, blue-black tongue. "Spert hungry. Mistress make porridge?"

CHAPTER TWO

ELVAR

Elvar watched Sighvat the Fat lay the last stone on Agnar's cairn. Her face twisted with the horror of it. Only yesterday, Agnar had led them on to the plain of Oskutreð, the great Ash Tree, and Elvar's heart had been full to bursting with the joy of the riches there. The thought of their fair-fame spreading around the world like a saga-tale; Agnar and his Battle-Grim, the finders of fabled Oskutreð, where the gods had fought and died, where gold and silver and the relics of the gods were supposed to hang from trees like bunches of ripe fruit, ready for the picking.

We found it, sure enough.

Elvar stood upon a grey-mantled plain, a gentle breeze sifting ash into swirling whorls like dark-flaked snow. All around were humped mounds, many of them skeletons, large and small, all smoothed by a thick-rimed cloak of ash. And elsewhere were fresher corpses, less than a day old. A handful of the Battle-Grim wrapped in cloaks and ready for their barrows, and over a dozen of Ilska's Raven-Feeders, still lying where they fell. Flies crawled on them and crows pecked at their flesh.

And we found more than we bargained for. We found battle and blood. We found death.

"Here lies Agnar Broksson; warrior, chief, friend," Sighvat intoned, his voice bellows-deep, a tremor croaking through the last word. "Battle-Grim, Fire-Fist, Slayer of Dragons." A tear rolled down Sighvat's cheek.

All true names, Elvar knew. The last of them brought a vivid-bright swell of fear and joy rising in her chest at the memory of Agnar's *holmganga* with Skrið, the Tainted dragon-born. Hulking and viper-fast, Skrið had been a fearsome foe. It had been a fight that skálds the world over should be singing of, where Agnar had fought a dragon-born and slain him, and Elvar had yelled herself hoarse at the weapons craft, courage and battle-cunning of her chief.

The Battle-Grim all added their voices to Sighvat's, grunts and heyas of agreement, even Grend, who stood at Elvar's shoulder like a storm-weathered cliff.

Elvar knelt and touched one of the stones of Agnar's cairn, grimaced with the pain in her shoulder at even that small movement, and with her other hand gripped the troll tusk that hung from a leather thong around her neck. Agnar had given it to her, for her part in the slaying of the troll back on Iskalt Island. That felt like a lifetime go.

"You will be missed, Agnar Battle-Grim," she breathed. "You already are." And then. "I will avenge you. Biórr will *die* for his betrayal."

Just the whisper of his name on her lips made Elvar shiver with rage. Biórr, her lover, who she had trusted, bound by oaths and battle and much, much more. And he had betrayed her, betrayed them all. Betrayed Agnar most foully with a spear-thrust through his throat as Agnar held out an arm to him.

She rose with a hiss of pain, Grend steadying her.

"So, what are we to do, now?" Sighvat said, looking around at them all.

They stood in silence, little more than thirty of them left, Sighvat staring back at them, his expression morose and unsure. Red weals and welts tracked lines across his exposed flesh, his face, wrists, forearms, where he had been bound by living vines that had burst from the ground at the Froa-spirit's command. Elvar glanced at the blackened stump that had been Vörn, the guardian of the Ash Tree. Ilska and her dragon-born kin had set her ablaze with their rune-magic and now she lay blackened and twisted like a dead branch thrown on the fire.

"What we came here for," Huld said with a shrug. She was youngest of the Battle-Grim after Elvar, dark-eyed and angry. "We have earned the battle-fame, now we take the treasure."

"Aye," said Sólín, steel-haired and wire-muscled, gap-toothed from their recent encounter with a nest of tennúr. "We take what we can and get out of here. That'th what we do."

Others of the Battle-Grim nodded and muttered their agreement.

"Agreed," Sighvat said. "What we find and can wear, we keep. The rest we pile in the wagons and share as an equal split."

Orv the Sneak, so-named on account of his light-footed stealth, nudged a small ash-covered mound at his foot, turning over bleached bones and revealing the glint of metal. He crouched and lifted an arm ring of age-blackened silver, then slipped it on to his arm, looked up and smiled.

The rest of the Battle-Grim began searching among the ash, all of them battered and carved up from their hard-fought battle with Ilska's Raven-Feeders.

Elvar turned away and strode back towards their makeshift camp, which was little more than a cluster of wagons, some tethered ponies and cloaks for pillows and blankets. Ash rose in puffs and whorls around her feet, and she heard the trudge of Grend following behind her. Ahead was the tide-line of yesterday's battle, where the corpses of their enemy still lay, marking where the Battle-Grim had formed their shield wall and stood against Ilska's warband. Elvar could remember the stink of it, the deafening battle-cries and clashing of steel, the crash and thud of shield against shield. She felt a swell of pride in her chest, to have stood with the Battle-Grim against such odds, and prevailed. They were hard men and women, these Battle-Grim, reavers and hewers, battle-scarred but unbowed. And they had been winning against the Raven-Feeder's greater numbers.

Until the dragon burst into our world.

She shook that memory away, trying to scatter it like flies from an open wound.

Uspa the Seiðr-witch was seated on the tailboard of a wagon, staring towards the great hole where the stump of the ash tree had been. Huge splinters reared up from the ground as long as the strakes of a sea-shattered *drakkar*, where Lik-Rifa the dragon-god had exploded from her underground gaol and scattered them all like chaff on the wind. Uspa's fair hair was braided and bound, rune-curving tattoos visible above the neck of her tunic and curling up to the line of her jaw. Her hands were clasped, knuckles white, fingers clenching and unclenching like a fist full of night-wyrms.

A figure lay on the ground at her feet. A woman with great rust-coloured wings and braided red hair, an empty sword scabbard at her hip. She was bound at wrists and ankles, and still unconscious. No one really knew who or what she was, other than Vörn the Froa-Spirit had mentioned her as one of three sisters, guardians of the dragon. All agreed that if she had been guarding a dragon for three hundred years that it would not be wisdom to just let her wake up unrestrained.

"She will likely be upset that Lik-Rifa has escaped," Huld had said.

"Aye, and that her sisters are dead," Orv the Sneak added.

Elvar had agreed to the right of that, and they had bound the winged woman with leather cords.

"We must be moving," Uspa said to Elvar as she drew close, Elvar walking to her pile of kit. A shattered shield, her rent coat of mail, a bloodied hole in it where a spear had burst the links and stabbed into Elvar's shoulder.

"Moving where?" Elvar muttered.

"After my Bjarn," Uspa said, eyes narrowing. "You made an oath."

"Aye, to get your son back from Ilska once you had guided us here, I know."

"And I have held my part of the bargain," Uspa said.

"Agnar dead and a corpse-ripping dragon set free in the world was not part of that bargain," Elvar said as she squatted and began rummaging through her kit.

"I warned you this would not end well," Uspa hissed.

"I did not think that meant fighting dragon-born and dead gods flying free in the skies."

"Once you unlock a door you cannot control what comes out

of it," Uspa spat. She sucked in a deep, shuddering breath. "None of it matters, anyway. We swore an oath and it is binding."

"Good luck with convincing them of that," Elvar said with a nod over her shoulder at the Battle-Grim. Shouts of discovery were ringing out. "They are doing what they came here for, searching for riches."

"You swore an *oath*," Uspa warned her.

"That was when Agnar still lived," Elvar snapped.

"*You* still live, and you swore the *blóð svarið*," Uspa answered, slow and calm and maddening. "And the *blóð svarið* does not care about the dead; only the living."

"Some oaths cannot be kept," Elvar muttered, but even as she entertained that thought, the breath of her words still lingering on her lips, she felt a flare of heat and pain in her wrist and forearm. She staggered back, gasping, and fell to the ground clutching her arm. The fine white tracery of scars that wrapped around it, burned there by Uspa's Seiðr-magic when they all swore her oath, were now flaring red, the skin blistering, weeping fat drops of fluid.

Grend snarled and drew his axe, strode to Uspa.

"Make it stop," he growled at Uspa, raising the axe over her head.

"I cannot," Uspa said. "Alive, dead, there is nothing I can do. Once set free the *blóð svarið* is like the ocean tide; there is no holding it back, no containing it. Only Elvar keeping the oath will end it. If she even *thinks* about breaking that oath, it will know, and it will act."

I take it back, I take it back, I will go after Bjarn, Elvar screamed inside her head and immediately the pain subsided, the heat in her veins hissing and vanishing as if Elvar's arm were fresh-forged iron that she had dunked in water.

"You see," Uspa said, her eyes full of grief, not holding any of the gloating that Elvar had expected to see in them. "The *blóð svarið* is like a living thing inside you, it knows your thoughts, knows your heart. There is no escaping it."

A shout of pain echoed out and Elvar twisted to stare, her hand snapping out for her weapons belt.

Sighvat was clutching his arm, staggering, dropping to one knee. Even from here Elvar could see the steam curling from his arm and hear the sizzling hiss of scalding flesh.

"I am thinking Sighvat is having second thoughts about this oath of ours, too," Grend said.

"I did not mean it, I did not mean it, I DID NOT MEAN IT," Sighvat bellowed at the sky and the red-glow of fire in his veins faded, the fat warrior remaining on his knees, head bowed and gasping.

"None of us can escape it," Uspa continued. "Sighvat, you, Grend, even me. We all took the oath. If any one of us give up then we break that oath; then we will die, our blood set to boiling in our veins; or had you forgotten?"

"If I had, I am well reminded of it now," Elvar snapped, glaring from her arm to Uspa, "but how do you suggest we get your son back when he is in the company of Lik-Rifa? A *god*? It was going to be a hard-enough task winning him back from Ilska and her Raven-Feeders. And now Agnar is dead . . ." She dropped her head, felt the weight of grief and frustration rearing in her and snarled away the rising tears. *This was not supposed to happen.* She had imagined finding Oskutreð, finding a hoard of wealth and tales of her fair-fame name spreading throughout all Vigrið, eventually reaching her father's ears in his hall in distant Snakavik. Then he would know that she had the strength and will to succeed without him. To succeed *despite* him and his twisted ways. Although she despised him, she still wanted him to *know*.

Footsteps as Sighvat stumped over to them.

"How do we get free of this oath," he said, holding his arm up. The veins in it were still red-raw, weeping pus.

Elvar held her own red-veined arm up and he blinked. Then glowered at Uspa.

"The only way is to fulfil your oath," Uspa said.

"There is a dragon-god loose, Seiðr-witch," Sighvat grumbled, "how can we take your son back from that?"

"I do not know," Uspa said, "but we have to try."

"Impossibl—" Sighvat began, but his arm began to hiss and steam, the veins changing colour and he grabbed it with his other hand, dropping to his knees. "I'll try, I'll try, I'll TRY," he bellowed. He looked up at Uspa with a thunder-cloud scowl as the pain faded, sweat beading his face. "I knew I should not have taken that oath," he grumbled. "Now Agnar is dead . . ." he looked suspiciously at his arm, "and a demon of fire is living in my arm."

"Not just your arm," Uspa said. "I did warn you; oath-breaking would end in pain."

"There are different types of pain," Sighvat muttered. "A stubbed toe. A boil on the arse. The squits after a bad stew. But this, it felt like my flesh and bones were *boiling* inside my skin." Shaking his head, he sat down with a sigh next to Uspa on the wagon's tailgate. "This is a bad business." He looked at Elvar and Grend. "So, what are we going to do? We will need a deep-cunning plan to come out of this with our lives, a Tainted *Berserkir*-child and no blood boiled in our veins."

"I was hoping you might have some ideas, there," Elvar said.

"Agnar was always the deep thinker. I just hit what he pointed me at."

"Uspa expects us to march off after Lik-Rifa and Ilska the Cruel and just take Bjarn back," Elvar said.

"That doesn't sound like deep cunning to me," Sighvat frowned. A silence between them.

"More chance if all the Battle-Grim were in," Grend said.

"Aye," Elvar nodded. "But they did not take the oath, only we four did. They are not obliged to come with us, and it is not as if they need the gold or silver now. If Agnar were here, they would follow him, but us . . ." She looked at them all. "Would you?"

"No," Sighvat said.

Elvar blew out a long breath. "Let them do their fortune-hunting," she said. "And when they are done, then we will talk with them, and see what is what."

"That will be a delay, in which my Bjarn is taken further away," Uspa pointed out.

"I am bound by this oath, I acknowledge that," Elvar said. "And I shall do all that I can to fulfil it and get your son back. But the *how* of it is my decision. And I say we need the Battle-Grim, and it does not take a deep-cunning thinker to see that if we asked them right now their answer would be *no*. So, we wait, and ask when they are glutted on silver." She looked around at them. "Agreed?"

"Heya," Grend and Sighvat said. Uspa stared at Elvar, then nodded.

"Might as well see what we can find," Sighvat said. "Who knows, there may be a dragon-killing spear lying around."

"That is more the spirit I am hoping for," Uspa said.

Elvar didn't answer, but she thought Sighvat was right. Might as well find what they could. Her shield was shattered and her mail rent from the battle. Maybe she could find some war gear used by a dead god. And if not, filling the wagons with as much wealth as they could find might help.

Perhaps we can use it to buy a warband of dragon-slayers. Even if the Battle-Grim walk away from this fight, there will be enough silver here to hire a thousand hard-faced warriors.

Elvar took her spear that was propped up over her shattered kit and began sifting through the ash-covered ground.

A cry rang out and she saw Orv the Sneak crouching, lifting something. A recurved bow, still strung.

How has the string not rotted in three hundred years, she thought? Then she realised: it had belonged to one of the winged women who had attacked the dragon. The one with the silver hair and white wings. Lik-Rifa had torn her head off and stamped her body to gruel. Before that, though, Elvar remembered seeing speckles of fire erupting from the dragon's hide as arrows shot from that bow had pierced Lik-Rifa's body.

Is it a Seiðr-bow, or rune-wrought, or was it the arrows?

Either way, Orv was the best of the Battle-Grim to find it; he was the closest they had to a huntsman.

Elvar carried on searching, her spear snagging on something and spiking a sharp pain in her shoulder. She had been spear-stabbed in the shield wall yesterday, Grend pulling her out of the front row. After Lik-Rifa had flown away and Ilska and her Raven-Feeders followed the dragon like crows trailing a warband, Grend had cleaned her wound, digging around in it for broken rings from her *brynja*, then pouring honey into the red-bleeding hole and stitching it with a curved fishhook. With a grimace she adjusted her grip on the spear and lifted what she had snagged. Ash fell away to reveal a skeletal arm covered in ring mail, dull silver rings jangling on the forearm. The white-boned fist gripped the shaft of an axe. Elvar squatted to lever the axe free and sucked in a gasp. The shaft was about as long as Elvar's forearm, studded with iron, silver wire wrapped winding from hilt to blade. The axe head was single-edged and bearded, as Grend favoured. Snarling-wolf knotwork coiled across the blade, which Elvar had never seen on an axe intended for battle, as this one obviously was, judging by the dark stains on it and the fact that it was half embedded in someone's shattered skull.

"Grend," Elvar called, looking up, and she saw he was standing about twenty paces away, not searching, just staring. At the mound they had investigated yesterday, when they had first arrived. At the skeleton of Ulfrir wolf-god, his bones draped with earth, his teeth as long as spears, jaws open in his death-howl.

"Huh," Grend grunted. He turned slowly and looked at her.

"This is for you," Elvar said, tugging at the axe. The skull crumbled as Elvar pulled the blade free and hefted it in her left hand. Since she was old enough to hold a stick Grend had taught her to fight with both hands, so her left side was not weak. The axe was well balanced and she threw it to Grend as he strode to her, the old warrior catching it easily. He felt the weight, gave it a turn with his wrist, grunted an approval. Slashed the air, a viper's hiss. Touched his thumb to the edge.

"Still sharp," he muttered. He looked down at Elvar, the touch of a smile twitching the hard line of his mouth.

He must love it, Elvar thought.

"That ring mail," Grend said, pointing at the *brynja* wrapped around the axe-wielding skeleton. "Would it fit you?"

"I can't lift it," Elvar said, grimacing from the pain in her shoulder as she tried.

Grend hooked the beard of his new axe blade under the coat's arm and pulled it up. Bones slid out of the *brynja*, crumbling and cracking, and Grend slipped his new axe into his belt and gripped the coat of mail by each shoulder, holding it up against Elvar. It was dull and coated with ash but Elvar could see no rust on it, the rings small and riveted, which was a good sign. The smaller the rings the tighter the weave, the greater the protection. The mail at neck, sleeve-rim and hem shimmered and Grend slapped the ash away, revealing three or four rows of brass rings.

"No thrall's *brynja*, this," Grend said. He looked at her and smiled, the cliff-crags of his face breaking up. "I have a new axe, and you a new ring-coat."

"You are happier over a good axe and a coat of mail than a wagon full of silver," Elvar said, feeling a smile tugging at her own mouth. The first since seeing Agnar fall.

"Better chance of living longer with these than a wagon of silver," Grend shrugged.

Elvar turned and stumbled over something; the clank of iron and she looked down and saw a collar on the ground.

A thrall-collar, and a set of keys.

She squatted and touched it.

"It is Kráka's, or Ilmur's," Grend muttered above her. A sear-bright memory of Biórr taking the keys from Agnar's belt flashed through her thought-cage. Of Biórr shouting to Kráka, the Battle-Grim's thralled Seiðr-witch and Ilmur, their *Hundur*-thrall, and the two of them running to Biórr. Of Kráka and Ilmur unlocking their collars and dropping them to the ground beside Agnar's still twitching body.

I liked Kráka, and Ilmur, Elvar thought. *But they are Tainted, and just like Biórr they have proved that the Tainted cannot be trusted.*

"Stay down," Sighvat shouted and Elvar stood, the collar and keys still in her fist.

Sighvat was standing beside the wagon, looking down at something on the ground. A cloud of ash swirling, something dark and red moving within it. Sighvat kicked it.

Elvar narrowed her eyes, trying to understand what she saw.

Wings. Rust-red wings shifting on the ground, stirring up the ash.

Sighvat shouted something as the figure on the ground moved. He dragged his axe from a loop at his belt as the woman rose. Her hands and feet were still bound, but her wings were stretched wide and beating, raising her up. A cloud of dust enveloped them both. A muffled shout.

Elvar broke into a run, Grend at her shoulder, forging ahead of her. Other Battle-Grim were moving.

Movement in the dust cloud. Sighvat exploded out from it, hurtling through the air and fell rolling on the ground, losing the grip on his axe, the winged woman appearing on beating wings and hovering over him. A straining of her muscles and she cried out, sharp as a hawk-screech, something feral and ancient and terrifying in her voice. The leather bonds at her wrists and ankles ripped, falling away. She reached down and swept up Sighvat's axe.

Grend slammed into her back, clubbing her with the haft of his new axe and the two of them fell tumbling to the ground, rolling in a storm of wings and ash. Elvar chased after them, Sighvat cursing as he rose, staggering to one knee, Sólín reaching him and helping him stand.

A crack like a branch breaking and Grend was flying through the air, blood sluicing from his nose. The red-haired woman stalked after him.

Elvar leaped, collided with the woman and pain exploded in her shoulder. They stumbled together, the winged woman tripping and crashing into a wagon, her head crunching into the rim of a wheel. She slumped, dazed, Elvar still clinging to her, gasping through her pain.

The woman blinked, eyes clearing, focusing on Elvar.

Elvar thrust the thrall-collar around the woman's neck, snapping it shut, fumbling with the keys, groaning as waves of pain spiked from her shoulder-wound. A click as she turned the key in the lock. She reached for the seax hanging at her belt, found the hilt.

A hand grabbed Elvar's throat, strong as iron, squeezed.

Elvar drew her seax and raked it across her hand, grabbed the iron collar and smeared her blood on to it.

"*Hold, blóð og bein, járnsmíðar kraga, þú ert bundinn núna, hlýddu mér,*" she croaked.

Flesh, blood and bone, iron-forged collar, you are bound now, obey me.

The fingers around her throat squeezed tighter, Elvar's lungs screaming for air.

"*Verkur,*" Elvar squawked from her constricted throat as dots of light burst in her vision. A flare of fire-glow from the thrall-collar and the red-haired woman screeched, letting go of Elvar, hands clawing at the iron collar about her neck.

Elvar threw herself away, staggered to her feet, Grend a presence at her side, blood pouring from his split nose.

The red-haired woman's wings beat, lifting her into the air as the collar glowed red.

"*VERKUR,*" Elvar shouted at her and the collar flared white-hot, the woman screaming and twisting in the air, legs kicking, hands ripping like talons at the collar.

"Do what I say, and the pain will stop," Elvar shouted up at her. "Land."

The winged woman glared at Elvar, savage and fierce, even as the skin of her neck began to hiss and bubble. A twist of her wings and she dropped to the ground, fell to her knees, hands still ripping at the iron collar.

"*Friður,*" Elvar said and the collar cooled.

The red-winged woman scowled up at Elvar, gasping for breath.

"What is your name?" Elvar asked her.

"Who are you to question me, you insignifi—"

"*Smíða hita,*" Elvar said and the collar flared red.

A scream of pain from the red-haired woman.

"Skuld," she hissed. "My name is Skuld."

"*Friður,*" Elvar said again and the collar cooled to dull iron. Skuld knelt there, glowering up at Elvar, gasping, her wings twitching.

"You are my thrall now, your life to be lived in service to me."

Skuld made a noise in her throat but bit back whatever words were forming.

"By Berser's hairy arse but I am sick of Seiðr-touched women throwing me around this gods-cursed place," Sighvat bellowed.

"Where is Lik-Rifa? Where are my sisters?" the winged woman said, looking from Elvar to the plain around them, taking in the shattered remains of Oskutreð.

"Your sisters are dead," Grend said. "They fought against Lik-Rifa and died."

"They fought well, died bravely," Elvar added.

A shiver ran through the winged woman, her mouth a snarl, tears running down her cheeks and she bowed her head.

Elvar blew out a long breath, looking around. The Battle-Grim were all around them in a loose circle, weapons levelled at Skuld.

"Why are you here?" Skuld snarled at them all. She saw the wagons being slowly piled high with treasure, with battle gear and silver. Her lips twisted with disgust. "You are scavengers come to pick scraps from the bones of your betters."

"We've earned this treasure," Huld snarled, stepping closer and levelling her sword-tip at Skuld, who just sneered at the dark-haired warrior.

"Where are the richest prizes?" Elvar asked red-winged Skuld.

Skuld looked around the ash plain, and then at the gaping hole that led into the depths of Oskutreð.

"This is nothing. The real treasure is down below," she said.

CHAPTER THREE

VARG

Varg shovelled earth with a spade that Røkia had found in one of the storage barns edging the Grimholt's courtyard. Orka Skullsplitter was swinging her long-axe, chopping into the hard-packed earth and others were shovelling it away, helping her dig out a shallow grave for the corpse that Orka had carried from the tower, now wrapped in a cloak and placed at the foot of the bloodstained steps.

I am helping Orka Skullsplitter dig a grave, and her one of the most fair-famed and feared warriors in the whole of Vigrið. Since the fight at the mine Varg had felt like he was walking in the midst of a saga-tale, and this only made that feeling all the stronger. Others were carrying stones from the riverbank, Einar Half-Troll heaving one the size of a man on to his shoulder and carrying it like a sack of grain. They filed from the river to where Orka was digging, piling the rocks beside the fresh-dug grave. Svik was stirring a big black pot that hung suspended over a fire, the scent of porridge drifting and making Varg's belly growl.

The tennúr Vesli was scraping loose earth away with her long-fingered hands, though occasionally she would stop and look up at the sky.

Lik-Rifa, corpse-tearer, dragon-god, and she is supposedly free from her gaol beneath the great Ash Tree. Much had changed in Varg's world in just a few days, discovering that he was Tainted, the blood of Ulfrir the wolf-god flowing in his veins, and that all of the Bloodsworn were Tainted, too. But now, being told that one of the gods he had only heard spoken of in saga-tales was free and roaming the skies, he struggled to believe it. Did not want to believe it. Something had slithered and uncoiled in his belly when the vaesen Spert had burst from the river and pronounced the truth of Lik-Rifa being free. Impossible to prove, but somehow, deep in his bones, Varg *felt* it. He had dreamed last night of dragon-wings and ash, and so had all else in the Bloodsworn, it seemed.

Orka stopped her chopping and stood back, leaning on her long-axe and allowing Varg, Røkia and the man who they had found at Orka's side when they rode into the Grimholt the previous day to clear the last of the loose soil from the shallow grave. Lif, Varg had heard him called. He did not look like a warrior. He looked . . . lost. Or perhaps it was his grief. The corpse wrapped in the cloak was his brother.

Without thought Varg reached out a hand and squeezed Lif's shoulder.

"Losing your brother, it is a hard thing," Varg said to Lif's questioning, red-rimmed eyes.

Lif nodded, a sharp twitch of a gesture. "You have lost a brother, too?" Lif said.

An image of his friend Torvik flashed into his mind. Of Yrsa stabbing Torvik as he sat with Varg, of Skalk watching, cold and indifferent.

Of Torvik calling him *brother.*

"I have," Varg said, though Torvik was no blood-kin to him, but he had been his friend, and as good a man as he could have hoped for as a brother.

Jökul stopped in his shovelling of earth and looked at Varg. "Torvik will be avenged," he growled through his greying beard.

"Aye," Varg muttered, then looked back to Lif. "And a sister." Frøya's face floated in his thought-cage. His oath to avenge her sat hunched upon his soul like some long-taloned, black-winged crow.

Have you forgotten me, brother? Frøya's grave-touched voice rasped.

"Why did you leave us, Skullsplitter?" Røkia said, dragging Varg out of his fech-haunted thoughts. "Us, who you had sworn to stand with. To shed blood with. To die with if needs be."

Orka turned her grey-green eyes on Røkia, the colour of a storm-wracked sea.

A silence stretched, Røkia weathering the storm in Orka's eyes where Varg thought most would wither and look away.

"I'd had my fill of blood and death," Orka finally said.

Røkia nodded. Then she looked around the courtyard, her eyes settling on the mound of the dead, most of them made that way by Orka and her long-axe.

"It does not look like blood and death have had their fill of you."

Orka turned and strode to the body of Lif's brother, stooping to scoop him up in her arms and then returning, kneeling and placing the corpse in the grave. She looked at Lif beside her, who was pale-faced, a muscle in his cheek twitching.

"Do you have some words, before we raise a barrow over your brother?" Orka asked him.

Lif looked up at her, then back at the shape of his brother, wrapped in the cloak. Varg could smell burned flesh.

"I will miss you, Mord Virksson," Lif said, his voice all tremor and whisper. Then, stronger. "My brother, my friend. A good man who never wanted any trouble. Never looked for it."

Drawing a seax at his belt, Lif wrapped a fist around the blade, drew it slowly out.

"Blood feud," he snarled. "Guðvarr will die by my hand, brother, and any who stand between him and me. I swear it and seal it with my blood." He held his hand out and clenched it into a fist. Blood oozed from between his fingers.

Orka grunted in approval. She crouched beside the grave, looked as if she would say something herself, but then lifted one of the rocks piled close by and placed it in the grave. Lif hefted another stone, and then Varg and Røkia and many of the Bloodsworn were helping to raise a barrow over the dead man.

When they were done Lif looked up at Orka.

"My thanks," he said, tears streaking his cheeks. He looked around at Varg and the others. "My thanks," he repeated, then walked away towards the river.

Varg sat on the stone steps and blew on his porridge.

Orka Skullsplitter was close by, two steaming bowls of porridge in front of her, the tennúr Vesli sitting perched on her knee, slurping two-handed from her own bowl of steaming oats. She smacked her lips and spread her wings, fluttering to the ground where she set the empty bowl down, then reached for a clay jar set in the shade of a step. The tennúr unstoppered the jar and reached in, pulled out a blood-crusted tooth, thin strips of flesh still hanging from it, and popped it into her mouth. Crunched, her jaws grinding.

Varg put his own porridge down, his appetite abruptly gone, and looked away.

In the courtyard Einar Half-Troll was playing with the score of children who had been found by Orka in one of the storage sheds. Einar was lying face down on the ground, pretending to be a sleeping troll as the children clambered and climbed all over him, as if he were a favourite tree. Einar yawned and sat up slowly, slapped his lips loudly as he wondered aloud how many children he would cook to break his fast. They squealed and ran like a pack of rats found hiding in a hay-bale.

Varg heard the rasp of a blade drawn and his eyes snapped back to Orka, who had pulled out her seax and was pricking her thumb. He watched in fascination as she squeezed a drop of blood and let it drip into one of the bowls. Then she spat in the same bowl and stirred the porridge, mixing the blood and spit with her seax. She wiped the weapon clean and sheathed it.

"Spert," Orka called and there was an explosion of water as the vaesen burst from the river and flew, wings buzzing, across the courtyard, alighting in front of her with its wings folding and disappearing beneath the chitinous segments of its body. Those segments narrowed to a slim, pointed tail, an oil-black, wicked-looking sting curving over the creature's back. It scurried close to

Orka on short, insect-like legs. Now that it was out of the water Varg saw it was about as long as his arm.

"There you go," Orka said, nudging the porridge with blood and spit with her boot and Spert sniffed.

Then his blue-black tongue was dipping into the bowl and he was making slurping, squelching noises as he ate.

Glornir strode over to them, Edel, Svik, Sulich and Røkia all following him.

"There is so much to speak on . . . too much," Glornir said to Orka as he stopped before her, looking up at the cloudless sky, as if he searched for dragon-wings. "Lik-Rifa free?" There was a tremor in his voice at those words, which scared Varg more than any nightmare could. Glornir shook his head and sat on a step beside Orka. "And I must be away, after Skalk and my Vol. But first I would know this," he said. "How did my brother die?"

A ripple shivered through Orka's face, twisting her lips. Then she blew out a long breath, the tension in her shoulders evaporating like the wind dying from a sail.

"We had built a steading, a new life in the hills to raise our son and live in peace," she said.

"Your son," Glornir said, shaking his head. "I have a nephew. His name is Breca?" Varg had never heard tenderness in his chief's voice before.

"Aye," Orka nodded. "Breca." A smile touched her lips as she said his name. "He is ten winters, a good boy. A deep-thinker. Too kind for this world, but that is Thorkel's fault." She was silent a moment, lost in her own thoughts.

"Vesli miss Breca," the little tennúr piped.

"Strange things were happening," Orka continued, ignoring the vaesen. "A steading close by raided, a thralled *Úlfhéðnar* arriving in a village close to us. A jarl talking of war. Thorkel and I decided it was time to move on. I went to the Froa-tree to seek her wisdom. She was dead, the Ash Tree hacked down, the Froa-spirit dead as a lightning-struck branch. When I was there, I heard the screams." A shudder passed through her. "When I got back to the steading it was burning, Thorkel down, Breca taken." She traced a white scar along her forearm, then her hand dropped to the hilt of one of the seaxes at her belt. She drew it, turning it over in her hand, blade and hilt as long as Orka's forearm. A fine weapon, thick-bladed and single-edged, a broken back tapering to a razored point. Carved knotwork spiralled around a hilt of ash, a cap of brass and a leather thong tied through a pin.

Varg felt a trickle of ice in his veins. He recognised that blade and looked down at the seax hanging horizontally from his own belt.

"I found this in Thorkel, and this one, too," Orka said, her other hand touching a seax hanging from her belt across her back, then she looked up and met Glornir's eyes. "I have spent the time from that day to this, searching for the man who left them in Thorkel, so that I can give them back to him." The snarl of Orka's voice sent a shiver tingling through Varg's blood.

"His name is Drekr," Orka said. "I caught up with him in Darl, but we were parted before our business was finished." She paused, sucked in a deep breath. "He is dragon-born."

Glornir blinked at that and those around them muttered.

"We fought a dragon-born, only four days gone," Glornir said.

Orka stiffened. "Black hair, and scars running across his face, as if he'd been swatted by a bear?" Orka said. "Thorkel left his mark on him."

"No," Glornir said, and Orka sagged, Varg not sure if she was disappointed or relieved. "The man we fought was older, bald, a white beard."

"Where is he?" Orka asked. "I must speak to him."

"He is in the ground," Glornir said. "A hard fight. Varg put him there."

Orka's hard stare swivelled to Varg, along with Vesli and Spert, and all the other Bloodsworn around him.

"A lucky blow," Varg muttered, uncomfortable. His hand went to his ribs, that still throbbed where the dragon-born had struck him with Orna's talon.

"Not luck. Courage," Jökul said.

"Aye, it was a wolf-brave blow," Glornir said, which made Varg's chest swell, though he shifted uneasily. Living all of your remembered life as a thrall did not make you a close friend with compliments. He gripped his seax and drew it.

"This seax," he said, "it has the same knotwork in the hilt." He lifted and turned the hilt for Orka to see. She leaned closer, scowling at the weapon. "It belonged to the dragon-born we fought."

"They could have been forged in the same fire, carved by the same hand," Røkia said, who was leaning close.

"And this Drekr dragon-born, he stole your son?" Glornir said to Orka. Her eyes lingered on the seax in Varg's fist for a moment, then rose to hold Varg's gaze before she looked back to Glornir.

"Aye," Orka nodded. "I found more stolen children in Darl, all Tainted, and then more here." She gestured to the bairns who were back to clambering all over Einar. "How did you find this dragon-born who held the twin of these blades at my belt?"

"We were hired by Queen Helka to track down something that was killing her people," Glornir said. "Vaesen, she thought. Turns out it was dragon-born stealing people and thralling them to dig out Rotta's chamber, though they had a troll and skraelings working with them. And there were signs that children had been kept there." He tugged on his grey beard, a thick-rope knot. "Three hundred years and no dragon-born have ever been seen. And now two appear, with seaxes carved by the same hand, and, if your . . . friends are to be believed," he said, glancing to Vesli and Spert, "then Lik-Rifa the dragon-god is free from the roots of Oskutreð."

"Dark deeds," Orka nodded, her eyes narrowed. "On the journey here, I passed an oath stone. An eagle had been sacrificed there, and Lik-Rifa's likeness scrawled on the broken stone. I am thinking that all these things are joined, like this serpent-knot," she said, tracing the serpent carved in coils around the hilt of her seax.

"Hmm," Glornir murmured, scowling. Then he blew out a short, sharp breath. "Vol first," he said, "before I walk down the road of hunting dragon-born and their corpse-tearing mother. Is there any more you can tell me of Skalk? What happened here?"

Orka closed her eyes a moment and pinched the bridge of her nose. "We were in the tower," she said. "Lif and Mord, me. All chained up after running into some frost-spiders up in the hills, being questioned by some arseling *drengrs* and the Galdurman, Skalk." She frowned. "There is some deal between Drekr and Hakon, Queen Helka's son. Hakon was allowing Drekr to bring his stolen children here. It was a surprise to Skalk the Galdurman, who is Helka's hound, I am thinking."

"He is," Glornir agreed.

"Skalk is injured," another voice said. Lif, sitting quietly on the steps close by.

"He is?" Orka said, frowning.

"Aye," Lif said with a small smile. "You put an axe in his shoulder. Not that one," he said, nodding at Orka's long-axe. "If you'd used that he wouldn't have an arm now. You threw your hand-axe at him when he spoke his words of power and his staff burst into flames. Took him in the shoulder and sent him falling out of the door and down the stairs."

"His staff?" Glornir asked Lif.

"He dropped it in the tower. It is ash and cinder, now."

"Ha," a voice barked, Svik, smiling grimly. "Good. Easier to catch and kill a Galdurman with no staff."

"He made it to one of the *snekkes* moored at the pier, and is rowing hard for Darl, I am thinking," Orka said.

"Did you see Vol?" Glornir asked. "Did you see him take her on the boat."

"No," Orka shook her head.

"Vesli saw a woman in mail, fierce, nasty face. She was carrying another, blue paint on her neck and chin," the tennúr said.

Glornir looked down at Vesli and nodded his thanks. Then he looked around those gathered about him, at the Bloodsworn.

"Then we are for Darl," Glornir growled.

CHAPTER FOUR

ELVAR

Elvar wrapped a strip of linen around the cut she had sliced in her palm, tying it off with her teeth as she stared at the gaping hole that led into the dark depths of Oskutreð.

"More treasure down there, you say?" Huld asked the red-winged woman.

"Aye," Skuld answered. "More than a hundred of those wagons could carry."

"Who *are* you, Skuld?" Elvar asked her. "*What* are you?"

Skuld glowered at her, the skin around her neck red and raw from where the thrall-collar had burned her. She flexed her wings and stared at Elvar and the Battle-Grim behind her.

"I am Skuld, daughter of Orna and Ulfrir," she said.

A hushed silence as that truth settled on them, giving Elvar an involuntary shudder, like walking through thick cobwebs in the dark.

Daughter of Orna and Ulfrir, Elvar thought. *Daughter of two gods, eagle and wolf. And she is my thrall.* A knot of fear clenched in her gut. *Can I control a god?*

"Let her kill the dragon while we take Uspa's bairn back," Sighvat muttered behind Elvar, "she hates Lik-Rifa enough."

"The dragon slew her two sisters," Elvar said, "what chance would she have on her own. We would need a warband of gods like her to slay Lik-Rifa." Her eyes drifted to the mound of Ulfrir-wolf's bones and she remembered an image from the oath stone that the

Battle-Grim had come across on their journey from Iskalt Island to Snakavik. An image of Ulfrir bound with chains, a horde of red-eyed warriors swarming over his body, stabbing him. "Or a warband of Tainted thralls," she added.

"Just an idea," Sighvat muttered with a shrug.

"Skuld, come here," Elvar said.

Skuld glared at Elvar, muscles in her face twitching. She was not used to being ordered. The iron collar about her neck shifted in colour, heating, and with a growl Skuld strode stiffly towards Elvar.

"How did you know the words of binding?" Sighvat whispered to Elvar. "Agnar did not even share them with me."

"I grew up in the hall of Jarl Störr, who has a Galdurwoman and over two score *Berserkir* thralls. You'll be surprised what an inquisitive child can overhear."

Sighvat rumbled approval in his throat.

"What is down there?" Elvar asked as Skuld drew near, pointing to the darkness that Lik-Rifa had burst from.

"Another world," Skuld said. "Vergelmir, Lik-Rifa's chamber, and many others." Her gaze swept the Battle-Grim. "A hoard of treasure."

"You will show me," Elvar said.

"You will show *us*," Huld said, frowning at Elvar. "If there is more treasure to be had then the Battle-Grim have earned it." Warriors murmured their agreement.

"Let's be doing it, then," Sighvat said. "We'll draw lots to decide who stays and guards what we have up here."

They set about making ready, drawing lots and checking their weapons.

Grend padded over to Elvar.

"You should put your new ring-coat on," he said quietly.

"I cannot lift my arm high enough," she said, jutting her chin at the wound in her shoulder, blooming fresh blood after her scuffle with Skáld. "You will have to be my coat of mail, for now."

"That is no new thing," Grend muttered.

"Battle-Grim," Sighvat called out and they gathered around him, twenty of the Battle-Grim, another ten staying behind to guard the treasure they had already collected. Sólín led a pony harnessed to an empty wagon, a tall, bright-bladed spear in her fist taken from the battlefield. Urt the Unwashed sat upon the driver's bench, a tall, willow-slender man with thinning, greasy, fair hair and a hooked nose. Sighvat looked at them all, then turned and strode towards the shattered tree of Oskutreð.

"Skuld, with me," Elvar said as she followed Sighvat. She threaded her way through huge splinters that reared tall as trees where Lik-Rifa had exploded into the world. Sighvat and others cleared a path for Sólín's wagon and soon they were all standing at the edge of a gaping hole that bored down into darkness.

"There," Skuld said, pointing and she spread her rust-red wings and beat them, rising from the ground and flying over to a sloping path that coiled around the edge of the vast hole. She strode down into the darkness and then there was the spark of flint and flare of fire as Skuld lifted a reed-torch that was set into a sconce, fire-light glowing.

Grend leaned and looked down.

Skuld stood with a torch held high and Elvar saw the ledge she was standing upon was wide enough for the wagon. The path spiralled down, hewn into the wall that circled the huge hole, like a giant well.

Uspa stepped out from the Battle-Grim and made her way towards Skuld, the others following. Elvar gave Grend a look and she followed, too, all of them gathering on the path before Skuld.

"Lead us on," Elvar said to Skuld.

They walked down into the darkness, Elvar striding beside Skuld. Even with her wings furled Skuld took up enough room for two. Every forty or fifty paces there was a new torch set in a sconce that was nailed into the rock. As they descended each one of them took a torch, lighting it from Skuld's, and as they spiralled down ever deeper Skuld lit the torches they passed by.

"This is an insult," Skuld muttered, one hand grasping at the collar around her neck. "I was worshipped by your kind, and now you would enslave me! Command me! It is unthinkable."

"The world has changed since you and your kind walked beneath the sun," Elvar said. "Your war almost destroyed humankind, and you and your kin are not loved for that. The gods are hated, now, and their offspring, too. Wherever they are found the Tainted are thralled, just like you."

"Tainted?" Skuld frowned.

"Those with the blood of the dead gods in their veins. Like those dragon-born who set Lik-Rifa free."

Skuld shook her head. "This is ludicrous," she muttered, "that the highest should become the lowest. The world has turned to madness."

"You should know some of the rules you are bound by," Elvar said to Skuld. "The collar is bound to me, now, will obey only me. If I am slain by your hand, it will know, and it will punish you for that. You cannot raise your hand against me. And the collar can hear my commands, whether I am standing next to you, or a hundred leagues away, so there is no escaping me."

Skuld stared straight ahead, glowering into the darkness.

"But it is not all bad, there are worse people you could be thralled to. My father, for one." Memories rose up of her father taking a whip to the backs of his thralls. Of his thin-lipped smile as the blood had sprayed. Of how he had ordered her to watch and slapped her when she looked away. She shuddered and pushed the memories away. "I shall treat you well and give you the chance to earn my respect."

"*Earn* it!" Skuld hissed, "I was born to it. To the blowing of horns and shouts of acclamation. I was worshipped."

"That is no longer the way of this world, and the sooner you accept that, the better it will be for you. You are hated and reviled, now. But with me you shall get the chance to avenge your sisters. We share a common cause: I seek Lik-Rifa's death."

"Why would you risk your life in that?" Skuld frowned at Elvar.

"Lik-Rifa has my son," Uspa said behind them, "and Elvar has sworn to get him back. Sworn the *blóð svarið*."

"Ha," Skuld exclaimed bitterly, "we share more than a common cause, then. We are both thralled."

"Huh," Elvar grunted, not liking the thought of that.

They walked on in silence, ever downwards.

Eventually they spilled on to level ground and Elvar paused to look up, saw the blue-white glare of sky high above and, circling the deep hole, torches flickered like red-gold stars spiralling through the darkness.

They were standing at the edge of a huge cavern or tunnel that disappeared into the crow-dark, as if a worm the size of a hill had burrowed its way through this ground. Torches burned in sconces, looking as small as pinheads and fading into the distance. Roots twisted and curled between rock and earth, thick as ancient oaks, damp soil oozing. Water dripped, echoing. The enormity of the chamber was overwhelming, Elvar feeling small and insignificant.

She took a few steps and stumbled on uneven footing, looked down to see that shattered wood, possibly smashed furniture, lay scattered across the ground, pots and pans thrown, weapons strewn, wooden chests heaped high at the cavern's edges like wreckage after a flood.

"Looks like a storm has raged through this cavern," Orv the Sneak muttered.

Or a dragon.

"Where is this treasure, then?" Huld said into the silence.

"Everywhere," Skuld said with a dismissive wave of her hand, taking in the scattered chests. "But the true treasure lies deeper."

Huld looked into the dark tunnel and sucked in a breath.

"No point standing around here," Elvar said as she walked forwards. Huld scowled at her and Grend followed her, Skuld's wings opening and beating.

They threaded their way through the wreckage of the tunnel, Sólín leading the pony by its bridle, Urt the Unwashed climbing down and helping to load chests of silver and gold on to the wagon. As they wound deeper into the tunnel Elvar saw the remains of a hearth fire, embers still glowing, and the spitted leg of a half-roasted deer. She gave Skuld an enquiring look.

"Our supper," Skuld said, "before the world was turned upside down."

"You have lived down here for three hundred years?" Elvar asked Skuld.

"Yes," Skuld said.

"How could you bear it down here, in the dark and the damp? How did you come by this meat? Where did you get your food from?"

"There are smaller tunnels, vents that lead up into the day. We would take it in turns, spend some time in the world above; to fly and hunt, to feel the wind in our hair, the sun on our face."

"That would make this place more bearable," Uspa said. "I am guessing that Lik-Rifa did not have such small pleasures?"

"She did not deserve any better," Skuld snarled. "Death would have been too good for her, after what she did to my sister." She sucked in a shuddering breath. "Lik-Rifa caused the war, caused the death of my father, my mother, all our kin. And now, my last two sisters."

"I imagine she would hold a different view," Uspa said as she moved through the chamber. Elvar watched her approach a loom, thick with weaves of woollen thread, and reach out a hand, finger-tips brushing threads. Beside the loom was a well, a bucket hanging suspended over it. A table close by, with a tafl board and pieces carved from white stone.

Even the gods must get bored.

"Lik-Rifa's opinion does not matter," Skuld said. "She was never to be trusted. She is unhinged, as if she has always seen the world through mist and smoke."

"Why did you stay down here? Why not kill Lik-Rifa, or just leave her to starve in her gaol?"

"We stayed because we swore an oath to our father. To ensure Lik-Rifa remained within her cage. She is not so easy to kill," Skuld muttered. "We tried in those first days, with arrow and spear, and when that did not work, we tried to starve her, but Lik-Rifa is . . . resourceful."

As the Battle-Grim moved through the chamber Elvar saw shafts of light spearing down through the roof high above. The torches flickered from unseen currents.

The vents Skuld spoke of.

There were other doorways, some just arches, others with wooden doors and iron hinges. Outside one was a table, tools scattered upon it, hammer, tongs, chisels, awls. Elvar lifted the latch on the door and peered in. The smell of iron and sulphur, charcoal and oil wafted out. She saw a pitted anvil and bellows, a hammer and tongs upon them.

"A forge," she murmured, and beside the table she saw bundles of arrows, iron-tipped and fletched with white feathers. She lifted up one of those bundles, tied like a sheaf of wheat. Uspa saw them and leaned close, touched an arrowhead with her finger. She shivered.

"What?" Elvar asked her.

"There is power in them," Uspa said.

"They were forged by Verdani, my sister," Skuld said.

Grend picked up another bundle.

"Orv," he called out, and threw them to the huntsman.

Orv reached out and caught them, the bow he had found on the field still in his fist.

Skuld looked Orv up and down, her eyes narrowing as she saw the weapon.

"That is my sister's," she said.

"Aye, well, she has no use for it, now," Orv replied, though he did not meet her gaze.

A shiver ran through Skuld, grief and anger chasing each other across her face.

She led them on, through the chamber, smaller doors and tunnels twisting away from it, until Elvar's head was whirling with the scale of this catacomb beneath the ground. It felt like a new world, one that went on for ever.

Something changed in the air, a coldness causing Elvar's breath to mist, but it was more than that, the hairs on the back of her neck standing on edge. It was a sensation Elvar knew well.

Fear.

A shattered door became discernible among the shadows, tall and wide as a hill. Splintered wood lay strewn across the ground and iron bars thick as mead hall posts protruded from the rock walls, twisted and broken. Darkness and malice leaked from the gaping hole like tendrils of mist.

"What is this place?" Sighvat growled.

"That is Vergelmir, Lik-Rifa's chamber," Skuld said.

Elvar stepped into the darkness, holding her torch high, and Grend hurried in front of her, his axe in one hand, torch in the other. The Battle-Grim followed after them.

The ground was slick underfoot, Elvar's boots sticking to some cloying substance. Bones and festering corpses littered the ground, in various stages of decay. The stench grew, of things long dead, of putrefaction, clawing its way into Elvar's throat like grasping fingers. Behind her Uspa retched.

Three hundred years locked in here. Lik-Rifa must have been driven insane.

Something moved, a shadow at the edge of their torches' reach, and Elvar stepped forward, though she could not draw a weapon and still hold on to her torch.

A shape stood on a mound, four-legged, pale as milk, its skin almost translucent. It was hairless, with a long muzzle and razored teeth like a rat's, though it was as big as a boar. Its body was low to the ground, a thick-corded tail twitching. Elvar could see the shadowed glow of organs pulsing within its translucent flesh. It looked at them, squinting at the torchlight.

"Looks like the wife you left behind in Iskidan, Sighvat," Huld said, and laughter rippled through the Battle-Grim, echoing and amplified.

"I crossed an ocean to get away from her," Sighvat grumbled.

"It's not her," Grend said, his face like stone, "that bald rat is far prettier."

More laughter, Sighvat laughing the hardest.

With a high-pitched squeal the creature turned and scurried away.

"Even when she was caged Lik-Rifa always liked to toy with life, to change and alter," Skuld said. "Never for the better."

"What is that?" Elvar said, pointing with her torch deeper into the chamber. There was a faint glow at the edge of Elvar's vision, like moonlight on mist.

"The treasure you seek," Skuld said.

Elvar made her way further into the chamber, Grend one side

of her, Uspa the other, and she saw the bulk of Sighvat and other Battle-Grim spreading wide, moving into the room. Things crunched beneath Elvar's feet and a sweep of her torch revealed fragments of chitinous shells, husked, insect-like bodies, though far bigger. A foot disappeared into what looked like a pool of slime, but she moved on, drawn to the glow at the chamber's edge, that moved and churned like a thick sea fog. Elvar thought she could see shadowed figures moving within the mist.

With every step Elvar sensed a change around her. The tunnel they had been travelling through had felt infinitely huge, but this chamber felt suffocating, constricting, a pressure all about Elvar, even though she could see no walls. The very air felt thick and stifling.

Uspa hissed and jolted to a stop, Elvar instinctively stopping beside the Seiðr-witch.

"What is it?" Elvar breathed, staring.

Pale mist swirled before them, churning like a slow-moving tide, and as Elvar stared figures became clear within it. They were pallid, ethereal, glowing with some inner light. Some wore mail and helm, dragged sword or axe or spear along the ground and bore the wounds of battle, gaping holes in chest or throat, while others walked in tattered tunics, limping, lurching, stumbling. Some were missing limbs, some appeared thin as reeds, emaciated from illness, their skin stretched and tight, features drawn. All walked with their heads bowed, travelling in the same direction.

"They are . . . dead," Sighvat rumbled.

"It is the soul road," Uspa whispered.

Mutters and curses rippled through the Battle-Grim, hands moving, making warding signs of protection.

"Lik-Rifa would savage them as they passed through her chamber," Skuld said. "Somehow, she learned how to take sustenance from them, from the ones who did not fight back, at least. That is why she is called corpse-tearer and soul-stealer."

All those tales I was told as a child, I thought they were to frighten me, to make me behave and obey. But they were true. Did my mother walk this road? Did Agnar?

The grim procession appeared to emerge from a wall of stone and earth, winding their way through the chamber and then disappearing through an ethereal gateway edged with corpses, bodies and limbs twisted about each other like roots.

The Corpse-Gate.

"Where are they going?" Urt the Unwashed rasped.

"To the halls of the dead," Skuld said, "though where or what they are, I do not know. Dread Snaka kept many secrets."

"I do not like it down here," Sighvat muttered.

Neither do I.

"The souls of the dead are not treasure that we can load on a wagon and sell," Elvar snapped at Skuld.

"This is not what I spoke of. The treasure you seek is deeper, that way," Skuld said, pointing, and Elvar saw another light, this one glowing red and amber, flickering like firelight in a breeze.

Elvar tore her eyes away from the soul road and the dead in their endless procession and walked on towards the red-glowing light. She heard the crunch of wagon wheels across the layer of remains that littered the ground. Her breath rasped in her throat, her heart thumping in her chest, a sense of dread growing and seeping into her with every step that she took towards the red light. Something moved at the edge of her torchlight, a flicker of shadow and the skittering of feet on the ground.

The rat-thing we saw?

"What are we walking on?" Elvar asked Skuld.

"Other things that Lik-Rifa found to eat," Skuld said with a disgusted twist of her lips. "The souls of the dead were not enough to sustain her, so she hunted the creatures that lurk in these deep, dark places. Creatures of carapace and of slime. And other things that Lik-Rifa's helpers brought to her."

"Helpers?"

"I told you, Lik-Rifa was ever trying to create, to alter, to subvert the natural life around her."

More movement around them, shadows flitting at the edge of their torchlight. The Battle-Grim drew instinctively closer, some shrugging shields from their backs, hefting weapons. Elvar gripped her torch tighter, and she saw Grend step nearer, drawing his new axe from his belt.

The light ahead grew brighter and clearer. Red runes flickering in the air, reminding Elvar of when Uspa had bound them all to the *blóð svarið*, runes of blood and fire-glow hovering before them. They formed an arch, high as two doors, wide as three, and spreading from and around the door a circle of flame-cast runes that enclosed a mound of rock and a pedestal. Upon the pedestal sat a black-bound book. As Elvar looked at it the air about the book shimmered and rippled, like steam from a pot.

"And what is that?" Huld said into the thick, reeking air.

"I do not know," Skuld said, "but I always wondered what Lik-Rifa got up to in the long dark of Oskutreð, and my sisters always suspected that she was dabbling in . . . wrongness." She shrugged. "Whatever it is, Lik-Rifa valued it enough to leave it protected with runes and guards around it." She spread her wings and rose into the air.

"Wrongness?" Sighvat muttered. "What does that even mean? And guards? What guards?" he said as Huld walked forwards and put a step across the boundary of the rune-marked doorway.

With a crack like the sound of a whip a concussive blast of air exploded outwards from the rune-circle, snuffing every torch out and hurling Elvar from her feet, the sound of bodies falling all about her.

Elvar lay on her back, a stab of pain in her wounded shoulder, looking up into the crow-black chamber.

"Elvar?" Grend grunted.

She spat and swore, looked around but the rune-glow of the doorway only made the darkness around it more solid and impenetrable.

The sound of flint scrapping, a spark of light as Sighvat lit his torch and raised it high.

"Battle-Grim?" he called out, and warriors answered, Elvar clambering to one knee.

Then something grey and slime-covered hurtled out of the darkness.

CHAPTER FIVE

BIÓRR

Biórr stood and smiled, a wide braid of a grin splitting his face. "Welcome back to us," Ilska said, her face sharp as a *drakkar's* prow, black hair sleek as raven-wings, though this close to her Biórr could see the threads of grey winding through it, like silver-seams in granite. She held out a night-black raven feather, a length of leather cord threaded through the quill. Biórr reached out and took it, tying the cord into the braid of his own black hair. Shouts rang out from the Raven-Feeders gathered about them.

"You are the reason we found the path to Oskutreð," Ilska continued. "The reason we were able to set Lik-Rifa free. And you slew Agnar Battle-Grim into the bargain." More shouting, warriors banging spear shafts on shields. Emotions flickered across Ilska's face at the mention of Agnar, for he had slain her brother, Skrið, which none had thought possible, Biórr among them. He felt his own face twist at the memory. Of Agnar kneeling in blood and ash, his shattered shield hanging from his arm, reaching out with his other hand for Biórr to help him rise. Of Biórr's spear snaking out . . .

"Well, do you not want it?" Ilska said, a frown pinching her brow. She was holding out an arm ring, twisted gold with serpent-head terminals, fangs bared.

Biórr blinked, pulling himself back into the Now and nodded.

"My thanks," he said, taking the ring and threading it around his arm, over the sleeve of his mail coat and squeezing it tight.

More shouting and spear thumping on shields, faces of old comrades grinning at Biórr, men and women he had grown up with, but that he had left close to three years ago, when he had been given his task of infiltrating Agnar's warrior band of Battle-Grim. He grinned again, sweeping away the image of Agnar's trusting eyes, shifting to shock. Ilska stared at him with her dark, unsettling gaze and he did his best to meet it, knowing what she thought of people who could not weather her searching eyes. "You'll find your old kit on one of our wagons. Myrk will show you where, no doubt." Then she nodded and walked away.

Other figures crowded around him, men and women he had grown up with, as close as kin. Grins all around him, mouths moving, hands slapping his back and shoulders as the Raven-Feeders welcomed him back to them.

Biórr grinned back at them all, turning this way and that, feeling the joy of being home seep into him. Not the home of a steading or mead hall, or any place, but here, among the people he had spent over half his life with. And yet, he felt . . . distant. Awkward.

It is only natural, after living among the untouched for so long. He rubbed his eyes and forehead.

A figure pushed through the crowd around him, laughing as she shoved warriors twice her size out of her way, and they all parted for her. The sight of her stirred memories and emotions in Biórr, feeling like a bird was fluttering its wings inside his chest. Another raven-haired woman with a sharp prow of a face, though she was younger than Ilska, younger than Biórr's twenty-three winters, too, and, unlike Ilska, the humour in her eyes softened the sharpness of her features. She wore an oil-dark *brynja*, sword, seax and axe all hanging from her weapons belt and she walked with the confidence and grace Biórr had seen in only a handful of warriors.

Like Agnar.

And Elvar . . . Images of her flooded his head, of her blue-eyed gaze, sharp and pure as a mountain stream, of her smile that felt like it cracked his heart, of her lips on his . . .

He grimaced and pushed the memories of her into the shadows of his thought-cage.

"Myrk," Biórr said, dipping his head to her, his smile stretching across his face.

"At last you come back to us," Myrk said, returning his smile and threading her arm through his, steering him out and away from the crowd.

They were sat on a rise of land surrounded by rolling hills and woodland, a circle of wagons to the north of the camp where the sound and stink of horses was thick in the air. To the west the slopes of Mount Eldrafell glowed in the strange ever-light of *sólstöður*, the long day, and Biórr knew that the vaesen pit and the Isbrún Bridge lay only a short march south from here. They had travelled hard and fast away from Oskutreð, a forced march for almost two days in their efforts to keep up with Lik-Rifa, the dragon-god now free from her underground gaol and revelling in the freedom of the skies.

And now Lik-Rifa was nowhere to be seen and the warband had finally staggered and stumbled to a halt, exhaustion overcoming them. Many were still sleeping, wrapped in cloaks, while others glanced through the thin canopy to the skies above, searching for Lik-Rifa's return.

"This way," Biórr said and they threaded their way through the camp.

"My sister likes you," Myrk said, nodding to the gold arm ring. "She guards her gold and silver like a hoard-sick dragon, so you are favoured."

"I am honoured," Biórr said.

"I like you more, though," Myrk said, nudging him with her elbow. "I am glad you're back. I'll give you more than an arm ring when we . . ." she smiled at him, a lazy, languorous stretching of her lips, Biórr finding it as unsettling as Ilska's hard gaze. "Hold a moment," Myrk said, grabbing his wrist, her grip even stronger than he remembered. He stopped and she leaned close, sniffing his cheek, his neck, close enough to smell the sour skyr on her breath, tinged with apple and honey.

"You smell of *them*," she said, pulling away, a twist of her lips.

For a moment he thought she could smell Elvar on him and he felt a flush of guilt.

"You smell *ordinary*," she frowned.

"Part of my disguise," he said, giving a weak smile and walking on.

"I will help you wash their stink from you," she grinned.

"I thought the new world we are fighting for will be one where we can all live together," Biórr said. "Us Tainted and the untouched, all in harmony."

"Oh, we will," Myrk said. "But there will be an order to things. There has to be, else all will be chaos. Lik-Rifa will be our queen, with her dragon-born as her captains. That means me." She flashed another grin. "And then will come the other Tainted, like you," she gave him a lip-twisting smirk, "and then will come the untouched. Those worshippers of Lik-Rifa and the dead gods who do not have the gift of god-blood in their veins." She glanced at a huddle of warriors, men and women with raven feathers in their hair, but sat apart. "They are untouched," Myrk said. "Part of the Dragon-Cult that is spreading through the land. My sister says we will need them, when the time comes." Myrk shrugged. "They fight well enough and do not wish to put a collar around my neck or sell me to the highest bidder, so I am not complaining, and my sister is the deep-cunning thinker, not I."

"I would agree with you there," he smiled.

Myrk punched his arm. A playful blow, but it staggered him a few paces.

"Where are we going?" Myrk asked him as they moved through the camp, approaching a line of wagons.

"Here," Biórr said as he rounded a wagon and stopped. A mass of children sat clumped together around a handful of fires, a few Raven-Feeders standing guard around them. Biórr searched and saw who he was looking for.

"Kráka, Ilmur," he said to two adults sitting among the children, dipping some hard bread into bowls of stew. Kráka sat with her knees hunched up, her black hair loose and hanging about her shoulders like crow-wings. Biórr could see the bones moving in her jaw as she chewed and slurped, blue-swirling tattoos coiling across one cheek and disappearing into the dark of her hair. She looked up at him and nodded.

Ilmur had his tattered sealskin cloak pulled tight around him, hair lank and stuck to his head, eyes sunken to pools.

"You two are free, now," Biórr said to them, touching a finger to his neck to remind them they no longer wore the thrall-collar.

"Aye," Ilmur said, nodding and grinning, though he still had the look of a kicked dog about him.

Biórr sat beside them, and Myrk kicked him to make room for her.

"This is Myrk, sister of Ilska," Biórr introduced her. "Also known as Sharp-Claw."

"My blades are my claws," Myrk said with a shrug, patting the weapons at her belt, "and they are always sharp. Welcome," she added, "I hope you have been well-looked-after. All has been a red-haze madness since Oskutreð, but I would be grieved if fellow Tainted had not been cared for by my Raven-Feeders."

Her Raven-Feeders! She has not changed.

"Yes, a good welcome," Kráka said quietly. "We have been given food and warm clothes, all that we could ask for."

"And no thrall-collars," Ilmur said, his hand going to the scarred skin around his neck. "We are *free*." He breathed the word as if it were formed of gold.

"Never again will you wear a thrall-collar, little hound," Myrk said. "Lik-Rifa's freedom is the first step to freeing *all* the thralled Tainted in Vigrið."

"And yet," Kráka said, lifting an arm and putting it around the shoulder of a boy sitting beside her. She stroked his brown hair with a wool-gloved hand. The boy had an iron collar around his neck and his eyes were filmed pearl-white, staring into nowhere. Bjarn, the son of Uspa, whom Biórr had given over to the Raven-Feeders when they had raided the Battle-Grim back in Snakavik. Part of Biórr had been looking forward to seeing the lad, for they had played some fine games of tafl and Biórr liked him.

"What's wrong with him?" Biórr asked, frowning.

"They are all like this," Kráka said, gesturing to the Tainted children sitting around them, close to a hundred of them. "And they all wear thrall-collars?"

"There was no choice," Myrk explained. "So many tried to run away, and Lik-Rifa could not have been freed without them. We have cast a Seiðr-spell to calm them, nothing more. But the collars will come off, once they learn the rightness of our cause."

Bjarn blinked, a shifting of colour in his eyes and he looked at Biórr, a glimmer of recognition for a moment.

"Tafl," Bjarn said, bringing a smile to Biórr's lips, but then Bjarn's eyes filmed over again.

"You have a new ring," Ilmur said into Biórr's scowl, a hand reaching out to touch the gold arm ring that Ilska had gifted him.

"For his great deeds," Myrk said, "not least of which is the slaying of Agnar Battle-Grim, the *niðing* who slew my battle-famed brother."

Biórr looked at Myrk with raised eyebrows.

"True enough, I did not like Skrið much, he would eat all my porridge when I was a bairn, and pinch me till I cried, just to see what path the tears would choose as they slid down my face. But he was my brother." She shrugged. "I loved him, and Agnar Battle-Grim was a worm compared to him."

Ilmur's face twisted at the mention of Agnar, a flicker of sadness that made Biórr frown.

He is not comfortable with all this talk of Agnar being a niðing. *But Agnar was Ilmur's master for so many years. Even the dog which is kicked and beaten will come to love the hand that feeds it.*

Kráka nodded.

"A mighty deed," she said, her face a hard-lined cliff, and Biórr's eyes narrowed.

Does she mock me?

"He was on his knees, bloody from his fight with Skrið, and I thrust my spear into Agnar's mouth as he held his arm out to me, thinking me a shield-brother come to help him," Biórr muttered, his own lips twisting at the shame of it. "It was no great saga-song of battle, no fair-fame victory," he said. "A poor death for anyone, that, let alone Agnar Battle-Grim." The shame of it robbed Biórr of the joy he should be feeling.

But he deserved a poor death, Biórr told himself. *He was nothing but a* niðing *slaver, making himself wealthy by trading in lives. In Tainted lives.*

"It was your blow that slew him," Myrk said, "and that is all that matters. Agnar Battle-Grim, who has chained and sold so many of our kind. Who slew my *brother*." She snarled, the faintest hint of the violent depths that Biórr knew lurked in her soul.

Something changed in the camp, a silence spreading, and above them branches creaked and sighed in a sudden wind. Heads looked up, and Biórr saw a shape in the pale sky, a dark shadow high above, growing larger as it circled lower.

"Lik-Rifa," someone said, the name whispered, then spoken and shouted, spreading through the Raven-Feeders like the sea-foamed wake of a *drakkar*.

The dragon sank lower and lower, spiralling down to them, her bulk growing to blot out the sky, Biórr and the others rising, walking across the camp to follow Lik-Rifa's descent. It became clear she had something gripped in the huge talons of her rear legs, something that hung dangling and limp.

Then trees were swaying, ripping at the roots in the storm of the dragon's wings and Lik-Rifa released the corpse in her claws. It crashed to the ground, a bear the size of the *Wave-Jarl*. The earth shook with its fall and it rolled and was still, head lolling, mouth open, eyes sightless. Red wounds gaped on its flanks and muzzle. Lik-Rifa landed upon it, more trees ripped from their roots and hurled like kindling as her head lunged forwards, jaws wide and she tore chunks of flesh from the dead bear, fur ripping, bones snapping, all of it disappearing into the great red maw of Lik-Rifa's mouth. Fur and flesh and bone erupted as the dragon tore and ate in a frenzy, and Biórr and the rest of the Raven-Feeders staggered back and stood in awestruck, horrified silence.

Lik-Rifa slowed in her gorging, and Biórr saw her emaciated belly filling before his eyes, red veins swelling across the striated muscles of her neck like a spiderweb and disappearing as they threaded beneath her pale, scabbed scales. The dragon took a lumbering step backwards, away from the torn carcass of the bear, leaving only its back legs uneaten.

The dragon shook and the air rippled and shimmered, mist or steam hissing from the bulk of her vast body, coiling around her as the outline of the dragon shifted and contracted, a series of cracks, like bones snapping, and then a dark-haired woman was standing before them, tall and regal in a grey-ash tunic hemmed with red, even if her body was pale and scabbed, patches of dark skin weeping pus. Red wounds gaped through her bloodstained tunic, across her belly, chest and throat, where she had fought at Oskutreð, against the two winged warriors, though Biórr could see the wounds were closed and healing faster than should be possible. Her lower jaw was red with gore from her feast, dripping in clots.

"I have brought you all a meal," she said in her too-deep voice that reverberated through the glade, a long-nailed finger pointing to the rear flanks of the bear. "A good mother will always provide for her children." She smiled, and picked her teeth, rooting out a strip of fur and a glob of fat and flicking it to the ground.

"Our thanks, mighty Dragon-Queen," Ilska said, dropping to one knee before Lik-Rifa. Ilska's claw-scarred brother, Drekr, stood beside her, Skrið's long-axe hanging over his shoulder, as well as all the other dragon-born who had survived the conflict at Oskutreð. Together they fell to their knees, bowing their heads. Lik-Rifa smiled, her eyes sweeping the clearing and Biórr felt Myrk beside him drop to one knee, felt his own legs tremble and before he knew it, he was kneeling, too, his head bowed in obeisance. All about him did the same.

"Good," Lik-Rifa purred. "Now, I must sleep," she said, her movements slow and languorous. "I must heal and regain my strength." All in the clearing slowly climbed back to their feet. Biórr could see Lik-Rifa's belly was bloated beneath her tunic, like some blood-gorged tick.

"My queen," Ilska said, stepping forwards.

"Yes," Lik-Rifa said, head snapping round, red eyes fixing on Ilska.

"What is our plan, my queen?" Ilska asked. Biórr found it strange to hear her speak with such awe and respect, almost fearful, when all he had known from Ilska was a will as hard as iron, and a heart to match.

Lik-Rifa shook, a ripple through her body. "The plan? To live," she said, a smile spreading across her face. "To fly, to hunt." She looked down at her arms, her hands bone-thin, the skin pale and translucent, and her fingers brushed over one of the scabbed wounds on her torso. "But I am weak, I need time to recover, to replenish my strength, before my enemies find me." Her head whipped around, eyes staring deep into the trees, as if seeing her foes sneaking up on her with sharp steel in their fists. She bared her teeth in a reptile snarl. Another shiver and ripple of her body. "My people must be summoned, gathered to me. And then, only then, shall I be safe." She looked back to Ilska, her snarl shifting to a smile. "And then, I shall rule."

"Where are your people to be summoned to?" Ilska asked. "Where are we going?"

"East, to my hall of Nastrandir," Lik-Rifa said. Her eyelids drooped. "A coastal strand shaped like a serpent. Like my father."

"I have heard tell of a place like that, though all that is there now is the Boneback Mountains and the icebound Sea," Ilska said, nodding. "If there is a hall there that still stands, it is buried beneath three hundred years of ice and snow, most likely just ruins."

"Like me," Lik-Rifa whispered, then shook herself. "It still stands. Now, I *must* sleep. You will guard me." It wasn't a question.

"Of course, my queen," Ilska said, dipping her head.

Lik-Rifa turned in a circle, digging at the ground with her feet, her dark cloak billowing like wings and then she was dropping to the ground and curling tight.

Ilska raised a hand, gesturing to warriors, setting up a perimeter of guards around the sleeping dragon-god. She saw Myrk and called her over. Biórr followed out of habit. He had always liked to listen to other people's conversations.

"You must go back to father at Rotta's chamber," Ilska said to Myrk. "Take ten with you, not Biórr," she added, seeing Myrk's sidelong glance.

"Why not?" Myrk scowled.

"He has only just returned to us, so I would not send him off again so soon. And he has brought guests, he needs to help them adjust to life among the Raven-Feeders."

Myrk kicked the ground with a toe.

"Tell Father to gather up all that we have found there and to bring it to the eastern edge of the Bonebacks. On the coast north of Svelgarth where the mountains meet the sea there is a promontory of land shaped like a serpent. The Corpse-Strand, Father calls it. He will know it." Ilska frowned and gave Myrk a hard look. "This is no lightly given errand. Father is there, and many treasures from the elder days. I am trusting you with this."

"I will not fail," Myrk said, brightening.

"Good. Leave as soon as you are ready," Ilska said.

"I will." Myrk began to turn away and Ilska grabbed her wrist, holding her tight.

"Be careful," Ilska said, releasing Myrk's wrist and raising a hand to stroke her cheek. "I have lost a brother. I would not lose a sister, too."

"I'm always careful," Myrk said, flashing a grin.

Ilska stared at her. "Hmm," she breathed, then turned and walked away.

"Don't look too down-hearted," Myrk said to Biórr as she took his hand, pulling him towards the trees. "I've still got time to hump you before I leave."

CHAPTER SIX

ELVAR

By the red light of rune-glow Elvar saw Sighvat fall in a tangle of limbs, something chitinous and clawed and big as a wolf clinging to him. All around her the Battle-Grim were crying out, blades hissing into fists, shields rising. Thuds and bellows, a swarm of creatures surging out of the impenetrable black. They were the things of nightmare, small, large, some slithering on segmented bodies, others scrambling on long-jointed legs, some dripping with slime, others clawed, fanged, pincers clacking, mandibled jaws snapping, some with many eyes, some with none, and they fell upon the Battle-Grim with hissing fury.

Something ran at Elvar, an abundance of legs, and it leaped, clinging to her neck and torso, serrated mandibles opening and closing, lunging at her face. She fell back, struck it with her extinguished torch to little effect, her empty fist punching into it. A hot pain across her cheek, stagnant, acrid breath washing her, and she felt a scream bubbling in her chest.

Then the creature exploded in a burst of chitinous shell and stinking slime and Grend was dragging her to her feet. She threw her torch at something with a mouth as big as a shield and far too many teeth and grasped her sword, clumsily dragging it free of its scabbard and slicing up into a slithering, sinuous body, skin thick and viscous, flesh parting, fluid thick as mucus oozing from the wound. The creature collapsed, its segmented body spasming and jerking.

Grend stood at her back, his new axe tracing red-glowing arcs in the rune-dark, Elvar hacking and slashing, glimpsing fractured images around her: Orv on one knee loosing arrows, their tips glowing, bursts of white-hot flame erupting as they sank into flesh or ripped through chitinous shells, Huld hacking something away from Urt's face as he rolled on the ground, Sighvat bellowing and chopping with his axe, explosions of legs, antennae, shells and slime all around him, Sólín standing by the wagon, her new-found spear glowing silver as she sliced and stabbed, carving something with clustered eyes and a multitude of legs from the pony.

Where is Skuld? Elvar thought. *She led us here, into a trap.*

"Skuld," Elvar cried, even as something tall and swaying with black, bulbous eyes came at her, legs as long as spears lashing out at her with hooked barbs on each foot, raking across her torso, red lines blooming through her torn woollen tunic. She hacked at it, sliced through a leg, a spurt of some dark ichor from the wound and the creature lurched, more legs lashing out at her.

"SKULD," Elvar bellowed and there was a turbulence of wings above, Skuld emerging from the shadow-dark heights of the chamber. The collar around her neck was glowing with veins of red and Skuld's face twisted in a snarl, as if raging against an invisible leash that dragged her downwards.

"Fight for us, you deceitful bitch," Elvar growled at Skuld as she ducked a slashing claw, and with a spasm rippling through Skuld's face she beat her wings and crashed into the many-legged thing that was attacking Elvar, Skuld ripping legs from its body with inhuman strength and punching through its hard shell, fluid spurting. She cast the juddering beast to the ground and stamped on its head, then flew at more creatures as they swarmed towards Elvar and Grend.

Screams all around Elvar, and she glimpsed a severed human leg cast through the air between two pincered creatures, as if they were sharing a piece of fruit.

We are going to die down here, in the stinking pit of Lik-Rifa's chamber, our bodies left to rot alongside those foul beasts that died before us, she thought, *no saga-songs or battle-fame to be sung about us.*

She snarled at that, a new rage rising up in her, slashing, hacking, stabbing, but the tide of creatures was too many.

"*Sólarljós, ég kalla á þig, blinda og brenna þessar verur af dimmum, rökum skuggum,*" a voice cried out, rising above the clamour of battle, above the screams and inhuman wails, and a light exploded, filling the chamber, bright as the sun. Elvar stumbled, putting her arm across her eyes, glimpsed their monstrous assailants staggering and flailing, dropping to the ground in paroxysms of limbs, twisting, shuddering, dying.

The light dimmed but did not fade, allowing Elvar to look around the chamber without risking being blinded.

Uspa stood before the rune-door, one hand held up high, a ball of glowing light in her palm.

Battle-Grim stood around her, bloodied, chests heaving, some still on the ground, blood leaking into the chamber's floor. The creatures that had assaulted them were either dead or had retreated beyond the reach of Uspa's light.

"*Opið fyrir mig, drekarúnir,*" Uspa growled as she strode through the rune-door and the glowing runes crackled, then hissed and evaporated like water in the sun.

Elvar saw Skuld and strode towards her.

"On your knees," Elvar snarled at the winged woman, whose face twisted in defiance, but the collar flared red and slowly Skuld dropped to her knees. Elvar backhanded her across the jaw, snapping Skuld's head back, blood and spittle flying from her mouth.

"You dare t—" Skuld hissed.

"Yes, I dare," Elvar shouted in Skuld's face, "and more." She hit Skuld again, this time with a fist, cracking her nose.

"You are mine; my thrall, to command, to maim, to kill, to do with as I please." She hit Skuld again, Skuld's head rocking back. Her fists clenched, muscles knotting and bunching in her arms and neck, but the collar glowed and flesh sizzled, Skuld crying out.

"Never try to betray me again," Elvar snarled, her sword-tip hovering over Skuld's eye. "Do you understand me?"

Skuld glared back at her long moments, then gave a small, curt nod.

"You were right, Skuld," Uspa's voice called out, a tremor in it. "This is a treasure far greater than anything we would find lying upon the plain above us. It is a weapon."

"What do you mean, a weapon?" Elvar asked Uspa, swiping blood away from a cut across her cheek. "What is that?" She stared up at Uspa as the Seiðr-witch leafed through the black book in her hands. Some of the Battle-Grim were gathering closer, those that could, others tending to their wounds, or the wounds of comrades. Others lay still and sightless in pools of their own blood, heaped corpses of Lik-Rifa's abominations piled around them.

"It is a Galdrabok," Uspa said, "written by Lik-Rifa."

"How is it a weapon?" Elvar asked Uspa.

"The spells . . ." Uspa breathed. "They are powerful, and terrifying."

"A weapon that could help us defeat a dragon-god?" Elvar pressed.

Uspa frowned. "Perhaps."

"How?" Sighvat said. He was bleeding from many wounds, but mention of freeing him from the *blóð svarið* caught his attention.

"Does it speak of resurrection?" Skuld said quietly.

Uspa's eyes narrowed. "It does."

Elvar's thoughts were scrambling, snatching at pieces of a puzzle. She could almost see it, like a tafl game playing out. Images of the ash-covered plain above flitted through her head, of the sharp-toothed mound that was Ulfrir-wolf's skeleton. Of the dull gleam of links buried in the ground about his skeleton.

He was slain by a Galdur-chain and a horde of Tainted dragon-born.

"Can this book raise a dead god?" she said to Uspa.

The Seiðr-witch's eyes flared.

"Bring my father back," Skuld breathed. "Please," she said. "If you do this, I shall serve you faithfully, for all eternity."

"Can your father defeat Lik-Rifa?" Elvar asked her.

"If any of the firstborn can, it is him," Skuld said.

"Uspa," Elvar's eyes snapped on to the Seiðr-witch, "does she speak true? Can this Galdrabok raise Ulfrir?"

"I think . . ." Uspa rasped, the words trailing away from her lips. She looked up and met Elvar's eyes. "Yes," she breathed.

The words forming in Elvar's throat sent fear rippling through her veins, but she could not hold them back.

"With a wolf-god on our side we would have a chance of facing Lik-Rifa, have a chance of getting Bjarn back."

"Wait a moment," Huld said, "what are you all talking about? Raising dead gods, fighting the dragon . . ." She looked at the Battle-Grim in the chamber. "We are here for the treasure, have fought for it and earned it, and now we would gather it and go and spend it."

"Heya," Urt, Orv and a handful of others agreed.

"I have sworn an oath," Elvar said. "As have Grend and Sighvat. It was the price for Uspa guiding us here, to Oskutreð; the price for gaining the wealth we have found here. Agnar swore it, too. He told you all, showed you his scars."

"But to raise Ulfrir-wolf," Orv said as he moved around the chamber, gathering his spent arrows, tugging them from corpses. "Surely that is madness. We all saw the dragon. This world is *not* a better place for her being loose in it. I am thinking it is best that the dead gods stay dead."

Murmurs of agreement rippled through the Battle-Grim.

"But as Orv says, the dragon is already loose in this world," Elvar said. "Do you think she will just slip quietly away to a life of peace and solitude?"

"No," said Sólín. "More likely she will cause death and destruction."

"She will want to rule," Skuld said.

"Rule where?" Huld asked her.

"Everywhere," Skuld said with a sweep of her hand.

"Do you think Vigrið is big enough to escape the wrath of a mad god," Elvar said.

"No," said Sighvat.

"The dragon must die," Uspa said.

The Battle-Grim stood silent.

"We are less than forty spears," Urt said, "we cannot slay a dragon-god."

"We have to try, us four," Elvar said with a wave of her hand at Grend, Sighvat and Uspa.

"To retrieve Bjarn for Uspa, we must face Ilska and her Raven-Feeders, and the dragon." She blew out a breath. "The blood oath is like a living thing inside us. It knows our thoughts, our intentions. If we do not try to fulfil our oath and get Bjarn back, it will boil the blood in our veins."

"And, believe me, that is not a good death," Sighvat muttered. "I have had a taste of it, and it has convinced me that facing Lik-Rifa is better."

"To kill a god, we need a god. Ulfrir must be resurrected," Elvar continued. "It is our greatest chance of coming out of this alive, and of saving Vigrið from destruction. But you Battle-Grim, you are not bound by our oath, and you are rich enough now for a score of lifetimes. If you choose to go your own way, I would not blame you." She shrugged. "In truth, if I were in your place, I would probably leave."

"You would not," Grend said quietly behind her.

"If you did return this wolf-god to life," Huld said, "how would you control him?"

"Links of the Galdur-chain that bound Ulfrir lay about his skeleton," Elvar said, "and it is fragments of that chain that are used to forge the thrall-collars and bind the Tainted." She pointed to the collar about Skuld's neck. "We use that chain to forge a new collar."

"That is some deep-cunning thinking," Sighvat said, blowing out a long breath and rubbing his head.

"And how will you do that?" frowned Huld.

"Skuld, I saw a forge out there," Elvar asked the winged woman; "is it functional?"

"Of course," Skuld said, a tremor of excitement in her voice. "My sisters and I used it to forge many things, including those arrowheads he is holding." She waved a hand at Orv.

Elvar looked to Uspa. "You can forge a thrall-collar for a god?"

"I can," Uspa said.

"*Will* you?" Elvar asked her.

Uspa stared back at her. "It is madness," she hissed.

"A mother's love is a powerful thing, you said to me not so long ago," Elvar said. "An instinct like no other, you said. You would let the world drown in blood if it would mean your Bjarn was safe and back in your arms again; *that* is what you said." Elvar walked close to Uspa, almost touching. "The question, Seiðr-witch, is did you *mean* it?"

Uspa drew in a long, ragged breath.

"To raise a dead god . . ."

"Will you do it?" Elvar asked her again.

"I will," Uspa whispered. "To save my Bjarn. But if I do this, you will free my husband as well."

Elvar scowled, sucked in a deep breath.

My life is becoming chained and weighted with oath upon oath.

"Berak is a *Berserkir* thralled to my father, so not a simple bargain to be made, but I will try," Elvar said.

Uspa stared, hesitant, looking deep into Elvar's eyes.

"You want another blood oath from me?" Elvar snapped. "I fear there will be no more room on my arm for the scars."

"No," Uspa said. "Just your word. And his." She nodded at Grend. He shared a hard look with Elvar, then nodded.

"That is enough for me," Uspa said. "Then, yes, with Lik-Rifa's Galdrabok I can forge a thrall-collar powerful enough to bind a god, and put flesh, blood and life back into his bones."

Elvar smiled, but looking around at the Battle-Grim she could see that they hovered on the knife's edge. "One more thing to think on, Battle-Grim," she said. "We have found many riches here, and won much fair-fame, as well. The Battle-Grim, first to find fabled Oskutreð; and we have stood against Ilska's Raven-Feeders, survived the coming of the dragon, and explored the caverns beneath the great tree, seen the soul road, fought Lik-Rifa's abominations. A good saga-tale for a jarl's hall, I am thinking."

"Heya," Huld said, pride-filled and grinning, others nodding.

"But think of the saga-tale that would be told if we were the ones to *slay* Lik-Rifa . . ."

CHAPTER SEVEN

ORKA

Orka lifted her *brynja* out in front of her. It was dark with patches of clotted blood and reeking, already rusting in spots. Flies crawled over it. She was stood in the open doors of a storage barn, in the courtyard behind her the Bloodsworn were making ready to leave. Horses were whinnying as they were tacked and saddled, the hearth fire being kicked out, everywhere economical movement.

"Hold the sack open," Orka muttered and Vesli did as she asked, an empty hemp sack at the tennúr's feet. Orka threaded the coat of mail into the sack, then took her seax and prised open the lid of a barrel full of sand and grit and salt, used for preserving shark meat. She tipped it up, pouring the sand into the sack. When she had covered her *brynja*, she set the barrel down and tied the hemp sack tight. Then she lifted the sack, shook it and swung it hard, thumping it on to the ground. And then she lifted it and did it again, and again, as if she were beating a sheepskin hearthrug.

"What are you doing?" Lif asked her.

"Cleaning my *brynja*," Orka grunted as she swung it high again, slamming the sack on to the ground. Then she kicked it, sending it rolling. She strode after it and kicked it again, then picked it up and resumed swinging it high and slamming it to the ground.

"*Cleaning* it," Lif said. "Looks more like you're trying to kill it."

"The sand, it scrapes all the shite away," Orka said as she swung the sack again. She paused and looked at him.

"You should go with Glornir and the Bloodsworn. They will be safe company to Darl, and I am thinking Guðvarr will be mixed up in this business with Skalk and Vol. You will most likely get a good chance to put some steel in his belly."

Lif looked at her, lips moving, though his words hovered in the dark cave of his mouth.

Footsteps, and they both turned to see Glornir striding towards them. He came alone this time, his long-axe slung across his shoulder. He walked past Orka, into the barn, and gestured for her to follow him. Orka dropped the sack.

"Wait here," she told Lif, then followed Glornir into the shadows.

"Will you come with us?" Glornir said as Orka stood before him.

She looked at him, words piling in her throat, so many things that she wanted to say, that she should say. Seeing Glornir and the Bloodsworn had stirred long-buried emotions. Of oaths, of bonds and of friendship. Of the Bloodsworn. And of shame. She had betrayed them, broken her oath and walked away without a word. She looked down at her hand, at a pale, faded scar that ran across her palm and she remembered the day she had made that scar, clenched a fist and cast her blood in a spattering line across a black-painted shield.

"You would have me back?" she croaked.

Glornir's face twitched. "Aye," he said. "Losing you and Thorkel, it was a hard blow, no denying." He swallowed. "We searched for days. Grieved for many more. And now to see you, to know that you just . . ." He trailed off, shaking his head. "It hurts again, like an old wound burst open. Part of me wants to weep and hold you, part of me wants to put my fist in your face."

Orka just watched him.

"But the past is done, no? And we have been through too much together to end it all in a *holmganga*. So, yes, I would have you back. The Bloodsworn would have you back, though not as our chief. Some are angrier than others. Mostly the ones who fought shield rim to shield rim with you, but they would still have you back. The younger ones are more forgiving, they look at you and gawp." He shrugged. "You have a fair-fame name." He looked her in the eye, their gazes almost level. Glornir was a big man, like his younger brother, Thorkel. "So, will you be coming with us?"

Orka sucked in a long breath.

"I cannot," she said, shaking her head and wincing as if from a sharp pain. "There is only Breca, in here." She tapped her chest. "Only room for him, now. And my oath to Thorkel, of vengeance."

A silence settled between them. Glornir nodded. "I understand," he said. "The world is changing, a dragon-god free and dragon-born loose in Vigrið, but all I can think on is Vol. But I think our paths are linked, think we will meet again, ere this is over. When I have my Vol back at my side, and you have your Breca. I would be a part of the vengeance dealt out for my brother."

Orka stood in silence.

"Where will you go, then?" Glornir asked her.

"West, to this mine where you fought a dragon-born. See if I can find anything, any clue to where they would have taken my Breca, or pick up a trail."

"Hmm," Glornir muttered. "Edel will take you to the mine."

"I can find it," Orka said. "If you are going to Darl you may have need of every shield."

"I am sending Edel and a few others back to the *Sea-Wolf*. It is moored and waiting for us on the River Slågen with an oar-light crew, and the mine is on the way, so," he shrugged. "It is no loss to me, and it will save you some time."

"My thanks," Orka said. "One thing," she added. "The Tainted children. Can you take them with you?"

"Are they not best finding their own way home?"

"They have no homes, now. Their parents are dead, murdered by Drekr and his hunters. Like Thorkel."

Another silence.

"I will take them as far as Darl," Glornir nodded through a frown.

Orka dipped her head, a thanks.

"One other thing," she said, looking out of the barn at Lif, who was trying to lift the sack with Orka's mail in it and failing. "His vengeance lies in Darl. The man who slew his brother fled on one of the *snekkes* with Skalk. Would you take him with you?"

Glornir looked to Lif. "Is he Tainted?"

"No," Orka said.

"But he knows that you have Ulfrir in your veins?"

"Aye," Orka nodded. "He saw it, no point denying it to him."

"You trust him? You know we have sent many on the soul road to keep our secret."

"I trust him," Orka said. "As much as I trust anyone."

Glornir made a rumbling sound, like a bear.

"Taking him puts the Bloodsworn at risk. If he were to find out what we really are . . . but, if you ask it of me." He shrugged. "I would take him to Darl. But I could still kill him, if he gave me reason not to trust him."

"That's fair," Orka said.

They regarded one another, the past thick as a mooring rope between them.

"I hope you find your Breca," Glornir said, breaking the silence. "I would like to meet my nephew."

"I hope for that, too," Orka said. "And I hope Vol is back with you soon."

"She will be, if Skalk and Helka know what is good for them," Glornir growled. He held his arm out and she gripped it.

"Kill your enemies," Glornir said.

"Aye, and make a mountain of their corpses," Orka finished.

Glornir smiled, a twitching hard-line of his mouth, and then he was walking away, back into the daylight towards the Bloodsworn.

Orka remained in the darkness a few moments, then strode out to Lif.

"Would you go with them?" Orka asked him. "Glornir will take you, if you wish it."

"Can I come with you?" Lif asked her.

Orka frowned.

"Why? I am walking away from Guðvarr and your revenge. Guðvarr is running south with Skalk, will be making for Darl and Jarl Sigrún, and I am travelling west. And I told you before, staying with me will likely get you killed." She looked over Lif's shoulder, at Mord's barrow. "It got your brother killed."

"You didn't get Mord killed," Lif said, his chin jutting. "The blame of that lies at Guðvarr's feet." His face twisted, anger and grief, tears welling in his eyes. He sucked in a deep breath. "I am not good enough to kill Guðvarr. Before I met you the only thing I'd ever skewered was a fish, and I know that you have taught me much, but . . . I am not ready. When I face him, I want to know, in here," he thumped his chest, "that I can finish him if the fight were fair. If it were a *holmganga*."

"Come with me and you may never get that chance," Orka warned. "You'll just as likely end up in a shallow grave with a pile of rocks over your corpse." She did not want him to come with her, did not want another innocent's blood on her hands, like his brother's, did not need anyone slowing her down. But she felt a debt to him. The brothers had saved her, in Darl, and no matter what Lif said, it had been Orka who led them into a frost-spiders' nest and got them captured. She felt the weight of that. Felt like she owed him for Mord.

"I will keep up, not slow you down," Lif said, as if he could read the words spiralling in her thought-cage. "Just carry on teaching me weapons craft, as you have been, and when we come back, with your Breca, well, if I am not ready by then to avenge my father and brother, after having been taught weapons craft by the Skullsplitter, then I deserve to die."

Orka sighed and shook her head. "The dead," she said, pointing to the pile of corpses. "Many were drengrs with good kit. Get yourself a coat of mail if you can, a belt, spear, axe, seax. And a good-fitting helm, if there is one. Find some food and provisions for us to take, a pot, our horses."

"A sword?" Lif said, excitement edging his voice.

"Swords are overrated."

"Plenty of these Bloodsworn have swords on their belts," Lif said.

"They have *earned* them. Taken them from the cold, stiff fingers of those they have slain," Orka said.

"Guðvarr has a sword," Lif said with a grimace.

"He will be just as dead with an axe in his skull as with a sword in his gut," Orka shrugged.

★

Orka gripped her reins and heaved herself up on to the back of her horse, Trúr, who she had ridden here all the way from Darl. A solid, broad-backed skewbald gelding. He whickered as she shifted her weight in the saddle and rolled her shoulders, adjusting her coat of mail, which was clean, now, sand-scoured and gleaming. Lif rode out of the stables, leading Mord's horse laden with barrels, sacks and a bundle of spears tied with walrus rope. He wore a coat of mail belted at the waist, and a seax and hand-axe were hanging from his belt. A simple leather helm hung from a saddle hook. A buzzing of wings and Spert whirled around her head and alighted on Orka's saddle pommel, wings disappearing beneath the segments of his outer shell and his sting arching over one shoulder. Vesli stood beside Trúr, holding her short spear in one fist.

"Ready, Bloodsworn," Glornir called out. He was sitting on a thick-muscled horse, his black, blood-spattered shield hanging from a saddle hook and his long-axe strapped beneath it.

Voices rang out in answer, forty or fifty warriors milling in the courtyard, many on horseback, some on foot, including a handful of scouts. Orka saw Røkia striding to the open gate of the Grimholt, Varg, the warrior who had slain the dragon-born walking beside her, a plain black shield slung across his back.

He has not taken the oath yet, then, Orka realised. A scattering of other scouts was with them, all lean, wire-honed muscle.

"Skullsplitter," Glornir said, and a silence fell over the courtyard. "I'll see you again, this side or the other," and he dipped his head to her.

Orka nodded.

"When I am done, I shall find you and tell you of how your brother has been avenged," she said with a snarl, and Glornir smiled at her through his grey beard.

"If you find Guðvarr," a reed-thin voice said, all heads turning in the courtyard. It was Lif, standing close by, pale as sour milk, but there was a fire in his eyes and a tremor in his jaw.

"If you find Guðvarr, a *drengr* of Jarl Sigrún," Lif said, "do me the favour of *not* killing him. And tell him that Lif will come for him."

Glornir looked at Lif a long moment and nodded approvingly. Then he was kicking his heels and dragging on his reins and the courtyard burst into movement. Røkia, Varg and the other scouts disappeared through the gates of the Grimholt, Glornir and the Bloodsworn following them in a cloud of dust. Einar Half-Troll sat on the bench seat of a wagon and flicked the reins, the Tainted children sitting on benches in the cart behind him. The wheels creaked and rumbled as the wagon rolled out after the Bloodsworn. Orka felt the urge to follow after them, invisible rope-bonds crafted from past oaths, from blood and sweat, from tears and laughter tugging at her.

"Ready, Skullsplitter?" a voice said. Silver-haired Edel standing close by, a spear in her fist and her two wolfhounds sitting at her feet. Nine others were around her, hard-looking men and women with their black shields all slung across their backs. Most were on foot, just two on horseback, and another horse laden with provisions.

Orka gave one last look at Glornir's back and the disappearing Bloodsworn.

Make a stone of your heart.

"Aye," Orka said.

Without a word Edel turned and broke into a jog, heading for the Grimholt's gates. Orka looked back at the ruined tower, all black-reaching timbers and holes gaping in the hall's roof.

"Breca, I am coming for you," Orka whispered, and she felt the wolf howl in her blood.

CHAPTER EIGHT

ELVAR

Sweat trickled into Elvar's eyes, stinging and blurring her vision. Smoke billowed and flames flared as she worked the bellows of a forge. Uspa was holding a glowing, twisted bar of iron in large tongs, shouting instructions at Grend and Sighvat who were both pounding rhythmically on the iron, each with a hammer in their fist. Incandescent sparks sprayed, lighting this forge deep within the bowels of Oskutreð in shifting flashes of flame and shadow. Skuld stood half hidden in a corner, her wings wrapped around her, staring at the rise and fall of the hammers, at the heated iron as it slowly took shape.

Into a thrall-collar for a god.

What am I doing?

It felt like Elvar was in a dream, hovering ephemeral and ethereal above her own body, watching all that happened as if she were just an observer. She glanced at her arm, the spiralling scars of her blood oath glistening and sweat-soaked.

This is the only way. That oath is like a parasite in my blood, a spy lurking in my veins. One that knows my very thoughts, and can kill me. I need it gone. The oath must be fulfilled.

Elvar's thoughts drifted as she pumped the huge bellows, feeding the charcoal and flame, her whole world the crash and ring of hammer blows, the crackle and hiss of sparks and flames.

She was unsure how long they had toiled here beneath the earth, half a day, longer, time had lost all meaning in this stifling, flame-filled subterranean world.

The collar was taking shape, now, black veins of dross already hammered from the white-glowing iron by Grend and Sighvat.

"Hold," Uspa shouted over the hammering and the two men stopped their pounding. She released the iron from the tongs, letting it sit on a wide anvil, heat radiating in waves, and then she was reaching for a seax at her belt, one that Elvar had seen her take from the ash-covered plain above. With a hiss she drew the blade and sliced the flesh of her palm, blood welling and pooling as she made a fist.

"Do the same," Uspa said to Elvar over the hiss and flare of the forge.

Elvar drew her seax and scored a line across her hand, cupping the blood as it leaked from the wound.

"Cast it on the collar," Uspa said as she lifted her fist and hurled her spilled blood on to the hot iron. Elvar did the same, the hiss and stink of metal as their blood coated the collar and sizzled.

"*Blóð Snaka ferskt úr æðum mínum, gefðu þessu dauða járn lífi, láttu það hlýða orði mínu og svaraðu skipun minni,*" Uspa called out, her words filling the room, echoing in Elvar's head.

"*Af blóði erum við bundin, tvö af holdi, í þetta járn. Hlýddu okkur.*"

The collar glowed white, a ripple passing through it as if it were a newborn creature taking its first breath. A spasm and it shifted, and then with the sound of a long exhalation it settled upon the anvil, just a thick ring of metal cooling to dull iron.

"It is done," Uspa said.

Sighvat frowned. "There is no lock, no key?"

Uspa looked at Elvar. "Command the collar to open, in the Galdur-tongue you have learned from your father's hall."

"*Opinn,*" Elvar breathed.

A crack as the collar split, a white-hot line glowing for a moment, and then it was sitting open on the anvil, as if it could turn on a hinge.

Elvar smiled.

"*Loka,*" she said, and the collar snapped shut, any sign or seam of its hinge and clasp gone, just a circle of smooth iron, like a ring crafted for a giant.

"Father is not going to like this," Skuld rasped from the shadows.

"Would you rather he stays dead?" Elvar asked.

A silence, then a shake of Skuld's head.

"No. I wish him to live."

"Then we are done here," Uspa said.

"Good," Sighvat said, wiping his brow and looking around. "Can we get out of here, now?"

The bright of day made Elvar squint, and for a moment all was a blend of darkness and glare. It seemed like a row of shadows stood around her as she emerged from the darkness below, taking shape, coalescing, and then she saw them, all of the Battle-Grim, standing rowed between the treasure-heaped wagons and Ulfrir's corpse. Elvar blew out a sigh of relief, as part of her had feared that they would be gone, having gathered their treasure and decided that dragon-slaying was not for them.

Huld stepped forward, lean muscled, her eyes wolf-hungry.

"Slaying a dragon sounds like a fine saga-tale to us," she said. "We are with you."

Elvar smiled.

"*And Agnar detherveth thome vengeanth,*" Sólín lisped.

The rest of the Battle-Grim rumbled their agreement.

"Well, that's a relief," Sighvat said.

Skuld flew out from the darkness of Oskutreð and winged over their heads, great beats of her rust-red wings, and she alighted beside the bones of her dead father, Ulfrir-wolf.

Elvar looked at the handful of wagons, piled high now with swords, axes, spears, seaxes, coats of mail, arm rings of silver and gold, as well as jewelled pendants on chains, cloak-pins, brooches, chests of silver and gold. Skeletons, empty-eyed skulls and ribcages, a mountain of bones. One of the wagons was filled with a huge tusk, yellowed and ridged.

Did that come from Svin, the boar god? We have collected treasure that no one in all Vigrið would believe. Relics of the gods.

A hoard of wealth that would make them all rich a thousand times over.

The Battle-Grim had not been idle. The layers of ash and earth had been scraped away to reveal the pale, grey-green bones of Ulfrir, the dead god. His skull was huge and thick, teeth as long as spears, ribs curved like the strakes of some giant *drakkar*.

Uspa walked past Elvar and strode towards the skeleton, the new-forged collar in her hand. Elvar, Grend and Sighvat followed her, the rest of the Battle-Grim joining them, until they were standing in a half-circle around Ulfrir's remains. Waves of rage pulsed from the dead bones, a lingering malice that set Elvar's blood tingling. A glance told her the other Battle-Grim felt it, too. Grend beside her was scowling, teeth clenched. One hand dropped to the shaft of his new-found axe, made a white-knuckled fist about it. Others stood with their hands gripping spears, swords, axes, all with that hard-eyed look and aura of blood-tingling fear and excitement that filled the air when battle was about to be joined.

If his mere bones have this effect on us, what will happen when he is flesh and blood?

"Best be getting on with it," Elvar said, eyes fixed on Uspa.

"For Bjarn and Berak," Uspa whispered, then she was snatching a spear from Huld's grip and carving lines into the ground. Eight lines like the spokes of a wheel, Ulfrir at their centre. Uspa stopped and leafed through pages in Lik-Rifa's Galdrabok, then set back to work again, cutting runes into the tip of each line.

"What is she doing?" Sighvat whispered to Elvar.

"I am making a *Guldurstafir*," Uspa muttered, "a runic-stave to channel and focus the power I will summon."

"Oh," Sighvat said.

Uspa finished her carving in the ground. She handed the spear back to Huld, then dropped to one knee, pulled her seax from her belt and drew the edge across her palm, opening up the wound she had made in the forge.

"*Jörð og klettur loft og himinn, kraftur blóðs og rúna, rís upp og fyllir bein Ulfrir,*" Uspa said as she placed her open palm on to a rune she had carved into the ground, her blood seeping into the ash and soil. A hiss and flare of heat and a thin line of flame spread through the rune, like molten metal poured into a cast. The thread of flame unrolled, etching the rune and then running along the line towards Ulfrir's body. Soon all of the lines and runes were flame-filled. Orv stepped quickly away as flames passed between his feet.

Uspa stood and looked up at the wolf skeleton, her lips twitching as she muttered unheard words. Then she was striding past the jaws and skull of the wolf and stepping through its ribs until she stood beneath the skeleton's spine, at the point where it met the skull.

"Sighvat, lift me up," Uspa said and the huge warrior lumbered forwards. He squatted, wrapped his arms around Uspa's legs and then stood, raising her high.

Uspa held the new thrall-collar up to the topmost vertebrae of the wolf's spine.

"It'th too thmall," Sólín frowned.

Elvar smiled, because that was what she had said to Uspa in the forge.

"Command the collar to open and grow," Uspa said to her.

"*Opna og vaxa, kraga bundin við mig*," Elvar said into the rage-tinged air.

Red veins of heat appeared on the collar, threading and spiralling through it, and then it rippled and shimmered, snapping open and growing as Uspa held it up, wrapping itself around the wolf-spine. The metal stretched and grew as if it were clay on a potter's wheel, until it comfortably surrounded the wolf's skeletal neck.

"Now command it to close, and to be bound to the skeleton; to the flesh, blood, sinew and soul of its new host," Uspa called down from Sighvat's arms. "And say his name. Say Ulfrir."

Elvar frowned, sifting through her memories of her youth in Snakavik, of Silrið, Jarl Störr's Galdurwoman, and of how she had lurked in the shadows as Silrið had taught her father the Galdur-words of power that bound the *Berserkirs* to him.

"*Kraga, lokaðu núna og vertu bundinn við þessa beinagrind, við hold, blóð, sin og sál nýja gestgjafans, úlfaguðsins, Ulfrir*," she called out, halt-ingly at first.

The collar closed with a snap, one last shimmering ripple, and then it was cold, hard iron again, though twenty-times the size of the collar Uspa had forged.

Sighvat lowered Uspa down and the Seiðr-witch took the red-skinned book from her belt. Skuld scowled at the book.

Made from the skin of her sister. I would despise that book, too. If I had a sister I loved. If it were carved from my brother Thorun's hide, that would not be such a terrible thing.

Uspa leafed through the brittle pages, the whisper of skin on parchment. Then she paused and stared at a page, her lips moving as she silently read to herself. She sucked in a long breath. A silence settled among them, Elvar sensing the enormity of what was about to be attempted. She felt the urge to scream at Uspa, to tell her to stop, that they would find another way.

Uspa dropped the book on the ash-layered ground and held up her still-bloody palm.

"*Blóð er lífið, gefin af ótta snaka, Krækjan sem bindur okkur öll, búin til af höggorminum, framleiðandanum og húsbóndanum,*" Uspa called out as blood welled.

"What is she saying?" Sighvat said, fear and awe shifting across his face. All of the Battle-Grim looked the same, frozen, uneasy, unable to look way.

"Something about blood and life, and Snaka the maker," Elvar said.

Uspa strode to the skull of the wolf and reached up, smearing her bloody palm across the upper teeth and muzzle of the dead god.

"*Ó mikli úlfur, heyrðu grát minn, finn aftur, andaðu, lyktu, þrumu.*"

"She says *great wolf*," Elvar said, "and other things I do not understand. Some of the words are *breathe, feel, smell, snarl.*"

"Ach, but I am getting a bad feeling about all of this," Sighvat grunted, shuffling his feet.

Uspa stepped back from the wolf's open jaws and dipped a finger into the blood in her palm, tracing lines in the air. "*Blóðflæði, hold og sinu prjónað,*" she cried out, and glowing, sharp-angled runes of flame and blood crackled into life in the air between Uspa and the skeleton, as if she were painting her blood-runes on to a solid surface.

Uspa turned and looked at the Battle-Grim. "All of you, add your blood to mine. Cut yourselves."

A frozen moment among them all. Grend was the first to move, stepping forwards and drawing his new axe, wrapping his fist around the blade. Blood leaked between his fingers. Then Elvar was following him, drawing a seax from her belt and slicing a red line across her hand. Sighvat followed her, and then all the Battle-Grim were stepping closer, gripping sharp steel.

"Cast your blood on to the bones of Ulfrir," Uspa called out, "do it now," and she hurled the blood welling in her fist at Ulfrir's skull. All of the Battle-Grim did the same, Elvar cupping her fist and casting it at the bones of the wolf, bleached yellow abruptly spattered with red.

"*Hjarta sló aftur*," Uspa called out, and then everything seemed to stop, as if the world around them was holding its breath.

The glowing rune that hovered in the air grew and elongated, stretching wider and wider like a monstrous spiderweb.

"*Kraftur orðs, kraftur blóðs, drekkur í dauða og lífgar*," Uspa chanted, at the same time gesturing with her hand at the wolf's bones and the rune of fire, huge now, moved through the air and settled like a great net upon Ulfrir's skeleton. As the lines of the rune touched the ancient bones the runes flared bright, tracing red and orange veins across the bleached skeleton, and then they faded.

A tremor in the ground beneath Elvar's feet, and the air about Ulfrir's skeleton changed, shimmering. Elvar shivered, her skin goose-fleshing. Skuld sucked in a sharp, hissing breath. A ripple passed through the bones of the dead wolf, like an animal dreaming, and then the bones began to change colour. No, something was forming *around* the bones, veins and arteries, slow at first, seeping upwards out of the soil like vines growing up around an ancient oak, twisting and coiling, and then faster, wrapping around the old bones, coating them in hues of red. Muscle appeared, sinew growing and stretching, Elvar glimpsing the viscous pink of lungs within the great ribcage, the slimy coils of intestines lower down. The skull shifted, flesh forming, the muzzle lengthening, ears growing, a liquid glint in what had been empty eye sockets, and then fur was sprouting, slate-grey, flecked with black, claws extending from paws. And the thrall-collar grew with it all, flaring red and white, expanding as flesh and muscle, blood and fur knotted and twisted around the neck of the wolf.

Elvar stood amazed, transfixed, her heart pounding as Ulfrir's form returned to him. And then it was done, a huge wolf lying on the ash-plain before them, wind ruffling its fur. The size of him took Elvar's breath away, almost as huge as her father's mead hall. Myriad wounds littered the creature's body, knitting slowly, patches of blood leaking here and there, elsewhere raw scabs and red, angry scars.

"He is still dead," Sighvat said into the silence, and Elvar saw that the wolf's body was still and cold, no movement of breath in its chest, no spark of light or life in its eyes.

"*HJARTA SLÓ AFTUR,*" Uspa bellowed, as she slammed her bloody palm upon the beast's chest.

"Heart, beat again," Elvar whispered. There was a crack like lightning splitting a tree and the dead wolf jerked, gasped, his huge jaws opening. Amber light flickered in its eyes and it blinked, legs twitching, shifting to take its weight and slowly, ponderously, the reborn wolf bunched its legs beneath it, rolled and then stood, towering over them all, casting them in its shadow. Its chest was thick-muscled and broader than any ordinary wolf's, its shoulders and neck hunched, its muzzle shorter and wider than any wolf Elvar had seen. Intelligence and malice flickered in its amber eyes. And then it raised its head to the sky and howled.

Elvar staggered back, lifting her hands to her ears as the ground shook beneath her and waves of sound buffeted her like a storm wind. Other Battle-Grim did the same, some dropping to their knees. Only Grend stood motionless, staring up at the giant wolf as it howled its fury and pain at the skies. Eventually the howl faded and died and the wolf slowly lowered his head, dropped it, and stared at the Battle-Grim.

"*Svo skal það vera,*" Uspa said into the silence.

"So shall it be," Elvar said, remembering Silrið's closing words after every Galdur-spell.

The wolf was panting, and Elvar saw the pain and weariness in its eyes. Its limbs trembled, blood still oozing from scores of wounds upon its body.

The wounds that slew Ulfrir, given to him by hundreds of Lik-Rifa's children, the dragon-born. They have not healed fully with his resurrection.

A ripple through his body and then Ulfrir's legs were buckling, folding, and the wolf collapsed to the ground, a cloud of ash exploding around him. The wolf howled again, but this time it was pain and exhaustion that radiated from him. The air shimmered and rippled as the wolf's body shifted, a series of cracks and snaps sounding like hammer blows as the wolf shrunk, its form closing in upon itself, the muzzle shortening, teeth shrinking, bones re-forming, until finally a man lay upon the ground. He wore a rent coat of mail, wounds and patches of half-congealed blood covering him, a wolf-pelt cloak around his shoulders. Empty scabbards for sword and seax hung at his belt. His dark hair hung long and lank about his face, amber eyes glaring out of sunken sockets, his face all sharp crags and deep shadows, a snarl of grey-black beard and the hint of sharp teeth behind his lips.

"Father," Skuld cried out and ran to the fallen god as he lay on the ground. She dropped to her knees, cradling his head in her lap.

"Skuld," Ulfrir wolf-god breathed, one dirt and bloodstained hand rising up to cup her cheek. "What has happened? Your mother, your sisters?"

"All dead," Skuld whispered, tears leaking from her eyes.

Grief and shock worked themselves into the crags of Ulfrir's face, he growled a snarl that turned into a wracking cough, his body spasming, and he hung his head, a line of blood and saliva dribbling from his lips to the ash-covered ground.

"How is *he* going to slay a dragon?" Sighvat asked.

CHAPTER NINE

BIÓRR

Biórr watched Myrk ride away, fifteen warriors with her, each leading a spare horse tied to their saddle pommels to speed their journey south. They faded into the woodland gloom and Biórr stood there long after they had disappeared from view.

The crackle of forest litter and a man came to stand beside him. Red Fain, tall and broad, thick-chested, white hair dragged back tight and tied in a knot at his crown, white beard braided into two forks.

"We'll see them soon," Red Fain said. "My son Kalv, and your woman, too."

"Myrk belongs to nobody," Biórr said.

"Ha, that is a truth," Fain laughed as he turned to regard Biórr. "It is good to see you, lad."

"It is good to see you, too, old man," Biórr said, trying to slip back into their old ways.

Red Fain frowned as he regarded Biórr. "You've the look of a startled colt about you, lad, worried that something is sneaking up on you." He raised a big, gnarled hand to cup Biórr's cheek, but Biórr pulled away.

Another frown from the big man. "Can't have been easy for you, living among the enemy, having to guard your tongue, your thoughts, your heart," Fain said, looking into Biórr's eyes as if he were reading his soul.

Biórr felt a swell of emotion in his chest, Fain's words unlocking something in him, as they always had. Fain had been the first living person to show Biórr kindness, back in the days when he had first come to the Raven-Feeders.

"Aye, well, there's plenty of time for that," Fain said, as if answering some unheard conversation. "Come and have a meal, my lad Storolf's missed you."

"Aye," Biórr said, "that'll be . . . good," and Fain steered him towards a hearth fire with a handful of warriors around it, a slab of bear meat turning on a spit.

"Storolf Wartooth," Biórr breathed as Storolf rose, a head taller than Biórr and nearly twice as wide, his blond hair and beard thick with braids, a black raven feather tied in one. He grinned at Biórr, showing the gap where some of his front teeth were missing, having been left in an enemy's shield when Storolf had bitten into it and ripped it out of the warrior's hands.

"Welcome home, brother," Storolf said, opening his arms wide and pulling Biórr into a bone-cracking embrace.

"I . . . can't . . . breathe," Biórr wheezed and Storolf released him, laughing and holding Biórr by his shoulders.

"You look weary, brother," Storolf said. "Is that because of three years living in secret among our enemy, knowing that you could be discovered at any moment, and that would mean your death?" He regarded Biórr with earnest compassion. There was a slight twitch at the corners of his mouth. "Or is it because Myrk has just humped you witless in the bushes?"

Laughter around the pit fire, Fain slapping Storolf's shoulder and men and women roaring, rocking and thumping their legs.

"Ha," Biórr laughed, having the good grace to blush. "She has missed me, what can I say."

"Aye, she made that well known," Fain said.

"You have a fair pair of lungs about you," Storolf added. "Our ears are still ringing." More laughter.

"Come, sit and eat. Our new queen has brought us some fine-tasting bear meat," and they all sat together, Biórr feeling some of his skittishness melt away.

"A lot of new faces," Biórr said, looking around the camp as he tore into a strip of hot meat. Grease and fat ran into his beard.

"Aye," Fain grunted. "Ilska says the time is close, so we need a bigger crew."

"Those all came with Drekr," Storolf said, nodding to where Drekr sat beside a fire, ten or twelve men and women about him. Some in mail, some in leather and furs. Biórr's eyes were drawn to a man, lean and weathered, a necklace of what looked like yellowed troll-tusks around his neck. Seax hilts jutted from many scabbards strapped and buckled to him.

"They're all handy in a scrap," Storolf said.

"Aye, they look it," Biórr mumbled as he huffed and chewed on hot meat.

There was a shift in the camp, those still laughing falling silent, and Biórr looked around to see that Lik-Rifa was stirring behind her guards. She had slept like the dead since she had returned with the dead bear. The dragon-god jerked and shifted on her makeshift bed. She snapped awake and scrambled to her feet, eyes flashing red. She was pale, a haunted look in her gaunt face, lip curling in something between fear and anger.

"Ulfrir," she muttered.

"Are you well, my queen," Ilska called as she strode across the camp, Drekr a hulking presence at her shoulder, the guards around Lik-Rifa parting to let Ilska through.

Lik-Rifa put a hand to her throat and picked at a raw, half-scabbed gash, one of the wounds the winged women had given her at Oskutreð.

"Ulfrir's jaws, around my throat," Lik-Rifa breathed. She blinked and shook her head, looked around, eyes wide, her lip twisting with a snarl. Slowly she focused on Ilska.

"Dark dreams," Ilska said, "Ulfrir is dead. We saw his corpse-mound on the plain of Oskutreð."

"He lives," Lik-Rifa snarled. "My stinking, mange-ridden, flea-bitten brother Ulfrir lives."

"Of the gods, only you live, my queen," Ilska said.

Lik-Rifa's face twitched, her eyes narrowing and the air around her seemed to ripple, to grow darker.

"I tell you, he LIVES!" she roared, her mouth growing, extending, razored teeth bursting into life, her body expanding, flesh shifting to scales, trees uprooted as she changed shape, her head snapping forward on a shifting, reptilian neck. Dragon-jaws opened wide and Drekr leaped forward, grabbing Ilska and falling to the ground. Lik-Rifa's jaws hissed over their heads, snapped around a guard who had been standing behind Ilska and slammed shut. A scream cut short as blood erupted and bones splintered, Lik-Rifa shaking her head like a dog with a rat. Blood fountained and a severed leg spun through the air, everyone leaping away, screams, shouts as Lik-Rifa's transformation into her dragon form filled the glade, wings spreading, cracking branches, bending trees.

Biórr stumbled away, though his eyes were still fixed on the scene. He saw Drekr rolling across the ground with Ilska in his arms, the huge warrior rising and dragging his sister away from Lik-Rifa as she tore the guardsman to ragged pieces.

Lik-Rifa lifted her head on a sinuous neck and swallowed, Biórr seeing human-shaped lumps undulating down her throat. She looked around, saw Drekr pulling Ilska away, Ilska looking back, stumbling.

"STOP," Lik-Rifa roared, the ground shaking and Ilska dropped to one knee.

Lik-Rifa took a huge step and was towering over Ilska, her head rearing back, jaws opening wide, strips of bloody flesh hanging from her teeth.

Drekr unslung his long-axe from his back and stood over Ilska, between her and the dragon.

Lik-Rifa paused, frozen for a moment as she hovered over Drekr and Ilska. Her mouth twitched, shifting into what looked like a smile to Biórr. Then the air was shimmering, and the dragon's form was changing, contracting with a series of bone-jarring snaps, and then Lik-Rifa was a woman again, tall and grim, standing before Drekr and Ilska.

"You would stand against me, your maker?" Lik-Rifa said to Drekr, who lowered his axe.

"She is my sister," he said, meeting her gaze.

Lik-Rifa threw her head back and laughed, her whole body

shaking. "*My* brothers and sisters did not share your sentiments," she said when she had her breath back. "I like this kind of loyalty." She frowned. "But you should show it to *me*. I should eat you for such defiance," she snarled, mouth shifting, growing, "but such loyalty to your sister, it is a treasure." Her face softened, and a solitary tear rolled from one red-burning eye. She reached out a hand and stroked Drekr's cheek.

"I want this devotion, I deserve it," she whispered.

"You have it, my queen," Ilska said, rising and bowing before Lik-Rifa. "My kin have toiled for generations to set you free."

"Yes, I see that," Lik-Rifa said. She looked at the remains of the guard she had eaten and sighed. "Too much of my father lives in me, I fear. He would eat his children, his creations, on a whim. I will try not to be him." She sucked in a deep, shuddering breath and reached a long-taloned finger up to her mouth, picked out a blood-wet strand of flesh.

You have just eaten someone, though, Biórr thought, but pointing out that fact did not seem like deep cunning to him, so he kept his lips stitched tight.

"And besides, you have served me well. You used my brother's book, the *Raudskinna*?"

"Yes, my queen," Ilska said. "We found his chamber."

"I loved Rotta, but he did not come when I needed him," Lik-Rifa murmured. "But he has saved me in the end, I suppose, with his book of runes. And you did well to find it. But you should not question me," Lik-Rifa said to Ilska. "Never question me, because I am right, my brother lives. I felt it. Felt my spell being used, felt him draw a shuddering breath, heard him howl." She gave Ilska an admonishing look. "I am always right. Best for you if you remember that."

"Yes, my queen," Ilska said. "But . . . how does he live? We saw his bones."

She has some stones, still to question this god after what we have just seen her do.

"My book," Lik-Rifa snarled. "It should have been safe, guarded by rune-spells and my children." A spasm of rage swept her face. "They must have killed my children," she spat.

"What would you have us do?" Ilska asked.

Lik-Rifa looked north, back along the path to Oskutreð, and then south.

"Back to this game between us, then, Ulfrir," she murmured. "But this time I shall not be so easily tricked, and this time you do not have Orna to guard your back." She looked up at Ilska and Drekr. "There is more than one way to catch a wolf," she said. "We shall travel south, with all haste, and cross the Isbrún Bridge. We must cross before *sólstöður* ends, or you will be imprisoned on this side of the vaesen pit."

"Yes, my queen," Ilska said.

"Well," Lik-Rifa frowned. "What are you waiting for?" She looked at all those gathered in the glade, staring at her. "Do I need to eat someone else to teach you the meaning of haste?"

The camp exploded into movement.

CHAPTER TEN

ORKA

The wolf in Orka's blood growled.

Danger, it snarled to her.

Her eyes snapped open. It was night, branches scraping above her, fractured strands of moonlight piercing the glade they were sleeping in. More growling, but this was in the world around her. Low, at the very edge of her hearing, and she rolled quietly, sat up, saw that Edel's two hounds were sitting with hackles raised and ears pointing forward, both staring into the impenetrable dark of woodland. Edel was stirring.

Orka stood, joints stiff with cold, and allowed the wolf within her to filter through her blood. Instantly the world around her changed, her scent sharper, her sight clearer, sounds more distinct. All in the glade were sleeping, except Edel, who was pushing herself up on an elbow and reaching for her spear, and one empty blanket: Lif's.

His guard shift?

The darkness parted for her wolf-eyes, trees becoming distinct, and she saw darker shapes moving among them, four, five, more. They made no sound, seemed to be floating, spectral and eerie. Further away there *was* a sound, deeper in the woodland, ragged, wheezing breaths, as if someone sucked air through a reed straw.

She took a deep breath, pine sap rich in the air, but there was something else, something old and rotting and corrupt, like a body long dead.

Night-hags.

"'WARE," Orka shouted, stooping to lift her long-axe from where it lay beside her, close as a lover, and she was moving through the glade, towards the sounds of ragged breathing. Indistinct shadows congealed, taking form, and something flowed towards her like mist, Orka glimpsing wide-staring eyes, a flat, skeletal nose and long black hair that swirled like knots of rope in a gale, writhing and whipping and blending with the mist. Ragged, tattered shreds of a cloak draped a skeletal form, pale skin visible through the rents, wrinkled in folds, sagging breasts stretched almost to the creature's hips. Clawed hands far too big for the body they were attached to reached for Orka on thin, branch-like arms, and tendrils of hair thick as twisted rope lashed out, coiling around Orka's waist and throat.

Orka swung her axe at the creature's head as the coils began to tighten around her throat and waist, dragging her towards the night-hag. The wolf within her revelled in that thought, wanted nothing else but to close with the creature and bite and rip and tear, but her axe passed through the night-hag as if it were so much mist and Orka stumbled after it, her momentum sending her crashing into a tree.

Fool, remember the Seiðr-words Uspa taught you.

The night-hag surged towards her on its mist-wraith body, although the tendrils of hair still coiled around Orka's throat felt real and hard as iron. They tightened about her, Orka gasping for breath. She wrenched her axe up.

"*Skuggar skilja,*" she snarled, swinging her long-axe and hacking it into the creature's chest, meeting resistance this time. The night-hag shrieked and shattered apart, its shadowy form exploding into dark shards like a thousand bats bursting from a cave. The pressure around Orka's throat was gone and she moved on, loping through the pinewoods towards the sounds she could still hear, of someone struggling for each laboured breath. The sounds were fainter, each one wider apart.

Edel shouted something and there was another shriek behind her, other voices echoing through the darkness, but Orka pressed on. Then she saw it. A black shadow slumped among the roots of a tree. Orka saw Lif half lying against a trunk, his face pale as silver in moonlight, mouth open, tongue black and eyes bulging. A night-hag was sitting upon his chest, huge hands and mist-like hair coiled around his throat. She was looking at Lif with an expression of deep-hearted love, like a mother at her sleeping child.

A burst of speed from Orka and she drew her axe back, slashed at the night-hag's back.

"*Skuggar skilja*," she cried as the night-hag twisted, face shifting from ecstatic joy to snarling, feral savagery, but it did not relinquish its tentacle-like grasp of Lif, which was a mistake. Orka's axe chopped into the night-hag's neck and it let out a piercing wail, bursting apart like mirrored shards of darkness.

Lif sucked in a deep breath, slumping and flopping like a landed fish. He let out a cry. Orka knelt beside him, grabbed his thrashing arms.

"It is gone," she said, and slowly he calmed, his breathing steadying, a hint of colour returning to his cheeks.

"What happened?" Orka growled at him.

A fluttering of wings and Vesli alighted on the ground, bleary-eyed, with her spear in her fist. She glared into the shadows.

"They are gone," Orka said to the tennúr. "Where is Spert?"

"Sleeping," Vesli croaked, voice still thick with sleep.

Other figures came crashing through the woods, Edel and her two hounds, and more of the Bloodsworn. They stood around Orka like a protective hand, eyes and weapons pointing into the darkness.

"I sat by the tree," Lif wheezed, "and then . . ."

"You slept?" Edel said.

Lif looked up at Edel, ashamed, then nodded.

Edel spat and turned away.

"You should not have done that," Orka said as she stood and helped Lif to his feet.

"I know that now," he rasped.

"Could have been all our lives," Edel said to him angrily. "We are fortunate that night-hags enjoy watching a slow death."

"I am . . . sorry," Lif said.

"Do not be sorry," Orka growled, "be *better*."

Lif nodded shamefacedly.

"Come, back to camp."

"Ingmar," Edel said, "you take next watch."

"Aye, chief," said a hulking, pale-faced and flaxen-haired man.

Orka guided Lif through the trees, Edel and the others spreading around them. Lif tripped over a root and Orka steadied him.

"How did you find me in this darkness?" Lif muttered to Orka.

"Where wolf's ears are, wolf's teeth are near," Orka said to him.

Orka woke with a start, gasping and reaching for her seax. Her thought-cage was full of snarling wolves and jaws ripping flesh. A wolf howl still echoed through her, reverberating in her head, so real that her eyes were searching the glade.

"You still have dark dreams, then," a voice said close by.

Orka whipped around, one of her seaxes hissing into her fist, and saw Edel sitting close by. She was prodding at the flames of a fire and tending to a bubbling pot.

"Huh," Orka snorted. That was a truth, but this one was . . . different. So vivid that it had felt real.

"Dreaming of night-hags?" Edel asked her.

No. Of a wolf. No, a man. She pinched the bridge of her nose. *No, a wolf.* It had been howling her name, calling to her. And part of her had wanted to go, to answer that call.

My oath binds me, she had said in her dream. Shouting Thorkel and Breca's names into the raging gale of the wolf howl as if the names of her dead husband and stolen son were words of rune-power, denying the wolf's powerful call.

Perhaps they are.

The camp was quiet and still, birdsong drifting on the breeze. It was hard to imagine that the attack in the night had ever happened.

One of Edel's wolfhounds growled at Orka, little more than a rumbling vibration in its chest.

"Easy, girl," Edel said, patting the hound. "Some porridge?" Edel offered, stirring the contents of the pot.

"No," Orka said, sitting and sheathing her seax.

Edel shrugged and spooned porridge into a bowl for herself.

Orka looked around, saw that Lif was sleeping close by, wrapped in his cloak, his chest rising and falling rhythmically. There were dark bruises around his throat. Vesli was curled up at Orka's feet, the tennúr snoring gently, and others of the Bloodsworn were lying about them. A stream chattered at the edge of the glade and Orka knew Spert had found a place among the rocks of the stream bed. Deep within the trees she saw the dense shadows of Ingmar standing guard.

"He is no warrior," Edel said, jutting her chin at Lif.

"We are none of us born warriors," Orka muttered. "It is the world that makes us so."

"Maybe," Edel said, "but if so, then the world has been too slow with him. He will be a burden to you."

"Time will be the judge of that," Orka sighed.

"We were almost in a night-hag's stew because of him," Edel reminded her.

Orka said nothing, knew she could not dispute that.

"Does he know?" Edel said. "About the wolf in your blood?"

"He saw it at the Grimholt," Orka said.

Edel nodded as she took a slurp of her porridge, then turned her one good eye to look at Orka. A scar ran through the other, leaving it a sunken, puckered hole.

"Does he know about us. About the Bloodsworn?"

"Have a care," Orka grunted, "he may be awake."

"No, he is sleeping still," Edel said. Orka nodded, knowing that Edel had the blood of Hundur the hound in her veins.

"I have not told him, if that is what you mean. That is not my place," Orka said.

"Good," Edel nodded.

"But he is no *hálfviti* fool. He knows I am *Úlfhéðnar*, and that I was the Skullsplitter, and that I was chief of the Bloodsworn. He knows that Thorkel was *Berserkir*. He'll wonder how Thorkel and I hid our Tainted blood from the other Bloodsworn."

"And he'll realise it would have been impossible."

"Aye," Orka nodded. "It is no great leap of wits to realise that maybe we didn't need to."

Edel blew on her porridge. A silence settled between them. "So," Edel said after a while. "We have kept our secret a long time. You know how." She gave Orka a hard look. "Might have been better if the night-hag had taken him."

Another silence, Orka feeling a twitching in her fingers, her fist aching for the grip of a weapon. Slowly she reached out and put a hand upon the haft of her long-axe, which lay beside her. "You would have to go through me to do that," Orka said, no anger or malice in her voice, just stating a fact. "I am in his debt, and he has my protection, whatever that is worth."

"It is worth a great deal, I would imagine," Edel nodded, as calm as Orka, as if they were discussing the consistency of her porridge. "And you would stand by him, one of the untouched, risk your life for him?"

Orka thought about that for a while.

"It is no less than he has done for me," she said.

"Hmm," Edel breathed. "And yet you walked away from *us*. The Bloodsworn, who you had sworn to stand with unto death, and sealed that oath with your blood."

Orka looked away, thought about all the answers she could give. That she wanted to give. The truth, that she had been weary and sick of the bloodshed, and that she had been with child and yearned to give her bairn a different life, but that she was sorry, that not a single day had passed from then until now that the faces of her brothers and sisters in the Bloodsworn had not floated through her thought-cage.

She looked back at Edel and met her one-eyed gaze, holding it. "That's right," she said.

A splash of water and a shape reared out of the stream, spraying glistening droplets.

"*Spert hungry*," the vaesen said.

Does he sleep through everything?

Orka held out a hand to Edel. "If you're not going to try and kill me, I'll have that bowl of porridge now."

CHAPTER ELEVEN

VARG

Varg fell on his arse with a thud and a clatter, his spear spinning from his grip, his shield rim crunching into his head.
Trees stood thick to one side of him, and a sharp drop to a white-
foaming river lay close on the other.

*A little too close, with Røkia intent on throwing me all across the
Bonebacks.*

"Up," Røkia said to him, holding her arm out.

Varg grimaced as he rolled away from the cliff edge and rose to
one knee. He gripped Røkia's offered wrist and she heaved him
back to his feet.

"You are letting me get too close," she explained as he searched
for his spear in the twilight haze of *sólstöður* that he had come to
associate with the time before dawn. "I only have a hand-axe, and
you have a spear with a longer reach. Use it."

"I am aware of that," Varg muttered, "but knowing a fact, and
doing something about it are two different things. Especially
when that fact is a snarling lunatic, trying to hit me with an axe,
and moving faster than Svik when cheese is being handed out
for free."

"A snarling lunatic?" Røkia asked, raising an eyebrow. Then she
shrugged. "No excuses. You cannot rely on the wolf in your blood
to save you from a skilled *drengr* with sharp steel in their fist, or
even from a *snarling lunatic* with an axe. You need weapons craft,

Varg No-Sense, to know how to react without thinking. It must become as simple as breathing to you."

"This is another fact that I am aware of," Varg sighed as he found his spear and stooped to grab it, "because you tell me so *at least* a hundred times each day."

In truth he felt slow and sluggish today. He had not slept well, and when he had, he had dreamed of wolves howling, a pack impossibly huge, and an amber-eyed, wolf-grey man standing at their centre, calling to him.

"You have a lump on your head," Røkia pointed out, and Varg nearly stabbed himself in the face with his spear as he raised a hand to feel it. Røkia snorted, half-laugh, half-disgust. "No-Sense," she muttered, shaking her head.

"I know I have a lump," Varg said, annoyed with himself. "You just gave it to me."

"No, *that* you gave to yourself when you chose to fall in a heap with no helmet on." She looked pointedly down at the helm hanging at his hip, buckled through his belt. It was the helm he had taken from the dragon-born he had slain back at Rotta's chamber, along with the old warrior's coat of mail, which he *was* wearing. He rolled his shoulders, shifting the weight of it.

"You are not wearing a helm," Varg retorted.

"I do not need to," Røkia answered.

Varg felt a stab of anger at that, but it shifted into humour. "That I cannot argue with," he smiled. "My helm is loose. I need to tighten the strap, add another hole for the buckle."

"Ah, well, now I know what to carve on the rune-stone of your barrow when we bury your cold corpse," Røkia replied. "This man died from a hole in his head, because he did not have the time to tighten his helm-strap."

She is infuriating.

"Did someone say free cheese?" a voice filtered up from their camp, twenty or thirty paces below them. Røkia had woken Varg with a booted toe and led him up to a grassy plateau to train before the rest of the Bloodsworn awoke. Their camp was nestled in the shelter of a steep slope, pine trees all around. Einar Half-Troll lay snoring loud enough to frighten birds from branches beside a wagon, the Tainted children were gathered around him sleeping in the wagon-bed. Nearby Varg saw the hulking form of Glornir sitting with his back to a tree. He was sharpening the blade of his long-axe with a whetstone. Varg did not think the blade needed sharpening. Glornir's face was set in hard lines, shadows lying deep in the grooves and valleys of his face.

As Varg watched him, Glornir put his whetstone away, stood and tested the edge of his axe with his thumb.

"Make ready," Glornir called out, and shapes on the ground shifted, warriors rising.

"No cheese," Varg said to Svik as the red-haired warrior climbed the slope to stand with them, and Svik frowned.

"Just cold biscuits and cold pickled herring again, then," Svik said morosely. He had run out of his own stores of cheese and, although they had taken many barrels of food from the Grimholt's stores, Svik had found no cheese among them.

They were three days south of the Grimholt now, still in the high ground of the Boneback Mountains, but Glornir had ordered no fires until they had caught up with Skalk the Galdurman and those who had fled the Grimholt.

"Røkia," Glornir called up to them, "lead us out as soon as you are ready."

"Aye, chief," Røkia called back. She had become their chief scout since Edel had left them to guide Orka Skullsplitter to Rotta's chamber.

"Give me that," Røkia said, pointing at Varg's helm, and he unbuckled it, hefted the weight for a moment, black shadows made by the eye sockets, the mail links of the aventail dark and slick with oil. He handed it to her.

"You have bone needles, which you bought in Liga, I remember," Røkia said, "but they are better for stitching linen, wool and flesh, not so good at putting holes in leather. But there are other ways to fix a strap." She lifted the helm, holding the strip of leather that threaded through the buckle close to her face, as if she were going to sniff it.

"What are you doing?" Varg said. Røkia's expression changed and he felt his skin prickle, as if someone had breathed gently across his neck.

"Another lesson," Svik said. "Everything from Røkia is a lesson."

The touch of a smile twisted Røkia's lips and Varg sensed a shift rippling through her. A tightening in her muscles, a tinge of amber flecking her eyes. Her lips drew back and Varg saw her teeth looked sharper, her canines longer. She bit down into the leather strap of Varg's helm, the click of teeth. A twist of her wrist as she worked the leather around her tooth, as if drilling a hole with an awl, and then she was opening her mouth and handing the helm back to Varg, a new hole in the strap.

"See if that fits better," Røkia said, her voice a guttural rasp. She shuddered, stretched her head left and right, neck clicking, and her teeth and eyes shifted back to normal.

"The beast in your blood must be made to serve you," Svik said. "There is a wolf in your veins, and it is vicious. Do not be its slave."

Varg took the helm and placed it on his head, buckling the strap. The fit was much better.

"How did you do that?" Varg said.

"Think of the beast in your blood as a river that has been sealed with a beaver's dam," Røkia said. "You must let it flow out steady, like a stream, not burst out like a floodwater."

"Teach me how," Varg said.

CHAPTER TWELVE

GUÐVARR

Guðvarr sniffed and wiped a ball of snot from his dripping nose. He was sitting on a bench within a *snekke* that was being rowed along the River Drammur, still breathing hard from his recent shift at an oar. A man was squeezed tightly beside him on the bench, one of Queen Helka's *drengrs* in a fine mail coat. He was slumped against the top-rail, asleep or unconscious. His face was a ragged wound, flesh torn by nails and teeth, leaking green pus, and on his neck was a red lump, at its centre a pinprick hole, put there by that repulsive little vaesen with a sting in its tail. Black veins radiated out from the wound like a mouldering cobweb. Yesterday the warrior had been pulling at an oar; now he was shivering, groaning and stinking.

Not long for this world, Guðvarr thought. *Another sent on the soul road by that mad bitch and her pet monster.* He looked down into his calloused, red-raw hands, face twisted into a sneering glower as he nursed his wounded pride.

I ran.

The one thought he had been trying to avoid, but it insisted on returning to his thought-cage, like a fat-bloated fly buzzing to shite. All his life he had wanted to be a warrior, and when his aunt, Jarl Sigrún, had proclaimed him a *drengr* and part of her honour-guard he thought his heart would burst with pride and happiness.

I am fierce, a skilled warrior, deserving of respect, he reminded himself.

I will leave no insult unanswered. Did I not fight that weasel-shite fish-erman, Virk, in the holmganga *ring for his insults?* He knew he did, but that had not turned out as well as he had hoped, so he did not dwell on that memory. *And did I not hunt down those* niðing *sons of his, Mord and Lif, and bury my sword in Mord's belly for the insult he dared give me?*

I did.

He sat straighter at that thought, feeling a glimmer of his pride return.

But you ran from her, a voice whispered in his thought-cage, and his shoulders slumped and his glower returned. He could not deny the truth of it, much as he had tried during the last four days of rowing.

"Some bread and cheese," Arild asked beside him, nudging his arm and offering a chunk of dark bread with goats' cheese already sliced and laid out neatly upon it.

"No," Guðvarr grunted. *I did not ask for any, you snivelling arse-kisser*, he thought, a habit he had picked up from his father, who in Guðvarr's memory would always insult any person he had spoken to. Guðvarr preferred to keep the insults inside his head, though. Partly because he had seen his father suffer a serious beating for insulting the wrong person, and partly because he found it amusing that he was dealing out his disrespect with the complete ignorance of the insulted. Not that he minded Arild's arse-kissing, as it was usually reserved for him alone. The way she looked at him, some-times he thought she would think even his shite was made from gold and smelled of juniper-scented mead. It made him feel good, and he needed some more of that right now.

His belly growled at the sight of the bread and cheese.

"Yes," he said and took the bread and bit into it.

Arild was squashed tight to him, which pressed him uncomfort-ably close to the stinking *drengr*. There were a score of bodies stuffed into this *snekke*, where twelve would have filled it. Eight were rowing, water spuming white around oar-blades as they dipped and pulled. Another similar sized *snekke* rowed close behind them, crammed with too many people, just like this one. A mixture of warriors, women and children, all the survivors of the slaughter at the Grimholt. Guðvarr forced himself not to think about that. He was haunted by fractured images of his terrified dash from the Grimholt's tower to the wooden pier and his leap into one of the moored *snekkes*, screams and howls filling the world behind him, every moment expecting that crazed woman's axe to hack into his back.

No, he told himself, choosing to look around him at the river-banks and the land beyond. The current was slower now, as they had moved out of the steep-sided valley that the River Drammur carved through the Boneback Mountains. All around Guðvarr were rolling hills and plains as the terrain slowly levelled towards the sea.

"We will be back in Darl soon," Arild said.

Guðvarr's eyes narrowed as he looked back at Arild, an unpleasant tightening in his belly and crotch at the thought of facing Jarl Sigrún.

Darl, where I will have to face my aunt, and tell her why I have failed to bring back the head of the woman who scarred her.

"Is that supposed to cheer me?" he said. *You witless idiot*, he thought.

"Why would it not?" Arild said. "Better to be there than crammed on this boat?"

Guðvarr pinched his nose. "Because Jarl Sigrún will not be happy with me," he said slowly, as if explaining to a bairn. "She is expecting me to bring Orka's head back to her. You know, the woman who put a hole in Jarl Sigrún's face and slew her lover. That *niðing* piece of weasel-shite." *Who slaughtered a score of* drengrs *and sent another two-score fleeing, including me.*

"What will you do when you see Jarl Sigrún?" Arild asked.

He wanted to say, *tell her that I am going back to finish what I started. That I am going to make Orka pay for her crimes and bring her head back in a sack.*

But nothing came out of his mouth. The thought of Orka, blood-drenched, snarling and wielding that long-axe had dried the spit from his mouth, closed his throat and shrivelled his stones.

"They will find you and kill you," a woman's voice said, Guðvarr's

head snapping round. It was the Galdurman's prisoner, her wrists
and ankles bound, a dark-haired Seiðr-witch, judging by the knot
of blue tattoos that wreathed her neck and lower jaw, and the iron
collar about her neck. She had been heaved into the *snekke* unconscious and bound at wrist and ankle. Four days on the river and
this was the first time Guðvarr had seen her stir.

"Shut up," said Yrsa, a *drengr* of Queen Helka, as she untied the
gag around the Seiðr-witch's mouth and forced the spout of a
leather water bottle between the woman's lips. A choking gurgle
as the woman tried to spit out the water, but there was a wiry
strength in Yrsa. You didn't get to be honour-guard to Queen Helka
and her Galdurman, Skalk, without some strength in your arms.
The prisoner gave in and drank, and Yrsa took the bottle away,
showed her a crust of bread and a slice of salted pork.

"You should eat, Vol," a man said, not unkindly. He was seated
opposite Guðvarr, broad-shouldered and fair-haired, skulls of birds
and rats tied into his blond braids. Skalk, Helka's Galdurman. "No
point starving yourself to death." He sat hunched over a chest, which
he had not left since he had stumbled into this boat. His shoulder
was bandaged, crusted blood staining the linen. Guðvarr remembered
seeing the Galdurman shout his words of power back in the top
room of the Grimholt's tower, remembered the crackle of flame as
his staff had ignited, and he remembered the axe hurled from *her*
hand as it had slammed into Skalk, sending him careening out through
the doorway and tumbling down the tower stairs in a spray of blood.

So much blood, he remembered with a shiver.

The Seiðr-witch looked at Skalk, such hatred in her eyes that
Guðvarr had to control the urge to stand up and leap into the
river, just to get further away from her.

"There is still a way out of this for you," Vol the Seiðr-witch
said. "Just let me go, and the Bloodsworn will not come for you."

Skalk waved his hand, a dismissive gesture, and his mouth twitched
in a smile.

"You are a lying witch," he said. "Why would the Bloodsworn
risk death and destruction to get *you* back. You are nothing but a
Tainted thrall. They can find more like you in a dozen thrall-markets."

"You do not steal from the Bloodsworn," Vol said. "Glornir will have your head on a spike."

"That old grey-beard, I saw him fall at the mine before that . . ." he paused, looking around. "He did not live up to his fair-fame reputation. I was disappointed."

Vol's lip curled in a sneer. "I will remind you of that when he catches up with you."

"Ha," Skalk smiled, shaking his head.

"I don't think you should be so haughty, Galdurman. You are . . . less, now, I can see your power is diminished." She looked around, then smiled. "Where is your staff?"

He did not answer, but his smile turned to a scowl.

"And who gave you that wound?" Vol looked from Skalk to the others in the boat, most bearing wounds of one type or another. "Are you sure the Bloodsworn have not already caught up with you?" she said. "It looks like you have fought a warband who have sent you all fleeing."

"Not the Bloodsworn. Not a warband," Skalk muttered.

A she-bitch from hell, Guðvarr thought. *And her nasty little monsters.* He looked at Skalk, who was scowling at Vol.

Even a Galdurman ran from her, there can be no shame in it for me, if even Queen Helka's most powerful rune-caster fled from her, too.

"How long before we reach Darl, Skapti?" Skalk directed at a white-haired warrior sitting at the tiller in the *snekke's* stern.

"One more day, lord," Skapti said, one side of his face a purple-green bruise and a chunk missing from one ear, blood crusted in his hair and neck. An old scar ran through a bulbous nose, which bobbed as he spoke.

"So, even if your Bloodsworn were so stupidly self-destructive as to chase after me for a thrall, they will never catch us before we reach Darl."

"That does not matter," Vol said. "Here or in Darl," she shrugged, "Glornir will find you and show you what happens to those who steal from the Bloodsworn."

"It will be too late for you," Skalk said, "because once we are in Darl you will have a new thrall-collar about your neck. You will be politer when you are my thrall. Once I put a collar of my own crafting about your neck there will be no going back for you."

Vol blinked, and for the first time Guðvarr saw a hint of fear in her eyes.

"You are a brave man," Vol said and Skalk smiled. "Or a fool." Skalk's smile withered.

"Yrsa, gag her, the sound of her voice is an annoyance."

Yrsa cuffed Vol and stuffed the gag back into the Seiðr-witch's mouth.

"What is that smell?" Arild said beside Guðvarr. He looked to his right, saw the wounded *drengr* had slipped so that he was half on the bench, half on the strakes of the boat's hull.

"Him," Guðvarr said, and nudged the man with his boot, trying to make some room. He leaned closer, heard the man's breathing was faint and uneven. Reaching out a hand he put it to the *drengr*'s throat, felt the ragged flutter of a pulse, like the beating of a moth's wings. A twist of his hand and he unclasped the silver eagle-winged brooch that pinned the warrior's cloak, slipping it into his fist.

"He is dead," Guðvarr said, *well, he will be dead soon. Why take up room on the boat, slow us down with his weight and offend me with his stench.* "Help me," he asked Arild, standing and gripping the man under his arms and lifting him up. Arild moved and took the man's ankles and together they heaved him up, had him balancing on the top-rail. His eyelids fluttered and Guðvarr moved to cover him from the rest of the boat's inhabitants.

With a grunt Guðvarr rolled him over the side and he slipped into the water, disappearing with hardly a splash. Guðvarr sat back down on the bench and stretched his legs out.

"That's better," Guðvarr said, resisting the urge to smile.

CHAPTER THIRTEEN

VARG

Varg slowed to a halt. Røkia stood forty or fifty paces ahead and to his left, her arm raised and her fist clenched. Sweat trickled into Varg's eye and he swiped it away, sucking in a deep breath. He'd been running for half the day and his lungs were burning, legs aching. There was a new scent in the air.

Smoke. And fish.

In the distance he could hear the river and through the trees he saw vertical streaks of grey in the blue-white haze of sky. Other scouts filtered in from left and right, gathering around Røkia and Varg followed them.

Soon Glornir and the other Bloodsworn appeared behind them, emerging from the tree-dappled gloom like a dark mist.

"What is it?" Glornir asked as he reined in his mount.

"There's a village ahead, chief," Røkia said.

"Svik, take someone and go and find out what you can," Glornir said.

"Aye," Svik nodded. He looked around the group, eyes settling on Varg. "No-Sense, you can keep me company."

Varg walked beside Svik on his horse and they moved down a steep slope, Svik's horse picking its way with care. The sound of the river grew louder, the trees thinning, and then they were stepping out on to a meadow. Sheep ran bleating.

Varg looked up at Svik, the red-haired warrior looking ahead at the path, unusually silent.

He has been like this since we left the Grimholt.

"Svik, is something troubling you?" Varg said.

"Huh," Svik said, looking down at Varg with a frown.

"You are . . . not yourself, since the Grimholt. You talk less."

"Some would say that is a good thing," Svik said with a smile that did not reach his eyes. Then he shook himself and reached a hand up to tug and twirl on the thick braid of his moustache. "Perhaps I am missing cheese to start each day," he said with a smile, though Varg didn't quite believe him.

They passed through the meadow, the ground levelling beyond it, a handful of buildings rearing up, curling along a bend of the river. Before the village lay a fresh-ploughed field, thralls bent and raking soil, dragging out stones. Men and women, some children, all shaven-haired, all willow-branch thin, patched, sweat-stained tunics hanging from their frames and iron thrall-collars around their necks. One paused and looked up at Svik and Varg as they entered the field, an old man with clumps of close-cropped white hair, gaunt and toothless.

The sight of the thralls caused Varg to pause, a flood of memories spiralling in his thought-cage.

That was me, not so long ago. His hand reached up to his neck, touched the silver scars left by his collar.

A sense of hopelessness seeped from the old thrall's eyes as he looked at Varg and Svik.

That was how I felt, as a thrall. Hopeless, a slave to another man's whim. Just a tool to be used up and worn out, to be cast aside, like that rake.

The old thrall blurted out a warning as he rose to his feet, turned and ran in the direction of the village, and in moments all the thralls in the field were following him.

"Why are they running?" Varg said.

"We are the Bloodsworn, as they have seen from my shield," Svik said from up in his saddle, his black, blood-spattered shield strapped to a hook. "We are armed and wearing mail. And we have a reputation."

Varg was not used to being looked at, or even noticed at all, let alone having a reputation.

"It is better this way," Svik said. "By the time we get to the village there will be a greeting party to meet us. No smiling at them," he added, "just be calm, leave your shield on your back, and let me do the talking."

"Why did you pick me to come with you?" Varg asked Svik as they approached the village.

"Because if I brought Einar Half-Troll down here, they'd all be running screaming from here to Darl, and Røkia scares people almost as much as Half-Troll. It's hard to talk to people who are running away from you." Svik glanced at Varg, looking him up and down. "You have just the right amount of fierce about you, enough to send them running back to the village, but hopefully not further. Enough to keep them wary, but not too much that you will set their teeth to chattering."

Varg frowned at that.

"Fierce? Me?"

"Ha, perhaps you have not seen your reflection, lately. A warrior in mail, sharp weapons at your belt, a hard look in your eyes. A silver ring about your arm, a jarl's gift for a strong deed. And you are starting to move like a warrior, now. Røkia's training has helped with that, no doubt, and now you know there is a wolf prowling in your blood . . ." Svik shrugged. "That always changes things."

"I do not feel like any of those things," Varg said. "I still feel like I am the one most likely to end up with chattering teeth," he muttered.

"Ha, so says the man who slew a dragon-born," Svik chuckled.

"It was a lucky blow," Varg said.

Svik laughed harder. "You do not kill a dragon-born with a lucky blow."

They drew near to the village, moving from uneven ground to a worn dirt track, buildings rearing up either side of them. A handful of smokehouses, a barn, some stinking pig pens. A score of pit-houses with their turfed roofs reaching down to the ground and dug-out interiors sprawled along one side of the dirt road, a handful of wooden piers built alongside the river on the other. Tattered nets flapped on timber frames, waiting to be repaired.

A half-dozen figures stood waiting for them, men and women. A few held spears, one a wood-axe. The old thrall was with them, talking and pointing at Svik and Varg. Behind them was a larger crowd, gathered around a man standing on a cart. He was clothed in ragged mail and a woollen cloak, his black hair bound in braids, hands raised in the air as if calling to some unseen being. Others stood around him, clearly his companions, all dressed the same, in tattered mail and leather, spears in their fists. The man on the cart was shouting, and the crowd were listening.

"What's going on here?" Varg said with a frown. Something about the man on the cart set his blood tingling.

"Let's go and find out," Svik said. "They have the look of *niðing* outlaws, to me, but then the villagers would not be standing around, listening to them."

A man stepped forwards from those waiting for them. Tall, thickset, blond-haired with a wild beard and wind-scoured face. A copper ring was wrapped around his neck.

"What passes for the jarl of this place, I am guessing," Svik spoke quietly to Varg.

"I'm Njal Olafsson, and I'll be knowing who you are and what your business is here," the blond man said as Svik reined in, Varg standing beside him.

"I am Svik Tangle-Hair, of the Bloodsworn," Svik said, touching his reins so that his mount took a step to the side, revealing his blood-spattered shield. "But we are just travellers passing through. I'd like to buy some news, if there is any. And some cheese." He slid a ring of silver from his arm.

Njal swallowed, the men and women around him staring wide-eyed. Varg suspected they had not seen a silver arm ring before, let alone come close to earning a hack-piece from one.

"What kind of news?" Njal said. "Nothing much new here, not that would interest the likes of the Bloodsworn. We sow the fields, fish the river, hunt the woods," he shrugged, though his eyes were fixed on the silver ring in Svik's hand.

"Anyone come down the river from the Grimholt, recently?" Svik asked.

Njal's eyes narrowed.

Svik tossed the arm ring in the air and caught it, the silver flashing in sunlight.

"Aye, two *snekkes* rowed through here, three or four days gone," Njal said.

"I'll need a little more than that, if I'm going to be carving some silver from this ring for you," Svik said amiably.

"Both *snekkes* were full to overflowing, warriors, women, bairns," Njal shrugged.

"Did they stop here?" Svik asked.

"Aye, briefly. For food. They gave us one of their dead to bury."

"Don't think there was a warrior among them not bleeding from some wound or another," a woman behind Njal said, lean and hard-looking, gripping a spear. "Though they weren't quick to tell us how they came by those wounds."

"There's been trouble at the Grimholt, then?" Njal asked Svik. "What kind of trouble?"

The Skullsplitting kind, thought Varg.

The man on the cart's voice rose in volume, Varg hearing him shouting something about judgement and death. His eyes were bulging and spittle spraying.

"That's what we are trying to find out," Svik said, louder, frowning at the man on the cart. "Where did you bury their dead?"

Njal pointed between two pit-houses to a field beyond the village.

"Anything else you can tell me? Did you see a woman, tattoos on her neck?"

Njal shook his head, shrugged. "They were here and gone, left their dead wrapped in cloaks, stole a few sacks of oats, some bread and cheese."

Svik winced.

"Left as quick as they could," Njal continued. "Ask me, they were scared that the warband that carved them up was following them."

Not a warband. Just one person. And a tooth-eating tennúr. And a vaesen with a nasty looking sting in its tail.

"All right," Svik nodded. "Do you have any cheese left after those *niðings* stole food from you?"

"What?" Njal said, putting a hand to his ear to hear over the man on the cart.

"Who *is* that?" Svik almost shouted.

"A dragon-worshipper, spouting troll-shite about the end of the world and a dragon for a queen."

"Huh," Svik snorted, "Queen Helka won't take too kindly to that."

"I tried to stop him, but he's not alone," Njal said, nodding to others in the crowd.

"God-worshippers are forbidden in Helka's lands," Svik pointed out. "You would be within the Althing Law to put a rope around his neck and dangle him from a tree."

"Aye, I told him that. But they're armed, so I'll let him say his piece and move on." He shrugged. "He's a sheep's bladder full of wind, and I'd not see any of my people bleed over their like."

"Sensible," Svik said with a shrug, though his narrowed eyes were fixed on the dragon-worshippers. "Be a good man and go and find me a round of cheese, if there's any left after those thieves from the Grimholt stole your food."

"Aye, we can find some cheese for you," Njal said.

"Good. As quick as you can," Svik said, twisting the ring in his hand.

Njal gestured at the old thrall who stood close to him, and the silver-haired slave turned and hurried off to one of the pit-houses.

Svik smiled and dropped the arm ring down to Varg.

"Carve Njal some hacksilver, will you, Varg," Svik said.

"Varg?!" a voice said from behind Njal, and a figure stepped forward, another thrall, a woman, grey hair clipped short, skin stretched tight on her face, the shift of her jaw clear as she chewed her lip. "I knew there was something familiar about you, but . . ." she hesitated, chewed her lip some more. "You've changed."

Varg had stabbed his spear into the earth and now was on one knee, the silver ring in one hand placed upon a lump of stone, his hand-axe in the other. He paused, staring at the thrall.

"Terna?" he asked. Felt the world contract in on itself, all else fading. Terna had been a thrall at Kolskegg's farm, and she had been sold along with Varg's sister, Frøya.

Varg chopped into the arm ring, slicing off a lump of hacksilver and threw it to Njal, who caught it deftly and secreted it away inside his cloak. Slowly, carefully, Varg stood, passed the rest of the ring back to Svik and took a step towards Terna, his eyes never leaving her.

She took a step backwards.

"Do you know who killed my sister?" he said, his voice a snarling rasp.

"Frøya's dead?" Terna said, eyes widening. "What are you doing with the Bloodsworn? Did Kolskegg sell you to them?" She hesitated. "You're not wearing your thrall-collar."

"Varg is no thrall," Svik said, "he is one of us."

Terna blinked, mouth open. "How?" she breathed.

"That does not matter," Varg said, stepping close to her. "How do you not know that Frøya is dead? You left Kolskegg's farm with her."

"She was alive when Brimil sold me to Njal," Terna blurted, taking a step back.

"Brimil?" Varg growled.

"The slaver that Kolskegg sold us to," Terna said.

"Where is this Brimil?"

Terna recoiled, something in what she heard in Varg's voice or saw in his face that sent her stumbling away.

"Stop scaring my thrall," Njal said. "I bought Terna at the thrall-market in Darl. Brimil is a respected slaver there."

Varg sucked in a ragged breath, emotions roiling inside him like a storm-whipped sea.

"How was Frøya, when you saw her last?" he managed to breathe, though he felt as if a belt was being pulled tight about his chest by Einar Half-Troll.

"Bruised," Terna shrugged. "Brimil beat her often, because she kept on trying to escape."

She was trying to get back to me. It is what I would have done if I were in her place.

"She spoke of you often," Terna said. "All the time. She worried for you."

Worried for me, Terna's words swirled in Varg's thought-cage. *Worried for me.* He felt a shiver rippling through his body, his limbs twitching. *I should have found her*, protected *her*.

Svik clicked his tongue and his horse walked forwards, Varg feeling the weight of Svik's hand on his shoulder.

"This is good information," Svik said. He squeezed Varg's shoulder. "We shall find this Brimil, brother."

"Find him and kill him," Varg snarled.

"Most likely," Svik said. "But only after he has answered your questions. Put the axe away."

Varg looked down, saw that his hand-axe was shaking in his white-knuckled fist. With a deep breath he slipped it into the iron loop on his belt.

"How did you come to leave Kolskegg's farm?" Terna asked Varg.

"I killed him and ran," Varg said.

A silence settled over them, Terna, Njal and those around him all staring at Varg.

The old thrall returned, hefting a large round of cheese wrapped in linen and tied with hemp twine. He passed it up to Svik, whose smile was genuine and broad.

"My than—" Svik began.

"YOU MUST BOW TO THE DRAGON," the man on the cart bellowed, drowning Svik out. "THE DAY DRAWS NEAR WHEN LIK-RIFA WILL FILL THE SKY, WILL BLOT OUT THE SUN, AND YOU WILL SEE HOW THE PETTY RULERS OF THIS NEW WORLD HAVE DECEIVED US."

Svik sucked in a deep breath.

"By Berser's Hairy arse, but will you SHUT UP," he yelled at the man on the cart. "I am trying to have a conversation over here."

"REPENT OR PERISH," the man on the cart screamed, pointing at Svik with veins bulging in his neck, eyes popping, spittle spraying.

"Be silent, or you will be the one who perishes, and much sooner," Svik said, hefting the round of cheese in one hand.

"YOU CANNOT SILENCE ME, I AM THE VOICE OF THE DRAG—" A thud and squawk as Svik's round of cheese connected with the dragon-worshipper's face, the man's nose splitting, blood spraying, and he stumbled back a step, then toppled off of the cart and into the crowd.

"Ach, now see what you've made me do," Svik said, shaking his head.

A spear hissed through the air, hurled by one of those with the dragon-worshipper. Svik swayed in his saddle, impossibly fast, and the spear sliced through empty air, thumping into a turfed roof behind them. Varg saw a hint of greenish-yellow in Svik's eyes.

"Well, that was a mistake, arseling," Svik said, tutting and lifting his spear from its saddle-cup.

Screams and screeches as a handful of shapes burst from the crowd, the other dragon-worshippers who had been scattered among the gathering. Varg saw four, five, six of them, men and women all in rusted mail with spears in their fists, one of them empty-handed, reaching for an axe at his belt. They ran screaming at Svik.

A surge of rage that had been boiling and bubbling at the thought of Frøya swept through Varg, and before he realised what he was doing he was running at them. Distantly he heard Svik calling his name, and behind that, the howling of a wolf.

The closest dragon-worshipper was tall and whip-thin, a wild beard thick across his chest. He saw Varg charging and blinked, slowed.

Varg leaped, his hand-axe lashing out, sweeping wild-beard's spear away and crashing into the man, the two of them tumbling to the ground, rolling. As they came to a halt Varg was scrambling on to the man's chest, his axe rising and falling and with a crack he clubbed his opponent on the temple with the cheek of his blade. The man collapsed like a boned fish, eyes rolling white. The hiss of air and Varg threw himself forwards, as a spear whistled through the space his head had just been occupying, a snarling woman spitting curses at him.

Varg took his weight on his free hand and kicked out, swiping his new attacker's feet from under her. She fell hard, losing her grip on her spear and lay there, dazed and winded, tried to rise and Varg's elbow crunched into her jaw, sending her back to the ground.

Varg leaped to his feet, a rush of strength flooding him, muscles bunching, speed pulsing through his twitching body. A wolf howled in his head and he could *feel* the beast in his blood, a power and malice lurking in his veins, snapping and snarling to be free. He remembered Røkia and Svik's words to him.

The beast in your blood must be made to serve you.

You must let it flow out like a stream, not a floodwater.

Dimly he was aware of Svik riding forward, his spear a blur, the crowd in the village heaving and scattering, screams and shouts ringing out. Njal and those with him were standing and staring, wide-eyed.

We are one, the wolf and I, he said to the beast in his blood, as Røkia had taught him. *Together we are more. But I am the chief, the jarl, the pack-leader, and you the wolf are bound to me, like an oathsworn warrior. Oathsworn obey.* He sucked in a deep breath, held it, felt its effect on the wolf in his veins.

Something crashed into Varg's back and he was airborne, his axe spinning away as he tried to twist in the air, realising someone was gripping him about the waist, and then he was slamming into the cart that the dragon-worshipper had been standing upon, a shaft of pain in his shoulder. He fell to the ground, the weight of a body upon him. Varg struggled, felt arms gripping him, pushing his head into the mud. He tried to breath, sucked in mud, coughed and spluttered. A blow to his ribs, he caught a glimpse of another figure standing over him, kicking him. A fresh spike of anger, the wolf snarling in his head and he was tearing free, lashing out with his fists, connecting with something, a wet slap and a grunt and the grip on him was gone. Then Varg was on his feet, hands raised like he was in the pugil-ring, bouncing on his toes, the pain in his ribs and shoulder dull and distant.

One man lay at his feet, groaning, one eye closed and swelling, blood sluicing from a broken nose. Before him stood a huge man in tattered mail, thick-muscled and small-eyed, hair matted. He held a club in one fist, iron nails hammered through it.

"You should not disrespect the dragon," he grunted and swung his club at Varg.

You and your wolf must work together. A stream, not a floodwater, he thought. Time seemed to slow for Varg and he ducked the swing easily, stepping under it and close to small-eyes, a flurry of blows to the man's midriff as the instinct of his pugil-ring days took over, but the coat of mail soaked up and dispersed the power of Varg's blows. Small-eyes grinned down at him and Varg kicked out, short and sharp into his opponent's knee. The big man bellowed in pain, wobbled and dropped as Varg reached to his belt, his hand searching for his seax or cleaver.

With a roar of rage and pain, small-eyes propelled himself from the ground, slamming into Varg. The two of them stumbled together, the dragon-worshipper lashing out with club and fist, Varg swaying and slapping the club away. His hand closed on cold iron at his belt, tugged and heaved but whatever he had gripped held fast. A savage wrench and it tore free of his belt and he was swinging it at small-eyes' head. A crunch as Varg's helm connected with his attacker's cheek and nose, a burst of blood and the big man stumbled away, tried to swing his club again. Varg swung the helm in his fist faster, shattering the man's wrist and he screamed, dropping his club as Varg powered in, using his helm like a hammer, punching and battering. Small-eyes fell to the mud, tried to raise his hands but the helm swung again, fingers snapping, then blood and teeth were spraying. The warrior crumpled, groaning and whimpering through torn, blood-frothed lips and curled up on the ground.

Varg stood over him, snarling, rage and malice flooding him, the urge to rip and tear and destroy filling his every fibre. He raised his arm to crush his skull.

"Brother," Varg heard a voice behind him. "Brother!" louder, closer, and a hand grabbed his raised wrist. Varg growled, turning to see Svik on his horse, leaning down and gripping Varg's wrist.

"Be the master, not the slave," Svik hissed at him. Then louder. "The likes of these *niðings* do not deserve our full wrath." Svik curled a lip. "Do not give them that honour."

A shuddering breath rippled through Varg as he felt his chest heaving, his nostrils flaring. The wolf in him howled for blood, for death.

Oathsworn obey, Varg told the beast, and slowly, incrementally, Varg felt the rage and bloodlust subside. He looked down at the man at his feet, saw a groaning mass of pulped flesh laying in the blood-slick mud, then he raised his gaze and looked around.

Bodies lay scattered about him, men and women in tattered mail, all bleeding into the mud, put down by him or Svik. Njal and his followers stood around a man on his knees, a spear held to his chest.

Most eyes were staring at Varg, fear and awe in their faces. Varg blew out a long breath and held his helm up, saw clots of blood smeared across it. The leather strap that Røkia had fixed for him was torn where he had ripped it from his belt.

"Good," Svik muttered and released Varg's wrist. He looked at Varg's helm.

"Røkia won't be best pleased with you," Svik said, a smile twitching his moustache. He looked up, towards the cart where the dragon-worshipper had stood. "Now, where's my cheese?"

"Njal, do you have any leather I could buy?" Varg called out, looking dejectedly at his helm-strap.

Svik's laughter echoed around the village.

Einar Half-Troll stooped over the barrow and lifted the last rock, dropping it on the turf with a thud.

Glornir stepped forwards and looked into the barrow, others of the Bloodsworn crowding behind him, peering at the dead warrior buried there. A man, dark-haired, clothed in mail with a bronze ring about his arm and a silver brooch fashioned to look like an eagle's wing. He held a hand-axe upon his chest in his dead grip. His face was torn and rent, strips of flesh hanging in tatters, bone-pale beneath the flesh. Maggots squirmed in his wounds. A night-wyrm slithered out of his mouth.

Looks like he has been mauled by an animal, Varg thought, his mind going back to Orka Skullsplitter sitting upon the steps of the Grimholt, blood-drenched, the dead piled all about her.

He glanced up and saw figures gathered between the houses of Njal's village, staring at them.

He looked away.

"Well, that is not Skalk," Einar pointed out, "so the Galdurman still lives."

"Good," grated Glornir, his face cold and hard, death in his eyes.

"Why good?" Einar frowned.

"It is good because Glornir wants to be the one to put Skalk in the ground, you oaf," Røkia hissed.

I am glad I am not Skalk. When we catch up with the Galdurman in Darl . . . Varg looked away from Glornir to the south, through the valley they were in to rolling hills and a tapestry of sparkling rivers, knowing that Darl lay there, somewhere beyond his eyesight.

And Skalk.

And Brimil the slaver. He felt his mouth curl into a snarl. *Brimil, it will not be a good day for you when I find you.*

CHAPTER FOURTEEN

BIÓRR

Biórr wiped sweat from his brow, heat radiating from the ground and, ahead, he saw the shimmering heat haze that marked the vaesen pit. They were winding out from high ground, leaving the Dark of Moon Hills behind them. To the west Mount Eldrafell throbbed and pulsed with lines of fire. Ilska led them across the Isbrún Bridge upon her black mare, looking to Biórr as if the horse were walking across a bank of sluggish, intangible mist. Her brother Drekr and the other dragon-born rode behind her, and behind them others marched in a loose column. Biórr walked among them, shield slung across his back and using his spear like a walking staff. Red Fain and Storolf Wartooth strode beside him, Ilmur as well, and behind them wagons creaked across the ground, filled with the Tainted bairns. Biórr glanced back, wondering how Bjarn was, and saw Kráka sitting on a wagon bench. She saw his glance and dipped her head to him.

It was not so long ago that Kráka, Ilmur and I were travelling in the other direction, with the Battle-Grim. Fractured memories of that journey came back to him, most of them involving Elvar, of her pulling him behind the wagons, of her hot breath and the feel of her skin against his.

No, he told himself, *forget her. She was happy to live a slaver's life. To be a slaver. But now Ilmur and Kráka are free of their collars.*

Even with that thought in his head, he could not dispel the

memories of Elvar, or how she had looked at him when he stabbed Agnar. The pain of his betrayal had been almost a physical thing leaking from her eyes.

"Thank you, Biórr," said Ilmur, who was walking at Biórr's heel.

"For what?" Biórr asked, shaking his head and grateful of the distraction from his memories.

"For saving me, setting me free from Agnar's thrall-collar."

"You are welcome," Biórr said. "That is not a life. I know."

"You have been a thrall?"

Biórr heard the crack of a whip in his head, felt the red-fire pain across his body, as if it were happening now. He grimaced.

"Aye, when I was very young," Biórr said. "I was lucky, escaped, and was found by Red Fain."

"Why do they treat us like animals?" Ilmur said.

"Because they fear us," Biórr said, feeling his age-old anger rise. "Strange, that their cruelty will bring about their own downfall." He glanced up to the sky and saw the shadow of Lik-Rifa high above. "Soon they will no longer be the lords of this world, or us Tainted the thralls."

"I am just happy for a kind word and a hot meal," Ilmur sighed.

"You are safe now, brother," Biórr said. "You are free. Enjoy that."

Biórr reached the edge of the vaesen pit, heat rising on thermals; it was like stepping out from the cool shelter of a longhouse into the midday heat. His stomach turned as he took his first step out over the gaping chasm with its river of molten rock churning below, and then he was walking on solid ground, the bridge hard underfoot. Colours shifted and glittered within it, looking like the swirling lights of the *guðljós*, the god-lights that could sometimes be seen in the dark night skies that some said were the spirits of the dead gods, fighting on in the skies for all eternity.

Apart from Lik-Rifa, the dragon, who lives and breathes and flies the skies of Vigrið again.

That thought gave Biórr a shiver, of both excitement and fear. *I am part of a new saga-song that will change the world, that will put a sword through the heart of the last three hundred years of slavery and prejudice.*

"I hate the north," Storolf said beside him. "First it is too cold, now it is too hot."

"Just like life," Fain said to his son, "it pleases itself, not us."

"The cold is good for you, makes you stronger," Biórr smiled, "it is just another enemy to defeat."

"Heya," Fain said.

Storolf looked at him, raised one thick eyebrow. "No one likes waking up with ice in their beard," he said, "or risking your stones freezing and snapping off when you take a shite."

"No fear of that here," Biórr said, nodding down at the churning river of fire below them, popping and hissing and sizzling.

How does this bridge of ice not melt? Biórr wondered, though he did not want to dwell on that thought, instead just tried to pick up his pace and get across the bridge quicker. Somewhere ahead of him the sound of horses' hooves crunching on ice shifted to the dull thud of hooves on turf and he saw Ilska leave the Isbrún Bridge and ride across a grassy plain towards a gentle hill. Biórr saw the fallen shape of a wagon in the grass, axles snapped and rotting, leather traces and harness dangling, and he remembered the tennúr that had swarmed out of a hill and swept over the Battle-Grim. Of the pony that had been pulling the wagon there was no sign, not a sliver of bone or a shred of skin.

Ilska was approaching that hill and riding up the gentle slope.

A moment as the consequences of that settled on Biórr.

"GET AWAY FROM THE HILL," he shouted, shouldering through the ranks in front of him.

Ilska reined in her horse and looked back to see what the noise was about, Drekr turning his horse and glowering as Biórr burst through the Raven-Feeders and ran across the plain towards them.

"THE HILL," he yelled as he pounded across the grass, remembering doing the same thing not so long ago, running towards Elvar as she stood over Grend's prone body. "IT'S A TENNÚR NEST."

A shadow enveloped Biórr, cast over the whole hill and a roar echoed from the sky, rattling him to his bones and sending him staggering to one knee. The horses whinnied and reared in terror, Ilska shouting for control and yanking on her reins as Biórr looked up and saw great wings above blotting out the sun, the silhouette of a serpent-neck and lashing tail.

The dragon roared again and it felt like the whole world was shaking.

Biórr struggled back to his feet, Ilska and the others all staring up at the dragon as she descended. Lik-Rifa's claws reached out and she landed at the base of the hill. The ground shook and many stumbled.

Lik-Rifa's jaws opened wide.

"*Komdu til mín, börnin mín,*" she said, deep and sonorous, Biórr feeling the dragon's voice reverberating in his chest.

Even from Biórr's position he could feel it, a vibration in the ground. Movement around the hooves of Ilska's horse, and Drekr's, a tremble and shiver in the soil as if they were standing on sand that shifted beneath them. Small-taloned fingers appeared, heads pushing out of the rippling ground, small figures with wings snapping out, spraying earth and exploding into the air. Pink, hairless bodies like newborn rats, thin-veined wings and too-large mouths.

"SHIELD WALL," a voice bellowed behind Biórr and he glanced back, saw Fain and Storolf organising the Raven-Feeders into a shield wall as they filtered off the Isbrún Bridge, the crack of linden wood echoing as shields came together.

"FORWARD," Fain shouted and the wall began to move at a fast walk, shields and axes beating time on shield rims. Biórr slipped his shield from his back and hefted his spear, looking backwards and then forwards, hesitating.

"*ELDHLÍF OKKUR,*" Ilska cried, Drekr and the other dragon-born adding their voices to her. Red-flamed runes burst into life in the air as they chanted, looking like shields of fire. As Biórr stared the small rune-shields hovering in the air began to expand, growing, joining, forming a dome of fire around Ilska.

The tennúr burst from the hill, leaping into the air, a crack of wings snapping wide and they were whirring away from Ilska and all around her, towards Lik-Rifa, swarming upon her. Ilska let out a battle cry and she kicked her horse into movement, the rune-shield evaporating with a hiss and she was riding down the hill,

Drekr and the other dragon-born following her. Biórr stood there, hefted his spear and ran after them.

There were so many tennúr that they were close to covering Lik-Rifa from view. Storolf led the shield wall around and began marching towards the dragon, Ilska, Drekr and the mounted dragon-born outpacing them. Ilska raised her sword and began shouting words of power, runes crackling to fiery life in the air before her.

"STOP," Lik-Rifa growled, head snapping round to fix on Ilska, and the chief of the Raven-Feeder's reined in her mount, turf flying as she skidded to a halt.

Biórr ran up behind the mounted warriors, stood and stared and the shield wall of Raven-Feeders stuttered to a halt.

"Do not touch my children," Lik-Rifa growled, lips pulling back in a snarl to reveal teeth long and curved as the ribs of a *drakkar* longship.

Children? Biórr thought, frowning, then he realised.

The tennúr. They were crawling thick on Lik-Rifa's skin, like lice in a beard, but they were not attacking. *They are vaesen; if the sagas are true then Lik-Rifa made them.* A sound came from Lik-Rifa, deep and rumbling, like a growl. *No, not a growl. She is . . . purring.*

Mist hissed and seethed around Lik-Rifa as her body started to shift, Biórr recognising the unsettling sounds of her transformation, a series of cracks and pops, as bones shifted and flesh morphed, contracting and reshaping, vaesen bursting away from the dragon like water droplets from a shaking dog and then Lik-Rifa was standing before them in her human form, tall, gaunt and regal, her grey tunic edged with red. The vaesen swooped back in, swirling around Lik-Rifa like a flock of starlings and she held her hands out, smiling as she touched and stroked them. She strode towards Ilska, who sheathed her sword and slid from her horse, dropping to one knee.

"My queen," Ilska said, bowing her head, Drekr and the other dragon-born doing the same. Biórr stood there, then he felt Lik-Rifa's eyes settle on him, realised he should be on one knee, too. He dropped clumsily, shield and spear still in his fists.

"Vaesen are my children, given form and breath and life by me, they are my creation," Lik-Rifa said, "as you are my children, descended from me by blood. So, we must all learn to get along together." She held her hand up and a tennúr landed on her forearm, translucent wings folding, and Lik-Rifa scratched the creature under its chin.

"*þú mátt ekki borða þessar manneskjur, þær eru líka börnin mín,*" Lik-Rifa said and the tennúr on her arm turned its head to regard Ilska and the others with a quizzical look.

"*Their teeth taste good,*" the vaesen said, its voice high and brittle, like dry leaves crackling underfoot. A line of saliva dribbled from its mouth, "*but if our Lady asks it, then we will obey.*"

Lik-Rifa laughed. She looked at Ilska. "See, vaesen can be reasonable."

Ilska looked at the tennúr, her lip curling in disgust, and Lik-Rifa's smile turned to a snarl, her mouth opening, a deep-throated growl issuing from her, Biórr feeling the rumble of it in his bones. Lik-Rifa's face twitched and juddered.

"I do not wish to give in to my . . . instincts," she said, her voice little more than a whisper, but carrying. Biórr saw that Ilska stood stiff and straight, though there was a tremor in one of her legs.

She is capable of feeling fear, then. I have often wondered.

"After all, so many of my children are gone, it would be a shame to eat the ones who are left, and so I have vowed to try and not eat you," she said, "but you are testing me on that vow, daughter. My vaesen are my children, just as you are, and they are our allies." A fresh tremor of barely contained rage shivered across her face. "You will treat them well."

A drawn-out silence, Biórr tensing, preparing for the possibility of snapping jaws and the spray of blood, ready to leap away.

"Yes, my queen," Ilska said.

Lik-Rifa nodded to herself. "Good," she said.

Biórr relaxed, marginally.

"*Farðu heim til þín og gættu þessarar brúar. Aðrir eru að koma, brúðir minn, úlfurinn. Þú mátt eta hann og allar tennúr hans og alla þá sem eru með honum,*" Lik-Rifa said to the tennúr swarming around her, her voice ringing out. The tennúr on her arm gave a little bow and its wings snapped out, the creature leaping into the air. Then the whole host of tennúr were swirling in a great cloud, rising high and then plunging back towards the hill. They crashed into it, clawing and scratching, burrowing and wriggling into the soil until they were all gone, myriad patches of loose soil the only evidence that they had been there. A few stones rolled and skittered down the hill.

Lik-Rifa turned and strode towards the Isbrún Bridge, halting before the granite boulder that marked the bridge's beginning. Steam hissed and rose from the edge of the vaesen pit. Lik-Rifa stared at the ice bridge. She placed her flat palm against the rock, within the cleft that resembled a huge claw. Biórr remembered Uspa placing her cut hand there and speaking her Seiðr-magic to reveal the bridge.

"*Brú, vertu innsigluð öllum sem fylgja. Vera áfram lokaður fyrir blóðtöfra,*" Lik-Rifa said, her voice seeming too loud and deep to be coming from her lips. White veins threaded out from her palm into the rock, and the Isbrún Bridge hissed, steam rising to engulf it in a great mist. When the steam evaporated the bridge was gone. Or, at least, Biórr could not see it.

Lik-Rifa smiled to herself and gave a curt nod. Then she turned and looked at Ilska for a long, uncomfortable time. Eventually she reached out and brushed Ilska's cheek with her long-taloned fingers. "I think I will rest a while in this form," she said and walked past Ilska, taking the reins of her black mare and climbing into the saddle. The horse neighed and shifted, ears going back, but Lik-Rifa whispered a few words and the mare calmed. She smiled down at Ilska. "We can talk as we travel. I have many questions, much that I would know of this new world."

"Of course," Ilska said, raising a hand to beckon for a new horse. A warrior from among the wagons ran to her, leading a harnessed horse by a roped bridle. Ilska mounted and drew close to Lik-Rifa.

"If these tennúr vaesen are our allies," Ilska said, "should they not travel with us. The more strength we have in crossing Vigrið, the better."

"They will join us later," Lik-Rifa said. "Once they have performed a task for me."

Biórr looked at the mound, then back at the Isbrún Bridge, fairly sure he had a good idea what that task might be.

"East, then, to Nastrandir," Lik-Rifa said, touched her heels to the mare and moved on.

CHAPTER FIFTEEN

ORKA

O rka pulled on her reins, slowing Trúr from a trot to a walk, signalling for Lif to do the same. The path they were following sloped down a wooded hillside, the ground becoming uneven and pitted, tree roots bursting from the ground in knotted, twisted tangles. Ahead of them Edel and her hounds loped at the edge of Orka's vision, disappearing among the tree-gloom, then re-emerging in bursts of daylight that sliced through the canopy above. The sun was high in a sheer, cloudless blue sky.

Spert lifted his head, shifting in front of Orka on the curve of Orka's saddle where the vaesen lay sleeping. His fat tongue flickered out as he woke.

"*Hungry*," he murmured.

"Only half a day has gone since you had your porridge," Orka said.

Spert sniffed, his many legs wriggling as he shifted, his tail twitching, the sting moving uncomfortably close to Orka's arm.

"Careful with that," Orka muttered.

"We are close to the mine," a woman said who jogged alongside Orka and Lif. Orka looked down at her. Halja Flat-Nose, a young warrior of the Bloodsworn, her red-gold hair bound and braided tight, her mail coat jingling with the rhythm of her movement. Pinewoods reared all about them, hills giving way to cliffs as they travelled along the edge of the Boneback Mountains.

Orka sniffed, a faint scent edging the fragrance of pine and rich soil that was thick about them. Something sweet and redolent, like milk that was beginning to curdle.

They travelled on in silence, the scent getting stronger.

Death, Orka realised. One hand dropped to the hilt of a seax hanging across her front, sitting balanced across her thighs as she rode.

Edel was closer now, standing on the edge of the pinewoods and looking out on to a treeless valley. Her hounds sat either side of her, panting, staring, ears pricked forward. Orka and Lif drew to a halt behind Edel, Halja Flat-Nose and the other Bloodsworn spreading out along the treeline, the few riders dismounting. Ten of them with their black, blood-spattered shields.

A blur of wings and Vesli dropped down from the canopy, Breca's half-spear in her fist. She perched upon Lif's saddle pommel, wings folding closed. "Vesli smell the dead," she said, her long nose twitching like a rat's.

"Behold Rotta's chamber," Edel said, spitting into the grass. "The home of a god."

"Doesn't look like much to me," Lif remarked.

Orka looked out on to an open glade of trampled, cracked mud, the far side bordered by more pinewoods that sloped sharply up towards rearing hills and cliffs. The eastern edge of the mud-trampled glade ended in a sheer cliff face, an arched, shadowed entrance sitting within it like a wide-gaping mouth. On the far side of the glade was a small hill of rubble and boulders, abandoned carts standing around it. The scent of death was stronger now, Orka's eyes drawn to another pile, this one covered by crows and formed of rotting bodies. The thick limbs of a huge troll were splayed on the ground, skin starting to collapse as the flesh rotted beneath it, where there was any flesh left to rot. Predators had been feeding. Crows stood on the dead troll's face, pecking and tearing at what was left of the soft flesh of lips and tongue. The eyes were red-bored empty sockets, its belly torn open and feasted upon. Other bodies had been laid out alongside the troll, skraelings and humans, the warriors stripped of weapons and war kit, all of them in similar states of decomposition and consumption. A handful of shields and spears were piled close to these dead, a few seaxes and belts.

War kit the Bloodsworn did not bother taking from the harvest of the slain.

Close to the pile of the dead lay a row of barrows, four of them, the rocks and boulders newly laid, as was clear by the absence of moss and lichen upon the rocks.

Edel whispered a word and her two hounds padded out into the glade, noses low, moving quiet and slow, like hunters. Crows exploded into the air, settling in branches of pine trees along the glade's edge and squawking their protest as the two hounds padded about the glade, one disappearing into the trees on the far side, the other loping into the shadowed entrance in the cliff face. Edel followed them, more of the Bloodsworn stepping into the glade. Orka dismounted and wrapped her reins around a low-hanging branch, lifted her long-axe from its saddle hook and strode into the glade. She heard Lif's footfalls as he followed her. Vesli launched into flight, whirring around the glade, and Spert's wings expanded as he slid from his sleeping place on Orka's saddle, descending to the floor and folding his wings, scuttling after Orka on his many-jointed legs.

Halja Flat-Nose walked straight across the glade and stopped before one of the barrows, stood staring down at it. Other Bloodsworn spread wide, searching the perimeter, some disappearing into the trees on the glade's northern edge, two striding down a track that led away from Rotta's chamber, another stepping into the shadowed entrance of the cave in the cliff face. Orka prowled around the open space, saw the ground was scarred and pitted, here and there dark stains. She walked past Halja but did not stop; by the set of the woman's shoulders and tight-lipped expression she was grieving the loss of someone. Orka moved past to regard a score of warriors, men and women, all stripped of their war gear, wax-pale apart from the dark wounds that had sent them on the soul road. Vesli whirred out of the trees, flew in a half-circle around Orka and alighted upon one of the dead, a woman, fair-haired, a black wound in her throat. Stabbing her spear into the ground Vesli crouched, reaching with her long, bony fingers into the woman's mouth and with a ripping, wet-tearing sound she wrenched a tooth from the dead woman's gums.

Lif made a gagging sound and Vesli stopped and looked around.

"She will not be needing them," the tennúr said with a shrug and popped the tooth into her mouth, a shred of flesh hanging from its root. Lif turned away as Vesli started crunching.

Orka walked slowly along the row of the dead, and then her flesh went cold and she stopped, the hairs on her arms and neck standing on end. She was staring down at a dead man.

A white beard, bald, a gaping wound in his skull. Tall and thick-muscled, his war kit had been stripped from him, the old man lying there in torn wool breeches and a bloodied, ripped tunic. Much of his face had been eaten; eyes, lips, ears all but gone, but despite his mauled condition Orka knew him. The edges of a blue tattoo were visible through tears in the man's tunic.

He is the dragon-born Glornir spoke of.

She squatted and reached out, her knuckles brushing the cold flesh of the dead man's arm and then gripping his tunic in her fist, ripping it open across his torso. A tattoo spiralled across the man's shoulder and chest, a twisting serpent, jaws gaping.

Not a serpent, a dragon, Orka realised, making out wings in the knotwork tattoo and remembering seeing the same image crawling across Drekr's shoulder, and carved into the oath stone she had come across on the journey to the Grimholt.

Do all the dragon-born wear this ink, or is it something else, something more?

"Vesli, take this one's teeth," Orka snarled.

Vesli paused in her work, where she was tearing tooth after tooth from the dead woman's gums and stuffing them into a leather pouch hanging from a belt she had buckled around her waist. Her wings flickered and she rose and dropped on to the white-bearded corpse and set to ripping his teeth from his mouth.

Spert appeared, scrambling on to the man's body and crawling over him, long antennae twitching, caressing and exploring the corpse like a blind man's touch. They found the gaping wound in his skull and delved inside, a soft, sucking sound.

Spert pulled his antennae from the dead man's skull, wet and glistening, and licked one of them with his fat, blue-black tongue. "This one is different," Spert said in his rasping voice. "Human, but not."

"He is dragon-born," Orka muttered, rising.

Spert shuffled to the next man and set to work examining this new corpse, a handful of wounds in the dead warrior's torso. Again, he inserted his antennae into a wound, then drew it out and sucked it clean.

"This one is human," Spert rasped, then shuffled on to the next corpse, a woman with her brown hair tied into one thick braid. A huge wound in her belly, made ragged by creatures which had gnawed on her flesh.

"Human, but not," Spert pronounced. "And different from the old man."

"Another Tainted," Orka murmured, "but not dragon-born." She turned away from the row of corpses and strode towards the dark entrance in the cliff face. Lif followed her, the whirr of Vesli's wings and the rhythmic scratching of Spert's many legs coming after her. Two of the Bloodsworn were standing in the shadows of the cave, a fair-haired man, tall and lean named Gunnar Prow, on account of his nose, which filled most of his face and curved like a prow-beast on a *drakkar*, and Revna Hare-Legs, because of her speed in battle. They were young, come to the Bloodsworn since Orka had left, and they were lovers, which they had made no secret of during their journey here from the Grimholt, much to Lif's red-cheeked embarrassment.

They were sifting through a wooden barrel and pulling out rush torches, bound with hemp. Revna drew out flint and a striking iron from a pouch and, in moments, sparks were spraying and the torches were crackling and hissing.

"Skullsplitter," Gunnar Prow said to Orka, offering her a torch and reaching into the barrel for another. Orka took it and held it high, saw other torches were mounted in iron sconces on the wall. She moved deeper into the tunnel, lighting the wall-mounted torches as she went, Lif, Gunnar and Revna following her. Vesli flitted above them and Spert followed behind, looking around with a frown on his thick, lined face, his antennae twitching in constant motion.

"So, this is Rotta's chamber," Lif said with a whistle as the tunnel sloped downwards. Entrances to rooms opened up on either side, Orka peering into them. Some had wooden doors, others were just shadow-filled holes. All the rooms were small, the walls damp and dripping. "I expected something . . . grander."

"It was a bolthole," Revna said, "Rotta was fleeing the wrath of his brother and sister."

"I've heard saga-tales telling of how he played a part in the murder of Orna's and Ulfrir's daughter," Lif said. "Is this where he came to hide from them?"

"That is what the saga-tales say," Revna said as she peered through another open entrance with her torch held high.

"Rotta slew Orna and Ulfrir's daughter, Valkyrie, and cast the blame upon Lik-Rifa," Gunnar said. "He strangled Valkyrie, skinned her and left her hanging from a tree. But Orna and Ulfrir saw through his deceit and so he fled from them. Came here, where he wrote the *Raudskinna*, his red-skinned book that holds the secrets of the gods, all of it carved into Valkyrie's flayed skin."

"Not a pleasant brother," Lif said, "to murder his niece."

"Trust is a rare thing, even among kin," Revna muttered, Gunnar Prow reaching out, his fingertips brushing the back of her hand.

"How many chambers are here?" Orka asked Gunnar.

"We did little exploring last time we were here," Gunnar said with a shrug, "other things to do. But from what I saw the whole chamber has not been fully excavated. It is like a warren. They were still working on it when we arrived, as the carts and rubble outside show. There is a central chamber ahead, and a few others that were clearly being used. I will show you." He strode ahead of Orka.

The tunnel bored ever downwards, roughly carved, all of them lighting the torches nailed into the walls as they went, and then they were stepping into a chamber, high and wide. Water dripped and echoed. Gunnar walked into the chamber's centre, holding his torch high to reveal a huge slab of rock, the top roughly levelled.

Four chains of iron links were embedded in the rock, dangling, each one ending in a shattered manacle wide enough to wrap around Orka's waist.

Vesli flew down out of the shadows and alighted beside Orka. Looking up at the slab she shivered.

"Vesli don't like it," the tennúr squeaked.

Orka stood and stared at the slab, saw it was pitted with black, spattered holes. Her skin was prickling, felt like the wolf in her veins prowled back and forth, growling a warning.

"Rotta's altar," Lif breathed as he drew alongside Orka.

Orka grunted.

"That is what Vol thought," Gunnar said. "The slab where Rotta was chained by Orna and Ulfrir. They said death was too quick for him, wanted a longer-lasting revenge."

"So he was sentenced to be burned and scalded each and every moment of his life by the venom of serpents, for all eternity," Revna finished.

"Say one thing for the dead gods; they were imaginative," Lif said. "I would like to do that to Guðvarr."

"Eternity did not last so long for Rotta," Orka said, looking from the shattered manacles at the end of each chain to the cavern's roof above them. It was wreathed in darkness, but that is where the saga-tale told that serpents born of Snaka were caged, their venom leaking and falling like rain upon the chained Rotta.

Spert scuttled up beside them and climbed up the side of the slab, his many feet sticking somehow to the rock. He clambered on to the top, his antennae sweeping before him, brushing over the surface and its black pitted scars.

"Nasty business, nasty business," he muttered as he walked across the slab.

"How did Rotta break free?" Revna said, nodding at the shattered manacles, "and he is not mentioned in the last battle of *Guðfalla* the gods-fall, not in any saga-tale I have been told."

"Well, he is not here, that is for sure," Orka said, blowing out a short breath and turning away. "What else did you find?" she asked Gunnar.

"This way," he said, leading them on.

Gunnar led them to a long, narrow chamber, another door at its far side. Scores of holes were carved into one wall, each the size of a fist, and rolled parchments protruded from them. There was a smashed table in one corner, clay jars of ink broken, sticks of carved bone for the writing of runes littered the ground.

"That was where Orna's talon was kept," Gunnar said, gesturing to the door on the far side of the room.

Orka grunted and walked forward, stepping over the smashed table. She saw a dark stain on the ground, sniffed congealed blood.

"This is where Vol was captured," Gunnar said. "Varg slew one of the *drengrs* with Skalk."

"Varg, the one who slew the dragon-born?" Orka said.

"Aye," grunted Gunnar.

Lif pulled a parchment out and broke the wax seal, unrolling it.

"What does it say?" Orka asked, peering over Lif's shoulder.

"Don't know," Lif said, passing the scroll to Orka, "I can't read. I'm a fisherman."

Gunnar took it.

"Here is a copy made from fragments of Rotta's Galdrabok," he read, then hastily rolled the parchment up and slotted it back into its hole in the wall. "Not something I want to know more of," he muttered.

"Not you, maybe, but you should still gather these up," Orka said to Gunnar and Revna. "Glornir may want them, and Vol definitely will, once you have her back."

"Aye, good idea," Revna said, pulling some of the scrolls out and gathering them under one arm. "There were many more in there," she continued. "Kept in a chest with Orna's talon. Skalk stole the chest when he captured Vol and ran."

Orka scowled at that, not liking the thought of Skalk having access to the secrets of a Galdrabok rune-carved by Rotta, no matter how fragmented they were.

"Is there anywhere else?" Orka asked.

"Aye, one more room we found that you should see," Revna said. She left the chamber and they all followed, soon stopping outside another. "We found this." Revna stepped inside and lit torches on the wall, revealing a large chamber. Straw mattresses were laid out upon the ground, scores of them crammed tightly together, the stench of urine and faeces thick in the air.

"Where they kept their thralls?" Lif said.

"No," Orka said, a muscle twitching in her jaw. "They kept children in here."

The mattresses were small, each one half the size of an adult. She had found a similar room with a similar scent in the loft above the inn at Darl, where she had found Breca's wood pendant of a sword. A pressure built in her chest and throat, tears stinging her eyes, and then she fought the urge to scream, felt that shift into a desire to howl and snarl and kill.

Vesli flew into the room and sped around it, and Spert bustled in, too, his antennae searching. He stopped at a small mattress near the centre of the chamber, antennae moving frenziedly, and Vesli swooped down and folded her wings, dropping to her hands and knees and pressing her long nose to the mattress.

"Breca was here," Spert said, looking back at Orka, confirming what she already sensed.

Orka padded forward, torch in one hand, long-axe in the other, and crouched beside the straw mattress that Spert and Vesli had singled out. She bowed her head and closed her eyes, memories of Breca flooding her thought-cage, his face, large eyes and raven-dark hair.

I will find you, she told him, over and over.

A cough from the chamber and Orka looked up through blurred eyes and saw Gunnar, Revna and Lif staring at her. She was unsure how long she had been kneeling beside Breca's mattress, but there was a tingling in her legs and ankles.

"We should go back to the others," Revna said, and Gunnar nodded.

"My belly is rumbling," he added. "Time to make a camp and cook something. Shall Revna tell the others we are making camp in the main chamber?" he asked Orka.

Orka looked back at him, frowning that he should be asking her.

"Best go and find Edel and ask her," she said and Gunnar nodded, started to turn away.

"I'd not make camp in here, though," Orka said. "Only one entrance, not a good spot to get caught in. Best to make camp out in the woods."

"Aye," Gunnar said and strode away, Revna and Lif following him. Lif paused and looked back at Orka.

"You coming?" he asked.

"Soon. I will search some more first," Orka said. Lif turned away and she wiped the tears from her eyes, looking back at the sweat-stained straw mattress.

CHAPTER SIXTEEN

GUÐVARR

Guðvarr sucked in a breath as they rowed along a sweeping curve of the River Drammur and Darl came into view, the sight of it causing him to lose the rhythm of his rowing. The man behind him spat a curse and swore at him as their oars clashed, and Guðvarr hastily steadied his rhythm.

Talk to me like that again and I will skewer you like a stuck pig, Guðvarr thought, though he refrained from voicing that, as his companion was a hard-looking man named Hrolf with cold eyes and scarred hands. Scarred hands were the sign of someone who spent a lot of time with a weapon in his fist, sparring, fighting. Guðvarr put his back into rowing, his eyes drifting back to Darl. A tight-packed cluster of buildings built upon the slopes of a hill and at the crown reared a wall that ringed a fortress. Huge, skeletal wings arched from the hall at the hill's peak, spreading wide over the buildings beneath them like protective hands. The first time Guðvarr had set eyes on Darl, and the skeleton of the dead god Orna rearing from it, he felt as if his breath would stop in his chest. Fear and awe had churned in his belly, squeezing out all else from his head.

As before, his first reaction now at seeing Darl and Orna's spread wings was a ripple of fear. But this time that spark of fear came from the thought of what Jarl Sigrún was going to do to him when he returned without Orka's head in a sack.

She does not like failure. What jarl does?

The river widened as they approached Darl, their two *snekkes* rowing almost side by side. Skalk stood in the prow of Guðvarr's *snekke*, Yrsa, his *drengr*, sitting behind him with their bound prisoner. Vol was staring at Skalk's back, malice leaking from her eyes.

Traffic was thickening upon the river as they approached the fortress, most of the many vessels being fat trading *knarrs*, though among them were a few *drakkars*, gliding like wolves prowling among sheep. Darl's dockside came into view, a snarl of hulls and masts and piers, and Skapti bellowed and cursed at other vessels from his place at the steering oar as he navigated a route to an empty pier. Figures hurried from the quayside as Skapti yelled for oars to be raised and the *snekke* coasted on dark waters, then bumped against the posts of the pier. A rope was thrown and caught, secured around a mooring post and then Skalk was standing and hefting the chest he had sat upon for their whole journey south, hoisting it on to his shoulder. He stepped over the top-rail and disembarked, began talking to the harbourmaster who had come to greet them as Yrsa dragged Vol to her feet and hauled her on to the pier. Guðvarr laid his oar down and clambered over the top-rail on to the wooden pier, pushing through those who stood between him and Skalk.

"Can I help you, my lord," he said to Skalk as the harbourmaster turned and left, sending one of his guards running ahead of them.

Skalk looked at Guðvarr, his eyes narrowing, focusing on Guðvarr's nose.

Guðvarr wiped it with the back of his hand, saw the glisten of snot as he took his hand away.

"Guthrum, isn't it?" Skalk said.

"Guðvarr, lord," Guðvarr said. "It was I who carried you from the Grimholt's hall to the *snekke*, when . . ." He trailed off, uncomfortable with the next words forming on his tongue. *When we ran for our lives.*

"Ah, yes."

"I found your *drengr* and told her of the danger," Guðvarr continued. *Told her we were all going to die unless we ran . . .*

Skalk regarded him for a few moments.

"You are not one of Helka's *drengrs*," he said. "Who are you?"

"Jarl Sigrún's nephew, my lord," Guðvarr said. "Sent after the woman and her companions. We did not know she was *Úlfhéðnar*."

"Well, Guðvarr, you have been of service," Skalk said. "I will not forget it."

"Thank you, my lord," Guðvarr said.

"And, yes, you can help. Carry this for me." Skalk gave Guðvarr the chest he was holding. "My shoulder is not yet recovered from that woman's axe."

Guðvarr took the chest, which was heavier than he had thought. With a grunt he hefted it on to his shoulder.

"Guard it well," Skalk said.

"With my life," Guðvarr said. *Never with my life*, he thought.

"Lose it and you will lose your life."

Guðvarr swallowed, abruptly wishing he had not offered his services. It was too late to back down now, though, so he just nodded. Besides, he had a feeling that Skalk might be his best path to avoiding the full brunt of his aunt's displeasure.

The second *snekke* ground against the pier.

Skalk stood waiting for everyone to disembark and then he was striding along the pier, Skapti gathering the survivors from the Grimholt about him and following after the Galdurman. Guðvarr hurried to keep close to Skalk, and Yrsa gave him a hard look when she saw the chest Guðvarr was carrying.

As Guðvarr stepped from the pier on to the dockside he heard shouting and saw another ship moored close by. A wide-bellied *knarr*, horses being led down a gangplank and on to the pier. Many horses, slim and tall, their manes knotted like warriors' beards, not at all like the stocky, big-boned workhorses he was used to seeing. And those leading them; men and women, all of them with dark, weathered skin and shaven-headed, apart from one long braid of thick-knotted hair. They were clothed in coats of small, iron plates stitched into leather, their breeches striped and baggy to the knee, wound tight from knee to ankle. Guðvarr remembered Queen Helka having such a man in her company, a Prince Jaromir from far-off Iskidan.

After the horses came a troop of warriors, and among them walked a man a head taller and half a man broader than the rest. His skin was darker than the others, almost crow-black, and his head was shaven with no braid, his neck thick as a bull's. He wore a thrall-collar. A woman walked beside him, cloaked and hooded, tattoos swirling up her hand and forearm, disappearing under the sleeve of her tunic.

A jab in the ribs and he jumped, Yrsa scowling at him.

"Keep up," she hissed, "or I shall find a new donkey for Lord Skalk."

Donkey! You're the donkey with a face like that, Guðvarr thought.

"Sorry," he said and hurried after Skalk and his followers.

Although the sky was bright it was late in the day, *sólstöður* stretching its hand throughout all Vigrið; a hint of darkness during the last two days lengthening as the Long Day drew towards its end. The streets of Darl were busy, heaving with traders shouting about their wares and sailors crowding into inns and brothels. They passed through the dockside streets into a wide, wood-paved road that spiralled up through the town towards the fortress at the hill's crown. The crowds thinned as they moved away from the river and docks, and then they were stepping into a market square that was remarkably quiet, all but empty. At its centre a wooden dais had been newly erected, thick posts jutting from it, like gallows. Seven black iron cages hung from the post, squeaking as they turned on chains. In each cage was a body. All of them were dead, in various stages of decomposition. Guðvarr saw a hand and forearm, what flesh was left upon it hanging in shredded tatters. Ravens squawked and fought as they feasted. A sign was nailed to the gallows post, black runes burned into it.

"*DREKA DÝRKENDUR*," Skalk said as they all paused before the squeaking cages. "Dragon-worshippers." He frowned, looking long and hard at the cages and the remains of their inhabitants.

Footsteps echoed from the far side of the market square and Guðvarr saw a procession of people striding towards them, close to a score, men and women, all wearing the same dark tunics as Skalk, pewter rings and animal skulls bound in their hair and beards.

A handful of warriors walked with them, all in bright *brynjas*, spears in their fists, eagle brooches pinning their cloaks.

"My lord," a woman said as she dipped her head to Skalk. Guðvarr saw a single blue tattoo on the back of each of her hands.

A Galdurwoman?

"Skapti," Skalk said. "You and your people will accompany Sturla." Skapti frowned, looking from Skalk to Sturla.

"Follow me," she said, but Skapti did not move.

"I should report to Queen Helka, and to Prince Hakon," he said.

"That is the last thing I want you to do," Skalk said. "I will do that."

"What are you doing?" Skapti said, frowning at Skalk. His hand slipped to the axe at his belt.

"I would not do that, if I were you," Sturla said, raising her tattooed hand. A flicker of fire rippled across her palm. The others with her, all Galdurmen and Galdurwomen, Guðvarr surmised, spread into a line behind her, and the warriors with them stepped around their flanks, spears levelled. Skapti froze, eyes taking them all in, shifting finally to Skalk. Some of the warriors from the Grimholt moved closer to Skapti, hands on weapons. Guðvarr saw big Hrolf among them, the tall man who had cursed Guðvarr for his poor rowing on the *snekke*.

Go on, draw your axe, Gangling Hrolf, he thought, *I would like to see what short work a Galdurman makes of you.*

"What are you doing?" Skapti directed at Skalk.

"I want Hakon to hear nothing of what happened at the Grimholt from anyone but me. And most of all, I do not want him to know that I have heard of his dealings with this Drekr. You are Hakon's man." Skalk shrugged, leaving the rest unsaid. "Show your wisdom, and no harm will come to you, on my word."

A long, tension-filled moment. Then Skapti sighed and nodded, his hand falling away from his weapons belt.

"Whatever you say, Lord Skalk," Skapti said.

"Wisdom can oft lead to a longer life," Skalk said with a smile. "Take them to the tower," he said to Sturla. Then he looked at Guðvarr.

Am I to be sent to the Galdur tower, too? I don't like the sound of that. He gulped.

Skalk's eyes shifted to Arild and the *drengrs* who had travelled with Guðvarr. "All will go with Sturla," Skalk said. "Except you, Guðvarr."

"Of course," Guðvarr said, just relieved that it wasn't him. "Go with them, Arild. All will be well," he said, giving her and his other companions his most reassuring smile. *Or perhaps it won't, but as long as I'm all right, truth be told I don't really care.*

Arild looked at him trustingly and nodded.

You should never trust anyone. Then the two groups were separating and leaving the market square by different streets, Guðvarr hurrying after Skalk, Yrsa and the Seiðr-witch.

Their path steepened and widened, the walls of Darl's fortress appearing above the rooftops before them, and then they were clear of buildings and approaching the gateway. A ditch had been dug around the hill's summit, steep-sided banks of earthwork ramparts built up, and at their top a palisaded wall ringed the fortress. One road led across the ditch to an open gateway, warriors standing in the open gate's shadows, all with Helka's eagle on their shields. They stood straighter as Skalk approached, bowing.

"Take me to the queen," Skalk said as he strode through the open gates. They passed through a torchlit tunnel that was carved through the earthwork rampart and strode into the fortress enclosure. Wooden planks formed a wide street, rows of buildings either side, each one as big as Jarl Sigrún's longhouse back at Fellur village. Soon a space opened up around a longhouse that dwarfed these other buildings, and out of its timbered rooftop rose the skeleton of an eagle. Wings arched high and wide, spreading up over the walls of the fortress. Rearing over the stepped entrance to the longhouse loomed the eagle's skull, its curved beak hooked, torches burning within the eye sockets. Looking up at those flaming eyes made Guðvarr's belly squirm, as if Orna the eagle-god was fixing him with her predatory stare.

More warriors stood at the top of a dozen steps, wide beams crossing over a doorway, eagle wings carved into them. Skalk was ushered inside and Guðvarr followed, their party passing through a corridor and stepping into a mead hall, long, rowed benches leading up to a dais where another bench sat crossways. The room was built within the curved bones of the eagle, ribs forming the arched supports, like the strake-ribs of a longship. Shaven-headed thralls were preparing for the evening meal as they lit fire pits and set skewered joints turning above the flames, laid baskets of fresh-baked bread and bowls of churned butter down upon the benches, others setting jugs of mead and ale alongside the food.

Guðvarr's belly rumbled at the smells wafting through the room and he looked longingly at the food, but Skalk led him on through the mead hall, up on to the dais and through a door at the hall's rear, into a corridor. Finally, he stopped as they reached a closed door.

A man and woman stood before it, both warriors, tall and lean-muscled, standing hunched like wolves with their hackles raised. The sides of their heads were shaved clean to reveal curling knot-works of tattoos, a thick strip of braided hair running from their foreheads across their crown and down their backs. Mail-coated with sharp steel at their belts, seax, sword, axe. Iron collars hung about their necks.

Úlfhéðnar, Guðvarr gulped. He had seen a handful of Queen Helka's *Úlfhéðnar* guard before and had even spent time and close company with one that she had gifted to his aunt, Jarl Sigrún. Vafri had been her name. But that was before he had seen what an *Úlfhéðnar* could do. Before he had seen the terrible slaughter Orka had committed at the Grimholt.

Are they all capable of becoming like her? Of wreaking such terrible, savage butchery? That thought made his belly constrict and his skin crawl.

One of the two *Úlfhéðnar* stepped closer to Skalk. The woman. She leaned close to him, took a deep, snorting sniff, a glimmer of amber flickering within her eyes.

"Lord Skalk," she said and stepped away, the other *Úlfhéðnar* opening the door and gesturing for Skalk to pass through. The Galdurman paused a moment, looking back at Guðvarr.

"Repeat one word of anything said in this room to anyone and I shall give you to them," he said, nodding at the two *Úlfhéðnar*. "And say nothing of the Grimholt, or of what happened there."

That will be my pleasure. I never want to think about what happened there again.

Guðvarr nodded, and then Skalk was striding through the open doorway, Guðvarr behind him, followed by Yrsa as she dragged the bound and gagged Seiðr-witch.

Guðvarr stepped into a large, richly furnished chamber. Oak tables with jugs and platters of food, fur-draped chairs and embroidered wool hangings. A hearth fire crackled, smoke filtering up to a smoke-hole in the shadowed eaves. Two great, skeletal feet hung suspended through the chamber's roof. Orna's claws, each one with curved talons long as a sword.

Torches burned on walls and shadows lay thick, like hanging drapes, because the room was windowless. Guðvarr spied shapes in those shadows, more *Úlfhéðnar* lurking, still and silent, Guðvarr feeling their eyes on him. Queen Helka sat in a high-backed chair, her black hair bound with gold wire, her face all sharp features and bright, intelligent eyes. She wore a red-wool dress, fine tablet weave at her collar, cuffs and hem, a belt with gold fittings about her waist, a small, scabbarded eating knife hanging across her lap, its hilt carved from walrus ivory.

A handful of people sat around her, thralls waiting on them. Guðvarr saw Prince Hakon, Helka's eldest son. Dark-haired, fine-boned and muscular. Where the queen wore gold, he wore silver. He was reclining in a chair with one leg draped over an arm. His expression shifted from boredom to alertness at the sight of Skalk and he sat a little straighter.

Others were seated in chairs around the queen. Guðvarr recognised most of them, Glunn Iron-Grip and Svard the Scratcher, both of them petty jarls who ruled swathes of land and had sworn their allegiances to Queen Helka, all clothed in fine wool tunics and breeches, rings of silver on their arms and glinting in the fittings on their belts. There was another man, different from the others. His skin weathered dark by the sun, his head shaved clean, apart from a long, thick braid of fair hair. He wore a green kaftan of wool and silk, and baggy breeches bound tight from knee to ankle with *winnigas* leg-wraps.

Jaromir, Guðvarr recalled, having met the man briefly when he had arrived in Darl with Jarl Sigrún on their search for Orka and the two brothers.

A prince of Iskidan, the queen's guest.

Last of all Guðvarr saw his aunt, Jarl Sigrún, sitting in a chair with a drinking horn in her hand. Guðvarr hid his grimace as he saw her, partly from his fear of this meeting, and partly because of her face. He had still not grown accustomed to her maiming. The scar had not healed well. His aunt had always been a hard-looking woman, but there had been a stark beauty to her. Now a red-raw scar cleaved her face, diagonally from forehead to chin, carving a chunk through the bridge of her nose and one side of her mouth. Guðvarr sucked in a deep breath and smiled at her, dipping his head. *Her face could look like boiled beeswax and I will still love her*, he told himself. She was the only person who had ever shown him a moment's kindness or respect that did not need to. And more importantly, she had put a sword in his hand and called him a *drengr*.

Sigrún blinked and smiled to see Guðvarr. The other jarls looked respectfully at Skalk, their gazes flickering to Guðvarr and the chest he carried, as well as the gagged and bound Vol.

"Welcome home, Galdurman," Queen Helka said, waving a hand, and thralls hurried to fill a drinking horn for Skalk. He took it and drank deep, the silence lengthening.

"Well," Queen Helka said. "What news from the north?"

Skalk opened the drawstring of a pouch at his belt and pulled something out, cast it on the rush-strewn ground. Two iron brooches, one fashioned in the head of a serpent, the other a tusked boar.

"It is as we feared, my queen," Skalk said. "Jarl Störr of Snakavik is behind the disappearance of your people along the northern border."

Some growls and grunts from the jarls.

"I will sound the horns and gather my *drengrs*," Glunn Iron-Grip growled as he stood, so violently that his chair fell over behind him.

Clumsy oaf, thought Guðvarr.

"I am grateful for your loyalty, Iron-Grip," Queen Helka said, "but no need to rush off to battle right now."

A thrall hurried to lift the fallen chair and with a glower and a grunt Jarl Glunn sat back down.

"Is there more?" Queen Helka asked.

"Aye, my queen," Skalk said. "The warriors I encountered were working in league with vaesen. Trolls and skraelings fought along-side them, like equals."

More gasps. Even Jarl Sigrún hissed a breath. Guðvarr found himself staring wide-eyed at Skalk. To work with vaesen was unheard of, an abomination. To use them like thralls, that was uncommon, but considered reasonable, if the foul creatures could be broken and tamed, but to treat them as *equals!*

"And what were Jarl Störr's forces doing on my land?" Helka asked.

"Searching," Skalk said. "For knowledge and power. And they have found it. We came upon them deep in the Boneback Mountains, digging. They have found Rotta's chamber."

"The rat god's lair," Jarl Svard snorted, scratching at his beard. "Just saga-tales, surely?"

"Aye, a saga-tale," Skalk said, brows bunching. He looked up at Orna's talons. "We live in a world surrounded by saga-tales."

"You saw it?" Jarl Glunn asked.

"Yes. I walked it, saw the altar that Rotta was bound to, saw the broken chains, and the altar burned with venom. But there is stronger evidence than that." Skalk looked at Guðvarr and the chest he held, and Guðvarr took a step forward.

"Where are the Bloodsworn?" a voice rasped, the accent strange to Guðvarr's ears. All eyes turned to Prince Jaromir, who stood up from his chair.

"I recognise their witch," Jaromir said, jutting his chin at Vol, "but where are the rest of them?"

"The Bloodsworn betrayed me, tried to steal what I discovered in Rotta's chamber," Skalk said with a snarl.

Vol grunted and tugged at her bonds, but Yrsa cuffed her hard across the head, knocking her to her knees.

"They wanted it for their own." Skalk shrugged. "I managed to escape their trap."

"And bring one of them with you," Queen Helka said, regarding Vol.

"She is Glornir's thrall, a Seiðr-witch of unusual ability," Skalk said. "She will be useful."

"This is not what was *promised*," Jaromir said, eyes flickering from Skalk to Queen Helka, his words clipped, halting. Guðvarr wasn't sure if it was because of his strange accent or because he was trembling with fury.

"As powerful as I am, I cannot predict the future," Queen Helka said calmly. "I hired the Bloodsworn to perform a task for me and told you that when they came to me for payment your concerns would be dealt with then. But if they are betrayers and murderers . . ." She shrugged.

"I will hunt them down for you, Mother," Prince Hakon said.

"No need, my prince, if this Seiðr-witch speaks the truth," Skalk said, smiling at Vol. "She has told me the Bloodsworn will be coming after me, because I have stolen their property." He looked from Vol to Prince Jaromir. "So, you may yet see the Bloodsworn."

"They would not be fool enough to come here now," Glunn Iron-Grip said. "To try and steal from Queen Helka's Galdurman, and then come to Darl. Only a fool would do that."

Not if you listen to the same fair-fame tales I've heard of the Bloodsworn, Guðvarr thought. He felt a worm of fear squirm in his belly at the thought of the famed Bloodsworn bursting through the door.

Am I choosing the right side, here? He looked to the shadowed forms of the *Úlfhéðnar* in the dark and felt reassured by their presence.

"I have to find them," Jaromir said. "If they are not coming here, then I will go in search of them."

"Let us see if they come to us," Queen Helka said. "If not, as they have chosen to become my enemy, I shall help you to hunt them down." She looked to Skalk. "And what was it that you discovered in Rotta's chamber?" she asked. "What is *so* valuable that the Bloodsworn would break their oath to me and risk becoming my enemy?" She looked at the chest that Guðvarr still held.

"Put it down," Skalk said, and Guðvarr set the chest down at the Galdurman's feet.

Skalk bent over and rested his hand upon the chest, pressing his palm hard against the lock.

"*þekki mig, læstu bringu og opnaðu*," Skalk murmured and the lock beneath his hands glowed red. There was a *click* and it snapped open. Skalk lifted the lid and reached inside. Guðvarr leaned, peering into the chest. He saw an assortment of rolled parchments, some tools forged of black iron and a scattering of large, grey-white bones, one long and curved, like a talon, another shorter, shaped like the blunt blade of an axe head. Skalk took hold of the biggest bone and lifted it out. Longer than a sword, slightly curved and tapering to a razored point. There was leather wrapped around the widest end, the leather sweat-stained, as if someone had used it as a grip. Skalk raised the bone as if it were a sword, for all to see. He ripped the leather away and strode forward.

The *Úlfhéðnar* in the room whined and growled.

"Is that . . .?" Hakon trailed off.

"The bone of a dead god," Skalk said. "Orna's missing talon."

Guðvarr shivered.

What have I got myself involved in? he thought, fear and excitement tremoring through him. *Dead gods, murderous* Úlfhéðnar, *a war between the most powerful jarls of Vigrið*

Skalk walked past Queen Helka and stood beneath the skeletal foot of Orna. He raised the talon high and slotted it into the knuckled cavity of bone above him.

"*Vera tengdur við líkama þinn, lengi fjarverandi beinbrot*," Skalk said. There was a red-white flash of flame, a hiss as of flesh being seared, and Skalk took his hands away, the talon remaining tight in the knuckle, fitting perfectly.

"After so many years of searching, Orna is at last complete," Helka said.

Skalk strode back to the box.

"What else did you find?" Prince Hakon said, peering excitedly into the chest. All in the room were trying to do the same, even Prince Jaromir, despite his obvious fury.

"Other bones, though they cannot be Orna's," Skalk said. "And copied manuscripts. These are not the originals," he said, reaching down to pull out a rolled parchment.

"Copies of what?" Helka asked.

"If I am not mistaken, of Rotta's famed rune-magic Galdrabok, the *Raudskinna*."

The Raudskinna . . .

All began talking at once, but Guðvarr just stared into the open chest at the rolled parchments and scattered bones. One word was swirling around his thought-cage, ringing loud like a struck bell and drowning out the babble of voices.

Opportunity.

CHAPTER SEVENTEEN

ELVAR

Elvar looked up at the sky. They had been marching without
pause for what felt like days, a leaden weariness in Elvar's
limbs, a burning behind her eyes.

Will we reach the Isbrún Bridge in time?

She was marching at the head of their party, the Battle-Grim
with their red shields slung across their backs. Grend strode close
to her, as always. They were threading their way out of the Dark
of Moon Hills on to the plain that led to the vaesen pit and the
Isbrún Bridge. To the west Mount Eldrafell glowed with its veins
of fire, and the Isbrún Bridge was almost within sight, but they
were moving far more slowly than they had on their journey to
Oskutreð, because now they had three wagons loaded with riches;
and also one wagon that was carrying a fevered wolf-god. Memories
of their journey going the other way, towards Oskutreð, insisted
on flitting through her head. Most of them were of Biórr, of his
dark eyes, the twist of his smile, of her fingertips tracing the scars
on his chest.

The niðing betrayer, she snarled in her head. *I trusted him, gave
myself to him . . .*

Elvar slowed her pace, dropping back from the head of their
column until she was walking alongside the wagon that held Ulfrir.
Uspa sat on the driver's bench, reins in her hands.

"How is your patient?" Elvar asked her.

"Healing," Uspa said. "Slowly."

Elvar looked into the wagon bed and saw Skuld sitting with her father. Her rust-red wings were furled tight across her back, looking like a great cloak of feathers. Ulfrir lay at her feet, wrapped in his wolf-pelt cloak, his new iron collar glinting about his neck. He was no longer shivering, which Elvar took to be a good sign, though his face was gaunt and pale, eyes sunken hollows, his grey-black beard a tangled snarl. Skuld and Uspa had dragged his rent coat of mail from his body and bathed his many wounds, cleaned them, smeared them with honey and bound them with linen lined with sage leaves. Even weak to the point of death, looking at Ulfrir gave Elvar a chill. A sense of power and malice leaked from him like an odour. As Elvar stared at him his eyes opened and he shifted, trying to rise on to his elbows.

"Careful, Father," Skuld said, wrapping her arms around him and helping him sit with his back to the wagon's side. She unstoppered a flask and held it to his lips, let him drink some water.

"Ah, my Skuld," Ulfrir breathed, voice a rasping growl. He patted her hand. "Orna dead, Verdani and Urd, too. Is this some terrible dream?"

"I wish it were," Skuld said.

"Ach, how have we come to this?"

"The blame of it all lies at Lik-Rifa's feet," Skuld hissed. "And great Snaka."

"My terrible father," Ulfrir said, shaking his head. "And Lik-Rifa, my demented sister." His lips curled, revealing the tips of sharp teeth. He looked around, saw Elvar and Grend walking beside the wagon.

"And who are you?" Ulfrir muttered, "that dares to look so boldly at a god?"

"She is our new master," Skuld said, glowering at Elvar.

Ulfrir blinked at that. Tried to sit straighter.

"I will show her who the master is," he growled, lips pulling back in a snarl that made Elvar want to leap away. She ignored the impulse, keeping her face calm.

"Do not, Father," Skuld said. "Or you will feel pain that even you cannot bear." She took his hand and placed it on the collar about his neck. "A rune-cast collar. You must obey her, or there will be a fire in your flesh."

Ulfrir felt the collar, pride and disbelief flickering across his face.

"I will treat you well, as long as you give me no cause to do other," Elvar said, forcing herself to return Ulfrir's hard gaze.

"I am a *god*," he said.

"Nevertheless," Elvar shrugged. "You are the one wearing a runed thrall-collar."

A silence, then Ulfrir looked away, barked out a stuttered laugh.

"The world is upside down," he said. "The strong made weak, the weak made strong." He looked back at Elvar, the amber of his eyes glinting in the shadows of his face. "But the tides ebb and flow, and then . . ." he did not need to finish his sentence, a swarm of unpleasant images flooding through Elvar's thought-cage, all involving sharp teeth and claws, and her being ripped to pieces.

"Do not threaten her," Grend grated, and Ulfrir turned his amber eyes upon the old warrior.

"You should not speak so to a god."

"I don't give a weasel's shite who or what you are," Grend said. "You were a pile of bones when we found you, and now you have breath in your lungs because of Elvar. You should be thanking her."

Elvar looked at Grend.

That is the most I have ever heard him say in one go.

"I *would* thank you for that, if I were free to do so, but a wolf is not meant to be chained," Ulfrir snarled. "And the lamb is not made to rule the wolf."

"Elvar is no lamb," Grend growled.

"We have common cause," Elvar said, jumping in before Grend ended up in a *holmganga* duel with a wolf-god. "Your sister, Lik-Rifa. I need to kill her."

A long silence as Ulfrir gazed at her from the dark pools of his eyes. Then he nodded.

"Perhaps we do have common ground," he acknowledged, then let out a wracking cough.

Uspa dragged on the reins, the wagon shuddering to a halt.

"What is it?" Elvar said, a hand resting on her sword hilt as she looked ahead, down the column.

The Battle-Grim were slowing, a crowd forming at the column's head, standing still, talking.

"What's happening?" Elvar said, striding along the column. Huld stepped out of the crowd.

"We're stopping for a rest," Huld said, her jet hair lank with sweat. "Been walking for four days, maybe more, who can tell in this gods-cursed land. We need to eat and sleep."

"We can eat as we walk," Elvar said. "There's no time to rest."

"Have I been sleepwalking, and woken to find the Battle-Grim have made you chief?" Huld said, jutting her chin out.

Elvar blinked at that. Normally, when a chief died others would put their names forward, and if more than one wanted the chief's job, then it would be decided by a *holmganga*. But things had happened so fast, changed so fast, that the idea of who would become the new chief of the Battle-Grim had not even entered Elvar's thought-cage.

"No," Elvar said. "But . . . we don't have time to stop."

"You may be a jarl's daughter, but that does not give you the right to go lording it with us," Huld said. One hand rested on the hilt of her sword, the other reaching up to the bear claw that hung around her neck.

"I . . ." Elvar said, but she found there were no words in her throat, just a fog in her head, and a building anger.

"Orv, you tired?" Huld said.

"Can't feel my toes, and it feels like my eyes are slithering down my face," he said.

"Sighvat, are you hungry?" Huld asked.

"Always," Sighvat mumbled.

"Then I say it's about time we stopped, ate something, slept a little, and then had a chat about who's going to take Agnar's place as the new chief of the Battle-Grim," Huld said. "We might all be in on this dragon-slaying job, but we still need a chief, and I for one think I could do better than a jarl's spoilt daughter."

Elvar's hand reached for her sword hilt, a moment later a fist wrapping around her wrist. She glared at Grend, who stood as solid and strong as a cliff.

"Tiredness is the father of mistakes," he breathed.

The creak of wheels as Uspa cracked her reins and drove her wagon up to them, warriors stepping out of her way.

"We need to move," Uspa said. "If you stop and camp here, you risk the Isbrún Bridge closing, and then we will be stuck here for half a year, until *langdagur*, the Long Night."

Huld glared at Uspa.

"I'm not in the business of being told what to do by a Tainted thrall," Huld said.

Elvar frowned at that. She had stopped thinking of Uspa as a thrall, even if she was their prisoner.

"I am no thrall," Uspa growled. "And whatever I am does not change the fact that the passage across the bridge will close soon. If you are still keen to chop someone up for the right to be chief of this crew, then why not do it the other side of the bridge?"

"Don't like the sound of being stuck this side of the pit," Sighvat said, looking up at the darkening sky. The *guðljós* whirled in brilliant hues, becoming brighter as the daylight faded.

"Me neither," Orv muttered.

"Uthpa ith speaking thenth," Sólín lisped.

Huld kicked the ground, then nodded.

Grend let go of Elvar's wrist, and she yanked it away.

"How can she think to be master of a god, when even her own kind do not obey her," Ulfrir rasped, many heads turning to look at him.

"I can't see it," Sighvat said. He was standing at the edge of the vaesen pit, heat rising and tugging at his thick rope-knot of a beard. "Are we too late?"

Elvar felt panic welling in her gut as she stood beside him. They were at the right place; she was stood beside a black granite rock, the same as the one she could see on the far side of the pit, that Uspa had said her Seiðr-magic say over to open the bridge, and on the plain beyond she could make out the rise of the hill where they had fought the tennúr swarm. But before her was only empty air and, far below, the hiss and crackle of molten rock, here and there an exploding burst of fire, like when fat dripped into a hearth fire.

I could not see the bridge before, though. It was not until Uspa stepped out into the abyss that the bridge was revealed.

She sucked in a deep breath and stepped out into thin air.

Her foot passed through the space where she expected, hoped, to meet resistance, and then she was teetering and falling, a sense of weightlessness as her arms windmilled. She sucked in a lungful of air to scream. A jolt and jerk about her neck and then she was hanging, suspended, feet dangling over a river of fire. She craned her neck, looked up and saw Grend looming over her with a fistful of her *brynja*, stretching over the land's edge, Sighvat gripping Grend's wrist. With a growl he heaved her up and dumped her down on solid ground.

"Idiot," he muttered.

She sat there, beginning to tremble, as Uspa climbed out of her wagon and strode over.

"What has happened to the bridge?" Uspa said.

"It's not there," Elvar hissed, feeling foolish and shaken.

"That cannot be," Uspa said, looking up at the sky. "*Sólstöður* is not yet over."

"Well, there's no bridge," Elvar muttered, still trembling from the realisation that she had willingly stepped into space over a river of molten fire.

Uspa lifted her leg and searched with her foot, only finding air. She frowned, then walked to the black rock and took a small eating knife from her belt. Pricking blood on her palm she pressed it to the rock.

"*Isbrú, opinberaðu þig, blóð guðanna skipar þér,*" Uspa said. Elvar saw Uspa's blood trickle in a line down the rock face. As before on the other side, a tremor passed through the boulder and the imprint of a huge pawprint appeared. But still the Isbrún Bridge did not appear.

Uspa stood there, staring, and Elvar felt panic fluttering in her belly.

We are stuck here.

"What are we going to do?" Sighvat said as the rest of the Battle-Grim spread along the line of the vaesen pit.

Murmured voices, all containing varying degrees of panic.

"I smell my sister's handiwork," a voice said, Ulfrir, struggling with Skuld's help to stand in the back of Uspa's cart. Uspa ran to him, calling to Sighvat, and they helped Ulfrir climb from the wagon. He stood there, swaying, looking like he would collapse at any moment, then he took some stumbling steps towards the black rock and sagged upon it, Skuld holding one arm, Sighvat the other. Ulfrir managed to stand straight and Elvar saw he was a head taller than even Sighvat.

"Cut me," he said, holding out one hand to the Battle-Grim.

Everyone looked at him, no one appearing to be particularly happy about drawing the blood of a god. Elvar clambered to her feet and drew her seax as she walked unsteadily to him. A small cut on his palm and she cleaned her blade on her breeches, then sheathed it.

Ulfrir looked at her, then pressed his bloodied palm against the rock.

Nothing happened.

"*Dreki, ég brýt innsigli þitt. Og þegar ég finn þig, skal ég rífa úr þér hálsinn,*" Ulfrir called out, more growl than words. The hiss of steam and great clouds of mist boiled on either side of the chasm, pouring out from each black rock. The two clouds bubbled and hissed, expanding, Elvar thinking she saw the likeness of a great wolf on her side of the pit, and a winged dragon on the other. Both images expanded, hissing and seething across the chasm of the vaesen pit, and then they slammed together. There was a concussive impact as wolf and dragon met in the centre of the abyss, a pressure building in Elvar's ears, though there was little sound. It was more like the echo of something distant, the dragon beating its mist-like wings, head arching on its sinuous neck, the wolf crouching, hackles raised, snarling. And then the wolf was bunching its legs, leaping, jaws clamping about the dragon's throat. With a savage wrench of its neck the wolf ripped the mist-dragon apart, its winged body evaporating into the air. The mist-wolf lifted its head and howled, and then it, too, was dissipating on the breeze. A ripple in the air and Elvar saw the Isbrún Bridge appear, lights flickering within its icy heart.

Ulfrir sagged against the rock.

"My sister knows I live," he breathed. He looked at Skuld.

"Good," Skuld said. "Let her know, and fear."

Not if she could see Ulfrir now.

Uspa hurried forward to take Ulfrir's arm and between them they guided him back to the cart.

"Quickly, across the bridge," Grend said. "Before it fades again."

He did not need to tell them twice. All the Battle-Grim crossed the bridge at a fast march, Elvar choosing not to look down as she strode across, ice crunching beneath her feet. She breathed a sigh of relief when the ground changed beneath her shoes and she stepped out on to the grassy plain. She walked on a few score paces, then turned to watch the rest of the Battle-Grim cross, the four carts bringing up the rear. They all spilled on to the plain.

"Make camp," Huld proclaimed, and Elvar glowered at her, still feeling the sting of Huld's words.

Spoilt jarl's daughter. With an effort she kept the snarl from her face.

"Not yet," Elvar said, "unless you want a swarm of tennúr picking at your teeth." She nodded at the hill where they had been attacked.

"No, I do not," Sólín said with passion.

The rotting remnants of a cart still lay on the plain, torn shreds of leather reins the only evidence that a pony had fallen with the cart.

Huld grudgingly nodded, and the Battle-Grim walked wearily on, skirting the hill.

Elvar was looking at Huld, feeling her anger bubbling within her, knew that her exhaustion was feeding it, like kindling to a fire, but she felt her fist hovering over her sword hilt.

Do I even want to be chief of the Battle-Grim? she asked herself. *I don't know* was the honest answer. But she did want to see Huld beaten and on her knees for her insult. Or dead.

I lived too long with the insults of my brother Thorun in my ears, and his beatings in the weapons court. I made a vow when I left Snakavik that my days of letting an insult go unanswered were done.

Elvar became aware of a change around her, blinked and looked around.

She swayed, thought it was from weariness, then she felt the ground tremble. A moment of confusion before she realised what it was.

"Oh no," she breathed. They were passing the hill, and as she looked at it she saw movement on the slope, soil shifting, a small figure clawing its way from beneath the ground, dirt spraying as wings snapped open. More tennúr were burrowing out of the hill and breaking into flight, and within moments the entire hill was a seething mass of movement, loose soil sliding, small, winged figures bursting from the ground like wasps from a kicked nest. They swooped above the hill, coming together like a thundercloud, and then they were surging towards the Battle-Grim.

"'WARE THE SKIES," Elvar shouted, unbuckling her helm from her belt and dragging it over her head. "SHIELD WALL."

A moment's horrified stillness as they all stared at the swarm of tennúr in the sky, and then the Battle-Grim were bursting into motion. Elvar fumbled her shield from her back, feeling muscles twinge and pull in her wounded shoulder, and then she was skidding among the Battle-Grim, shoulders jostling as they formed a shield wall, three rows deep. She drew her sword as Grend shoved his way to stand beside her.

"SHIELDS," he bellowed, and their shields came up, slamming together with a *crack* as the Battle-Grim shuffled close. A stab of pain in Elvar's shoulder but she ground her teeth and tried to ignore it. Fear was helping her do that, the whirring of the tennúr wings growing in volume, filling Elvar's senses and reminding her of the last time, fractured images of fighting through the storm of tooth and claw, of Grend lying unconscious at her feet. The tennúr were close enough now for her to pick out their sharp-taloned fingers and gnashing teeth in their too-large mouths. She was aware of Grend on her left side, knew that he was pushing close, trying to take some of the weight of her shield from her shoulder, and Huld was standing on her other side, all thought of *holmgangas* gone as they faced the vaesen swarm. Behind her she heard Sighvat bellow a wordless challenge. An arrow hissed over her head, Orv at the rear of the wall, loosing into the boiling cloud of wings and talons and teeth. A shriek and a skewered tennúr crashed to the ground, rolling and flopping.

They were almost upon them and Elvar pushed her shoulder into her shield, bracing for the impact she knew was coming.

And then the tennúr were flying overhead, passing above them in a hissing blur of wings. Elvar looked up, confused, as the entire swarm of tennúr sped above them, for a few heartbeats blotting out the light. She turned to follow their course, other Battle-Grim shuffling and moving. Behind them the tennúr spiralled up, high into the sky, coming tighter together and then with a terrible shrieking they were speeding back to the ground, crashing into one of the wagons at the rear of the Battle-Grim's column. Elvar glimpsed rust-red wings, heard a high-pitched screaming, below it a deeper growling.

"Ulfrir," she said. "They are going for Ulfrir."

She pushed and shoved her way through the Battle-Grim, began running towards the besieged wagon. The drum of feet behind her, Grend following, others realising what was happening and joining them.

The tennúr flew in a screeching swarm of claws and teeth around the wagon, hundreds of them. There was an ear-splitting howl, and then the tennúr were exploding outwards, spinning through the air, hurled in all directions. Ulfrir stood in wolf form, hunched and snarling. Blood dotted his fur coat in a hundred spots, and a winged figure lay prone between his paws. Many of the tennúr hit the ground and did not rise, but far more of them swirled, regaining their balance and surging back in, shrieking and clawing, whirring about the great wolf like a swarm of flies. Ulfrir snarled, his jaws snapping and biting, claws swiping, and tennúr fell in eviscerated globs of meat and bone. Skuld rose into the air, her wings beating, lashing out with her fists, tennúr seething around her.

Elvar shouted a wordless cry as she ran.

Ulfrir cannot die, we need him.

Uspa appeared from behind a cart, her mouth moving, uttering words that Elvar could not hear and a shield of flaming runes appeared in the air before the Seiðr-witch. It spun, rolling towards the tennúr, spitting flames, carving a burning swathe through the bunched tennúr. Shrieks of agony and tennúr dropped, wings and bodies charred. Elvar stabbed her sword down into one, trampled another, and then she was beneath them, shield raised, stabbing and hacking. She glanced up to see the tennúr swarming around Ulfrir, dozens of them clinging to one of his long fangs, screeching in a frenzy as they tried to rip the huge tooth from his jaw. The great wolf snarled and roared, the crunch of his jaws biting, tiny bones cracking, another swipe of his raking claws and more body parts spattered the ground. And then the remaining tennúr were wheeling away, only a handful of them left, wailing as they flew.

Ulfrir stood there, pieces of tennúr stuck between his teeth, blood dripping and streaming from a hundred tiny wounds. Skuld lay on the ground. Her wings twitched and she pushed herself up on to one knee. Ulfrir raised his head to the sky and howled as the Battle-Grim picked their way among tennúr dead.

"Looks like that's the last we'll see of them," Sighvat said, watching the handful of surviving tennúr disappear into the distance as he stepped over piles of the dead vaesen.

"Good," Sólín said, kicking a tennúr's corpse. "I hate thoth nathty little bathterds."

CHAPTER EIGHTEEN

ORKA

Orka woke to the sound of Edel scraping out the fire pit. It was raining, drops dripping from pine branches above them. The one-eyed huntress glanced at Orka.

"You spent a long time in Rotta's chamber last night. Did you find what you need?"

"My son was kept down there," Orka ground the words out through tight lips as she rolled on to her side and pushed herself up, rubbed at her eyes. She pulled her cloak about her, a barrier to keep the rain from her mail coat. "But I found no clue how to find him." There was a knot in her chest, a tightness in her shoulders, despair threatening to overwhelm her. The need to do violence shivered in her blood. "I will look again this morning," she said slowly, trying to calm the tremor in her veins, "and if there is nothing down there that will help me then I shall scour the land for tracks and keep searching until I find something."

Edel nodded, saying nothing. They both knew that could be a long and fruitless task, but Orka did not know what else to do.

"We'll leave you, soon," Edel said. "Glornir wants the *Sea-Wolf* in Darl, so there is no delaying for me." She took a step towards Orka and squatted, old knees clicking, and just stared at Orka a long moment.

"Been a shock, seeing you walking and talking when I thought all these years that you were food for fish," Edel eventually said.

"But . . ." she paused, silent again. Then she stood, sniffed and spat. "I could get used to having you around again. Hope you find your son. And put something sharp in the heart of whoever ended Thorkel. Always had a soft spot for him."

Others in the camp were stirring, and Ingmar Ice emerged from the shadows, returning from his shift on guard duty.

"Start a fire," Edel said to him, "and I'll fetch us some salmon."

Ingmar grinned at the mention of food. He was a thick-muscled, flat-faced warrior, hair so fair it was almost white, his eyes blue as a mountain stream. He had been with the Bloodsworn many years, Orka knowing him from when she had been their chief and remembered he was always happiest with a bowl or trencher of food in his hand. He was bynamed Ice because of the coldness that came upon him in battle. No *Berserkir* rage for Ingmar, even though Berser the bear flowed in his veins. His was an ice-cold fury, and it was terrifying to his enemies.

Orka climbed to her feet and stretched, bones clicking, aching joints complaining. She lifted her rolled-up weapons belt that she'd used as a pillow and buckled it about her waist, taking some of the weight of her ring-coat from her shoulders. She shrugged off the pain of her aching joints and strode to Lif, who lay curled beneath his cloak.

"Up," she said, nudging Lif with her toe. He mumbled something and tried to roll over, so she nudged him harder, reached down and dragged his cloak away.

"Up," she said. "You're not going to learn weapons craft in your dreams."

Lif blinked, scrubbed the sleep from his eyes and sat up, reached for his spear and hauled himself to his feet.

"What, now?" he mumbled.

"Yes, now," Orka snapped. "Do you think your enemies will wait until you are up, fed and washed before they attack you. Be ready to fight in a heartbeat. So, defend yourself." She drew one of her seaxes and slashed at his belly. Lif stumbled away, clumsily deflecting the seax with the shaft of his spear. Orka followed after him, feinted left and sliced right, her seax grating against the rings of Lif's mail coat and he brought his spear round to strike at her head. She ducked and slammed into him with her shoulder, sent him tumbling to the ground, swept his flailing spear away and put her boot on his neck.

Gunnar Prow laughed. "Orka Skullsplitter is ready to fight from the moment she opens her eyes."

Edel rolled her one eye at Gunnar's praise. "You should learn how to use a shield," she commented to Lif, who was still pinned beneath Orka's boot. "Only fools searching for a quick death fight without a shield."

"*I* fight without a shield," Orka said, glowering at Edel.

"I know," Edel said, gave Orka her one-eyed stare and smiled. A few grunts around the Bloodsworn, a few ripples of laughter. Some shocked stares.

"The Skullsplitter does not need a shield," Revna said.

"Ha," Edel barked a laugh, "see how fair-fame can make a warrior invincible. It should be weapons craft and the battle-fray that does that."

"I am not invincible," Orka said, "but I am still alive, and though I do not seek out battle, that does not mean that battle does not still find me."

Edel dipped her head, acknowledging Orka's words like she would a good hit in sparring.

Lif grunted, still on the ground. Orka took her boot from his throat and offered her hand, heaving him back to his feet.

"Practise your weapons craft on me," Gunnar said, fetching his spear.

Lif looked nervous, glancing at Orka.

"Be careful of his big nose," Ingmar Ice said, "he is more likely to stab you with that than with a spear."

Laughter at that, Gunnar included.

"Fight him," Orka said. "Every warrior has their own style; it will be a good lesson for you."

"Your fair-fame will spread through the land," Revna said, "taught weapons craft by the Skullsplitter and Gunnar Prow of the Bloodsworn."

"Fair-fame is not always a good friend," Edel muttered, stirring the fire with a stick.

"I don't want fair-fame," Lif said. "I just want to put Guðvarr Snot-Nose in the ground."

"The man who slew your brother?" Gunnar asked him.

"Aye," Lif nodded. "While my brother was shackled to a wall."

Growls at that, warriors muttering about the dishonour of slaying a bound, unarmed man.

"Niðing," Edel grunted as she spat on the fire.

"He is," Lif agreed. He looked at Halja Flat-Nose, sitting silently in the shadows, sharpening her sword with a whetstone.

"You have lost kin?" he asked her. "I saw you at the barrow."

Halja looked up at him. "My brother," she said.

"Losing a loved one, it is a wound like no other," Lif said.

Halja did not answer Lif, but Orka saw her look at the young man as if seeing him for the first time.

"Come on, then," Gunnar Prow said, "let's see how you like fighting me and my big nose."

"Safer than fighting the Skullsplitter, most likely," Revna Hare-Legs said, to further laughter among the other Bloodsworn.

"Of that there's no doubt," Gunnar said. He set his feet and raised his spear at Lif. "I shall be a fool and fight you without a shield." He winked at Edel.

Lif lunged in, a straight stab at Gunnar's belly while he was still looking at Edel, which Orka approved of, but Gunnar moved fast as an eel, slipping to the right, letting Lif's spear hiss harmlessly past him. He wrapped a fist around the shaft and tugged, pulling Lif towards him, his own spear darting out to touch Lif's chest.

"Well, that was quick," Ingmar Ice commented.

"Something Gunnar is well acquainted with," Revna said wryly, to some raucous laughter and leg-slapping.

"If you had a shield, you could have blocked that," Edel said to Lif.

"Enough about the shields," Orka said, throwing her hands up. "It is clear there is only one way to make this old woman stop squawking like a crow. Lif, there are shields to be had in the glade. Go and fetch one and I shall teach you how to use it."

"The sensible thing to do," Edel sniffed.

Lif nodded and hurried away, a grin on his face.

"Well, all this excitement is too much for my old heart," Edel said. "I'm off to pull some fish from the lake for our breakfast."

"Spert slept there. Give him a poke and let him know his porridge is in a pot?" Orka asked her. Edel nodded, gave a whispered word to her two hounds, which were curled around the dead fire, and then the three of them were loping off into the woods.

A crunching sound up above and Orka looked up to see Vesli sitting on a branch, her pouch on her lap as she reached in and pulled out a tooth, popped it into her mouth and ground her jaws. Ingmar swore as he scraped sparks into kindling, the drip of rain hissing. The rest of the Bloodsworn set about packing up their kit.

Footsteps and Lif was back, red-cheeked from the cold, carrying a round shield with an iron boss. Orka took it from him and inspected it, saw it was crafted from planks of linden wood, a linen covering and leather-hide edge. The front was painted a colourless grey, like those dark moments just before dawn, with no emblem upon it. There were a few scrapes upon it, a dent in the iron boss and a slice taken out of the leather edge.

"Good enough," Orka grunted an approval.

Ingmar had the fire crackling, a pot of oats in water hanging over it and a flat stone warming ready for the salmon.

"Come on, Edel, I'm hungry," he said, slapping his hands together.

"Grip your shield like this," Orka said to Lif, finding a space away from the fire. Gunnar Prow, Revna Hare-Legs and the other Bloodsworn all stopped packing their kit away to watch. Orka slipped her fist around the wooden grip behind the protection of the iron boss. "Hold it away from your body, so that you will not be skewered by any weapon that pierces the shield. Cover your body like so," she said, hefting the shield so that it covered her from thighs to neck. "And once in a fight, never hide your face behind it so that you lose sight of your enemy."

"Unless arrows are coming at you," Ingmar put in, helpfully.

"Yes, of course," Orka frowned.

"Or a hurled spear," Gunnar Prow added.

Orka glowered at him.

"Keep your shield slung across your back unless you need it," Orka said, "shields are heavy and will drain the arm of strength more than a sword, spear or axe. Once you have it in your fist, let it hang until you need it, or better still rest it on the ground."

"Your arm and shoulder will thank you later," Ingmar said from the fire.

"And remember," Orka continued, "a shield is a weapon as well as a defensive tool. The rim can crush a windpipe or smash teeth out."

Vesli made an approving sound from the branches above them.

"And the boss will crack bones, break a jaw or crush a skull. So," Orka said, "come and kill me."

"Shouldn't I be the one with the shield?" Lif said nervously.

"First I will show you something of what can be done with a shield," Orka said.

Lif looked at her, frowned.

"You don't have a weapon."

"I just told you, a shield is a weapon," Orka said and strode at him, tired of waiting.

Lif raised his spear and jabbed it at her face. Orka twitched her wrist and swatted the blade away, made a quick step inside Lif's guard, but he shuffled back, keeping the spear blade levelled at her.

Good, she thought.

Lif rotated his wrist, changing grip and stabbed up at her, angled beneath the shield rim and aiming for the vein in her thigh that would give a quick kill. Orka slammed the shield rim down, knocking the spear into the soft ground, took a few quick steps forward and twisted her wrist, punched the upper rim into Lif's gut, doubling him over, then touched the boss to his temple, at the same time hooking her foot behind Lif's ankle and pushing him over. He crashed to the ground with a grunt.

"Oh ho, and Lif's dead," Ingmar cried, laughing and clapping his huge hands together.

"Three uses of the shield there," Orka said, "blocking a spear-thrust, using the rim for a counter-strike and the boss to end it."

"I was too busy feeling pain and falling to see what you did," Lif wheezed as he climbed back to his feet. Revna laughed so hard she had to steady herself against a tree.

"Huh," Orka snorted. "Perhaps you should just watch, then. Ingmar," she called. "Come and kill me."

Ingmar blinked, then shrugged and stood. He drew his sword and went to wrap his cloak around it.

"No need for that," Orka said.

Some of the Bloodsworn chuckled.

Ingmar grinned, fetched his own shield from his pile of kit, hefted it and strode at Orka, shield held ready, sword held high behind it. He was tall and wide, though not as tall as Orka, thickset with long arms. Orka remembered training him when he first came to the Bloodsworn. He was strong and fast even then, and Orka had been fifteen years younger. As he drew within range of Orka he stepped to the right, sword darting out, stabbing at her face, but Orka stepped away, the sword hissing past her, and Ingmar dipped his head. Hoots and heyas echoed around the Bloodsworn as they formed a loose ring, enjoying the spectacle.

Ingmar continued moving right, trying to circle Orka, instinctively keeping away from her right side, even though she was holding no weapon in her fist. Orka took a few shuffling steps back, then pushed left, closing the gap between them and Ingmar's sword stabbed out, punched into the rim of Orka's shield, pushing it back, and behind it he slammed his shield into hers, but Orka was already moving, twisting her shield wrist to guide Ingmar's sword high and away, stepping inside his guard, taking the force of his shield-blow as it crunched against hers, then she was stepping right, around the edge of his shield and she swung a hook with her right fist, hidden until the last moment by her own shield. It caught Ingmar flush on the jaw. He tottered back a few steps, then dropped on to his backside.

A silence, then the ring of Bloodsworn exploded in laughter, slapping their legs, leaning over for breath.

Orka stood over Ingmar, who sat on the ground looking up at her.

"What was the first lesson I taught you?" she said to him.

"The blow not seen is the one that ends the fight," he said, then gave her a rueful grin, rubbing his jaw. "I should have remembered that."

She offered him her arm and pulled him back to his feet.

"Again, again," some of the Bloodsworn called out, laughter still echoing through the trees.

Vesli appeared in a blur of wings, flying among them.

"*Riders are coming, riders are coming,*" she cried out.

They all froze, heads cocked, listening. Sure enough, Orka heard the drum of hooves, approaching from the west. The Bloodsworn shifted as if at an unseen command, all moving to their kit, lifting shields, checking weapons. Some buckled on helmets. Ingmar strode to the fire and kicked dirt over it, putting the flames out with a guttering hiss.

Orka gave Lif his shield and strode to her long-axe where it lay next to the spot she had slept and swept it up.

"Buckle on your helm," Orka said to Lif, nodding at the leather cap hanging at his belt. Then she strode down the hill through the trees, towards Rotta's chamber, stopping in the shadows of the last trees.

The sound of horses' hooves grew louder, a rhythmic rumble, coming up the track from the west. A branch creaked overhead as Vesli landed upon it, and she heard Lif approach behind her. The Bloodsworn moved through the gloom like shadows, all with black, blood-spattered shields in their fists.

Riders spilled from the track into the glade, the ground soft with rain, mud spraying. Each rider led a spare horse tied to their saddles.

They have been intent on travelling fast.

The rider leading them was a woman, black-haired, a raven's feather braided into it with silver wire. She had pale, sharp features, her eyes dark pools, and she was smiling. A sword hung at her hip, her belt buckled about an oil-dark *brynja*, a seax hanging across her lap. An iron helm bounced at her belt. Orka saw the bulk of another seax protruding from her boot. The rim of a shield was visible, hanging on a saddle hook on the horse's far flank. More than a dozen riders followed the woman into the glade, men and women, all grim looking, all in mail, sharp iron hanging from their belts, sealskin cloaks to protect their *brynjas*, many with spears in their fists.

Orka glimpsed a shield, saw it was painted grey with black wings spread upon it.

A hissed breath from behind her, Halja Flat-Nose.

"Raven-Feeders," Halja breathed, though Orka already knew. She had seen their raven-winged shields before, seen their warriors with feathers bound in their hair, heard the fair-fame tales of Ilska the Cruel and her band of hard warriors.

Orka took the leather cover from the blade of her long-axe and let it drop to the ground.

The woman leading the riders opened her mouth to call out, but as she did so her eyes came to rest upon the pile of corpses. She dragged on her reins, her horse skidding to a halt, and she sat in her saddle and stared, eyes fixing on the limbs of the dead troll that protruded from the heaped dead. Her smile withered. Then she was dismounting and running, straight to the mound of corpses. She dropped to her knees before one of the corpses, threw her head back and screamed.

Orka knew that sound. The echo of it still rang through her soul, every time she thought of Thorkel. Grief and rage mingled.

The other warriors were dismounting, running to stare at the mound of the dead. Some spread around the glade, two striding towards the dark entrance of Rotta's chamber, disappearing quickly into the gloom. Orka saw the flicker of torches kindled, orange glow receding into the darkness.

The woman on her knees stood, turned, her cheeks bright with tears, a snarl of fury twisting her face. She stepped away from the pile of the dead, looking around the empty glade.

Orka took a step but a big fist wrapped around her wrist and she looked to see Ingmar holding her.

"What are you doing?" he breathed at her.

"I'm going to ask her where they took my son," Orka snarled, holding Ingmar's gaze. After a moment he released his grip on her arm. "Stay here, this is not your fight," Orka said to him, and then she stepped out from the treeline into the glade.

CHAPTER NINETEEN

VARG

Varg jogged out of the wooded hills, open grassland before him, a bridge up ahead. It crossed a deep-sided ravine and he heard the hiss and roar of a river far below, one of the many tributaries to the River Drammur. He took a moment to slow his breathing, closed his eyes, focusing on the wolf in his blood as Røkia had been teaching him, then listened. Sounds came, sharp and clear. The patter of rain on leaves, birdsong, the raucous cry of crows. The rustle of wind blowing through grass. Steps to his right and his head snapped round. He saw Røkia emerge from the treeline, fifty or sixty paces away, a spear in her fist. He nodded to her, and then they were both stepping out on to the plain, moving slowly, warily.

The bridge loomed closer, Varg seeing it had been newly repaired, fresh timber posts and planks, on some of the older timber the black scars of old flames. Water foamed white far below. On the far side of the bridge a track led away, winding around a rocky spur. Røkia crossed first, Varg focusing on the path ahead of her. He could see or hear no sign of life, other than a hedgepig snuffling in the undergrowth.

Røkia reached the other side, and walked on a few score paces, stopping as the track curved around a spur of land.

She raised a hand, indicating all was clear.

Varg turned to look back at the treeline. He lifted his spear high, and then the Bloodsworn were emerging from the shadowed gloom.

Glornir first, riding his black horse, with Svik at his side, then a wide column of warriors, a few pack-ponies and finally a horse-drawn cart. Einar Half-Troll sat on the driving bench, which was bending under his weight. Over a dozen children sat in the back of the cart.

Varg crossed the bridge, jogging to Røkia. The ground sloped away in undulating ridges, mostly close-cropped grass dotted with heather and fern, here and there pockets of wind-blasted trees, a long, gentle descent to the River Drammur. Varg could see the river, growing wide and sluggish compared to the torrent it had been as it flowed out of the Bonebacks. It coiled across the plain like a glistening, black-skinned serpent, curling around a town built upon a hill.

"Is that Darl?" Varg asked. Even at this distance it looked huge, filling the horizon. A walled fortress built around the hill's peak, a tumble of buildings on the slopes and spreading out into the land alongside the riverside and into the plains behind, and a forest of masts crammed on the river, thick and dense as the pinewoods Varg had been travelling through. Sullen smoke hung like a cloud above the fortress.

"Aye," Røkia said, "and a bigger shite-hole in all of Vigrið you will not be finding."

A multitude of scents assailed him: cooked fish, rotting vegetables, sweat, urine, smoke.

"You do realise when you call the wolf that your eyes change colour?" Røkia said.

Varg blinked at her. She had told him, but he'd forgotten.

"Be careful when you summon the wolf," Røkia said. "If you did that in the presence of the untouched, they would know that you are Tainted. Then . . ." She shrugged.

"A thrall-collar, or left in a cage to rot," Varg said. "I will be careful. But it is safe, now. I am among . . . friends."

It still felt strange, using that term, when apart from his sister he had been friendless his whole life. It gave him a warmth in his belly that he had never known. He stared back at Darl, using his wolf's vision to study the fortress.

He stared at the piled earthworks, the palisaded wall atop it, and within the fortress boundaries were orderly lines of buildings constructed in quadrangles, four of them, each with their own courtyard, the four of them spread evenly around a central longhouse that dwarfed the other buildings. On the far side of the hill, beyond the fortress wall, Varg saw a tower looming, rearing tall like a black nail into the sky, but his eyes were drawn back to that central longhouse. There was something there that he could not quite understand, something pale that he kept staring at. Frowning, he squinted, straining his eyes.

"Are those . . ."

"Wings," Røkia said. "The fortress on the hill is built around Orna's skeleton. The bone-sword that left its mark on you; that was one of Orna's talons."

Varg put a hand to his ribs, which were still tender to the touch. Just the memory of the pain he'd felt made him wince. "That's why Skalk wanted it so badly?"

Røkia shrugged. "Who knows the mind of that *niðing* Galdurman."

The tramp of feet, jangle of mail and harness, the creak of wheels.

"Ah, the sweet stink of civilisation," Svik said as he reined in his mount to stop beside Varg and stared at Darl. "How I've *missed* it."

Glornir strode on a few paces, gripping his long-axe like a walking staff, his black, blood-spattered shield slung across his back. The Bloodsworn spread along the path, looking down at the smear of Darl that spread like a bloodstain upon the land.

"We'll make camp here, for now. In those woods," Glornir said, nodding to a copse of hawthorn and spruce sitting in a dip of land. "I'm going to take a closer look."

The Bloodsworn shifted from the path into the cover of the trees, Einar helping the children to unload a barrel and lever it open with the edge of his axe. Apples, cold salted pork and cheese was handed out, Svik happily taking a plate of cheese.

Varg took an apple and sat beside him, the two of them sitting in silence and watching as the children talked Einar into a game of dodge-the-troll, Einar playing the part of a hungry troll and the wagon being the homestead. With a dramatic roar Einar grabbed a squealing boy as he tried to run around his legs, lifted him up by an arm and pretended to eat him. The boy laughed and laughed, and then Einar set him down again, the boy standing with Einar as he was now troll-touched, and so had to help Einar capture more children for food.

Most of the Bloodsworn sat around eating, drinking, tending to their kit and watching Einar pretend he was too slow to catch the children, allowing them to run between his legs, dodge around him and even climb over him when he fell over, laughing and pretending he was too short of breath to move.

Røkia was standing beside Varg and Svik, and she huffed a frustrated sigh and stalked out to stand beside Einar.

"I will help you," she said, giving the children a hard stare.

Einar looked at her with a raised eyebrow.

Svik snorted a laugh.

"What?" Varg asked him.

"Røkia doesn't know how to play. Watch."

The game began again, almost twenty children running, Einar swinging his arms ponderously in a half-hearted attempt to catch them. Røkia moved faster than Varg could follow, and in her wake children were left lying on the ground. One started to cry. Four children made it to the safety of the wagon.

"What are you doing?" Einar said to Røkia.

"Helping you win," Røkia said. "You are clearly *useless* at this game."

Einar walked over to her, leaned close, but Varg still heard his whisper.

"I have been letting them win," Einar explained.

"*Letting* them win!" Røkia exclaimed, "are you insane?"

"It makes them happy," Einar shrugged.

"Happy?" Røkia said, spitting the word out as if it tasted bad. "Happy?" She stalked away, shaking her head.

Glornir walked into their camp, looking around at them all.

"What's the plan then, chief?" Einar asked him.

A long silence, Glornir looking back over his shoulder where he could still see the tower on Darl's summit. He looked up at the sky through twisted branches, which was growing paler, the sun a weak stain behind bloated rainclouds, then back at the tower.

"The *Sea-Wolf* won't be close, yet," Svik said, talking about the Bloodsworn's *drakkar* longship.

"No," Glornir agreed.

"Should we wait for it?" Svik asked.

"No," Glornir growled. "When we have Vol we'll head south, follow the river until we meet the *Sea-Wolf*."

Svik nodded.

"Chief," Einar said, his voice a rumble.

"Aye," Glornir grunted.

"What about the children?"

"I gave my word to Orka that I would get them to Darl. And I have done that," Glornir said.

"But they're only bairns," Einar said.

Glornir tore his eyes away from the tower on the hill to look at Einar. "They can stay with us today, sleep here when we move out. Then make their own way into Darl tomorrow. There's enough work for them to find in Darl."

"But," Einar said, looking back at the cart full of children, "they're Tainted, with no parents to protect them. They'll be found out, end up with collars around their necks, or worse."

"That is the best I can do for them," Glornir said with a grimace.

"But they are helpful, Chief . . ." Einar said, shuffling his feet.

Glornir looked a long moment at the children, then back to Einar.

"Once we have Vol back, we will need to move fast. They have slowed us down too much, already."

"But—" Einar began.

"Enough," Glornir growled.

Einar opened his mouth to say something else but Svik squeezed his arm and he clamped his mouth shut, shoulders slumping.

A collar around their necks, Varg scowled, looking back at the children. *I know what that feels like. I wish I could melt every thrall-collar and bloody the nose of every thrall-owner. And the first one I'll deal with will be that* niðing *thrall-seller, Brimil.*

CHAPTER TWENTY

ORKA

Orka stepped out into the muddy glade before Rotta's chamber. Heads snapped around, weapons hissing into the fists of warriors as she strode into the clearing.

Footsteps behind her, Lif hurrying to catch up.

"Go back," Orka snapped at him. Lif didn't answer, just walked on beside her. She could hear his breathing; short, fast breaths, and there was a tremor in his hands, his knuckles white as he gripped his spear and new shield.

"Who are you?" the dark-haired woman leading these warriors called out, striding towards them. She had left her shield strapped to her horse, but her hands hovered close to her weapons belt, where her sword and seax hung.

Orka stopped walking, waited for this woman to come to her. The rain was fading, more like a fine mist in the air now. She saw the other warriors spreading wide around her, shields held loosely, spears half levelled. Twelve of them, including their leader, and two more gone into the darkness of Rotta's chamber. Orka felt the wolf in her blood growl, hackles rising, that moment before violence when everything became heightened. The wolf coursed through her, as if straining at a leash, ready to leap and tear and rend.

Soon, Orka promised the beast.

"What's the plan?" Lif whispered.

"To kill them all, save one," Orka breathed.

"I should have known," he muttered.

"When it starts, stay behind me," Orka said. "Try to take small steps, the ground will be slippery. And watch for the two in the chamber."

"I was hoping we might reason with them," Lif whispered.

"No," Orka said.

The black-haired woman stopped a handful of paces from Orka, out of range of Orka's long-axe, which she was holding loosely in two hands across her body.

"Who are you?" the woman repeated. Tears were bright in her eyes, a muscle twitching in her cheek, her grief and anger raw, shivering through her. She was younger than Orka had first thought, maybe twenty-five years on her shoulders, no more. She moved well. Confident and smooth, a warrior's gait.

"Did you kill my father?" the woman asked.

Father? The old man? Then she is dragon-born, too.

"No," Orka said.

"Who did?"

"Someone better than him," Orka said with a shrug.

A grimace from the woman at that and her fingers twitched.

A warrior stepped forward, fair hair, a flat, wide face, silver rings in his braided beard, and an axe in his fist.

"You do not speak to Myrk Sharp-Claw like that. Show some respect or I shall teach it to you."

Orka gave him a long stare, shifted to take in the warriors spread around her. She saw the questions in their eyes, asking who she was, why was she here, but she saw their confidence, too, in their abilities, in their numbers. They had no concern that Orka was a threat to them. Orka looked back to Myrk, the silence lengthening.

The whirr of wings and Vesli alighted on the other side of Orka, glaring at Myrk and her warriors. Someone laughed.

"An old woman, a boy too young to grow a real beard, and a rat with wings," flat-face sneered.

Vesli looked at the man's teeth.

Myrk took a step forward, her eyes narrowing. "Did you eat my father's teeth?" she growled at Vesli. The tennúr gave her a sharp-toothed grin.

"Where is my son?" Orka asked Myrk.

Myrk frowned. "Are you moon-touched, old woman?" she asked, "what business is your son to me?"

"My son was kept in those chambers. Where is he now?" Orka felt the shift happening within her, felt the wolf breaking its shackles. Last time, at the Grimholt, the wolf had come in a flood, a storm of tooth and claw, of rage and blood.

Wait. Soon, she told the wolf again, even as she felt the change happening, time slowing, a sharpening of her senses between one heartbeat and the next. The anger that always bubbled away beneath the surface changed within her, like a forge fire moving from red flames to white incandescence. A flush of strength flooded her muscles. Orka looked down at the ground, closing her eyes.

"What happened here?" Myrk said. "I will not ask you again." Her hand closed around the hilt of her sword.

"Drekr," Orka said.

A pause.

"How do you know Drekr?" Myrk asked.

Orka kept her head lowered, said nothing. She had learned enough from Myrk's answer, from the shift in her voice. She knew Drekr, and well. Orka felt the trembling in her blood, heard the wolf prowling in her veins.

"Take them," Orka heard Myrk command, "and I shall beat some answers out of them."

Now, Orka told the wolf and she looked up.

Flat-face was coming at her, smiling, a few others behind him. He faltered as he saw her face, Orka knowing that her eyes were now amber, her teeth longer and sharper. In the moment he paused she was moving, impossibly fast, lunging forward, long-axe swinging up. The blade sheared into his lower jaw, carved through flesh and bone and burst free in an explosion of blood and teeth. Flat-face collapsed, gurgling. Orka kept moving, the long-axe held high. She punched the butt-end into another warrior's face, a red-haired woman, her nose bursting and she stumbled back, crashed into

Myrk behind her. Orka set her feet and swung the axe around her head, hacking down into the next warrior charging at her, a blonde-haired woman, chopping deep into the meat between neck and shoulder. The crack of bone splintering and the woman dropped. Orka yanked on the axe haft but the blade was snared in bone, so she let it go, ducked and pivoted as a spear flickered through the space where her head had been, came slipping out of the pivot with a seax in one fist, hand-axe in the other, pushed forward and buried the seax in someone's belly as they crashed into her, iron rings of a *brynja* splitting, blood gushing, hot on her fist. She twisted the blade, heard a high-pitched scream and shoved the warrior away, ripping her seax free. Stood there, chest heaving, nostrils flaring, three corpses at her feet. It had all happened so quickly, twenty heartbeats, no more, and most of the other warriors were standing frozen, staring. Then they were all moving.

Screams to her left, a snatched glance at Lif backing away, stumbling on the slippery ground, stabbing his spear at a mailed woman, his shield raised. The woman was pressing him hard, chopping chunks out of his shield with a hand-axe.

"Help him," Orka growled to Vesli and in a blur of wings the tennúr sped away, dropping to the ground before the woman attacking Lif, raising her spear and stabbing it forward, into the meat of the woman's calf. A scream and a gush of blood as Vesli dragged the spear free, the woman staggering. Lif stepped forward, punched his blade into the wounded woman's open mouth, in and out, adder-fast, her scream turning to a choked gurgle as she fell. Another warrior looming, sword raised over Vesli and Orka threw her hand-axe, the blade whistling as it flew turning through the air, a wet slap as it connected with the warrior's head and he was falling away.

"Bitch," someone snarled and Orka turned, sliced a wild parry with her seax at whatever was coming, felt a blow to her shoulder and she was stumbling away, snarling and spitting curses. Myrk was coming at her, a warrior either side. They knew what they were doing, the two either side of Myrk had their shields raised, sword and spear levelled at Orka, spreading wide to open up angles on her, moving carefully across the mud-slick ground. Myrk had a sword in one fist, seax in the other, her eyes glowing red, teeth pointed, strength pulsing from her in waves. The other two had eyes of amber and gold.

Orka glanced at her shoulder, pain throbbing, saw some links of her mail were broken, but there was no blood. She snarled, bunched her legs ready to leap at them. As she did so a blur flashed past on her left and something collided with one of Myrk's shield men, the shield splintering and the man flying through the air. A woman stood there, fair-haired, clothed in mail with a black shield upon her back, blood-spatters cast across it.

Revna, Orka registered through the red rage filling her.

More screams and battle-cries behind Orka, Myrk's eyes staring past her as the Bloodsworn came charging from the treeline. The wolf in Orka's blood howled and she was surging at Myrk. They met with a flurry of blows, Orka grabbing the other seax sheathed across her back and drawing it, sparks grating as sword and seaxes clashed, Myrk swinging and stabbing simultaneously, Orka parrying, chopping, stabbing, and then Myrk was stepping away, smiling, a line of blood flowing down one cheek. Orka blinked sweat from her eyes, swiped at it, realised it was blood. All around her figures fought, screams, the clash of steel striking steel. She glimpsed Ingmar lunging inside a spear-thrust, grabbing the shield held by his attacker and ripping it from the warrior's grip, lunging forward with open jaws. The sound of flesh ripping followed by high-pitched screams.

Then Myrk was coming at her again. Another flurry of blows, strikes and parries, a grunt from Myrk as her sword spun from her grip. She stepped away, reached down and dragged another seax from her boot, then they were close again, slicing, the clang of steel.

Movement in Orka's periphery, the drum of feet and she ducked, too late as something slammed into her and she was airborne, flying through the air, crunching to the ground, a weight upon her, a man, heavily muscled, teeth snapping, frothing bloody foam where he had chewed his own lips. Orka lost one of her seaxes as they rolled together, the man coming out of the roll on top, one knee pinning Orka's wrist and last seax. He raised a fist and hammered it down on to Orka's chest as she tried to rise, hurling her back to the ground, then wrapped a huge fist around her throat and started to squeeze.

"Hold her," a voice shouted: Myrk?

Berserkir, Orka realised as she looked up at the warrior, his teeth sharp, veins bulging. She choked and spluttered, sounds muted as she bucked and writhed in the mud, punched him with her free hand. Blood spurted from his jaw, a tooth flying loose, but he did not let go, almost as if he did not feel Orka's blows. She kicked him in the back, grabbed his fist around her throat with her free hand, clawed and raked at it, her new-grown claws tearing his flesh, grating on bone, but his strength was iron, his eyes wild and frenzied. Black dots burst in Orka's vision. Myrk appeared above them, her face bruised and bloody. She had retrieved her sword.

"How do you know Drekr?" Myrk shouted at her, barely audible over the *Berserkir*, who was roaring, eyes bulging, veins close to bursting in his neck. Orka heard the wolf howling in her veins, snapping and snarling, frantic as if it were caught in a hunter's trap. Dimly she was aware of screams all around, shrieks, battle-cries, the thud of weapons on shields.

Myrk raised her sword high.

A blur of wings and Spert alighted on the *Berserkir's* shoulder, a flash of movement. The *Berserkir* frowned, and looked at Spert, who leaped back into the air and darted away, then black veins were spreading from a point on the *Berserkir's* cheek, up behind his eyes, down into his neck and his grip around Orka was gone, his hands reaching to his own throat as he choked for breath. His tongue protruded from his mouth, black and swelling.

A hound slammed into the *Berserkir*, jaws snapping, hurling the big man off Orka.

Myrk swore and stabbed down with her sword, Orka rolling and kicking out, sweeping Myrk's feet away and she was falling, Orka grappling her, punching. They scrambled across the mud together, Myrk's teeth biting into Orka's shoulder, the grate of iron, pain, a spurt of blood and then Orka had one of Myrk's arms in a lock.

A savage wrench and she heard the crack of bone. A scream from Myrk.

"*Drekablóð, brennt þessa tík, bræðið hold hennar úr beinum,*" Myrk hissed, spitting Orka's blood, close enough for Orka to smell her sour breath, and Orka saw a circle of rune-fire crackle into life in the air before her. It rolled in the air like a wheel, spitting flames, and swirled towards Orka. The sizzle of flesh as it touched her cheek and she hurled herself away, saw Myrk stagger to her knees, one arm hanging limp, the other gesturing in the air.

"*Brenna hana, brenna hana,*" Myrk screeched and the flaming runes surged towards Orka like a fiery net.

Orka ran at the onrushing runes, screamed a rage-filled roar and leaped, dropping to the ground beneath the runes as they hissed over her head. She rolled, came out of it in front of Myrk and slammed her elbow into the woman's jaw. Her eyes rolled white and she fell. A hiss in the air as the fire-rune evaporated, sparks drifting on the breeze.

Orka knelt there, breathing hard, blinking blood from her eyes. Spert fluttered down beside Orka.

"*Mistress all right?*" the vaesen muttered, his antennae brushing across Orka's face, concentrating on where the blood was flowing from a wound on her head.

The wolf in her veins was surging within her, the need for violence shivering through her muscles, the desire for more enemies to tear and kill.

Enough, Orka told the wolf, *our enemies are dead, they are all dead*, and she felt the beast reluctantly begin to calm.

"I'm fine," she muttered to Spert, brushing the antennae away and staggering to her feet. She swiped blood from her eyes, felt a flap of skin hanging on her forehead. Various pains throbbed in her body, worst where Myrk had bitten her. She touched the wound, mail rings torn and blood seeping.

Dragon-born have sharp, strong teeth.

She looked around the glade, saw Halja Flat-Nose standing over a Raven-Feeder, eyes blazing, as she chopped her sword into the warrior's head. A scream cut short, heels drumming as the man died. Then it was over, Bloodsworn standing, chests heaving, their Tainted blood still surging. Gunnar Prow swayed and sat down in the mud, his black eyes returning to blue. One leg was soaked with blood below the knee. Revna Hare-Legs hurried to him. Edel was standing over a dead warrior, scowling at Orka.

"I leave you alone for a few moments," she said, shaking her head. Her hounds stood either side of her, red-mawed and panting.

Lif was stood pale and wide-eyed, staring around the clearing. His hands were trembling, and his new shield was battered, blood on his spear blade. Vesli alighted beside him, a wide smile splitting her face as she looked around at the dead.

"What are you so happy about?" Edel snapped at the vaesen.

"*All the teeth*," Vesli grinned.

CHAPTER TWENTY-ONE

GUÐVARR

Guðvarr strode down the centre of the mead hall, the benches either side of him crammed with warriors. Food, ale and mead lay thick on the tables, and the warriors were shouting his name, thumping a war-beat on the benches, making jugs of ale topple.

"Guðvarr," they shouted.

So long he had waited for this moment. All his life he had known he was special, that he was destined for greatness.

He smiled at the table ahead of him, eyes fixed on Queen Helka, raven-haired, dark-eyed, red-lipped. His aunt, Jarl Sigrún, sat one side of the queen, and Hakon, Helka's son, sat the other, but they blurred in his vision, only Helka bright and vivid. Guðvarr stepped up on to the raised dais and stood before the queen's table. She rose elegantly and drew the sword at her hip, took a ring of gold from her arm and threaded it on to her sword, then held it out over the table to him.

"For your great deeds of bravery, Jarl Guðvarr," Queen Helka said as the crowd quietened, "you slew the *Úlfhéðnar*, protected my realm," and she angled her sword so that the arm ring slid down its blade, falling into Guðvarr's outstretched hand.

I am a jarl. I am proclaimed a hero by a queen and gifted gold, Guðvarr thought, *it is no more than I deserve.*

"Guðvarr, Guðvarr," Queen Helka's *drengr* warriors cried.

"Is there a finer man in all of Vigrið?" Helka said, gesturing to Guðvarr, smiling at him with her red lips.

"Guðvarr," the crowd roared.

"Is there a man braver, more fierce or skilled in combat? So honoured and respected as Guðvarr?"

"Guðvarr", his name echoed through the hall, shaking the rafters and bones of Orna above them.

"And that is why I will take Guðvarr as my husband," Queen Helka called out. "The only man equal and deserving of me in all Vigrið."

More shouts of acclamation, deafening, pounding in his head.

Guðvarr blinked at that, though as the words still hovered in the air he realised it was the obvious thing to do. He was born to rule, and, besides, Helka was a fine-looking woman. Perhaps a little grey at the temples, and lined around the eyes, but he'd never let that get in the way of advancement before, so why start now.

"Guðvarr," the crowd acclaimed him.

Queen Helka stepped around the table and took him in an embrace, pulled him close, but as her lips drew nearer, they changed, drawing back from sharp, jagged teeth in a snarl, eyes flaring amber, hair growing fairer, streaked with grey.

Orka, but I killed you. He tried to pull away, his heart pounding like a hammer on a smith's anvil.

"Guðvarr, Guðvarr," the crowd still roared.

Orka grabbed him, her strength savage, her jaws opening unnaturally wide, lunging forwards and her teeth bit into his throat.

"Guðvarr," the crowd roared.

He opened his eyes, coming awake with a jolt, and realised he could not see.

I'm blind. A rush of fear. He opened his mouth to suck in a breath and found he could hardly breathe, air hissing through a tangle of something in his mouth. The war-drum beat again, bang, bang, bang, pounding.

"Guðvarr," a voice cried, "open this door."

He squeaked out a strangled cry and jerked, thrust out his hands, felt something warm.

A woman beside him, snoring. His face had been squashed into her hair.

"What's wrong?" the woman mumbled, a tangle of red-hair and soft, pale flesh.

Guðvarr frowned, fractured memories filtering through his thought-cage; of pulling her on to his lap in Helka's mead hall, laughing, slapping her arse. Of giving her a silver coin. She pushed herself up, blinking, pale and naked, a hand reaching for her tunic and hangerock, which were hung on a nail hammered into a post. They were in a dark room, straw on the ground, a sloping roof above.

"Where am I?" Guðvarr rasped.

"The hayloft of *The Dead Drengr*," the red-haired woman said. "Who's banging on the trapdoor?"

Queen Helka and all her Úlfhéðnar, along with all the dead gods reborn. How should I know, I cannot see through doors you niðing idiot? I don't even know who you are, and you're in my bed.

"I don't know," Guðvarr mumbled as he rolled off a straw mattress and half fell, tripping over breeches that were gathered around his ankles. He cracked his head on a roof-beam, swore and leaped back up.

"Coming," he squeaked, hopping as he dragged his breeches up and searched for his tunic, flushed with shame at the fear he'd felt when he woke. *It was only a dream.* He stubbed his toe, squawked with pain and wished he was still asleep, dreaming of his acclamation. Then he remembered Orka, her teeth savaging his throat.

I'm glad I'm awake.

He tugged on his tunic and stumbled to the trapdoor, head pounding, his belly churning, head thumping.

Too much mead last night.

He lifted the latch and pulled the trapdoor open.

Yrsa, Skalk's *drengr*, stood in a stairwell, looking up at him, fair and cold as winter's sun. He tried to stand straighter, saw her staring at his nose and he wiped it.

"Queen Helka wants to see you," she said, a frown creeping on to her face as she looked him up and down. She sniffed, the corners of her mouth turning down in disgust.

"When?" Guðvarr said, his voice a croak.

I'm never drinking fire-mead again.

"Now," Yrsa said. "Get dressed."

I can't go now, you moron, I need more than a few moments to dress and prepare for a queen.

"Yes," Guðvarr squawked and dropped the trapdoor.

"The queen wants to see me," he hissed at the red-haired whore, glaring at her as if it were her fault that he had drunk enough ale to sink a *drakkar* last night. "Help me dress."

Guðvarr followed Yrsa as they strode through Queen Helka's empty mead hall, only a few thralls flitting around the chamber, scrapping half-dried vomit from the ground, sweeping up ale and urine-soaked rushes, scooping out the black ash from hearth fires. It was a different place from the room Guðvarr had feasted in last night, full of boasting warriors, skálds singing, and what felt like a flowing river of ale and mead. The smell was not helping the churning in his stomach. A crow cawed from a shadowed rafter and bird-shite spattered his boot. He saw two figures sitting half shadowed on a bench, shaven-haired with long braids, like Prince Jaromir, a man and woman, both with dark-weathered skin, and both wearing coats of lamellar plate. They looked at Guðvarr with cold, flat-eyed stares, and Guðvarr pretended to ignore them.

"What did you say this is about?" Guðvarr asked Yrsa.

"I didn't," Yrsa grunted as she led him through the room, up on to the dais and into the corridor to Queen Helka's chamber. Two *Úlfhéðnar* stood outside the door, tattoos visible through stubble on the sides of their shaven heads, thick braids of hair running down the centre of their heads.

"Yrsa," one of the *Úlfhéðnar* said, black-haired and dark-eyed.

"Frek," Yrsa said.

The *Úlfhéðnar's* eyes flickered amber as he turned his gaze on to Guðvarr, stepping close and breathing deep, sniffing.

A flash of his dream filled his thought-cage, an image of Orka's amber eyes and sharp-toothed bite, caused him to take a step back. The other *Úlfhéðnar* snorted a laugh.

"This is Guðvarr, the one Queen Helka sent me to find," Yrsa said.

Frek just nodded.

"Queen Helka has company," the other *Úlfhéðnar* said.

The sound of voices, muffled, then one rising in volume. Guðvarr thought he heard the words *give*, and *Seiðr-witch*. More muffled words and then footsteps and the door was being dragged open, Prince Jaromir standing there, his face twitching with rage.

That man always seems to be angry.

He pushed past Guðvarr and stormed down the corridor towards the mead hall.

"*Drengr* Yrsa and . . . Guðvarr," Frek the *Úlfhéðnar* announced through the open door.

"I am a *drengr*, too," Guðvarr corrected the *Úlfhéðnar*, but Frek just stared back at him.

"Come," Queen Helka called out and Yrsa strode in. Guðvarr took a deep breath, then followed.

Queen Helka was seated in her high-backed chair, reindeer furs spread across it, and Skalk stood beside her. There was another chair beside Helka's, a dark-haired young woman sitting in it in a tunic of deep blue, edged with silver-dyed wool. Estrid, youngest child of Queen Helka. Guðvarr stood straighter as he saw the princess.

Perhaps we are to be betrothed? His eyes took her in, noticing a strong frame beneath her tunic, even slumped in her chair as she was. *I would not complain if that is why Helka has summoned me,* Guðvarr thought. Estrid met his gaze, giving him such a withering look of contempt that he almost turned around and left. Then her eyes swept up to regard the eagle claws of dead Orna hanging suspended above them, as if old bones were more interesting than anything else in the room.

Spoilt bitch, Guðvarr thought.

Both Queen Helka and Skalk had drinking horns in their hands, and Skalk was picking at a bunch of grapes on a table. Shadowed forms lurked in the shadows, and Guðvarr thought he heard a growl.

"Ale?" Skalk offered.

"No, thank you, my lord," Guðvarr said, feeling his stomach lurch, *unless you want the contents of my stomach deposited at your feet.*

"Skalk tells me you saved his life," Helka said, her direct gaze making Guðvarr feel uncomfortable.

"I did," Guðvarr said, feeling himself stand a little straighter. This was a subject he liked, his own greatness. His eyes flickered to Estrid, but she was still looking up at Orna's claws, as if there was no one else in the room.

Rude.

"Skalk was injured, and his recollection of the incident is vague," Helka went on, "but Yrsa agrees."

"I saw Guðvarr carry Skalk from the Grimholt's hall," Yrsa said. "And he carried him to me, warned me of the danger, and then to the *snekke* that we escaped on."

Guðvarr nodded. *All the while terrified for my life and hoping that I would not soil myself, but there's no need to mention that.*

"So, it would appear that I owe you my thanks," Helka said. "Skalk is dear to me. I value his life." She stood and took a ring of gold from her arm, then held it out to Guðvarr.

Guðvarr blinked and rubbed his eyes. This was far too similar to his dream for his liking.

A silence lengthened, Guðvarr half expecting Queen Helka to transform into a blood-crazed *Úlfhéðnar* and rip his throat out.

Stop being an idiot, this is what you wanted. Recognition, opportunity.

"M-my thanks, my queen," Guðvarr mumbled as he stepped forward and took the ring.

"Mama, I'm bored," Estrid said, tapping a finger on the arm of her chair.

"Not all about ruling is excitement," Helka said.

"I have learned that lesson," Estrid puffed, her gaze flittering across Guðvarr, her lip curling as if he were a steaming lump of shite on her shoe. "Can Frek teach me some weapons craft? I prefer it to . . . this." She looked at Guðvarr again.

Perhaps I haven't been summoned for a betrothal.

Queen Helka sighed. "Very well," she said with a wave of her hand and Estrid jumped to her feet and swept from the room.

"Tell me of this Orka," Skalk asked him as Queen Helka took a sip from her ale-horn.

Tell you of that moon-touched, axe-wielding lunatic. He sucked in a deep breath. *Good, this will give me a chance to rehearse what I must say to my aunt.* Although Guðvarr had seen his aunt last night, and she had embraced him and welcomed him back, he had avoided giving her any kind of account of what had happened at the Grimholt, and, more importantly, avoided telling her about the running away. That was the part he thought she would find least impressive.

"There's not much to tell," Guðvarr said, "Orka lived in the hills close to Fellur village, with her husband Thorkel and their son, Breca. They would come to the village to trade; skins, mostly. They found a steading close to theirs in the hills raided, a man and woman dead, their son taken. Orka brought the bodies to Fellur, and I told her we would hunt the killers."

"Did you?" Skalk asked.

"Did I what?"

"Find the killers."

"I led a search party, but, no, we did not find them. They were gone, disappeared. Used the rivers around the fjord." He shrugged. "The couple murdered were loners, outsiders with no kin. And the next thing I knew of Orka was when I heard a scream from Jarl Sigrún's chamber in the dead of night." He chose to leave out any telling of the Althing at the Oath Rock, or of his *holmganga* with Virk. Not his finest moment. "I was first into the room," he continued, puffing out his chest, "and saw Jarl Sigrún's lover dead, the jarl fallen, and your *Úlfhéðnar*, Vafri, with a hole in her belly."

A series of growls rippled from the shadows around the chamber, Queen Helka's *Úlfhéðnar* pacing and restless.

"That was a sore loss," Helka said. "Vafri was dear to me, and pack to my *Úlfhéðnar*. She was no small gift to your aunt, a sign of how much I value her."

"Vafri was . . . fierce," Guðvarr said, remembering his *holmganga* with Virk, how pain had exploded in his shoulder and he had fallen flailing to the ground, his shoulder spurting blood. How he had looked to see Vafri hurtling at Virk, snarling, teeth bared, eyes blazing, the sound of her seaxes punching into Virk's flesh, again and again and again.

"And yet, this Orka slew Vafri," Skalk said. "Did you not think then that Orka was *Úlfhéðnar*?"

"No," Guðvarr said, "I just thought she crept into a dark room like a *niðing* and stabbed people while they slept."

Queen Helka tapped her fingers on a table.

"Why did she do that?" Helka asked. "Creep into your aunt's chamber?"

"I . . . don't know," Guðvarr said. "A fire had been seen in the hills earlier that day and my aunt sent riders to investigate. They returned the next day, told us that Orka's steading was burned out, and that there was a new barrow raised in the courtyard with her man in it: Thorkel. Perhaps Orka thought that Jarl Sigrún had something to do with it all." He shrugged. "Who knows the mind of a moon-touched lunatic."

"But her son was not buried at the steading?" Skalk said.

"No, Lord Skalk. Not her son."

Skalk looked at Queen Helka. "Orka was chained in the Grimholt, being put to the question. She told us that her son had been stolen, and that she was hunting those who had taken him. It was hearing a child's cry in the Grimholt that brought out the wolf in her."

"She appears to be no ordinary woman, this Orka," Helka said. "She is *Úlfhéðnar*, and has curious friends: vaesen, and giant ravens."

Guðvarr nodded.

"I would like this Orka brought before me," Helka said, iron in her voice. Grunts and murmurs from the shadows.

"I will go after her and bring her back to you, my queen," Guðvarr said, though even as the words left his mouth, he regretted them. Just the sight of the *Úlfhéðnar* in this room turned his skin to gooseflesh. He'd rather dive into a fjord full of Sjávarorm serpents than meet Orka face to face again.

Queen Helka smiled coldly.

"You have courage, to undertake such a task," Helka said. "But I do not want you to do that, Guðvarr."

Thank the dead gods.

The relief he felt was palpable, like a physical thing.

Queen Helka looked at Skalk.

"Well?" she said to him.

Skalk looked from Helka to Guðvarr, then back to Helka. He nodded.

"There is something you can do for me, though, that is closer to home," Helka said.

"Anything, my queen," Guðvarr said.

Anything that does not have me risking my life.

"Follow me," Skalk said.

CHAPTER TWENTY-TWO

ORKA

Orka sat on a boulder as Vesli cleaned and tended the wound on her forehead, washing the blood away with a rolled-up rag that the tennúr had dipped in water. The blood did not seem to want to stop flowing, dripping into Orka's eye. Vesli's face was taut with concentration, her pink tongue poking out between her thin lips.

Orka was only half aware of the tennúr, because she was staring at a seax in her fist. One of Myrk's weapons. It was thick at the guard, single-edged and wide-bladed, with a sudden taper towards the blade's tips. The hilt was carved from ash, serpent knotwork spiralling around it. Orka had two identical blades hanging from her weapons belt. Drekr's seaxes, the ones Orka had found in Thorkel's body. The only difference being that Myrk's seax was lighter, being shorter and slimmer in the blade.

"*Mistress Orka, put your finger here,*" Vesli said, tugging at one of Orka's hands with her small, thin fingers, and she placed one of Orka's fingers on her forehead, holding a flap of skin in place. Then Vesli made some coughing sounds, bending over, and spat a glob of something green into the palm of her hand, like a bird regurgitating for its young. She kneaded the ball of spit and phlegm between her hands and it became thicker, pulling it out like slimy dough, and then Vesli was plastering it on to Orka's forehead, working it into the wound. At first it felt warm, and then Orka couldn't feel the wound at all.

Vesli took a step back and smiled at her handiwork.

"*Mistress Orka's head fixed,*" Vesli pronounced. She looked at the wound in Orka's shoulder, where Myrk had torn through iron links in Orka's *brynja*, blood starting to congeal.

"*Mistress need that cleaned quickly. Iron in wound, nasty,*" Vesli said, shaking her head.

"Aye," Orka nodded, knowing Vesli was right. She stood, unbuckled her weapons belt and then winced as she wriggled out of her coat of mail. A frown as she examined the broken links, and then Vesli was ushering her back on to the boulder, ripping Orka's tunic away and pouring a bottle of water over the wound. She leaned close, tutting, and began to pick bits of shattered iron links out of the wound with the long, needle-like talons on her fingers.

It had stopped raining, the day damp and still now, almost impossible to believe that only a short while ago the silence had been torn and fractured by the din of battle. If not for the bodies that littered the ground, blood pooled in ruts of mud. All about her the Bloodsworn were tending to their wounds, stripping the dead of their kit, cleaning weapons. None of them had fallen in the battle, though all of them were bleeding from some wound or another, apart from Edel. Lif was sitting with his back to a tree, shaking like a branch in a storm. A few moments ago, he had been bent over, vomiting. Gunnar Prow was sitting close to Lif, and Revna Hare-Legs was cutting away his blood-soaked breeches to get a better look at the wound in his leg.

All the dead lay where they'd fallen, Edel crouched and going through their belts, searching pouches and kit. Close to them lay Myrk, bound and gagged, still unconscious.

A dragon-born, who has some kind of Seiðr or Galdur-magic. A dangerous woman. Orka hissed as Vesli probed deep into her wound. *A dragon-born with strong, sharp teeth.* Then Vesli was dropping her blood-soaked rag on the ground and she was coughing and heaving again, spitting up her green pile of whatever it was, and kneading it like a frenzied baker. The familiar warm sensation as Vesli pressed it on to Orka's injury, working it deep into the wound, a sharp stab of pain, and then a tingling spreading through her shoulder, fading to numbness.

"*Done*," Vesli said, fluttering her wings to fly and hover in front of Orka.

"My thanks," Orka grunted. She looked at Gunnar Prow. "Will you see if you can help him?"

"*If mistress Orka wants me to*," Vesli said.

"He fought with us," she said, "though he did not have to," and Vesli nodded. Her wings whirred and she flew to Gunnar and Revna.

"*Let Vesli see*," Orka heard the tennúr squeak.

Orka stood, sweeping up her weapons belt, seaxes and a pouch hanging from it. The axe-loop was empty, Orka vaguely remembering hurling her hand-axe during the fight. She slung the belt over her shoulder. Spert uncoiled from where he had dug a damp place in the mud, where the boulder met the ground.

"*Spert hungry*," the vaesen muttered.

"Soon," Orka said absently, walking away, striding to Lif and standing over him. Spert's many legs extended, and the vaesen followed Orka, his sting curled high over his back.

"Are you all right?" Orka asked Lif.

He looked at her with wide eyes, a tremor in his lips. A dribble of vomit was drying in his spindly beard.

"Any wounds?" Orka said.

"Just this," Lif said, lifting his arm to show a cut along the back of his spear hand.

"Good," Orka said. "You are in shock. Drink something. Mead is best. There's a barrel up in the camp."

Lif stood, reached down and took up his shield.

"You won't need that," Orka said, "they're all dead."

Lif looked at the shield and held it up. It was splintered, chunks of wood hacked away and torn out.

"Told you a shield was a good idea," Edel said as she crouched beside a dead woman.

"I'd have been dead a dozen times without it," Lif said.

"That one's not got much more life-saving in it, though," Edel said, looking at the battered shield. "Just pick another, you have plenty to choose from."

"Mead first," Orka said, "and bring the barrel back with you."

Lif nodded, dropped the shield and trudged up the slope into the trees. He swayed and tottered, put a hand on a tree and vomited again.

"I'll get the mead," Ingmar Ice said, "I could do with a drink. And some food." Lif sat back down and Ingmar's bulk disappeared into the tree-gloom.

Orka heard Vesli coughing and retching, spitting up her healing slime.

"You are not putting *that* anywhere near me," Gunnar Prow said.

"*It will help, make you better, quicker,*" Vesli said, sounding irritated and looking insulted.

"It smells bad," Gunnar protested.

"Listen to Vesli," Orka said.

Gunnar Prow frowned. "I think I'd rather die," he muttered, not able to take his eyes from the green sticky mass in Vesli's hands.

"Ignore him, just do it," Revna said to Vesli and the vaesen pressed the green slime on to a gash in Gunnar's thigh, just below the rim of his mail shirt.

Orka turned around and walked to Myrk, boots squelching in the mud, Spert still following, and stood over her. The dragon-born's sword lay close by, fine made with a five-lobed pommel and silver wire wrapped tight around the hilt.

A sword fit for a jarl. She thinks highly of herself, this Myrk Sharp-Claw. Orka pushed the sword away, made sure it was well out of Myrk's reach, and put the seax still in her hand beside it, then she squatted, checking the bonds at Myrk's wrists and ankles. Bound with thick cords of twisted leather, and then with hemp rope. A gag of linen had been rolled and stuffed into her mouth, again tied in place with twisted leather.

A pouch hung from Myrk's weapons belt and Orka ripped it free, hefted it and heard the jingle of coin. It was heavy. She opened it and saw the glint of gold and silver. There was more silver on Myrk's arms, twisted rings with serpent heads. Orka took them all.

Blood leaked from a cut on Myrk's cheek. Orka tore a strip of linen from the hem of her tunic, poured some water from the bottle at her belt over the wound, then daubed the blood away. She stood and stuffed the bloodied linen into the pouch hanging on her own belt.

Vesli flew over.

"*Vesli helped all your friends,*" the tennúr said.

"Good," Orka grunted. "Now go and help yourself to some teeth."

Vesli grinned, revealing her own two rows of teeth, outer ones sharp as needles, inner ones flat and wide, like grindstones at a mill, and she whirred away to the closest of the dead.

"Wake up," Orka said, and nudged the unconscious woman with her toe. Myrk groaned, eyelids flickering.

Edel came closer, her two hounds following her. Their muzzles were dark with drying blood. Halja Flat-Nose and others of the Bloodsworn gathered around them.

"Wake up," Orka said again, kicked Myrk in the ribs this time.

A grunt and Myrk's eyes snapped open, flaring red. Her muscles tensed, seemed to expand as she thrashed and strained at her bonds, but they held. Sounds leaked from Myrk's mouth, spit dribbling down her chin, but words were impossible.

"You are the only one of your company still breathing, all your warriors are dead," Orka said. "I'm going to take the gag away, but try any Seiðr-tricks and you'll be joining them quick enough."

Myrk glared at Orka, eyes red as coals.

"Tell the dragon in your blood to behave." Orka drew a seax from her belt and touched it to Myrk's throat. Slowly the red-glow faded in Myrk's eyes, shifting to blue.

Orka sliced leather and pulled the wad of linen out of Myrk's mouth.

"You are a dead woman walking," Myrk hissed, voice hoarse.

"Where is my son?" Orka asked her, not wasting her time on trading insults. *Insults are for fools and cowards.*

Myrk looked around, saw the Bloodsworn looming all around her, Edel sitting and stroking her hounds.

"What are the Bloodsworn doing here?" she asked. "We will kill you all."

Edel laughed. "I think your lot just tried that," she said.

"If you hadn't noticed, it did not end well for them," Halja Flat-Nose added.

"Which one of you weasel-shite *niðings* slew my father?" Myrk snapped.

Orka sighed and lifted the linen gag. "You are the prisoner, which means you answer the questions, not ask them."

"Fight me. I challenge you to a *holmganga*," Myrk said.

Some of the Bloodsworn laughed.

"I just did fight you," Orka said, "and you are the one on your back, trussed like a hog for the skewer, not me."

Myrk's mouth twisted. "You had help," she growled, eyes fixing on Spert, who looked back at her and raised his sting, twitching it. The vaesen smiled. It was not a pleasant sight. More laughter rippled among the Bloodsworn.

"You will not be laughing when Lik-Rifa is picking your bones from her teeth," Myrk snarled.

A silence at that. Frowns and scowls among the Bloodsworn. One of Edel's hounds growled.

Has Thorkel's death and Breca's abduction got anything to do with Lik-Rifa's return? Orka thought.

"Where is my son?" Orka said. "You are alive because I need answers. No answers . . ." She hefted her seax.

Myrk clamped her lips shut.

Orka sighed, feeling her patience fraying, her temper rising.

There is no one left breathing to ask. Be calm, she knows the way to Breca.

"I know much about you already," Orka said. "Your name is Myrk Sharp-Claw. You are one of Ilska's Raven-Feeders. No doubt you are a fair-fame warrior among them, to lead these others. You are Tainted, a dragon-born. And all the Raven-Feeders are Tainted, too." Orka stared at Myrk a while, seeing her words sinking in.

Myrk looked around at all the faces staring at her.

"I have learned something, too," Myrk said. "That the famed Bloodsworn are also Tainted." She nodded, seeing the reactions on the Bloodsworn, a smile splitting her lips.

Edel put a hand to the axe at her belt.

"And you know Drekr," Orka said, wanting to dig for her answers before Edel or someone else put an axe in Myrk's skull. She held up the seax in her fist, one of Drekr's, then reached over and lifted Myrk's seax, held them both close together, showing the same craftsmanship and knotwork. "I have been looking for him."

"How did you get that?" Myrk said, a flare of her eyes as she stared at Drekr's seax.

"I found it in my husband's body," Orka snarled, quiet as a whisper.

Myrk smiled.

Orka felt her fingers twitch and fought the urge to pound this woman's face until it was soft. Or stab her seax into Myrk's throat until she felt it grate on bone. She took a long, shuddering breath.

This woman knows where Breca is. I would happily slice parts of her away until there was nothing left of her, but I think it will be a long road to crack this one's shell. I suspect she is one of the rare ones that do not break, only die. I need her to answer my questions and pain is not the way to loosen this one's tongue.

"Drekr has some new scars," Orka said, brushing her spread fingers diagonally across her face, "as if he has been clawed by a bear. My husband did that to him."

A scowl across Myrk's face, replaced by a smirk. "But Drekr is the one still breathing," she said, "while your husband is cold in the ground." Another smile.

"Drekr has a new scar, here," Orka continued, trying to blot out Myrk's smile, trying not to think of Thorkel in his barrow, trying to control the red mist that was starting to creep behind her eyes. She touched a hand to her shoulder, remembering where she had blooded Drekr during their fight in Darl. "I gave it to him. And a broken thumb."

Myrk blinked. Scowled again. "He told me about you." Her eyes narrowed. "He said you walked into *The Dead Drengr* on your own, against twelve. He said you are moon-touched."

Lif snorted a laugh.

"I will ask you again. Where is my son?" Orka said.

"Who killed my father?" Myrk spat back.

"Where is BRECA?" Orka bellowed and she slammed her fist into Myrk's jaw, pulled her arm back, punched her again, and again, screaming her question with each blow. Hands wrapped around her wrist and arm, Edel, Halja Flat-Nose, Revna, all hanging on to her.

"She can't hear you," Edel said.

Myrk lay with her face pulped and oozing blood.

No, Orka said in her thought-cage. She shook her head. *I need this one alive.* Myrk's chest rose and fell with shallow breaths. Orka stood and walked away.

Orka tightened the girth of her saddle-strap and patted Trúr's neck. She rolled her injured shoulder, her mail shirt back on now, and over it a sealskin cloak taken from one of the dead Raven-Feeders. There was no pain from her more serious wounds, thanks to Vesli, though her body was stiff and ached from a hundred lesser bruises. Close by Lif was tending to his own mount. He was looking better now and he, too, wore a sealskin cloak across his shoulders taken from the dead. Ingmar had returned with the barrel of mead, as well as their pot and a sack of oats, so they had all sipped some mead while porridge boiled over a fire. The horses were saddled and ready for riding, standing patiently in the glade before Rotta's chamber, all the camp packed away, the Bloodsworn almost ready to move out. Spert was sitting beside a rock, and Vesli was whizzing from corpse to corpse, glutting herself on teeth and filling her pouch.

Footsteps, and Orka turned, Ingmar Ice striding towards her, two bowls of porridge in his big hands. He sat beside her and gave her a bowl.

"Good scrap," he said as he slurped a mouthful.

She said nothing, but did eat a mouthful of porridge.

"Good to fight with you again, Skullsplitter," he added. "You've been missed." He looked at her. "Thorkel was a good man. A good friend."

She opened her mouth, but words could not squeeze past the constriction that was abruptly in her throat. Ingmar patted her leg and went back to eating his porridge.

Spert looked up from his muddy pool and in a burst of wings he was at Orka's feet, eyeing her bowl of porridge.

Orka took another mouthful, then she set the bowl down, drew her seax and pricked her thumb, squeezing a drop of blood into the porridge. She hawked and spat a glob of phlegm into the bowl, then stirred in the blood and spit with her spoon.

"There you are," Orka said, pushing the bowl towards Spert and he fell upon it, slurping and sucking.

Ingmar looked at the vaesen with his spoon of porridge halfway to his mouth. He put the spoon down and looked away.

More footsteps, Edel approaching.

"What will you do?" Edel said as she squatted down beside them.

"Follow their tracks as far as I can," Orka said, nodding to the pile of the dead. "And try asking Myrk again, when she wakes up." They looked at Myrk, who was trussed and gagged again, draped over her own horse, tied tight to the saddle like a dead reindeer.

"It may be a while before you can understand what she says," Edel said. "She has fewer teeth now than when she rode into this glade, and her face is swollen like rotten fruit."

Orka shrugged, knowing she had made a mistake, losing her temper. If not for Edel and the others it would have been worse.

"I was at the lake when they rode past," Edel said. "They came from the north-west, following the Bonebacks. Follow that path long enough and it takes you to Lake Horndal and the trading town of Starl. I don't know if that is where they came from, but that is where I would head." She looked away. "I cannot come with you. I would if I could."

Orka blinked at that.

"I did not expect you to," she said. "Glornir needs the *Sea-Wolf*. But, my thanks."

Edel looked back at Orka and nodded. Orka was shocked to see tears in the old woman's eyes.

"But there are some who can come with you," Edel said. She raised her arm and figures moved across the glade. Halja Flat-Nose, Gunnar Prow limping and Revna Hare-Legs. "They have asked to go with you, if you'll have them."

Orka frowned. More hands in a scrap would be helpful, and there was no question there would be more fighting ahead, especially now that things had changed. Ilska's Raven-Feeders were involved in this somehow, and fighting Ilska's whole warband might prove a problem, even for her. But she had betrayed the Bloodsworn, turned her back on them, and her oath. How could she ask or allow any of the Bloodsworn to risk their lives for her now?

They already have, a voice in her thought-cage said. *You would likely not be breathing if they had not joined in the fight against Myrk and her Raven-Feeders.*

"Glornir said the *Sea-Wolf* is crew light," Orka mumbled. "You'll need every arm at an oar."

"We can manage," Edel said. "Three less will make little difference. Ingmar rows hard enough for three, anyway."

"I do," Ingmar grinned.

"But . . ." Orka said.

"There is something in this that makes my skin crawl," Edel continued, frowning. "Raven-Feeders, dragon-born, dark dreams of Lik-Rifa . . ." She looked at Orka. "I am scared, and something is whispering to me that your son is deep in the weave of it all. Glornir will want to find out what is going on." She smiled and blew out a short breath. "That is what my thought-cage is telling me, anyway, and I am chief of this crew for now, so the decision is mine." She nodded as if all was decided and made to walk away. Orka reached out and gripped her wrist.

"I walked away from the Bloodsworn, turned my back on you," Orka said, the words thick in her throat, sticking. "I do not deserve . . ." the words dried and turned to ash in her mouth.

"Deserve has nothing to do with it," Edel said, looking deep into Orka's eyes. She turned away. "Here are your new crew," she said more loudly as the three Bloodsworn drew near. "They're not worth much, but better than nothing, I suppose."

"Thanks for that, chief," Revna said.

"You don't have to do this," Orka said to them. "My path is dark and most likely full of death. Maybe your death, if you come with me. As I keep telling Lif, you may not come back from it."

"She does," Lif agreed, nodding.

"We are Bloodsworn," Revna Hare-Legs shrugged. "Death is a companion we are well-used to."

"Why would you come with me?" Orka asked them.

"My brother fell here," Halja Flat-Nose said. "Slain by a troll who fought for the dragon-born." She gestured to the corpse of the man that Myrk had called father. "The troll is dead, but I would see those who set this in motion. I would put them in the ground, if I can."

Vengeance, I understand that well enough. She looked at Gunnar Prow and Revna Hare-Legs.

"Better than breaking my back at an oar-bench on the *Sea-Wolf*," Gunnar Prow smiled.

"He'll only slow us down, with that leg," Edel said. "I will be setting a fast pace through these hills until we are on the *Sea-Wolf*'s deck."

Orka knew the lie of that. They had thirty horses between them now, with those taken from the Raven-Feeders, so Gunnar could ride, and with spare mounts they could ride hard for days without stopping.

"And you?" Orka asked Revna.

"You are the Skullsplitter," Revna said with a shrug. "A walking saga-tale back from the dead. I'm thinking you're in the weave of a skáld-song that will be sung from one end of Vigrið to the other." She grinned. "I'd like to be in that song."

"All right, then," Orka said, puffing her cheeks out. "We'll leave as soon as we're ready."

A wail drew all their eyes to Vesli, who was stood atop a dead Raven-Feeder, a pile of bloody teeth between her cupped palms, trying to force them into the pouch at her belt. She froze, as if realising that all in the glade were staring at her, and looked up.

"What's wrong?" Orka asked the tennúr.

"*Too many teeth for my pouch,*" she said, shoulders slumping. "*Vesli going to need a bigger bag.*"

CHAPTER TWENTY-THREE

GUÐVARR

Guðvarr followed Skalk out of Queen Helka's chamber and into the corridor, where the *Úlfhéðnar* guards stood, still and menacing. Skalk turned left instead of right, which would have taken them back to the mead hall, and walked down the corridor. Guðvarr followed, and Yrsa followed him. Soon Skalk stopped before a timber wall.

"Close your eyes and turn around," Skalk said, and Guðvarr did. Normally he would have been tempted to open his eyes a crack, to try and see what was hidden, but he was with a Galdurman, who could reputedly conjure fire in the palm of his hand and sear flesh from bones. Skalk was a man that Guðvarr did not want to offend. Also, Yrsa was staring intently at him, and her cold gaze unnerved him. He heard Skalk's voice, muttering incomprehensible words, and then there was a grating sound and a breeze, as if someone had opened a window.

"Turn around and open your eyes," Skalk told him.

There was a hole in the ground, steps leading down into darkness, torches flickering.

"Follow me," Skalk said, striding down the steps. Guðvarr hesitated a moment, never liking the thought of being in a place where he felt trapped, where he was not confident of a quick escape. He felt something prod his back, Yrsa poking him. He followed after Skalk. Looking around he saw they were in a tunnel, wide enough for two abreast, braced with timber. Torches crackled. As the ground levelled, he heard a scraping sound behind him and looked back, saw that Yrsa was closing the entrance to the tunnel, like the last stone placed upon a barrow.

No going back now, then.

"I am showing you considerable trust, here," Skalk said as they walked. "Very few know of this tunnel, but I consider myself a good judge of character. I see qualities in you that I like. That could be mutually beneficial."

Guðvarr found himself nodding and smiling.

"You are a warrior of some skill, to be a named *drengr*, but there are too many of them around here for that to be considered anything other than ordinary. More importantly, I think you have a sharp mind, with some wit and cunning."

You see much, and have great wisdom, that is clear, Guðvarr thought, walking a little straighter, a little taller.

"You are ambitious, I can see that in your eyes, and your actions."

Yes. Yes, I am, Guðvarr agreed.

"And brave. The way you chose to help me at the Grimholt. When blood was spraying and warriors dying, that was not the easiest choice."

I am brave, Guðvarr thought. *Exceptionally so.*

"It is true, in my village I am counted among the bravest, though I am loath to admit it," he said.

A grunt from behind, Yrsa clearing her throat.

"And humble, too," Skalk said.

"I find the greatest warriors do not need to sing their own praises," Guðvarr said. "That is what the Skálds are for." *And one day soon they shall be singing of me.*

"Yes, true enough," Skalk said. "And you have a strong sense of self-preservation."

Guðvarr frowned, his smile faltering. Where he came from, that could be considered another way of saying *cowardly*.

"You are a survivor," Skalk clarified.

That's more like it, Guðvarr thought. *To be a survivor is the opposite of being a fool. Staying and fighting at the Grimholt was the fool's choice.*

Retreat and live to fight again, that is the deep-cunning mark of a strat-egist, and that's what I did at the Grimholt. Seize the opportunities presented to you, that's what I say.

You ran because you were scared, another voice whispered in his thought-cage.

"Because I see these qualities in you," Skalk continued, "I am giving you an opportunity, which is what you want, yes?"

"Um, yes," Guðvarr said. *Can he read my mind,* he thought, feeling uncomfortable, desperately trying to remember all he had thought while in the company of this Galdurman.

Skalk drew to an abrupt halt and turned around, Guðvarr skid-ding to a stop. He felt Yrsa's presence behind him.

"Of course, if you prove to be untrustworthy," Skalk said, leaning forward, brows knitting, their noses almost touching, "then I will introduce you to pain you could not begin to imagine; I will turn your eyeballs to skyr, melt the flesh from your bones, and grind them into dust." He held a hand out. "*Eldur,*" he whispered, and a spark of flame flickered into life on the Galdurman's palm, curled hungrily.

Guðvarr gulped, tried to take a step back, but Yrsa's solid presence was a wall behind him.

"Your aunt could search for you for the rest of her life, and never find one single hair from your head."

A silence settled between them, Skalk holding Guðvarr's gaze. He tried not to gulp. He felt a wetness running down his nose.

Skalk's fist closed with a snap, snuffing the flame out.

"Do we understand each other?" he said.

I am a man of honour, and I find your slurs and threats insulting, he thought.

"Yes," Guðvarr squeaked.

"Excellent," Skalk smiled, then turned on a heel and walked on. Guðvarr followed, a little reluctantly, but Yrsa's presence behind him felt like an unseen hand, pushing him on.

"Of course, I have my own reasons for taking this risk with you," Skalk continued, "and they are not entirely altruistic. I want you to befriend Prince Hakon."

"Prince Hakon?" Guðvarr said, still unsettled from Skalk's unpleasant threats.

"Yes. I have reason to believe that he is . . . concealing things from his mother."

Nothing wrong with that, Guðvarr thought. *Who doesn't?*

"Things that could put this realm at risk."

Ah, not so good. And it sounds like it could possibly be dangerous. Deeds in the shadows, knives in the back, bodies thrown in the river.

"If I may ask, Lord Skalk, why have you chosen me for this task?"

"Because of the qualities I have seen in you," Skalk said, "and because you are an unknown here. Hakon knows my people in Darl, and his mother's, and he would not trust them. You are an unknown; a young, ambitious warrior, related to a powerful woman. You have common ground. I think he will like you."

Of course he will, Guðvarr thought. *That's not the issue. Staying alive is the issue.*

"Tell me what to do, and I shall give it my all," Guðvarr said.

"Good man," said Skalk as he slowed. Steps appeared ahead and Skalk climbed them, coming to a wooden door. He turned the latch and stepped through the open door, Guðvarr following him. As he drew close to the threshold he felt a resistance, a feathery touch on his skin, like walking through a cobweb, growing thicker, denser with every moment, until he was held immobile, hovering, one foot raised over the entrance. He tried to speak, but even his lips were frozen.

Has he lured me here to kill me? Some kind of Galdur-sacrifice to his dark arts? He felt his bladder twitch as fear flooded through him, but he was so completely immobilised that even his own urine could not escape his body.

Behind him he heard a muffled snort of laughter from Yrsa.

"*Leyfðu honum að líða,*" Skalk said, and the pressure was abruptly gone, Guðvarr stumbling through the doorway and into a large room. Yrsa walked through behind him.

"Welcome to the Galdur tower of Darl," Skalk said.

Guðvarr gazed round. The chamber was high-vaulted, flaming

braziers crackling. It was clearly an entrance chamber, huge oak doors on the far side of the room, a thick timber bar across it, scrollwork carved into the wood, and two warriors stood either side of the door, clothed in bright *brynjas*, shields slung across their backs, spears held loosely. A stairwell curled around the rear wall, climbing up into the shadows.

"Lord Skalk," the two guards said, bowing their heads.

A muffled horn call rang out from beyond the barred gate and the two guards lifted the oak bar and slid it to one side, then pushed the doors open. Pale sunlight stabbed into the entrance hall, making Guðvarr blink. Skalk strode forward and stood in the doorway, Guðvarr close behind him. He looked out into a courtyard, a timber wall circling it, the tops of buildings visible beyond the wall. Guðvarr turned around, trying to get his bearings, and saw the earthwork rampart of Darl's fortress.

The tunnel has taken us out of the fortress and back into the town, he realised. In the courtyard there was a clatter of hooves as a handful of riders rode through an open gateway. All the riders were wearing bone and pewter in their hair, all in the dark tunics that marked them out as Galdurmen and -women. Guðvarr recognised dark-haired Sturla, the Galdurwoman from the night they had arrived. She was as pale as milk, her skin drawn tight like a hide across a tanning frame, a bruise purpling across one side of her face. Others swayed in their saddles, some with bloodied faces, and one rider was leading another horse, a body lying across the saddle, tied in place, tunic torn, one hand hanging limp. Something was being dragged behind Sturla's horse, attached to the saddle with rope and chain. It looked at first to Guðvarr like a new-felled tree, but as he looked closer he saw details among the bark and branches: hair, arms, a face.

A wooden statue? he thought.

"We have her," Sturla said as she reined in before Skalk, "though the cost was heavy. I fear Kuru might die."

Skalk walked past Sturla and stood staring at the statue of wood attached to Sturla's saddle. He reached out and touched it, Guðvarr shuffling closer and seeing a carved face in the timber, the details so intricately crafted as to look almost lifelike. A woman, mouth open in a scream of pain and rage, face distorted, eyes wide, tendons rigid in her neck.

"Is that . . ."

"A Froa-spirit," Skalk said. "Well. She was, before Sturla and my apprentices killed her tree. You have done well," he added, glancing up at Sturla, a smile spreading across his face. "Quickly, bring her." He turned and strode back into the Galdur tower, Yrsa at his heel.

Guðvarr just stood there as Skalk and the others passed through the tower's wide gates. He heard a screech above him and looked up, saw a hawk circling in the pale sky. It spiralled down and alighted upon the tower's stockade wall, its head twisting to regard him with a liquid eye. Guðvarr frowned. He didn't like the way the bird was looking at him, as if he were its prey. A sense of unease had been growing in his belly since he'd stepped into Skalk's tunnel, and now there was a looseness in his bowels that felt more like fear than the effects of last night's fire-mead.

If I wait a few moments I could just slip away, out through that gate and go back to my bed. I wonder if that whore is still there, keeping it warm?

"Guðvarr, what are you doing?" Skalk called, peering through the door at him. "Keep up."

"Yes, my lord," Guðvarr sighed and followed the Galdurman.

Sturla and the other apprentices had all dismounted, stable hands hurrying to take reins and lead horses away. Only Sturla led her own horse into the tower, still dragging the dead Froa-spirit as she followed Skalk. Skalk opened another door and disappeared through it, Guðvarr hurrying to catch up and finding himself in a long corridor, on each side rooms sealed with iron bars. Some were empty, others had people inside. Guðvarr saw big-nosed Skapti and gangling Hrolf from the Grimholt in one.

Is Arild locked up somewhere in here with my aunt's drengrs?

They approached the end of the corridor, another door set into the wall. As Guðvarr drew closer to it he felt his skin start to prickle, sweat beading on his forehead. Skalk stopped at the last chamber before the door and one of his apprentices slipped an iron key into the lock and opened the iron-barred door. A woman was inside, lying on a cot, her hands bound with iron shackles. It was Vol, the Seiðr-witch. Guðvarr took a step back at the sight of her. The blue tattoos on her neck and jaw were hard to distinguish for the mottled bruising that covered her. One eye was swollen shut; blood caked on a gash on her forehead. But it was to her mouth that Guðvarr's eyes were drawn in horrified fascination.

They had been stitched shut, the stitch holes red-raw and swollen, some leaking watery pus, linen thread caked with clotted blood.

"She has given us some trouble," Skalk said by way of explanation. "Vol, on your feet," he said. The Seiðr-witch looked at him through one bloodshot eye, and beaten and battered as she was Guðvarr still felt the urge to back away, this time from fear rather than revulsion.

You have made an enemy there, my lord, he thought. *If I were you, I would hope she is never free to practise her Seiðr-art against you.*

With a muffled grunt Vol staggered to her feet and stood there glowering at Skalk.

"Bring her," Skalk said, four of his apprentices moving cautiously to surround Vol. She mumbled something, spit and blood frothing on her stitched lips, dribbling down her chin and then her chains were grabbed and they were dragging her from the chamber.

Skalk walked to the single door at the end of the corridor and placed his palm upon it.

"*Opinn*," he said, and with a hiss the door creaked open. Skalk walked through, the door tall and wide enough for Sturla to lead the horse and its cargo after him. Guðvarr darted forward and stumbled to a halt. He was standing in a wide, circular room, high-vaulted with thick crossbeams, a pale glow high in the darkness showing the smoke-hole. People in dark tunics sat at benches around the edges of the room, carving runes into wood, bark and wax tablets. More of these were piled in high banks of shelves that climbed the wall, looking like the inside of a beehive. On a table beside the rune-carvers sat the chest that Guðvarr had carried from the docks to Helka's chamber. The lid was open, and he saw the glint of bone within. Parchments had been unrolled and weighted down, the rune-carvers copying what they saw on to their bark tablets. Elsewhere were clay jars, hundreds of them, of varying sizes, piled one upon the other, and rows of barrels, each with a rune carved into it. Cages were stacked and piled on one side of the room, Guðvarr seeing movement within some of them. A grey-striped serpent uncoiled and hissed, giving Guðvarr a dead-eyed stare; a pale-furred lynx padded endlessly back and forth in its cage; in another a tennúr was sitting and staring into space with its wings loose and draped on the ground. A larger cage, tall as two men, with a dense-leaved bush inside it. Guðvarr saw green eyes staring out and, as he watched, a creature emerged, smaller than a man, thin as a sapling, hair like a snarl of leaves, skin dark and grained like wax-polished wood, patches of moss and lichen dappling its body. Its fingers were curled and sharp as thorns. It gripped the bars of its cage and curled its lips at Guðvarr.

"*Arseling*," the creature snarled at him.

"What's that?" Guðvarr muttered, taking a step back and scowling at the creature.

"A faunir," Skalk said.

"It's rude," Guðvarr muttered, "and would not be so brave and foolish as to insult me if those bars were not there to protect it."

I'm glad those bars are there to protect me, he thought. A flicker of movement drew his eyes to a pool that was dug into the ground, the water black and oily. A ripple revealed the presence of something beneath the surface.

"Stay away from the water's edge," Skalk advised as Guðvarr took a few steps closer. "There's a Näcken in there."

This is a place of monsters! Guðvarr thought, his skin crawling.

On the far side of the pool there was a tree, though it looked dead, its branches bare, and around the trunk's waist there was a protuberance, like a fat man's belly spilling over his breeches. It glittered with flickering colours, amber and green and gold shifting through it like sunlight through rain. As Guðvarr stared at it he saw the surface was moving. Crawling with . . .

"What is that?" Guðvarr murmured.

"A hyrndur's nest," Skalk said as he directed Sturla, who was unclipping the chains that held the dead Froa from her saddle. The chains fell to the ground with a rattle.

Guðvarr took a few paces back. Hyrndur were kin to wasps, but far larger and far more aggressive. A sting from one could paralyse you for a few moments, and when you returned to your senses the pain was supposed to be unbearable. Worse than that, though, was the fact that the females liked to burrow into your flesh and hibernate there, only waking to lay their egg-sacks within your pulsing blood. His aunt Sigrún had told Guðvarr a terrible tale of a man whose neck had swollen while he was sitting listening to sagas at a hearth fire, and before the story was over his skin was ripping and bursting like ripe fruit, a hundred hyrndur swarming out of his veins, wet and bloated with blood. Guðvarr winced and stepped away, making sure that Skalk stood between him and the nest.

At the room's centre was what looked like a giant link of chain, black and pitted with age. Half of it was embedded within the ground, and beside it was a table, iron rings and leather straps bolted into the wood. Dark patches were stained into the table, looking suspiciously like blood.

"What *is* this place?" Guðvarr said, unable to keep the disgust from his voice or face. "And is it safe in here?" He wished he was somewhere else. *Anywhere* else.

"Of course it's safe," Skalk said, "everything in here knows not to disobey me." He looked around the room, a beatific smile spreading across his face. "This is the beating heart of my tower." He nodded towards the chain in the centre of the room. "And that is a shard of Ulfrir's chain, that bound him on the *Guðfalla*. A shaving of that is forged into every thrall-collar that we use upon the Tainted." He looked at Vol, his smile fading. "Take her to the table," he said and Yrsa grabbed her chains and pulled her towards the table. "Guðvarr, help us with this," Skalk asked as he gripped one of the chains attached to the dead Froa-spirit. Guðvarr took one of the chains in his fists, other Galdur-apprentices hurrying to help, and together they dragged the dead Froa across the chamber, setting her down with a thud next to the central table.

Yrsa had secured Vol's chains to one of the iron rings set in the table, Skalk stepping close to the Seiðr-witch and raising a hand to touch the iron collar around her neck.

"You see I have a Froa to carve a new staff from and, once that is done, I will have the power to remove this collar and replace it with one of my own. Once I have my collar around your neck, I think we'll get along far better. I'll have the stitches cut from your lips."

I am sure she would be gushing with thanks, if she could only open her lips and speak, Guðvarr thought.

Skalk turned his cold gaze on to Guðvarr.

"Strap him to the table," he said.

What?

He looked around, thinking Skalk must be talking about someone else, but many hands grabbed him, Yrsa first among them, a thin smile on her lips. Sturla grabbed him as well, and he was pulled towards the table.

"What? No," Guðvarr squeaked, struggling, "there must be some mistake." His voice rose in pitch. "Put me down." He was lifted from the ground and slammed on to the table. "LET ME GO," he shouted, his voice quavering between scream and shriek.

Chains rattled, locks clicking, and leather buckles were wrenched tight about his wrists and ankles, Guðvarr finding himself staring up into the eaves of the room, where shadows were thick. He saw a rat scuttling across one of the roof-beams.

Skalk leaned over him.

"Please don't kill me," Guðvarr whispered, feeling panic building in his chest, a sob welling in his throat.

"I'm not going to kill you," Skalk said pleasantly.

"W-what are you doing, then?"

Skalk looked over his shoulder and lifted his hand, palm flat and open.

"*Hyrndur, komdu til mín*," Skalk called out, his voice deep and loud, filling the room. A silence, Guðvarr frowning, trying to turn his head to see what Skalk was looking at, but there were too many people in the way. He saw Vol looking at him, a sadness in her eyes.

She has been beaten bloody and had her lips stitched together, and yet she still feels sadness for my *plight?* Now he was truly scared.

A sound in the silence, faint, growing. A buzzing. A shape flew above Skalk's outstretched palm, circled and landed upon his hand, opaque wings whirring and folding over a creature's back. A creature with six jointed legs, a hairy body and an orange-striped, tapering abdomen that ended in a hooked, glistening sting. Its head had two large, black eyes, twitching antennae and razored mandibles. A hyrndur.

Skalk nodded to Yrsa and she pulled the sleeve of Guðvarr's tunic up his arm.

"Remember, in your home you are counted among the bravest," Yrsa said, her thin smile spreading.

No, Guðvarr thought, his throat constricting, unable to find breath to form words.

Skalk lowered his palm, bringing the hyrndur closer to Guðvarr's face. It was bigger than Skalk's thumb, taking up most of the Galdurman's palm.

"Please, no," Guðvarr managed to breathe. He swallowed, trying to control the fear. *I will not weep. This is a test; it must be. He will stop in a moment. Any moment now. Show your courage.*

"This is a female hyrndur," Skalk said, matter-of-factly, as if he were discussing the weather. "She is ready to burrow, and then lay her eggs." He lowered his hand, angled it so that the hyrndur walked on to Guðvarr's forearm, just above his wrist, its antennae touching his skin, searching. It walked forward, barbed feet digging into Guðvarr's flesh, leaving faint droplets of blood in its path, and stopped at the joint of his elbow. It lowered its head and *clacked* its mandibles with an audible snap.

"Do not try and shake her off," Skalk warned. "That will not work, her feet have barbs in them that hook into your skin. You would only make her angry."

It's a test. It's a test, it's a test, Guðvarr told himself, feeling his limbs begin to shake uncontrollably.

"I have given you a task that involves the fate of a prince and possibly a realm, shown you a secret tunnel into the queen's chambers, brought you into the ancient Galdur tower of Darl and invited you into my inner sanctum," Skalk said. "You did not think that I was just going to *trust* you, did you?"

Actually, I did, you deceitful bastard, Guðvarr thought, feeling his grasp on whatever resolve and determination he had left begin to crumble. He could not draw his eyes or attention away from the monster on his arm for long enough to form any kind of comprehensible response.

"Now, let me tell you what is going to happen, so that you do not panic and make this worse for yourself. I am going to tell this hyrndur to burrow into your flesh, and to find a nice warm spot close to your heart. She will be my spy within a spy, if you will." He smiled at his own joke. Guðvarr let out a little whimper. "In your dealings with Prince Hakon, and in all things, she will know if you are true to me, or if you are betraying me. No harm will come to you if you stay true to me; well, no permanent harm, anyway. I won't lie, this *is* going to hurt, and this will be no quick-sting-and-then-it's-over. It will take a while for the hyrndur to reach her resting place. But, pain fades, and you will still have your life. Consider her my reassurance. And when your task is completed, I shall ask her to return to me." Skalk pulled a face. "That will hurt as well, but," he shrugged, "better than death, no?"

"Please, please, please," Guðvarr begged, unable to stop the words pouring from his lips, tears streaming from his eyes, snot rolling down his nose, trickling down his face. All thought of holding his courage was a vague and distant memory. Dimly he was aware of someone sniggering.

"*Hyrndur, búðu heimili þitt í holdi hans og bíddu eftir orði mínu*," Skalk said and the hyrndur's mandibles opened wide, the creature dipping its head towards Guðvarr's flesh.

"PLEASE," Guðvarr cried and then the hyrndur's mandibles tore into his arm, ripping, gouging, burrowing, and Guðvarr screamed, thrashing his head, his body rigid as agony seared through him. He felt a pressure in his arm, looked down and saw that the hyrndur was half buried in his flesh, just its orange-striped abdomen and sting still visible among a pool of his own blood. He sucked in a lungful of air and cried out again, eyes bulging, staring up into the darkness overhead. A hawk was sitting upon a beam straight above him, watching him. It opened its beak and screeched, though Guðvarr could not hear it for the sound of his own screaming.

CHAPTER TWENTY-FOUR

VARG

Varg tried to stop himself staring as he walked through the streets of Darl.

I thought Liga must have been the biggest town in all Vigrið, he thought. *I was wrong.* Sounds and scents assailed him, the crush of buildings looming either side and people funnelled like rats in a tunnel crushed tight all around him. Walls reared high, the sky a strip of grey above him. It was almost overwhelming. Glornir had split the Bloodsworn into a dozen small bands of three or four, all of them filtering into the town from differing directions over a period of time, the plan to make their way slowly to the Galdur tower that sat at the rear of the fortress. Varg's group, led by Svik and including Jökul and a short, squat, fair-haired woman called Æsa had entered the town from the west, where buildings sprawled among the canals and tributary rivers that fed into the body of the River Drammur. The stench had been overwhelming as they'd moved through waterways surrounded by slaughterhouses and tanneries, blood running in streams across the ground, offal floating in the stagnant canals. Svik had led them on, higher up the hill, and now they were passing through the trading quarter of the town, which ran like a central ring around the slopes of Darl's hill. Traders lined the muddy streets, tables set out with all manner of goods. Skins and furs, jewellery, belts, pouches, axes, knives, spear-heads, seaxes, bolts of cloth and wool, bundles of walrus ivory and elk antler, others with food, pots of bubbling soup, skewered meat turning on spits, fresh-baked bread. Varg eyed the food, slowing as the scent of frying onions and pork drew him.

"Keep up," Svik said over his shoulder and Varg hurried on. *Habits of a thrall*, he thought. He was not particularly hungry, but life as a thrall on Kolskegg's farm had taught him to take food as and when it came to him.

"Smells good," Æsa said to him, offering a biscuit to Varg from her pouch. He took it without thinking, nodded his thanks.

"Always best to go into a scrap with something in your belly," Æsa said, a grin on her face. She did not look much like a warrior, but Varg had sparred with her while they had been camped in the woods, and she was fast and slippery as an eel. She seemed to feel no pain, either. Quite the opposite. She'd laughed when Varg had struck her on the head by accident with the butt of his spear.

Varg looked up as he nibbled on his biscuit, saw that day was fading, twilight filtering into the world.

The time is close. He felt his pulse quicken, a nervous excitement rippling through him. The black spike of the Galdur tower loomed ahead, rising over the other buildings of the town, and behind it Varg saw the earthwork ramparts of the fortress, a stockade wall at its summit, the glint of steel from guards walking upon it. Beyond that he glimpsed the arch of Orna's skeletal wings, spreading wide over the summit of the hill. He felt the dead god's presence in his bones, a slow, steady pulse, like a drumbeat, growing with every step he took up the hill.

"Where is the thrall-market in this town?" he asked Æsa.

"On the east side, close to the docks," Æsa said, gesturing at and over the fortress.

Varg frowned at that. He had hoped their path would take them through the slaver's quarter.

"Mind on the job," Svik said, overhearing Varg and looking back at him with a frown. He wore a wool cloak, a hood pulled up over his head and tight over his *brynja*, no shield upon his back. All of them had left their shields behind, stacked in the wagon with the children from the Grimholt.

"*We can give no sign that the Bloodsworn are marching into Darl*," Glornir had said. "*No shields. Hide mail and weapons under cloaks, and take your time in making your way to the Galdur tower. As long as you are all there for sunset. That will be when Helka sits in her feast-hall for the evening meal with her oathsworn and guests about her.*"

"Aye," Varg grunted, though knowing that the slaver who had sold his sister on to her death could be so close gnawed at him.

Svik slowed and stepped into the shadows of a space between two buildings. Jökul, Æsa and Varg followed him into the darkness.

"Remember the plan," Svik said quietly to them as they all shuffled close. "Wait for Glornir to move, then we all go. In and out, fast as we can. Speed is our friend, here."

Varg knew that. Glornir had told them the problems they would face. Gaining entry into a rune-guarded Galdur tower, facing an unknown number of Galdurmen and -women, all without the help of any Seiðr-witch to balance their runic powers. Finding Vol once they were inside. And that was without the risk of rousing Queen Helka's *drengrs*.

"*Skalk has his own warrior-retinue, as well as a number of apprentices, all of varying Galdur-power,*" Glornir had told them.

"Anyone gets into a scrap, end it quick," Svik said. "Stay close together, help each other. Only call on your beast if you have to, if the only other outcome is your death, and make sure any that see you do not live to tell the tale. We are Bloodsworn, we are Tainted, but the world cannot know that."

Grunts and nods.

"You know the meeting place if we get separated, if things go wrong?"

"Aye," Varg said.

"That won't happen," Æsa said, smiling as if they were talking about a name-day blot. "These arselings won't know what's hit them."

Svik smiled, the glint of his white teeth in the shadows.

"Well then," he said. "The tower is close, and so is dusk. Check your kit and we'll move."

Svik pushed the hood of his cloak back and checked over the braid of his beard, then smoothed his moustaches, pulled his hair tight to his nape and bound it with leather.

Varg leaned his spear against a wall and reached for his seax, checked the draw from its scabbard, then brushed his hand over his hand-axe and cleaver, both hanging at his belt. They had all left their helms back in the wagon, knowing that a band of mailed and helmeted warriors moving on the Galdur tower would raise suspicion.

Æsa blew snot from her nostrils, then slapped her face hard, leaving a red mark.

"Pain wakes me up," she said to Varg's look. "Makes me sharp. I like it."

"Like it?" Varg repeated.

"Ha," she said at the look on his face, part laugh, part snarl.

Jökul dropped to one knee and placed his palm on to the ground, scooped a handful of mud, then stood and rubbed his hands together. He wiped his hands on the pitted leather apron that he wore over his *brynja*, then lifted the head of his hammer that sat in a loop on his belt, let it slip back into place.

"Why do you do that?" Varg asked him.

Jökul stood straight, slapping his hands together.

"The sagas tell us that Snaka made us from the mud of the world, moulding us like a potter moulds clay and, when he was pleased with our form, that he breathed his Seiðr-breath into us, giving us life. When we die, it does not take long for us to go back to the ground, to become what we were, once the spark of life has left us. So, I do this to remind me, of where we came from, of where we are headed, and that this life is fleeting. Best to make the most of it. To fight hard and fierce." He shrugged, pulling the pitted, iron-headed hammer from his belt and hefting it. "It also helps my grip."

"This is not the time for sitting comfortably and listening to saga-tales, No-Sense," Svik said, slapping him on the shoulder. "This is the time to *make* the saga-tale."

"This will be a song, and no denying," Æsa grinned. "How the

Bloodsworn walked into the Galdur tower of Darl and took back one of their own."

Varg looked down at his hands. They were shaking. His mouth was dry, a fluttering in his belly; fear, anticipation.

Will I ever get used to this?

A hand gripped his wrist, Jökul. "It is normal before a fight, brother," he said.

Brother. How have I had such good fortune to find these people, after so many years of loneliness and pain?

Varg nodded, remembering those moments before his bouts in the pugil-ring.

"The *drengr* who slew Torvik," Jökul said. "Yrsa. She is Skalk's oathsworn, so we may well cross paths with her."

"Aye," Varg said.

"It will be good to avenge Torvik if we have the chance," Jökul said. "He was a good lad."

"He was," Varg agreed, remembering Yrsa stabbing her sword into Torvik's throat, how he had held his friend's hand as the life had faded from his eyes. How the wolf in his blood had howled for vengeance.

He felt the presence of the wolf in his blood now, a shadow prowling within him. Felt it growl, a silent shudder rippling through him.

No, he told it. *Wait until you are called.*

He reached out and gripped his spear, pulled the leather cover off the blade and tucked it into his belt.

"With me," Svik said, and stepped out of the shadows.

The streets quietened as they moved out of the traders' ring and passed along a road that reeked of iron and charcoal. Varg heard a hiss and jumped, saw a cloud of steam boil out of a doorway. Jökul touched Varg's arm.

"Blacksmiths," he said, teeth glinting in a grin through his white-streaked beard.

Varg blew out a breath, trying to calm his nerves.

The tower loomed huge and black now, only a few rows of buildings separating them.

A scream rang out. A solitary wail cut short by a thud.

Then shouting, the clang of steel. Horses neighing and the drum of hooves.

A concussive explosion, shaking Varg and all the others, Jökul stumbling and steadying himself against a building.

They all shared a look and broke into a run.

CHAPTER TWENTY-FIVE

GUÐVARR

Guðvarr lay gasping upon the table. His chest was heaving, tears and sweat mingled, stinging his eyes, his body slick with it. The pain was still there, worst in his arm, a rhythmic throbbing where the hyrndur had bored its way into his flesh, and there was a pulsing trail through his body where he had felt it squirming and burrowing up his arm and into his chest. But the pain he felt now was nothing compared to what he had just been through.

Unimaginable, unthinkable pain. Agony. Torment. He heard someone whimpering, realised it was his own voice. *It's over, it's over*, he told himself, knowing that the creature had stopped moving now. He could still feel it, though, a pressure, deep inside.

It has made a home of my flesh; it is living within me.

The thought was horrific and terrifying in equal measure. If he had had the strength left, he would have screamed again, just at the thought of it, but he was too exhausted, his body drained, throat raw, his voice little more than a rasping croak.

Other pains filtered into his consciousness; his wrists and ankles where he had fought and thrashed against his bonds of leather and iron. The smell of urine wafted up to him.

Did I . . .? He didn't even have the energy to feel ashamed. Blinking sweat, he found he was staring up, into the darkness of the roof, a pinprick of fading light marking the smoke-hole.

It was brighter when I was first strapped here, he thought. The hawk was still there, sitting half in shadow on a cross beam, regarding him and all in the room.

A face loomed over him, blotting out the hawk.

"You see," Skalk said. "You still live. I told you; you are a survivor." He smiled, and Guðvarr wanted to rip the man's throat out with his bare hands. He looked away, tears stinging his eyes and saw Vol the Seiðr-witch was still shackled to the table. She was looking at him with sad, pitying eyes.

The hawk in the rafters screeched again, and Skalk twisted to look up at the bird.

A faint scream, distant.

Outside?

A crash shook the room, Guðvarr feeling it in his bones.

"What?" Skalk said. A moment's silence. Then. "We are under attack."

Movement, people bursting into motion, blurs in Guðvarr's peripheral vision. He glimpsed Yrsa shrugging the shield from her back and drawing her sword.

A second crash, far louder than the first, the ground shaking, rattling the table Guðvarr was strapped upon. People around him fell. He flopped his head to stare.

A hole in the wall, daylight leaking through, cracks rippling out from it like a cobweb. Galdur-apprentices spread in a line between Guðvarr's table and the wall. Creatures in cages growled, hissed and screeched. A splash of water in the Näcken pool. The sound of shouting, the clash of steel filtered through the crack in the wall.

A third concussive crash and the wall exploded inwards, something smashing its way through and falling sprawling on the ground. Timber sprayed, splinters raining down around Guðvarr, one stabbing like a spear into the wood between his legs. He whimpered. Looked back at the hole again.

A man rose slowly from the ground. Black-skinned, shaven-haired, a tunic torn and tattered, his physique impossibly muscled, shoulders and back hunched. He wore a thick iron collar about his neck. Two lumps grew from his forehead, like the beginning of horns, and he was breathing heavily, breath snorting from his nostrils in clouds.

He looks like a bull.

The huge man opened his mouth and bellowed. Dust shook in a cloud from the rafters.

Other figures filled the great hole in the wall behind him. Figures on horseback, bows in their hands, pouring through in a clatter of hooves and horseflesh. The twang and hiss as arrows were loosed, screams and people fell.

"*Eldskjöldur rís upp, verndaðu okkur,*" Skalk cried, a shield of runes and flames hissing into being in the air before him. Those Galdurmen and -women still standing drew close about him.

"*Eldskjöldur rís upp, verndaðu okkur,*" they called out together, and then a shield wall of flaming runes crackled into life. The snap of bowstrings as another volley of arrows was loosed, more riders pushing through the gaping hole in the Galdur tower's wall. A sizzling hiss as the arrows hit the rune-wall and they burst into flames, wood popping and charring, feathers evaporating in a hiss.

"*Eldur skar hann til beina,*" Skalk snarled, standing close to Guðvarr, and a spike of flame appeared in the Galdurman's fist. He hurled it like a knife, and it sped through the air, stabbed into the face of a rider wearing a horsehair-plumed helm. The rider screamed, dropping her bow and tearing at her face as flames rippled across her eyes, consuming her flesh. Other riders were pushing around the man who had smashed a hole in the wall, spreading into the room, trying to find angles around the rune-wall of flames for their arrows. More barbs of fire were hurled at them from the Galdur-apprentices, less powerful than Skalk's, but still causing a ripple of screams across the room. One horse and rider passed close to the pool and the slime-slick tentacles of a Näcken slithered out, wrapping around the horse's legs. The horse neighed wildly as it was dragged to the pool's edge, the rider loosing arrow after arrow into the tentacles, but if the Näcken felt them, it did not show it. A savage wrench and then the horse was toppling into the pool, water erupting in a fountain, the rider scrambling to leap from his saddle, but another tentacle snaked out, gripping his ankle and with a choking scream he was dragged beneath the water.

The huge man who had smashed the wall down let out another deafening roar and ran at Skalk and the wall of flaming runes. He tucked his head down, charging like a bull, and slammed into the rune-shield. An explosive crack as the wall of flames buckled, two of the Galdur-apprentices hurled from their feet, and some of the rune-shields hissed, stuttered and went out. Fire caught in the bull man's tunic, crackling hungrily, and the bull man roared and stumbled, slapping at the flames as they spread across his body. Another flight of arrows, most of them incinerated by the flames, but some slipping through the gaps the bull man had made. More screams among the Galdurmen and -women.

Skalk glowered at his fallen apprentices and looked over to the hyrndur nest.

"*Hyrndur, heyrðu kall mitt, hlýddu mér núna. Snúðu reiði þinni að þessum boðflenna,*" he yelled, gesturing at the nest, veins of red light rippling across his hand, and there was a furious buzzing filling the room, hyrndur bursting from the nest in a seething mass, hovering and circling for a moment, then launching themselves at the intruders.

"*Stinga þá, rífa þá, drepa þá,*" Skalk roared as the hyrndur reached the first of the mounted warriors, enveloping them like an orange-veined cloud. Screams, rising in pitch, horses neighing, blurred shapes falling, crashing to the ground, the hyrndur swarming and seething in a furious storm of wings and mandibles and stings.

The clatter of hooves and a rider broke around the flank of the Galdurmen and -women, spurring her mount at Skalk, a long spear levelled at his chest.

Yrsa leaped in front of the Galdurman and swept the spear wide with her shield, stepped around the charging horse and stabbed up with her sword. A gurgled scream as the rider toppled backwards, blood spurting from her throat.

A screeching from above and Guðvarr looked up to see the hawk swooping down, talons outstretched. It slammed on to Skalk's head, talons tearing and ripping at him. Skalk screamed, staggering, hands grabbing at the hawk as its talons tore his flesh, its beak stabbing down. He grabbed a leg, tore the bird from his face and hurled it away, Guðvarr seeing rivulets of blood pouring down Skalk's face, flesh flapping, one of his eyes a blood-filled hole.

The hyrndur's buzzing changed and Guðvarr saw their swarm break up, the winged creatures flying in all directions. They still attacked anything in their way with a frightening ferocity, but their attacks were random now, no longer a controlled, cohesive swarm moving together. Guðvarr saw some of them flying out through the hole in the wall and disappearing.

A new figure stepped through the ruin of the wall, a woman, hood thrown back, her head shaved, covered in a snarl of coiled tattoos, more tattoos swirling up her arms and disappearing up the sleeves of her tunic. She, too, wore an iron thrall-collar about her neck. She walked beside a rider, Prince Jaromir sitting tall in his saddle, clothed in his gleaming coat of lamellar plate, a curved sword hanging at his hip. He held his arm out and whistled, and the hawk spiralled down to him.

Skalk was leaning against the table, Sturla supporting him, the Galdurman holding his face as blood welled between his fingers.

I hope it hurts, you arseling, Guðvarr thought, though he would have been happier if he was not shackled to a table in the middle of a battle. Although he had a new and deep-burning hatred for Skalk, he realised in this situation it might be better the monster you know. He knew that Skalk was not going to kill him immediately, because the Galdurman had plans for him. But these new arrivals . . . they seemed the type to kill first and ask questions later.

Jaromir reined his horse in, standing silhouetted in the grey of dusk, and the woman strode forward a few paces.

"*Ís og eldur, logar byrjuðu,*" she said, not breaking her stride as she walked towards Skalk and the beleaguered rune-shield. What appeared to be a fine mist swept from her mouth, seething out like wind-blown clouds across the room, encompassing the bull man who had fallen to his knees, his tunic blazing like a torch, and on into the wall of flaming runes. A hissing filled the room, clouds of smoke and steam boiling as the runic flames sputtered and died.

Guðvarr heard shouting, Skalk's voice, and then the cloud of steam was evaporating, clearing and Guðvarr saw the tattooed woman still striding across the room.

Skalk saw her, pointed a hand and sucked in a breath.

"*Jörð opnast, gleypið þessa aumingjalegu orma,*" the woman called out, stamping a foot upon the ground. A great, groaning sound and a fissure opened up at her feet, speeding away from her like ice cracking on a fjord, towards Skalk and the other Galdurmen and -women. The crack opened, growing wider as it moved towards Skalk, the ground shifting, walls creaking, and then Skalk was staggering and sinking. Guðvarr felt the table lurch, craned his head to look down and saw the ground opening beneath them, jagged rocks, shifting soil, all falling into darkness. Sturla dropped from sight, disappearing with a wail. Skalk stumbled and fell with a cry of rage and Yrsa leaped after him. Guðvarr screamed as the table pitched and swayed like a ship in a storm. An ear-splitting crack and the table splintered, Guðvarr's back arching, limbs feeling as if they were being torn from his sockets. He screamed again, and again.

Slowly he realised the table had stopped moving. He was angled down, blood rushing to his head, and he glimpsed Vol still shackled to an iron ring on the table. He could see a black chasm in the ground, heard distant, echoing cries filtering up.

The sound of hooves, the twang, hiss and slap of arrows loosed and thumping into flesh. More screams, the remaining Galdurmen and -women breaking and running. A horse and rider filled Guðvarr's vision, Prince Jaromir with his hawk upon his arm. The tattooed woman walked at his side. She was holding the hand of the bull man, leading him like a child. He was hideously burned and blistered from the Galdur-fire and making small, whimpering sounds.

"Worms," Jaromir said, peering down into the black chasm. "Their grasp of rune-work is not even a match for the Seiðr and Tainted thralls of Iskidan. They are fortunate I did not bring a rune-trained necromancer here with me to this dung heap of a town." His gaze shifted to Vol. "I know what you are, woman," he said. "Glornir's whore." He waved a hand. "Iva, take her," he said, and the tattooed woman placed her hand on the iron ring on the table that Vol was bound to.

"*Járn, þú þolir ekki kraft aldanna, sprungið og brotið,*" Iva the Seiðr-woman said. The iron groaned beneath her hand, rust that would have taken decades to build accumulating and eating into the iron like maggots in flesh. Then with a twist of her hand the iron collar was crumbling away, a handful of rust, and Vol fell free of the table, Iva grabbing her arm and hauling her upright. Jaromir saw Vol's stitched lips and grunted.

"At last, something they do right in this cold-cursed land." He looked around, his mounted warriors filling the room, pursuing the survivors fleeing the chamber. The cries of battle echoed in from outside, and Guðvarr heard warriors shouting in the corridor beyond this room.

"Find the chest," Jaromir called out. He stroked his hawk's head as he waited. "Well done," he said, lovingly as a mother to her child. The hawk's beak was blood-flecked, its talons red.

Hooves, and a woman rode up, clothed in a coat of lamellar plate, a horsehair helm on her head and a curved sword in her fist. With her other hand she was balancing a wooden chest across her saddle. "My lord," she said, balancing it and pulling the lid open.

Jaromir smiled. "That is it," he said. "These fools, to not even know the bones of great Hraeg when they see it. My father will make us rich beyond compare when we put this at his blessed feet."

Ilia grinned back at him and closed the chest with a snap.

The sounds of fighting were louder, fiercer, both in the corridor and beyond the hole in the wall.

"We should be away, my prince," Ilia the warrior said.

"Here," Jaromir said, holding a hand out to Iva. The Seiðr-woman wrapped an arm around Vol and heaved her up over Prince Jaromir's saddle, far stronger than her frame would suggest. Then Jaromir was twitching his reins and his horse was moving, turning and he was riding for the hole in the wall, Ilia following, shouting an order to the other riders in the room and within moments they were all disappearing through it.

Iva walked to the bull man.

"Taras hurt," the man said, his voice deep, echoing in Guðvarr's chest. He put a huge hand to his burned face.

"I know," Iva said. "I will make it better, but first we must get far away from here."

Taras the Bull nodded and Iva took his hand, leading him through the wreckage of the room and out through the hole that he had made.

Guðvarr lay on the table, just breathing, amazed still to be alive. He tugged on his bonds and found that two of the leather straps had snapped. He pulled one hand free and swung himself up and reached over, awkwardly unbuckling the arm that had been bored into by the hyrndur. He sat up on the table, moving slowly, not wanting to dislodge it and send it sliding into the black chasm that loomed beneath him. Pain was shooting up his injured arm. He flexed his fingers, testing them, and slowly bent his arm. A wave of nauseating pain rolled through him and sweat prickled his brow. He sat there a few moments, getting his breathing under control, and pulled the rolled-up sleeve of his tunic down, so that he did not have to see the blood and torn flesh of his arm. Then he leaned forwards and slowly unbuckled the last leather strap around one ankle.

As it came free the table shifted and started to slide into the chasm. With a cry he heaved himself off the table and slammed to the ground, bit back a scream as he took the weight on his injured arm, and lay there, panting.

The sounds of battle outside grew louder and he pushed himself upright.

The room was in ruins. Parts of the splintered wall everywhere, other sections of the room burned and charred. Barrels, tables, jars, cages, were all strewn and scattered as if an angry giant had lost a game of knucklebone and upturned the room. Something rippled beneath the surface of the Näcken pool, and the faunir that had called him an arseling was standing in its cage, staring at him with a nasty little smile on its face.

Best be off, Guðvarr thought. He looked to the hole in the wall, but sounds of combat were loud from that direction, and as he stared, he saw a bald man in mail swinging a great long-axe over his head, hacking into one of the Galdur tower's guardsmen. Blood was spraying.

Not that way, then, he thought and began picking his way through the wreckage of the room. He stepped between the legs of a dead horse, saw the rider still in the saddle, male or female he could not tell, as the face was swollen black and yellow from hyrndur stings. Clay pots were shattered across the floor, and iron-ribbed barrels smashed to pieces. Fluid leaked from them, pooling on the floor, a stench that bit into his throat and made his eyes water. He saw body parts spilled from broken barrels; the hand and forearm of what looked like a troll, a skraeling's head, a barrel full of black-nailed toes and large, blue-veined ears.

Then he stopped, staring at the remains of a broken barrel and what had spilled from it. A human body, bones broken and twisted unnaturally so that it could be folded and squashed into the barrel. He crouched, reached out tentative fingers.

It was Arild.

Her dead eyes were staring at him, her mouth twisted in fear and pain.

After the first flush of shock and horror faded, one thought filled his thought-cage.

That could have been me. He felt relieved. That he had approached Skalk and offered his help. *If not for that I could have ended up with my body broken and stuffed into a barrel. Like her.*

He could not tear his gaze away from Arild's distorted face.

"At least your suffering is over," he told Arild's corpse as he stumbled away, found the door to the corridor and half fell through it.

There were riders at the far end of the corridor, battling with guards of the tower on foot. A horse reared, screaming, and crashed to the ground, rolling, but the tower warriors were being pushed back. Slowly Guðvarr followed them.

"Let us out," a voice hissed, Guðvarr looking to see Skapti, gangling Hrolf and the other warriors who had survived the Grimholt.

Let you out? Don't you think I've got more important things to do than try and help you, you bunch of niðing *idiots,* he thought. *Like saving myself.*

"Sorry, no keys," Guðvarr said, slapping his belt. "I'll try and find them," and then he was hurrying past their cell, ignoring the hissed pleas and threats, and he was approaching the door that led into the entrance chamber. There was a whirl of combat by the gates, but as Guðvarr watched it swept out of the entrance chamber, through the doorway and out into the courtyard, where the shouting and screaming were louder. He picked his way across the entrance chamber, hugging a wall, and peered around the open doorway.

It was almost dark now, a red glow streaking the western sky as the sun bled into the horizon. Braziers flared and crackled in the courtyard, flames snatched by a sharp wind, sending shadows flickering and dancing. Guðvarr had snatched glimpses of combat: a handful of Jaromir's riders loosing arrows, stabbing with spears, chopping down with their curved swords at the guards of the Galdur tower. The red flare of rune-magic flickered and consumed a rider in flames, showing that at least one Galdur-apprentice still fought on. But Guðvarr saw others, too. Indistinct figures in cloaks, the gleam of mail in firelight. A mass of shadows swarmed over the courtyard's wall and leaped into the courtyard, a short, fair-haired woman hitting the ground running, charging at a tower guard and skewering him with a spear. She was laughing as she did it. Others came after her, a solidly built man wielding a blacksmith's hammer, crunching it down on to a tower guard's helm.

Guðvarr looked to the gateway, saw that it was blocked, choked with battle, and there was more combat in front of it, a red-haired warrior with a sword and seax, another with him, lean and savage, a hand-axe in one fist, what looked like a butcher's cleaver in the other. They were attacking both the tower guard and one of Jaromir's riders.

"Need to get out of here," Guðvarr muttered, looking back over his shoulder across the tower's wide entrance chamber and seeing the small door he had entered by. That felt like a long time ago.

Grunts and swearing close by and he twisted back to see two

men stumbling across the courtyard towards him, a tower guard trading blows with the man he had seen with the hammer. He had a moment to suck in a breath and then they crashed into him, the three of them falling to the ground in a tangle of limbs. Something crunched into Guðvarr's nose and he heard a loud crack, tasted blood. He thrashed and writhed and then he was free, rolling across the ground and rising to one knee, blood sheeting from his nose.

The other two still fought on, the man with the hammer punching the tower guard in the face as his other hand searched for his hammer, which lay close by on the ground.

Guðvarr took a few strides, swept up the hammer and with a shriek of vented rage crunched it down on to hammer-man's head. A wet crack, the man's skull breaking open and brains leaking out. He flopped on top of the tower guard, who lay there, pinned and panting.

"I've had enough of pain," Guðvarr spat, wiping blood from his nose with the back of his hand. The guard grunted a thanks and heaved the dead man off him.

A scream from the courtyard drew Guðvarr's attention. The man he had seen with the cleaver was staring at him, wild-eyed, veins bulging in his neck as he screamed something. Guðvarr couldn't hear the words, but he did not need to hear them to know that the man he had just killed must have been cleaver's friend. Shock and grief swept cleaver's face, quickly replaced with rage. He raised his hand-axe high and hurled it.

"Troll shite," Guðvarr hissed, frozen, unable to move, his eyes fixed on the hand-axe that spun towards him.

The tower guard staggered to his feet. A thud and squawk as the axe crunched into the back of his head and he fell into Guðvarr, showering him in fragments of bone and brain.

Guðvarr shoved the dead man away, saw cleaver break into a run towards him and leaped back out of view, into the entrance hall. He looked wildly around, desperate to get away, and he saw the door on the back wall that led to the tunnel. He ran to it, fearing that the Galdur-power that had snared him on his way in would stop him from leaving. He grasped the latch, lifted it and heaved, and the door flew open, Guðvarr falling back on to his arse.

He clambered back to his feet, pain shooting down his arm, and looked into the darkness of the tunnel. The sound of feet slapping in the courtyard, growing louder. A surge of fear.

That arseling with the meat cleaver is almost upon me.

He ran through the open doorway, no hint or trace of Galdur-power slowing him.

Maybe it has been broken with Skalk's fall, or perhaps it only works on the way in, to keep people out of the tower?

Footsteps echoing in the gateway and he ran on, tugging the door closed behind him. Torches flickered on the wall and he fled into the darkness.

CHAPTER TWENTY-SIX

VARG

V arg ran through the courtyard, cleaver in his fist, a hot rage pounding through his body. He'd left his spear buried in a man's chest. Svik was behind him, to his right, up on the back of a horse and cutting the throat of its rider. Æsa was laughing as she fought. None of them had seen Jökul fall.

He had been confused, trying to understand what was going on here. They had heard the screams and crashes as they'd run for the Galdur tower, thinking that Glornir had started his attack early. When they had sped out of a street into the road that circled the tower, though, they had seen riders filling the open gateway to the Galdur tower's courtyard, fighting with what seemed to be the guards of the tower. And to add to the confusion, he had recognised the riders, had fought their like before, back in Liga.

Druzhina of Iskidan, under the command of Prince Jaromir, come here from far-off shores in search of Sulich, one of the Bloodsworn. The last Varg had seen of them they had been standing on the docks of Liga as he had helped the Bloodsworn row the *Sea-Wolf* out into the fjord. Prince Jaromir had been in the mead hall in talks with Queen Helka.

People were screaming and Varg felt a stab of worry for Røkia, knowing she was leading another of the small Bloodsworn crews. He had asked Svik what was going on, what should they do, but by then Svik was pointing to a snarl of figures stepping from the shadowed streets. Glornir and his small band of the Bloodsworn, Sulich among them. Glornir had hefted his long-axe and just marched into the open gateway, swinging his axe and carving into the fighting like a woodsman felling trees.

"There's your answer," Svik had grinned. He'd dragged Æsa back by the cloak as she'd started to run towards the gateway.

"Too crowded," Svik had said. "We'll go over the wall."

So, they had run to the stockaded wall, Varg hesitating a moment as he tried to control the wolf in his blood, Æsa up and over before Varg had caught up, the woman light on her feet and balanced as a mountain goat. Svik cupped his hands and heaved Jökul up, but Varg was feeling the strength and speed of the wolf pulsing through his body so he had just leaped and scrambled up the wall, swinging his legs and tumbling over on to the flat roof of an outbuilding, rolling and falling to the hard-packed earth.

Battle had been raging, mounted *druzhina*, Galdur tower guards, and Glornir and the Bloodsworn surging into the fray.

Æsa was already among them before Svik and Jökul were on the ground. A shared look and they were charging, Varg stabbing with his spear.

The rest had all been fractured, swirling moments of blood and iron, the clang of steel, snarling faces, screams, snorting horses and hooves stamping, Varg falling, tumbling, climbing back to his feet, stabbing a tower guard with his spear as the man aimed an axe blow at Svik's head, a thud in his back as Jökul sent a warrior flying into him, the smith dragging him back to his feet, swinging his hammer and crushing the guardsman's skull. The wolf was raging in Varg's blood, but somehow he was holding it in check, like a lunging, snapping hound on a leash. Allowing it to feed his strength, speed and senses but maintaining the thinnest edge of control.

And then he had seen Jökul fall. Seen a dark-haired, sharp-nosed man sweep Jökul's hammer up from the ground and slam it into his friend's head.

Another friend slain in front of my eyes.

He'd felt a rush of horror, of grief, and then a wave of rage. Friends were new to Varg and he prized them beyond all gold. To see Jökul slain with a cowardly blow . . . it sent the wolf in his blood into a ravening frenzy. He sped towards the open doors of the tower, intent on finding the dark-haired man and ripping his throat out.

The thud of hooves and he twisted to see a man riding at him, sword raised, the horse intent on trampling him. He leaped to the side, crashed into a tower guard, at the same time glimpsed Svik leaping up on to the back of the horse, behind the rider, ripping his seax across the *druzhina's* throat. The tower guard Varg collided with cursed and swung his shield at him, trying to push him away and bring his spear to bear, but Varg hooked his cleaver on to the shield rim, dragged himself close to the warrior and stabbed the cleaver forward, slicing deep into the guard's throat. He fell away gurgling and grasping at the wound, blood spurting through his fingers. Varg ran on, across the courtyard and away from the swirl of combat, pounding across an open space toward the tower's open doors.

The Galdur tower loomed above him. This close Varg realised it was built from wood, rather than the polished black stone it had appeared as from a distance. He slowed as he approached the doors, saw Jökul's body slumped across the threshold and skidded to a halt beside him, dropping to his knees. Just a moment's glance confirmed what he had seen, a pulped wound on the top of Jökul's head, bone and brain leaking from it. With a snarl Varg scrambled to his feet, ripped his hand-axe from the skull of the tower guard's corpse and burst into the entrance chamber, twisting left and right, checking for hidden enemies, and searching for the dark-haired man.

No one was there, the chamber huge, battle from the courtyard echoing and swirling in the vaulted roof.

Where had he gone?

There was a closed door to the right, and a stairwell that spiralled up the tower. A door left ajar on the back wall. He padded across the room to the half-open door, hooked the latch with his hand-axe and eased it open, cleaver raised in his other fist. There were planked steps, descending, torches flickering on a wall. He moved closer, stood on the first step and heard the sound of slapping feet echoing down to him through a tunnel.

"Varg," a voice called and there was the drum of hooves behind him. He twisted, crouching, weapons raised, but it was Svik on his new-found horse. A fine animal, slim and tall, its mane braided like Svik's beard. Æsa ran one side of Svik.

"Jökul," Varg called to them, pointing, and he saw Svik and Æsa look down at the fallen guard and Jökul's body, Svik dragging on his reins, leaping to the ground and dropping to his knees. Æsa skidded to a halt and looked down, unbelieving.

"I saw who did it," Varg called to them. "I think he fled into this tunnel."

Varg and Æsa were with him in heartbeats, peering through the open door.

"Let's kill the *niðing*," Æsa snarled.

"Yes," Svik growled and took a step into the tunnel.

Muffled sounds of combat and a crash behind them, a door splintering apart and bodies falling through it, rolling and laying still, limbs twisted. More tower guards. Glornir strode through the door, long-axe held two-handed. Sulich followed him, more of the Bloodsworn behind him.

"Search everywhere," Glornir said, and a handful of Bloodsworn ran for the stairs, Sulich leading them, disappearing into the shadowed eaves. The sound of feet drumming on timber floorboards above them.

"What have you found?" Glornir growled as he strode into the chamber.

"Jökul is slain, and the man who did it fled this way," Varg said. "It's a tunnel, leading . . . east, I think."

Glornir stood over Jökul's corpse. A muscle twitched in his cheek and he strode over to Varg and the others.

More Bloodsworn were entering the chamber now. Varg saw Røkia, her face blood-spattered, her spear blade red. He nodded to her, felt a flush of relief to see her. Einar Half-Troll walked behind her.

"Where does it go?" Æsa said, looking into the tunnel.

"Helka's fortress," Glornir said. "That is all that is east of this tower."

Feet on the stairs, descending.

"She's not here, chief," Sulich called.

"Skalk?" Glornir growled.

Another Bloodsworn appeared from another corridor. "No sign of her, chief," he said.

"Nowhere," another voice said.

"What were *druzhina* of Iskidan doing here?" Svik asked.

More feet thudding, all the Bloodsworn gathered close now, some taking guard, watching over the courtyard, others standing by the doorway Glornir had smashed. Horns were blowing in the distance, in the streets beyond the courtyard. Somewhere a bell was ringing.

"Well, the hornet's nest has been kicked. Won't be long before *drengrs* come buzzing," Æsa said. She sounded happy about that.

We are losing the advantage of surprise and speed, Varg thought, knowing that had been the heart of Glornir's plan.

"What's the plan, chief?" Svik asked Glornir.

Glornir's face twitched, a vein pulsing in his temple. He blew out a sharp breath.

"I don't like what we've walked into, don't understand it," he said. "But Skalk slew one of our own, and," his face rippled, muscles shifting, teeth growing, a flicker of green in his eyes, "and he took Vol." He shivered, growled. "I'm not leaving without her."

Heyas and grunts of agreement for the Bloodsworn.

"And Jökul's killer is at the end of that tunnel," Varg said.

Angry muttering from the Bloodsworn.

Glornir looked around at all those gathered in the chamber. "We find Skalk. If he's not here then he's most likely at Helka's side. The time for stealth is done. We hit Helka's hall, hard as a hammer."

"Yes," Æsa said, grinning, and the Bloodsworn shifted into motion.

"With me," Glornir said and strode through the open door, down the steps and into the tunnel. Varg followed, Sulich, Svik and Æsa close behind. Varg heard Einar grumbling that he had to stoop as he entered the tunnel, Røkia telling him to stop complaining.

The tunnel levelled out. It was well-lit, torches pinned to supporting beams and crackling from some draught of air. They marched in silence, the tramp of feet, the rhythmic grate and clink of mail coats, and then Glornir was climbing steps upwards. He stopped, some kind of trapdoor above him. Varg looked but couldn't see any kind of bolt or handle. He felt a moment of worry, that they were going to be trapped down here, enemies behind them. Then he felt something, a shift in the air around him, the hackles on his neck standing up. Glornir was hunched over and twitching. As Varg watched the big man seemed to swell, a ripple passing through him. Then he raised his head and Varg saw his eyes glowed green in the firelight, his teeth sharp-tipped through a snarl in his grey beard. He let out an ear-splitting roar and smashed a sharp-clawed hand up at the trapdoor. Wood splintered and exploded, raining down around them and then Glornir was striding up the steps. Varg followed him, Svik behind, and they stepped into a wide hall. Varg felt a pulsing in his head, a rhythmic beat, like waking up after a night of too much mead. Glornir jerked and tremored, Varg seeing his claws shrink back to normal, his eyes returning to his normal hazel brown.

That is the control Røkia has been trying to teach me.

Without a word Glornir strode on, down the hall. He pointed to the first door and Svik opened it and swept in, Æsa with him, but the room was empty. Glornir marched on, the Bloodsworn filling the corridor behind him as they emerged from the tunnel. Glornir and Varg turned a corner in the corridor. Up ahead stood a solitary *drengr*, leaning against a wall, a woman with blonde braided hair. She saw Glornir, Varg and the other Bloodsworn appearing. A moment's hesitation and then her mouth was opening and she was reaching for the sword at her belt. A hiss, something slicing past Varg's ear, and a spear punched into the guard's chest, piercing mail and flesh. She let out a gurgling hiss as she slid to the floor.

Røkia ran past Varg and wrenched her spear out of the dead warrior, Glornir, Varg and the rest joining her. The *drengr* had been stood outside a door.

Varg hearing noises within. Creaking. And grunting.

Røkia kicked the door in and strode into the room, Svik, Æsa and Varg the next behind her. It was large and richly decorated, a hearth fire roaring, wool tapestries hanging. Silver candlesticks on a table before a bed thick with furs. Where a man and woman were humping, a pale arse rising and falling.

"What . . .?" the man said, spinning over. Dark-haired, a warrior's build, sharp, fine-boned features, his beard oiled and braided, bound with silver.

"Prince Hakon," Svik said with a grin and a bow.

"Get out, this is an outrage," Hakon said. "Yana," he called.

"Get up," Røkia said, levelling her blood-dripping spear at his chest.

Hakon's expression shifted, from indignation to confusion, perhaps a flicker of fear.

"What do you think you're doing?" he snarled. "I am Prince of Darl. My mother will have your heads for this. Yana?" he called, louder, shifting to look out of the door. Then he saw his *drengr*'s boots, a pool of blood spreading about them.

"Where's Skalk?" Glornir said, stepping close.

Hakon blinked, his skin paling.

"Glornir," he said, recognition in his eyes as he scrambled away from the woman on his bed and pulled furs over his waist. "The thrall Seiðr-witch said you would come for Skalk, but he didn't believe her."

"Where is the Galdurman, and Vol?" Glornir growled.

"I . . . I don't know. The tower?" Hakon said.

"We've tried there," Svik said with a sigh.

"I don't know, then," Hakon said. "I've been . . . busy."

"So we can see," Svik smiled.

"Bring him," Glornir said, turning and striding out of the room.

"Up. On your feet, humper," Røkia snarled at him, prodding him with her spear and leaving a smear of his dead guard's blood on his belly.

"Now, hold on a moment," Hakon said. "You can't just—"

Røkia twirled her spear and cracked the butt-end into Hakon's jaw, sending him rolling off the bed. She walked after him. "If you want to keep breathing, get on your feet," Røkia snarled. Hakon climbed unsteadily to his feet, his jaw purpling, a mixture of affronted rage, shock and fear spasming across his face.

"Out," Røkia said, slapping Hakon's bare arse with the flat of her spear blade and he hopped forward with a squawk. Svik blew a kiss to the naked woman trying to hide beneath the furs as they all left the room.

Varg followed Glornir as he strode along the corridor, a doorway open ahead of them. The pounding in his head was louder, deeper, causing a ripple of nausea in his belly. Firelight and raised voices echoed through the open doorway, the scents of food, mead and ale thick in the air. Glornir did not break stride, walked through the open door and out on to a dais, a long-table there, looking out on to a mead hall full of feasting, smoke heavy in the air, and above them pale curved bones hung instead of roof beams.

The bones of Orna the eagle-god. The pain in Varg's head was coming in waves now. He shook his head, sucked in a breath.

Glornir paused.

Varg saw Queen Helka sitting there, gazing out into the hall. A man stood in the space between the benches in the mead hall and Queen Helka's table, pale and dark-haired, face slick with sweat and grime, his long nose glistening with snot. He wore a fine wool tunic, though one sleeve was torn and bloody, and he held Jökul's hammer in his fist. He made to step into the hall, but Svik pulled him back.

"That's him," Varg hissed, pointing his cleaver at the snot-nosed man.

"I see him," Svik said with a winter's cold hiss. "But we wait for Glornir."

Men and women sat either side of Queen Helka, all in embroidered wool tunics, rings of silver and gold on their arms. One woman's face had a long scar running diagonally from forehead to cheek. *Drengr* warriors were on their feet in the mead hall, shouting, and other warriors prowled the dais like a curled fist around Queen Helka.

Úlfhéðnar, Varg realised. A ripple of fear shivered up his spine, the hairs on his neck rising. The wolf in his blood knew them, saw them as a threat, a challenge, like a rival pack, but Varg also felt a sense of sorrow for them, enslaved, with iron thrall-collars about their necks. The wolf in him snarled, wanting to rip Helka's throat out for doing this to his wolf-kin.

Varg took all of this in during the few heartbeats he stood there, then Glornir was stepping out on to the dais and the Bloodsworn followed.

The *Úlfhéðnar* sensed them first, shifting fluidly about Helka, turning to face the Bloodsworn, and Varg heard someone cry out, pointing a finger; it was the dark-haired man who stood before Queen Helka, but by then Glornir's axe was swinging and blood was spraying as he hacked into the neck of a turning *Úlfhéðnar*. Screams and howls rang out and a dozen *Úlfhéðnar* sprang forward, a roar from the mead benches as *drengrs* rose to their feet, scrambling for weapons.

Einar Half-Troll chopped into an *Úlfhéðnar* as she leaped at Glornir, so enraged and frenzied that she hadn't even drawn a weapon, sharp-clawed hands reaching, jaws opening. Einar's hand-axe hacked into the woman's upper back, *brynja* rings and blood spraying as the *Úlfhéðnar* was slammed to the ground. She twisted and howled, trying to bite Einar's leg.

Svik and Sulich stepped forward, guarding Glornir's flanks as his long-axe rose and fell again, Varg stepping deeper into the room, hefting his hand-axe and cleaver. An *Úlfhéðnar* saw him and came at him, drawing two seaxes from her belt, all frothing, snarling teeth and amber eyes. She ran at him, no pause to appraise or test Varg's ability, no feint and thrust, just a rush of feral violence in her eyes. Varg's instinct was to leap away, but he felt frozen a moment, just staring at the *Úlfhéðnar*. Her seaxes slashed and stabbed as she barrelled into him and he swung his hand-axe wildly, parrying one seax, his body twisting so that the other grated on the rings of his *brynja*. Then she was slamming into him and Varg was hurled back, crashing into a wall, his head ringing, white stars bursting in his vision, and he slipped to the ground, a seax stabbing deep into the wall where his throat had just been. Varg lashed out with his cleaver and chopped it into the woman's foot, carving through flesh and bone, deep into the timber floorboard beneath. The *Úlfhéðnar* howled, let go of the seax buried in the wall and slashed down at him with her other seax, the tip skimming his cheek, the sharp tang of blood as she bent and grabbed the cleaver's handle, ripping it out of the floorboard and her foot. Varg kicked out at her legs, sweeping her into the air and she fell hard, losing her grip on the seax and cleaver. Varg twisted on the floor and rolled away, but she was scrambling after him, dragging herself up his body, one hand clamping around his throat, pulling his face towards her, her jaws wide, sharp teeth gnashing. Varg pulled and writhed, but he had no leverage to put any strength into his movements. He could smell her breath, hot and sour, felt panic surge through him as the tips of her canines touched his cheek. The wolf in his blood howled for release, and a part of him knew that if he held the wolf back, he would die.

Her jaws lunged at his face and he tried to throw himself away, but all he managed to do was turn his head. Felt her teeth rip into the side of his head and ear, heard her hot, slavering breath and a ripping, tearing sound. Sharp, excruciating pain.

An explosion of blood and bone and gore splashing his face, and the *Úlfhéðnar* was slumping upon Varg, pinning him down, her breath a gurgled rattle. Someone dragged the *Úlfhéðnar's* body off him and he saw Sulich standing over him, hand outstretched to Varg. He took it and was heaved upright, spitting the woman's blood out of his mouth. Sulich spun away, ducking a spear-thrust from a *drengr* and slashing his curved sword across the man's belly.

Varg put a hand to the side of his head, pain pulsing and radiating in nauseous waves, felt his fingers slick with blood, felt grooves in his flesh where the *Úlfhéðnar's* teeth had raked him. He jerked his hand away, something feeling . . . wrong. He looked down at the dead *Úlfhéðnar*, saw a lump of something in her open mouth, a torn and pulped lump of flesh.

She bit my ear off.

He swayed, reached out and steadied himself on a wall and looked about, saw the dais was heaving with combat, a handful of *Úlfhéðnar* gathered around Queen Helka, the rest fighting the Bloodsworn. *Drengrs* from the feast-hall were clambering on to the dais, moving more cautiously than the *Úlfhéðnar*. Varg saw Einar swinging his axe and bellowing, Glornir hacking and chopping his way towards

Helka, his movement slowed by *Úlfhéðnar* and the growing number of *drengrs*, as if he were wading through waist-deep water. Svik was being pushed back by an *Úlfhéðnar*, Æsa leaping on to the table to stab left and right with her spear. But wherever he looked the Bloodsworn were being held or pushed back, swamped by numbers as more warriors poured on to the dais. Wherever the *Úlfhéðnar* fought they had the upper hand now, as the Bloodsworn were keeping their Tainted blood hidden.

"STOP," a voice yelled, loud and commanding, and instantly the *Úlfhéðnar* were disengaging from combat and backing away, hunched and snarling. "STOP," Queen Helka shouted again, and when a *drengr* ignored her, his blood still fired with battle, an *Úlfhéðnar* lashed out and knocked him to the ground.

Then Varg saw why Helka had screamed for a halt to the battle.

Røkia was walking out into the dais, the naked Prince Hakon held tight in front of her, the blade of a seax at his throat.

CHAPTER TWENTY-SEVEN

GUÐVARR

Guðvarr leaned against a long bench in the mead hall. He had seen the silent warriors pour through the doorway on to the dais, recognised the bald grey-beard with the axe from Skalk's courtyard, and the lean, savage-looking man with the cleaver who had chased him. He had stared in horror as the grey-beard had marched out into a room full of warriors and started carving up *Úlfhéðnar* with his long-axe.

What kind of lunatic is he?

He looked to Helka, a handful of *Úlfhéðnar* wrapped tight about her and her daughter, Estrid, who was looking at the chaos with a glitter of excitement in her eyes. Further along the table was Jarl Sigrún, Guðvarr's aunt. Really, he should have rushed to her side when battle erupted, to defend her. Instead, he had sagged against a table, exhausted.

I have had a bad day. He looked at his arm and shivered. *And when I stumbled into this feast-hall, instead of thanking me for the warning and giving me a chair and a horn of mead, Helka wants to interrogate me! I told her the Galdur tower was under attack. If she'd have just listened to me perhaps she wouldn't have been caught by surprise by these lunatics.*

As quickly as battle had erupted it had now ceased, a stillness filling the dais as warriors froze at Queen Helka's command, *Úlfhéðnar* moving back towards their queen, *drengrs* shuffling away from these new warriors.

Who are they?

They were not Jaromir's warriors, that was clear. All of them were dressed like *drengrs* in mail and wool, well-armed, many of them carrying swords. But they wore no helms and carried no shields to show their allegiance.

Guðvarr's eyes skimmed across them, taking in the hard faces, scars, weapons, blood and mail.

A nasty looking bunch of arselings, if ever there was one, he thought, but his gaze was drawn to the grey-beard, standing tall and broad, bald head glistening with sweat, blood spattered across his face and beard, his mail, blood dripping from the long-axe in his fists. His brows were knotted like a thundercloud as he glowered at Helka. But she was watching the blonde-haired warrior who had walked out on to the dais with a seax held to the throat of a naked Prince Hakon.

Well, he's been caught with his breeches down.

"Let him go," Helka said.

"Where is Skalk?" the bald man asked. A pause, a shudder passing through the muscle of his neck, shoulders and back. "Where is *Vol?*"

"Glornir, you dare do this?" Helka snarled.

"Skalk and Vol," Glornir repeated.

"Skalk? He went to the tower," Queen Helka said.

"We've looked for him at the tower, and he's not there," one of the band on the dais said. A slim, red-haired man, beard and moustache braided and oiled.

"Well, he is not here," Helka said. She fixed the old grey-beard with her hard stare. "Glornir, you cannot hope to leave here alive. You have attacked me in my feast-hall, are holding a blade to my son." She shook her head. "Are you insane?"

My thoughts exactly, Guðvarr thought. *Hold on. Glornir! The Bloodsworn's Glornir Shield-Breaker? Well, that would explain a few things.*

"I will leave here with Vol, or this will be Hakon's last day of life," Glornir shrugged. "We Bloodsworn may die here; but we will not die alone." His eyes flickered across the hall full of warriors, touching on Guðvarr's for a brief moment, but long enough for

Guðvarr to feel a trembling in his knees and a looseness in his bowels.

"I cannot give you your Seiðr-witch when I do not know where she is," Queen Helka said.

I have had enough of being a whisper away from death today.

"Jaromir took her," Guðvarr said. Every single eye in the hall turned to stare at him. He saw Glornir fix him with dark eyes, saw the old warrior's gaze move down him, and he looked to see he was still clutching the hammer he'd taken and used to crush that arseling's head. He dropped it with a clatter.

"What?" Queen Helka said.

Guðvarr sucked in a deep breath.

"Jaromir took the Seiðr-witch and the chest that Lord Skalk brought here. The one with the god bones in it," he said. "Jaromir said something about Hraeg's bones?"

"How do you know this?" Glornir snarled.

"I . . . was there," Guðvarr said. "I saw it. Jaromir carried the Seiðr-witch across his own saddle."

Growls and mutters among the Bloodsworn. Glornir became unnaturally still, apart from a pulsing vein in his bald head.

"He was in the tower," cleaver-man said nodding at Guðvarr. One side of his head was gouged with teeth marks, sheeted with blood. "He killed Jökul like a *niðing* coward, then fled." He took a step towards Guðvarr, but Glornir held a hand up, stopping him.

"I did not flee," Guðvarr said haughtily, trying to stand a little straighter and resisting the urge to put some more space between him and cleaver-man. "I came to warn my queen of danger."

"You see then, Glornir. I cannot find your Seiðr-witch for you. She is already gone," Helka said.

"Bring me Skalk then," Glornir said.

Helka sighed. "This is going in circles," she said. "And what do you intend to do if I manage to find Skalk and bring him before you? You will still not leave Darl alive."

"I will see Skalk, or your son will die," Glornir said. "Your heir, as he has told us a thousand times."

"I have a spare," Helka said with a thin-lipped smile.

"*Mother!*" Hakon squeaked.

Guðvarr saw Estrid smile.

Glornir looked to Røkia and her arm tensed.

"*Please*, Mother, do as he asks," Hakon blurted, tears welling in his eyes. Helka gave him a long, calm stare.

"I am *negotiating*," she said.

"Let him die," Estrid said with a shrug, "I'd make a better job of ruling than him."

"Quiet, daughter," Helka said.

"Please, Mother . . . I am getting cold," Hakon said, a tremor in his voice, though he glared at Estrid.

"So we can see," a short, broad-framed woman among the Bloodsworn said, smiling as she stared pointedly at his nakedness. Other warriors laughed, and not just among the Bloodsworn.

"Tell me, my son. How is it that you are naked?"

"He was humping," the same warrior said. "So loudly that he didn't hear us kicking his door in." She smiled. More laughter stuttering around the room.

Guðvarr heard voices and the slap of feet coming from the far end of the hall. He turned to see figures entering the mead hall. Yrsa and Sturla. They were both supporting a figure between them.

Skalk.

He was managing to walk, though he dragged one leg and his face was sheeted with blood. Someone had torn a strip of linen from a tunic and wrapped it around Skalk's head, covering the mess that Guðvarr had seen the hawk make of his eye.

The three of them walked down the centre of the hall, between two long benches, approaching Queen Helka.

"My queen," Skalk said.

"Well, you look like you have seen better days," she said. "I am glad you are here. You have saved me a search." She gestured to Glornir and the Bloodsworn, and last to Hakon. "Glornir and his Bloodsworn would like me to trade you for my son. I believe they wish to kill you. Is this correct?" she looked to Glornir.

"Yes," Glornir said glaring at Skalk.

Good, Guðvarr thought. *Hand him over, hand him over now; let me see Glornir kill the lying, torturing piece of weasel-shite.*

"And her," another voice said. The man with the cleaver. He was staring at Yrsa with a look of malice. "She killed Torvik in Rotta's chamber. Put a sword in him as he sat next to me." He took a step towards Yrsa.

"Hold," Glornir said, and cleaver paused.

Skalk looked from Glornir to Helka.

"They have come for your Seiðr-witch, as she said they would," Queen Helka said.

"She is gone," Skalk rasped.

"Yes, we know. Guðvarr has told us. Prince Jaromir, I understand."

"Aye. He had a Seiðr-witch, and a Tainted thrall," Skalk said. "They were . . ." he swayed, Yrsa and Sturla supporting him. "Powerful."

"*Mother*," Hakon said. "Can you just hand Skalk over, please."

Queen Helka looked at her son a long moment.

"No," she said thoughtfully. "Glornir, if I give you Skalk, then you will kill him, and then my *Úlfhéðnar* and *drengrs* will kill you."

"Perhaps," Glornir shrugged.

Helka laughed. "You and your Bloodsworn are fair-famed, but forty against two hundred? I don't think there is any question of the outcome here. But there is a second option."

Glornir just stared at her.

"Prince Jaromir has insulted me. Arguably as much as you have. More, even, as he was my guest. I want him caught and punished for this insult. And here you are, a mercenary band; spears for hire. And there is more in it for you than just the chest of silver I will give you. Jaromir has your Seiðr-witch." She paused a moment, letting her words sink in. "So, my Galdurman will live. You will give my son back, and you will be paid to hunt down and capture our shared enemy. And in the bargain you get your Seiðr-witch back. How does that sound to you?"

No, no, no, let him kill Skalk. Please.

"You can have your Galdurman a while longer," Glornir said after a while. He turned his gaze to Skalk. "I *will* kill you. But not yet." He looked back to Helka. "We will keep Hakon until we are out of Darl; forgive me if I do not just take your word on this. Hakon will be our surety. I will release him when we are clear of here. And you will pay half now, and half when I bring you Jaromir. Or his head."

Helka pursed her lips. "How do I know you will let Hakon go?"

"You don't. But it is in my interest. As you say, Jaromir has what I want, and why would I choose to nursemaid your son while I am chasing *druzhina* across Vigrið?"

Helka tapped her chin with a long finger.

"And I will need a *drakkar*," Glornir said.

"Mother, you can't seriously be considering this foo—"

"Agreed," Helka said.

Hakon spluttered his protests, but Guðvarr saw some of the tension leak out of the warriors in the room.

"You will take one of my *Úlfheðnar* with you, as my son's guardian," Helka told him.

Glornir shrugged and nodded.

Skalk sat on a mead bench and looked at Guðvarr.

Something shifted, deep in Guðvarr's torso, a sharp pain like a pinch, but *inside* his body and he gasped, clutched at his chest.

The hyrndur, I think it just moved. It was a reminder to Guðvarr of the task Skalk had given him.

Befriend Prince Hakon. Damn fool that he is.

Guðvarr walked towards the dais and leaned down, taking the cloak from a dead *drengr*.

"What are you doing?" Queen Helka frowned at Guðvarr.

"No closer," said Glornir.

"The prince is cold, and deserves some dignity," Guðvarr said. "It is no crime to be caught humping. Quite the opposite."

A few laughs at that.

"Depends who it is you're caught humping with," someone said.

Helka looked to Glornir and raised her eyebrows. "He will have to be clothed at some point. You cannot march him through Darl like that."

Glornir nodded and Helka waved a hand at Guðvarr. He strode

on to the dais and threaded his way through *drengrs* until he was face to face with Prince Hakon.

"My prince," he said. The blonde woman raised her seax a fraction, allowing Guðvarr to slip the cloak around Hakon's shoulders.

"My thanks," Hakon mumbled and Guðvarr stepped away.

"Well, let us be getting on with this," Queen Helka said, clapping her hands. "A chest of silver and a *drakkar* longship for our visitors. And food and drink while we wait."

Warriors moved away from the dais, shifting back towards the mead benches. Guðvarr turned to walk away, but a hand clamped his wrist, pulling him around. Guðvarr looked back to see cleaver-man staring at him, little more than a handspan between them. He was taller than Guðvarr, making him look up into his face, which was twitching with barely contained rage. He had a short beard, his face lean and sharp, his torn ear just a few lumps of tattered flesh. Guðvarr tugged but the grip was like iron. "What do you want?" he piped.

"Are you Guðvarr?" the man asked him.

How do you know that? As if I would tell you, you snivelling oaf.

The man's eyes bored into him with a fierce intensity.

"Yes," he rasped.

The man nodded to himself.

"A friend asked me not to kill you. But he sent you a message. To say that Lif is coming for you."

"Lif," Guðvarr snorted. "That *niðing* could not kill anyone, even if they were wrapped in chains."

"Like you killed his brother," cleaver-man said with a curl of his lip, "and hit Jökul from behind. You are making a name for yourself, coward."

I should challenge you to a holmganga *for your insolence. But I am in no state to fight, a monster has recently chewed its way into my chest.*

"Take your hand off me, arseling," Guðvarr snarled.

"I do not know if I can keep my promise to Lif," cleaver-man said. "For I do not know how long I will be able to stop myself from killing you." His face juddered and spasmed, veins pulsing. Guðvarr pulled away but he could not break free of the man's grip.

He was aware of others gathering about them, a slim red-haired man with an annoying smirk on his face, a woman squat and broad, and another man big and ugly as a troll.

"You should have a care who you insult, no-ear," Guðvarr spat, "I have challenged people to *holmganga* for far less."

"Challenge me, then. Please," cleaver-man said.

"Yes, I think you should challenge him," the slim red-haired man said. "Your honour demands it." He smiled unpleasantly.

"No more blood will be shed this night," Queen Helka said.

Thank the dead gods, Guðvarr thought.

"You are fortunate, no-ear," Guðvarr said.

Still cleaver-man would not release his wrist.

"Let him go, Varg. Now is not the time," a voice said, Glornir, and cleaver-man opened his fist, Guðvarr stumbling away.

Varg. I shall remember you.

CHAPTER TWENTY-EIGHT

ELVAR

"My thanks," Elvar said to Uspa. The Seiðr-witch nodded, her face all pale ridges and ravines of dark shadow in the pre-dawn grey. With a long, exhaled breath Uspa rose to her feet and walked away, pulling her cloak tight about her shoulders.

Elvar gazed into the fire a while, then pulled a whetstone from a pouch on her scabbard, drew her sword and set to scraping the stone along her blade's edge.

After the tennúr attack they had decided to put some distance between them and the tennúr hill and had marched a fair distance from the vaesen pit. Darkness was cloaking the world when they set about making a new camp, and it had not been long before most of the Battle-Grim were lying in their cloaks, snoring with their bellies full. Several days and nights of solid marching combined with the tennúr attack had taken its toll.

Elvar had woken early, daylight just a hint on the horizon. She had scraped out the ash and embers of last night's fire and lit new kindling, heaping on dry wood until a fire was crackling, fetching water from a nearby stream and setting a pot to boiling. Then she had walked to Uspa's cloak-wrapped, sleeping form, crouched and put a hand on her shoulder.

"How's your shoulder?" Grend asked her as he returned from last watch. He walked past Uspa, nodding to the Seiðr-witch as she made her way to the wagon where Ulfrir and Skuld lay. She had tended their wounds after the tennúr attack, and the two gods had slept throughout the Battle-Grim's march and all through the night. They were still sleeping now, Elvar had already checked on them.

Elvar shrugged and rolled her left shoulder. She had felt the muscles complain when she'd raised her shield in the shield wall yesterday. She knew why he was asking.

"Well enough," she said.

"You don't have to do it," he said.

Elvar didn't answer, just looked at the gleam of her blade as she ran her whetstone along its edge.

Others were rising now, Orv the Sneak climbing to his feet, stretching and buckling on his weapons belt, a quiver and bow case hanging from it. He nodded to them as he walked out beyond the wagons to empty his bladder. He returned with a sack of oats that he poured into the boiling pot.

Sighvat sat up and belched, stood and scratched his arse, his red hair and beard looking like a bush that two angry cats had fought in.

"Morning," he said.

A red smear appeared across the rim of the world as the sun crested the horizon, and a figure walked between Elvar and the fire pit, casting a long shadow.

"I call an Althing," Huld said, her eyes locked on Elvar, "for the Battle-Grim to decide who will be their next chief and fill the boots of Agnar Fire-Fist." She pulled back her jet-black hair and tied it at the nape, as if she were preparing for a fight.

Elvar stopped the rasp and grind of her sword sharpening, slipped the whetstone back into its leather pocket on her scabbard, and sheathed her sword.

Here it is, then, she thought.

Any still sleeping woke now, Huld shouting out the call to an Althing, and it was not long before all the Battle-Grim were gathered around the fire.

"Hurry up, Sighvat," Huld snapped as Sighvat stood over the pot, filling his bowl with porridge.

"This Althing could take a while," Sighvat grumbled, "and I don't like to talk or think on an empty stomach." He heaped another ladle into his bowl, then turned and found a place in their circle.

"We all know what this is about," Sighvat said, "so let's get to the choosing. Who here puts themselves forward as chief of the Battle-Grim?"

"I do," said Huld, sitting with a hand clasped around the bear-claw at her neck.

A silence settled over the gathering, broken by Sighvat slurping on his porridge.

"How about you, big man?" Orv said to Sighvat. "You were Agnar's man, his second, and you're a right good man to have at the front of any scrap, is my thinking."

Sighvat dipped his head to Orv. "I'm grateful for that, Sneak," he said. "But I'm no deep-cunning thinker, and that is what our chief needs to be. Point me at a shield wall, or a troll, or a skraeling, or anything else that can put up a fight and I'm your man. But making deep-cunning plans," he tapped his temple. "I'd rather eat porridge and fight." He grinned. "How about you, though?" Sighvat said, looking at Grend.

"Me?" Grend said, blinking, looking as surprised as Elvar had ever seen him.

"Aye, you," Sighvat said. "Probably the only man or woman here who can take me in a scrap. Not an arm-wrestle, mind you," he winked at Grend. "But put cold steel in your fist and you're a hard man to beat, and no denying. And you're a thinker. A calm head that sees the paths through or around a tangle." There were grunts and murmurs of agreement among the Battle-Grim.

"No," Grend said. He shook his head. "No," he repeated. All the Battle-Grim were staring at him, a silence stretching. "I'm here for her." He nodded to Elvar. "If she stays, I stay. If she goes; or dies, I'm gone."

"Fair enough," Sighvat shrugged.

"Anyone elth put their name forward?" Sólín said.

A further silence settled over them, broken once again by Sighvat's slurping.

Do I even want to be chief of the Battle-Grim? Elvar thought. *Once the answer would have been yes, without hesitation. It would give me what I've wanted all my life. Recognition and battle-fame carved by my own hand rather than offered it by my silver-rich jarl of a father. But do I still want that now, after I have sworn the* blóð svarið, *and am committed to rescuing Uspa's son? To be chief of the Battle-Grim.* She rolled the title around her head, tasting it like sweet mead in the mouth. *To be their gold-giver, their ring-giver. To put food in their bellies and silver on their arms. But if I have any chance of fulfilling this cursed blood oath then I need the Battle-Grim, though they are not cattle to be led to slaughter . . .* The argument swirled back and forth in her thought-cage.

And then Huld's words rose up, shouting loud over them all, drowning all else out.

You are a spoilt jarl's daughter.

That is the reputation I have spent the last four years trying to escape, and yet Huld still thinks it of me. One of the Battle-Grim, one of my sword-sisters. What do I have to do to prove that there is more to me than my father's blood?

Carve the lesson into her flesh. Win. Lead, came the answer in her head.

"I put my name forward," Elvar said into the silence.

She felt Grend's eyes boring into her.

"Then it must be a *holmganga* to decide," Sighvat said with a sigh.

"You sure you want to do this?" Orv asked them both. "You've both got a good arm, and we've got a dragon to kill. Would be a shame to be one warrior light."

"Elvar can always stand aside," Huld said.

"No," Elvar said.

"Elvar is injured," Grend said. "I will fight in her place."

"No," Elvar said again, standing and stretching. She bent and picked up her weapons belt, rolled her shoulders to shift the weight of her *brynja*, then buckled on her belt. Made sure it was tight, to take the weight of the ring mail from her injured shoulder. Finally, she looked at Huld. "Let's get this done."

Huld smiled grimly and stood. The Battle-Grim broke into

motion, apart from Sighvat, who stayed to finish his bowl of porridge. Lacking a hazel tree nearby to make the rods, warriors of the Battle-Grim marked out a square with their spears. Elvar looked at Grend.

"Will you be my second?" she asked him.

"As if you have to ask, idiot," he muttered.

Elvar stooped and lifted her shield, holding it loosely, her arm dangling, not taking any of the weight with her shoulder.

They walked to the edge of the *holmganga* square.

Huld was there waiting, shield in one fist, her sword already drawn. A seax hung from her weapons belt. She looked at Elvar and sliced the air, rolling her wrist, warming up muscles and tendons. A tall, willow-slender man stood with her, thinning, greasy fair hair and a hooked nose. Urt the Unwashed. He stood over two more shields, ready for Huld if she should need them, as the rules of *holmganga* allowed.

"You can use my shield, if you need it," Grend said.

Elvar lifted her own shield and tested its weight. She winced and lowered it quickly, Grend seeing the flicker in her eyes.

"You must end this quickly," he said quietly, a worried frown creasing his brow.

Elvar nodded.

"She is fast, and skilled," Grend said, his voice reminding Elvar of those long-gone, countless days in the courtyard of Snakavik, where Grend had schooled her in weapons craft beneath her mother's window. "Do not underestimate her," he continued. "She attacks like a summer storm, fast and violent. If you were not injured, I would counsel you to weather that storm, wait for her to start sucking air, and then finish her. But," he looked at her shoulder, "you might not be able to last that long. So, finish her quick."

Elvar nodded, as she listened her hand wrapping around her sword hilt, drawing it a short way, checking the blade was not sticking, then let it slide back down. Another old habit that Grend had ground into her.

Sighvat stepped into the spear-square and beckoned for Elvar and Huld to join him.

"The rules of *holmganga* must be abided by," he said, the Battle-Grim gathering around the square. "When the fight is done there is no blood feud or weregild for friend or kin to pursue." He looked at Grend. "You hear that?"

Grend stared at him, lips tight together.

"You hear that, brother?" Sighvat repeated, louder and sterner.

"Aye," Grend ground through his clenched teeth.

"Good. Now, the two combatants must agree. First wound, submission, or death?"

"Death," Huld said, eyes fixed on Elvar's.

Some of the Battle-Grim muttered at this.

"Not a good choice, if you ask me," Sighvat said. "You two are both handy in a scrap, and I have the feeling the Battle-Grim are going to need every blade and strong arm we have."

"Death," Elvar said, looking into Huld's eyes.

Sighvat sighed and nodded. "Let us see who will fill the place of Agnar, then."

Elvar's hand rose to the troll's tusk hanging around her neck, given her by Agnar. She squeezed it tight, knuckles whitening.

I miss you, Agnar.

Sighvat walked away and stepped over the line of spears. Grend hovered a moment, and so Urt the Unwashed did, too.

"Go," Elvar said to Grend, though she did not take her eyes from Huld. "I'll see you in a moment."

Huld snorted and stepped back a few paces, eyes fixed on Elvar.

Grend still hesitated, then turned and walked away, Urt doing the same. Elvar saw a flicker of movement in the line of the Battle-Grim behind Huld, saw people shuffling aside and then Skuld and Ulfrir were there, watching her.

Two gods, watching me fight a holmganga. *Surely there is a skáld-song to be made from this.* She felt her heart pounding, blood tingling, a smile clawing across her face. *Do not think on things like that,* she told herself, *focus, else you may not live to hear the skáld-song sung.*

"Are we ready?" Sighvat called out.

"Aye," Huld said.

Elvar turned to look at Grend. She drew her sword and raised it to him, touched her lips to the flat of the blade.

Grend tapped his temple, and mouthed the word *think*.

Elvar turned back to face Huld, who stood waiting a dozen paces away.

"Aye," Elvar called out.

"Then begin," Sighvat bellowed.

The rasp of leather soles on patchy grass, Huld approaching fast. Elvar spread her feet, light on her toes, and half raised her shield. Winced. Huld covered ten paces in a heartbeat, her own shield rising, and as she closed within striking range she stepped to Elvar's left, sword swinging hard at Elvar's head, too fast to evade, leaving Elvar no choice but to meet the blow with her own shield. She felt the strike shiver through the linden wood and up her arm, into her shoulder, stumbled back a step, grimacing, and Huld followed, fast as Grend had predicted. A flurry of strikes, high and low, Elvar blocking with her shield, her own sword held high, looking for an opportunity, but there were none. Huld's shield was solid as a wall, perfectly positioned, and the power of her blows drove Elvar back, breaking her balance and sapping her ability to counter-strike.

Elvar stepped left, trying to bring Huld around and move her off Elvar's shield side, took another blow on her shield but stepped through it, stabbed straight and fast at Huld's face. Huld flicked her shield up, the rim knocking Elvar's sword high, and Huld was barging in, punching her shield boss at Elvar's face, another savage swing of her sword aimed at Elvar's ribs only just deflected by Elvar's shield. Splinters of wood sprayed and Elvar stumbled away, ducking Huld's iron boss, her eyes narrowed as she winced and grimaced.

Huld grinned and pressed her attack. Stepped to her right and swung at Elvar's left side, hard enough to fell a bull, and Elvar caught the blow on her shield and cried out, staggered, half lowered her battered shield, fought to raise it just in time as Huld stormed forward, raining blow after furious blow on to Elvar's shield side. Splinters flew, the linden wood cracking, and Elvar stepped in close again, struck low, at Huld's legs, but she danced backwards, grinning.

"I learned to fight in the streets of Svelgarth," Huld snarled, "against men and women who would cut your throat just to warm their hands on your blood, not in some privileged weapons court with thralls all about me to mop my brow when I broke sweat."

"You bleat like a goat," Elvar rasped, sucking in deep breaths, trying to prolong this break.

"A goat that's going to take that shiny gold ring from your cold corpse," Huld said, motioning to the gold arm ring that Agnar had given Elvar. Huld rolled her shoulders and lifted her shield, raised her sword. Elvar saw her eyes flicker to Elvar's shoulder and sagging shield, even as Huld was moving, sword arm lashing out.

Elvar hefted her shield, raising it with ease and stepped into Huld's strike, taking the blow on the flat of her shield, just above the boss, and twisting her arm and wrist so that Huld's sword was guided across Huld's chest and pinned tight on her own shield.

A frozen moment as Huld stared into Elvar's eyes, realisation dawning. A flare of shock, then fear. Then Elvar struck, her blade crunching into Huld's face, cutting deep into her mouth, crunching on bone, blood and teeth spraying. A gurgling, blood-choked gasp and Huld was falling, tumbling to the ground, Elvar standing over her, Huld's blood spattered in streaks across her face. Huld's hand searched the ground for the hilt of her sword. Elvar stood on Huld's wrist and stabbed down, piercing Huld's throat, carving through her spine and stabbing deep into the ground beneath her.

A moment of silence, then roars from the Battle-Grim and Elvar was dragging her sword free, turning, raising her sword and shield, punching the air.

Grend was the first to step over the *holmganga* line, striding towards her on long legs. He stopped before her, face part frown, part smile.

"That was well done," he said.

Elvar gave him a grin.

"And your shoulder? Did you feel *any* pain? Was it all a feint?"

"No pain," Elvar said. She looked to Uspa, who was talking with Skuld and Ulfrir. "Uspa said some of her Seiðr-runes over it, before dawn. It's never felt better." She grinned again, feeling the first touch of the joy and relief that follows any fight where your life has been at risk.

I'm alive. Her hands began to tremble, quickly spreading through her body, and clumsily she cleaned her blade on Huld's cloak, then, with difficulty, she sheathed her sword.

Sighvat lumbered up to them, carrying something across one arm. Agnar's bearskin cloak. Sighvat shook it out and spread it around Elvar's shoulders, then pinned it with a gold brooch.

"A chief's cloak," Sighvat said. "Our chief's cloak. "He gripped Elvar's wrist and held her arm high.

"Elvar Fire-Fist, chief of the Battle-Grim," he bellowed, and the Battle-Grim added their voices to it. Elvar looked around, saw their faces shouting her name, and felt a shift in her chest. Her eyes came to rest on Ulfrir. He gave her a sharp-toothed smile and dipped his head. She grinned back at him.

As the cheering subsided Sighvat looked at her.

"So, what now? Where to, chief?" he asked her.

Elvar blinked.

Chief! That's going to take some getting used to.

"First, we shall raise a barrow over Huld. She was Battle-Grim and fought well, died well."

Heyas of agreement at that.

And where should we go? I need a plan.

By the tracks they had found at the Isbrún Bridge, Ilska and her Raven-Feeders were heading east.

But do I want to follow straight after them? Ulfrir is far from healed, and we are less than forty spears.

She stood straight, making her decision.

"We are heading south, back to the *Wave-Jarl*."

CHAPTER TWENTY-NINE

VARG

V arg stepped out of the dockside barracks that Queen Helka had allocated the Bloodsworn, into a chill, pale day, ephemeral clouds scattered across the sky. He felt a weariness deep as his bones after last night's fight, and a churning sense of grief at the loss of Jökul. Pain throbbed in one side of his head and he put a hand to the bandage that was wrapped around it. A strange, nauseous feeling as he touched where his ear should have been.

"*It's an improvement,*" Røkia had said as she'd held him down, Glornir pressing a white-hot knife to the wound to cauterise it. He'd remembered screaming for a brief moment.

A dozen of Queen Helka's *drengrs* stood a few paces away, warming their hands over a crackling brazier and staring suspiciously at Varg. Hands reached for weapons when Einar Half-Troll emerged through the doorway behind him, followed by Svik and Røkia.

"Morning," Svik said cheerfully to the *drengrs*. Røkia glowered at them.

"We are off to buy some provisions for the *drakkar*," Svik said to the warriors.

"Which way?" Varg said.

"Follow me," Svik said, walking away. "Quickly, we haven't got all day."

That is a truth, Varg thought. He was still shocked that Glornir had given Varg his permission to do this.

After the agreement in Helka's feast-hall she had put food and drink in front of the Bloodsworn, and while they were cautiously eating, and the dead were being carried from the hall a chest had been carried in and set before Glornir. Two *drengrs* had pulled the lid open, revealing a pile of silver that had snatched Varg's breath away: all manner and size of coins, rings and twisted arm rings, brooches, pendants, necklaces. Glornir had frowned and shut the chest lid with his long-axe. Then Helka had offered them accommodation within the fortress. Glornir had declined, and they had settled upon a barrack building close to the docks, where a *drakkar* was being prepared to sail in the morning. They had marched there in the dead of night, carrying Jökul and three others who had fallen against Helka's *Úlfhéðnar*, wrapped in their cloaks. The whole journey Røkia had kept her seax tight to Prince Hakon's throat. He was being watched over by Æsa now, who was enjoying tormenting him about his nakedness and humping skills.

Svik led them away from the riverside docks and the stink and din of a hundred bobbing, grating ships, where goods arriving from all over Vigrið were being unloaded and haggled over by a swarm of merchants. The streets of Darl began to awake as they made their way deeper into the town, steadily climbing. Men and women, most with the look of warriors, fishermen and seafarers about them appearing from doorways, blinking and bleary-eyed as they left the inns and brothels where they had spent the night, most of them searching for alleyways where they dropped their breeches to urinate. Svik led them on, through a marketplace where dead bodies swung in high cages and traders were setting up trestle-tables and starting fires for cookpots to feed the snarl of humanity that would soon be filling the market. They left the square behind, Einar sniffing and looking longingly at steaks sizzling on a charcoal brazier, and then they were moving through narrow, twisting streets, feet drumming across wooden bridges spanning canals that fed into the River Drammur, and then they were spilling into another market square. This one was larger than the first, a wooden dais at its far end, and all around the edges of the square were wooden stalls and pens, like the ones Varg had tended most of his life on Kolskegg's farm, built for goats, sheep, pigs and oxen. But in these pens were people.

Hundreds of them, crammed and huddled like cattle. The sharp tang of urine and faeces was thick in the air, clawing into Varg's throat. All of them were shaven-haired, iron collars around their necks, wrists and ankles bound with rope or iron, wearing tattered, dirty tunics of linen or hemp or homespun wool. Flat, empty stares looked out into the square. Varg felt a lurch of nausea in his belly, followed quickly by a sense of guilt. That he was free, where they were slaves. He had been one of them, not so long ago. A spark of horror and futile anger in his gut, that he lived in a world where people were treated like this.

Men and women stood at the gates of each pen and enclosure, all with hard stares, wearing boiled leather and holding clubs in their fists.

Svik led them across the square, pushing through a thickening crowd as they approached the dais, where a row of thralls stood tied together, one of the thralls stripped naked and standing in front of them as a tall, fat-bellied auctioneer shouted out the skills and abilities of the thrall.

Varg stuttered to a halt, just staring at the thralls on the dais. They were all dark-skinned, as close to black as the pitch pine painted on the *Sea-Wolf*'s hull.

"What's wrong?" Svik said, stopping and turning. He followed Varg's amazed stare.

"Oh, have you never seen a Bruised Man before?"

"Bruised Man?" Varg mumbled. "They're not bruised, they're black."

"Their tongues are blue, and their skin changes colour in different lights, or when it's wet, like a magpie's wing, or oil," Svik said.

Varg just shook his head. "Where are they from?"

"Iskidan," Røkia said.

"They don't look like Jaromir and his *druzhina* to me," Varg said.

"Iskidan is a big place," Svik said. "The bruised men are from the south, whereas Jaromir and his *druzhina* are from the north."

Varg frowned. "People from the north of Vigrið look much the same as those from the south," he said.

"Think of it like this," Svik said. "Imagine a boil on Einar's arse."

"Not a pleasant thought," Røkia muttered.

"I don't have any boils on my arse," Einar said with a hurt frown.

"I said *imagine*," Svik said. "You know, using your thought-cage," he tapped his temple. "So, *imagine* Einar has a boil on his arse. Vigrið would be the boil, and Iskidan would be the whole of Einar's arse."

Varg puffed his cheeks and blew out a whistle. "I thought Liga was the biggest town in the world, and then I came here, and thought that Darl must clearly be the biggest town in the world."

"Ha," Svik said. "No. Wait until you see Snakavik, and even that is like an outhouse compared to Gravka, city of Iskidan's emperor."

As they were talking, the Bruised Man on the dais was sold, and for a price Varg found inconceivable for a thrall. A tunic was thrust over the man and he was led from the dais, coin exchanging hands, and another of the thralls was brought forward, a woman this time. Her tunic was pulled roughly from her and the next auction began.

"This makes me sick," Varg growled.

"The world is cruel and full of pain and dark deeds," Røkia said quietly, Varg not sure if she were talking to him or to herself, but her words hung in his thought-cage, reminding why he had asked Glornir's permission to come here.

"How do we find Brimil?" Varg asked.

"Like this," Svik said. "Do you still have your thrall-collar?"

"Aye," muttered Varg. He reached inside his cloak, felt the cold weight of it within a stitched, hidden pocket.

"And the key?"

"Aye," Varg said.

"Good. Put the collar on."

Varg's eyes flared at the thought of it, a ripple of fear and shame shivering through him, a flood of unwanted memories.

"Trust me, brother," Svik said gently.

Varg breathed deep and nodded, putting the collar around his neck and closing it with a snap. It was tighter than he remembered, and heavier, rubbing on his skin. He felt his lips curl in a snarl, heard the wolf growl in his blood.

"Won't be for long," Svik said. "Røkia, act like Varg is our prisoner."

She gave a thin smile.

Svik walked off, threading his way through the crowd to approach the dais. He stopped in front of the fat auctioneer and asked something. The auctioneer pointed to his right, and then Svik was beckoning to them. Røkia touched Varg's back with the tip of her spear and they followed after Svik, Varg giving one last look to the Bruised Men on the dais as he followed Svik into a street that exited the square. The street sloped downwards, back towards the river. Wooden, planked paths had been laid on either side of the road, which was mud-churned and slippery. Ahead of them Svik stopped outside an inn and spoke to a thickset man leaning on a long club. As Varg drew nearer the man looked him up and down, curled his lip and opened the door. Varg saw the inn's windows looked as if they had been recently repaired, a sign hanging over them, creaking in the breeze.

The Dead Drengr.

Svik gave the guard one of his dazzling smiles and walked into the inn.

"Get on, thrall," Røkia said and pushed Varg's shoulder. He walked forward, meeting the guard's gaze and returning it.

"Best you take your dirty thrall-eyes off of me," the guard growled, "else you'll feel the kiss of my girl, here." He hefted his club and patted it in one palm.

Varg felt the urge to tear the man's throat out. He looked away and walked into the inn, Røkia following him. Einar stooped to fit through the doorway.

Varg walked into a dark room, torches flickering, pots of walrus-oil burning, thick and salty in the air. A handful of tables with chairs, and a bar, a grey-haired, balding man pouring ale into a row of tall jugs. The rest of the room was empty apart from one man sitting at a table, bald head gleaming in the firelight, a grey-streaked beard bound with gold rings. He was thickset, muscled shoulders and arms, looked like he could look after himself though his belly rolled over his belt. He was counting a pile of coins on the table. A woman stood behind him, clearly his guard, her arms folded, clothed in wool and boiled leather, a seax and hand-axe at her belt.

"Who are you?" the bald man asked, looking up at Svik.

"Got a thrall to sell. A runaway," Svik said, gesturing to Varg. "I'm looking for Brimil, have been told he's a good man to see about that."

The bald man looked Varg up and down, Varg feeling his skin crawl and hackles rise, as if a serpent were slithering across him.

"I'm Brimil, and you've been told right," Brimil said. "No one better with runaways than me." He looked to the bartender and raised a hand.

"Rog, some ale for my guests." The bartender nodded and set one of the jugs he'd just poured on to a tray, then began hunting out some clay cups.

"But runaways are a pain in the arse," Brimil continued. "Once they think they can slip their chains, they're forever looking for a chance. And this one looks like he's got *difficult* tattooed across his forehead." He leaned back in his chair and glowered at Varg. "Suggest you point those insolent eyes somewhere else, 'fore I take one of them out to teach you a lesson," he said, calm as can be, then spat on the floor. "Can't give you much for him, with an attitude like that," he said to Svik.

"Ah," Svik said, "it's nothing I'm sure you can't beat out of him. I was told that's your talent. Taming unruly thralls."

Brimil puffed his chest out. "It has been known," he smiled.

An image of Frøya rose up in Varg's thought-cage. Her sad eyes looking at him as she had cleaned his cut, swollen face after a bout in Kolskegg's pugil-ring. And then Terna's words, back at the village in the Boneback Mountains. "*Brimil beat her often, because she kept on trying to escape.*"

The wolf snarled in Varg's blood, and he welcomed it.

The bartender, limping, a bandage around one ankle, was bringing his tray of ale and cups.

Varg exploded into motion, crashing into the bartender as he leaped at Brimil, sending the man spinning and cracking his head on the edge of a table, upending it so that the table crashed on to his body as he hit the ground. The bartender did not move. The tray flew through the air, the jug smashing and raining ale over them all. Brimil fell backwards in his chair, Varg on top of him, hands around his throat. The guard stood frozen a moment, then stumbled back, reaching for her axe and seax as Røkia leaped forwards and stabbed the woman in a shoulder with her spear. The woman cried out, tumbled back, crunching against the wall, Røkia's spear blade hovering at her throat.

"You *niðing*—" snarled Brimil, but then Varg's fist connected with his mouth, mashing the words as well as his lips. He sat on top of Brimil, punching and punching, the man's head rocking back.

"I think he might be ready to talk," Svik said, putting a hand on Varg's shoulder.

"Huh," Varg grunted, one fist raised.

Brimil had one eye swollen closed, his lips torn, nose bent and bloody, a few teeth missing.

"You came here for answers, remember," Svik said.

"Control," Røkia said, her eyes and spear still fixed on the guard.

Varg stood, sucked in a deep breath and blew it out slowly. He grabbed the arms of Brimil's chair and hauled it up, Brimil still in the chair. He groaned.

The creak of a door.

"You all right, boss?" the guard outside said as he stepped into the room. Paused as he took in the scene.

Einar's fist crashed into the guard's jaw and he dropped, unconscious before he hit the ground.

"Not a very good guard," Einar observed, nudging the unconscious man with his boot.

"Ask your questions, then," Svik said.

Varg closed his eyes and clenched his teeth as he wrestled with the wolf in his blood, forcing it to calm. He opened his eyes and looked at Brimil, who was lolling in the chair, semi-conscious.

"I want to talk to you about two thralls you bought from Kolskegg's farm," Varg said.

"Guh," Brimil wheezed through blood-frothed lips, his head lolling and eyes rolling.

"Wait a moment," Svik said and walked across the wreckage of the room to the bar, fetched a jug of ale and threw it over the slaver, Brimil coughing and spluttering. The slaver held his head straighter, eyes clearing.

"Thralls from Kolskegg's farm," Varg said again. "Two women, around a year ago."

"Kolskegg," Brimil nodded. "Aye," he mumbled.

"One you sold to Njal Olafsson, jarl of a village in the Bonebacks. Her name was Terna."

"I remember her," Brimil said. "A good thrall. Knew her place." He smiled through bloody teeth.

"The other; Frøya . . ." Varg felt his throat constrict, just saying her name out loud stirred so much within him.

And this man beat her.

The wolf in his veins prowled back and forth, growling, wanting to taste Brimil's blood.

"Frøya," he said again.

"I remember her," Brimil said. "A runaway. Caught her, though, every time. What of her?"

"And you punished her for that, didn't you," Varg growled.

A hand on his shoulder, Svik.

"Brother," he cautioned.

"Had to, she was a defiant bitch," Brimil said. He hawked and spat phlegm and blood. "She needed teaching her place. Sometimes you have to hump the defiance out of them."

"What . . .?"

A flood of rage, the wolf surging up in him, uncontrollable, a red mist falling, and he was lunging forward, teeth snapping. Dimly he heard Brimil scream, felt arms wrapping around him, dragging him away. He twisted and writhed, gnashing and snarling.

"Easy, brother, easy," Einar's voice in his ear, thick arms around him like a vice. Slowly Varg calmed, felt the red mist fade, the wolf slinking back into a corner of his soul.

"All right," Varg breathed.

Einar let him go and he walked back to Brimil, Svik standing behind the slaver, one hand pressed on his shoulder to keep him in his chair. A chunk of Brimil's cheek was hanging, blood pulsing from ragged teeth marks. He looked at Varg with frightened eyes.

"Frøya," Varg said slowly. "Who did you sell her to?"

"Brák . . . Brák Trolls-Bane," Brimil said, quick and trembling, not wanting to meet Varg's eyes.

"And where will I find this Brák Trolls-Bane?" Varg asked. "Is he here in Darl?"

"On and off," Brimil said, now gushing information like a river bursting a beaver's dam. "He's a trapper. A hunter for hire, too. He's out of town right now."

"Anything else you can tell me?" Varg asked him.

"He drinks here, when he's in town, at *The Dead Drengr*. That's all I know."

Svik moved between one heartbeat and the next, dragging his seax across Brimil's throat. A spurt of blood, Brimil choking, spluttering, sagging. Behind Svik came a gurgling screech as Røkia punched her spear into the guard's mouth, a red stain on the wall as the guard slipped to the ground. A crunch behind Varg and he twisted to see Einar wrenching his axe out of the unconscious guard's skull.

"What?" Varg said.

"He saw the wolf in you," Svik said. "Saw your eyes change. No one can know your secret. Our secret."

Varg nodded, feeling numb. It had all happened so quickly. He wasn't sure how he felt: Guilty? That he was responsible for these people's deaths. Angry, that Brimil had not died by his hand? The wolf inside him snarled, wanting more blood.

It is done, now.

"We should go," Røkia said, wiping her spear blade clean on the fallen guard's breeches and walking to the door.

"Aye, Glornir is waiting," Einar rumbled.

Svik sheathed his seax and strode to the door, Einar and Røkia already through it. He stopped at the doorway and looked back.

"Come on, Varg," he said. "We've got a *drakkar* to catch. And then we can talk about how we'll find this *niðing* Brák Troll's-Turd."

Varg reached inside his cloak and pulled out the key to the collar about his neck. He tried to fit it into the lock, but his hand was shaking.

"Here," Røkia said, stepping close and taking his hand in hers. Her hands were warm and rough. "You're no thrall," she breathed as she guided the key into the lock, turned it and then he was ripping the collar from his neck and shoving it back inside his cloak.

"My thanks," he muttered.

A touch of a smile across Røkia's lips.

Einar was looking at them all.

"I have a favour to ask," Half-Troll said.

The screech of gulls grew louder as they reached the dockside, moving quickly even through the crush of people. Most were quick to move out of Einar's way, not just because of his size, but because he was leading oxen harnessed to a wagon. He led them to the *drakkar* Queen Helka was loaning the Bloodsworn, Svik sitting on the driver's bench, Varg and Røkia walking behind.

Varg's head was full of Brimil and his words, the startled look in his eyes as Svik had cut his throat, the stench of his blood still in Varg's nostrils. A whispered name curled amid the images, echoing in his thought-cage like the scrape of branches in the dead of night.

Brák Trolls-Bane.

The sound of Brimil's guard as Røkia stabbed her, and the crunch of Einar's axe into the unconscious guardsman.

I caused their deaths, by my lack of control. I may still have killed Brimil, though I do not know if I could have done it there, like that: to kill an unarmed prisoner . . .

"They deserved to die," Røkia said.

Varg looked at her, dragged away from his thoughts.

"Can you read my thought-cage?" he asked her with a frown.

"You do not hide your feelings well," she shrugged. "The slaver deserved to die, and so did the other two: *niðings* who took coin to protect a man like him." She curled a lip. "But you forced the decision by losing control. No harm has been done, this time. But you cannot let that happen again. What if it were in a marketplace, or in a mead hall, or on this street . . ."

"I know," Varg said. "I am sorry."

"Don't be sorry; be better." She gave him a hard look. "A mistake like that could mean the death of us all, or Galdur-collars around our necks."

Varg nodded, a shiver running through him at the thought of that. He put a hand to where his collar had been around his neck. It was gone now, but still felt like it was there. He thought of the dead-eyed thralls in slavers square.

I will never go back to being a thrall.

Varg saw that they had reached the pier where the *drakkar* was moored. Smaller than the *Sea-Wolf*, it was black-hulled with twenty oars, so the Bloodsworn would be able to row in shifts if there was no wind for the sail.

The pier was crowded, warriors of the Bloodsworn thick upon it, boarding the *drakkar* across a gangplank. They carried four corpses wrapped in linen shrouds upon their shoulders, Jökel and three warriors who had fallen during the fight in Helka's mead hall.

Einar walked round to the back of the wagon, joining Varg and Røkia, and Svik jumped down from the driver's bench. Einar unbolted the tailgate and then they were hefting barrels on to their shoulders and striding on to the pier. Svik led them, walking across the gangplank, jumping down into the *drakkar* and depositing the barrel on his shoulder close to the mast-hole. Varg and the others did the same, the ship rocking when Einar jumped in.

"Did you find what you needed?" a voice said behind Varg and he turned, saw Glornir standing there, tall and broad, a small, scabbed cut across his cheek the only sign that he had been in combat yesterday. He was leaning on his long-axe.

"Yes," Varg said. "My thanks."

He knew Glornir had taken a risk, allowing him to go in search of Brimil.

"Heard of a *niðing* turd named Brák Trolls-Bane?" Svik asked quietly as he walked past Glornir and headed back to the gangplank, going to fetch another barrel from the wagon.

"Brimil sold my sister to him," Varg said.

"I've not heard the name," Glornir said, his brows knitting. He reached out and put a hand on Varg's shoulder. "We must be away now, Varg. But you are one of us, and this Brák will have a reckoning."

Varg mumbled his thanks and nodded as he walked away to help Svik and the others with the barrels, still not used to being offered help and friendship.

But it feels . . . good.

They brought another load of barrels back to the *drakkar*, and then returned for the rest, while others prepared the ship, checking sails and rigging, pinning and securing the steering oar in place, spreading the weight of provisions.

A horn blew as Varg was carrying the last barrel along the pier; he looked back, saw a wide column of *drengrs* march towards them. Queen Helka at their centre.

Varg hurried up the gangplank, set the last barrel down then took an oar from a rack along the galley, finally finding an empty sea-chest where he sat, waiting.

Queen Helka stopped at the gangplank, a dozen of her *Úlfhéðnar* surrounding her, the *drengrs* forming a line along the dockside. Glornir nodded to her.

"Where is my son?" Queen Helka said.

Glornir pointed.

Prince Hakon was seated in the shadowed curl of the prow, with Æsa beside him, a spear in her fist. She raised a hand to Queen Helka and gave her a broad smile.

"He has been well looked after," Glornir said. "Fed and clothed."

"More's the pity about the clothing," Æsa said, prodding Hakon with a grin, "I was starting to like the look of his snake."

"More like a wyrm," Røkia said, rolling her eyes.

The Bloodsworn fell into fits of laughter, Svik slapping his thigh. Even Varg felt the tug of a smile at his lips.

Helka's silence and dour stare eventually brought the laughter to a stuttering halt.

"As agreed, one of my *Úlfhéðnar* shall accompany my son," Helka said. She raised a hand. "Frek."

A man stepped out of the group of *Úlfheðnar*, dark hair tied in a knotted braid across the centre of his head, tattoos swirling across shaved sides. He wore mail and a sword, seax and axe hung at his belt. And, of course, a collar of iron around his throat.

Glornir stepped aside, allowing Frek to walk across the gangplank and jump into the boat. Without a word or backward glance, he strode to Hakon in the prow and stood beside Æsa, ignoring her smiling attempts at a greeting.

"I wish you good hunting for Jaromir," Queen Helka said, "and I will have another chest of silver waiting for you when you bring him to me. Make sure you come to collect it."

"You'll be seeing me again," Glornir said. "I'll be back for the silver. And for Skalk." He looked along the pier. "He is not with you, then?"

"He has injuries," Helka said with a shrug and Glornir's lip curled. "Release my son, and soon," Helka called out, loud for all of the Bloodsworn to hear. "He *will* return to me unharmed, or you will all spend the rest of your short lives running."

"I gave you my word," Glornir said as he pulled the gangplank in with a rope. "Cast off," he called out, and the mooring rope was untied and cast on to the *drakkar*, Bloodsworn on the starboard side pushing off from the pier with their oars.

Varg rotated the leather oar-stop that covered the oar-hole and threaded his oar through. "OARS," Einar shouted and began to beat a rhythm on a barrel-lid with the butt of his axe, then oars were dipping into the dark waters and the *drakkar* was slipping into the current of the River Drammur.

"Svik," Varg said to the red-haired warrior sitting on an oar-chest in front of him, "why are we in a ship when Jaromir has fled on horseback? He could be anywhere in Vigrið."

Sulich was sitting on the oar-bench behind Varg and he heard his question. "Because Jaromir will be making for Iskidan as fast as he can," he said. "And his ships are docked at Liga. They are his only way out of Vigrið. If we're fast, we can catch him there."

Svik gave Varg a broad grin. "Better get rowing then, No-Sense."

CHAPTER THIRTY

BIÓRR

Biórr's shadow stretched before him, the sinking sun at his back. He was marching in a loose column with Ilska's Raven-Feeders, Red Fain and Storolf Wartooth at his side. At the head of the column rode Ilska and Lik-Rifa and, at the rear, came the untouched dragon-worshippers and the wagons full of children. Lik-Rifa had remained in her human form for days now, as they'd journeyed ever eastwards. She had an unquenchable thirst for information and knowledge, and the cadence of her voice had felt like a constant throughout every moment of their long march.

She has three hundred years of news to catch up on.

Biórr had been close enough to overhear most of the conversations. Ilska had answered Lik-Rifa's steady stream of questions with as much detail as she could, describing the history of Vigrið since the *Guðfalla* and Snaka's fall; the rise of humankind and the emergence of Galdurmen and -women, of the early days where the Tainted had been hunted, their total destruction the goal, and then the discoveries of Ulfrir's fragmented chain and the forging of the Galdur-collars. Of the days of slavery and servitude that followed, which they were still living through. Lik-Rifa had asked about the hierarchy of the world, and Ilska had told her of Vigrið, of the petty jarls who would be kings and queens of this new era, of the growing powers; Jarl Störr of Snakavik, Queen Helka of Darl, and Jarl Orlyg of Svelgarth who were either gathering the other petty jarls of Vigrið to their sides or swallowing them. She also spoke of the Dividing Sea and the land of Iskidan, far to the south, and of their unfamiliar gods, who had also died during the *Guðfalla*, leaving behind a vast kingdom that was ruled now by one emperor, Kirill the Magnificent.

Ilska raised a hand and behind her Drekr put a horn to his lips and blew, calling the end to another day's march. The column stuttered to a halt, men and women breaking ranks, beginning to make camp. Even though they were far in the north of Vigrið and the days of summer were leaking from the land, it was still warm, green grass on the ground, streams sparkling golden in the sun's last rays and trees thick with leaves. Biórr looked north and saw what looked like a second sunset, a thin strip of glowing red across the horizon that marked the vaesen pit. They had marched parallel to the molten river, far enough from it not to be sweating each day, but close enough that they could still feel the warmth in the ground and keep the cold at bay.

"Come on, lad," Fain said, "standing there gawping won't put a meal in your belly."

Biórr smiled, nodded and set to work with the rest of the warband, digging out pits for fires, gathering kindling and dead wood, filling waterskins and barrels from the wagons. He saw Kráka and Ilmur helping organise the children, still entranced, all moving slow and stiff-limbed, as if they were half asleep.

Scents started to drift through the camp as fires crackled and pots boiled. Spitted elk hearts and haunches roasting, tracked and killed two days before, porridge bubbling, the sharp tang of pickled stockfish as barrels were opened.

Soon they were settling into small groups seated around the many fires, Biórr with Fain and Storolf and a few other Raven-Feeders. He sat in silence, not listening to the conversation around him, lost in his own thoughts. Images of Agnar on his knees haunted Biórr. How he had looked up at Biórr with trust and friendship.

And then I put a spear in his mouth.

Most days one of the Raven-Feeders would slap his back and commend him for the slaying of Agnar Battle-Grim, but all Biórr wanted to do was forget the act.

Agnar was the one who fought a holmganga, against that brute Skrið. Who would have thought that Agnar would win? Impossible. That was something to sing a saga-skáld about. All I did was murder someone who trusted me.

And betray my lover.

He would often wake from distorted dreams in the night, gasping and sweating, Elvar's face stark in his thought-cage, staring at him accusingly as he stood over Agnar's twitching body.

"You've less to say these days than before," Storolf said to Biórr. Fain gave his son a look, a slight shake of his head.

"In his own time," Fain said.

Biórr just shrugged and filled his bowl with skyr.

"Or did Myrk just hump all of the talk out of you before she rode south?" Storolf said.

A ripple of laughter around the fire at that.

"She's a lot of woman," Biórr said with a half-smile. "I'm just conserving my strength for her return."

More laughter, louder at that. Storolf wheezed and nodded, and Biórr went back to eating.

"Eyes up," Fain said.

Biórr looked up to see Lik-Rifa standing in the centre of their camp, tall, regal and terrifying. Ilska stood one side of her, thin and cruel as a whip, and on the other side stood Drekr, made to look short beside Lik-Rifa, though he was taller than anyone else in the camp. He was still broader than her, though.

"Bring the children to me," Lik-Rifa called out in her too-deep voice. Behind them stood the rest of the dragon-born, maybe another score of warriors.

Voices shouted, the tramp of feet and the children were led through the camp to stand before Lik-Rifa. Almost a hundred of them, all with the glint of cold iron around their necks. Thrall-collars, which made Biórr feel uncomfortable. Myrk had explained to him that the collars were only temporary, that they had been necessary to stop children running away; that the Tainted children had been vital for the rune-spell that freed Lik-Rifa. But still . . .

We are fighting those who would enslave us Tainted, and yet we have gone and done it to our own. Do the ends always truly justify the means?

Biórr grimaced, trying to push those thoughts away.

What is wrong with me? He growled at himself in his thought-cage. *I was happy here, before. Then I spend a year among the untouched and now I see conflict in everything.*

Warriors walked among the children, shouting orders, pushing, some leading children by the hand. Biórr saw Kráka was one of those; she held Bjarn's hand, though he did not look like he knew where he was, but Biórr was glad of Kráka's presence. He had a soft spot for the lad.

Lik-Rifa waited until they were all standing in loose rows before her.

"Take their collars off," Lik-Rifa said.

Ilska and the other dragon-born walked forward. They held keys in one hand and were chanting in their Galdur-tongue.

"*Rúne-álög stjórnunar, dofna, láta vilja sinn og styrk snúa aftur,*" Ilska and her dragon-born kin chanted as they walked among the thralled children, turning locks in collars and letting them fall to the ground. As they passed through the crowd the children behind them who had been freed stretched and looked around, blinking. "Papa?" one called out, another began to cry, another screamed.

Ilska and the others took collars from the last of the children and walked out into a space behind them.

"Silence," Lik-Rifa said as the murmuring and crying among the children spread, rising in volume. Some stared at Lik-Rifa, but most were too bemused or unsettled to take any notice of her.

It must be like going to sleep safe in one place, and waking in an entirely different place, no one and nothing familiar around you, Biórr thought, feeling sorry for them.

"SILENCE," Lik-Rifa roared, mist swirling around her, the crackle of bone as her body shifted and grew, jaws expanding, teeth sprouting, skin becoming scale and wings arching from her back. The children screamed. And then Lik-Rifa was shrinking, morphing back into human shape, the mist evaporating. She stood there staring at the gathered children, and they stood there, frozen, staring back at her. Not a sound could be heard, not a whimper or a sniff.

"I am Lik-Rifa, the dragon-god," Lik-Rifa said, "second-born and most favoured of Dread Snaka, maker of all."

Another silence, the children either terrified or enraptured, Biórr was not sure which.

"The first lesson you must learn is that your parents have lied to you, all the years of your life. You are Tainted, though that should never be considered an insult. It is an honour. The blood of the dead gods runs in your veins, and your parents have kept that hidden from you." She paused a moment and sniffed, allowing her words to sink in.

"I am your family, now. I am your *all*. Your past is gone. There is only me and this moment, and all that follows after it. Unlike this world that would enslave you just for being descended from a god, you have nothing to fear from *me*. I will be your queen, I will love you, lead you, protect you, provide food and wealth for you, and in return all that I ask is that you be LOYAL." She roared the last word, her dragon-voice sounding like a thunderclap, her eyes blazing. A tremor passed through her as she calmed. A solitary whimper drifted from among the children. "I shall *love* you as a mother loves her children, and you shall love me in return." It was a command, not a request. She walked closer to them, her eyes raking them, holding their gaze one by one, and then she was walking among them, holding her hands out to brush across heads, cheeks, shoulders. Some of the children shuffled closer to her, wanting to be touched, others shuffled further away.

"These men and women you see," Lik-Rifa said, gesturing to Ilska and the dragon-born standing behind the children, "they are my children, and so they are your family, too. And all these others," Lik-Rifa waved a hand at the Raven-Feeders and untouched sitting around their fires. "You are all my people, my followers. Together, we are going to change this world."

A hushed silence.

"LIK-RIFA," Ilska shouted, "LIK-RIFA."

Drekr and the other dragon-born joined their voices to Ilska's, and then Storolf and the other Raven-Feeders around Biórr were standing and shouting out. Slowly Biórr put his bowl of skyr down and stood with the others, adding his voices to the crowd.

Among it all he heard the high-pitched, discordant voices of children joining in the shouted cry.

"LIK-RIFA, LIK-RIFA."

Biórr awoke to the wailing of a child. He sat up and rubbed his eyes. The sky above was a blush of pink and orange as the sun crept over the horizon, pushing back the darkness. Storolf snored close by, another half-dozen Raven-Feeders sleeping around the cold ash of last night's fire. Biórr looked around and saw two men walking into the camp, one of them dragging a child who bucked and kicked and screamed in his grasp. The first man loped ahead and Biórr realised that it was Ilmur. The Hundur saw Biórr and grinned at him, beckoning him over, so he stood, cracked his neck, buckled on his weapons belt and strode towards Ilmur.

"Had my first job," Ilmur smiled at Biórr.

"Have you? And what was that?" Biórr asked him, putting a hand on Ilmur's shoulder. He still had that beaten, subservient look about him that many who had been thralls for a long time clung to. Eager to please, as if Ilska and the Raven-Feeders were his new masters, rather than his liberators.

"Tracking a runaway," Ilmur said, pointing over his shoulder.

The other man was labouring through thick scrub, one of Drekr's crew, a black raven feather bound in his dark hair and a necklace of long, curved teeth or tusks hung about his neck. His skin was weathered and worn, like the bark of a wind-battered tree. Of average height and slender, clothed in boiled leathers and furs, a weapons belt bristling with a multitude of knives. A sword hung at his hip, slim and long. He was dragging a child, a pale-faced boy of roughly ten or eleven winters. As Biórr looked the boy managed to find his feet and balance, twist himself in the man's grip and sink his teeth into his captor's hand.

A shriek and the man let the boy go, jerking his hand away. The boy stumbled and fell, but in a heartbeat was back on his feet and running. He was at least twenty paces away when a scabbarded knife crunched into his head and he fell in a rolling, boneless tangle.

The man strode after him, flicking blood from his hand and muttering curses. He reached the boy and put a boot in the lad's belly, sending him rolling over, followed after him and kicked him again. Then reached down and grabbed a handful of tunic, pulled the lad half-back to his feet and then backhanded him, snapping his head back. Biórr heard the distinctive crack of the boy's nose breaking. He found his feet were hurrying him towards the man and boy.

"Think he's had enough," Biórr said as he drew close, the man pausing with his fist back. The boy was still conscious, crying and snarling at the same time. His mouth and chin were slick with blood pouring from his nose.

The man looked at Biórr, eyes narrowing.

"You're the rat in Agnar's Battle-Grim," he said.

Biórr ignored that. "Think you've knocked the running out of him," he said instead.

"He's a runaway," the man grunted, "needs to be taught a lesson." His eyes stayed fixed on Biórr as he slapped the lad again.

"Aye, but the dead can't learn any lessons."

"Ha," the man grinned, "that's a fair point."

The hiss of a knife drawn from a scabbard and Biórr looked down to see the lad had found the sheathed knife thrown at him and had drawn it. He slashed at the huntsman, who jumped back, the blade scoring a thin line through the leather and linen on his arm. He grunted a curse, dodged another wild slash and stepped agilely in, a punch faster than Biórr could track whipping out and crunching on to the lad's chin. He collapsed, wheezing and the man stamped on the hand that clutched the knife. The *snap* of bones breaking, and the boy cried out.

The man crouched down and took his knife back from the lad's fist.

"What's your name, boy?" the man said.

"Guh," the boy mumbled.

The man slapped him, open palmed, across the face.

"What's your name?"

"B . . . B . . . Breca," the boy wheezed. He sucked in air, eyes focusing, and glared at the man. "Breca Thorkelsson."

"Just Breca now," the man said. "Remember what Lik-Rifa said last night. Your parents and past are gone."

"Breca Thorkelsson," the boy said again.

The man smiled, pinned Breca with a knee across his throat and chest, gripped the boy's crow-black hair in one fist and sliced a line across his cheek, deep, just under his eye. Breca whimpered.

"Well, Breca Thorkelsson," the man said, "you're going to have a scar on your face from this cut for the rest of your life. So next time you think about running away, you put your hand to this scar, and you remember what happens to runaways. And you remember who gave it to you. My name's Brák Trolls-Bane, and don't you go forgetting it."

"I won't," snarled Breca.

CHAPTER THIRTY-ONE

ORKA

Orka cut the rag that was tied around Myrk's mouth.

"Time we had another chat," Orka said.

Myrk looked at her with hate-filled eyes. She was leaning propped against a tree, her wrists and ankles bound with leather cord.

"Need a hand, chief?" Revna Hare-Legs called out. She was sparring with Lif beside a fast-flowing stream, the *clack, clack, clack* of their spear shafts sending woodpigeons bursting into flight from the pinewoods close by.

I'm not your chief, Orka thought. She had pointed that fact out over a score of times during the last few days' travel, and not just to Revna Hare-Legs, but she was reaching the point where she was close to giving up.

"No," Orka said. Spert and Vesli were positioned either side of Myrk, Spert with his sting raised and twitching, and Vesli staring at Myrk's mouth and teeth with an unsettling intensity.

"You *would* need help if my hands and ankles were not tied," Myrk snarled, though her face was still too swollen from the beating Orka had given her for the intended menace to be communicated.

Spert scuttled a little closer, his antennae touching Myrk's leg and his sting curling over his back.

"Get away from me, you disgusting little vaesen," Myrk hissed.

Spert smiled at her, which was never a pleasant sight.

"*Maður woman rude*," Vesli commented.

"And you can shut your flapping lips," Myrk said to Vesli, "you're nothing but a bald rat with wings."

Vesli's wings twitched and she hissed at Myrk, revealing her two rows of teeth.

Orka sniffed and looked around. Although they had ridden hard from Rotta's chamber and covered a lot of ground, following the trail that Myrk and her Raven-Feeders had left on their journey to the chamber, they were still nestled in the foothills of the Bonebacks, the sinking sun bathing the landscape of slopes and ravines in golden light and deep shadows, swathes of pinewoods and snowmelt rivers and streams laid across the land like gold and silver thread in a weaver's tapestry. Myrk and her crew had not been diligent in covering their tracks and so the remnants of burned-out fires, flattened grass and piles of horse dung had told Orka every day that they were on the right course. That trail had taken them north-west, as Edel had suspected, hugging the Bonebacks and leading them ever closer to Lake Horndal.

"You don't have to answer my questions," Orka said. "I can just follow your trail back and see where it takes me. To Drekr, I suspect, and my son."

"So why bother to ask me at all?" Myrk said.

"Here you go, chief," Gunnar Prow said as he limped up, handing Orka a wooden bowl filled with hard cheese, pickled onion, a chunk of rye bread and slices of salted pork.

I'm not your chief.

She took the bowl with a scowl and set it down beside her. Gunnar sat on a rock nearby with his own bowl of food and grinned at Myrk. "How does it feel to have a face that's swollen as a ten-day dead pig?" he asked her.

"Better than having a *drakkar* prow for a nose," Myrk muttered, to which Gunnar almost rolled off the rock he was sitting on, he laughed so hard.

"You'll have to do better than that to win a *flyting* word-war with me," he said. "I *like* my prow of a nose."

"I *love* your prow of a nose," Revna Hare-Legs called out as she battered Lif back to the edge of the stream.

"I'm asking you, because you might save me some time," Orka said to Myrk. "I am getting tired of dragging your hide all across Vigrið and setting a guard over you each night. It might be easier just to cut your throat and roll you into that stream."

"Food for the fish," Gunnar smiled through a mouthful of cheese.

"Nibble, nibble, nibble," Revna Hare-Legs called out from the streambank as she parried a spear lunge from Lif.

"So, where is my son?" Orka asked.

"Who killed my father?" Myrk snapped.

Orka sighed. "This could end badly for you," she said. "Remember the last time you answered a question with a question?"

Myrk smiled, opening her mouth and sticking her tongue into a gap where a tooth had been. "How could I forget," she said.

"Then answer my question," Orka snarled.

"Cut me loose and fight me," Myrk snarled back.

Gunnar choked on some cheese. "Chief, she's not right in the head," he said.

"Do a trade," another voice called out, Halja Flat-Nose striding towards them, having just untacked and rubbed down all of their horses. "The location of Orka's son, for the name Myrk wants. Of the Bloodsworn who slew her *niðing* father."

Myrk glared at Halja. "Call my father a *niðing* again and I'll kill you," she snarled.

"He was a *niðing* and died squealing," Halja said, her face flat and emotionless as a cliff.

Myrk jerked and twisted in her bonds, gnashing her teeth; blood frothed on her lips and there was a flare of red within her eyes.

A hiss and blur of movement and Orka had a seax at Myrk's throat. Spert's sting was hovering a finger's span from one of her eyes and Vesli's spear-point was touching Myrk's heart.

Myrk froze. The flush of red behind her eyes faded.

"*Good Maður*," Spert grated.

"*Fight on*," Vesli piped. "*Please. Your teeth look tasty.*"

Myrk glared at the two vaesen.

"You're not helping," Orka frowned at Halja. "And how can I tell her who slew her father? I would not betray one of the Bloodsworn."

"It's no betrayal," Halja said with a shrug as she walked to the wool blanket where Gunnar had set out their evening meal and began helping herself to food. "There'll be skáld-songs in every mead hall about it soon enough. And if Myrk were to seek out her father's slayer," Halja gave a cold smile, "I think she would be joining her father in the ground."

Orka nodded, thinking that through. "Gunnar, Revna, do you agree?"

"Aye," Gunnar nodded.

"I agree-ooph," Revna grunted, Lif catching her in the gut with the butt of his spear.

"Cheat," she smiled at him, like a proud mother.

Lif looked about as happy as it was possible for a man to be.

"I hit you!" he grinned.

Revna attacked him, her spear a blur and he stumbled back, fell with a shriek and a splash into the stream as Revna stood on the bank grinning.

"All right," Orka said, looking at Myrk. "A trade? Answer my questions and I shall tell you who slew your father."

"You think me a *hálfviti* idiot?" Myrk said. "As soon as I tell you, that seax will be scrapping across my throat."

"If you talk, I will not kill you until I find my son," Orka said. "Then I will set you free and we can have the *holmganga* you keep asking for."

"Oh, and I'm just going to believe you, am I? Just going to *trust* you?" Myrk laughed and shook her head.

Orka lifted her seax and drew it slowly across the heel of her palm, blood welling. "I swear it, on the life of my son, and seal it with my blood," Orka said.

A silence, Myrk looking at the blood dripping from Orka's hand.

"All right, then," Myrk smiled. "Why not," she shrugged. "You're all going to die, anyway. Whether you kill me, follow my trail, or carve some answers from me; it will all end the same. You and your followers ending up as meat and bones for Lik-Rifa to crunch."

"You have mentioned Lik-Rifa before. And we have all felt the dragon's presence."

Myrk nodded with a rabid smile. "We have freed her from her gaol beneath Oskutreð. Lik-Rifa will change the world. She's going to *eat* you."

"That sounds . . . far-fetched," Gunnar Prow said.

"Did you see inside Rotta's chamber?" Myrk said.

"Aye," Orka nodded.

"Then you saw the room with the rune-scrolls?"

"Huh." Orka had a bad feeling growing in the pit of her belly.

"We found the *Raudskinna*," Myrk said, a whispered hiss. "The secrets, the power." She shook her head. "It told of a way to break the seal on Lik-Rifa's prison. Among other things."

"That sounds too easy," Gunnar Prow said.

"Well, I'm simplifying things, of course. For one thing, we needed a lot of Tainted blood for the spell." Another slow smile at Orka.

"Breca," Orka breathed. An image in her thought-cage of Myrk holding Breca, slicing one of her seaxes across his throat.

This bitch is toying with me, thinks me a mouse and she the cat.

Orka grabbed a fistful of Myrk's hair, dragged her head back and smashed the hilt of her seax into Myrk's eye, ripped it out with a burst of blood and eye-jelly, and threw Myrk back on to the ground.

Myrk screamed and writhed, her body convulsing with pain.

Orka waited, controlling the wolf in her blood, the red mist in her thought-cage.

Slowly Myrk's wailing shifted into something else. It took a few moments for Orka to realise what it was. Laughter.

"Gunnar's right," Revna said, "she's not right in the head."

"He's . . . alive," Myrk wheezed, sitting up, blood and slime leaking down one cheek.

"As are you, for now," Orka growled.

"Your face, though," Myrk said, "ah, but that was a sight to see."

"Not as much of a sight as yours is now," Revna Hare-Legs said.

"Breca's alive?" Orka said, the fire in her blood shifting to something colder.

"None of the Tainted children died, so, yes, he must be," Myrk rasped, wiping blood from her cheek with her arm. She shivered, a ripple of pain or rage, Orka did not care. "Not that I know if one of those brats was yours."

"Why children?" Halja asked as she came back with a plate of food.

"We tried older Tainted, but that didn't end well," Myrk said. Blood was pooling in the socket of her ruined eye and dripping down her cheek. "Children are easier to control. Especially if you know how to blend a little Seiðr and Galdur-power."

Orka sat back, flexing her fingers. The thought of Breca under some Seiðr-spell made her want to put out Myrk's other eye, want to rip her throat out and taste her lifeblood. She sucked in a deep breath, held it a few moments, then blew out slowly.

"So, where is Breca now?" Orka asked her.

Myrk paused, looked from Orka to the others, all gathered around now, even Lif, who stood dripping wet.

Halja passed Lif a wool blanket. "You should take your ring mail off and dry it, else you'll rust stiff like a tin pot."

Lif nodded and attempted to wriggle and heave out of the mail coat, getting stuck for a few moments before it slithered into a heap on the ground.

"When I left Lik-Rifa and my sister, they were north of the vaesen pit, so they had to march south and cross the Isbrún Bridge before the end of *sólstöður*."

"Pfah," Halja snorted. "The Isbrún Bridge! You are telling us a saga-tale for your own amusement."

"It's true," Myrk said. "A Seiðr-witch thralled to the Battle-Grim opened the bridge, and we followed them across, followed them all the way to Oskutreð."

"I know of the Battle-Grim," Revna said. "Their Seiðr-witch is Kráka, and she does not have the power to go around opening god-bridges."

"Kráka has joined us, now," Myrk smiled. "But it was not her who opened the bridge. It was another Seiðr-witch, named Uspa."

A stunned silence.

Vol's sister. How is Uspa a thrall to the Battle-Grim, and what of Berak? He would never have allowed such a thing to happen. Unless he were dead. Orka saw the appalled, angry faces of the Bloodsworn.

"You know this Uspa, then," Myrk smiled.

"Where is she now?" Gunnar asked, his voice cold as iron.

Myrk shrugged. "Dead, maybe. Or alive, with the few Battle-Grim still breathing. We left Oskutreð in a hurry, did not stop to count the dead or living that Lik-Rifa left behind." She looked at them all. "I've told you much, and no word of a lie. So, tell me, who killed my father?"

"You still have not told me where my son is," Orka said.

"When I left, he was with my sister, Ilska, north of the bridge."

"Where were they going? Where are you to meet them?" Orka snarled.

"The plan was to cross the bridge and head west, to the coast off of the Iskalt Islands."

Orka frowned. "Why there?"

"I do not know the mind of a god," Myrk said with a shrug. "Lik-Rifa told me to bring my father there, that is all I know."

Orka sat back.

The Iskalt Islands. The relief of *knowing* was a palpable, physical thing. Finally, a destination to aim for. She looked suspiciously at Myrk, sitting there bleeding and smirking. *Is she telling me the truth?*

"Tell me, then," Myrk said. "Who killed my father?"

"His name is Varg," Halja said.

"Varg," Myrk breathed, tasting the name as if it were poison. She looked east, back towards Rotta's chamber. "Well, Varg, enjoy what is left of your short life while you can."

CHAPTER THIRTY-TWO

VARG

V arg stretched, feeling stiff muscles in his back and shoulders pull tight, bones grinding. The *drakkar* coasted on dark waters as in the stern Einar lifted the anchor-stone and dropped it overboard with a splash. The *drakkar* slowed and stopped, the river current foaming white as it cut around the hull. Day was waning, the sun just a red strip across the edge of the world and a fading glow reflected high above on undulating clouds.

Glornir shouted for food to be shared out, cold from stored barrels, as they would be sleeping on the ship. Some of the Bloodsworn set to securing an awning over the rear of the deck, as a means of shelter in case of rain.

Varg stood and stowed his oar in a rack along the centre of the deck as Glornir walked to the stowed barrels, resting an elbow on one.

"What's for our evening meal, then," Glornir said. He rapped his knuckles on the barrel and took a seax from his belt, digging the point of it into the barrel-lid.

"Not that one," Einar said, hurrying down the deck, making the *drakkar* sway.

Glornir stopped and looked at Einar. Raised an eyebrow.

"Why not?" Glornir said.

Einar stuttered to a halt before him, then looked sheepishly at his feet.

"Perhaps because we don't want to be eating cold children for our evening meal?" Glornir said, working the lid off and reaching inside, hauling out a bedraggled-looking boy, about eight or nine winters old.

"Can we come out, now, Einar?" the boy said.

Glornir put the boy down on the deck.

"I'm hungry," the boy said as he walked up to Einar and hugged his tree-trunk leg.

"Best get them all out, before they starve to death," Glornir said, walking away. Varg saw the big man's moustache twitch, just for a moment the vaguest hint of a smile.

"Yes, chief, thank you, chief," Einar said as he set to opening the barrels he had brought from the wagon. Varg helped, working lids loose with his seax and dragging out children. Svik and Sulich were opening other barrels, these ones with actual food inside, and the children were soon being presented with bowls of pickled herring and hard bread. Røkia unstoppered a barrel of mead and horns were filled, bellies beginning to warm.

"I'm not eating that filth, I need something hot," a voice said. Prince Hakon, pushing past the last few children in search of food. His guard, Frek the *Úlfhéðnar*, walked behind him like a silent shadow, Æsa close to them both.

"No fires as we are sleeping on the ship tonight," Glornir said, "so no hot food."

"Poor little prince," Æsa said mockingly, which elicited a scattering of laughter and a scowl from Hakon.

"But why?" Hakon asked Glornir.

"Because I do not trust you, or your mother," Glornir said. "Far easier to slip away in the dark when you're on land than to escape from a *drakkar* anchored in a river."

"Why would I want to escape tonight when you're letting me go tomorrow?" Hakon frowned.

"I'm not letting you go tomorrow," Glornir said.

"You should rethink that decision," Frek the *Úlfhéðnar* said. There was no hint of anger or movement to any weapons from Frek, but Varg felt the hairs of his neck stand, a sudden tension filling the air. He saw Æsa stand straighter, her eyes fixed on Frek.

"I will not let you go tomorrow, because then your mother's warriors would soon fall upon us," Glornir said to Hakon. "Both the force she has sent on land, and the *drakkars* that are shadowing us on the river."

"I've not seen any *drakkars*," Hakon said.

Glornir shrugged. "They are there," he said. "So, I will set you down at Liga." He looked at Frek. "Do not die here for nothing, child of Ulfrir. I will not harm the prince, unless he tries to escape. And he will be free as soon as we reach Liga. You have my word on that."

Frek held Glornir's gaze, as if there were no one else on the *drakkar* but them. Eventually he shrugged. "I am here to protect the prince, and to see that he is set free, so I will find out how good your word is, grey-beard."

"Hold on a moment," Hakon said, "don't I have a say in this?"

"No," growled Glornir.

"But, but, that's not fair," Hakon said.

"Fair?" Glornir snorted. "Fair has nothing to do with it; fair is not the way of this world. Ask him." He looked at Frek, his iron collar glinting gold in the last rays of day.

Hakon looked from Glornir to Frek, then back at Glornir again.

"But . . ." the prince began.

Glornir turned his back on Hakon and walked away.

"An outrage," Hakon muttered to himself, but still helped himself to a bowl of pickled herring and bread.

"Don't worry, pretty boy, I'll keep you company," Æsa said, grinning.

"Svik," Einar called out, "give us a story to pass the time, and distract these children." Four boys and six girls were hanging on Einar's legs, trying to wrestle him. "Stop that; if I fall, we'll tip this little boat over, and I'm in trouble enough," he whispered to them, though his whisper was loud enough for all on the *drakkar* to hear him.

"A tale?" Svik said.

"Yes, a tale," Einar called out, and others added their voices until Svik nodded, holding his hands up. He put the lid back on one of the barrels and sat on it with a horn of mead in his hand.

"All right, then." He looked around the *drakkar*, eyes settling upon Hakon and Frek. "I shall tell you about the boy, the widow, the wolf and the troll; and the way of the world."

Einar clapped his slab-like hands together and laughed, then sat on the deck of the *drakkar*. All the children swarmed to him, treating him like a boulder or tree, clambering over him until they found a comfortable spot.

Varg went and sat on his oar-chest with a bowl full of food and a horn of mead as the rest of the Bloodsworn pulled barrels up or found places to sit, apart from those who Glornir had assigned first watch.

A hush settled across the *drakkar*, even Glornir sitting quietly in the prow and watching.

"There was a widowed woman who went into the woods," Svik began, "as she needed to cut poles for a new fence; let us call her . . ." Svik put a finger to his chin, as if thinking hard. "Helka," he said with a smile. Prince Hakon blinked.

"So, Helka went walking into the woods in search of wood to chop for fence poles, but wherever she went, the trees were too thick or too twisted, so she walked deeper and deeper. Eventually she found a tree to her liking but, as she lifted her axe to start chopping, she heard a sound. A terrible groaning; a whimpering wail that stirred her pity, so she went in search of the wailing's owner. After a time, she came to a great heap of rocks at the bottom of a cliff, where the groaning and wailing was louder, and bending down on her hands and knees, she saw that a huge, thick-skinned troll was trapped beneath a flat stone. Let us call him . . . Einar."

A burst of laughter among the Bloodsworn at that, Einar smiling.

"Don't worry, I'm not really a troll," Einar said to the children surrounding him.

"Einar the troll was in a pitiful state," Svik continued. "Trapped and exhausted, weak and thin from hunger, he did not look like he had much time left in this world.

"'Help me'," pleaded Einar the troll to Helka.

"'Hmm'," said the woman, and she got to her feet and walked away. Einar wailed as he saw the woman's feet disappearing, but, after a while, he saw them returning. Helka had gone to a tree and cut a stout branch with her axe, trimmed it and now she was wedging it beneath the stone. With a jump and a heave, she levered the stone high enough for Einar the troll to crawl out from beneath it.

"He stood slowly, and Helka saw that he was tall and broad and all of his skin was sagging like a melted candle, as much of his muscle had wasted away from being stuck under a stone.

"A great rumbling sound filled the air, and Helka looked around, fearing another rockfall that might trap them both, but it was just Einar's belly rumbling because it was empty."

"It does that all the time," one of the children sitting on Einar said.

Einar nodded happily. "It does," he agreed.

"'I am so hungry,'" Einar the troll said, and he reached out his hands to grab Helka.

"'What are you doing?'" Helka cried out.

"'I'm hungry, so I am going to eat you,'" Einar the troll said.

"'Well, of all the ungrateful acts, this is the worst I have ever heard of. How is this fair treatment? This is shameful thanklessness,'" said Helka."

There were mutters and nods of agreement among the Bloodsworn.

"She has a point," Sulich said.

"'I am sorry,'" Einar the troll said, 'but life is far from fair and I'm afraid that is the way of the world,' and he reached out his long arms to grab her.

"Seeing that the troll meant what he said, Helka fell to her knees and pleaded for her life."

"Doesn't sound at all like my mother," Hakon said, to which he received a great round of laughter, much to his pleasure. He smiled.

"Helka fell to her knees and pleaded for her life," Svik repeated, frowning at Hakon for interrupting him. "'Let us decide this by an Althing,' Helka begged, 'because we have a difference of opinion here. I believe I deserve to go on my way without being eaten, while you think that you can devour me because it is the way of the world.'

"Einar the troll paused at Helka's words and frowned." Svik leaned conspiratorially forward and said in a hushed voice, "Einar was a troll and not the owner of much clever." He tapped his temple, then sat straighter and spoke louder.

"'All right,' Einar the troll said. 'If you can find someone or something here to judge our case.'

"It just so happened that at that exact moment a hound came bounding along. He was old, with filmed eyes and white fur in his muzzle. Helka and the troll hailed him, and when he stopped, they explained their predicament to him, and asked if he would judge their case.

"'I have served my master faithfully since I was a pup,' said the hound. 'I have hunted for him, guarded him, fought thieves and robbers to protect him. Shown him the way home when he was lost in a storm. But now I am old and half-blind and useless, and so he wants to cut my throat and feed me to his pigs rather than feed *me* any more.' He looked morosely at Helka. 'I am sorry, but the troll is right. Life is not fair. He should eat you; it is the way of the world.'

"The hound went on his way.

"'See,' said Einar the troll. 'It is nothing personal, it is just the way of the world', and he reached out his long arms to grab her.

"'This is too important a matter for just one old, half-blind hound to decide,' Helka pleaded. 'Let us ask another to be the judge. Pleeeeeeeaaassse.'"

The children sitting on Einar giggled at Svik's wail.

"Einar the troll shrugged. 'All right!' he said. He was certain that whoever they asked, the answer would be the same, because, of course, it *was* the way of the world. They looked around for another judge.

"At that exact moment a lame horse came limping through the woods. Helka and the troll hailed him and explained their predicament to her, and she agreed to be their judge.

"'I am sorry,'" she said to Helka after she had heard both of their cases. 'Since I was a foal, I have served my mistress. I have allowed her to put a saddle on my back and carried her wherever she asked me to go. I have pulled carts for her and ploughed the land for her. But now that I am old and lame, she says that I am not worth the oats and hay to keep me, and so she plans to cut my throat and put me in a stew.' The horse shrugged and neighed. 'Life is not fair and the troll should eat you; it is just the way of the world.' And with that the horse trotted off.

"'You see?'" said Einar the troll, 'it is perfectly reasonable for me to eat you in these circumstances. I am sorry, but it must be done; I am so hungry I can hardly think.'

"Helka fell on to her knees and held her hands up to the troll. 'One last judge. Three times for all,' she begged.

"The troll sighed and nodded. 'Very well,' he said, 'if that will help you come to terms with me eating you; one more judge. But this is the last time.'

"They looked around for another judge, and at that exact moment a black-furred wolf came loping through the woods. Let us call him . . ." Svik stopped and looked around the deck, his eyes settling upon Hakon's *Úlfhéðnar*. "Frek."

Chuckles among the Bloodsworn, Varg smiling along with them all, though Frek did not so much as blink. Hakon smiled. "You're in the story," he said, nudging Frek with his elbow.

"Helka and the troll hailed the wolf called Frek," Svik continued, "and he came to them and listened as they told him both sides of their story. As they finished Einar the troll swayed and sat down, his belly rumbling loud as thunder. He put his head in his hands. 'See how hungry I am,' he said and sniffed, tears rolling down his cheeks."

"Poor Einar," one of the children said, and dabbed Einar Half-Troll's cheek.

"It's not me," Einar whispered.

"As Einar the troll wept, Frek the wolf called Helka aside.

"'What will you give me if I help you with this troll?' Frek the wolf whispered.

"'I have a flock of sheep on good pasture,' Helka whispered back to him. 'If you help me here, I shall give you a whole night of freedom with them, from sunset to sunrise.'

"The wolf grinned a toothy smile.

"'Einar the troll,' Frek the wolf said, 'I have heard both your cases, but before I can concentrate on this matter, there is something I don't understand that I hope you can help me with.'

"'What is that?' asked Einar the troll, sniffing and wiping his eyes.

"'Well, you are a big troll, and that is a small hole. I do not see how you could have been trapped in such a small space.' The wolf narrowed his eyes. 'Is this all some kind of jest?'

"'No, it is most serious,' Einar said. 'And the absolute truth. I was trapped in that hole for days.'

"'I'm sorry,' the wolf said, shaking his head. 'But I just can't believe it. It seems impossible and I feel that I am being taken for a fool. I think I am going to leave now, and who knows how long it will be before another judge comes along.'

"'No, no,' said Einar, 'please don't leave. Look,' and Einar stood wearily and staggered to the hole. He dropped to his knees, then rolled into the space he had been trapped. 'See, I do fit in here.'

"As soon as he did so Helka and Frek leaped on to the cut branch holding the stone and ripped it free. The stone slammed down and pinned Einar the troll, just as it had before Helka arrived. Einar let out a terrible wail.

"'I am sorry,' said Frek the wolf, 'but life is far from fair; it is the way of the world.'"

The Bloodsworn fell about laughing, slapping their legs, apart from the children, who had all got it into their heads that the Einar they were sitting on was actually the troll in the story. Some of them sniffed, holding back tears, their lips quivering.

"I don't like this tale, it doesn't seem very fair," Hakon said.

"It's the way of the world," someone called out, setting the laughter off again.

"Ah," Svik said, holding a finger up and waiting for the laughter to die down. "But that is not the end of the story."

"Ah-ha," said Hakon, smiling. "I knew there must be more to it."

"Yes," said Svik. "Soon after, once Helka had returned to her homestead and the wolf had loped back into the forest, the wolf felt hungry and so he thought it was time to take Helka up on her offer. He sniffed out her trail and found her homestead, and he saw the flock of sheep grazing on the hill. His belly rumbled. He waited until the sun had gone down, and then he ran up to the hill and made a feast of the sheep and lambs. He ate so much that night, more than he had ever eaten in his life, that he fell into a gorged, deep, deep sleep. He did not awake with the coming of the dawn. In fact, he only awoke when he felt the first shepherd's stick whack him on the nose. He awoke with a howl, but he was surrounded by Helka's workers, all with sticks or farm tools in their hands, and they gave him a good beating. It was not long before he found himself lying on the ground, pain everywhere, as the farmhands sent for Helka. She came soon, and she had a son with her, a lad of say fourteen or fifteen winters. Let us call him . . . Hakon.''

Hoots and laughter from the Bloodsworn sat all around Svik. Varg's jaw was aching from laughing so much. Hakon's face twitched, not knowing whether to smile or frown.

'''Well, if it isn't Frek the wolf,' said Helka. 'You have broken our bargain and stayed too long. Sunset to sunrise, I said.'

'''Please, have mercy,' Frek said. 'Fair's fair, I saved you from the troll.'

"Helka looked at him and shook her head. 'Life is far from fair,' she said. 'It is the way of the world, I'm afraid. I am going to get my axe, to finish you quick.' She ordered her farmhands to dig a pit at the bottom of the hill to bury Frek's body, and set her son, Hakon, to guard over Frek until she returned with her axe.

"Frek lay there moaning, in pain and misery, too injured even to crawl away. Then he felt strong hands lift him up. He opened his eyes and saw that Hakon was carrying him up and over the hill, out of sight from the farmhands, and down into woodland. Hakon walked for a long while, carrying Frek deep into the woods and eventually set the wolf down on soft grass, close to a stream.

'''Thank you,' Frek managed to say through his pain. 'I thought I was done for then. After all, it is the way of the world.'

'''You silly old wolf,' said Hakon. 'There is no such thing as the way of the world. There is only this,' and he tapped a finger to his head. Then Hakon got up and walked away."

Svik sat there, a silence heavy all around him, and then people began to smile and nod. Some hooms and heyas of agreement as understanding rippled through them all.

"Well told, well told," Sulich said.

"I don't understand?" Hakon frowned.

Varg saw that Frek was sitting in shadow, looking down at his hands, which were bunched into fists, knotted and twisted like rope.

CHAPTER THIRTY-THREE

GUÐVARR

Guðvarr walked morosely through the streets of Darl and looked up to see the Galdur tower looming in front of him. It was the last place he wanted to see, and yet here he was, walking willingly towards it.

Well, not entirely willingly, he thought, glancing to see the *drengr* Yrsa one side of him, and the dark-haired Galdur-apprentice Sturla on the other.

Bitches.

It brought him a small amount of comfort and pleasure to see that Sturla was walking with a limp and that one hand was covered in blisters, and that Yrsa had a scabbed, puckered gash across her forehead.

They had found him in the hayloft of *The Dead Drengr* with the red-haired whore, Vilja. It was less than two days since the Bloodsworn had sailed away from Darl and Guðvarr was still wracked with pain; in his arm, from the hyrndur's tearing mandibles, in his wrists and ankles, from his thrashing while bound to Skalk's table, and in his thought-cage, from the recurring nightmares of buzzing wings and blood and broken bodies stuffed in barrels. After the horror he had been through he felt he deserved some cheering up, and Vilja had been doing a good job of that. Yrsa and Sturla hammering on the hayloft trapdoor had put an end to that, though; and then they had stood there like two night-hags, watching him and hurrying him along as he dressed, telling him only that Lord Skalk had asked for him. He glanced at his arm, covered now with a new tunic of green wool, the gold ring Helka had given him glinting in the sunlight, but beneath the gold and wool he could feel the scabs pulling where the hyrndur had burrowed into his flesh.

The tower loomed above them, the timber wall around it charred and blackened in places by fire. The gates stood open as Sturla and Yrsa led Guðvarr through them, a swarm of men and women sawing and hammering at repairs around the courtyard. Guðvarr saw dark stains upon the hard-packed earth and, in one corner, he glimpsed a pile of bodies stacked high, horses among them. He tried not to look at it, feeling his stomach spasm, and rested one hand on the sword hanging from his belt, as if it might somehow calm his churning stomach. It didn't, but it did remind him that he was a *drengr* walking among a courtyard of freedmen and women.

I am better than them, he told himself.

On into the tower, guards opening the doors and dipping their heads to Sturla. She led Guðvarr across the entrance hall, Yrsa falling in behind him. He noticed that the door leading through the cells to Skalk's chamber was smashed, a new door now being fitted by a team of carpenters. The corridor beyond was silent, the cell door open where Skapti, Hrolf and the others had been kept.

Perhaps they have been murdered, their bodies broken and stuffed into barrels, like Arild. Much as he had tried not to think on it, a vision of her dead-eyed stare had insisted on filling his thought-cage at the most unwelcome moments, both sleeping and waking.

Sturla led him up a winding stairwell, passing archways to corridors as they climbed higher, eventually stepping into an empty corridor, stopping to knock on a door.

"Enter," an all too familiar voice called from the other side of the door.

I hate that man.

Skalk stood hunched over a table in a circular chamber, racks of tools and rolled parchments all about him. Guðvarr noticed a number of barrels piled together and felt a trickle of fear down his spine.

No, he doesn't want me dead, yet. He has use of me, first.

Sturla walked around Skalk to another table and poured ale from a jug, handing the cup to Skalk.

"You have finished it, Lord Skalk," Sturla said, wonder in her voice. She was looking at something on the table and, as Guðvarr walked deeper into the room, he saw a staff of grey ash-wood laid out upon it. Yrsa closed the door with a disheartening thud behind him.

"I have," Skalk said, running his fingertips across the staff. Ripples of light flickered across the grain in the wood at the Galdurman's touch. Skalk saw the staff's head was thicker, and he could make out faint features. A curl of hair. The hint of eyes, a nose and mouth, and abruptly Guðvarr realised what it was.

The Froa-spirit that Sturla and the other Galdur-apprentices slew. Or what is left of it.

Skalk turned to look at him and Guðvarr forced himself to meet the Galdurman's gaze. Skalk's face was a lattice of bandaged wounds, long red strips where the hawk had raked him with its talons, and where one eye had been there was now a red hole.

"Ah, my spy," Skalk said, and smiled at him, more a grimace as missing flesh bunched and writhed.

I wish you had never crawled out of that hole the Seiðr-witch from Iskidan threw you into.

"My Lord Skalk," Guðvarr said, looking away after a few moments, down at the floor.

"We all have our scars," Skalk said, "do we not?"

You would know that better than most, as you commanded a hyrndur to eat its way into my body.

"Not all of us have a hyrndur sleeping in our chest, though," Skalk said.

"I would rather not think on that," Guðvarr muttered, a swell of hatred burning through his veins.

But at least I still have two eyes. He could not keep the hatred from his glare as he looked at Skalk, gritting his teeth and clamping his mouth shut to make sure that the words in his thought-cage did not leak out of his lips.

"Ah, do I see a spark of defiance?" Skalk said with another twist of his lips. Whether it was a smile or a snarl, Guðvarr was not sure. "Do not think that because a Seiðr-witch and a Tainted thrall bested me that *you* can. And now that I have a new staff, if they returned things would end differently."

We can all say brave words when the danger is passed. I should know, that is my speciality. A memory of Skalk squawking as the ground cracked and opened beneath his feet filled Guðvarr's head, the Galdurman swaying and toppling with a shriek into darkness. A smirk escaped on to his face.

Skalk snatched the staff from the table and pointed it at Guðvarr.

"*Hyrndur, heyr húsbónda þinn, hreyfðu þig í holdi hans,*" Skalk rasped.

The Froa-spirit's eyes in Skalk's staff flared green, the mouth seeming to shift, and there was a sharp, stabbing pain in Guðvarr's chest as something moved deep within him, snatching his breath away and making his gorge rise. He gasped and stumbled, his legs going weak and he half fell, Yrsa behind him grabbing him beneath an arm and hauling him upright.

"*Hyrndur, farðu aftur að sofa,*" Skalk said and the movement within Guðvarr was abruptly gone, the pain a fading ripple through him.

"Just a reminder," Skalk said, "that you are mine. That was just a whisper of what will happen to you if you displease me." He stepped close to Guðvarr, glowering with his one eye. "Do you understand me?"

"Y-yes, Lord Skalk," Guðvarr said with a reluctant whimper. Behind him Yrsa snorted her disgust.

I would like to see how you behave with a monster living in your chest, Guðvarr thought bitterly.

"You did well, in Helka's hall," Skalk said, as if talking to an old friend as he rested the butt of his new staff on the ground. "To take the cloak to Hakon. He will remember that; will be grateful to you. Make sure you use that, when he returns."

"Yes, Lord Skalk," Guðvarr wheezed, the memory of pain in his chest lingering and leaving him feeling shaky.

"And Yrsa tells me you are a frequent visitor to *The Dead Drengr.*"

"I . . . am," Guðvarr muttered.

"Your friend Orka told me that Hakon met with Drekr there. I have asked questions about *The Dead Drengr* since I have been back in Darl, and it seems that Hakon visited the inn on many occasions, in the dead of night, or early, before the inn opened its doors to customers. As you spend so much time in the place, you may find an opportunity to become better acquainted with Hakon."

"I will do as you say, Lord Skalk."

"Good. Now get out."

The door creaked as Yrsa opened it and Guðvarr turned and walked out of the room as fast as his unsteady legs would carry him.

Guðvarr walked through the fortress of Darl, feet thudding on the wooden walkway. After leaving the Galdur tower he had fully intended to go straight back to the embrace of Vilja in the hayloft of *The Dead Drengr* and resolutely attempt to forget all about what had just happened to him.

But there is no forgetting this, he thought, jabbing at his chest and muttering under his breath. And so his feet had carried him through the streets of Darl to the gates of the fortress at its summit. He had shown the gold arm ring Queen Helka had given him and been allowed to pass through, and now he was marching across the wooden walkway, muttering to himself. *Drengrs* sitting on the steps of a longhouse looked at him and nudged one another.

I am not moon-touched, he snapped at them in his head, *just cursed by your Galdurman.*

He thought about Vilja's warm embrace again, and the oblivion to be found in flesh. *No, I have to try and do something, before it is too late. I have no illusion that Skalk will keep me alive for a single moment after I have performed his task for him. I'll end up with my body broken and stuffed inside one of Skalk's barrels.*

He looked up and marched on, stopping before a turf-roofed longhouse close to the fortress walls. A *drengr* stood on guard, a young man with a spear clutched in his fist, a patchy beard and ears too big for his nálbinding cap.

"Járn," Guðvarr nodded to the *drengr* as he climbed the steps. "Is my aunt here?"

"Aye, and Jarl Sigrún has been asking for you. She's not best pleased."

Guðvarr glowered and stepped around the *drengr* into the longhouse. He paused a moment, letting his eyes adjust to the gloom.

A long, single room, a hearth fire crackling at its centre. Thralls were sweeping, one stirring a barrel of ale and at the far end, Guðvarr saw his aunt sitting in a chair, clothed in a fine tunic hemmed and embroidered with tablet weave, a seax hanging from her belt lying across her lap. Her dark hair looked slick in the torchlight and the scar that Orka had given her was a black-shadowed valley across her face. A handful of servants and *drengrs* were around her, listening attentively to the jarl. Sigrún stopped talking as she saw Guðvarr approaching and held up a hand to silence any questions.

"Where have *you* been?" Sigrún said to him, her voice cold and hard. She shifted in her chair, torchlight catching her scar and turning it silver.

"At the Galdur tower," he said.

Sigrún frowned, a bunching of shadow across her brow. "And before? You know I have been asking for you since before Jaromir fled. You have been avoiding me."

Guðvarr looked down at the ground and scrapped a toe in the fresh rushes that had been laid down before the evening meal. The truth was that his aunt was right. At first, he had avoided her because he did not want to talk about how he had run from Orka at the Grimholt, but since his ordeal in the Galdur tower he had just wanted to avoid *everything*.

"I need to talk to you," Guðvarr said, looking up at Jarl Sigrún.

"That is what you are doing," Jarl Sigrún scowled.

"Alone."

His aunt pursed her lips, staring at him a few moments.

"Out," she said with a wave of her hand and those around her walked away.

"What is it? What has happened?" she said to him.

Guðvarr waited until he was sure that there were no flapping ears close enough to hear him.

"I've got myself into some trouble," he said with a tremor in his bottom lip.

CHAPTER THIRTY-FOUR

ELVAR

Elvar led the Battle-Grim through dense woods. She had noticed the ground becoming softer, the trees of ash and elm shifting to alder and willow and ahead of her there were flashes and glimmers of sparkling water between the trees, Lake Horndal finally within sight.

She felt different, since the *holmganga* with Huld, as if a weight had settled upon her shoulders along with Agnar's bearskin cloak. Her thoughts often returned to her fight with Huld. She should not have enjoyed killing her, a woman she had fought alongside, stood with shoulder to shoulder in the shield wall, but the truth of it was that she *had* enjoyed it. She had enjoyed *winning*, enjoyed the roar of the Battle-Grim, enjoyed the thrill of *being alive* when it was done, and her fractured memory of the duel was of her blood pounding in her veins, a rush of pure joy as she had sensed Huld believing her deception with her wounded shoulder, growing like a wave building towards its rolling crash as she had lured Huld into her trap, tricked her and then put her on the ground. But despite all that, every day since then as she had led the Battle-Grim south, she had felt a growing sense of unease.

"What is wrong?" Grend said beside her.

She gave him a frown.

"What do you mean?"

"You are different," he said with a shrug.

She decided to tell him the truth.

"I find that I am no longer thinking of how to win my reputation and battle-fame," she said. "My thought-cage is too crammed with the problems and doubts of each day."

"Doubts? Problems?" Grend asked her, his hand going to his axe as if any problem was an enemy that could be killed.

"Am I leading us in the right direction? Will our food and water last us the day? Where can we re-stock? Who shall I send out as scouts each day? Who will take the vanguard and rearguard today? Am I making the right choice, or am I going to get us all killed? What have I forgotten?" She scowled and tapped her temple. "There are a lot more thoughts like that swirling around in here."

Grend's face twitched, and then he was roaring with laughter, a sight both annoying and unsettling, as Elvar had hardly heard him laugh during the whole of her life, and certainly never like this. He slowed and bent over, had to rest a hand on his knee.

"What's the joke?" Sighvat asked as he lumbered up.

Grend stood straighter and wiped tears of laughter from his eyes.

"Elvar is growing up," he said.

Elvar scowled at him and walked on.

A figure appeared out of the trees ahead, Orv the Sneak looking at her.

"What is it?" Elvar snapped at him.

"The *Wave-Jarl*," Orv said, a grin splitting his face.

Elvar checked over her weapons in the firelight, all of them laid out on her cloak before her. Spear, sword, seax. She was scouring a spot of rust from her sword with sand and a linen cloth, keeping half an eye on the Battle-Grim around her.

The *Wave-Jarl* was a joy to behold and she glanced at it now, its long, sleek strakes gleaming in the moonlight as it sat in the river like some sleeping serpent, moored to a willow tree.

It is my ship now. She felt a thrill shiver through her at that thought, excitement and unease blended. The *Wave-Jarl* was testament to what she had accomplished, but also a reminder of what was ahead of her, and of her responsibilities to her crew.

I am their gold-giver now, the one they look to, the one who decides the way forward, who takes on the task of putting meat in their bellies, mead in their drinking horns and silver about their arms. And in return they will follow me, fight for me, die for me, if needs be.

She blew out a long breath.

This is the weight of responsibility my father must feel every single day. But that does not excuse him for being a treacherous, wife-beating niðing.

Memories of her mother's screams rose up in her head, her brother Thorun's arm around Elvar, holding her back as she had tried to run to her mother's aid. Of his laughter in her ear. The thuds of Grend kicking the door in, bursting in and lunging at her father; and of Elvar's mother shouting, ordering Grend to stand down. It had been one of her father's many tests, seeing if he could push Grend into drawing a blade against his jarl, an offence that would have been punishable by death. Grend had listened to Elvar's mother, stood stiff as stone and then made to leave, but Jarl Störr had ordered him to stay and watch while he beat Elvar's mother some more.

Elvar grimaced at the memory, felt her fists clenching and with an act of will she pushed it back into the shadowed corners of her thought-cage. She looked around, saw the Battle-Grim sitting, eating, drinking, those who had stayed to guard the *Wave-Jarl* asking question after question about the adventures at Oskutreð.

Ketil the Silent, named on account of him having flapping lips and rarely ever being silent, was sitting before Skuld and Ulfrir, gazing at them with a mixture of awe and disbelief on his wide, flat face. Elvar suppressed a laugh at the sight of it.

I have become accustomed to living in a saga, she thought. *Accustomed to travelling in the company of gods.*

Sitting here, in this glade reminded her of when she had last been here, listening to Agnar telling the Battle-Grim why they had sailed across Lake Horndal, telling them that they had come in search of fabled Oskutreð and showing them the scars of his blood oath. She had felt elated, as if she stood on the precipice of battle-fame and fortune.

That was the night Biórr first kissed me.

More memories surged up inside her, of Biórr, of the tender moments they had shared.

"He is a liar and a betrayer, and if I ever have the good fortune to meet him again, I shall cut his black *niðing* heart from his chest," she spat under her breath as she scrubbed furiously at her sword. Footsteps on dry leaves and she looked up to see Uspa walking towards her. The Seiðr-witch sat down beside Elvar, offering her a plate of bread and cheese, an onion and a few cuts of salted pork.

"My thanks," Elvar said, wiping her sword clean and sheathing it in her scabbard.

"You are welcome," Uspa said. "A leader needs to eat, to keep their strength up."

"Been talking to Grend?" Elvar snapped. She had assigned Grend first watch, mostly because his face insisted on twisting into a smile every time she looked at him, and she did not want to see that.

"A little," Uspa said with a half-smile. "Much has changed for you, and you have achieved much," she said, her face serious, now. "Leading is no easy task, and, for what it is worth, I think you are doing well."

"My . . . thanks," said Elvar, taking the plate of food and drawing a short, sharp eating knife from its sheath on her belt. She skewered a slice of pork and chewed.

"I have been thinking," Elvar mumbled through her food, "of the fight at Oskutreð, against Ilska. She spoke to you as if she knew you."

"Yes," Uspa nodded. She was silent a while, just looking down at her hands. "You are right, I know Ilska. She invited me to join her. Me and my husband, Berak, because we are Tainted. For a while we travelled with her and the Raven-Feeders, but the longer we stayed, the clearer it was that Ilska was on a dark path." She sighed. "The wrong path. She talks of righting the wrong, of ending the enslaving of the Tainted, but at her heart she wants vengeance and death, not justice. She would replace one twisted way of life with another. So Berak and I stole the *Graskinna* from her, and set about destroying it, thinking it would end her plans and madness."

"That is what you were doing when we found you on Iskalt Island?" Elvar remembered seeing Uspa throw a book into the pool of fire.

"Yes," Uspa said. "Thinking that I was saving the world from Ilska's madness, thinking that I was saving people like you from a life of slavery, torture and death." She looked Elvar in the eye. "And then you captured us, beat my husband to his knees, put a collar around his neck and sold him to the highest bidder. And treated me and my son as thralls, as cattle to be bartered. Or slaughtered."

Elvar looked away, unable to meet Uspa's gaze.

"I . . ." she mumbled, feeling the need to apologise, but unable to speak the words. "It is the way of the world," she muttered instead.

"Nonsense," Uspa growled. "That is a fool's answer. *We* decide what is the way of the world. Us. People. It is not imposed upon us by some greater force. Once the gods ruled and humans were as slaves to them. Now humans command and the offspring of the gods are slaves."

"See, that is what I mean," Elvar said.

"No," Uspa said. "We decide what is right, up here," she tapped her temple with a curved finger, "and here," she prodded her heart. "And then we do it. I decided to live a life of peace and solitude with my husband and son, and only came out of that solitude to try and help your kind."

"And look how that ended up," Elvar breathed.

"But it doesn't have to be this way," Uspa said. "If more made that choice, in their head and hearts, to live a peaceful life with those they love and value, and just allow others to do the same."

"But there is no one else out there who feels as you do," Elvar said. "If there are, I have never met them."

"There are," Uspa said. "There are many who know that life is not about power and greed, about battle-fame." She looked at Elvar with a raised brow. "And there are those who agree with me, but just haven't realised it yet." She gave Elvar another hard look.

Elvar spat out a half-hearted laugh. "I am struggling with the responsibility of leading forty warriors, and now you want me to lead the whole world; to end thralldom and convince the jarls and rulers to lay down their swords!" She stood up, buckling on her weapons belt, and shrugging her sword and baldric over one shoulder. "My thanks for the food," she said and walked away, striding towards Ketil the Silent, who had a circle of the Battle-Grim around him as he talked to Sighvat.

"So, you walk out of the northern wilderness with bad news and good news," Ketil was saying with a grin. "The bad news is that you have let a dragon loose upon the world, and the good news is that you have amassed more wealth than could ever be spent in a hundred lifetimes."

"That's right, but there is more to it than that," Sighvat said.

"Ah yes, I am forgetting," Ketil said. "There was more bad news and more good news. The bad being that we have to fight and kill the dragon, and the good news that *he* is the one who will be helping us with that dragon killing." He pointed a finger at Ulfrir, who sat huddled in his wolfskin cloak, his head in darkness. "Even though he doesn't look fit to fight his way out of his own cloak."

Elvar heard a deep-throated growl rumble out of the shadows of Ulfrir's hood.

"Aye, that's about the whole of it," Sighvat said with a smile.

"I will also help with the dragon-killing," Skuld said, the firelight reflecting like molten flames in her hair.

"Ah, that is so much better," Ketil said. "Now I feel reassured."

Ketil looked up at Elvar as she joined them.

"Oh, and the other news is that we have a new chief, the youngest among us, not grown much passed being bounced on her father's knee."

"I've fought one *holmganga* to prove my worth, Ketil the Silent," Elvar said to him, calm as if she were talking about the weather, "it makes no difference to me if I fight another." She stood over him, one hand resting casually on her sword hilt.

"Oh ho, there will be no chance of that," Ketil said, holding his palms up. "I am too old and stiff to be challenging for Agnar's bearskin, and I am happy enough as I am, without the task of working out how to kill a dragon, or to lead this band of rogues and cut-throats."

"Thpeak for yourthelf," Sólín lisped, spraying spittle between her missing teeth as she sharpened her sword, a single-edged longseax.

"Ha, that's enough cheek from you, Sólín Spittle, you couldn't even come back from the north with all your teeth, let alone the clever to kill a dragon."

Laughter rippled around the Battle-Grim at that.

"Sólín Spittle," Sighvat chuckled, slapping his knee.

Elvar sat down between Sólín and Sighvat.

"I have faith in Ulfrir," Elvar said, feeling that it needed to be said in front of the Battle-Grim, even if she did not fully believe it herself.

"You're the chief, and that's good enough for me," Ketil said, "though, to be fair, I haven't seen this dragon. Perhaps she is smaller than she looks in my imagination and will not be so hard to kill."

"She is huge," Urt the Unwashed said. "Big enough to blot out the sun."

"You're not helping me here, Urt," Ketil said good-naturedly.

"She is insane, and needs to be put down," Ulfrir growled.

Ketil shifted to look harder at Ulfrir.

"So, you are Ulfrir wolf-god, who slew a hundred dragon-born and hung them in the Gallows Wood," he said to Ulfrir, who went back to his silence, face masked in shadow.

"More like five hundred of Lik-Rifa's children," Skuld said with a snort of derision.

"And you are the Ulfrir who fought a dozen Sjávarorm serpents during a swimming competition against your brother, Berser?"

"Ha, it was fifty serpents, and the competition was not against Berser, he is a bad swimmer," Skuld said. "It was against Krodil, one of the gods from the south, who often bragged that he was the greatest swimmer in the world." She looked at Ulfrir and smiled. "He was not."

"And you are the Ulfrir who lured Lik-Rifa into the chambers of Oskutreð and locked her there?" Ketil said.

"That was mother," Skuld said.

"Mother?" Ketil asked.

"Orna, the eagle," Skuld said proudly, her wings twitching. "She knew how to lure Lik-Rifa into the depths of Oskutreð."

"How?" Ketil asked.

"The soul road," Skuld breathed. "Mother found it, and she knew that Lik-Rifa would not be able to resist looking upon the road of the dead. She was ever obsessed with life and death, and the barriers that separated the living from the dead."

"But why did you need to do it, why was there war between Lik-Rifa and Orna?"

"Lik-Rifa is insane, jealous, paranoid. She needs no reason to go to war. And she was building an army of creatures, her vaesen. She thought they were hidden, that they were secret, but we knew. Rotta told us. She was preparing to overwhelm and kill us all in one swift move on the tafl board of the gods."

Ketil nodded slowly, and Elvar saw that all the Battle-Grim were leaning in and silent, listening to a god talk of times that belonged in sagas.

"So, Ulfrir, you are the one who wrestled a clan of a hundred giants and won their allegiance."

"Ach, enough of this," Ulfrir growled, breaking his silence. "It was only one giant, and I bit his hand off." He shifted, firelight reflecting from his sharp-angled face, glinting from his teeth and eyes. "It appears that you know nothing of the *Guðfalla*, or the time before it. Next you will be telling me that you have not heard of Snaka's sister, Skuggar."

Gasps around the glade, all the Battle-Grim stunned, Elvar's voice joining them in a sharp hiss of breath.

What?

Snaka's sister!

"No, we have not," Uspa said. "Dread Snaka had a sister?"

"Aye, Skuggar, but perhaps it is not so much of a surprise that you have not heard of her. Skuggar was always one for the shadows, where Snaka would love the world to watch him. Snaka was the maker, Skuggar the unmaker."

Elvar opened her mouth to ask a question, but then she heard the thud of feet and Grend was bursting into the glade.

"Something comes," he said, and then the trees were swaying behind him, a shadow tall as the trees lurching out of the gloom.

A vibration in the ground and a figure emerged from the woodland, tall and slender, a dark-skinned woman, hair swirling about her like vines, long arms knotted and thick as twisted rope. Her head swayed back and forth, green eyes blazing.

"Where are you, wolf-god?" she rasped in a voice that creaked and rustled, reminding Elvar of wind soughing through leaves and branches.

"FROA-SPIRIT," one of the Battle-Grim cried and then the glade exploded into movement, warriors leaping to their feet, drawing weapons.

Ketil swept up his spear by his side, set his feet and threw it, the blade arcing high, glinting in the moonlight and then slamming into the Froa-spirit's chest. Others rushed at her, hacking into her root-like legs with axes.

"YOU DARE?" she roared, lashing out with one arm and sending a handful of the Battle-Grim flying through the air.

Ketil grabbed a burning branch from the fire and ran at the Froa-spirit.

A howl shook the glade and all paused for a heartbeat, looking to see Ulfrir standing, his body shifting, expanding, bones cracking and popping as he grew, muzzle lengthening, muscles thickening, until he towered above them all, even the Froa-spirit. He snarled at the Battle-Grim and then his head was lunging down, jaws wide, and he grabbed Ketil around the waist and heaved him into the air. A savage shake of his head, Elvar hearing flesh tearing, bones snapping and then half of Ketil's severed body thumped on to the ground, Ulfrir lifting his head and swallowing the rest of the dead warrior in a gulp.

All stared up at the giant wolf.

He looked down at them, amber eyes blazing, lips drawn back in a snarl to reveal spear-long teeth.

"You shall not harm the Froa-spirit," he growled at them.

The Froa strode to Ulfrir on her trunk-like legs, toes spreading like vines through the soil, and she stopped before him, with a creak and crack of wood she dropped to one knee.

"You have come back to us, then, great Ulfrir, friend of the woods and trees," she said in her inhuman voice.

Ulfrir regarded her a moment, then leaned down to sniff and nuzzle her thick-barked skin.

"I have," he growled, "though things are . . . changed." He twisted his head, the collar about his neck glinting in the firelight.

"The seasons may change," the Froa said, "the seas dry up and the mountains crumble, but the loyalty of the Froa will never waver."

"That is good to know, my friend," the wolf rumbled.

The Froa-spirit rose to her feet, looked around the glade and gave the Battle-Grim a contemptuous glance, and then she was striding off into the trees, disappearing into the gloom in a few heartbeats.

"The Froa are my friends," Ulfrir said, looking down at the Battle-Grim.

"And the Battle-Grim are my crew," Elvar snarled, striding forward to stand before Ulfrir, looking up like at him. "You do not just start *eating* them."

"I am a god," Ulfrir snarled back, malice leaking from him in waves.

"*Eldsverkur,*" Elvar shouted and the collar about Ulfrir's throat glowed red, veins of white heat rippling through it. The wolf threw his head back and howled, twisted and snapped, branches snapping, trees ripping up from their roots.

Skuld spread her wings and flew up to Ulfrir, shouted over the howl of his pain.

"Submit, Father, you must submit to her," Skuld cried out.

The wolf's body spasmed and writhed, a mist leaking and twisting around it as his bones crackled and shortened, his fur fading, muzzle shrinking, until he was kneeling upon the grass and forest litter before Elvar. He looked up at her and snarled.

"You must obey me, wolf-god," Elvar said to him. "And that includes no spontaneous eating of my crew."

Ulfrir merely glared at her, lips curling in defiance.

"Skuld, kneel before me," Elvar said, and the winged woman flew down and alighted before Elvar, dropped to her knees.

"You and your daughter are mine," Elvar said. "Obey me and all will be well. Disobey and there shall be consequences." She looked at Skuld.

"Skuld, gouge one of your eyes out."

Skuld looked up at her, a tremor in her face. Her collar glowed red and she lifted a hand to her face, a long-taloned finger moving towards her eye.

"No," Ulfrir said, reaching to grab Skuld's arm.

"*Sársauki*," Elvar said and Ulfrir fell back, howling in agony.

"It stops when I say it stops, not you," Elvar said over Ulfrir's pain. "You must learn this."

Skuld's talon moved ever closer to her eye.

"Please," Ulfrir hissed.

"Skuld, stop," Elvar said, and Skuld's hand fell away from her face.

"*Sársauki endar*," Elvar said to Ulfrir, and his collar dulled to black iron. He stood there, gasping, chest heaving, looking from Skuld to Elvar.

"This is the way of this new world, Father," Skuld said, "at least for now." She stepped to him. "But at least you live. And we have Lik-Rifa to kill, Mother to avenge."

Slowly he nodded and stood straighter. Looked at Elvar.

"I will eat no more of your Battle-Grim," he said. He reached into his mouth and dug out a glob of red flesh and torn skin, flicked it to the ground.

"Well, looks like he's feeling better," Sighvat said into the silence.

CHAPTER THIRTY-FIVE

BIÓRR

Biórr turned his back on the vaesen pit as Lik-Rifa and Ilska led their band south. To the east reared sharp crags that marked the eastern edge of Vigrið, beyond them the Icebound Sea, and they were going to follow those crags south for the last leg of their journey, until they joined the eastern tip of the Boneback Mountains.

"One last sprint to finish the race," Fain said to Biórr and Storolf as they set their eyes south, in the distance the land shifting from green to grey to white.

To snow.

"A sprint will be best," Biórr said, "to keep the blood warm."

"Aye, and to stop our stones from freezing, snapping off and rolling down our breeches," Storolf said.

"You seem uncommonly worried about such a thing," Biórr said.

"If your stones were as big as mine, you'd be worried, too," Storolf grinned.

Biórr chuckled and took one last glance over his shoulder at the orange glow and shimmering heat haze that marked the molten river of the vaesen pit. At the rear of the column he saw Kráka sitting on the driving bench of a wagon, two children next to her. One was Bjarn, and the other was Breca Thorkelsson, the boy who had had the bones of his hand broken by Brák Trolls-Bane. Biórr could see the gleam of linen bandaging around Breca's hand.

Biórr had not spoken to Bjarn yet, although he had been tempted

to seek the lad out. But guilt held him back. He had arranged
Bjarn's abduction back in Snakavik, was responsible for the lad's
separation from Uspa, his mother. And finding him with a thrall-
collar about his neck had not helped ease his guilt.

The collar is gone now, though.

I'll talk to Bjarn tonight, see if he wants a game of tafl, Biórr thought.
He pulled his cloak tighter about him, feeling the bite of an east-
erly wind, and trudged on.

Biórr finished the bowl of fish stew and checked the pocket of his
cloak, feeling the weight of his pouch full of tafl pieces, then set
off, picking his way through the camp. Voices called out to him
from different fires, friends from the past, though he still felt like
they were a distant memory, his days with Agnar and the Battle-
Grim feeling like a wall between him and his old bonds.

Ahead of him were the wagons used for carrying the children
as well as their stores of food and drink. He saw Kráka sitting
among a handful of children by a fire, her black hair glistening like
oil in the reflected light.

"Biórr," Kráka said to him as he stepped into the firelight. She
shuffled to her left, making room for him to sit. He saw that Bjarn
was sitting the other side of her, the lad Breca next to him and
another boy beside him, fair-haired, squat and wide, looking like a
boulder. After Brák had dragged Breca back into the camp, the lad's
hand broken and a deep cut on his cheek still sheeting blood, there
had been no more attempts by the children to run away. Though
whether that meant they were coming to terms with their new
lives among Ilska's Raven-Feeders, or just that Breca's beating had
cowed them, Biórr could not tell.

But at least here they will not be hunted and thralled for their Tainted blood.

"Bjarn," Biórr said, smiling.

Bjarn looked up at Biórr.

"Biórr, what are you doing here?" Bjarn said.

"These are my people," Biórr said, gesturing to the camp behind
him. "You are safe here."

"With a dragon?" one of the other lads muttered. Breca Thorkelsson.

"A god," Biórr corrected. He put his hand into the pocket in his cloak and pulled out the pouch with tafl pieces. He opened it and pulled out a carved warrior.

"Game of tafl, Bjarn?" he said.

A wisp of a smile crept across Bjarn's face, but then he looked away, as if he'd forgotten that Biórr was standing there.

"Bjarn, are you well?" Biórr asked him. Bjarn smiled but did not answer. "What's wrong with him?" Biórr asked Kráka.

The Seiðr-witch shrugged. "Some are back to themselves, others . . . not so much. I'm hoping that it is just the effects of the Seiðr in them and that it will fade; like too much mead in the blood."

"I'll play tafl with you," Breca Thorkelsson said.

"What, with only one hand?" Biórr said. He could see splints of wood bound within the linen bandage, to set the broken bones.

"It's a game of wits, not limbs," Breca said.

"All right, then," Biórr said and sat. He emptied his pouch and rolled out a strip of linen marked with the positions for tafl, and the two of them set to placing the figures in their places. A jarl and his oathsworn in the centre, and a raiding warband of superior numbers encircling them.

"Jarl, or raider?" Biórr asked Breca.

"Jarl, of course. I need all the practice I can get at escaping," Breca said with a twist of a smile. The fair-haired boulder of a boy beside him laughed.

"Don't make jokes like that, Breca," Kráka said, frowning at him.

"Wasn't a joke," Breca muttered.

"Talk like that will get your other hand broken," Kráka whispered. "That's not brave, just stupid."

"You sound like my papa," Breca said. He looked into the fire a moment, then his lip started to tremble and Biórr saw a fat tear leak down his cheek.

"Drink some of this," Biórr said, unstoppering his ale-barrel. Kráka produced leather cups and he poured for all of them. "Where's Ilmur?" Biórr asked Kráka.

"He has made new friends," Kráka said. She jutted her chin towards a campfire and Biórr saw Ilmur sitting with Brák Trolls-Bane and a few others. He saw the hulking figure of Drekr there, too, an array of weapons set out around him as he sharpened blades.

He felt a seed of worry for Ilmur. He knew the Hundur was fragile, having lived as a thrall for so many years, and he needed some kindness to bring him back to life as a free man. He wasn't sure the company of Drekr and this Brák would help with that.

"Let's play," Breca said.

"Begin," Biórr dipped his head.

The game did not last long. Breca struck hard at Biórr's raiders, and though he made some early victories and took some of Biórr's *drengrs*, it was not long before Biórr had Breca's jarl surrounded and unable to move.

"You are too aggressive," Biórr said. "This is a game of deep-cunning. Of strategy and position. You must outmanoeuvre me with fewer pieces to escape. It can be done, but not by charging my lines like a boar with his snout down. Brave, but foolish."

Breca scowled, studying the board.

"Again?" he said.

"Of course," Biórr said with a smile.

A ripple of murmuring drew Biórr's eye and he saw that Lik-Rifa was walking through the camp towards Biórr and the wagons. She climbed up and sat upon a grey-bleached boulder close to them, looking down upon the children. Ilska walked behind her, like a guard.

Though Lik-Rifa needs guarding from no one.

A hush settled over the camp, all of the children staring at Lik-Rifa, even Bjarn.

"My children," Lik-Rifa said, a smile stretching across her lips. "I have told you that you are Tainted, and that your parents have long hidden that fact from you. But, of course, you must not just take my word for this. I will help you discover the truth for your-self. Firstly, do you all know what Tainted means?"

A silence greeted Lik-Rifa's question.

"Ah, you are all shy," Lik-Rifa said.

What would you expect? I imagine they have never spoken to a dragon-god, before.

"Well, let me tell you," Lik-Rifa continued. "Tainted means that you have the blood of a god running in your veins. Most of the gods are dead now, but their ancestors live on, and this ridiculous new world has the impudence to call an ancestor of the gods *Tainted*! As if it were something to be ashamed of. The arrogance! Ilska tells me that if you have a god's blood flowing in your veins then you are considered *less*; that you are hunted and enslaved, used like animals. This is MADNESS!" She screamed the last word, a hint of her dragon form shimmering in the air, her eyes glowing red, teeth and jaws growing, and Biórr felt the children around him tense, some shifting, as if on the verge of fleeing. But then Lik-Rifa shivered and twitched and juddered, and the human Lik-Rifa was back, sitting on the boulder. She brushed a strand of her hair from her face and tucked it behind an ear. "You should be called the Fortunate Ones, or some such title." She waved a hand in the air, dismissing the stupidity of humankind. "So, each and every one of you has the blood of a god in your veins, and that makes you special. That makes you *powerful*."

Biórr felt a ripple of excitement at Lik-Rifa's words, and of pride, and that was a strange feeling. He had spent so many years feeling afraid and ashamed of his heritage; bore the wounds of his blood-line in the whip scars across his chest. But the way Lik-Rifa spoke, he felt as if no one else was here; that she was speaking to him alone, and she stirred something deep within him. A sense of worth.

"Ilska, show them," Lik-Rifa said.

Ilska stepped forward into firelight. She dipped her head, and when she looked up again her eyes were glowing red, like two coals of fire. She raised a hand and Biórr saw her nails stretch and grow into claws, and then she opened her mouth, lips curling back to reveal long, sharp teeth. The children gasped and hissed around Biórr.

"Thank you, my child," Lik-Rifa said and Ilska stepped back into the shadows, the fire in her eyes fading.

"Ilska has my blood running through her veins. She is dragon-born, and so can manifest something of me within her. Strength and fury, among other things. Your abilities will be different, depending on which god is your ancestor. But which god flows within you? That is the question," Lik-Rifa said. "There were many gods: Snaka the serpent. Me, the dragon." She paused and ran a palm across her sleek hair. "Orna the eagle," she sneered. "Ulfrir the wolf, Berser the bear, Rotta the rat, Svin the boar, Hundur the hound, and many, many others. We were all kin. Did not always get along, if I am honest, but that's families, I suppose." She smiled.

"And each bloodline has different strengths and abilities. You may have the sharp sight of an eagle, or the sense of smell and hearing of a hound. The *Berserkir* strength of a bear, the savagery of a wolf, or the deep cunning of a fox." She shrugged. "The sooner you discover which god lingers in your blood, the sooner you will learn to use and harness your true potential. To be the best you can be." She smiled widely at them all, like a kindly mother teaching them a wonderful truth.

"How do we do that, then?" the broad lad called Harek piped up from beside Breca.

"Close your eyes, each and every one of you," Lik-Rifa said. "This will be difficult for you, but you must do it. It is vital to understanding yourself."

Biórr saw all the children gathered around close their eyes and bow their heads, even Breca beside him.

"Ilska tells me how all of you were taken from your families," Lik-Rifa said. "From your mother and father. Remember that moment. When you were taken, ripped away from them. Some of you may have seen your parents die. Remember that, too."

Biórr heard sniffing, saw that the lad Harek was crying, his shoulders shaking. Breca had his eyes screwed tightly shut, tears leaking, his unbroken hand clenched in a white-knuckled fist. Bjarn was the only one who seemed calm and still.

He already knew what his parents were; must have known he was Tainted. This is not a shock to him, as it is to these others.

"Emotion brings out the beast within you. Do you feel it?" Lik-Rifa said. "A whisper in your blood? A growl, a screech or a hiss, perhaps?"

"Yes," breathed Harek, his shoulders not shaking any more. Breca made a grunting, growling noise.

"That is the beast in your blood. The god. Speak to it, in your thought-cage," Lik-Rifa said. "Become acquainted. You are one and the same, so the sooner you accept that and welcome this creature that is prowling in your veins and heart, the sooner you will be complete."

A heavy silence settled over the camp, the children lost in their own thought-cages, the rest of the camp looking on, recognising that something momentous was happening. The air seemed to tingle.

"Now, open your eyes and speak out which animal lurks in the shadowed places of your soul," Lik-Rifa commanded them.

Bjarn looked up immediately.

"Bear," he said.

Harek opened his eyes and gave a shy smile. "Boar," he whispered. All around Biórr he heard the whispered voices of children. Lik-Rifa sat, patiently waiting, listening to the murmured voices.

Breca's face twitched and spasmed. He was last to open his eyes, and he looked up at Kráka.

"Wolf, *and* bear," he said.

Kráka's eyes widened, and Biórr blinked. Usually only the bloodline from one of your parents would dominate your blood and it was rare for someone to feel the beast of both parents in their veins. Rare, but not unheard of. And those with two animals in the blood were valued higher than any other *Tainted* among the jarls and powers of Vigrið.

Wolf and bear are a powerful combination. This boy will grow into something fierce. Strong and savage and cunning.

Kráka reached out and squeezed Breca's unbroken hand.

"And remember this," Lik-Rifa called out loudly. "Your parents lied to you your whole life. Kept hidden from you your true nature, as if you were too foolish and pathetic to deserve this truth. The grief and sorrow you are feeling; they do not deserve it. I am your family now, and I will always tell you the truth and treat you with the respect you deserve."

Lik-Rifa stood abruptly, looking to the west, though all Biórr could see beyond their campfire glow was impenetrable darkness.

Lik-Rifa jumped down from the rock and walked a few paces, then froze.

Biórr heard them first. A whirring, hissing sound on the air, like a breeze rubbing branches and dry autumn leaves together in a forest. Then the flicker of movement, a deeper shadow in the darkness, fire-glow reflecting off something in the air.

All in the camp leaped to their feet, Biórr reaching for his seax, wishing he'd not left his spear at Storolf's fireside.

Drekr strode to Ilska, hefting his long-axe, the other dragon-born gathering around her, and then they were shouting words of power and rune-fire was crackling into life.

"No need," Lik-Rifa called out, holding a warning hand out to Ilska. She smiled. "It is my children returning to me."

And then creatures were swarming in the air above them, shapes flickering and swirling around Lik-Rifa. She stood there, holding her arms wide as tennúr flew around her, some landing on her arms and shoulders, others settling on the ground at her feet or hovering in the air. They were speaking to Lik-Rifa in a gaggle of voices, Biórr unable to make sense of it all.

Lik-Rifa's face shifted, from beatific smile to twitching, growling rage.

"My *niðing* brother has crossed the Isbrún Bridge," she snarled.

CHAPTER THIRTY-SIX

ORKA

Orka reined in Trúr and looked ahead. The path they had been following through a narrow, winding ravine had spilled out on to an open plain. To the east the Boneback Mountains reared, white-capped and lost in cloud. Ahead of Orka and her companions, to the north-west, Lake Horndal sat like liquid silver, shimmering in the sun between two mountains, and sprawling along the lake's southern bank was Starl, a market-town grown fat on the southern travellers and traders who would venture north beyond the Boneback Mountains and those from the north who would sell their goods to merchants from the south. Ships dotted the River Hvítá that wound southwards from the lake, ferrying cargo bound for the town of Snakavik that sat at the river's mouth.

Lif, Gunnar and Revna spread either side of Orka, all of them mounted, as well as Myrk, who sat in the saddle of her horse now, rather than draped across it like a dead deer. She was still bound at wrist and ankle, with rags wrapped around her mouth, and she was trussed into the saddle, Orka leading her horse by a rope. A whirr of wings as Vesli hovered above them, clutching Breca's spear, a fat bag of teeth hanging at her belt.

"Did you ride around the lake, or sail across it?" Orka said as she leaned to pull the rag from Myrk's mouth.

Myrk stretched her jaw and spat.

"We booked passage on a *knarr* and sailed across," she said. "It's faster."

"Huh," Orka grunted, looking back at the town and lake.

Sailing is the quicker route to the northern shore of the lake. But, if Myrk is lying, then we will lose her trail and may never pick it back up again.

"*Stopping for food?*" Spert asked hopefully, shifting from where he lay across Orka's saddle to look up at her.

"No," Orka said.

A figure loped across the plain towards them – Halja Flat-Nose.

"The Raven-Feeders' tracks lead to Starl, not to the path around the lake, chief," she said to Orka as she drew near.

Orka nodded.

"See," Myrk said.

Orka leaned over and tugged the cloth back up over Myrk's mouth, making sure it was tight and secure.

"Spert, Vesli, you cannot come into the town with us," Orka said. "They would kill you. Find a safe place near the lake, where you can see the vessels coming in and out. Look for us on the water. We'll be no more than a day."

"*Yes, mistress,*" Vesli said.

"*What about Spert's porridge?*" Spert grumbled.

"Life is sacrifice," Orka shrugged. Then she touched her heels to Trúr's flanks, and they were moving on, Spert's wings snapping and whirring, lifting him from the saddle and into the sky with Vesli. The two vaesen flew north, Spert's grumbling drifting back to them on the cold wind.

Orka rode Trúr at a slow walk through the streets of Starl. Dogs and children ran at their heels, the children begging and the dogs yapping and snapping at the horses. Orka gave them a dark look and the dogs ran off, whining.

They had ridden through open gates set in a stockaded wall that ran in a horseshoe around the town, the eastern flank of the town running up to steep cliffs, the north of Starl bordered by Lake

Horndal. Guards had stood at the gates, men and women hired by the most powerful traders in Starl, a merchant group who ran the town. There was no jarl here. The guard had looked at Orka and her companions, and looked harder at Myrk, trussed and bound like an outlaw, but they had asked no questions. The Bloodsworn's distinctive shields had most likely helped with that.

The streets were planked with wood, mud oozing through the gaps, the ground either side slick and treacherous, people on foot slipping and sliding to move out of Orka's way. She saw an inn with stables and dismounted, led Trúr to the door and tied him to a rail, then entered the inn. A dark room lit with seal oil, smoke thick and salty in the air. Orka found the landlord and negotiated for stables and a meal, handed over a silver coin from Myrk's pouch and then guided her companions into a courtyard next to the inn. There was a tangle of buildings edging the courtyard, one flowing into the next: a brewhouse, a barn for stabling, a handful of storage sheds and a paddock more mud than grass.

"Food and water for the horses," Orka said as the Bloodsworn rode into the courtyard. Each of them led a second horse, and there were two more packhorses that they had taken from the Raven-Feeders, laden with sacks and barrels. Orka dismounted and led Trúr into the stable barn, the Bloodsworn following behind her. Two stable hands met them, helping to settle each horse. Myrk was dragged down from her saddle and tied to a post beside the stables. Orka took Myrk's horse, a tall, bay gelding, into a stable and unbuckled his girth, sliding the saddle from his back and setting it on a dividing wall. She drew a seax from her belt and cut a strip of linen from the hem of her under-tunic, then she nicked the horse's shoulder, a few beads of blood blooming. The horse just looked at her. Orka wiped the blood away with the strip of linen, which she folded and put in the pouch at her belt. Walking out of the stable she reached for her long-axe, which was leaning against bales of hay.

"A meal will be brought out soon enough from the inn," Orka said. "Don't take your eyes off her." She nodded at Myrk.

"Where are you going?" asked Lif.

"To re-stock our provisions and buy passage across the lake."

"Want some company, chief?" Halja Flat-Nose said.

"All right. Come on then," and then she was turning and striding from the stable barn.

The market district of Starl was the beating heart of the town and Orka and Halja found it soon enough, a succession of squares and connecting streets selling all manner of goods situated like a buffer before the docks and piers that stretched out into Lake Horndal. The first market square was selling tools and weapons, leather, furs, undyed linen and wool. Weavers shouted their wares, belts of tablet-weave hanging from hooks. Orka strode past a stall stacked with walrus ivory, sealskin and bear furs without a glance, through a connecting street and into the next square. This one was thick with competing aromas, food, drink, spices from all over Vigrið. Orka slowed here and took her time choosing a trader, settled on one and began to haggle. Halja wandered through the square, listening to the gossip. Soon Orka was telling the trader where to deliver his goods and counting out coin from Myrk's pouch.

"You could save money by buying from different traders," Halja said as she rejoined Orka.

"I could," Orka agreed as she walked away, "but that would take time, and I want to be out of here as fast as possible."

Halja nodded.

"What is the news?" Orka asked as she led Halja out of the square.

"Talk of a winged beast seen in the far north. Some say a dragon. Some are scared, some laugh at it," Halja said.

Orka felt a shiver ripple down her spine. It was one thing to have dark dreams of dragon wings, but it was another to hear traders speak of it in the light of day. They walked into the next market-place. The stench of sweat and urine and faeces hit Orka before she saw the thrall-stalls and heard an auctioneer shouting out prices from a wooden platform.

Orka slowed a moment, looking around, then strode to a guard as wide as a wall with an iron-bound club in his fist.

"Any slavers here deal in *Tainted*?" Orka asked him.

"Haga, over there," the guard grunted, pointing with his club to a grey-haired woman. Orka gave the guard a sliver of hack-silver and walked away, towards Haga. The woman was standing with a handful of guards around her, dressed in bright orange wool with silver around her neck. Her hair was pulled tight into a single braid that ran down her back. Tattoos were scrawled across the backs of her hands.

"What are you doing?" Halja hissed.

"Buying a *Tainted* thrall, I hope," Orka said.

"But we are——" Halja hissed again.

"I know," Orka growled back at her, "but it must be done."

Halja shook her head. "I don't like it," she muttered.

Neither do I, thought Orka.

Two guards stepped in front of Orka as she drew close to Haga, both of them eying Orka's long-axe.

"Need to buy a *Tainted* thrall," Orka said. She hefted the pouch at her belt, coins chinking.

"Let her through," Haga said. She was a head shorter than Orka and looked her up and down. "And what would you be wanting with a *Tainted* thrall?" she asked.

"Should be obvious, though it's none of your business," Orka said. "The blacksmith doesn't ask what you're going to do with his axe. But this *is* your business," and she took her pouch from her belt and gave it a shake, coins jangling.

Haga was silent a long moment.

"What are you looking for?" she said.

Orka leaned forward and whispered in Haga's ear.

"Just so happens I can help you out," Haga said.

Orka walked away from the thrall-square putting a key inside a pouch at her belt. The pouch where she kept Breca's wooden sword pendant. A tall woman followed her, thin to the point of emaciation. She had mouse-brown hair shaved to stubble and wore a mud-spattered, threadbare linen tunic. Her feet were bare, and an iron collar glinted around her neck, red blisters weeping where it had worn at her skin.

"Name's Orka, and she's Halja," Orka said to the thrall.

"I am Sæunn," the thrall said.

Orka led them away from the thrall-square and the dockside of Starl opened up before them, the lake glistening in the sun, a forest of masts bobbing along the quays and piers. The stink of pitch-pine was a welcome change as they left the stench of slavery behind them.

A crowd was gathered on one side of the street, listening to a woman who was standing on a barrel. She was dressed in tattered mail, her lank, greasy hair braided many times, bound with rings of pewter and copper. Other men and women dressed like her were scattered among the crowd, some with spears in their fists. Orka frowned as she drew closer.

"The time of judgement is coming," the woman shouted, "when the dragon will fill the sky. She will sear the wicked and greedy from this world and set the downtrodden free. You must choose a side."

Some in the crowd cheered, though Orka heard one man laughing. The ones in the crowd clothed like the woman on the barrel shifted their way closer to the laughing man.

Halja nudged Orka.

"I know," Orka said as she walked past the crowd, a sense of unease churning in her gut. The woman's shouting faded behind her. She stopped at a stall on the dockside and haggled for a seal-skin cloak, a wool tunic, a linen under-tunic, nålbinding socks, elk-hide turn shoes and grey wool *winnigas* leg-wraps.

"Here," Orka said, handing the clothes to Sæunn.

The thrall took them. "Yes, mistress," she said, bobbing her head and holding them in her arms.

"They're for you to wear, not carry," Orka explained.

Sæunn just looked at her a moment, confused.

"Put them on," Halja said.

Sæunn set the clothes aside and tugged her linen tunic off, standing naked in the bright, cold sunshine. Her pale, skinny body was a multitude of scars, many white and faded, some new, some red and raw.

"I meant, *find* somewhere to change," Halja said as people around them stared and muttered at the sight of Sæunn.

"Sorry, so sorry," Sæunn said, starting to put her old tunic back on.

"No, just get it done," Orka said.

As Sæunn dressed herself Orka turned and looked out at the lake. It was vast, the northern shore far beyond even Orka's *Tainted* wolfish eyesight. Either side of Starl's docks and piers the lakeshore was thick with reeds. Swans and geese swam among them. Crakes waded in the shallows and lapwings flitted in the sky. The Boneback Mountains reared high to the east and west, and over the lake Orka could see the grey-green arch of one of dread Snaka's ribs. She felt a pulsing in her head.

Snaka's bones; his power still lingers, she thought.

But as she looked out on to the lake the pulsing in her head grew stronger, and she heard the faint howl of a wolf. Her eyes narrowed and she stared harder, saw a *drakkar* appear on the lake, sail full of a cold northerly wind. The hull was newly caulked and pitched, a serpent-headed prow rearing proud as it sliced through the white-spuming water. Its hull lay deep in the water, as if it carried a heavy cargo. As Orka watched the *drakkar* the sail was dropped and furled, figures working at the mast, pulling out the pins from the mast-lock and lowering the mast. Oars snaked out like Spert's many legs and dipped into the water, the *drakkar* slowing and making for an empty pier on Starl's dockside. As the ship drew closer Orka saw the design on shields stacked along the top-rail. Black crossed spear and axe on a blood-red field. The howling in her head grew louder, like a wolf calling to its pack.

"That *drakkar*," Orka said to Halja, pointing. "Do you recognise their shields?"

Halja stared, then sucked in a sharp breath.

"Aye. They are the Battle-Grim."

CHAPTER THIRTY-SEVEN

VARG

Varg stacked his oar along with thirty other rowers and their *drakkar* coasted the remaining distance across the fjord to a pier, grating on wood as mooring ropes were cast to men and women standing ready. The town of Liga sprawled along the fjord's bank, reeking and seething with life like a kicked anthill.

When Varg had first come here, an outlaw fleeing the son of his recently deceased slave-master, Liga had seemed like the biggest town in the world, the sights, sounds and scents almost overwhelming, but now that Varg had seen Darl, he saw Liga for what it was. A fair-sized port and trading town. The whole dockside was busy with the business of buying and selling; merchant ships unloading goods, harbour officials collecting mooring fees, lines of traders with their wares laid out on trestle-tables, tallymen here and there sitting with their scales and weights, sharp knives ready for carving numbers and runes into birch-bark tablets.

Before the mooring ropes were tied off Glornir climbed up on to the top-rail of the *drakkar*, his shield slung across his back and his long-axe in one fist, and leaped across the fjord's green-dark water to the pier. Røkia was a heartbeat behind him, and then the hull was grinding against timber and the boarding-plank was being lowered, more of the Bloodsworn disembarking. A harbour official was approaching down the pier, a handful of guards at his back, but he stuttered to a stop as he saw Glornir striding towards him, an aura of glowering malice and menace leaking from the Bloodsworn's chief.

"Jaromir and his *druzhina*?" Glornir called out as he drew nearer.

The harbour official blinked. A tall, thin man with a fur-trimmed cap on his head, a rich wool tunic of deep red and a thick silver ring around one arm. Confusion fluttered across his face as he stared up at Glornir.

Clearly a man not used to being spoken to like that, Varg thought as he hurried across the gangplank, one hand hovering close to the axe at his belt. His eyes scanned the crowded dockside, searching for the tell-tale horsehair helms of Jaromir's *druzhina*.

"Your mooring fee—" the harbour official began.

"Prince Jaromir of Iskidan; is he in Liga?" Glornir growled.

"We should settle your account before you—"

"We won't be stopping if he's not here, so is he or not?" Glornir interrupted.

"Harbour fees are my task, not answering your questions," the harbour official said.

Glornir's hand snapped out, grabbed the harbour official by his throat and dragged him forward, lifting him from the ground. The guards around him spread wide, three men and two women, all reaching for weapons. One lifted a horn to their lips and blew.

"I would not do that if I were you," Svik said casually, a half-smile twitching his moustache as he stepped around Glornir's side. Einar Half-Troll loomed behind him, Varg and a dozen more of the Bloodsworn pressing close. Røkia appeared on Glornir's other side, shield slung across her back, her spear in her fist and Sulich filled the space behind her. Not one of the Bloodsworn had drawn a blade, but Varg could feel the imminence of violence, tasted it in the air like a scent.

The guards looked to the harbour official, feet dangling above the wooden boards of the pier, waiting for his order.

"This is an outra—"

"Yes, an outrage, we know," Svik said. "Now tell the big man what he wants to know before your painful death replaces your outrage."

"Jaromir?" Glornir snarled, starting to squeeze.

"I . . . don't . . . know," the harbour official squeaked.

Glornir threw the man to the ground, where he gasped and coughed, rising slowly to one knee.

"Jarl Logur shall hear of this," the harbour official wheezed.

"Good. Send for Logur now," Glornir said.

"I think they already have," Svik said wryly.

People milled at the end of the pier, Varg seeing in the crowd a handful of blue-painted shields, red sails upon them. Other figures were pushing through, and then a silver-haired woman was striding on to the pier, two large hounds loping either side of her. Varg saw Ingmar Ice behind her, pale-skinned, broad and thickset, his fair hair gleaming white in the sunshine. The big man grinned at the Bloodsworn.

"Edel," Glornir said, striding past the harbour official, the guards stepping aside for him. "Have you seen any sign of Jaromir or his *druzhina*?"

"No," Edel said, shaking her head, we've only just docked with the *Sea-Wolf*. Why?"

"He has Vol."

Voices from the dockside, a horn blowing and more blue-shields appeared, crowds parting for a score of warriors. Jarl Logur strode among them, grey-haired, barrel-chested and broad-bellied. He grinned to see Glornir, his smile fading as he took in Glornir and his harbour official still kneeling on the pier.

"I'd say well met," Logur said as he reached them. "But . . . is there a problem?" He looked from Glornir to the harbour official, who was rising back to his feet.

"Thank goodness you are here, Jarl Logur. These brigands are refusing to pay their harbour fees; they have assaulted me; *me*, one of your chosen men," the man said, his voice shrill and hoarse.

"I meant, are *you* causing my friend a problem, Palrun?" Jarl Logur snapped at the official.

"B . . . b . . . but," the official stammered.

"Jaromir has Vol," Glornir said to Jarl Logur, ignoring the official. "Is he here?"

A moment's silence as Logur took that in.

"No," Jarl Logur said. "He arrived a few days ago, re-stocked his ships and sailed with the tide."

"Ach," Glornir growled, bowing his head.

"What can I do to help, my friend," Logur said, laying a hand on Glornir's arm.

Glornir trembled, then looked up, blowing out a long breath. "Help my crew to re-stock the *Sea-Wolf*, and take this *drakkar* off of my hands. It is one of Helka's."

Jarl Logur raised an eyebrow at that.

"She will have warriors arriving soon, so you will not have it taking up space on your docks for long."

"Been causing trouble, have you?" Logur said.

"You could say that," Glornir said with a shrug. "And one other favour. Look after this man for me. Give him back to Helka along with her longship." Glornir turned to point at Prince Hakon, who was being led on to the pier, Frek the *Úlfhéðnar* at his heel, Æsa walking close to them.

Jarl Logur looked at Hakon, then threw his head back and laughed. It was loud and booming and infectious, so that soon Varg felt a chuckle in his own belly and others in the Bloodsworn were grinning.

"Of course, my friend," Jarl Logur said, wiping his eyes when he had found his breath. "Palrun, you will oversee the stocking of my friend Glornir's longship. See that they have all they need."

"Yes, lord," Palrun said sulkily.

"Good. Now, Glornir, while the *Sea-Wolf* is being loaded you will come and drink with me in my hall, and tell me how you have ended with Helka's firstborn on your ship, and him with a face like someone has pulled his breeches down and slapped his arse."

Glornir frowned at that, though others in the Bloodsworn laughed.

"You cannot sail until the tide turns anyway, so there is time," Logur said. "I would hear of what you have been up to and how Vol has ended up in that arrogant *niðing*'s hands. And I will send for any word of Jaromir while we wait. Who knows, there may be some news that will help you."

Glornir gave a curt nod. "My thanks," he said. "Svik, keep an eye on him," Glornir jutted his chin at Palrun, the harbour official.

"That will be my pleasure," Svik smiled, and then Glornir was striding down the pier alongside Jarl Logur, the jarl's oathsworn men settling around them.

Svik looked at Palrun and smiled.

"Lead on, then, my good man, and let's see if we can empty Liga of cheese."

Palrun blinked. "Cheese?" he said.

"I am joking," Svik said, then looked back over his shoulder at Varg and shook his head, whispered, "no I'm not."

"What about me?" Hakon said, looking indignant at being left out. "Huh, am I invisible?" he muttered when no one answered him.

"You could stay here and show me how good you are at humping, I'd wager I'm better," Æsa said, grinning at the prince. He blinked and took a step away from her.

Palrun turned and led Svik down the pier, his guards following. Most of the Bloodsworn set to emptying the *drakkar*, and Einar whistled to the children they had escorted from the Grimholt, who came swarming over the gangplank like a pack of wolf cubs, swirling around Einar, some of them climbing up on to his shoulders.

"You'll have to start helping if you want Glornir to let you stay," Einar said, and set them to fetching what stores they had left from the longship's deck.

Feet drummed on the pier and Varg saw four of Logur's blue-shields jogging back to them.

"Prince Hakon," one of them said, an auburn-haired woman with a scar beneath her left eye. "Jarl Logur requests your company."

"Humph," Hakon muttered. "About time."

"Please, follow us," the woman said.

"With pleasure," Hakon said, scowling at the Bloodsworn and hurrying away from Æsa.

Æsa blew Hakon a kiss. "You're missing out," she called after him.

As Prince Hakon walked past them Varg reached out and touched Frek's arm. The *Úlfhéðnar* stopped and looked at Varg, pulling his arm away.

"I have been a thrall," Varg said. "And I never thought I would be anything other."

Frek looked at him a long moment, a weight of despair swirling in his eyes. Then he shrugged and walked on after Hakon.

"You should stow your coat of mail in your oar-chest," Røkia said to Varg as they boarded the *Sea-Wolf.*

"Why?" Varg said. He had become used to the weight of the coat now, and felt safer for it. "I thought I might keep it on."

"Because the sea rots metal faster than Svik eats cheese," Røkia said.

"The sea?" Varg said.

"Aye. You know, that water over there," she pointed with her spear at the horizon to the south, where there was a gap between the steep cliffs of the fjord, water shimmering in the sun.

"I know what the sea is," Varg said, "but we are not on it."

"We will be, though," Røkia said, "sure as day follows night. Jaromir is running for Iskidan, and we will be chasing after him."

"Oh," Varg said, not liking the thought of sailing across the open sea. He had become used to rowing and sailing on a *drakkar*, but on a river where land was always reassuringly visible. Even when they had sailed out of the fjord, they had hugged the coast northwards, land always in sight, and that had only been for half a day, until they had turned into the estuary of the River Slågen.

Varg shrugged. "The sea, a river, what's the difference."

Røkia only smiled in answer and walked away shaking her head, muttering, "No-Sense."

He strode down the deck, placed his spear in a rack and secured his shield in the rim pegged to the top-rail, then found his old oar-chest. He stood there a moment, looking down at it, remembering the last time he had closed the lid. It felt a long time ago now, when he had disembarked from the *Sea-Wolf* and set off with Skalk and the Bloodsworn in search of whatever was killing Queen Helka's people.

He opened the chest, hinges stiff, and saw a hemp sack. He leaned in and opened it, seeing all that he had left behind.

A coat of lamellar plate, a decorated helm plumed with horsehair, a fine belt with a long knife and scabbarded sabre, an unstrung bow, a quiver of grey-feathered arrows and a bow case.

All taken from the druzhina *I killed on the docks.* A flood of fractured memories dominated by the sensation of fear. The *druzhina* charging at him, his spear blow with the leather cap still on the blade, leaping on to the back of the horse, stabbing with his seax. Blood slick on his hand. At the time Varg had felt repulsed at the thought of taking possessions from the dead, but he understood more clearly now what it meant. *The tale of my battle-fame. Who I have bested in combat.* He looked down at the coat of mail he was wearing, the helm and seax hanging at his belt, all taken from the dragon-born he had slain at Rotta's chamber. It did not feel wrong to wear these things.

But I have too much kit, now. And I have never used a bow in my life. He looked around the deck, then reached into the chest and pulled out the hemp sack, hefted it over his shoulder and walked away, swaying. He stopped beside another oar-bench where Sulich was storing his own war gear, though he did not seem to own much. No coat of mail, just a plain nasal helm and a curved sword.

"I owe you a blood-debt," Varg said to Sulich. "You saved my life, back in Darl."

Sulich frowned. "Did I?"

"Aye. From an *Úlfhéðnar* in Helka's hall." He put a hand to the side of his head, touched the ragged nub of flesh that had been his ear. "I would repay you."

"We are Bloodsworn, sworn to each other. And perhaps you will return the favour sometime," Sulich shrugged. "I am thinking you will have many opportunities where we are going."

"I could save your life by giving you this," Varg said, dumping the hemp sack on the ground and opening it. He held his hand up as Sulich's face clouded. "I offered it to you once before, I know, without realising the insult," Varg said, "and I am sorry for that. But now I owe you a life; *my* life, and here is kit that could save yours. A coat of lamellar plate, a fine helm, bow and quiver, arrows that may save me once again, if you put those arrows into my enemy." He smiled, though looking at Sulich's face he was not sure if he had insulted the man again.

"You earned that kit, it is yours," Sulich said.

Well, he is scowling, but he isn't walking away. Or hitting me. That's a good sign, surely?

"Yes," Varg agreed. "Mine to do with as I will. To wear and use, or to pay a debt." He shrugged. "That is what I choose to do. I owe you, and this will clear that debt. And besides," he added, gesturing to the *brynja* he was wearing. "I have also won this coat of mail and this helm, and I do not need two of each."

A silence as Sulich's eyes narrowed.

"Ha," a voice boomed behind them, Einar Half-Troll. "Listen to Varg No-Sense bragging of his battle-fame."

"That is not what I mean— oooff," Varg grunted as Einar slapped him on the back.

"Take the mail, Sulich," Einar said. "It is well earned, and there is no doubt that Varg will need his hide saved by you again."

Sulich looked from Einar to Varg to the bag of kit, a frown knitting his brows, then he looked back to Varg and smiled.

"I accept," Sulich said, his drooping moustache twitching with his grin.

"You . . . do?" Varg said. "Good. Good." He smiled, too.

Sulich delved into the hemp sack and took out the unstrung bow. "I need a bowstring," Sulich said.

"You're in the best place to buy one in all of Vigrið," Røkia called over to them, gesturing to the dense snarl of traders on Liga's dockside. Sulich grinned again and then he was hurrying along the deck and leaping on to the pier, breaking into a run towards the docks.

"That was well done," Einar said with a nod. "He's a proud one, is Sulich. For a moment there I thought he might stab you."

"So did I," Varg breathed.

Einar laughed.

Varg saw Svik appear at the pier's end, Palrun with him, and a score of men and women following them, their arms piled

high with heaped goods. Hurrying back to his open oar-chest
Varg unbuckled his helm from his belt and placed it in his
chest, then unbuckled his weapons belt and rolled it up around
his seax, cleaver and axe, putting that in the chest, too. He leaned
forward, jumped and wriggled out of his *brynja*, the coat of mail
falling on to the deck like a shed skin. He wrapped it in his
sealskin cloak and set it in the chest as Svik reached the *Sea-Wolf*
and ushered those behind him on to the *drakkar*.

Men and women boarded the *Sea-Wolf* heavily laden with sacks
of salt and oats, barrels of water and ale and whey. Svik walked
down the boarding plank leading four people carrying heaped rounds
of cheese wrapped in linen. Svik saw Varg and winked at him. More
people followed the cheese-carriers, a multitude of barrels and chests
carried aboard; stockfish and pickled herring, salted pork, iron nails
and rivets, reams of linen thread and leather cord for the repairing
of kit; thick rolls of walrus rope and even a folded sail of wool.

"That is everything," Palrun the harbour official said as his
followers deposited the goods on the *Sea-Wolf*'s deck. "An expen-
sive journey you are making."

"Just give your tally to Jarl Logur," Svik said. "The Bloodsworn
are good for it."

"Yes, well," Palrun croaked as he stood there a moment, looking
as if he would like to disagree about that, but the red marks around
his throat were turning to purple bruises, and his voice was still
hoarse from Glornir's squeezing. He pursed his lips and walked
away, his helpers following him.

"Do you think you've bought enough cheese, Tangle-Hair?"
Ingmar Ice said with a smile.

Svik shrugged. "You never know when you are going to meet
a troll in the woods," he said, and Einar chuckled. "Glad to have
you back with us, Ice. A good journey?"

"Aye, good enough," Ingmar said. "Quiet, apart from some back-
breaking rowing to get the *Sea-Wolf* here, but we had a good scrap
at Rotta's chamber to break things up."

"A scrap?" Røkia said. She looked to Edel. "Is all well? Not
everyone is here. Gunnar Prow and Revna Hare-Legs."

"And Flat-Nose," Varg said, looking around for Halja.

"All still breathing," Edel said. "Gunnar'll have a nice new scar on his leg, but that's all. Gunnar, Revna and Halja are keeping the Skullsplitter company."

Varg saw Svik's smile falter and fade.

"Orka is . . . well?" Svik asked.

"Oh, aye," Ingmar Ice said. "It's those she picked a scrap with that aren't."

"Good," Svik said quietly.

"Sounds like Skullsplitter," Røkia said.

"What happened?" Svik pressed.

"Some of Ilska's Raven-Feeders rode up to Rotta's chamber as we were making ready to leave," Edel said as she sat on her oar-chest and tugged at the ear of one of her hounds. "Led by a vicious little lass who turned out to be Ilska the Cruel's sister, and that old man that Varg left his cleaver in; he was their father."

Hisses of indrawn breath and mutters among the Bloodsworn at that.

Varg frowned at that.

"I killed the father of Ilska the Cruel," he said.

"Ha," Ingmar laughed, clapping Varg on the shoulder and sending him stumbling, "no need to look so worried, you are one of us, now." He looked at Varg's scarred head and the lack of an ear. "Looks like you have a tale of your own, No-Sense, you didn't try to kiss Røkia, did you? There is no-sense, and then there is insanity."

Røkia scowled at Ingmar.

"No, I did not!" Varg said, feeling heat flush his cheeks.

"One of Helka's *Úlfhéðnar*," Sulich said.

"Ah," Ingmar nodded. "I will hear more of this tale with a horn of ale in my hand, I am thinking."

"He should be worried about dragon-born," Edel said dourly, "all of us should. Apparently Ilska has the company of a god."

"Lik-Rifa?" Svik asked.

"Aye," Edel said, "so this Myrk told us. The Raven-Feeders are deep in this, somehow." She shrugged. "Things are going to get bloody, I'm thinking, so it won't hurt for a few of ours to tag along with Orka and see what's going on. And Halja is set on carving some revenge for her brother."

Varg remembered standing in the shield wall with Halja and her brother, Vali Horse-Breath. The troll at Rotta's chamber had turned Vali's bones to gruel with a blow from his club. It made him think of his own sister, Frøya.

Kin and blood feud. I am not the only one to feel its pull.

The tramp of feet and Glornir came striding down the pier, Jarl Logur and a dozen of his oathsworn warriors about them. At the boarding ramp Glornir gripped Logur's forearm and they exchanged a few words, then Glornir was thudding across the boarding ramp on to the *Sea-Wolf*'s deck. He stood there a moment, eyes closed, and ran one big hand along the top-rail, took in a deep breath and held it, as if savouring some precious memory. Then his eyes snapped open. He paused as he took in the small figures running around the deck, helping to stow the goods Svik had purchased, and then he looked to Einar.

"They will be a help, not a hindrance, chief," Einar pleaded.

"They'd better be," Glornir said, glowering at the dozen or so children. "I hope they can row."

"I can," a fair-haired girl said, maybe eleven or twelve winters on her shoulders. She held her palms up, showing calloused hands. "I've got strong hands."

"What is your name?" Glornir asked her.

"Refna," the girl said.

"Well, Refna Strong-Hands, show me," said Glornir and the girl grinned, hefted an oar and found an empty oar-chest.

"Make ready to sail," Glornir shouted, and all the Bloodsworn were moving, taking oars from racks, settling on to oar-chests. Røkia and Sulich had fitted the steering oar in place, hammering securing pegs into holes. Glornir walked down the deck to the prow and turned to face them all.

"Jaromir arrived here three days ago."

Some of the Bloodsworn muttered and growled at that. Three days was a big head start.

"But Jaromir waited for another day, and two more parties of *druzhina* rode into Liga. Jaromir and the rest of them rowed out of here two days ago, in three *drakkar* and two *knarr* that caried his horses. He is running for his home, so we are after him. We will teach him what happens to those who steal from the Bloodsworn; we are sailing for Iskidan."

A wordless roar from the Bloodsworn as oars were threaded through oar-holes and the mooring ropes were slipped and thrown on to the *Sea-Wolf*'s deck. Einar and Ingmar used spears to push away from the pier and Glornir took his position in the stern, gripping the steering oar as oars dipped into the fjord's black waters.

Svik turned on his sea-chest and looked at Varg.

"Your first seafaring then," he said, and laughed.

"What is so funny?" Varg said. "Røkia was just laughing about the same thing."

"I am just happy," Svik said. "There is no joy like sailing the whale road."

Varg bent his back as his oar dipped below the fjord's surface and he pulled.

CHAPTER THIRTY-EIGHT

ELVAR

Elvar stood in the shadow of the *Wave-Jarl's* prow, Agnar's bearskin cloak pulled tight about her shoulders to ward off the cold wind that had filled their sail and speeded their journey across Lake Horndal. The sail was furled and stowed now, the mast down and the lock-pin hammered in place, oars rising and falling to the rhythm Sighvat was beating on an empty barrel. The *drakkar* felt unusually sluggish, sitting low in the water with the weight of gold and silver they had loaded from Oskutreð.

Once Elvar had made the decision to travel south to the *Wave-Jarl* they had made good time. Now that she was chief of the Battle-Grim and the decisions were hers, good or bad, she felt as if a burden had been lifted. She knew what the *blóð svarið* expected of her, and added to that there was her vow to Uspa, to try and free the Seiðr-witch's husband, Berak. To her mind now she had a course charted, like sailing from Vigrið to Iskidan. She could see the path of the rope through the tangled knot.

Now the task is to stay alive while I untie the knot, and not just me, but the Battle-Grim, as well. I might die along the way, but I know the way forward. It is the best hope of succeeding and ridding myself of this Seiðr-magic that lurks in my blood.

It was not all going to be battle, brave deeds and saga-songs around a hearth fire, though. There was the issue of empty bellies, as their store of food and drink was close to empty. She looked at

Starl, a dark stain on the lakeside, growing larger with every stroke of the oars. Elvar could see humanity moving and seething within the town like maggots in shite.

"Is this wise?" Grend said beside her, a solid presence, as always.

"I'd rather sail on, straight down the Hvítá, but there will be mutiny if I do not feed our crew," she said. "Oats and ale are gone, and not much of anything else left. We have to re-stock."

She saw Grend's deep-knit frown and knew why. They had two gods sitting on their longship, and a saga-tale fortune heaped and stowed on the deck, hidden under an awning of spare sail, and Elvar knew what the Battle-Grim were like when they docked at a town. Any town. Knew where they would go.

"Ale and whores," Elvar muttered.

"Make for loose lips," Grend grunted.

Elvar nodded. She turned to look along the deck of the *Wave-Jarl*.

Sólín was standing at the steering oar, guiding the *drakkar* towards a space on a pier. Elvar looked at the crew.

My crew.

She liked that, though some said that leadership weighed down the soul and gnawed at the thought-cage, sending a warrior to an early grave. *Now that I have tasted that, I would not argue the point.* The Battle-Grim looked to her as their chief and she felt the weight of that, but there was something else growing inside her, too. A depth of joy she had never known before. Like when she had first put on the *brynja* she was now wearing, the one she had found on Oskutreð's plain. It had fitted like no coat of mail she had ever worn before, sliding over her shoulders and torso like liquid silver, making her feel like she was wearing a tunic, not a thousand rings of riveted iron. It had felt like *hers*, as if it were made for her, and her alone. And that was how she was beginning to feel about being chief of the Battle-Grim, not from the moment Sighvat had placed Agnar's bearskin cloak around her shoulders and lifted her still bloody sword in the air, but from when she had brought Ulfrir to heel, in the wooded glade by the *Wave-Jarl*.

"Listen up," she called out as the crew rowed towards Starl's docks. "We are stopping to buy ale and food."

A ragged cheer echoed across the deck.

"But only Sighvat, Orv and Urt are to leave the ship, the rest of us are staying on the *Wave-Jarl*."

Some groans and scowls and shouts at that.

"I know what you *niðing* goat-humpers are like," Elvar said. "You'll make for the dockside inns like crows to corpses, and we know what ale and whores make."

"Loothe lipth," shouted Sólín Spittle from the steering oar.

"That's right," Elvar grinned as laughter echoed around the deck. "And I have two gods and a dragon's hoard of gold and silver that I'd rather all of Vigrið didn't know about. Not yet, anyway." She looked to Ulfrir and Skuld, who sat near the stern with Uspa. Skuld had her head bowed, huddled under a cloak, but Ulfrir was gazing at Starl's dockside.

"OARS," Sighvat yelled and Elvar turned to see they were gliding towards the empty pier. Oars came out of the water and slid back through oar-holes as Sólín steered the *drakkar* into position, Sighvat hefting a roll of walrus rope and hurling it across the water to a woman on the pier, part of Starl's harbour crew.

Grend touched Elvar's wrist and nodded towards the dockside.

Figures appeared at the end of the pier, three women. They strode towards the *Wave-Jarl* as it was moored and the boarding plank set in place. One was a thrall, judging by the iron collar around her neck, though she was clothed better than most thralls. The other two were both warriors in ring mail, one with red hair and a broad, flat nose, looking like she'd stopped a fist with her nose too many times. A sword hung at her hip, but Elvar's eyes were drawn to the other woman. Taller than the other two, and broader, too, thick-muscled around the shoulders and back, lean at the waist. Older than the other two, fair hair going to grey, bound into a braid. She wore a coat of mail and held a long-axe in one hand, a fine-looking seax hanging from her belt. Something about her set Elvar's skin prickling. Beside her Grend made a sound in his throat, like a hound's warning growl and his hand rested upon his new axe.

Elvar walked down the deck of the *Wave-Jarl* and climbed up on to the boarding plank, where she stood, watching the three women approach. Grend was close behind her, and Sighvat followed.

"You are the Battle-Grim," the red-haired woman said, looking up at Elvar. It wasn't a question.

"We are," Elvar answered. She felt the older woman's eyes boring into her and met her gaze. Grey-green eyes, a hard, flat stare. The eyes of a killer, Elvar knew. She felt her skin prickle again, like spiders crawling down her neck, but she stared back, refused to look away.

"Where is Agnar?" Red-Hair asked. "We would talk with your chief."

"Agnar is dead," Elvar said. "I am chief of the Battle-Grim, now. And who are you?"

Red-Hair looked up at Elvar. "I am Halja of the Bloodsworn. And what is your name?"

The Bloodsworn! Elvar had heard tales of them and their fair-fame; who had not? Songs were sung of them around the hearth fire. Of the bloody days of the Skullsplitter, and of their new chief, Glornir Shield-Breaker.

I have even heard tales told of Halja Flat-Nose, and her brother, Vali Horse-Breath.

"She is Elvar Troll-Slayer, Elvar Fire-Fist," Sighvat shouted out behind Elvar.

Halja snorted. "Never heard of you."

"You will," Grend said, quieter than Sighvat, but something in his voice caused Halja to pause a moment.

"We are here for Uspa," the older woman said, breaking her silence. Her voice was a flat, rasping growl, as dead as her stare.

"Is Uspa here, or dead in the north?" Halja asked.

The north! What do they know?

Elvar blinked a moment. This was something unexpected. One hand drifted to her sword-hilt, the older woman's eyes tracking the movement.

"Give Uspa to us, if you have her," the older woman said. She bent her head left and then right, bones clicking. "It will go better for you."

Grend took a step forward.

Behind Elvar, Sighvat laughed.

"You are *mad*," he said. "We have a crew of forty behind us, and you are three. Respect for the size of your stones, though."

"Get out of the way, you fat pile of whale blubber," Halja said.

Sighvat scowled, then laughed again. "Ha, I like you. It would be a shame to kill you."

"Make your choice, fat man," Halja said. "Life or death?"

Sighvat laughed again. "Who do you think you are, the Skullsplitter?"

Halja snorted a laugh, her eyes flickering to the older woman for a heartbeat.

Footsteps behind Elvar, on the deck of the *Wave-Jarl.*

"Halja Flat-Nose," a voice called out, Uspa clambering up on to the top-rail beside the boarding ramp. "What are you doing here?"

"Right now, I'm looking for *you*," Halja said with a smile. Uspa smiled back, a look of deep and genuine joy flittering across her face, and Elvar realised she had not seen the Seiðr-witch truly smile before.

"Well, you have found me," Uspa said.

"Step over and come with us," Halja said.

As Elvar watched, Uspa's eyes shifted to the older woman beside Halja. Elvar saw the look of joy evaporate from Uspa's face, replaced with shock.

"Orka," Uspa breathed. "I . . . I thought you were dead?"

"Not yet," the older woman said.

"Orka," Elvar mouthed, the name triggering some dim memory, as if she should know it.

"Come with us, Uspa," Orka said.

"That is not going to happen," Elvar said. She took a short step across the boarding plank and shrugged her bearskin cloak back, freeing her right arm and her sword.

Orka's gaze returned to her, flat, emotionless. She gave a short nod, as if accepting the inevitable, and lifted her long-axe.

"Hold," a voice called out and Elvar looked around to see Ulfrir walking down the *Wave-Jarl*'s deck, Skuld behind him. She had a wool cloak cast about her wings, making her look freakishly muscled and hunched.

Ulfrir walked to the boarding plank and stopped, just stood looking at Orka. He closed his eyes and drew in a long, deep breath. Then he opened his eyes and smiled.

"You have come, then, wolf-child," Ulfrir said.

CHAPTER THIRTY-NINE

ORKA

Orka stared at the man on the longship. Long, dark hair flecked with grey, he was regarding her with amber eyes. Unequivocally, beyond all doubt, she knew him, even though it was impossible.

I have heard him howl in my soul, heard his wolf-call echoing through my blood. I still hear it now. The wolf within her prowled and paced.

He is Ulfrir, the wolf-god.

But he is . . . dead; slain during the Guðfalla. Then Orka saw the glint of iron around the man's neck, saw the thrall-collar sitting there.

Ulfrir gave her a cold twist of a smile, savage and cunning and bleak.

The wolf has been chained.

Orka looked up at Elvar.

"What have you *done?*" she said.

Elvar scowled at her. "What is going on here?" she said, her gaze shifting from Orka to Ulfrir.

"She is my child; she has my protection," Ulfrir said, taking his amber gaze from Orka to look up at the chief of the Battle-Grim.

"I do not need your protection," Orka growled.

"No, you do not," Ulfrir agreed. "You are fierce and strong. But you have it, nonetheless."

That sent a shiver through Orka.

"Come aboard," Ulfrir said, beckoning to Orka, "we have much to talk about."

Orka felt her feet moving before she realised she had taken a step. With an act of will she forced herself to stop. "On there? Among the Battle-Grim who have put a collar about my friend?" Orka said, looking at Uspa.

Friend. That word tasted strange on her lips.

"I am not shy for a scrap, but that would be like stepping into the wolf's jaws," she said.

Ulfrir looked at her, then roared his laughter. The red-haired woman at Ulfrir's shoulder grinned and laughed, too, and soon others on the *drakkar* were chuckling. Eventually Ulfrir stopped laughing and wiped his eyes.

"You will be safe, Orka," he said, laughter lines still creasing his eyes. "You have my word, and that is not lightly given. Come aboard."

"Hold on a moment," Elvar said. "I give the orders and invitations here. And the promise of safe passage." She gave Ulfrir a hard stare, his mirth evaporating, lips twisting.

"You cannot have Uspa," Elvar said to Orka and Halja. The thrall Sæunn stood behind them, meek and silent. "I need her, and she would not go with you even if she were free to choose. So, we have nothing to talk about."

"That's where you are wrong," Halja said.

"Oh?" Elvar took her eyes from Ulfrir and looked back to them.

"We have a dragon-born prisoner, recently come from Oskutreð," Orka said.

Elvar blinked at that. Orka saw the young woman's thought-cage working.

"A conversation could be mutually beneficial," Halja said with a wink.

Elvar stared at them a long moment, then nodded.

"Agreed," Elvar said. "We have a truce, then. Be welcome on my ship, and know that you will not be harmed, unless you break that truce." She took a step back, jumping back down on to the deck of her ship, though the warrior at her shoulder did not move. Tall and broad, black hair turning to grey, his eyes were fixed on Orka. She noted the faded white scars on his cheek, on the backs of his hands that marked him as a veteran of battle, saw one fist resting on a fine-looking hand-axe.

He is dangerous, that one.

"Something to say?" Orka growled at him.

"I'll be watching you," he said.

"A lot of good that will do you," Halja said.

"Sæunn, stay close to me," Orka said as she strode up the boarding plank, coming to a stop in front of the dark-haired warrior, his face cragged like a weathered cliff. He was shorter than Orka by a handspan, but broader. They shared a hard look and then he stepped back, jumping sure-footed on to the longship's deck. Orka followed him.

"Daughter, follow me," Ulfrir said to Orka, turning and walking away.

Daughter. Orka frowned at Ulfrir's back, not liking the sound of that, not liking the way his presence was making her feel. Unsettled, as if she were standing on tide-swept sand. The wolf in her blood paced and whined.

Halja dropped lightly on to the deck and embraced Uspa. Sæunn jumped down beside them.

Elvar barked out orders as she strode down the deck and warriors stood to move sea-chests. Ulfrir sat on one, the red-haired woman always at his shoulder sitting next to him. Elvar gestured for Orka, Halja and Sæunn to sit, but Sæunn walked to stand behind Orka. Elvar sat, along with the fat one. The crag-faced man stood behind Elvar. The rest of the Battle-Grim shifted around them.

"Introductions for our new friends," Ulfrir said with a sharp-toothed smile. "As you know, Orka, I am Ulfrir."

Hearing him say it out loud seemed to make it more real, sending shivers skittering down Orka's spine.

"This is my daughter, Skuld," Ulfrir continued. "You have met Elvar, chief of the Battle-Grim."

"And I am Sighvat, sometimes called the Fat," the fat man said as he shifted on his sea-chest. It creaked. Halja snorted another laugh. "And the friendly one is Grend," Sighvat said with a wave of his hand to crag-face, standing behind Elvar.

"You have raised and thralled a dead god," Orka said, looking from Elvar to Uspa and then back to Elvar.

"Yes," Elvar said.

"Are you insane?" Halja asked.

"You need a god to slay a god," Uspa said, to which she received a hard stare from Elvar.

"They can be trusted," Uspa said to Elvar. "And besides, they have one of the dragon-born from Oskutreð as a prisoner. They will know of Lik-Rifa already."

"This is a truth," Orka said.

"There is talk in the streets of Starl about a dragon seen in the skies," Halja said. "Lik-Rifa free from her cage is not a secret that can be kept hidden."

Orka saw Elvar listening, saw the intelligence behind the young woman's eyes. Saw her give a small, imperceptible nod to herself.

"Let us agree to be open, then," Elvar said, looking at Orka and Halja.

"Agreed," Orka said, and Halja nodded.

"Orka, why are you here?" Uspa asked her.

Orka sucked in a deep breath and made a choice.

"I am looking for my son," she said, her eyes fixed on Uspa. "He was taken, Thorkel slain by those who took him." A crackle of pain at saying the words out loud. It was as if the grief were an ocean within her, swirling beneath a layer of ice, always there, lurking.

Uspa's eyes creased, sadness, sympathy, something more.

"My son, Bjarn, has been taken, too."

It took a few moments for understanding to leak through Orka's thought-cage.

They are together; my Breca and your Bjarn. Taken by these dragon-born to use in the ritual that freed Lik-Rifa.

"You should come with me," Orka said. "I am going to get Breca back."

Sighvat laughed at that.

"What, just like that?" he chuckled. "You are forgetting the small matter of a dragon, and her dragon-born offspring, and more, besides."

Orka turned her gaze on to Sighvat. "I have not forgotten that," she said.

"Ha, both of these shieldmaidens think they are the Skullsplitter," Sighvat laughed, rocking on his oar-chest.

Halja laughed at that and Orka ignored him, looking back to Uspa. "Come with me."

"I cannot," Uspa said. She pulled back the sleeve of her tunic and revealed a coil of white scars around her wrist and forearm. Elvar, Sighvat and Grend did the same. "We have sworn the *blóð svarið*, to get my Bjarn back." She looked to Elvar. "Elvar has a deep-cunning plan. It is no easy task ahead of us, but if there is any way to get my Bjarn back, I think it will be to follow Elvar's plan." She looked at Orka and shook her head. "But what you are doing, it is madness. You are likely a match for any living warrior, Orka, that I do not doubt. But a dragon-god and a warband of dragon-born? Not even you can win alone."

Orka shrugged. "There is only one way to find out," she said.

Sighvat chuckled. "I like this woman," he said.

"You should come with *us*," Ulfrir said. His voice was more like a rasped growl. "You should come with *me*. My blood runs in your veins; my children should be around me." He reached out a hand and patted the arm of Skuld beside him.

Orka saw images in her head of travelling with this crew, of walking at Ulfrir's side. It felt . . . intoxicating, and fitting, like a sword slipping into a well-made scabbard. And then Breca's face was there, his shock of black hair and sharp nose, his jaw, and his grey-green eyes, looking at her.

"No," Orka said, though it took an effort of will to disagree with Ulfrir. "Whatever plan you have, however cunning it is, I will not be separated from my son a moment more than I have to be."

"In essence, I am your father," Ulfrir said. "Your place is at my side."

"My father beat me for the joy of it," Orka said. "I killed him and left my home when I was twelve summers old."

Ulfrir smiled. "I am like no other father," he said.

She felt his power radiating from him, and she knew the wolf in her blood wanted to go with him. To follow him. To be *pack*.

"Still no," Orka growled.

Ulfrir's amber eyes bored into her and Orka glared back at him. He dipped his head and leaned back.

"How will you find your son without us?" Sighvat said.

"They have a dragon-born prisoner," Elvar said.

"Ah, I remember, now," Sighvat said.

"You may be a big man, but there is not much clever going on in that big head of yours, is there?" Halja said.

"That is a fair observation," Sighvat said. "Deep cunning is not my strength, which is why she is chief, not me." He jutted a chin at Elvar. "But I'd beat you in a wrestling match. Want to try?" He winked at Halja.

"I do not wrestle whales, I stick them with my spear," Halja said, and laughter erupted along the deck, the Battle-Grim hooting and howling. Even Sighvat smiled.

"So," said Uspa, tapping her iron collar thoughtfully with one nail. "I understand why you are here, Orka. But you, Halja, one of the Bloodsworn. Why are *you* here?"

A twitch of Halja's cheek, her jaws bunching. "Vali was slain by those that Orka is hunting. I would carve some vengeance into those responsible for that."

"Ah," Uspa nodded. She reached out and squeezed Halja's hand. "Vali was a good man."

"Aye," Halja grunted.

"How did you come by your dragon-born prisoner?" Elvar asked.

"We found her in the Bonebacks," Halja said. "At a place that me and some of the Bloodsworn took Orka to. We think it was Rotta's chamber."

"Rotta?" Ulfrir hissed. "Rotta, that *niðing* piece of troll-shite," he snarled, lips pulling back and jaws snapping. "Describe this place to me?"

"It is all beneath the ground, now," Halja said. "I do not know if that is because of Snaka's ruin, or whether it was always like that."

She shrugged. "A catacomb of tunnels and chambers. One with a slab of rock at its centre, iron collar and chains hammered into it. The rock was pitted and blackened, as if spattered with something that had burned it."

"That is Rotta's chamber," Ulfrir growled, "Rotta's bolthole, but he could not hide from us. We would have hunted him to the ends of the world for what he did to my Valkyrie."

Orka saw tears well in Ulfrir's eyes, muscles in his cheek and jaw twitching. "It was I who hammered those iron chains into the rock. I smiled when the serpent's venom burned him."

Orka and the others stared at Ulfrir, all of them unsettled by the depth of savagery and malice in his voice.

Halja coughed and continued. "There was another room of rune-carvings and parchments. Pages copied from a Galdrabok. We thought it might have been the *Raudskinna*."

"That is where they found it, then," Uspa breathed. "That is what they used to break Lik-Rifa's bonds at Oskutreð."

"Not good to have the *Raudskinna* loose in this world, and in the hands of Lik-Rifa and her dragon-born," Halja said.

"No, it is not," Uspa agreed.

"There were fragments of the Galdrabok still in Rotta's chamber, and other things," Halja said. "Some of them were taken by Skalk, Queen Helka's Galdurman."

Elvar frowned at that. "What other things?" she asked.

"Orna's talon, for one, or so we think," Halja said.

"Orna," Ulfrir breathed. "Ah, my beautiful, proud, fierce Orna." He cuffed another tear from his eye, and Skuld beside him shivered, a tremor rippling through the cloak about her shoulders.

"Mother," Skuld whispered. She looked at Elvar. "You could bring her back, too?"

Elvar ignored her. "This does not answer my question. How did you come by your dragon-born prisoner?"

"That is a long story," Halja said.

"Well, I'm comfortable," Sighvat said. "Though my belly is starting to rumble."

"Tell us," Elvar prompted Halja.

Orka sat back and looked around as Halja explained how the Bloodsworn had been hired by Queen Helka to discover who or what was making her people disappear. How they had discovered that the dragon-born were stealing Queen Helka's people to thrall them and send them digging out the ancient chambers.

Ulfrir was sitting with his shoulders hunched beneath wolf-pelts, his face in shadow, eyes gleaming amber. She knew he was looking at her, she saw the glint of teeth as his mouth spread in a smile.

Daughter, she heard his voice in her head, felt his presence in her blood. She tore her eyes from him and looked at the woman beside him, Skuld, who was staring at her, too, her gaze intense and piercing, like that of a predatory hawk. She nodded to Orka, as if they were old friends.

Skuld. Is she the Skuld from the saga-tales? One of the three sisters set to guard Lik-Rifa's chamber? I have walked into a saga-tale.

Orka looked away from Skuld's piercing gaze. Much of the deck was piled high, whatever was beneath it covered with a spare sail. Orka saw the glint of silver poking beneath it.

"We found the chamber," Halja continued, "fought and slew who was there, freed the thralls and left in a hurry, chasing Skalk; he stole Orna's talon, fragments of the *Raudskinna*, and . . ." Halja paused, looking at Uspa. "Vol. He has taken your sister."

"What?" Uspa breathed, going pale.

"Aye. Skalk took her and fled. Glornir is after him. Most likely has caught up with him, by now."

Uspa shook her head, lines of worry deep in her brow.

"Carry on," Elvar said, though she was looking thoughtfully at Uspa.

"That's when we met Orka," Halja said. "Looking for her son. So, some of us took her back to Rotta's chamber. One of the chambers was full of small mattresses, as if many children had been kept there. While we were there, a dragon-born rode up with a small crew at her back."

"Her name is Myrk, and she is sister to Ilska the Cruel, chief of the Raven-Feeders," Orka said. "She was sent to the chamber to collect the dragon-born still there and lead them to Ilska and

Lik-Rifa. She is still alive because she is guiding me to that meeting point."

"And where is this meeting point?" Elvar asked Orka.

"She will not tell me; she's no fool, knows that is the only reason she is still breathing. But she has said it is in the west, close to the Iskalt Islands."

"She is lying," Elvar said with a frown.

"What?" Orka said, feeling a stab of worry in her gut and a pulse of rage in her temple.

"Ilska and her Raven-Feeders are travelling east," said Elvar. "We saw their tracks turn that way at the Isbrún Bridge."

"This is true," Sighvat said.

Orka's jaw clenched, her knuckles whitening around the haft of her long-axe.

"You are sure," she growled.

"Their tracks lead east, no question," Elvar said.

"Nastrandir was in the east," Ulfrir growled. "My sister's halls. Whether they still stand after my father's destruction, I cannot say, but Lik-Rifa is a creature of habit; she is weak after three hundred years beneath the ground. She will want to go somewhere that feels familiar, where she feels safe to rest and recover her strength."

"Rotta's chamber still stands. Buried, but not destroyed," Halja said. "Perhaps this Nastrandir is the same."

"Good," Sighvat said. "Then we shall find Lik-Rifa at Nastrandir."

"Whether it still stands or not, that is not helpful if we don't know where it is," Elvar said.

"Another good point," Sighvat muttered.

"We may not know where this Nastrandir lies," Elvar said, quietly, as if talking to herself, then her gaze fixed on Orka, "but we know it was in the east, and that is where Lik-Rifa is headed now. Not west, as your prisoner has told you. So, your trail is dead to you."

I will kill Myrk. Squeeze the life from her and smile as I hear her last choking breath, Orka thought. She took a shuddering breath, calming the rage bubbling in her belly.

No. I must find Breca, and Myrk knows where he is, even if she has not told me. Yet.

"You could do something to help me," Orka said.

Elvar raised an eyebrow. "Where I come from, a favour is returned with a favour."

"Agreed," Orka said.

CHAPTER FORTY

BIÓRR

Biórr trudged through a track of snow and slush, his breath misting, moisture in his beard and the last flakes of a heavy snowfall drifting softly around him. Hints of blue sky broke through grey-clustered cloud. Beside him Storolf puffed, red-cheeked and grinning, using his long spear to steady himself on the slippery ground.

"What are you so happy about?" Biórr asked him, each breath a cloud.

"That," Storolf said, pointing ahead, and Biórr followed his gaze, saw through the clearing snow haze a wall of steep-sloped cliffs and glimpsed high, snow-capped peaks.

"The Boneback Mountains," he breathed.

"Aye, and never have I been so happy to see a pile of giant rocks," Storolf chuckled.

Biórr agreed, because seeing the Bonebacks meant they were near the end of their journey. Since they had left the warmth of the vaesen pit behind them, each day had been harder than the one before. The cold had grown sharper, a wind from the east felt like it was hurling shards of ice from the Icebound Sea at them, and then, late last night, the snow had come, swirling in a white-hazed blizzard. When he woke that morning, he had found a layer of snow over him, deep as his fist, and he had been glad for his sealskin cloak and sheepskin blanket. His beard and eyebrows had crackled with frost but marching half a day through deep snow warmed the blood and melted the frost on his face. Now he was sweating.

Ahead of him carts laboured through the slush-churned ground, many of the children they had been carrying walking alongside the carts. Partly because the carts had been getting stuck in the slush with too much weight in them, but also because it was warmer for the children to move, if they could keep the pace. Biórr saw the lad Breca, one hand still bandaged with splints and linen, walking with his squat friend, Harek. They were travelling on a track carved through knee-deep snow by Ilska and her dragon-born kin, who had used their Galdur-rune powers to melt a wide path, though it was slow going. Lik-Rifa had not helped, just sat upon her horse, looking ahead with a frown on her pale, smooth-skinned face.

Horns blew up ahead, drifting on the snow-flecked wind, signalling a brief halt for their midday meal.

They all stopped in their tracks, cartwheels creaking, horses stamping and snorting, and Biórr strode on a dozen more paces to come alongside one of the carts.

"Biórr," a voice said, and he saw Bjarn looking out at him, huddled and shivering beneath a blanket. For the first time Bjarn's eyes looked clear and bright, as Biórr remembered the lad.

Has the Seiðr-magic left his veins, now?

"Good to see you, Bjarn," Biórr said with a smile.

"I'm hungry," Bjarn said, and he gave Biórr a wan smile.

"Me, too," Storolf said as he and his father joined them. "Kráka, open a barrel, before I start gnawing at my own toes," he called out.

"You'll wait your turn," Kráka snapped back at him, though Biórr saw the hint of a smile in her eyes and a twitching at the edges of her lips. He realised he'd never seen Kráka smile before. She stood on the driver's bench and stepped over into the cart, rummaging through a row of piled barrels and crates. Settling on one, she tried to pull it free but swore when it would not move.

"Here, you need a strong arm to help you," Storolf said, clambering up into the cart, though Biórr saw the back wheel sink into the slush with his great weight.

Kráka spat an insult at Storolf but she allowed him to tug a barrel free and lift it up on to his shoulder as if it were a roll of wool. He jumped out of the cart and set the barrel down, Kráka joining them and levering the lid open with a seax at her belt.

"Bjarn, he is more himself," Biórr said to Kráka as she worked the lid loose.

"He is," she said, glancing at Bjarn. Her eyes creased and she rubbed her arm through thick layers of wool and linen.

"I was worried for him," Biórr said.

"Well, I think the Seiðr is out of him, now," she said as she went back to opening the barrel. The lid came off and then Kráka was handing out apples and slicing wedges from a round of cheese. "Here," she said to Storolf as she handed him a hard wedge, "though I do not know how you will eat that, with so many of your teeth missing. Perhaps you should wait for some porridge or skyr?"

"They don't call me Wartooth for nothing," Storolf said with a wink. "It is true that I left a few teeth in a shield once, but I think the ones I have left should be able to deal with some cheese," and he tore a large chunk off the wedge, to prove his point, then grinned, crumbs falling out through the gaps his missing teeth had left.

Kráka hid a smile and turned away, handing more food out to the children. Breca and Harek took some. "Take a lesson from this man," Kráka said to them, waving at Storolf. "Try to keep your teeth in your head, then you will not spill half of what is in your mouth on to the ground with every meal."

Storolf laughed and got down on to his knees in the slush, started snuffling around for the crumbs he had spilled. "I have Svin the boar in me," he said, looking up at them as the children fell about laughing, "I do not mind rooting around in the mud for my supper."

"Aye, well, each to their own," Kráka said.

"You should come down here and join me," Storolf said to her. "You have Snaka in your veins, a bit of slithering should be no hardship to you."

Kráka kicked at him playfully, and Storolf snorted and pretended to tusk her foot, more laughter ringing out.

"I don't know what you are laughing at," Storolf said to Harek, who had tears of laughter streaming down his cheeks. Even Breca, who was always dour-faced, had a smile tugging at his lips, the red-wealed scar under his eye twitching. "You have Svin in your veins, as you well know, so you should be getting used to this."

Fain offered his son an arm and Storolf took it, clambering back up to two feet, slipping in the slush as he did so, arms windmilling for balance and Fain caught his arm, to more laughter.

Storolf grinned and tousled Harek's hair. "You are doing well, lad," he said, "all of you are, in getting to know the god in your veins."

Since Lik-Rifa had taught them to recognise the beast in their blood, each night after their evening meal she had continued to teach the children how to understand their hidden strengths. They had been split into smaller groups, each child assigned to one of the Raven-Feeder Tainted, and so Storolf had been teaching a handful of children who had Svin the boar's blood in their veins.

"You will do even better when my brother, Kalv returns to us, eh, Papa?" Storolf said to Fain. "He is a better teacher than I am."

"That they will," Fain said, "though to my mind you're as good a teacher as any." Fain ruffled Storolf's red hair just as Storolf had done to Harek.

Something drew Biórr's eye and he looked ahead of their long column. A cloud in the distance. As it drew closer Biórr saw it was not a cloud, but the surviving tennúr, looking like a swirling flock of starlings at this distance. They moved fast and soon they were swooping down to Lik-Rifa at the head of the column, whirling and eddying around her like leaves in a storm.

"They have found something," Kráka murmured.

Biórr crested a ridge and slowed, a wall of biting wind almost throwing him back down the slope he had just climbed. The path ahead sloped downwards, an icy trail that wound through a serpent-shaped promontory of sharp-faced crags, bordered to the south by a towering escarpment of cliffs wreathed in cloud. At the feet of those cliffs rolled huge waves, each one taller than a mead hall, smashing and churning against the battered cliffs in an endless assault, white-tipped and savage. The constant roar of the sea filled Biórr's ears, punctuated by the mournful calling of gulls.

"The Icebound Sea," he murmured.

Lik-Rifa was riding at the head of their column, the swarm of tennúr hovering over her like some dark cloud. Ilska and Drekr rode either side of Lik-Rifa, the other dragon-born in a thin line behind them, and then marched the bulk of Ilska's Raven-Feeders. Behind them the carts trundled, juddering across the rocky peninsula. Biórr, Fain and Storolf had taken to walking in the company of the carts. Biórr spent much of his time chatting with Bjarn, who seemed almost back to the lad he had been in Snakavik. Storolf didn't complain either, as he seemed to be enjoying trading words with Kráka.

"Come on, stand still too long and your stones might freeze," Storolf called over the howling wind, looking back over his shoulder at Biórr.

"Always worrying about your stones freezing," Biórr muttered.

The scrape of many feet behind him and Biórr glanced back to see the last of their column crest the ridge, the score or so of dragon-worshippers. He pulled his cloak tighter around him and trudged on. Somewhere ahead he heard a horn call and the column shuddered to a halt.

"Biórr, what's happening?" Bjarn called to him from the back of Kráka's cart, his voice snatched and strangled by the constant wind.

"I don't know," he muttered and walked on, finding a path through warriors, children and carts until he turned a bend in the winding track and had a better view.

Lik-Rifa had reined in her horse and dismounted. She was walking on ahead, a sharp word and upheld hand stopping Ilska and Drekr from following her. She strode along an icy path, a hundred, two hundred paces, more, until she was just a dark spike walking through foam-flecked spume. Towering cliffs rose before her, patched with scree and twisted, wind-blasted trees scattered across the slopes. Lik-Rifa stopped before them, gazing up at the cloud-wreathed heights.

The air shimmered around Lik-Rifa, like a heat haze, and then her body was shifting, growing, neck stretching, wings sprouting and elongating, a sinuous tail lashing. She grew and grew, Biórr newly staggered by the size and majesty of Lik-Rifa in her dragon form. Her scales were slick and shining with sea-spray and Biórr saw that she looked even more fearsome than when she had burst from Oskutreð's depths. Scars still latticed her body and neck, but they were not scabbed or weeping pus now, and her bones were not standing out stark and rigid through her pale, scaled skin. She looked strong.

As Biórr and the rest of them stood and stared Lik-Rifa's wings stretched wide, blotting out the sea. Her serpentine neck arched, huge jaws opening, and she let out a bellowing, bone-shaking roar. The ground beneath Biórr's feet trembled, rocks and scree on the cliff face tumbling and hissing in a landslide that crashed into the sea, sending up gouts of white foam.

"NASTRANDIR," Lik-Rifa roared, shaking the mountains, echoing on and on. When finally the roar faded Biórr saw Lik-Rifa's jaws moving and heard her voice ululating on the wind, sounding more like a saga-song that a skáld would sing around the hearth fire.

"*Ormsalur, hristu af Þér Þennan klettahylk, farðu aftur til mín,*" the dragon sang, over and over, her voice echoing among the cliffs and crags, rising and falling on the wind. Slowly Biórr became aware of a vibrating beneath his feet. The cliffs before Lik-Rifa, dwarfing even her bulk, began to shimmer and ripple. A cloud of dust burst from them, like a dog shaking off water, and then great explosions of earth and rock were launched into the air, huge boulders and slabs of rock hurled up into the sky, raining down into the sea and crashing around Lik-Rifa. It felt like the world was ending and Biórr was thrown to the ground, all around him people dropping, horses neighing and rearing, carts groaning and creaking. Sea-spray and dust merged into a rapidly unfolding wall that masked Lik-Rifa from view and swept over the promontory, enveloping the whole column of travellers. Biórr pushed himself up on to hands and knees, turned but could only see shadowy shapes in the damp murk.

Slowly the cloud settled about him, the wind tearing and ripping at it, the sea still roaring. Biórr climbed unsteadily to his feet, wiping sea-spray and dust from his face.

Lik-Rifa stood before the cliff face, although it was not a cliff any more. Huge doors of black granite towered before Lik-Rifa, taller and wider than the dragon, edged in glistening silver. Around the doors the rock of the cliff face was moving, untold stone serpents carved into the face undulating and twisting, each one wide as a tower, their heads of fanged granite rearing and hissing, fangs bared. All of them loomed high and then swept low, bowing before Lik-Rifa.

The dragon turned to look down at Ilska and the rest of the column.

"Welcome to my home," she said, her deep-chested voice rumbling across the promontory.

CHAPTER FORTY-ONE

GUÐVARR

"I am sorry," Guðvarr said.

"For what?" Jarl Sigrún said, a raised eyebrow twisting the scar that ran through her face. They were sitting in a chamber at the rear of the longhouse that Queen Helka had provided for Jarl Sigrún and her retinue. It was the only place where they had anything resembling privacy, although even here Jarl Sigrún had warned Guðvarr to speak cautiously and quietly.

"I am sorry for not bringing Orka's head back to you," Guðvarr said. "I tried, was close, but . . ." Images of Orka's blood-soaked face, amber eyes blazing, sharp teeth snarling. He blinked and shook his head. "She is more than she seemed; Orka. Tainted. And she had unnatural help. Vaesen. We were lucky to escape with our lives."

"I know," Jarl Sigrún said. A single torch burned in the chamber, bathing his aunt's face in flickering orange and dark shadow.

"You deserve her head, deserve your revenge," Guðvarr snarled, despising himself for a moment.

Everything I have, my aunt has given me, and I could not do this one thing for her.

"Revenge? I do not care so much about that," Jarl Sigrún said.

Guðvarr frowned. "How can you not? She has left you scarred; she slew your lover."

"Aye," Sigrún sighed. "But there are other lovers to be had, and I still breathe."

"Then why did you send me after her, if not for your revenge?" Guðvarr asked.

"Because Orka made me appear weak, and that I *cannot* allow. I became jarl of Fellur by my own strength, both of body and wit; by grit and bloody-minded determination, and to appear weak, especially among this pack of snapping, scavenging dogs . . ." She shook her head.

"Who?" Guðvarr frowned.

"Helka and her petty jarls: Glunn Iron-Grip, Svard the Scratcher, Illur Storm-Crow. They are all here, thinking they can smell my weakness, like blood in the water. They would all like my lands added to their own."

"I will kill them," Guðvarr snapped.

"Aye, perhaps you will," Jarl Sigrún said. "But only when I ask you to," she added, giving him a hard look. "But there is more to being jarl than brute strength. There is guile. In a *holmganga* duel, many a contest is won by guile and deceit. A feint that opens up your enemy to your sharp edge."

Guðvarr nodded. "It is often the unseen blow that ends the fight," he murmured, repeating the words that Sigrún had drummed into him in the weapons yard.

"Just so," Jarl Sigrún said, her lips twisting in what now passed for a smile. "Orka's head in a sack would have been helpful, but it is not the end. Perhaps this is a time for guile, rather than brute strength."

"I wish we could go home, back to Fellur," Guðvarr said. *I hate this place and its people, that smile at you and say honeyed words, and then plant monsters in your flesh.*

"You cannot leave Darl, now. Skalk has your life in his fist."

"I know," growled Guðvarr, hating the reminder. "Why do you not just go to Helka and demand that she order Skalk to release me?" *It seems like the obvious, and most pain-free option.*

"Because I am not certain that she would do as I ask," Sigrún said. "The fact that Skalk has the audacity to do this to you, and to kill Arild and my other *drengrs*," she shook her head. "It suggests he thinks he can act with impunity. I am important to Helka and her plans, but I am not indispensable. What if she chose Skalk over me? It would not be long before we were all being stuffed into barrels. Best not to step out into the marshland until the path ahead is clear."

Guðvarr nodded, though he seethed inside. *I hate Skalk, and Helka, and this place.*

"But, even if we did not have your . . . circumstances to deal with," Jarl Sigrún continued, "I could not go back to Fellur. Queen Helka has asked me, and her other jarls, to stay. She has invited Jarl Orlyg of Svelgarth for a meeting. He has sent messengers to say he is coming."

"Jarl Orlyg!" Guðvarr said. "Queen Helka's enemy."

Jarl Sigrún nodded.

"And he is coming? Why stick your head into this den of vipers?"

"A good question," Sigrún said. "Perhaps Helka is offering peace, or a pact? She has Jarl Störr on her western border and Jarl Orlyg on her eastern. She cannot move decisively against one without leaving her back open for a sharp blade from the other."

"So, befriend one enemy so that she can slay the other."

Jarl Sigrún smiled. "Guile," she said.

Guðvarr heard horns blowing throughout the fortress and looked at his aunt.

"Well, someone important is new-come to Darl," Sigrún said, "those horns don't blow for everyone. They didn't blow for me." She looked at Guðvarr. "Let's go and see." She stood and walked out of the chamber and through the gloom of the longhouse's main hall out into the light of day, a handful of her guards following.

They had only walked a short way towards the fortress gates when a procession appeared; two score of Helka's *drengrs* escorting two men.

Jarl Sigrún stepped aside, allowing the procession to pass her by. Guðvarr caught up with her and peered at the warriors marching through the fortress.

The two men the *drengrs* were escorting were Prince Hakon and the *Úlfhéðnar*, Frek. Hakon looked far better than the last time Guðvarr had seen him.

He has some clothes on, at least, and he is still wearing the cloak I put around his shoulders. Caught humping while the Bloodsworn were storming the fortress; I'm not sure whether to respect him or scorn him.

Jarl Sigrún jabbed an elbow into Guðvarr's ribs.

Get the job done.

"Welcome home, great prince," Guðvarr called out, drawing Hakon's eye.

The prince stared at Guðvarr a moment, clearly not knowing who it was that called his name, but then Guðvarr was sure he saw a glimmer of recognition in Hakon's eye. The prince gave him a curt nod. Frek the *Úlfhéðnar* looked at Guðvarr with flat, dead eyes.

Then the procession was passing them by.

"Good," Jarl Sigrún breathed, and then she was walking after the prince. Guðvarr and her guards followed her.

As they marched to Helka's mead hall, the great skeletal wings of Orna spreading wide over them, a crowd gathered behind the prince's escort; warriors and thralls, craftsmen and whores, all come to watch the prince's return.

The *drengr* escort led Hakon and Frek through the open doors of the mead hall, Jarl Sigrún and Guðvarr first behind them, many more following behind.

Queen Helka was seated in a chair on the dais of the main hall, listening to a handful of merchants. As Hakon strode through his escort to stand before her the merchants fell silent and Queen Helka stood and walked down to him.

"Welcome home, my son," Queen Helka said, and allowed him to kiss her hand. Then she looked at the crowd gathered in the hall.

"We shall feast tonight," she said, "to celebrate the safe return of my son."

The crowd roared its appreciation.

Everyone loves a feast, Guðvarr thought. *None more than I.*

CHAPTER FORTY-TWO

BIÓRR

Biórr stood on the tip of the icy promontory and stared up at the entrance to Nastrandir, which reared tall and wide before him. A huge black hole gaping in the side of a mountain, although it did not seem to be a mountain any more, but a seething, writhing nest of granite serpents. Each serpent slithered and twisted around the gateway, like animated statues, each one as wide and thick as Lik-Rifa in her dragon form.

It made Biórr uncomfortable about stepping over the threshold and entering the dark hall beyond, and, judging by Fain's and Storolf's gawping faces, Biórr was not the only one who felt that way. The tramp of feet behind urged him on. Fain nudged Storolf and the three of them stepped into the darkness side by side.

"*Logi, logandi bjartur,*" Lik-Rifa said from somewhere ahead. She was back in her human form now, wreathed in shadow, and then flames were bursting into life, crackling from within enormous braziers wider than shields, some placed on pedestals, others looking like they were carved at various heights into the rough-hewn walls. Biórr saw they were walking into a huge hall, wide and high enough for a score of dragons to walk or fly. The thud of hooves, creak of cartwheels and scrape of shoes echoed on dry stone. Rows of thick serpent-carved pillars stretched upwards and onwards into a dense, vertiginous blackness high above. Lik-Rifa strode along an aisle between two wide rows of pillars, Ilska, Drekr and the

Raven-Feeders following at a distance behind her. Biórr looked around him as he followed, the immensity of this one hall making him feel dizzy. Here and there shafts of light sliced down from high walls, beams of daylight arcing through cracks and fissures in the walls. Long tables and benches were scattered around the hall, clustered around empty, ash-filled hearth-fire pits.

The last of their column entered the chamber and the great doors swung closed with a reverberating crash.

Ahead of them Lik-Rifa came to a handful of steps cut into the stone. She climbed them and sat in a stone-carved chair; as she leaned back into it the stone shifting around her, sinuous movements as the high-backed chair divided into serpents, smaller versions of the ones that guarded the gateway. Lik-Rifa reached out a hand and stroked a scaly head, mouth opening to let out a rasping hiss.

"Welcome to Nastrandir, my hall," she said as Ilska and the Raven-Feeders stood before her. "Rest now, for you are under my protection here. We are all safe here; it is a good place to recover and gather our strength. And to plan the way forward." She looked around. "A little careworn, perhaps, for lack of a tending hand, but we shall put some life and warmth back into this place soon enough." She opened her mouth to say something else, then paused as one of the stone serpents that coiled around her chair hovered before her ear, mouth open, stone tongue flickering. Lik-Rifa cocked her head, like a hound listening to a sound that humans could not hear.

Lik-Rifa's face darkened into a scowl and she stood, turned and looked down at her chair.

"Someone has been here," she snarled. Then she was striding down the steps and marching towards the rear of the great cavern, barking orders, and more braziers of flame came crackling to life before her, lighting her way. The tennúr swirled above, flitting in and out of the shadows like bats at dusk. Biórr and everyone else followed, Biórr shrugging his shield from his back and gripping his spear a little tighter.

They left this giant chamber by a tunnel that was still broad and tall enough for Lik-Rifa's dragon to walk or fly through it. She led them on through a series of chambers and tunnels, past a stone pier and a line of moored boats that rose and fell on the swell of ice-touched water, Biórr seeing two serpent-prowed *drakkars* among a handful of *snekkes*. Lik-Rifa led them on, until she stood before closed doors. Light leaked through gaps.

"*Opinn*," Lik-Rifa roared, and the two great doors were hurled inwards, as if kicked by a bull troll.

Biórr stood and stared, feet set, shield and spear raised. All around him stood in mute astonishment.

They were looking into another chamber, not as expansive as the one with Lik-Rifa's throne, but still large enough to accommodate a full-grown dragon. Hearth fires burned and the scents of a hundred different foods drifted tantalisingly in the air. Deer and boar turned on spits and dripped fat on to fires, food of all manner laid out on long tables: warm bread, rounds of cheese, platters of fresh fish, heaped bowls of turnip and kale, jugs of ale and mead, pots of honey.

People moved in the chamber, a score or so men and women tending to the tables and turning meat on spits, music filtering from a group gathered at the back of the hall, the sweet notes of a lyre and the rhythmic humming buzz of mouth harps. The music faded as all in the hall stopped and stared at Lik-Rifa.

A man sat on a bench close to the open doorway. Even though he was seated, Biórr could tell that he was exceptionally tall and lean, with long brown hair oiled and tied neatly into braids that were fixed with a long silver pin. His beard was close-cropped and oiled. Dark, bright-glistening eyes sat in a starkly handsome, slightly stretched face, tips of teeth protruding beneath a wide mouth, as if he had too many of them for his lips to contain. He was leaning back and grinning, and the grin did not falter as he stood and took a few steps towards Lik-Rifa, his arms opening wide.

"Welcome home, sister," he said.

"Rotta!" Lik-Rifa breathed.

"Hope you don't mind," Rotta said. "I've been looking after the place while you were away."

CHAPTER FORTY-THREE

GUÐVARR

Guðvarr sat at a bench in the mead hall and drank from a horn of ale. It was good, dark and salty, and Guðvarr held it out for a thrall to refill.

The hall was crowded and hot, a boar turning on a spit over the hearth fire, smoke from rush torches and oil burning, churning sluggishly in the eaves around Orna's pale-gleaming bones. Men and women were eating and drinking, though most of the eating was now over, trenchers and bowls of food half empty, racks of bones half gnawed. Hounds snapped and snarled beneath the benches as they fought over scraps. The hall was full of warriors laughing and talking, some wrestling, occasionally fighting, though Queen Helka's *Úlfhéðnar* were a presence that helped to temper any serious bloodletting. Queen Helka sat at the top table, her son Hakon one side of her and her daughter Estrid the other. Further along the top bench sat Skalk, his head all bandaged and his one eye glowering out at the hall of feasting *drengrs*. Jarl Sigrún was seated next to him, as were the other petty jarls still in Darl: Glunn Iron-Grip and Svard the Scratcher. Guðvarr saw that his aunt was looking at him as he raised a fresh-filled horn to his lips and saw a frown flicker across her face.

"Don't let drink cloud my wits", she would tell me if she were sitting next to me. He smiled at her. *But she isn't sitting next to me, and I have been through a difficult time, with almost certainly darker times still to come.* He raised the horn to her in a mock-toast and drank deep.

Jarl Sigrún's frown deepened, but Guðvarr looked away.

He saw two men enter the hall and make their way to Queen Helka's table, only stopping as Helka's *Úlfhéðnar* emerged to bar their way.

One of the men was tall and broad, a thick snarl of black beard on a weathered face. A scar ran down one cheek and through his lips. He had the look of a merchant or a wealthy farmer about him, wearing a wool hat trimmed with fur, a fine cloak of red wool and an embroidered woollen tunic, a seax hanging at his belt. The other was a warrior, dressed in mail with an axe and seax at his belt. His fair hair was lank and greasy, tied at his nape, his beard thin and wispy. His eyes were pale to the point of opaqueness and watering in the smoke-thick hall. He had a shield slung across his back, Guðvarr glimpsing an eye painted in golden scrollwork upon it.

Their voices rose over the *Úlfhéðnar* who were blocking their way to the queen and Guðvarr leaned forward in his chair to hear better.

"Just a moment is all I ask," the man with the black beard was saying, "just to ask one question of my queen."

"Let him through," Helka said with an annoyed wave of her hand and the *Úlfhéðnar* shifted to let black-beard through, but closed up before the other man could join him.

"This is no Justice Day," Helka said, referring to when she would sit in judgement on all matters and disputes brought before her.

"No dispute, my queen, I only hoped that you would grant me your ear, as evidence of your joy and celebration at your son's safe return," the man with the black beard said, pulling off his fur cap and dipping his head.

Helka gave the man a long, hard look, then her lips twisted in the glimmer of a smile, and she dipped her head.

"Say what you have come to say," she said.

"My name is Leif Kolskeggson. I am a farmer in your district and pay my taxes. I am here to ask permission to hunt an outlaw. A man who is both my enemy and yours, I have been told."

"And who is this man?" Helka said.

"A man named Varg."

Varg! The arseling with the cleaver.

"He is a thrall from my farm who murdered my father, stole his silver and fled."

I knew he was no good.

"Of course you may hunt him," Helka said with a frown and a flick of her hand. "Murderers and thieves must be punished. Why are you even asking?"

"Because this *niðing*, troll-shite, goat-humping . . ." he trailed off into incomprehensible, wordless snarls, his face purpling, veins bulging, then sucked in a deep breath. "Sorry, my queen. The death of my father weighs heavy on me. I am here before you because this Varg has come under the protection of the Bloodsworn. He is one of them. I heard that they were your enemy, had dared to attack you in your own hall, but that they had also taken a job from you. I do not wish to do something that would displease you."

"You mean, you don't want to hunt and kill him, only for me to have your neck stretched and corpse picked clean by crows," Helka said.

"Uh, yes," Leif Kolskeggson said.

"Plain talk, Leif, that is always the best way forward," Helka said. "And my answer to your question is this; hunt this Varg. Maim him, hang him, boil him alive in his own blood for all I care. The Bloodsworn took my son as hostage, but as you can see, he is back beside me now. I wish nothing but ill upon the Bloodsworn. But you are a farmer, you say. The Bloodsworn are . . . formidable. How do you think you can take one of theirs?"

Formidable? I killed one of them without too much trouble.

"You are right, my queen, I am a humble farmer, not a trained warrior or killer of men. But I know right from wrong, and I am the owner of a wealthy farm and a chest of silver that will fund that justice." He looked over his shoulder at the pale-eyed man. "I have hired him to help me. Sterkur death-in-the-eye, and his band of mercenaries."

Guðvarr blinked at that, staring at the pale-eyed man with renewed interest. He had heard skálds sing of Sterkur, of his feats of strength and cunning. Of his prowess in the *holmganga* ring.

He does not look much like a saga-hero to me, but, then, if I've learned one thing since leaving Fellur village, it is that looks can be deceiving.

Queen Helka looked from Leif to Sterkur.

"I wish you well. Hunt this Varg with my blessing."

You have my blessing also. Hunt him down and kill him like the piece of weasel-shite he is.

"And here is some information that may help you," Helka continued. "The Bloodsworn have sailed from Liga, in pursuit of a prince of Iskidan. Jaromir is his name. I suspect they are all somewhere in Iskidan, by now."

"My thanks, great queen," Leif said as he bowed low to Helka. Then he was turning on his heel and striding away, the *Úlfhéðnar* letting him through and Sterkur following him out of the hall.

A scraping of wood as Queen Helka stood, a handful of *Úlfhéðnar* slipping out of the shadows behind her to stand closer. Silence settled over the hall.

"A challenge to welcome my son back to us, before I have a host of people filling my hall with their requests," Helka said. She turned to look at Hakon. "It's your feast, so you choose."

Guðvarr sat straighter in his bench. He loved a good feast, but it was a challenge at the end that always made it memorable, whether it was a *flyting* war of words, wrestling, axe-throwing or any other chance to show off.

Hakon tugged at his short beard as he looked around the hall, silence heavy as all waited for his decision.

"The shield-dance," Hakon said and the hall erupted with cheers and shouting. Guðvarr leaped to his feet, grinning, and swayed. Many hands set to dragging the benches back and *drengrs* reached for their shields where they had been left leaning against the hall's walls.

"Who will compete?" Queen Helka cried out and Guðvarr thrust himself forward.

"I will," Jarl Glunn Iron-Grip shouted, a squat, broad man with legs like tree trunks. He was fair-haired and young, not many more years on his shoulders than Guðvarr. "If the prince will race against me?" He smiled at Hakon, who looked to his mother, then gave Glunn a curt nod.

Guðvarr shoved and twisted through a crowd of forty or fifty, knowing that Hakon would only choose a dozen more.

The prince stepped from behind his table and stood at the edge of the dais, looking out over the crowd of volunteers while others set to preparing the hall.

"Hafrun, Bersi, Gunilla," Hakon called out, pointing into the jostling, laughing crowd. All three stepped up on to the dais, grinning.

He is choosing those he knows, Guðvarr realised. He kicked the woman in front of him in the back of the knee and, as she stumbled, he slipped through the gap to stand in front of her, then twisted sideways and pushed through two more until he was standing in the second row. All the while Hakon was calling out more names and the dais around the prince was filling with chosen competitors.

"Welcome home, Prince Hakon," Guðvarr yelled, cupping his hands to his mouth.

Hakon heard him and paused, eyes searching Guðvarr out. He put a hand to the cloak he was wearing and Guðvarr nodded.

"You," Hakon said, pointing to Guðvarr. With relief and excitement flooding him he stepped up on to the dais. Ten others were standing around him, and Hakon looked into the crowd to choose the final challenger.

"I'm in," a languid voice said behind Guðvarr and he turned to see Estrid tying her hair into a tight braid as she walked up to her brother.

"My feast, my choice," Hakon said.

"Hakon," Queen Helka said, giving him a look.

Hakon's lips twisted and Estrid smiled.

"Afraid I might beat you, big brother?" she asked him.

"No," he snapped.

Queen Helka clapped her hands.

"Shields," she cried out.

Guðvarr saw two rows of warriors arrayed in a loose, double

circle around the hall. They raised a shield between them, resting the rims on their shoulders, so that the shields were like floating stepping stones across a stream. The shield-dance was a challenge often performed in the training yard, one of the first ways of preparing young warriors for the oar-dance on a *drakkar*. This was easier, and there was no threat of getting wet if you fell, but with a few horns of ale in each contestant's belly it would feel more like they were on a swaying longship than in a mead hall.

Hakon led the way to the first shield, where a handful of thralls and freedmen and women stood, all holding drinking horns and jugs of ale. Hakon took a horn full of frothing ale and drank it back, smacking his lips, laughing and climbing up on to a bench and then leaping up on to the first shield, where he stood, swaying and finding his balance as the two warriors holding the shield adjusted their stance to take his weight.

"Begin," Queen Helka shouted.

Hakon leaped from the first shield to the next, legs bent as the shield wobbled, and then on to the next. Estrid had emptied her drinking horn and was climbing up on to the first shield, leaping on without a pause. Jarl Glunn was next to climb up, the *drengrs* holding the first shield grunting under his weight. He laughed as he leaped to the next shield, well balanced and light on his feet for his mass. Two more were standing before Guðvarr and they hastily drained their drinking horns and clambered up on to the shield, leaping away. One landed too far to the left, slipped and went crashing to the ground as the hall erupted with hoots of laughter.

Guðvarr held his horn out to be filled, his eyes fixed on the first shield. His blood was thrumming, heart pounding with excitement.

"Drink up," a voice said, and he looked to see that it was red-haired Vilja who was filling his drinking horn. She smiled at him, leaned forward and stroked the inside of his leg.

"Winners get a prize," she whispered into his ear.

He drained his horn, grinned, wiped his nose and clambered up on to the first shield. He stood there a moment, finding his balance, and then he was off, leaping nimbly from one shield to the next.

He laughed with the joy of it, because he knew he was good at this, had always won the shield-dance tournament in Fellur village, and the oar-dance on Sigrún's *drakkar*. The hall was full of noise, the warriors holding the shields thumping a rhythm on them, the crowd filling the hall shouting and roaring encouragement. As Guðvarr slowed and leaned to round the first half-circle he glimpsed Queen Helka standing on the dais, Sigrún close to her. His aunt gave him an encouraging smile, but beside her Skalk was glowering and he remembered the hyrndur buried in his chest. He swayed and tottered a moment, one arm flailing and the roar of the crowd rose as they readied for another fall, but he managed to find his balance and complete the turn, leaping on towards the starting point. Hakon had already passed it, sweeping up a new-filled drinking horn and gulping as he leaped. Estrid was three shields behind him and Jarl Glunn one shield behind her, then there was a gap of five or six to the next contestant. Shields thudded behind Guðvarr as other contestants leaped after him. He heard a mistimed thud behind him, a squawk and a crash, followed by another roar of the crowd as another challenger fell.

Ha, how embarrassing, he thought as he leaped on. Quickly Guðvarr caught up with the warrior in front of him, a whip-thin man with black hair tied at the nape. He quickened his pace and landed on the next shield as the man in front of him was leaping off it. The shield rim bucked upwards and clipped the dark-haired warrior's heel, ruining his landing and then he was tumbling to the ground in a splay of limbs. Guðvarr laughed as he hurtled past him.

As he neared the starting point, he bent his legs and stooped, snatching up the drinking horn that Vilja held up to him, her eyes alight with promise. He ran on, surefooted and nimble, drawing ever closer to Jarl Glunn, and swilled more ale as he landed on the next shield, half of it running down his chin into his beard, drained the rest of the horn and threw it as he pushed off, landed again. Only one shield separated him from Glunn Iron-Grip now. The man was heavy and slow, but his balance was excellent and Guðvarr could see him carrying on round the shield ring until the sun rose, whereas Guðvarr's chest was already heaving, his lungs burning.

Another crash behind him and he snatched a glance back, saw three figures flying through the air, others tottering and swaying as shields bucked and rippled, more bodies crunching into them. Ahead Hakon was catching up to the last challengers and he leaped and pushed the warrior in front of him, sending the man spinning and squawking, crashing to the ground amid a roar of laughter from the crowd.

Got to get past Iron-Grip, the fat ox, Guðvarr thought, *or I'm never going to catch Hakon*. He jumped just as Iron-Grip was bunching his legs for his next leap, landed on the jarl's shield, sending him rocking and swaying, stepped nimbly around Glunn while he was slack-jawed, gaping and shocked, and then leaped away as the jarl snarled and lashed out, trying to grab Guðvarr's arm.

Guðvarr landed on the next shield, laughing, while behind him Glunn shouted curses and all around them the crowd howled their appreciation.

Sweat was dripping into his eyes, the heat and smoke in the room suffocating, his lungs burning, but Guðvarr hardly felt any of it. It had been a long time since he had smiled or laughed, but now he felt invincible, as surefooted as the dead god Rotta. Ahead of him Estrid drew closer, leaping, landing, leaping again, drinking from her horn in mid-leap to thunderous cheers from the crowd. She was so close to Hakon, just an eye-blink between them, and from the angle of her head and the set of her shoulders Guðvarr could tell she was close to doing exactly what he had just done to Glunn Iron-Grip. He risked a backward glance and saw that all the challengers had fallen apart from Jarl Glunn, who followed as doggedly and resolutely as a hound, though there were eight or nine shields separating them now.

He looked ahead and saw the muscles in Estrid's legs bunch and so he leaped, harder and faster, flying through the air, then thumping down on to her shield and crashing into the princess just as her feet left the shield. The two of them careened through the air, limbs flailing, and Guðvarr caught a fractured glimpse of Jarl Glunn staring at them and missing his footing, falling, and then Guðvarr was crunching on to the ground, rolling in the rushes, feet and legs all around him. He came to a halt and just lay there, looking up at the bones of Orna in the eaves, his chest heaving. A hound's head appeared over him and licked his nose.

He heard a shout of anger and felt hands gripping him, hauling him upright and then he was looking into the face of Estrid.

"You stupid *hálfviti* idiot," she snarled at him, straw poking from her hair.

Don't call me stupid.

"Sorry, my lady," he mumbled.

Her eyes narrowed. "You did it on purpose. Is Hakon paying you, or are you just another snivelling, arse-kissing groveller?"

I wish I were getting paid, but I'm only doing this because there's a monster living in my chest.

Then the crowd was roaring and they both turned to see Hakon leap past the starting and finishing point. He stumbled to a halt, stood swaying on a shield, thrust his arms in the air and yelled a victory cry. The noise of the crowd became deafening and Guðvarr took the opportunity to slip away from the irate princess.

He shoved his way through the crowd as Hakon leaped to the ground and was immediately handed a horn of ale, which he slurped noisily. Queen Helka stepped to the front of the dais and the hall quietened. She beckoned to Hakon, who jumped up beside her, red-faced and grinning, and then calls were going out to the other contestants, calling them up on to the dais. Guðvarr stepped up to join them. Glunn Iron-Grip appeared beside him, shorter than Guðvarr but broader and thick-muscled.

"A fine move," Jarl Glunn said, a smile on his face, and Guðvarr nodded a thanks.

Estrid pushed past Guðvarr, glaring at him as she did so, and stood in second place beside Hakon.

"You did well, sister," Hakon said with a grin. "Keep practising and perhaps one day you'll be as good as me."

"Shut up," Estrid snapped. "I'd not be surprised to find out you paid that stupid snot-nosed oaf to trip me."

I said, don't call me stupid, Guðvarr thought. *Wait a moment . . . "snot-nosed"?* Absently he wiped his nose with the back of his hand.

"It was an accident, my lady," Guðvarr said. "I passed Jarl Glunn on the shields doing the same manoeuvre, but alas, I mistimed it with you." He leaned forwards to look at Hakon. "Well run, Prince Hakon, a masterful display."

"My thanks," Hakon said, grinning. "Yes, it was." He grinned harder, looking at Estrid, who stared out at the crowd.

Thralls walked along the line of contestants, handing out fresh horns of ale.

A silence settled as Queen Helka took Hakon's wrist in her hand and lifted his arm.

"To the winner," Queen Helka called out.

Hakon drank deep.

The crowd cheered, ale and mead flowing.

I wonder if Hakon will end up at The Dead Drengr *tonight?*

"To Hakon the Humper," someone shouted out, sending laughter rippling through the hall. Hakon looked as if he were unsure whether to feel insulted or complimented, finally deciding it was not a fair-fame name to be ashamed of, and grinned.

Talking of The Dead Drengr *and humping*, Guðvarr thought, *where's Vilja?* He scanned the crowd and saw her. She was smiling at him. He emptied his drinking horn and threw it over his shoulder.

CHAPTER FORTY-FOUR

BIÓRR

Biórr stared at the man standing in the chamber's entrance, tall and lean, wearing a pale blue tunic with fine tablet weave at its hems, a seax and hand-axe at his belt and rings of gold and silver on his arms.

"Rotta, what are you doing here?" Lik-Rifa said.

Rotta! The god Rotta? Rotta the rat? But . . . he's dead.

Rotta shrugged, still smiling. "Thought I'd prepare a fitting welcome for you." He gave an elaborate bow.

"But you're dead," Lik-Rifa said.

"Rumours of my demise have been greatly exaggerated," Rotta said, smiling even more widely, revealing white-gleaming teeth.

"When did you escape your prison?" she asked him.

Rotta's smile faded.

"Before or after the *Guðfalla*?" Lik-Rifa pressed, an edge to her voice that made Biórr uncomfortable. "Before or *after* I was imprisoned."

A silence, then Lik-Rifa took a step forward, her fists bunching. Rotta took a step back.

"Do not lie to me," Lik-Rifa snarled.

"I think, if we are going to be completely accurate, it was *during* the *Guðfalla*," he said.

"You should have come to me, fought for me," Lik-Rifa said, that edge still in her voice.

I won't be surprised if she eats you, Rotta, Biórr thought, making sure he was light on his toes and ready to leap away.

"I did think about it," Rotta said. "I wanted to, even."

"Then why did you not come?" Lik-Rifa said, anger in her voice, but something else, too. *Hurt? Disappointment?*

Rotta's smile faded and withered. "I was . . . scared," he said. "Look what they did to me. Orna and Ulfrir. *Afhjúpa*," he said as he waved a hand across his face. The air seemed to shimmer and ripple around him and then his face was changing, shifting, the beard withering away, his fine cheekbones sinking, holes and ragged tears appearing in his flesh, pus weeping, his jaw shrinking, lips drooping like a drained skin of ale.

"They chained me to a rock, and caged poisonous serpents above me, enchanting them so that their venom dripped and burned me every moment of every day and night." His voice quivered as he spoke, a tear rolling down his cheek and long lines of saliva dripping from his ruined mouth. "Every day I live in pain," he hissed, tremors twitching through his face and body. "*Leyna,*" he said, casting his hand across his face and the air rippled again, this time his face shifting back to the handsome, neat-bearded man he had appeared when the doors had opened.

"I wanted to come and help you, and fight those *niðing* . . ." his voice trailed off, became an unintelligible, white-frothing snarl. "Orna and Ulfrir," he said with a shudder, breathing deep. "I wanted my *vengeance* on them, but I was scared of losing, scared that they would chain me up again. And then, after the battle was done, I discovered that those three bitches, Skuld, Urd and Verdani, were guarding your chamber, and you know how they hated me," he added, smiling again.

"You killed their sister, skinned her alive and used her blood to write your Galdrabok," Lik-Rifa said with a shrug.

"Yes, yes, I know that," Rotta said. "I didn't say they didn't have good cause to hate me, but nevertheless, they were not three people I wanted to come face to face with. Especially after what their cursed mother and father had done to me." He shivered. "Those three bitches are the reason I have stayed clear of Oskutreð all these years."

"I ate them," Lik-Rifa smiled. "Well, one of them, anyway. Ilska and Drekr slew another, what good children they are. As for Skuld . . ." Lik-Rifa frowned. "I don't recall."

"Good that two of those bitches are dead," Rotta said.

"But you should have come to me. I needed you," Lik-Rifa said, though the flicker of violence had drained from her voice.

"I am sorry," Rotta said and took a tentative step forward. "Please believe me when I say I wanted to come. Fear is a terrible thing. But," he grinned again, "on the brighter side, you are free now. So, all's well that ends well."

"This is not over yet," Lik-Rifa said. "Ulfrir lives."

"What?" Rotta said, his face twisting with a ripple of fear and hate.

"I have written my own Galdrabok. Three hundred years in the dark beneath Oskutreð is a lot of time to fill," Lik-Rifa growled. "Unfortunately, it has fallen into the wrong hands."

Rotta bit back words, let out a twisted sound, then sucked in a deep breath. "Well, no use dwelling on past mistakes," Rotta said. "I am here now, and will stand with you, this time. Together we will end Ulfrir, for all time." He gave her a hesitant smile. "I have missed you, sister," he said, and stepped closer to Lik-Rifa, his arms opening. "And, look, I have prepared a warm homecoming for you."

Lik-Rifa said nothing, just stood there, and slowly, gently, Rotta wrapped his arms around her and hugged her. At first Lik-Rifa stood rigid and frozen, but then, equally slowly, her arms rose to hold him, and she seemed to sink into his embrace.

"I have missed you, too," Biórr heard her whisper.

Biórr sat on a bench, eating and drinking, Fain and Storolf beside him. He had not felt so full of fine food and ale for as long as he could remember. But added to the sense of contentment seeping through his body was the fact that he was sitting on a bench before Rotta, the rat god. *His* god. The father of his bloodline.

Rotta's blood runs in my veins, and he is sitting right there, eating and drinking and laughing with Lik-Rifa the dragon. Strangely, it felt *right*, as if without realising it Biórr had been waiting for this moment his whole life. He leaned back on his bench and laughed out loud. No one looked at him as if it were out of place, because everyone was smiling and laughing, the ale flowing and music playing, echoing through the shadow-shrouded, cavernous hall. The only two faces Biórr saw that were not smiling were Kráka and Bjarn. Kráka was leaning and whispering in Bjarn's ear, and Bjarn was staring down at his hands while she spoke, eyes round and serious.

A whirr of wings and one of the tennúr landed on the table in front of Storolf, who was slurping on a bowl of fish stew. He was the tennúr who seemed to speak most often to Lik-Rifa, and so Biórr assumed that he was their chief. The tennúr folded his wings and walked along the centre of the table, inspecting each bowl and trencher of food, peering and sniffing, a frown growing deeper across his pale-skinned forehead with every moment. Dark veins stood out stark against his pink, hairless skin.

"What's wrong with you," Storolf called out to the tennúr.

The tennúr stopped in his inspection and turned to regard Storolf.

"No teeth," he scowled.

Storolf looked at him open-mouthed for a moment, then roared his laughter.

"I'd give you one of mine," Storolf said when his laughter subsided and he was wiping his eyes, "but I've not got enough in my head as it is." He grinned and poked a finger at the gap in his teeth.

"Get off the table, you filthy little rat," the man sitting beside Storolf said. His name was Oleif, one of Drekr's crew, new-come to the Raven-Feeders. He took a long draught of mead from his drinking horn and swayed a little.

The tennúr spread his wings but Storolf held out a hand.

"Hold on," Storolf said. "You're part of Lik-Rifa's crew, same as the rest of us," he said. "Seems to me you're as entitled to this feast as the rest of us."

"Have you lost your wits as well as your teeth?" Oleif slurred at Storolf, clearly well into his cups. "It's nothing but a rat with wings."

Faster than Biórr could track Storolf twisted on his bench, his fist crunching into Oleif's jaw. The man flew backwards off the bench, heels in the air, unconscious before he hit the ground.

Storolf shrugged his shoulders and glowered at Oleif's companions.

"Anyone else got something to say about my lack of teeth, or who I choose to talk to?"

No one did, so Storolf turned back to the tennúr on the table.

"What's your name, little vaesen?" Storolf asked the tennúr.

"Tannbursta," the tennúr said.

"Well, hold on a moment, Tannbursta," Storolf said as he swung a leg over the bench and leaned down next to Oleif's motionless form. There was a crack and a ripping sound, and then Storolf sat back up and threw the tennúr something. Tannbursta caught it in a long-fingered hand and looked down at a tooth in his palm, a sliver of red flesh clinging to it.

Tannbursta looked up and grinned at Storolf, then put the tooth in his mouth and crunched down on it.

Biórr nearly fell off the bench for laughing so hard.

A hand fell on Biórr's shoulder and he looked round to see Rotta standing over him. Seeing him this close Rotta was even taller than Biórr had thought. A sense of power leaked from him, and friendship. Biórr found himself smiling up at the god.

"My blood runs in your veins, I can feel it," Rotta said to him.

"It, it does . . ." Biórr mumbled, finding himself unsure what to call this man in front of him. *Lord. God. Rat?*

"Call me Rotta," he said, looking deep into Biórr's eyes, his grip on Biórr's shoulder squeezing tight. Rotta closed his eyes for long moments, head cocked to one side as if he were listening to some whispered voice. Then his eyes snapped open, his gaze intense. "You have been through many hardships, borne much pain, because of your heritage," Rotta said. "Because you are descended from me."

Biórr nodded, abruptly remembering so much of it, the hard words and whippings and fire, the fear and pain. He felt his throat constrict with emotion, his eyes blurring with tears.

"I am sorry for all that you have suffered, merely because you had the misfortune to be born from my bloodline," Rotta said, patting Biórr's shoulder, his many arm rings jangling. "But I am here now and will do what I can to make it right."

A silence settled over the hall and Rotta looked away, Biórr following his gaze to see that Lik-Rifa was rising from her seat and looking out over them all.

"It is good to be here," she said. "Good to feast. Good to see my brother." She looked along the hall to Rotta, who smiled back at her. "But we must remember, we have a task to do. To right the wrongs that have happened in this world, since the *Guðfalla*. To restore our place, and the place of our children, our bloodlines, in this shattered world." She paused a moment. "And to kill my twice-cursed brother, Ulfrir."

"Yes," Rotta breathed above Biórr.

Cheers rang out from all in the hall, Raven-Feeders, dragon-worshippers, tennúr. Biórr even saw some of the children cheering, Harek among them, though Breca sat next to his friend glowering.

"But there is much to do," Lik-Rifa said, "and we are too few. I will change that now." She opened her mouth and began to sing.

"*Komdu til mín, börn mín sem búa til. Börn úr föndri mínu kallar móðir þín til þín. Komdu til mín. Komdu til mín. Komdu til mín,*" Lik-Rifa sang, repeating the last few words over and over. The hall filled with the sound of her voice, growing in volume, becoming louder than a hundred horns, swirling and rising until it filled Biórr's senses, nothing else existing. He could almost see the words leaving the chamber, a thousand tendrils twisting and turning in an endless procession through the open doorway and on, out into the world.

Slowly the words faded, just the crackle of hearth fires left to break the silence.

"What did you do?" Ilska asked from her seat close to Lik-Rifa.

"She has called her children to her," Rotta said. "The vaesen that she created and bred; my sister has called them to her."

CHAPTER FORTY-FIVE

ORKA

Orka sat on a bale of hay and dragged a whetstone across the blade of her long-axe. It was late, moonlight silvering the half-open door of the stable, distant sounds of Starl drifting on a cold wind.

"I'm cold," Myrk said. She was close by, sitting on the ground, her back to the post her wrists were tied around. In the stable behind her Orka could hear Myrk's horse tugging hay from a rack.

Orka ignored her.

Myrk muttered and snarled under her breath.

The rest of the Bloodsworn were going quietly about tasks before they settled down for sleep. Halja Flat-Nose was stitching a torn seam on her tunic and close to her Lif scoured at a spot of rust on his spearhead. Gunnar Prow was standing with his breeches around his ankles while Revna Hare-Legs unwound the bandage about his thigh, checking his wound. A part of Orka was aware of all that was going on, but most of her thought-cage was filled with the events of the day.

I have met a god.

Rasp, rasp went the whetstone.

And not just any god. Ulfrir, the wolf-god. The sire of my bloodline.

Walking away from Ulfrir and the Battle-Grim she had felt his loss, like walking away from the heat of a fire into a winter's ice-touched night. Every step it had grown more pronounced, but she had kept on walking. Knew that to take up his offer and go with him would mean to lose a part of herself. The wolf within her had whined and paced, and Orka still felt that restlessness in her blood.

I am your father, he had said to her.

I do not want a father, or have time for one, she snarled at the voice in her head. *There is only Breca.* She saw her son's face, black hair spiked and scruffy, serious, grey-green eyes set in a pale face.

I will never stop looking for you. Not while blood flows in my veins.

"You know my brother will kill you," a voice said, dragging Orka from her thoughts. She looked down at Myrk and stopped sharpening her axe.

"There is only one way to find out," Orka said with a shrug.

"You are a pathetic maggot compared to him. He will carve you up and feed you to your son."

A muscle twitched in Orka's eye at the mention of Breca.

Myrk smiled. "After all, that is what he did with your man."

Orka put her whetstone away. Dimly she was aware that the others in the stable had all stopped what they were doing and were watching.

"You waste a lot of breath," Orka said with a sigh. She reached into the sack at her feet and pulled out Myrk's seax, sheathed in its elaborately carved scabbard. A rasp of leather as she drew it and ran her thumb across its edge.

"A fine blade," Orka said. "When you have led me to your brother then I will give it back to you."

"Perhaps Drekr will let me kill you," Myrk said, pursing her lips in mock thought. "He has always enjoyed watching me in a *holmganga*."

"So did we, back at Rotta's chamber," Revna said with a snort. "When Orka put you on your arse and trussed you like a hog."

The others laughed, Gunnar stumbling and falling because he hadn't pulled his breeches back up.

Myrk's teeth drew back and she hissed at them, straining at her bonds. Veins pulsed in her neck and temple and motes of red fire danced in her eyes.

"Enough of that," Orka said, touching Myrk's seax to her throat.

"*Eldur*," Myrk growled, and sparks of flame flickered in the air.

Orka gave a flick of her wrist and opened a red line across Myrk's neck. She raised the seax for Myrk to see.

"Another word and you'll have a second smile," Orka said.

Myrk calmed, the red in her eyes receding and she slumped in her bonds.

Orka wiped the blood from the seax on a hem of tunic that poked beneath her coat of mail.

"I am glad to be leading you to my brother," Myrk snarled. "I look forward to seeing you all die. It is like leading lambs to the slaughter."

"But these lambs have sharp teeth and claws," Revna Hare-Legs said, and clicked her teeth together. "Bite, bite, bite," she said, and Gunnar laughed so hard he fell over again.

Orka reached down and pulled Myrk's gag up before she could snarl another answer.

"Lif, give us a song," Gunnar Prow called out as he tugged his breeches up. "I need something to take away the memory of Myrk's screeching. It is ringing in my ears like a night-hag."

"Me?" Lif said.

"A song would be good," Revna said. Lif looked to Halja, who didn't say anything, but she stopped her stitching and sat back.

"All right," Lif nodded, giving his spearhead one last wipe and putting the leather sheath back over it. He sat quietly a few moments, thinking, and then opened his mouth and began to sing.

His voice was soft and mournful as he wove a tale of two brothers and of vengeance. Orka felt herself drifting on the ebb and flow of Lif's voice, a sense of melancholy seeping into her, Lif singing of love and loyalty, of friendship and loss. She set Myrk's seax down beside her and lay back on to the bale of hay, allowing her eyes to close. Her last image was of Halja, her eyes glistening with tears as she stared at Lif.

The sound of footfalls and Orka opened her eyes. She had been dreaming, of wolves and dragons and a child's cry. The stable door creaked and Orka saw dark silhouettes framed against the moonlight. The glint of steel.

"'Ware," she croaked as she lumbered to her feet, snatching up her long-axe, sleep falling away like a shroud.

Eight, ten figures were slipping into the stable, more behind them, all of them cloaked and hooded. Orka saw steel in their fists and the glimmer of mail beneath their cloaks.

"Step away, old woman," said a voice in the darkness. "We just want your horses. No need for you to die tonight."

"It'll not be her who's doing the dying," Halja said as she came to stand at Orka's shoulder, shield and spear in her fists.

One of the horse-thieves gave a bellowing roar and a dense shadow separated from the rest, hurtling forward, Orka hardly having time to bring her axe up before the huge figure crashed into her, sending her flying backwards, slamming to the straw-covered ground and rolling. Shouts erupted around her, the clash and grate of steel. Orka rolled, kicked out and heard a grunt of pain, heaved herself back to her feet with her long-axe. The figure that had knocked her flying was limping after her, all around the Bloodsworn fighting, weapons tracing silver blurs in the moonlight, but Orka could see they were outnumbered, maybe three to one. She hefted her long-axe, holding it two-handed across her body. Then the figure in front of her was upon her, a hand-axe hissing at her head. Orka stepped right and thumped the butt of her axe into the figure's side, a grunt of pain and exhalation of air but the figure still managed to swing a slab-like shoulder and slammed Orka in the chest, sending her stumbling back half a dozen paces. To her right she glimpsed Lif with shield raised and spear stabbing. He shuffled back as two cloaked figures struck at him. All the Bloodsworn were retreating to the rear of the barn, Gunnar and Revna fighting shield to shield, Halja swirling among a handful of attackers. Horses neighed and Orka stepped back a few more paces, giving herself room to swing her long-axe. She roared as she struck, the huge warrior still following her ducking, lashing out with his hand-axe, Orka jumping back, then lunging forwards. Meaty fists grabbed the haft of her axe and she wrestled back and forth, tripped over a bale of hay and the two fell, Orka landing on her side, feeling her axe head hiss a finger's width from her nose. She smashed her head into her attacker's cloak-shadowed face, heard a squawk of pain and the meaty hands fell away from her axe haft. Then Orka was clambering to her feet and raising her axe over her head.

A wild neighing and the drum of hooves and Orka looked up to see Myrk on her horse's back, the two of them thundering out through the stable doors. Hooves clattered across the courtyard and then they were gone into the night.

Orka stood there a moment, frozen, while her attacker groaned at her feet and all around her the Bloodsworn fought on.

"HOLD," Orka bellowed, and the fighting around her slowed and stopped. She held a hand out to the figure on the ground and pulled him upright.

Sighvat the Fat pushed back the hood of his cloak, blood streaming from his nose.

"Didn't have to go so hard at it," he mumbled through swelling lips.

"Had to make it look real," Orka said with a shrug. "Besides, I held back."

"Huh," Sighvat grunted.

Orka looked around, saw that the Bloodsworn had lowered their weapons. Lif stood frozen, shield and spear still raised, pale-faced and trembling.

"It's all right, lad, you can put that pig-sticker down now," another cloaked warrior said as he pushed his cloak hood down. "We are friends. Pleased to meet you, name's Orv the Sneak."

"Friends?" Lif said. "Strangest friends I've ever had."

Sighvat laughed through his bloody nose at that, and the laughter spread.

"Sorry," Halja Flat-Nose said to Lif, "we didn't have an opportunity to tell you."

Lif blinked, looking around as the other cloaked figures pushed their hoods back. Orka saw Elvar, her fair hair tied into a tight braid, and Grend at her shoulder.

"But, but," Lif stammered. "Myrk has escaped."

"That was the idea," Orka said, striding through the barn. She nodded a greeting to Elvar as she passed her, looked at the post where Myrk had been tied and saw that the seax she had left by the hay bale was gone. Orka reached the stable doors, put her fingers between her lips and whistled. A slim figure emerged from the shadows and stepped into the stable, moonlight gleaming on an iron thrall-collar.

"This is Sæunn," Orka said to Lif and the Bloodsworn, who were gathering around her. She opened the pouch at her belt and took out the rag she had used to wipe blood from Myrk's horse, then ripped off the hem of her tunic, where she had cleaned Myrk's seax of her blood.

"Sæunn is Tainted," Orka said, "the blood of Hundur the hound runs in her veins. Sæunn, here is the blood of the horse and rider that I need you to track. Can you do this?"

Sæunn took the two strips of fabric and sniffed one, then the other with deep, lung-filling snorts.

"Of course, mistress," Sæunn said.

"I am Orka, not mistress," Orka said.

"Of course, mistress Orka," Sæunn said.

"Ach," Orka sighed.

"I'll saddle the horses," Lif said, lowering his trembling shield.

"Wait a while," Orka said. "I don't want to catch Myrk."

"Eh?" Lif frowned.

"I want to *follow* her. Myrk lied to me, has been leading us on a false trail. But now ⸱ . . Now, she will lead us all the way to my son."

Elvar came to stand by Orka, looking out into the night. Grend followed, and then Sighvat. He grinned at Halja, blood on his teeth.

"My thanks," Orka said to Elvar.

"Our pleasure," Elvar said. "Always good to have a scrap in the middle of the night." She looked up at Orka. "And that favour we spoke of . . ."

"Aye. You want word sent to Glornir and the Bloodsworn."

"Yes. Tell them I wish to hire them, and that I will pay double what they ask. Give them this as a measure of my regard." She reached inside her cloak and took out an arm ring of pure silver. It was thick, strands twisted to fit an arm easily as large as Sighvat's. The terminals were two bear heads, jaws snarling.

"From the Battle-Plain of Oskutreð," Elvar said. "It may even have belonged to Berser himself, or one of his children."

"Glornir will like that," Gunnar Prow said as he came limping up. "But it may take a while to get word to Glornir and the rest of the Bloodsworn. We don't know where they are. Maybe Darl."

Elvar shrugged. "I have kept my part of the bargain," she said, eyes fixed on Orka. "How you fulfil your part is your business, but the sooner the better."

"It will happen," Orka said. "Where do you want them to meet you?"

Elvar looked back out into the night.

"Tell them to come to Snakavik."

CHAPTER FORTY-SIX

GUÐVARR

Guðvarr woke with a pounding in his head.

"Where am I?" he breathed, his voice a dry croak, his breath sour and rotten, so bad he moved his head in an attempt to escape the putrid stench.

Moving his head was a bad idea, feeling like a clan of trolls were trapped inside his skull and were attempting to thump and pound their way out. Waves of nausea pulsed through his neck and into his belly. His stomach lurched.

"Bucket's over there," a voice said, husky and slurred with sleep.

Guðvarr rolled and sat up, found that he was on a straw mattress in a dark room, the walls sloping. A sharp beam of light pierced a crack, motes of dust floating.

No, not walls, a roof.

He realised where he was, fractured memories of last night appearing in his thought-cage. Of the shield-dance, of falling with Estrid. Of drinking with Vilja. Lots of drinking. And then back here to *The Dead Drengr* for a hump, though he had no memory of whether that had happened or not. Judging by his lack of clothes, perhaps it had. He ran his tongue around his mouth and decided not to do that again.

Tastes like something has crawled into my mouth to die.

The glimmer of a memory, a sense of needing to be here, at *The Dead Drengr.*

Well, obviously. The humping is good.

But there was more to it than that, and then he remembered.

Hakon. Skalk told me the prince is often here, and especially early, before the doors are opened to the inn's customers.

He saw his breeches in the gloom and slowly set about pulling them on. He stood and cracked his head on a roof-beam, cursed and almost wept with the added pain.

"Shush," Vilja muttered, "I'm sleeping."

He scowled at her, though he could not quite make out where her face was, hidden behind a tangle of red curls. Her pale shoulder was poking out from beneath a wool blanket.

"You can come back, if you like," she said, stretching and patting the mattress. She stuck a bare leg out to him, toes tugging at his breeches. "I'll give you a bargain price."

"Need to piss first," he muttered, feeling like his bladder was close to bursting. His tongue stuck to the roof of his mouth.

And I need to look for Hakon, and scour the dead, rotting creature from out of my mouth. Maybe a drink will help?

Guðvarr found his turn shoes and tunic and pulled them all on, though it took him a while, then looked for his weapons belt. It was thrown in the corner, sword half covered with straw. He slung the belt over his shoulder and stumbled his way to a door that led to a stairwell. Timber creaked as he made his way down. He came out into a small room, crates and barrels of ale, mead and food stacked high. The door to the yard was on his right and he stumbled blinking out into the light of day. It was early, quiet lying heavy across Darl, just the sound of slow-flowing water in the canal behind the inn's courtyard breaking the silence. He found the latrine, just a shed with a bigger bucket, and groaned as he emptied his bladder.

"Much better," he mumbled to himself. *Now I can think straight, I'll have a cup of ale to wash the rot out of my mouth and see if there's been any sign of Hakon. If not I suppose I'll just have to go back up to Vilja.* He chuckled to himself. *It's a hard life.*

Slipping back into the inn he heard chairs scrape and a voice to his right, coming through the open door that led into the inn's drinking room. A voice that he recognised.

Hakon.

He stood and listened.

"Rog, some ale for me and my friend, and some food if you have it."

"Always got ale, my lord," another voice said, old and grating. "Food's a different matter. What were you thinking of?"

"Eggs, oatcakes, bacon. I celebrated a win on the shields last night, and I find there is nothing like a meal of eggs and bacon after a night of ale, don't you agree?"

Guðvarr took a slow, silent step to the open doorway and peered in.

Prince Hakon was sitting at a table close to Guðvarr and the back of the inn, his black hair tied low with a strip of leather. Another figure sat with him who wore a dark, stained cloak, the hood pulled up high. A *drengr* was seated at another table beside a crackling hearth fire, her back to the corner so she could see the entrance to the inn and the rest of the room. An older man behind a bar was pouring ale from a jug into two wood-carved cups. He had a dirty linen bandage tied around his head, thinning grey hair and a straggly beard.

"I'm sure I've got some eggs and ham out back," Rog the barkeep said as he started pouring another cup.

"I've been waiting for you," the figure in the cloak said, voice a husked rasp. "For days."

"Well, I've been away, Kalv," Prince Hakon said. "Couldn't be helped. But I'm back now." He looked hard at the cloaked man. "I'll remind you that I'm a prince, and that you will talk to me with the respect I am due."

"Respect is earned," Kalv grated.

Hakon blinked. "And I have earned it, else Drekr would not be sending you to me."

Kalv grunted and shifted, Guðvarr glimpsing broad shoulders and a thick torso beneath the man's cloak.

"Drekr said you would prove your commitment. He said for you to show me, before I speak his message."

"Oh, he did, did he? Well, I resent your lack of faith, and his.

But . . ." Hakon drummed fingers on the table. He leaned forward and put a hand to the back of his head, lifting his hair high. Kalv leaned in close, and Guðvarr strained his eyes to see. It looked like a strip of Hakon's hair had been recently shaved and had only grown back a little way. There was a shadow beneath the skin, like the swirling lines of the tattoos Queen Helka's *Úlfhéðnar* wore.

Hakon has a tattoo? Drekr? That name rang some kind of distant memory in Guðvarr's skull, but it was still too full of pounding trolls for him to sift it out.

Prince Hakon leaned in close to Kalv and spoke quietly, though because of his proximity Guðvarr could still hear him clearly.

"No doubt you have a message for me, then? What is the word from Drekr?" Hakon whispered.

Kalv pushed his hood back. A fair-haired man, a thick braid binding it tight, and a short-cropped beard with streaks of grey. He had small, narrow eyes, as if permanently squinting. His jaw was wide, face all sharp angles, his skin looking like it had been rune-carved. Guðvarr saw the hint of mail beneath his cloak.

"Drekr says the job is done. That the day is coming. He says to make sure that you are ready."

Hakon tensed at that, and Guðvarr heard him suck in a sharp hiss.

"Well, that's something," Hakon said, and ran a hand through his hair. His face had drained of colour and he shook his head. "You mean, she is free?"

"Aye, the world is changed, though few realise it yet," Kalv said.

"The day is coming," Hakon repeated Kalv's words. "When?"

Kalv leaned closer and whispered into Hakon's ear.

The barkeeper put the two cups of ale on to a tray and walked out from behind the bar, limping towards Prince Hakon and his companion.

He's going to come out here for the food, Guðvarr realised, feeling a jolt of panic.

He took a step back towards the stairwell, then sucked in a breath and stumbled through the open door into the inn, bouncing off the doorframe.

Chairs scraped as all turned to look at him and before he could take another step Guðvarr found a sword point at his throat. Hakon's *drengr*, her eyes cold and hard. She had risen from her chair, drawn her sword and covered the half-dozen paces to Guðvarr in a heartbeat or two.

"Lord?" the *drengr* said, and Guðvarr knew full well what she was asking.

"Prince Hakon," Guðvarr said, trying to keep the fear that was shrivelling his stones to the size of two peas from putting a tremor in his voice. "Congratulations on your win last night. You were an inspiration."

Hakon frowned, then recognition dawned in his eyes.

"You are the one who knocked Estrid into the straw," he smiled.

"A dubious honour, but yes," Guðvarr said. "I gave you that cloak, too," he added.

"Ah, yes," Hakon said, a hand going to the cloak about his shoulders. His eyes narrowed.

"What are you doing here?"

"I've been humping Vilja in the hayloft," Guðvarr said as he scratched his head. "I think I did, anyway. A little too much ale and mead last night, memory is a bit of a blur." He tried to ignore the sword tip that was still hovering less than a finger's width from his throat.

"Ha, I know how that feels," Hakon said, and smiled. "Humping, eh? Well, good for you. But what are you doing in *here*?" Hakon gestured around the room. "The sun hasn't been up long, and the inn isn't even open."

"Just been to empty my bladder and my mouth tastes like a weasel has crawled into it and died," Guðvarr said. "I was hoping a cup of Rog's ale might help scour the bad taste from my gums." He looked at the barkeeper, who stared back at him.

"Give the man a drink, Rog," Prince Hakon said. "And Gudrun, put your sword down," he ordered. She gave Guðvarr one last, cold look and took the blade way, sheathing it and stepping back, though Guðvarr noted she did not sit back in her chair.

"A cup of ale," Rog muttered and walked back to the bar, pouring a cup and bringing it back.

"My thanks," Guðvarr said.

"I'll put it on the tab," Rog said as he walked to the storeroom. *Tab? I didn't know I had a tab!*

"Guðvarr, come and sit," Prince Hakon said, nodding to an empty chair at his table. "Drink with me."

"I would not want to . . . interrupt," Guðvarr said, looking from the prince to Kalv.

"No interruption, just a chance meeting, eh, Kalv," Prince Hakon said, smiling, though Kalv's glower gave Guðvarr the distinct impression that Kalv did not agree.

"Well, then, my thanks," Guðvarr said, and sat in the empty chair.

Rog emerged from the storeroom with a crate in his arms and strode to the hearth fire, where he set about carving strips of ham and cracking eggs, laying them on an iron griddle suspended above the fire. Guðvarr's belly rumbled as fat hissed.

"You ran well, last night," Hakon said, raising his cup to Guðvarr.

"Not as well as you, Prince Hakon," Guðvarr said, touching his cup of ale to Hakon's and drinking. He swilled the ale around his mouth before swallowing, then smacked his lips. It tasted surprisingly good.

"Ha, nothing like the tail of the wolf, eh?" Prince Hakon said. He looked at Guðvarr intently. "Where are you from, Guðvarr? Why are you here in Darl?"

"My aunt is Jarl Sigrún, from the Fellur district," Guðvarr said.

"Ah," Hakon said, "the one with . . ." He ran a finger down his face, drawing the scar Orka had given Sigrún.

"Yes. She will have her vengeance. I will make sure of that." Lately he was feeling braver when he thought of Orka and the Grimholt.

Hakon frowned. "Are you a friend to Skalk, the Galdurman?"

"That *niðing*? No," Guðvarr spat. No pretence was required.

"That *niðing* is my mother's counsellor," Prince Hakon said, his face flat and stern.

"My apologies, I did not mean to offend," Guðvarr spluttered.

Hakon was straight-faced for a few drawn-out heartbeats, then he smiled. "He *is* a *niðing*," the prince said. His smile faded. "Only,

I remember now when I first saw you. Carrying Orna's talon, for Skalk."

Guðvarr felt a rush of fear, like a fist being clenched in his gut.

"I was chasing the woman who scarred my jarl," he blurted, "and that trail took me northwards, where my path crossed with Skalk's," Guðvarr said with a shrug, trying to appear nonchalant. "He took command of my crew and ordered us to escort him back to Darl, much against my wishes. He is an arrogant pig."

Hakon leaned back in his chair, giving Guðvarr a long, appraising look. Beside him Kalv shifted, and Guðvarr saw the man's hand rest casually upon the hilt of a seax that lay across his lap.

I should have gone back upstairs and humped Vilja, Guðvarr thought. He felt his nose running and wiped snot way.

"I agree, he *is* an arrogant pig," Hakon said, breaking the silence, and took another sip of his ale. "I think, Guðvarr, that you and I could be friends."

"That . . . that would be an honour, my prince," Guðvarr said, trying to keep the relief and fear from his voice.

Rog appeared, putting trenchers of steaming food on the table, eggs and cooked ham, oatcakes and skyr, a pot of honey, along with wooden bowls and plates. He put one before Guðvarr, too.

"Be my guest, eat with me, Guðvarr," Prince Hakon said.

Guðvarr did not need asking twice. He filled his plate with ham and eggs and drew his eating knife from his belt, eating hungrily.

I could get used to this, Guðvarr thought. *And I think that Hakon and I could be friends. For the first time I feel that I am in the company of equals, where I belong. I was made to be the friend of princes.* He had to stop the smile spreading across his face. *Somehow, I just have to deal with Skalk, and make sure that Hakon never knows I have been connected with the Galdurman. Guile, as my aunt said. I have a rare gift for it, so it should not be too difficult.*

There was a knock at the inn's door and Rog limped to the entrance. He lifted the latch and opened the door a crack. Guðvarr glimpsed shadowed figures and heard muffled voices, but thought little of it, too busy stuffing a slice of ham into his mouth.

Rog stepped back, opening the door wide.

Two men walked in, both with cloaks and hoods pulled high. Guðvarr glimpsed a white beard in the cowl of the first, the man behind tall and lean.

"More friends of yours, Lord Hakon," Rog said, and the two men pulled their hoods back.

Guðvarr stared at them both, mouth open and full of food.

It was Skapti and Hrolf from the Grimholt.

CHAPTER FORTY-SEVEN

VARG

Varg leaned over the top-rail of the *Sea-Wolf* and vomited into the green-black sea, only to have a gust of wind hurl most of it back into his face. He tasted pickled herring, peas and skyr. He vomited again, to the sound of Svik and Røkia's laughter.

I'm going to die, he thought, hanging on to the top-rail like a drowning man. The deck rose and swayed as another wave rocked the *Sea-Wolf*, Varg feeling like he was on the back of some crazed, bucking beast. He looked over his shoulder to see Svik and Røkia staring at him. Røkia sat on her oar-chest, looking at him like he was the worst kind of fool. Svik was laughing so hard tears were streaming down his cheeks.

Two days they had been at sea and, almost from the moment he had lost sight of land and a cold wind had swept in from the east, he had been emptying his stomach over the side of the *drakkar*.

"I'm going to die," he mumbled at Røkia and Svik, feeling a string of thick saliva hanging across his chin.

"Don't be absurd," Røkia snapped at him.

Svik bent over, hands on knees as he wept his laughter.

"When will it end?" Varg wheezed, almost pleading.

"Soon it will pass," Røkia said.

"You said that yesterday."

Røkia shrugged. "Most are stronger than you, it must be said."

His stomach churned and clenched, a fresh spasm seizing him, and he retched over the side, a mixture of bile and half-digested peas. His throat burned.

He swiped drool away and looked back at Svik.

"You told me to try some breakfast," Varg glared at Svik. "'It will make you feel better,' you said."

"I thought it might," Svik spluttered. He stood straighter, holding his sides. "I am going to have to walk away, else I fear I will die from laughter."

"Arseling," Varg mumbled as Svik walked away, chuckling.

Glornir was bellowing orders and most of the Bloodsworn were wrestling pine-tarred ropes, struggling to fill the *Sea-Wolf's* sail as the longship tacked across a strong south-easterly wind. The last half-day had been hard going, zigzagging across the open sea like a switchback trail up a mountain, but it was either that or row into a headwind. Varg would rather have been doing that than emptying his insides over the rail.

"Even if you do not stop this foolishness, we should make land in another day," Røkia said, "so that should definitely be an end to it."

"Another day!"

"Perhaps a day and a half."

Varg wept inside.

He retched and heaved and spat the contents of his stomach into the foam-flecked sea. After a while he looked up to see Røkia still sitting there, watching him. He felt his stomach settle for a moment, like the calm between two waves.

"At least my pain has restored Svik's good humour," he said.

She raised an eyebrow at him. "You noticed that, then."

"Aye. Ever since the Grimholt he has been . . . quiet. Do you know why?"

"I would tell you to ask him yourself," Røkia said, looking at Svik's retreating back. "But he would never tell you." She stood and walked over to him, leaned against the top-rail and looked out at the endless rolling sea.

"It is because of Orka," she said.

"The Skullsplitter?" Varg said.

"Aye, Skullsplitter," Røkia said. "Svik may tell you many a tale

of how he came to be part of the Bloodsworn; how he saved
Glornir from a clan of trolls, how he rode into the Bloodsworn's
camp on a wagon pulled by a dozen skraeling, how he was fleeing
from a swarm of hyrndur." A flicker of a smile touched her lips.
"That *is* a good tale, but it is not the truth. None of them are."

"What is the truth then?" Varg said, his voice hoarse from the
constant retching.

"Orka found him hiding under a bush, cold and weeping, bloody
from the lash. A runaway thrall, like you." She shrugged. "He had
seen ten winters. He tried to bite her hand off when she lifted him
up, the beast in his blood was running wild."

Varg blinked at that.

"Orka took him in. Well, the Bloodsworn took him in, but Orka
was chief and it was Orka's decision, Orka who trained him, taught
him to be human again. Gave him his pride and dignity back. So,
when she died, he took it hard. Or, when we *thought* she'd died. It
was a battle on the *Sea-Wolf*, we were set upon by three longships
as we rowed out of a bay. A long, hard fight. At the end of it Orka
was gone, and so was Thorkel, who was her man and Glornir's
brother. We stayed and searched for them; checked the beaches to
see if the tide had washed either of them up. Swam the seabed."
She looked at Varg. "When you fight in a coat of mail and you go
over the side, you are done. Mail's too heavy, it will drag you down
to your grave. Svik found others, but not Orka, or Thorkel. We
thought currents had swept them away." She shrugged. "It was a
dark day for the Bloodsworn, and for Svik more than most. He
loved her like a mother. We all did."

Røkia was silent a while, eyes distant, sifting through her memories. Varg wanted to know more but he kept his lips pressed tight,
knowing that Røkia would either speak or she would not. No
amount of prompting would change that. Eventually Røkia began
to talk again.

"So, seeing Skullsplitter at the Grimholt, it was a shock, and no
denying. And Svik will be thinking 'Why did she leave us?'

"She swore an oath to us all, as we did to her. To stand, unto
death." Røkia shrugged. "Life is full of disappointments. But my

guess is Svik seeing her alive like that. Well, it's like ripping out the stitches of a wound."

"I understand," Varg said.

"Svik should be more like me," Røkia continued. "He should make a stone of his heart."

"I can see that would help avoid the pain of betrayal, true enough, but it also stops you feeling the joy of friendship or love," Varg mumbled.

Røkia raised an eyebrow at him.

"Should I trust words of wisdom from a man called No-Sense?"

He tried to say more but a fresh spasming in his belly had him leaning over the side again, just as the *Sea-Wolf* rose high on a huge swell and then dipped, slicing down the wave's back.

Varg felt something touch his face and looked up to see the child, Refna, standing there with a rag and a drinking horn. She wiped at his chin with the rag and offered him the cup.

"Fresh water, to wash your mouth out," she said.

Varg took a sip and swilled his mouth, then spat it out. He wanted to gulp the water down, but the churning in his belly warned him off.

"My thanks, Strong-Hands," he said. Glornir's name for the girl had stuck after she had sat at an oar-bench for the first shift rowing out of Liga and kept pace with the Bloodsworn around her. She was as thin as a fish bone, looked like a gust of wind could snatch her up and fling her overboard, but she was strong, mostly muscle and gristle. She smiled at Varg as he gave her the cup back.

"A helping hand goes a long way, my big brother used to say," she said.

"Your brother was wise beyond his years," Varg said. He frowned. "Where is he now?"

Refna's smile wobbled, and a tear rolled down one cheek.

"He is dead," she said.

"Ah, I am sorry to hear that," he said, thinking of his own sister, Frøya. He remembered Einar Half-Troll saying that these children had lost all their kin. "Your brother, was he with you, when you were taken?"

"Yes," Refna said. "They killed Mama and Papa, and took me and Kel."

"What happened to Kel, little one," Røkia said, stroking Refna's hair.

Is that the first act of kindness I have seen from Røkia?

"He . . . he kept on trying to escape. The last time he tried I went with him and fell, hurt my ankle. He stayed, would not leave me. When they found us, Brák nailed Kel to a wagon and cut his throat; said he would be an example to the rest of us." Her lip trembled and tears popped out of her eyes.

Røkia looked at Varg. He was staring at Refna, gripping on to the rail with white-knuckled fists.

"This Brák," he said. "Did they call him Troll-Slayer?"

"Aye," Refna said. Her face screwed up, disgust, rage, terror all flickering behind her eyes. "I hate him."

Varg felt as if the world was falling away beneath him like crumbling rock at the edge of a cliff and he swayed, a moment of vertigo.

"Brák Troll-Slayer was the one who took you from your parents?" Varg asked her.

"One of them," Refna sniffed. "Not the chief. That was Drekr."

Røkia sucked in a breath at that name.

"Drekr," Varg repeated. "The one Skullsplitter is hunting."

"Aye," Røkia whispered. She looked at Varg. "I think we will be crossing paths with Orka Skullsplitter again."

Footsteps, and Sulich came to stand beside them, but he said nothing, did not even look at them. He was staring out into the open sea. Varg saw that his eyes were flecked with gold.

"What is it?" Røkia asked him.

"There," Sulich said, staring. Røkia followed his gaze.

"What? Where?" Varg said.

"There," Røkia said, pointing south, to the horizon. Varg squinted, shielded his eyes from the glare of the sun on white-spumed waves, and then he saw it. At the edge of his sight, on the horizon that looked like the rim of the world, two small strips of colour appeared, growing taller as he stared, like trees or hills emerging from out of the waves.

"Is that . . . land?" he said, hardly daring to hope it.

"CHIEF," Røkia called and Glornir handed the tiller to Æsa and came striding over. "What is it?" he said.

Røkia pointed and Glornir squinted. Then he scowled.

"WEAPONS," he bellowed.

Then Varg realised what it was. Not land. Sails.

CHAPTER FORTY-EIGHT

GUÐVARR

Guðvarr sat at the table and stared at Skapti and Hrolf.
I am a dead man.

"My prince, it is good to see you back, Skalk is up to dark deeds," Skapti said, then his gaze fixed on Guðvarr and his eyes narrowed.

There's no talking my way out of this.

Guðvarr lurched to his feet, upending the table into Prince Hakon and he hurled his cup of ale into Kalv's face. Hakon yelled as hot food spilled into his lap and the table crunched into him. Kalv spat ale and spluttered a curse as he stood, drawing his seax. Guðvarr sensed movement off to his right, Hakon's *drengr*, but he was already moving, stumbling backwards, turning and sprinting for the back door. He crashed through it, his shoulder clipping the doorframe and sending him careening into a stack of barrels and boxes. He stumbled on, righting himself, one hand dragging at the barrels and sending them crashing to the ground behind him, just as the *drengr* appeared in the doorway. She cracked her shins into a barrel and fell, cursing, as Guðvarr burst through the back door and out into *The Dead Drengr's* rear courtyard. He sprinted through it, past the outhouse latrine and smashed through a pair of rotting gates, splinters of wood spraying, ran stumbling on and looked back over his shoulder. Kalv was emerging from the inn's back door, the *drengr* close behind. Fear gave him a burst of speed and he looked ahead, shrieked as he skidded and stood teetering on the edge of a canal-bank, arms windmilling. He looked left and to his horror saw white-haired Skapti emerge from an alley, looked right and saw tall Hrolf loping towards him.

Death behind and to either side. Only one choice is no choice at all.

He leaped into the canal with a splash and slipped beneath the water. It was dark and oily, things floating in it that Guðvarr did not want to think about, though the stench gave him a good idea what was all about him. He struck out with arms and legs, his weapons belt tangled about him, snaring an arm. He struggled, freed his arm and swam underwater in what he hoped was the right direction, away from Kalv and his pursuers for thirty or forty heartbeats. When his lungs were bursting, he surfaced in a spray of water, spluttering and gasping for breath, spitting slime and filth. He saw that he was close to the far bank and twisted to see Kalv, Skapti and the *drengr*. They saw him and pointed, and he turned and struck out for the bank, clawed himself up through reeds and thick mud, then flopped on to the canal-side and rolled, lay there gasping for a few moments. He caught his breath and climbed to his feet, grinned to see Kalv, Skapti and the *drengr* still standing on the far bank.

Ha, see, I am a man who will do what it takes to survive. Don't want to get your feet wet, eh?

He heard a rhythmic creak and splash, then saw a small rowing boat appear, Hrolf sitting on the bench, rowing up to Kalv and the others. They jumped into the boat and lifted oars.

Guðvarr let out a whimper, turned and looked around wildly. Saw a tangle of barns and buildings around him, looked up to see the fortress high above, Orna's skeletal wings spread wide, and the outline of the Galdur tower behind them.

He ran, knowing now that his only hope was Skalk.

Behind him he heard the thud and scrape of the rowing boat grating against the canal's bank, then the slap of feet on hard-packed earth. Fear gave his feet wings and he sped through the streets of Darl, twisting and turning through alleys, crashing through a tanner's yard, skins stretched taut on frames to be scraped of fat, and he ran

on, leaping a fence, tripping, falling, scrambling back to his feet and
then he was spilling into a wider street, wooden planks laid for a
path and he veered right, climbing ever uphill. Faces gawped and
scowled at him as the town came to life, but they were gone too
quickly to give any thought to.

Perhaps I have outrun them, he hoped. He risked a glance as he
rounded a corner and saw Kalv behind him, Hrolf only a few strides
behind Kalv. They were less than twenty paces away. Guðvarr could
not contain a shriek and he dug deeper, trying to find new strength
and speed.

Each breath burned, air rasping from his lungs, legs feeling like
lead, but he kept on running, knew that to slow or stop was most
likely to die.

He saw the walls of the fortress looming, ran on, following a
road that wound around the high walls.

Have to get to Skalk. Have to get to Skalk.

The pounding in his head was unbearable now, sending waves
of nausea deep into his gut. Hot bile burned his throat and he
retched, spitting it out. He turned a bend and saw the Galdur tower
ahead, figures standing in its gateway.

"Help," he wheezed. He was a hundred paces away from the
gates, now, then ninety, eighty. He sucked in a stinging breath and
opened his mouth to call out again. Something crashed into his
back, sending him flying, weightless through the air. He hit the
ground with a thud, gasping as every shred of breath was crushed
from his lungs, rolled and flopped and crunched into the wheel of
a cart.

"Got you now, you little weasel," a voice growled and Guðvarr
felt a hand clamp around his ankle. He pulled away, glimpsed Kalv's
fair beard and small, dark eyes. Lashed out and kicked him in the
face, saw blood spurt and the grip on his ankle lessened. Guðvarr
clawed his way up the cart and back to his feet. Saw people standing
around, staring, Kalv lurched upright, blood streaming from his
nose, staining his beard. Behind him Hrolf loomed.

"Help!" Guðvarr pleaded.

"What is happening here?" a man said to Guðvarr, stepping

forward and putting a hand on his arm. He was black-bearded and dressed in a trapper's furs and leather.

"Step away," Kalv snarled and Guðvarr grabbed the trapper and hurled him into Kalv, broke into a staggering, stumbling run. He heard a yell behind him, looked back to see Kalv pushing a body away, his seax red.

"HELP!" Guðvarr screamed and saw the guards at the Galdur tower's gates looking. Something crunched into his head and he fell like a stone, white lights exploding behind his eyes. He lay on the ground, blinking, looking up, saw the bones of dead Orna's wings spread high above, a pale blue sky smeared with tattered white clouds beyond. Hrolf's face appeared over him and he saw the man bend and snatch up a hand-axe, the iron poll slick with blood.

"Lucky for you I'm no good with a throwing axe," Hrolf said with a frown, hefting the axe.

"Get it done," a voice rasped.

Hrolf raised the axe high and Guðvarr covered his face with his hands.

A thud and scream, something spattering across Guðvarr's hands. He peered through his splayed fingers and saw that Hrolf was gone. Guðvarr rolled on the ground and came face to face with Hrolf's lifeless eyes. He pushed himself to his knees, saw Hrolf lying on his back, skewered with a spear, blood spreading and soaking into the ground. Kalv stood a few paces away, scowling, eyes fixed over Guðvarr's shoulder.

Voices shouted behind him, footsteps drumming as guards ran from the tower gate. Skalk appeared behind them, striding with his new staff in his fist.

Kalv looked between Guðvarr and Skalk, and Guðvarr saw something change about the man. His eyes shifted, becoming darker, iris and pupil changing, as if ink were leaking through them, and his shoulders and neck seemed to broaden and thicken. Teeth curled from his lower jaw. Then with a roar Kalv was running at Guðvarr, his head down, his seax slashing for Guðvarr's belly.

He is Tainted. Guðvarr felt his bladder loosen. He couldn't move, limbs frozen with shock and fear.

"*Bindið hann,*" a voice cried out and Guðvarr glimpsed a flare of red light, heard the crackle of flame and then a net made of fiery threads was hurtling into view, settling and coiling around Kalv. He cried out, tried to hack at it with his seax, but the net drew tighter, Kalv staggering and falling to the ground. He thrashed and rolled, face purple with strain, tendons and veins thick as corded rope. There was the stench of scorched flesh and red weals burned themselves into Kalv. The Galdur-guards appeared, eight or ten, forming a circle around him, spears levelled, and then Skalk was there.

The Galdurman looked down at Kalv with his one eye, his lip curling back in a sneer. He was no longer bandaged and red-raw scars raked his face and head, patches of his skull showing where his hair no longer grew.

"The more you struggle, the tighter the net will become," Skalk said, "so you see, you are only making it worse," but it looked to Guðvarr like Kalv didn't really care about that. He was roaring and screeching, ink-black eyes bulging, teeth gnashing.

This man really doesn't like being trapped.

"Who is he?" Skalk said as Guðvarr staggered to his feet, the world shifting unsteadily around him. He felt blood trickling down the back of his head and neck as he stood looking down at Kalv. Waves of heat radiated from the net as the man struggled and writhed, his skin bubbling.

Good, that will teach you for the race you have given me, and then to try and gut me!

"His name is Kalv," Guðvarr wheezed. "He is a messenger sent to Prince Hakon; from a man called . . . Drekr."

Skalk's expression shifted, looking down at Kalv with more interest and less disgust now.

Kalv screamed as he pressed his face against the ever-tightening fiery net.

"I . . . I think he's trying to kill himself," Guðvarr said.

"Well, we can't have that." Skalk raised his staff, cracked it down on to Kalv's head and the Tainted man grunted, slowed in his thrashing. Skalk frowned and hit him again and Kalv went limp. The hiss of burning flesh receded as the net loosened a little.

"*Eldur slökktur,*" Skalk said and there was a great hissing sound, a cloud of steam rising up around them, as if the fiery net had been doused with water. When the steam cleared Guðvarr saw that the net was now just thin cord.

"Bring him," Skalk said and the guards bent to lift Kalv.

Skalk looked at Guðvarr and sniffed, Guðvarr becoming painfully aware of the urine-soaked stain in his breeches.

"Follow me," Skalk said.

CHAPTER FORTY-NINE

ELVAR

Elvar looked up at Orka as she climbed into her saddle, all of the Bloodsworn already mounted. Daylight poured into the barn through the open gates. Elvar and her crew had stayed the rest of the night with Orka and her handful of warriors, talking quietly through the night and into the first light of day.

"I wish you well," Elvar said to Orka. She paused a long moment, still undecided on whether to pass on Ulfrir's message to this woman. In the end she shrugged.

What harm will it do? None. It is only that there was something . . . unsettling about them, when they were together. "And I have a message to you, from Ulfrir," she said.

Orka just looked down at her, grey-green eyes hard and emotion-less.

"He asked me to bid you good hunting, and to say that he will see you again."

"Huh," Orka grunted.

"And *I* have a message for *you*," Sighvat said to the red-haired warrior of the Bloodsworn, Halja Flat-Nose.

Halja just looked at Sighvat with a curled lip.

"If you're ever in need of a good hump, come and find me."

The young lad who sat on his horse alongside the Bloodsworn shot Sighvat an outraged glare.

"I would be old and grey before you could find your snake,

buried beneath all those bellies," Halja said with a smirk, "and by then you would have forgotten what to do with it anyway." Raucous laughter erupted from both the Bloodsworn and the Battle-Grim. Even Sighvat was chuckling.

Orka tugged on her reins, turning her horse. "Sæunn, are you ready?"

"Yes, mistress Orka," the *Hundur*-thrall said, standing at the barn's entrance.

"Then lead us on," Orka asked.

"Don't forget your part of the bargain," Elvar called up to Orka as Sæunn took a deep sniffing breath from the two bloodstained rags in her fist, her eyes closed.

"The Bloodsworn will hear of your offer," Orka said. "Whether they choose to take you up on it is their business."

"Fair enough," Elvar said.

And then Sæunn was moving off at a loping run. Orka touched her heels to her horse and she rode out of the barn after the Hundur woman, the others following with their shields slung over their backs and weapons jangling, each one leading a packhorse, laden with sacks and barrels. They rode through the inn's courtyard and on to the streets of Starl, disappearing in a cloud of dust.

"Ah, but I'm going to miss them," Sighvat said as he came to stand beside Elvar.

"Miss them?" she frowned.

Sighvat shrugged. "You get a feeling about people," he said. "I'd not mind them standing in the shield wall with us."

"Aye, or lying under the furth with one of them, I don't doubt," Sólín Spittle lisped, standing close by.

"Fine women are a rare thing and hard to find," Sighvat said, then ducked a swipe of Sólín's fist.

"Come," said Elvar, walking out of the barn and through the courtyard. "Back to the *Wave-Jarl.*"

Elvar walked on to the pier, the *Wave-Jarl* moored at its end, and saw a wagon full of provisions being unloaded on to her *drakkar*.

My drakkar. She was still not used to thinking of herself as chief of the Battle-Grim, but slowly it was settling on to her shoulders, like a new coat of mail. Grend a shadow at her side.

"You all right?" Elvar asked him.

"Uh," Grend grunted.

"You have seemed different. Tense. Since we met Orka and her crew?"

Grend shrugged, a ripple of mail. "She is . . . dangerous. It rolled off her in waves."

"What did?" Elvar asked.

"The scent of death."

"Ha," barked Elvar. "This from you? The man who has slain more foes than a tally-stick can hold notches, who has seen Lik-Rifa burst from Oskutreð, and who has sailed with Ulfrir the wolf-god."

"Ulfrir is thralled to you, and Lik-Rifa was flying away, so you were safe."

"Ah, so this is about my safety? Do you not think you are being a little over-protective?"

A hint of a smile cracked Grend's lips. "Perhaps," he acknowledged.

"Come then, faithful protector," Elvar said, "and protect me across this boarding plank," and she ran across the plank and leaped on to the deck of the *Wave-Jarl*. Grend followed her with his familiar scowl back in place.

"Make ready," she called out. "Sighvat, you take the tiller."

"Yes, chief," Sighvat said and walked down the deck to the stern.

All the goods she had sent Uspa to buy in Starl's markets had been unloaded and stowed on the deck, and all about her the Battle-Grim were seeing to their kit and sea-chests. Some were already sitting with oars ready. Elvar strode to the prow, where she found Uspa, Ulfrir and Skuld. They were staring out across the waters of Lake Horndal.

"Uspa, you did well with the stores."

"Easier than stocking a longhouse and running a farm," Uspa murmured, gaze still fixed on the lake.

"You ran a farm?" Elvar said, somehow unable to imagine Uspa leading such a monotonous and dreary life.

"Aye," Uspa said, almost wistfully. "Once. Another lifetime it feels now."

"We are making ready to leave, you should go back to your seats in the stern," she said to them all.

Skuld's gaze turned from the lake to glare at Elvar.

She is still not used to being told what to do. Somehow, I think she will never get used to it.

"Did you give her my message," Ulfrir said. Still gazing out on to the lake.

"Orka, aye," Elvar nodded. "She gave you no answer, though."

"Ha," Ulfrir laughed, "that does not surprise me."

"I liked her," Skuld said.

I liked her, too, Elvar thought, *even if she worried Grend. Perhaps because she worried Grend. I would not want her as an enemy.*

"Why are you all looking at Lake Horndal?" Elvar said, wondering why all three of them were still staring out over the water. She tracked their gaze and saw that they weren't looking at the water, they were watching movement on the lake's shore. Narrowing her eyes she stared hard, then saw a pinprick line of riders following a track that passed between the lake's edge and the tree-shrouded slopes of the Boneback Mountains.

"Orka," Elvar whispered.

"Yes, it's her," Ulfrir said.

The small column of riders stopped, and Elvar had the distinct feeling that they were looking back at her. Ulfrir stood unnaturally still, like a wolf before it pounced upon its prey, the world deathly quiet for a long, frozen moment. And then he sighed, shaking himself.

"We shall see her again," Ulfrir said as he turned and walked down the deck, Skuld following him.

Elvar did not doubt him.

"MAKE READY," Elvar cried out as she stepped into the hollow before the prow, one hand leaning on the carved serpent's head. "CAST OFF," and the mooring rope was untied and thrown aboard, Sólín leaping from the pier to the top-rail of the *Wave-Jarl*. Oars on the starboard pushed the *drakkar* clear of the pier and then they were dipping in ice-bright water and the *Wave-Jarl* was moving, sluggishly at first, then gathering momentum, white foam skimming as the prow carved through water. Elvar smiled as a cold wind caressed her face and birds squawked and shrieked in the sky above, Sighvat steering the *drakkar* towards a river's mouth on the southern edge of the Lake.

"The River Hvítá," Elvar murmured, "and then Snakavik."

And my father.

CHAPTER FIFTY

ORKA

Orka sat upon Trúr's back and looked across the lake to the docks of Starl. She allowed a flicker of her wolf to seep through her blood, and immediately she felt her senses change, her sight sharper, smell keener.

She picked out the *Wave-Jarl*, small figures bustling upon it, oars slipping into oar-holes. And at the prow she saw him. Ulfrir, with Skuld and Uspa beside him. He could see her, she knew in a heartbeat, was watching her as she watched him. And then, his voice was in her head.

A new age has dawned, the wolf-god's voice howled in her thought-cage. *A wolf age, a sword age, and blood will flow in rivers. Remember, I am no dream to blink away with the coming of day; I will see you again, my fierce wolf-child.*

And then he was gone, and Orka felt a moment of despair and fear, like a child abandoned.

Stay out of my way, and out of my head, she snarled back at him, though she had no idea if he had heard her or not. The *Wave-Jarl* was moving now, droplets of water glittering as oar-blades sliced in and out of the water. She watched it for a few more heartbeats, then tore her eyes away.

"Chief, why have we stopped?" a voice said, distant at first. Orka shook her head, tethering the wolf in her blood, and looked around, saw Lif and the Bloodsworn gathered behind her, some of the horses dropping their heads to crop at grass by the side of the track. Sæunn came running back down the track, where she had loped on for a while, not realising that Orka and the others had stopped.

"For this," Orka said. She put two fingers to her mouth and whistled. Then waited.

A splash from the water to their left, and a whirring of wings from among trees to the right, and then Spert and Vesli were there, Spert dripping with water as he clambered out of the lake on to the shore, and Vesli hovering above them, Breca's short spear in her fist.

"*Mistress Orka said to watch the docks,*" Spert rasped an admonishment, his old man's drooping face looking like it had swallowed a wasp.

"*Vesli worried,*" the tennúr squeaked, "*Vesli thought we'd missed your ship, that we'd lost you again.*"

"Been a change of plan," Orka grunted.

"Myrk was about to lead us on a false trail," Lif added, "so we've let her think she's escaped, and now we are tracking her."

Vesli grinned, showing her two rows of teeth. "*That is deep-cunning,*" she said. "*Vesli like it.*"

"Orka's idea," Lif said with a shrug.

Spert's antennae twitched and his mouth moved, jaws grinding.

"What's wrong?" Orka asked him.

"*Nothing,*" Spert muttered.

Orka looked from Spert to Vesli. "What has happened?" she said with a frown.

Vesli's mouth twisted and she looked at Spert a moment, then looked back to Orka.

"*Our maker called us,*" Vesli said. "*In the darkness. Summoned us to her.*"

"What do you mean?" Gunnar Prow said. "What maker?"

"*Lik-Rifa,*" Spert muttered, "*the dragon.*"

"What? How?" Lif asked.

"*Don't know how,*" Spert said, his segmented body shifting in what looked like a shrug. "*Spert just heard her, in Spert's head.*"

"*Vesli, too,*" Vesli added.

Orka looked from Spert to Vesli. *As I have just heard Ulfrir. Have been hearing him in my dreams.*

"Explain," she said.

"*We are vaesen,*" Vesli said, "*and Lik-Rifa made us, or made our kin, who spawned us. In the night, when Vesli sleeping, her voice came, like a song. She called us, told us to come to her, told us that the world was changed, and we would be part of great and terrible deeds.*"

Orka shifted in her saddle. It sounded uncomfortably close to the experience she had just had with Ulfrir.

"Then why are you still here?" Orka grunted. "Why did you not go?" *Can I trust these two now, when their master is my enemy?*

"*Because Spert swore an oath, to mistress Orka. Because we have a pact.*"

"I released you from that," Orka said.

"*So,*" Spert snapped, "*Spert didn't agree.*" He sounded angry with her, but that wasn't unusual.

Orka looked to Vesli. "Why did you not go?" she asked the vaesen.

"*Because mistress Orka and Breca saved Vesli, when even her own kin cast her out,*" Vesli said, her mouth twisting. She looked . . . hurt. "*It was . . . hard, to resist Lik-Rifa's call, but our oath to you, our pact to find Breca, they gave us strength to say no.*"

Orka frowned at them both. Part of her could understand what Spert and Vesli meant. She had felt Ulfrir's call, and an automatic compulsion to go to him. It was her promise to find Breca and avenge Thorkel that had stopped her, that had given her the strength to resist the compulsion she'd felt.

"All right," Orka nodded.

"Good to know we've still got you two with us," Revna said, "but I don't like the sound of this."

"What do you mean?" Lif asked her.

"Lik-Rifa calling the vaesen to her. Not just Spert and Vesli. *All* the vaesen. What does she want them for?"

A silence settled among them, as they all chewed that over in their thought-cages.

"War," Orka growled.

CHAPTER FIFTY-ONE

VARG

Varg stared into his sea-chest as all around him the Bloodsworn were in motion, making ready. Tying loose hair back, dressing in mail, buckling on weapons belts. Spears were being swept up from the inboard racks, shields from the top-rail rack. Glornir had ordered for the sail to be furled when he had seen the two long-ships approaching.

"*Perhaps they are friendly,*" Varg had said to Røkia.

"*We have no friends,*" Røkia had told him. "*And these waters are thick with pirates, picking at the trade in and out of Iskidan.*"

"*Can't we just sail away from them?*" Varg had asked.

"*No,*" she said, and told Varg it was impossible to outrun the ships because they had the wind behind them, while the *Sea-Wolf* was fighting into it, and that to try would tie up a score of the Bloodsworn on ropes and sail as they tacked into the wind. Best to lower the sail and prepare for the enemy to close, rather than come under attack with warriors caught hauling on the rigging or rushing to their sea-chests.

So, all about him the Bloodsworn were making ready for battle, but not Varg. He was frozen, his thought-cage full of a single name, echoing louder and louder, consuming him; Brák Troll-Slayer, Refna's words swirling like a loud blown horn call ringing through his head.

"No-Sense?" a voice said, a hand slapping him on his shoulder, and he looked up to see Svik standing beside him, dragging a horn-carved comb through the snarl of his red beard.

"Best get moving," Svik said, "or they'll be climbing over the top-rail before you're dressed for the occasion."

"Uh," Varg nodded.

"You all right?" Svik asked him, frowning. "This is no time to be heaving your guts over the side."

"No, I feel better, now," Varg mumbled. *Apparently, there's nothing like the imminence of a spear through the belly to cure seasickness.*

"Good. Then get ready." Svik finished braiding his beard and tied it off with a thin strip of leather. He opened his own sea-chest and pulled out a bundle of sheepskin, unrolled his coat of mail from it, slick with greasy oil from the sheepskin to keep out the sea-rot.

"Should you wear mail?" Varg asked. "Røkia told me if you fall into the sea, you're as good as dead."

"That's true," Svik said with a grin as he wriggled into his ring mail. "So, don't fall over the side." He gave his body a last shake, settling the mail, and rolled his shoulders. "We're going to have a scrap, against people with sharp steel who mean to put holes in your body." He shrugged. "It's a question of priorities. Of course, it's each warrior's choice, but look around you."

Varg did and saw all of the Bloodsworn in mail. Even Sulich was buckling up the coat of lamellar plate that Varg had given him.

Varg reached into his oar-chest and pulled out his own coat of mail, dark with oil.

"Good. Maybe No-Sense is finally getting some sense," Svik laughed.

Varg dressed quickly, pulling on mail and buckling on his weapons belt. The weight of axe and cleaver and seax on his hips no longer felt strange, more like a familiar friend now, a reassuring presence. He pulled out a nålbinding cap and dragged it tight on to his head, then reached back into the chest and lifted his helm, settled it on his head, feeling strangely unbalanced with only one ear. He spread the curtain of mail over the back of his neck and shoulders and buckled it under his chin. Checked his vision through the eye sockets. Some of his beard got caught in the buckle and he pulled it free, realised his beard was the longest it had ever been. Thralls were not allowed beards. He hefted his shield from the top-rail rack, then swayed and stumbled along the deck to snatch his spear from the inboard rack, tugging off the blade's leather cover and tucking it into his belt.

He stood straight and looked out to sea.

The two ships were much closer. Longships, though both smaller than the *Sea-Wolf*, perhaps thirty to forty oars on each ship. They were flying towards the *Sea-Wolf* with the wind in their sails and white spume spraying about prows that carved through the waves. Varg could see warriors clustered on the decks, steel glinting. A raven-haired man dressed in thick furs stood in the prow of the closest longship, a long-axe in his fist.

"Bloodsworn, show these *niðings* what, we are," Glornir called out, standing in the prow draped in mail, his long-axe in his fist. Æsa banged her spear on her shield and laughed.

"No cutting their ropes, let them think we are cowering in our ship's belly, an easy feast for them. Then let your beast free; we shall leave no survivors." He looked back at Varg. "No-Sense, it is time for you to run with the wolf," he said, and Varg saw the hint of green prickle across Glornir's eyes.

Varg nodded and felt the wolf inside him howl. The Bloodsworn shuffled tighter together in the centre of the deck, two lines back-to-back, facing port and starboard. He found himself between Sulich and Svik. Einar Half-Troll had herded the children into the gap between the Bloodsworn's two lines.

"Stay down," Einar grunted at them as he hefted his huge shield and axe.

Varg saw the sails on the approaching *drakkars* come down, heard the creak and splash of oars as the two ships separated, rowing to attack the *Sea-Wolf* from both starboard and portside.

Røkia shoved herself in close to Varg, pushing Sulich aside.

"Try to keep your head, No-Sense," she said to him.

"I'll do my best," he said.

A hissing sound.

"SHIELDS," roared Glornir and the Bloodsworn raised their shields high, Røkia snarling at Varg. He jerked his shield up, and a heartbeat later there was a thud of impact, an arrow quivering in his shield.

Svik grinned at him and laughed as he snapped the arrow in Varg's shield with his sword.

"Almost time," he cackled.

On Varg's other side Røkia let out a low, rumbling growl. He could see the hint of sharp teeth in her snarl.

The scrape of timber on the *Sea-Wolf's* hull, a ship sliding alongside. The *Sea-Wolf* was bigger and sat higher in the water. Varg glimpsed iron helms and spear-tips. A handful of grapple hooks flew over the top-rail, landing with a clatter, pulled back, scraping on timber and some snared on thwarts.

Varg tried to swallow, his mouth abruptly dry. Fear sent a tremor rippling through his chest. He had lived with violence, though, and he snarled a curse at the fear. Felt the wolf in his blood growl at it. All his life the wolf had been there, a red mist that gave him strength, and speed, and savagery when he had fought in the pugil-ring for Kolskegg. But somehow, he had kept the beast at bay, knew that he could not let the bloodlust rule him. Knew that he could not kill his opponents in the pugil-ring. Now, though . . .

We will do this together, he told the wolf in his veins, and it growled its answer. *Kill, tear, rend.*

Hands appeared on the top-rail, mailed heads, bodies flopping over the side and on to the deck.

"SHIELDS," Glornir roared, though he stood out from the line, with his shield slung across his back and his long-axe gripped two-handed. The Bloodsworn raised their shields, the crack of timber as they locked them tight together, Varg's shield overlapping Røkia's on his right, his shield rim tight to her iron boss, and Svik doing the same on his other side. Røkia glanced at him, saw he had his arm from knuckles to elbow pressed tight to the back of his shield, holding it firm. In his right fist he held his spear in an underhand grip. It meant he had reduced range, but his grip was stronger and the spear was more manoeuvrable in the crush of the shield wall.

"Huh," she snorted, which was high praise from her.

Varg heard the thud and grate behind him as the other longship scraped along the *Sea-Wolf*'s hull and he twisted, trying to look over his shoulder, saw the mailed back of Ingmar Ice.

"Eyes ahead, No-Sense," Røkia's voice said in his ear, "trust the Bloodsworn to guard your back, as they are trusting you."

A dozen figures scrambled over the *Sea-Wolf*'s rail, more swarming behind them. Some landed staggering on their feet, others fell and clambered upright. Men and women, most clothed in wool and leather, some in tattered mail. Shields were shrugged from backs, spears and axes hefted and more bodies swelled their ranks. They stood there, dead-eyed and silent, staring at the Bloodsworn, and Varg frowned. There was something wrong with these people. Unsettling.

I expected a screaming rush.

Then the silent warriors came on in a stumbling, stuttering rush, only the scrape of leather shoes on timber, the thud and rasp of shields knocking.

Glornir stepped forward with a roar, swinging his long-axe around his head and chopping down, hacked through a raised shield and into the meat and bones behind it. A wet slap, like cutting damp wood, the crack of bone and a spray of blood as Glornir wrenched the axe free, the man he'd struck toppling with a gurgling hiss.

Varg stared, transfixed and unnerved by these mute warriors, and then a spear was stabbing at his face. He moved his head to the right, felt the spearhead hiss past his cheek and instinctively he stabbed back, felt the blade grind on the bone of her spine. He tugged the spear back, a gout of dark blood spurting. The woman's mouth opened but no sound came out, only a river of blood. She swayed, but struck again. Varg stood, not expecting her to be fighting on with a blood-spurting hole in her neck, and could only watch the woman's spear stabbing at his eye. There was the crack of wood as spear shafts met, Røkia's weapon moving impossibly fast and smashing the woman's away, a raking, backward slice opening her face from cheek to cheek and then the woman stumbled away and disappeared in the crush behind her.

"Keep fighting till they're down," Røkia snarled at him.

Figures loomed, a great mass pushing into the Bloodsworn's shield wall, battering, spears stabbing, axes hacking. A blow crunched into Varg's helm, rocking him and sending the world spinning, but he shook it off and kept his shield up. Dimly he heard Svik laughing, glanced and saw him stabbing over his shield rim with his gore-dripping sword, almost too fast for Varg to track. The wolf in Varg's blood was slavering and snarling, desperate to be let loose, but Varg kept the red mist at bay.

As he stabbed and grunted behind his shield, he felt something touch his foot, kicked out, thinking it was a fallen body, but the pressure remained, and grew, squeezing. He ducked behind his shield and looked down, saw that a hand was grasping his ankle. He shook his leg, but the hand did not let go, instead clung on to him like a drowning man clutching at a branch in a river. The hand squeezed and the arm moved, a body sliding over the blood-slick deck and he saw it was the woman he had stabbed through the throat. She flopped and rolled, flat, dead eyes staring up at him, mouth a red well. He felt a rush of fear and stabbed down at her, again and again, slashing her face, slicing into her mouth until all that was left was strips of flesh, white bone gleaming beneath. With a last, choking sigh the woman stiffened and her grip loosened, her hand falling away to flop on the deck. Varg shuddered and stood straight, felt a blow on his shield and sucked in a trembling breath.

"They really don't want to die," he heaved at Røkia.

"Make them," she growled back at him as she stabbed a man through the eye.

Varg's shield arm and shoulder were burning, sweat stinging his eyes, but there seemed to be no end to their foe. All around he heard the grunts and snarls of the Bloodsworn, heard Einar bellowing, Glornir roaring, all against the silent onslaught of their attackers.

He stabbed again, downwards, his spear arcing over a shield rim, through wool and linen and into a man's chest, the crack of ribs breaking, and his spear carved on, deeper. Varg tugged at his blade but it snared on bone and he dropped it as the man he had stabbed swung a lurching axe blow at Varg's head. He swayed back and reached for his seax, dragged it free. Saw the man with the spear in his chest reach out and grab Varg's shield rim, dragging it down. He stumbled forward, felt a moment of panic at being pulled from the safety of the shield wall. Blows rained at him, blades turned by his helm and mail, hands pulling, spears and axes flashing, and he swung his shield and slashed his seax. He felt his blade bite, kept stabbing, blood slick on his hand, but the enemy swarmed around him, grabbing, pulling. Dimly he heard Røkia's savage snarl, heard Svik shouting his name, but he was in a world alone, these unnatural, silent warriors all around. His shield was ripped from his fist, hands grasping and pinning his seax, and then a face was looming in front of him, a man with thin, greasy hair and pock-marked skin.

The man hissed, and his mouth opened wide, breath smelling like rotted seaweed and behind his jagged, brown teeth Varg saw the man's tongue move. It was thick and broad and covered with viscous-like slime, moving sinuously, like a snake, and as Varg stared he saw the tip of the tongue separate, opening up as if it had its own mouth with small, needle-like teeth.

Varg screamed, and deep within him his wolf howled.

Be free, save me, Varg told the wolf.

The world changed in between one heartbeat and the next. Scents became sharper, his vision clearer, sounds more distinct, strength flooded his muscles and rage pulsed through his veins. He ripped free of the grasping hands, his own hands suddenly becoming claws, raking flesh around him, and he headbutted the open-mouthed man before him, saw blood spurt, the man's head snapping back, saw him stumble away and he leaped after him, jaws wide, biting into the man's throat, his seax stabbing up into his belly, ripping and twisting the blade, tearing it out, then stabbing again and again. They fell to the ground, the pockmarked man shuddering and jerking, gasping and hissing as Varg stabbed and clawed and bit. Something thudded into his back and he leaped to his feet, slashing and snarling, blood spraying as he carved into the bodies around him.

Rend, tear, kill, the wolf inside him snarled, over and over.

And then, abruptly, there was no one left in front of him to kill. They were gone, Varg standing on a mound of corpses, the deck slick with blood. He stood on his dead prey, looked up to the slate-grey skies above and howled.

CHAPTER FIFTY-TWO

GUÐVARR

Guðvarr stood in a chamber of the Galdur tower and shifted uncomfortably. The smell of urine was drifting up from his still damp breeches and close by Sturla sniffed and looked at him with a curl of her lip. Guðvarr ignored her, looking away, but that inevitably brought his eyes to Skalk, who stood leaning over a table.

I hate that man.

Beside the Galdurman, Kalv was bound with chains at wrist and ankle and strapped into a chair.

The table Skalk was leaning over was littered with all manner of unpleasant looking tools: saws, tongs, an array of different-sized hammers, knives, a small axe. A fire crackled in a brazier in which he saw the hilt of a narrow-bladed knife poking out, the blade stabbed into the glowing charcoal. Seeing the table brought back memories that Guðvarr had tried hard to forget. As glad as he was to be alive, Guðvarr had not wanted to set foot back inside this Galdur tower.

No matter how hard I try to get away from this place, every path seems to lead me back here. He rubbed his arm, nothing but a white-ridged scar there now to mark where the hyrndur had sliced its way into his body.

But the little monster is still in there somewhere, lurking deep inside me. He shuddered at the thought of it.

Still, it could be worse, he thought, looking at Kalv. *I could be him.*

Kalv twitched and shuddered with pain. His tunic had been burned almost to tatters, red-blistered weals across his torso, a flap of his tunic hanging to reveal a knotwork tattoo etched across his shoulder and one side of his chest. A serpent, or dragon, Guðvarr thought. Strips of Kalv's hair had been burned away, leaving weeping red tracks across his skull, and he looked like he had been blinded in one eye, a jelly-like substance leaking down his cheek from one eye socket.

He looks worse than Skalk after that hawk gave him a mauling, and that is no easy feat.

Despite his obvious pain, though, Kalv was glaring at Guðvarr, waves of palpable rage leaking from him. He muttered and cursed under his breath, fingers opening and closing, as if he were imagining wrapping his hands around Guðvarr's throat.

Guðvarr took a shuffling step away from Kalv.

"So," Skalk said, turning away from the table to look at Kalv. "You were chasing my friend Guðvarr because of what he overheard in your meeting with Prince Hakon. What exactly did you tell the prince?"

Friend? Guðvarr thought, *if I am your friend, I would hate to see how you would treat your enemy.*

Kalv continued to look at Guðvarr, twitching and muttering and hissing under his breath.

Skalk looked at Sturla.

"Get his attention, please."

Sturla took a small hammer from the table, bent down and pulled one of Kalv's shoes off, then raised the hammer and smashed it down on to one of Kalv's toes.

He roared with pain and threw himself back in the chair, but it was bolted to the ground and the bonds around his wrists and ankles were iron. Skalk waited for his thrashing to slow, his shouts to quieten.

"What did you say to Hakon?"

Kalv glowered up at Skalk, his lips pressed tight. Skalk nodded to Sturla and she smashed another of Kalv's toes to bloody pulp.

More screams, ending with a long, breathless wail.

"He told Hakon that Drekr said the job was done, and to be ready," Guðvarr said. Kalv's screams were making his head ache and the sounds of toes being bludgeoned was not helping the churning in Guðvarr's belly. He wanted it all to stop.

Skalk looked up at Guðvarr. "So you tell me, but I would rather hear it from the boar's mouth. That is what you are, Kalv, is it not? You are Tainted, and the blood of Svin the boar runs in your veins?"

Kalv clenched his teeth together and Skalk sighed and looked down at Sturla.

Sturla raised her small hammer and smashed it down.

Guðvarr fought the urge to squeeze his eyes shut and clamp his hands over his ears. He felt his stomach heave and he retched at the sight of Kalv's smashed toes, just a mashed puddle of flesh and blood and bone now, beneath Sturla's hammer. It had not been that long ago that he'd been sitting down to a cup of ale and a cooked breakfast with this man.

Cooked breakfast: don't think of it, don't think of it.

He gagged and retched again.

"Kalv, you are running out of toes," Skalk observed, once the retching and screaming was over. "And once that happens you must know that I will not stop there. Not when we have your ankles, your knees, your *stones* to take the hammer to. And once that is done, I shall introduce you to the touch of this knife," he gestured to the knife blade in the brazier, now starting to glow. "And if that does not loosen your tongue, then you shall become acquainted with the power of my Galdur-staff. The pain of the hammer is nothing compared to that. So, you must see, there is only one way to end your pain. Talk to me."

"Do your worst," Kalv grunted, "enjoy what you have left of your *niðing* life."

"Sturla," Skalk said, and she raised her hammer.

Guðvarr heard footsteps in the corridor.

"Hold," Skalk said and Sturla's hammer hovered in the air.

A knock and then the door opened. Yrsa walked in, and behind her strode Queen Helka, Prince Hakon at her side. He faltered and paled as he saw Guðvarr, Kalv and Skalk. *Úlfhéðnar* loomed behind them, Guðvarr recognising Frek among them.

"My queen, my prince," Skalk said, smiling as if he were talking about the price of vegetables on market day.

"Well?" Queen Helka said.

"I believe this is an acquaintance of yours, Prince Hakon," Skalk said, gesturing to Kalv.

"No," Hakon said calmly. "I have never seen him before in my life." He looked at Guðvarr. "You look familiar, though." He snapped his fingers. "I remember. The shield-dance last night."

The lying shite! Guðvarr thought, outraged. *Mind you, I would probably do the same if I were in his position.*

"I shared a cup of ale with you at *The Dead Drengr* this morning, my prince," Guðvarr said. "Where you were meeting with this man, Kalv."

"You are clearly no better than a lying thrall," Hakon snorted, "to concoct such an outrageous lie. And who is Kalv?"

Guðvarr fought the urge to draw his sword and hack Hakon down in front of his mother.

I have been through a great deal today, just to stay alive. To stand here and listen to desperate lies from a pompous princeling feels like a step too far.

Queen Helka looked from Hakon to Kalv and his mangled toes, finally to Skalk.

"What has he told you?"

Skalk shrugged. "Nothing yet, but we have only just begun," he said.

"Kalv gave your son a message from Drekr, whoever that is, my queen," Guðvarr said, wanting to speed this along as much as possible. He wanted to go and change his breeches and find a jug of ale. "He told the prince that the job was done, and to be ready."

Hakon gasped, feigning outrage. "And what evidence of that do you have?" Hakon said. "None, of course, because you are a *liar*. I shall have the skin peeled from your flesh and a cup made from your skull for this."

Guðvarr did not like the thought of that, and a seed of worry blossomed in the pit of his belly, because it seemed that no matter what Skalk did to Kalv, the stupid idiot would not talk. That was clear from the way he had put up with his toes being turned to gruel.

"I hope I will see some evidence, here," Queen Helka said. "You are accusing my eldest, my heir. The testimony of some backwater jarl's snot-nosed nephew is not enough."

"My point exactly," Prince Hakon smiled.

Guðvarr looked hopefully to Skalk, but the Galdurman was frowning at him, so he looked to Kalv, but there was no hope to be found there. The moron was actually smiling at Guðvarr, even in the state he was in, with smashed toes, face burned like ham on a griddle and his tunic and body torn and shredded.

Then Guðvarr remembered something.

"Hakon has a mark on his head," he said.

"What are you talking about?" Helka snapped.

"In *The Dead Drengr* Kalv would not pass on his message until Prince Hakon showed him. He said it was Drekr's command, that Kalv not pass on the message until Prince Hakon had proved his commitment to the cause."

"Ridiculous," Hakon half snorted, half laughed, but his eyes flitted from Guðvarr to the door. "This arseling lies."

"Prove it," Guðvarr said, "lift your hair and show them, like you did to Kalv."

"This is insulting," Hakon said. "I am not going to stand here and listen to this—"

"Show me," Queen Helka said quietly.

Hakon took a step away, towards the door, one hand twitching to the seax at his belt.

"Frek," Queen Helka said.

The *Úlfhéðnar* moved faster than Guðvarr could track, and in a heartbeat or two Prince Hakon was held in an iron grip.

"Get off me," Hakon grunted. "Mother, this is ridicu—"

"Be silent, Hakon. I will look and if there is no mark then this Guðvarr will be next in Skalk's chair and you will be free to go."

"It is an insult," Hakon grunted, his voice rising in pitch as he struggled, but Frek's grip held him immovable.

"Where is this mark?" Queen Helka asked Guðvarr.

"On the back of his head, close to his neck beneath his long hair," Guðvarr said.

Frek twisted Hakon so that he was bent forward and Helka stepped close, gripped his long black hair in her fist and yanked it up.

"Ouch," Hakon grunted.

There was a patch of hair that had been recently shaved and was now growing back to stubble. Even from where Guðvarr was standing he could see a dark stain beneath the stubble, like a birth mark.

Helka frowned, her eyes narrowing. She drew a small knife from her belt and put the knife to Hakon's head. He hissed and struggled.

"Stay still, else I will cut you," Helka said, voice sharp and cold as frost.

Hakon whimpered and stilled.

"Please, mother," he pleaded.

The knife scraped on skin and hair drifted to the floor. Guðvarr shuffled to get a better view over Helka's shoulder. Scrape, scrape, scrape. The queen paused, stared and sucked in a sharp breath. And then Guðvarr saw what was on Hakon's head. A tattoo, newly done, the skin green-black, cracked and peeling, but the image was still clear. A dragon, wings spread, jaws wide. He looked to Kalv and saw the same image scrawled across his shoulder and chest.

Helka stepped back and slapped Hakon across the cheek, snapping his head back.

"You fool," she hissed at him.

"Mother, you don't understand," he said, blinking, a red mark appearing on his cheek.

"I understand you have the tattoo of a dead god on your head," she snarled, the knife in her hand twitching. "You have defied *all* that I stand for, thrown everything away." She raised her hand and struck him again. "Why?" she said.

Hakon clenched his lips tightly shut.

Queen Helka took a step back, closed her eyes and shuddered, then opened them. "Know this, Hakon. Being my son will not save you here. I will have my answers, one way or another." She looked at Skalk and nodded.

With a rasping hiss Skalk slid the knife from the brazier out of the coals and strode towards Hakon, holding the knife high. Heat rippled from it in waves.

"Skalk, stop right there," Hakon said. Skalk ignored him, stood in front of him and slowly brought the knife closer to Hakon's face.

"Answer my questions," Helka said.

"I . . . can't," Hakon breathed. "Drekr is . . ." he mumbled something unintelligible.

"Drekr is what?" Helka asked.

"To be feared," Hakon whispered.

Helka barked a surprised laugh. "And I am not? You do not know me, if you think I will spare you out of some kind of motherly sentiment. You have deceived me, Hakon, conspired and plotted against me." She shook her head. "Skalk."

The knife came closer, hissing as it hovered a finger's width from Hakon's cheek.

"Please, don't," Hakon whimpered.

"Answer my question then. Why have you done this?"

"Say nothing," Kalv gurgled.

"Skalk, do it," Helka said. The knife moved.

"Because she is risen," Hakon blurted in a half-whispered hiss.

Skalk froze, the knife singeing the fine hairs on Hakon's cheek. Guðvarr caught the reek of burned hair.

"What?" Helka said. "Who is risen?"

"Lik-Rifa, the dragon. She has been set free from her gaol beneath Oskutreð."

"Don't be ridiculous," Helka said.

"It is true," Hakon said, almost weeping. "Ask him." His eyes moved to Kalv.

"Him? You ask me to trust a Tainted *niðing*?"

"It is a truth," Kalv wheezed from his chair. "The great dragon is free. If you do not believe me, ask them." He jutted his chin at Frek and the other *Úlfhéðnar*.

"Frek, what is he talking about?" Queen Helka asked.

Frek frowned, the other *Úlfhéðnar* shifting uncomfortably.

"We have had dark dreams," Frek admitted. "All of us. Of a dragon, wings beating a storm."

Queen Helka snorted. "Dark dreams, this is my evidence."

"How?" Skalk said to Hakon. "How has the dragon been freed?"

"I will tell you. Just move that knife away," Hakon said.

"Do it," Helka ordered and Skalk stepped back.

"How has Lik-Rifa been freed from beneath Oskutreð?" Helka asked her son.

Hakon shrugged. "The dragon-born are real," he said, almost a whisper, as if he feared who might be listening. "I have seen them. Drekr, and others. They are many, their servants are all around us, and they have found a way to free Lik-Rifa."

"What way?" Skalk prompted.

Hakon shrugged. "Something to do with Rotta's chamber," he said. "Drekr and his dragon-born kin found it, in the Boneback Mountains, and you know that to be true," he said to Skalk, "you have seen it with your own eyes. They found a Galdrabok hidden there with a spell capable of breaking the bonds that held Lik-Rifa captive in Oskutreð. But they needed Tainted children."

Orka is involved in this, Guðvarr thought. *She came north searching for her brat, Breca.* He did not like all this talk of dragon-born and dragons, of spells and Tainted children.

Skalk looked worried. "Rotta's chamber; the place where we found Orna's talon," he said. "I have told you, my queen, how the Bloodsworn fought a man there who was Tainted. He was dragon-born. And in the chambers beneath the ground, you know I found copied pages from a Galdrabok, you have seen them." Absently he picked at one of the many scabs on his head. "I think it was the *Raudskinna.*"

"Yes, I know this," Helka hissed, "but do you think there is truth in Hakon's words? That Lik-Rifa the dragon is free in the skies of Vigrið?"

"It is . . . plausible," Skalk said. "When Orka was being interrogated in the Grimholt she spoke of a man named Drekr. She said he had abducted her son and taken him north. As we discovered, she was *Úlfhéðnar*, so her son would be Tainted." He tugged on the braid in his blond beard. "And Skapti, the Grimholt's captain, said that he allowed Drekr to come and go, that Drekr was transporting children into the north, and that he had Hakon's protection." He smiled at the prince. "It is like the pieces on a tafl board coming together."

Helka sagged, like a sail emptied of wind. "No," she breathed.

"The dragon is coming," Kalv said, "and she will change the world." He began to laugh, a bubbling, wheezing rattle. "She's going to *eat* you."

"Shut up, worm," Skalk said absently. "Where are they now?" he asked Hakon.

"Uh, what?" Hakon said.

"Lik-Rifa and her dragon-born. Where are they now? And what is their plan?"

"Say *nothing*," Kalv snarled, bucking and writhing in his chains, the chair creaking and rattling. There was a crack of wood, one arm and a leg of the chair splintering, and Kalv half rose, his other arm and leg still bound to the chair.

"Frek," Queen Helka snapped.

The *Úlfhéðnar* released Prince Hakon and swept through the room, the hiss of a drawn blade and then Kalv was slumping back into the chair, blood bubbling from his throat and out of his mouth. Frek stood before him, blood dripping from a seax in his fist.

"Good, some peace so I can hear myself think," Helka said, standing straighter, some of her strength returning. "Hakon, Skalk asked you a question. Where is the dragon and this Drekr?"

Hakon was silent a long, drawn-out moment.

"Do I need to make it clear to you that the choices you make here will determine your future."

"Somewhere in the north," Hakon said, dropping his head. "Kalv said . . . Nastrandir?"

"Nastrandir," Skalk murmured. "The sagas tell that Nastrandir was Lik-Rifa's hall, before Snaka fell and broke the world."

"But surely it no longer stands," Helka said.

"They found Rotta's chamber," Skalk answered. "Buried, but still standing. These places were built by gods, remember; perhaps they have some kind of . . . protection." He shrugged, then fixed his eyes on Hakon. "Where is it?" he said. "Kalv would have been travelling back there, with a message from you, no doubt."

Hakon sucked in a shuddering breath.

"Kalv said it is to be found on the north-eastern tip of the Boneback Mountains, three days north of Svelgarth," he said.

How the spoilt prince is spilling his guts, just at the threat of a hot knife. Pathetic. I should be thankful, though, because for a moment I thought it would be his word against mine, and I had a good idea of how that would turn out. He looked at Kalv, slumped in the chair, his throat cut. *My body broken, stuffed into a barrel. But I have fulfilled my oath to Skalk now. Become Hakon's friend and brought about this, the discovery of his secrets.* He felt a weight lift from his shoulders and took in a deep, long breath, filling his chest. *Skalk will remove the hyrndur from my body now, that is the bargain.* But then he remembered his aunt's words to him. *"If you are of no more use to him, he may just remove you from the tafl board."* He gulped.

"Hakon, why have you done this?" Queen Helka asked her son.

"Because Lik-Rifa changes everything," he said desperately. "Your plans for power, to defeat Jarl Störr and Jarl Orlyg, and to rule Vigrið. Lik-Rifa makes them all dust. There is a new power loose in the world, and there can be no standing against it. Better to join it than be *destroyed* by it."

"And why did you not come to me about this? Why betray me?"

"I was going to come to you," Hakon said, "but your hatred for the dead gods, the way you treat those who worship them, hanging them in cages to starve and rot . . ." he shook his head. "I was . . . scared, of how you would react. So I left it, and the longer I waited, the harder the thought of talking to you about it became."

Queen Helka shook her head. "You are a fool, and a staggering disappointment. You have left me weakened, open to attack and unprepared."

"There is a safe path through this, Mother," Hakon said.

"Oh, really, my son of great wisdom, and what is that?"

"Join her. Join Lik-Rifa."

"I kneel to no one," Helka snarled. "Even a god." She looked to Skalk. "What is the way forward here?"

"If Nastrandir is to be found north of the Bonebacks," Skalk said, tugging at his beard, "that is a long journey. The quickest route is through Jarl Orlyg's realm, but in the numbers we would need that would be impossible. Perhaps after Orlyg's visit to Darl and your offer of a pact?" he said to Queen Helka.

Ha, so my aunt was right. You hope to win Jarl Orlyg over.

"And what would we do if we could get there?" Queen Helka said. "How can we fight a dragon?"

"The gods were killed before," Skalk said.

"Yes, by each other," Helka said.

"Yes," Skalk muttered, "you are right. And who was Lik-Rifa's greatest enemy?"

"Her sister, Orna; you know this. The sagas are full of their hatred."

"Orna, whose wings enfold us even now," Skalk nodded. "Orna's skeleton is complete, since I returned her talon," he said. "And the fragments that I found copied from the *Raudskinna*, they talk of resurrection spells."

A silence hung in the room.

"And I have a link of Ulfrir's chain, that can thrall any creature of flesh and blood."

"You cannot be serious," Helka said.

"We could raise dead Orna, thrall her with the chain, and with her as your servant we could slay a dragon." A light was gleaming in Skalk's eyes.

"A god as my thrall," Helka whispered. "That is a sight I would like Jarl Störr to see." A smile touched the edges of her mouth. "Perhaps," she whispered, nodding. "Perhaps. How long would this take?"

"I do not know," Skalk shrugged. "I would have to scour the *Raudskinna* fragments, ensure there are no gaps in the spells, test the Galdur-runes. Forge a thrall-collar for a god. Days. Many days."

"And what if Lik-Rifa moves against us before you are ready?"

Guðvarr was growing increasingly uncomfortable as he stood there, feeling more and more like an eavesdropper to momentous decisions.

They have forgotten I am here, otherwise they would not talk so freely in front of me. Then an unpleasant thought struck him. *Unless Skalk is confident that I will not be leaving the room alive.* He felt his bladder twitch at that thought, and his stones shrivel with fear. *I need to give Skalk a reason to keep me alive. I need to remain useful.*

Guile, he remembered Jarl Sigrún say to him, and a seed of an idea took root in his thought-cage.

Not all courage is found with a sword in your fist, he thought.

Guðvarr gulped. "Send *me* to Nastrandir," he said.

"What?" Skalk and Helka said in unison, turning to look at him with surprise, confirming Guðvarr's suspicion that they had both forgotten he was there. Helka's lips twisted as if she had just caught the scent of a steaming pile of troll shite. "What are you talking about?" she said.

"Send me to Nastrandir, as Prince Hakon's messenger," Guðvarr said. "You said they will be expecting Kalv. Send me instead. I could say Kalv was caught and slain, which is no word of a lie, and that Prince Hakon sent me in his stead. You need to know what they plan. Drekr's message told Hakon *to be ready*. Ready for what? If I take a message to them, surely they will give me a message to bring back."

Skalk's eyes narrowed.

"You are not half the fool I thought you to be," he said.

CHAPTER FIFTY-THREE

VARG

Varg shuddered, eyes sweeping the blood-soaked deck of the *Sea-Wolf*, the wolf in his blood wanting more flesh to rend, more blood to spill, more foes to slay. A hand touched his shoulder and he whipped around, snarling.

"Easy, brother, easy," Svik said, and Varg saw the beast in his friend's eyes, saw the flicker of green colour fade back to blue. "Control your wolf," Svik said.

Enough, Varg told the wolf in his blood. He heard it snap and snarl, the desire to rip and tear white fire surging through him. *Enough*, he growled again in his thought-cage, and slowly the wolf listened, the red mist retreating, the fury in his veins dimming. He shuddered, his arms dropping, shoulders slumping, feeling abruptly exhausted, too weary to raise a hand. On the far side of the deck he saw Ingmar Ice punch his shield into a man, hurling him to the ground, Ingmar's arm rising and falling, his axe chopping. Nearby Edel stabbed her sword down into a body, her two hounds pinning it. He heard the creak and splash of oars and saw one of the *drakkars* that had attacked them crawling away like a wounded animal.

Glornir stood with a mound of corpses around him, his eyes flickering green-brown, teeth sharp. He let out a low-rumbling growl and shook himself, Varg seeing the bear in his blood fade and Glornir the man return.

"Are you all right, brother?" Svik was asking him.

"Uh,"Varg grunted, nodded, spat blood. He looked at the corpses around them and remembered the man with the wide-open mouth, and his slithering, sinuous tongue.

"What were they?" he breathed.

Svik's mouth twisted in disgust.

A crunch drew their eyes and they looked to see Glornir's foot smash down on to the neck of a body at his feet. A man with a gaping hole in his back, ribs hacked away, the wet, pink glisten of a lung visible. He was obviously dead, could not still be alive. And yet he moved. A hand clenched and unclenched, and his head jerked, mouth snapping open and shut, over and over again.

Glornir reached down and shoved his hand into the man's opening mouth, gripped something and pulled, leaning back, using all his strength. The head and shoulders lifted from the ground and Glornir put a boot on the man's forehead, holding it down, and pulled harder. There was a wet, tearing, sucking sound, and Glornir's fist appeared, gripping the man's tongue. Except that it just kept on coming, impossibly long, a thick, twitching length of muscle, dripping with sticky mucus. Varg saw rows of tiny, hook-like barbs running along the length of its body. Glornir tugged and heaved and still more appeared from the man's mouth, the muscle splitting into thinner strands that curled and whipped at Glornir. Eventually, with a sickening rip of tissue, the tongue came free, the man's head flopping back to the deck. He no longer moved.

Glornir held the tongue up in front of him, looking at it with an expression of disgust, and he squeezed. The tip of the tongue, fat and bloated and slimy, twisted and writhed, and Varg saw a mouth appear, opening up to reveal rows of tiny needle-sharp teeth glistening with mucus. Two black eyes were visible.

"What *is* that?" Varg breathed, feeling sick.

"A *tungumatur*, a tongue-eater," Sulich said, coming to stand with Varg and Svik and staring at the thing in Glornir's fist.

"A *what*?" Varg said, feeling his stomach churn.

"They are parasites, smaller than fleas when they are young; they live in stagnant water."

"By the dead gods,"Varg muttered. "How did it get into his *mouth*?"

"Swimming in a lake or pond, maybe," Sulich shrugged. "Or just taking a drink from the water. Once they are in your mouth they latch on to your tongue, see the hundreds of claws on its body, like hooks. And then, slowly, they start to eat your tongue, bit by bit, until it is gone, and they have grown enough to replace it."

"That can't be true," Varg said, hoping it wasn't. "I think I would know if something were eating my tongue."

"They inject something into you, so that you do not feel it. Like when a mosquito sucks your blood," Sulich said. He was smiling, seemed to be enjoying Varg's horrified response. "Then, once they are full grown and your tongue is gone, when you eat food, they share it with you. They have a little, and push the rest down your throat, to keep their host alive."

"That is *disgusting*," Varg said, feeling like his tongue was swelling in his mouth, his throat closing. He gagged and retched and spat.

"And then, when they are fully grown," Sulich continued, still smiling, "they grow tails up into your thought-cage." He frowned. "See them, there," he pointed. Varg nodded. "Somehow, do not ask me how, they slowly take control of their host, like a master pulling a puppet on strings. But their host does not live long after that. Which is why they begin the search for a new host."

Varg remembered the pockmarked man lunging at him, mouth open, the tongue-eater in his mouth moving.

It was trying to pass over to me!

"But how did so many become infected?" Varg asked, looking around at the dead littering the floor, and then at the fleeing longship. "There must have been sixty or seventy of them."

"Sharing a water barrel, or a jug of ale, or mead. A kiss. Humping. There are many ways," Sulich said. "These parasites are common in Iskidan, and there are pirates that hide in the islands between us and Iskidan; if just one of them were to become infected it is not so hard to imagine the parasites spreading among a whole crew or warband. Like lice in Ingmar's beard."

"I do not have lice," Ingmar shouted.

Varg shook his head. "This is why I will never live in Iskidan," he muttered.

The tongue-eater in Glornir's hand screeched and writhed, its head lashing out at him, needle-teeth snapping. Glornir's veins bulged as he squeezed harder, and then the thing exploded in his fist, a spray of meat and blood, and it flopped, hanging loose like a dead snake. Glornir threw it over the side, looked around the deck, and then turned to stare at the fleeing longship.

After a long moment he turned to look at the Bloodsworn.

"After them," he growled.

Varg pulled on his oar, sweat beading on his brow, muscles in his back and shoulders burning.

Glornir stood and wrestled at the tiller, guiding the *Sea-Wolf*.

The dead had been heaved over the side into the sea, their blood washed away with buckets of seawater. Varg would have been happy to let the parasite-infected longship row away from them, but Glornir was determined to stamp out the infected. Varg was unsure how long they had been rowing, but it was before noon when he had sat at his bench and threaded an oar through an oar-hole, and now the sun was sinking towards the sea.

Abruptly the rowing became easier and the *Sea-Wolf*'s pace picked up. Varg looked up from his labour to see they were passing through a snarl of green-backed islands that were breaking the wind and calming the waves, and the longship they were chasing was close. Maybe three or four hundred paces away. The *Sea-Wolf*'s prow was cutting through their wake.

"Row, you goat-humpers," Svik shouted out, "and we'll be eating supper and drinking ale before sunset," and Varg set back to rowing with renewed energy.

"OARS," Glornir shouted and as one the Bloodsworn raised their oars, water spraying like a fountain, sparkling gold and bronze in the sinking sun. With a scrape of timber Varg dragged his oar inboard.

"MAKE READY," Glornir bellowed, the *Sea-Wolf* coasting through the calm waters of a bay. Varg stood and reached for his shield, slung it over his head and shoulder, then buckled on his helm and reached for his spear. The rest of his war kit, mail and weapons belt, he'd kept on. Ahead of them the fleeing longship was grating on sand as the hull slid partway up a beach, its inhabitants leaping from its deck and running in stuttering jerks up a sloping beach towards a huddle of buildings nestled in the curve of a treeline.

Einar threw the anchor stone over the side and the *Sea-Wolf* lurched to a halt. Glornir leaped from the stern and splashed thigh-deep through the surf, Svik and Røkia close behind him, Edel and her two hounds leaping after them.

"Stay here," Einar Half-Troll said to Refna and the other children and then he leaped over the top-rail, sending up a gout of white-spumed spray as he crashed into the water. Varg followed after him, gasping as the cold sea soaked him. He waded through the water, holding his spear high and splashed out on to the sandy beach, broke into a run, passing Einar and chasing after Glornir and a dozen of the Bloodsworn ahead of him. The beach steepened and Varg climbed a shifting slope towards the treeline where buildings huddled. Glornir was already there, Varg seeing his long-axe rising and falling, heard the sound of flesh and bone being cleaved.

The ground levelled and Varg ran past a strip of animal pens and then he was in a courtyard of sorts, ringed by turf-roofed buildings spread in a loose half-circle, nestled beneath the first trees of a beechwood that spread into the distance. A well stood at the centre of the courtyard and, all about it, the Bloodsworn were carving a bloody ruin.

Many of the warriors they had chased had turned and were fighting, though they were no match for the Bloodsworn. Everywhere Varg looked they were falling, and he felt a wave of sympathy for these people. They were most likely thieves and raiders, but no one deserved the half-life they were living with these tongue-eating parasites in their bodies. Killing them was an act of mercy.

As Varg stood there, staring, Einar lumbered past him, hefting his shield and axe, and chopped into the neck of a man who had leaped on to Svik's back and was trying to chew his way through Svik's iron helm. Einar's axe almost took his head off, the man falling

away, blood spurting, his head dangling by a thin sliver of flesh.
More figures lurched out of the shadows of a building, stabbing
with spears at Einar and Svik. Varg leaped in, feeling the wolf surge
through his veins, and stabbed one of them through the throat,
ripped his blade free, sending the injured man stumbling, half turning
to look at Varg and swing a hand-axe. Varg swayed away from the
blade, then followed after the wounded man, stabbed him in the
belly, tore his spear free, slashed it across the man's chest, stepped
around him and sliced his spear blade across the back of his leg,
hamstringing him. The man stumbled and dropped to one knee,
grasped at Varg, his mouth opening, the tongue-eater in his mouth
flexing and hissing at him. Varg stabbed his spear into the thick
muscle of the parasite, twisted his blade, carving through blood-
bloated muscle and kicked the man in the chest, sending him
crashing to the ground. He stood over him, stabbing down into
the bloody maw of his mouth, skewering and slicing the *tungumatur*
again and again, until the man on the ground lay still, his face a
ruin of flesh, blood soaking into the ground. Varg stood over him,
chest heaving.

"I think he's dead," Æsa said as she ran past him, grinning wildly
as she sprinted after a handful of men and women who were
running from the settlement, fleeing into the gloom of the beechwood beyond.

"Best be after them," she said, "don't think we want any of these
parasite-spreading *niðings* getting out of here," and without waiting
she was running after them. Varg broke into a run after Æsa, Einar
saw them and followed.

Trees closed around them, their trunks thick with moss and vine,
the sounds of battle from the settlement quickly fading. Æsa was
just a flitting shadow ahead, then they heard her shouting, the sound
of steel cleaving flesh, and Æsa screamed.

A surge of speed from Varg as he let his wolf flood through him,
pulling away from Einar, and then he was bursting into a clearing,
a dark pool in front of him, thick with green algae and rotting
reeds. The smell of decay was thick and pungent. He skidded to a
halt, struggling to understand what he was seeing. Einar crashed

into the clearing and stumbled to a halt beside Varg, both of them staring.

There were at least a dozen of the infected spread about the rim of the pool, a few lying dead on the ground, some wrestling with Æsa, throwing her to her knees and trying to bind her wrists with rope. And there were others, too. Tied to trees. Varg saw a handful of *druzhina*, recognising them instantly by their shaved heads and thick braids, their drooping moustaches, coats of lamellar armour and baggy breeches. Some of them were slack and staring, others screaming, struggling with their bonds as they stared in terror at something that reared from the pool's edge.

A mucus-slick body, wider than Einar and taller. It looked like one thick strand of muscle, green and slime-covered, dark veins like worms writhing beneath its glutinous skin, rising out of the pool like some giant serpent. Small black eyes and a head that opened into one huge mouth, many rows of small, razored teeth and a thick-thrashing tongue that whipped and cracked.

It is a giant tongue-eater, Varg realised, *bigger than a bear.*

One of the *druzhina* was being dragged towards the creature and as Varg watched in wide-eyed horror the giant tongue-eater reared back and swooped down upon him, its huge mouth opening wide, enveloping the *druzhina's* head and shoulders, mouth clamping around him.

The *druzhina* screamed and thrashed, the tongue-people letting go of him as the giant creature sucked and slurped its mouth over the *druzhina's* torso, then lifted him up, ripples spreading through the creature's muscular body as it swallowed the *druzhina* whole. And then only the *druzhina's* boots were visible.

The tongue-people dragged Æsa before it, Æsa cursing and struggling like a wild thing.

Varg and Einar moved at the same time, charging towards the pool. Einar hacked tongue-people to the ground, trampled them.

Something moved to Varg's left and he swung his shield, caught a clumsy axe blow and stabbed instinctively with his spear, the blade punching into a man's belly. He folded over the blade, dropped his axe and grabbed the spear shaft with both hands, pulling himself along it, towards Varg, his mouth opening horribly wide, the creature in his mouth writhing and hissing. Varg released the spear as if it were scalding hot and staggered back a step, grasped for a weapon at his belt and found the cleaver's handle, ripped it out and sliced, hacking into the man's head. A wet crack and the man collapsed, spinning grotesquely as the blade of the spear piercing his body stabbed into the ground. Varg stood over him and hacked down into his neck, blood spraying. The tongue-eater in his mouth squirmed out from between the man's jaws, its mucus-dripping head looking around, searching for Varg. It saw him and lunged, its slime-dripping mouth opening wide, needle-teeth glistening. Varg chopped again, severing the creature's head and it flopped on the hard-packed earth. The man's feet drummed, then he was still.

Einar roared. Varg spun around to see him scattering the attackers holding Æsa and she leaped to her feet, dragging an axe from her belt and hacking around her in a frenzy. A woman lunged forward, stabbing a spear deep into Æsa's thigh. Einar took her jaw off with his axe, the woman spinning away.

A shadow over Einar and Æsa, both of them turning and looking up as the giant tongue-eater struck at them. They leaped apart, the thick-bloated body crashing to the ground between them, lashing out and wrapping around Einar's waist, pinning one arm and lifting him up into the sky.

Varg ran at it, leaped, crashed into its back and hacked with his cleaver, opening up great rents in its body, thick, white, mucus-like liquid spurting.

The giant tongue-eater threw Einar spinning through the air and he hit a tree with a crack, dropped to the ground and did not move, then the tongue-eater's head was whipping around, mouth gaping, trying to swallow Varg. Æsa screamed, lurched forward with a spear and buried it deep in the creature's body. It bucked and screeched. Varg clinging to it, still hacking and chopping. More shouts and screams, Varg glimpsing Glornir entering the glade, Ingmar and Svik behind him, other shadowed figures.

The tongue-eater gave a savage wrench and hurled Varg into the shallows of the pool among rotting reeds and reared over him, its mouth spread wide.

Glornir's long-axe chopped into its head with a wet slap, the blade buried deep. The creature shivered and spasmed and dropped, half in the water, half on the ground.

Varg clawed his way out of the pool, gasping as he had closed his mouth tight and held his breath, stumbled to his feet and ran to Einar, dropped to the ground beside him, lifting the big man's head to rest it in his lap.

Einar was breathing, unconscious, a huge dent in the side of his helm and blood trickling into his beard. Varg unbuckled the helm and pulled it off, saw a tangle of blood-matted hair on the back of Einar's head. His arm was twisted at an unnatural angle and a glint of bone showing. Varg felt a weightlessness in the pit of his stomach, a rush of fear greater than anything he had felt in battle, that Einar might die.

"No, no, no," Svik cried as he rushed to Varg's side, dropping to the ground and putting two fingers to Einar's neck. Others loomed over them. Svik's hand moved to inspect Einar's injury, gently pulling strands of hair away. Blood pulsed slowly from the wound and Svik probed it gently.

"His skull's cracked," he muttered, "and his arm's broken. Maybe more bones besides."

"Ach," Glornir spat somewhere behind and above.

A hand on Varg's shoulder. "Out of the way, No-Sense," Røkia said, and Varg stood numbly, Røkia taking his place. "I need water, but none from this cursed place," she said. "A barrel from the Sea-Wolf. A bolt of linen."

Ingmar turned and ran out of the glade.

Røkia drew her seax and sliced a strip of linen from the hem of her under-tunic and began dabbing gently at Einar's wound.

"Chief," Sulich called. "Think you should see this."

"Look after him," Glornir growled at Røkia. "Edel, make sure there are no more of these tongue-eaters lurking." Edel grunted and left the glade, her hounds at her heels. Glornir strode away, Varg following.

"Looks like we weren't the first ship these fools raided," Sulich said to Glornir.

They were stood looking down at the men and women tied to trees.

"Is Jaromir here?" Glornir growled as he stood over them.

The men and women looked at Glornir. Some stared flatly at him, others writhed and squirmed. Blood trickled from their mouths. One of them was coughing and spitting blood, his mouth cracked. He opened his mouth, trying to say something, but his tongue was thick and swollen, blood oozing from it.

Looks like he has tried to chew his own tongue off.

"Kill us," the swollen-mouthed man mumbled, looking up at Glornir. There was grey in his braided hair and long moustache.

"Why?" Glornir asked.

"That thing," he said, jutting a chin at the dead creature flopped at the pool's edge. "Some of us it just ate, swallowed whole. Others it . . . infected, wrapped it's disgusting mouth around us and filled our mouths and noses with its slime." He let out a strangled sob. "Put its filth into us."

"You are Jaromir's *druzhina*?" Glornir said.

"Aye," the man nodded.

"Where is he?"

The man was silent.

"I can walk away, leave you here with those things in your mouth," Glornir said. "Or I could help you. Do as you ask."

The bound man looked up at Glornir, lips clamped shut, eyes pleading.

"Come, Sulich," Glornir said, turning and walking away.

"Prince Jaromir was not on our ship," the bound man blurted. "We were on a *knarr* with the horses and became separated from Jaromir's *drakkar* in a sea-mist. When the sun burned it away, we found ourselves floating among the islands and those . . ." his mouth twisted, and he jerked his chin at the bodies of dead tongue-eaters scattered around the glade. "They came hard at us."

"Huh," Glornir grunted. "You know who I am? Why I am searching for your prince?"

"The Bloodsworn. You are their chief," the *druzhina* said. "Prince Jaromir has your woman."

A tremor rippled through Glornir. "Where is he going with Vol?"

"I am the prince's man," the *druzhina* said.

Glornir squatted down, his knees clicking. "That thing in your mouth, you know what it will do to you? It will eat your tongue, and then it will infect your thought-cage, until you are nothing but an empty husk. Is that the death you want? A proud, fierce *druzhina* of Iskidan?"

The *druzhina*'s face twitched.

"Jaromir is taking your woman to Valdai," he said.

CHAPTER FIFTY-FOUR

BIÓRR

Biórr stepped to the side, pivoting on his front foot as he raised his shield and caught a blow from the blade of a long-axe on his shield boss, a dull thud, and he deflected the blow wide, stepping inside the range of the axe man and stabbing his seax up, into Storolf's belly. Or would have, if the blade of his seax had not been wrapped in sheepskin.

"And he's dead," Biórr said, stepping away from Storolf and looking at the row of children staring at him. To complete the display Storolf dropped to his knees and toppled to the cold stone floor, grunting and twitching. Some of the children sniggered.

They were standing in the huge hall where they had first entered Nastrandir, shadows flickering and the walls echoing with the *clack* and *thud* of practice weapons. Some of the Raven-Feeders were teaching the older Tainted children, other Raven-Feeders were teaching the dragon-worshippers, and others were sparring among themselves. Ilska had set them to a hard-working regime from the day after their feast in Rotta's hall, as they had all come to call it.

"*We are preparing for war,*" Ilska had said. "*The time is almost upon us, where we will march out as Lik-Rifa's apostles. We must be worthy of her name.*"

"Storolf had the long-axe, with the longer range," Biórr said to the dozen or so children watching him as he offered his arm to his friend, pulling him back to his feet. Despite his fooling for the children, Storolf seemed different today. Quiet and with-drawn.

"So how did I manage to kill Storolf, with just this little knife?" Biórr held up his seax and spun it in his fist.

"You stabbed him with it," Harek said, looking at Biórr as if he was half-witted. Some of the children laughed.

"Yes, Harek, but how did I get close enough to stab him with such a small weapon, when Storolf was swinging his long-axe at me?"

Harek scratched his head.

"You used your shield to make an opening," another voice said, Breca, standing between Harek and Bjarn.

"Good lad," Biórr said, "that's right, and once you're inside the range of the axe head, Storolf is unprotected. It is the same with other long weapons, like a spear."

"What about a sword," Breca asked.

"Ah, a sword is a different matter. You can't just deflect it and step inside its range with no fear of a further blow. Even the hilt of a sword is a weapon. It can crack a skull or cave in your face, smash your teeth, pulp your eye."

"This is why I wish to learn sword-craft," Breca said with a shrug, "not seax or spear or axe. The sword."

"Swords are the weapon of the rich or the skilled," Biórr said. "They cost more than any other weapon, so only the rich own them, or those who are good enough to kill someone who has one." He shrugged. "If you want a sword, learn your weapons craft, or wed a rich jarl."

Children laughed.

"*You* have a sword," Breca said with a scowl, nodding to the blade hanging at Biórr's hip.

"I have," Biórr nodded.

"How did you get it?" Breca asked him.

"Well, I will just say, I have never been rich, and nor have I married a jarl."

"Then how—" began Harek, frowning, but Breca nudged him with an elbow.

"He won it in combat," Breca said. "Took it from his dead enemy."

"Ah," Harek frowned, then smiled, nodding. "That's what you will have to do, then, Breca."

"I intend to," Breca said, and his gaze drifted to where a handful of Raven-Feeders were sparring. Brák Trolls-Bane was there, his slim sword in his fist, wrapped in wool, crouched and ready as another warrior came at him, a big woman with a long-axe. Faster than Biórr could track, she was on her back and Brák had a foot on her chest, sword at her throat and a grin on his face.

"Let that go," Storolf said to Breca, "we are all on the same side, now. Pick up your shields and your practice weapons and get into twos. One with a spear, one with a hand-axe or seax."

Breca scowled but kept his lips pressed together, and then the group of children were sweeping up practice weapons and shields from racks. Once they were organised into pairs, Biórr called out for them to begin, and he and Storolf walked among them, correcting grips and stance, talking through footwork and balance.

"Forget the fancy moves you've heard in the sagas," a new voice rang out and Biórr turned to see Rotta striding over to them, two seaxes hanging at his belt, an axe and sword, too. "Hack their feet and ankles," he snarled, face twisting, "stab them up in their stones, chop their fingers off, put a hole in their throat or mouth. A seax in the eye. If your enemy is wearing mail don't aim there, go for the soft parts, the unprotected parts. Do whatever it takes to be the only one still breathing."

Biórr felt his beast surface in his veins as Rotta drew close to him, the rat excited and eager for blood and chaos. With an effort he calmed it.

The children paused for a moment, enraptured as a god walked among them, and then set upon each other with a renewed fervour. Biórr saw their aggression grow, rising in them like bread in the oven. There were more thuds of weapons hitting flesh, yelps of pain, snarls of anger.

Rotta came to stand by Biórr and Storolf.

"Fierce little monsters, aren't they," Rotta said with a large-toothed smile, all the violence gone from his voice now.

"They all have the blood of a dead god in their veins," Storolf shrugged. "They'll make good fighters."

"Not all of us gods are dead," Rotta grinned and winked, and clapped Biórr on the shoulder. "Keep up the good work," he said, making Biórr's chest swell, and then he was walking away to inspect a different group of children.

Biórr looked around the hall, seeing warriors sparring, laughing, cooking, stitching, some of them Tainted, others untouched by the blood of the gods, all safe within the thick walls of Nastrandir, and among them sat Lik-Rifa.

He gave a smile and patted Storolf on the shoulder. "Look, my friend, this is all we have hoped for. Our friends, our family, fighting for a new world."

He heard Storolf sniffing and was shocked to see a tear leaking down the big man's cheek.

"What's wrong, my friend?" Biórr asked him.

"My brother Kalv," Storolf breathed. "I had dark dreams about him, but told myself they were just dreams. Now, though . . ." his face screwed up in pain and he punched his chest, over his heart. "I cannot feel him. He is my brother, and I cannot feel him." He looked around, searching for his father. Fain was striding away from a group of dragon-worshippers he had been training towards Storolf, the lines of age looking deeper in his face.

"I'm worried about Kalv, Papa," Storolf said.

"I am, too," Fain said, wrapping his son in his big arms.

Biórr said nothing, just put a hand on Storolf's arm. He knew the bonds between Tainted kin and knew that what Storolf felt meant that Kalv had probably died.

Horns blew and the great doors creaked and began to open, a shaft of light lancing in, wind and lashing rain swirling into the hall, making the braziers of flame hiss and crackle. Strange silhouettes stood against the pale grey of day, many-legged and scuttling. Biórr saw the glint of clustered eyes and the glitter of ice on blue-tinged fangs.

"Frost-spiders," Storolf muttered, wiping his eyes with the back of his hand.

More than a score of the creatures skittered into the hall, moving in a tight pack, barbed claws scraping on the ancient stone, and Lik-Rifa rose from her serpent throne to greet them. They were not the first vaesen to arrive at Nastrandir in answer to Lik-Rifa's call. More tennúr swirled in the shadowed heights of the cavernous chamber and a score of thick-muscled skraeling moved around Lik-Rifa like a protective fist, their grey-melted flesh clothed in furs and rough-stitched leather, crude, heavy-iron weapons hanging from belts and baldrics. On the edge of shadow, spread between high columns in the hall, Biórr could just make out the glimmer of webs, thread as thick as rope where other frost-spiders had already arrived spun their webs, and attached to another column he saw a nest made by a swarm of hyrndur that had swept buzzing into the hall. Even hulking Drekr had looked uncomfortable when that happened. In a corner of the chamber a clan of trolls had made their home, a dozen of them sitting around a giant cauldron of porridge, the sharp ammonia tang of their urine and dung seeping into every part of the chamber. Lik-Rifa had given one chamber to a coven of night-hags, because they preferred to live in darkness. Biórr had shivered when they had passed close by him, ethereal and floating like mist.

But they are all the creations of Lik-Rifa, born and bred in the darkness of the vaesen pit, before Snaka's fall broke Mount Eldrafell and set the rivers of fire loose, sending the vaesen crawling and scuttling for the safety of the open world.

Lik-Rifa dropped on to one knee as the frost-spiders approached her, one of them scurrying out from the group, its body thick-haired and scarred, forelegs raised and probing, caressing Lik-Rifa's face and body.

"Ah, little ones," Lik-Rifa crooned, and the rest of the spiders scuttled about her, Lik-Rifa disappearing from view as they pressed close to her with their bloated, hairy bodies. Biórr heard Lik-Rifa's voice, though the words were indistinct, and then the spiders were moving away, gathering around a snake-carved column and climbing it. They disappeared into the gloom where ice-touched webs were hanging.

Lik-Rifa rose and nodded to one of the skraeling who stood close by, like some kind of guardsman, and he raised a horn to his twisted lips and blew on it, the sound of it wavering and echoing eerily through the cavernous hall.

"It is time to talk of war," Lik-Rifa said.

Biórr stood in a large crowd, Fain and Storolf and Ilmur pressed close to him, all of the Raven-Feeders and dragon-worshippers gathered in a half-circle before Lik-Rifa on her serpent throne. Most of the children were scattered among them, as well as a few score skraelings, clouds of tennúr and a handful of trolls. At the rear of the cavern he saw the shadowed forms of night-hags floating, and spread around the edges of the hall were a few spertus, standing still as stone with their wax-melted faces and black-dripping stings curled over their backs. Much to Biórr's relief the frost-spiders and hyrndur did not seem to be interested in the details of Lik-Rifa's plans for war, though Biórr did catch the hint of shadowed movement in the murk above him, just beyond the reach of the firelight, and the glint of flames reflected in clustered eyes.

"I am feeling stronger, and rested," Lik-Rifa said, smiling and stretching languorously, like a cat after it had feasted on mouse or bird. "And I feel better for having my vaesen gathering to me." She gestured to the vaesen about the hall, "As well as those with my blood running in their veins." She gave Ilska a wide, lazy smile. "And, of course, I have my brother beside me again." She reached out a fist and grabbed the hand of Rotta, who stood at her left side. "These are things I've dreamed of, over the long, lonely years that I have been caged in the bowels of Oskutreð." She shivered and Biórr saw the hint of rage that never seemed to be far from the surface of Lik-Rifa's emotions. Her face twitched, a hint of dragon-scales and teeth, but then she blew out a long breath and relaxed back into her chair.

"But, as pleasant as this is, we cannot stay here forever. For one reason, this new world has committed a great injustice, both to my bloodline and the bloodlines of my brothers and sisters." She looked up at Rotta and smiled. "I mean to PUNISH THEM for that," she screamed, eyes bulging.

Biórr's hand rose to hover over the scars on his chest and he sucked in a deep breath, imagining how the world was about to change. *No more enslaving the Tainted*, he thought, *an end to the beatings and depravation, to the hate and shame.* Just the thought of it made him stand straighter, hold his head higher. *To be part of the sword that brings this freedom, I am proud to be here.* It made all he had been through, all of the pain and sacrifice, worthwhile. And those dark deeds that haunted him, too. The lies and false-hoods, the betrayals and killings. Agnar's face hovered in his mind, kneeling in the ash of Oskutreð's plain as he held out a hand to Biórr.

"And the other reason why we must act," Lik-Rifa continued, her composure returned, "is Ulfrir. My *niðing* brother is out there, somewhere, lurking and plotting. He is wolf-cunning and will be thinking only of how he is going to put his jaws around my throat." She shifted in her chair, the stone serpents writhing and hissing as she twisted her head left and right. "I will be the one to rip *his* furry head from his body," she snarled.

"We will fight until he is back in the ground," Ilska said from the crowd.

"Yes," Lik-Rifa said, smiling at Ilska, "you will. But it is finding him. So, we shall tear Vigrið apart until he is revealed. Ilska, tell me again of the world beyond my halls."

"To the south," Ilska said, "not more than a few days' march from here, lies Svelgarth. There you will find Jarl Orlyg, one of the three powers in Vigrið. He is old but hale, and warlike, though weaker than his two rivals. On his borders he fights with Helka, who calls herself queen—"

"The deluded cur," Lik-Rifa snarled, "there is only one queen in Vigrið."

"Helka is most likely the strongest of the three," Ilska continued, "if we are thinking of the number of petty jarls, *drengrs* and warriors at her command. Her land stretches to the banks of the River Slågen, and everything west of that river comes under Jarl Störr's sway. All of them are ambitious and strong in their own way. Orlyg a warrior, Helka ruthless, Störr a deep-thinker."

"So, sister, what is the plan?" Rotta asked Lik-Rifa.

"We will kill them all," Lik-Rifa said with a nonchalant shrug. "This Orlyg at Svelgarth first, then Helka, and finally on to Störr. And I shall free your Tainted kin as we go and take the warbands from these petty jarls and pretenders, until we find Ulfrir skulking in his den. And then we will kill him."

CHAPTER FIFTY-FIVE

ORKA

Orka kicked dirt over their small fire as they made ready to ride out. Over the last two days Sæunn had tracked Myrk north along the edge of Lake Horndal, and then followed her trail eastwards, skirting the northern tree-shrouded slopes of the Boneback Mountains. Elvar had spoken the truth: Breca was being taken east, not west, as Myrk had sworn to Orka. A bubbling of anger in her veins, and the distant growl of a wolf as she thought on that. Images of blood and ripping flesh flooded her thought-cage.

Wait, she told the wolf in her blood. *We shall see Myrk again* . . .

Slurping noises drew Orka's eye and she saw Spert's fat black tongue licking the last of his porridge from a bowl. Vesli was frowning as she sat on a boulder hefting her sack of teeth, which looked far lighter than when they had left Rotta's chamber.

"Which of you two is the better flier?" Orka asked them.

The two vaesen stopped what they were doing and looked at Orka.

"*She is*," Spert rasped, one of his antennae pointing at Vesli.

"Is he telling the truth?" Orka asked Vesli.

The tennúr nodded. "*Spert fatter than Vesli*," she said with a sniff. Spert muttered something unintelligible.

"I need you to do something for me," Orka said, reaching inside her cloak and taking out the silver arm ring that Elvar had given to her. "I need you to find the Bloodsworn, and give Glornir a message. And this arm ring, too." She hefted it and threw it to Vesli, whose wings snapped open and became a blur, raising her up so that she caught the arm ring in one of her hook-clawed feet. She dropped a little in the air with the weight of it. Orka frowned at that.

"How far can you travel in a day, with the extra weight?" Orka asked her, still frowning.

"*Don't know*," Vesli shrugged. "*But Vesli will do it for mistress, no matter how long it takes her. What is the message, mistress?*" Vesli asked her, though an anxious twist flickered across her sharp-boned face.

"A message from Elvar, chief of the Battle-Grim," Orka said. She paused a moment, puffing her cheeks out as she looked at the line of mountains they were following. "Wait on it," she said, "I will give it some thought." She held out her hand and Vesli dropped the arm ring back to her.

A jangle of hooves and harness and Lif was leading his horse and Trúr over to Orka. She nodded her thanks, took the reins and climbed into the saddle, bones stiff from the cold.

"Sæunn," Orka said and the *Hundur*-thrall broke into her loping run, leading them ever eastward on Myrk's trail.

Orka shifted in her saddle and pulled her cloak tighter about her. It was getting colder, the further north and east they travelled. In the distance she could just make out Sæunn. The Hundur-blood was crouched low to the ground, looking at something. The track they were following cut through woodlands of dense pine as they skirted the northern foothills of the Boneback Mountains, the ground spongy with needles, but as Orka drew closer she saw that the trees thinned and ended as the ground rose, climbing into an expanse of green meadows dotted with black-stone boulders. Sæunn was crouching at the edge of the treeline, eyes focused on the ground before her.

"What is it?" Orka said as she reined in.

Sæunn stood and pointed at the ground, where a large swathe

of grass was torn and scratched, as if someone had dragged a spiked tree trunk behind them. Orka followed the trail and saw it rose up through the meadow, dipping with the land and disappearing into more trees in the distance.

"What did this?" Gunnar Prow asked as he and the others reined in.

They had seen many tracks during the last few days of travel, all of differing species of vaesen: skraeling, trolls, faunir, all of them heading eastwards.

"I have not seen these kinds of tracks before," Sæunn frowned. "Whatever did it, there was more than one of them. Many more." She brushed her hand across the churned ground, and it came away with a faint glow, almost invisible hairs glistening with dew in the sunlight. Sæunn lifted her palm to her face and took a long, deep breath. Then her mouth twisted, and she wiped her hand on her tunic.

"Frost-spiders," she said.

A grunt from Lif as he twisted in his saddle and looked up at the trees behind him, his spear gripped in white-knuckled fists and pointing at shadows.

He has bad memories of frost-spiders, Orka thought as she looked, too, and saw a glint of sunlight on a thick strand of ice-tinged web hanging between branches.

"*They answer Lik-Rifa's call*," Spert muttered, looking up from where he slept across Orka's saddle.

The thought of countless vaesen flocking to Lik-Rifa was not a good one and did not bode well for the future of Vigrið.

I cannot think on that. There is only Breca.

They set off again, moving across the meadow, butterflies taking to wing before their horses' hooves. To the north the world dipped towards an undulating plain, cracked with rivers and dark-seamed chasms, and dotted with clusters of sharp crags and swathes of dense woodland. Here and there smoke rose from isolated steadings and farms. North of the Bonebacks was a different world from the south. In the south vaesen roamed, but they kept to the shadows, lurking in the mountains and the dark hearts of forests, and people thrived in their fortresses and villages and lived in great numbers. North of the Bonebacks it was the opposite. Vaesen roamed unafraid of being hunted by humankind, the only people to be found here living in isolation, a steading here, a farm there.

People like me, who want a life alone.

They crossed the open meadows quickly, Orka feeling exposed out in the open, but they slowed and moved more cautiously into the treeline on the meadow's far edge. The ground returned to normal and Sæunn found marks and traces of web on the bark of trees.

"They crawled back into the canopy," she said, and Orka let the wolf seep through her, sharpening her sight and smell and hearing, but she could see or smell nothing.

"See anything?" Orka asked Halja, who had Orna the eagle in her blood, and so was the keenest sighted among them. A shimmer of air around her and Orka saw Halja's eyes shift to flecks of tawny gold.

"Webs, lots of webs," Halja said, "but it is loose, swinging in the breeze. The spiders are long gone from here."

"And travelling in the same direction as us," Revna Hare-Legs murmured, looking ahead, through the pine-cloaked slopes.

"Aye, be vigilant," Orka said, "keep your weapons close, and loose in their scabbards. And Sæunn, be careful. Don't want you ending up as a frost-spider's supper."

"Yes, mistress Orka," Sæunn said, and then she was moving off again.

They moved on, their passage through the pinewoods feeling uncomfortably loud in the oppressive silence. Orka touched on her reins to slow Trúr's pace to ride alongside Lif, who was constantly scanning the boughs above them.

"Your brother was a brave man," Orka said to him.

Lif frowned, taking a few moments for those words to sink in.

"I always thought so," Lif said, "but why do *you* say so?"

"Because when you were lying on the ground, twitching and frothing ice with frost-spider venom in your veins, Mord stood over you and fought. He slew many spiders."

"Did he?" Lif asked, his face softening. "I don't remember any of that. Until the tower . . ."

"I saw how scared he was to enter the woods, knowing that frost-spiders might be in the branches above us, and yet he stayed. He stood and fought his fear. There is much to respect in that," Orka said.

"Aye," Lif nodded, tears leaking down his cheeks, silent for a while. "I thought you would think Mord a coward," he sniffed, "because of how scared he was."

Orka remembered the words Thorkel had often said to Breca, could almost hear his bear-deep voice in her thought-cage. *Real courage is to feel fear, but to stand and face it, not run from it.*

"No," Orka grunted, "I did not think him a coward. Everyone feels fear, there is no shame in it."

"You don't," Lif snorted.

I feel fear every day. Almost every waking moment. Fear that I will fail Breca, never find him, never see his face again, touch his cheek, never hold him or kiss him again. Fear that Thorkel will lie cold in his barrow unavenged. A chill shivered through her body, almost physical pain, like a fist clenching around her heart.

They rode in silence awhile, Orka lost in the dark-tinged dread of failure.

"Why did you lead us into that nest of frost-spiders?" Lif asked her, pulling Orka from her dark thoughts. "Why did you help those ravens trapped in the frost-spiders' web?"

"Because I'm an idiot," Orka grunted.

"You are many things, Orka Skullsplitter," Lif said, "but I would not count idiot among them."

"Huh," Orka snorted.

"So, why?"

Orka sighed.

"Because of Breca," she said, remembering the night before he had been taken, when he had saved a moth snared in a spiderweb. She told Lif about it. "'That is not a good death, Mama,' he said to me. 'And to stand by and just let it happen,' he said." Orka shrugged.

"I understand," Lif said, nodding.

Another silence settled over them.

"Are you lonely?" Lif asked her.

Orka scowled at him and did not answer.

To grieve is to be trapped in a world of loneliness.

"I am," Lif said. "Do you ever think of comfort, hope for it?"

Aye, when I see my boy again.

"I will find comfort when Drekr's corpse is twitching at my feet," she growled, a hand going to one of the dragon-born's seaxes, sheathed across her lap.

"And I in Guðvarr's death," Lif agreed. "But I mean something else, something more." He glanced at Halja Flat-Nose, who was riding well ahead of them, keeping Sæunn in her eagle-touched sight.

"Ah," Orka said, understanding.

"But she must think me weak and pathetic," Lif said morosely.

"If she thinks of you at all," Orka agreed.

Lif blinked at that. "Well, my thanks for the encouragement . . ."

Orka felt the twinge of a smile, which was a rare thing these days.

"You share common ground, and companionship often begins there," Orka said.

"Common ground?" Lif said.

"Grief," Orka muttered. "Grief is your common ground."

"Yes," Lif agreed. "We do share that."

"And she likes your singing," Revna Hare-Legs said behind them.

Lif jumped and twisted in his saddle.

"You are eavesdropping!" he said, blushing.

"Riding day after day is boring; finally, something interesting to talk about. I could be helpful." She grinned at Lif, and Gunnar Prow chuckled.

"You are forgetting one thing," Gunnar said. "Halja only humps women."

"There was that man in Liga, though," Revna said with a frown. "She humped him."

"Aye, but then she killed him."

Revna's frown deepened. "That was because he cheated at tafl, not because he had a snake between his legs."

"Are you sure?"

"No," Revna shrugged. She looked at Lif. "Ignore Gunnar, I'll help you with Halja."

"I like Halja," Lif said, "but it sounds a bit . . ."

"Dangerous?" Gunnar finished for him, shaking his head and smiling.

Revna just grinned and winked at Lif.

Up ahead Orka saw a dark mound on the path, a foul-clawing stench seeping into her throat as Trúr stepped over it.

"What is that *smell*?" Lif wheezed, putting the back of his hand to his nose, lips twisting downwards in disgust.

"Skraeling shite," Revna said.

"I hate skraelings," Gunnar grunted.

A sound echoed through the woodland, a deep, reverberating horn call that sent a tremor through the canopy above.

"What in the dead gods is that?" Lif asked with a worried frown.

Orka touched her heels to Trúr's side and clicked her tongue, picking up the pace. They turned a corner in their path and saw Halja and Sæunn standing on the edge of another rolling meadow, pale sunlight dappling the ground through swaying branches. Orka didn't need to ask why they had stopped. They stared out, northwards, down the slope and rolling meadow to a stockaded farm nestled against woodland. The deep-bellied horn calls were rolling out from the steading, and faintly behind the blowing of the horn Orka heard screams drifting on the breeze. Black smoke billowed into the sky.

"Best we take a look, don't you think, chief?" Halja Flat-Nose said.

Others' misfortune is not my business, Orka thought. *This is a world of tooth and claw.* She looked up at the sky and twisted in her saddle to find the sun. It was long past midday, the sun sinking into the west behind them. *But I don't want anything creeping up behind us in the night.*

"Aye, we'll take a look," Orka agreed.

CHAPTER FIFTY-SIX

ELVAR

Elvar bent her back and pulled on her oar. Lean and pull, lean and pull. She liked to row, although some of the Battle-Grim had raised an eyebrow when she had sat at her old oar-chest. Agnar had never rowed, their old chief much happier at the tiller of the *Wave-Jarl*, the position of power, steering and controlling their direction. Elvar had tried that, but she found she did not like it so much.

Strange, because once I dreamed of being chief and able to stand at the steering oar, dreamed of being free of the exhaustion and mundanity of the oar-bench. But standing at the tiller had made her feel isolated and gave her too much time to think; about Lik-Rifa and her oath, about where she was going and about who she would see, all too soon. So she had handed the tiller over to Sighvat and gone back to the oar bench, where she could become lost in the rhythm of her work, in the burn of muscle and rasp of lung.

"OARS," Sighvat yelled and, as one, all those on the oar-benches raised their oars from the clear water, a sparkling curtain of ice-shard droplets, then the crew were shipping and stowing their oars in deck-racks. The *Wave-Jarl* coasted on, the current helping keep their momentum as the second shift of rowers settled on to their benches, threading their own oars through oarlocks.

"READY," Sighvat bellowed and then shouted, "ROW," and oars were once again dipping into the river and powering them on.

Elvar straightened and stretched her back, standing and stepping out into the deck. Since leaving Starl they had made good time down the River Hvítá, and the decision to row in two shifts of half-crews had helped that. It meant that twenty-four oars were constantly propelling them towards their goal from dawn until they stopped at night to make camp, but it also meant that her crew wouldn't be exhausted when they reached Snakavik.

We may well need our strength.

"Here," Grend said, offering Elvar his leather-carved water bottle and she drank deep, feeling the cold breeze already cooling her sweat. She picked up Agnar's bear-cloak.

My bear-cloak.

And wrapped it around her shoulders, then turned and strode down the deck towards Sighvat.

"Making good time, chief," he said as she drew near. Ulfrir was sitting in shadow among a stack of chests and barrels, a cloak pulled up over his shadowed face. Skuld stood and stared out at the land around them.

"Aye," Elvar said to Sighvat, feeling both excitement and apprehension at that.

A step closer to getting this blood oath out of my veins, but that means . . .

She shook her head, not wanting to think about the consequences of that.

Downriver Elvar saw a fat merchant *knarr* rowing towards the *Wave-Jarl*, the crew pulling and making slow headway against the current and the wind.

The River Hvítá had widened since they had left Lake Horndal, the land around them shifting from mountains and hills to rolling plains as the river coiled deep into the heart of Vigrið and her father's realm. Large swathes of dark woods and rolling meadows dotted with towns and villages. All she could see came under the iron fist of Jarl Störr, her father. And now the river was curling back to the west, the white-capped Bonebacks growing larger, taking her ever closer to Jarl Störr and her birthplace. Glimmers of grey-green bone broke through the soil and trees that cloaked the skeleton within the Bonebacks.

Back to the beginning. My beginning. Back to Snakavik.

The merchant *knarr* was closer now and had veered across to the far bank of the river, taking a course as far removed from the *Wave-Jarl* as possible.

They like the look of a sleek drakkar about as much as a sheep likes the look of the approaching wolf.

"Sighvat," Elvar said, "bring us close to that fat-wallowing sow."

"Aye, chief," Sighvat grunted.

"OARS, HALF-TIME," he bellowed, and the *Wave-Jarl* slowed as Sighvat steered them across the river.

Elvar stood with her hands on the top-rail, watching the merchant ship. As soon as the *Wave-Jarl* altered its course to head the merchant ship off she saw movement on its broad deck, and within a few heartbeats the sun was glinting on spear-tips and mail, a dozen warriors lining up along the ship's portside.

The merchant's hired guards. Must be a prize worth protecting, and if I were Agnar we'd be making ready to board the fat sow and stain her decks red.

They were close enough for Elvar to see individual features now. She saw a slim, richly dressed woman with a fur-trimmed hat standing in the prow, a gold-tooled pouch hanging from her gold-buckled belt.

An arrow hissed into the air and disappeared into the river with a faint splash.

"They dare raise weapons against me, born of Ulfrir and Orna!" Skuld said at Elvar's shoulder. "I will crush them for their impudence. I will kill them all, rip them to pieces, drown them in their own blood—"

"You kill them when I tell you to kill them," Elvar snarled at Skuld. Then she raised her hands to her mouth. "WHAT NEWS FROM SNAKAVIK?" Elvar yelled at the gold-draped woman.

The *Wave-Jarl* moved ever closer, into arrow range.

"OARS," Elvar cried out and her crew raised and shipped their oars, the *Wave-Jarl* hissing through water, slowing.

"We'll make you pay in blood and lives if you board us," the woman called back.

"I don't want your cargo, I want your news, and am happy to pay for it," Elvar shouted. She took a silver ring from her arm and hurled it across the gap between the ships, saw it clatter on the deck by the merchant's feet. She scooped it up, bit it, examined it, her eyes widening.

That arm ring is probably worth as much as your cargo, Elvar thought, *but I need news, not more gold or silver.*

"Well?" Elvar cried out. "Don't make me come over there to get my arm ring back."

"The news is Jarl Störr gathers his *drengrs,*" the merchant called across the water.

"Why?" Elvar shouted.

"For war," the merchant shouted back. "Against Helka. Jarl Orlyg of Svelgarth is bound for Darl, and Jarl Störr suspects an alliance. He means to strike at Helka before she is ready." The woman shrugged. "That is what Jarl Störr's *drengrs* are whispering to whores anyway."

Elvar dipped her head to the merchant. "My thanks," she said. "Sighvat, take us back on course."

"Aye, chief," he said, grunting as he moved the tiller, the steering oar guiding the longship away from the riverbank and then the *Wave-Jarl* was gliding past the merchant *knarr* and carving a wake through deeper water.

Towards Snakavik. Towards war.

A touch on Elvar's shoulder as she stood in the prow, brooding. It was Grend.

"What?" she snapped at him.

He pointed, south and west, to the western bank of the Hvítá. A flicker of movement drew her attention and she saw people moving on the steep-sided bank on their starboard side, heading towards a wooden bridge that spanned the river. Thirty or forty men and women moving in loose formation, the glint of spear blades and mail among them.

More drengrs *answering my father's call?*

Elvar saw wagons piled with stores, oxen pulling them, and as the *Wave-Jarl* drew closer she saw children dotted among the crowd. They began to cross the bridge.

They are heading east, away from Snakavik.

Closer still and she saw that they were not *drengrs*, or, if they were, they should be ashamed of themselves, because their mail was tattered and rusting, their spear blades dull. Then she saw their shields.

A grey dragon painted in a white sky.

Elvar blinked, stunned by the audacity of these people.

A presence at her shoulder and she turned to see Skuld standing there, staring. Ulfrir was a hulking presence behind her. He pushed the hood of his cloak back, head raised high, sniffing the air.

"They serve my sister," he growled.

"Dragon-worshippers, marching across my father's land in the bright light of day, without a worry or care!" Elvar breathed. She remembered the dragon-worshippers she had seen swinging in the cages of Snakavik, or what was left of them after the ravens had had their fill. She barked out a shocked laugh at the thought of her father's face if he could see them.

He would choke with rage, to be so disrespected.

"We could land and put them in the ground," Grend said as the *Wave-Jarl* drew close to the bridge, the sound of tramping feet and grating of wheels sending dust falling from the underside of the bridge.

Elvar stared up at them, and then looked east, in the direction they were heading.

"No, let them go," Elvar said. "One battle at a time."

And then in a few heartbeats they passed beneath the bridge's shadow, out the other side and were turning a sweeping bend in the river.

Ulfrir hissed a breath as he stared into the distance.

"Father," he said.

The great skull of Snaka stood outlined in the distance, a black silhouette of fang and eye sockets, and upon the dead serpent's skull stood the fortress of Snakavik.

CHAPTER FIFTY-SEVEN

ORKA

Orka crawled up a slope of forest litter and thick-winding roots and eased her head over the ridge, peering between pine trees.

The homestead lay a few score paces below them. A stockade of rough-sawn pine that ringed a half-dozen buildings, longhouse, barn, pig and chicken pens, charcoal kiln, a brewhouse, a forge. There was only one gateway that Orka could see. A stream ran through the steading and Orka saw the timber where the stream entered it had been hacked into a broader hole. One of the main gates was swinging by one hinge. The other gate lay flat and trampled in the mud. In a wide, muddy courtyard there was a strange sight. At its centre stood a huge pile of felled trees, looking as if they'd been thrown there by some giant.

What is that?

Beside this mound of wood stood a timber frame, a huge horn hanging from it. Two bodies lay on the ground about the horn, blood pooling black into the mud around them. One of the bodies was being skinned by a skraeling with a thin-bladed knife, and dismembered by another skraeling with a crude iron weapon that looked like a long cleaver. Other skraeling were sifting through a pile of spilled offal. The other body was being stripped of weapons and boots by three more skraeling. Flames crackled through the roof of a barn and black clouds of smoke were billowing.

Muffled screams rang from inside a grass-turfed longhouse, pulling Orka's eyes away from the strange pile of timber. The doors were smashed open, and on the roof Orka saw that a gaping hole had been carved through turf and the timber framework beneath.

A surge of blood-tinged memory in her thought-cage, of running through woodland, the screams of Breca drifting on the air, her home in flames. She felt abruptly breathless, a low-snarling growl echoing through her blood. She stopped herself from standing and running down the slope.

They are not my kin.

Another scream rang out.

"We must help them," said Lif, who had crawled up on Orka's right. The Bloodsworn were spread along the ridge either side of her, all of them looking down on the scene of slaughter.

"No," Orka said.

"Remember Breca's compassion; the moth and the spider," Lif said. "The raven and the frost-spiders."

"Your brother died because of that foolishness," Orka said. "We are not a saga-tale."

"But it is wrong," Lif muttered, "and we could help."

"A thousand injustices happen every day," Orka growled. "And to run down there is to risk your own death. No vengeance for Mord, no finding Breca, just a shallow-dug barrow, if anyone who cares enough is left to dig it. Life is a knife's edge, and all can change with the thrust of a blade."

Lif was silent. More screams echoed and a cloud of smoke drifted up across them, acrid in Orka's throat.

"If it were Breca and Thorkel, and someone could have saved them . . ." Lif said.

Orka rolled and grabbed Lif by his coat of mail, dragging him towards her, a snarl pulling her lips back from her teeth, rage flooding through her. Lif just looked back at her, a hint of fear in his eyes, but he made no move to resist her.

"Chief," a voice said, a hand touching her shoulder. Halja Flat-Nose, though it felt like she spoke from some great distance.

"Ach," Orka spat, releasing Lif and sliding back out of sight of the steading.

"I'm not your chief," she growled, shaking her head. "All have a choice, here." She looked at them, all staring back at her.

"I hate skraelings," Gunnar Prow said with a shrug. "And they're going to Lik-Rifa anyway. I say we carve them up now, there'll be a few less to worry about when we find your boy."

"Huh," Orka scowled. She had thought about that, too. "Flat-Nose?" she said.

"Skraeling were at Rotta's chamber when my brother died. They work with the *niðing* dragon-born." She spat in the mud. "I'll gladly kill them all, for Vali's sake."

"Revna?" Orka said.

"Makes a change from riding all day long," she said. "My arse is aching from it." She grinned. "Besides, I'd rather put these vaesen in the ground now, than have them creep up on us in the night."

Orka sucked in a long breath.

"All right," she said, already striding down the slope to where Sæunn stood minding the horses. She walked to Trúr, unclipped her cloak-pin and took her cloak off, laying it across her saddle, then unstrapped her long-axe, slipping the leather blade cover off and tucking it into a saddle strap.

"Gunnar, how is your leg?"

"It's good," he said, putting weight on it to prove his point. "Whatever is in Vesli's spit," he pulled a disgusted face, "it works."

Vesli grinned from where she was sitting on Orka's saddle alongside Spert. "You and Revna work round to the east, where the stream enters the steading. Flat-Nose and Lif, you're with me. We'll go in the front door." She looked at Gunnar and Revna. "You two meet us in the middle."

"*What about us, mistress?*" Vesli squeaked.

"Fight, don't fight," Orka said, "do as you wish."

Spert stretched across Orka's saddle. "*Spert will fight*," he muttered.

"*Vesli will fight, too*," Vesli said, and flew off to the packhorse where her short spear was strapped.

Orka nodded. "Just don't get yourselves killed."

"*Spert will not be the one doing the dying,*" he said, his wax-melted face twisting with malevolence.

"What are your orders, mistress Orka?" Sæunn asked her.

"Stay here and guard the horses," Orka said. She walked to a packhorse, pulled a spare spear from its binding and threw it to Sæunn. "Know how to use this?"

Sæunn caught it deftly in one hand and spun it, reversing her grip. "I will guard them with my life."

"Good."

All around her the Bloodsworn were making ready, unstrapping their black and blood-spattered shields from saddles, tying back their hair, fetching spears, loosening blades in scabbards, buckling on helms. Orka watched Lif move to his horse and make ready, buckling on his iron cap and hefting his shield. Tightening his weapons belt. A slight tremor in his grip gave away his nerves. Orka turned away and pulled a nålbinding cap on to her head, then buckled on her nasal helm, rolling her shoulders to settle the curtain of mail across her neck. She checked her seaxes, drawing them in their scabbards and letting them slip back in.

She hefted her long-axe and looked at them all.

"Ready?" Nods and grunts. "Stay in your groups. Work together. Lif, skraeling are strong, inhumanly strong, so use your wits and weapon-craft." Lif nodded, sweat beading his brow.

"Right," Orka rumbled. "Let's do this."

"We'll see you after," Revna said with a grin as Gunnar strode off through the trees.

"Lif, have another look over that ridge, check where the skraeling are," Orka said.

Lif nodded and hurried up the slope, moving a little too fast, jerks and tremors in his limbs.

"Spert, Vesli," Orka muttered quietly, "keep an eye on Lif. I want him still breathing when this is done."

"*Yes, mistress,*" the two vaesen answered.

Then she was striding up the ridge, Halja at her shoulder, Spert and Vesli whirring up into the canopy above.

"Seven of them in the courtyard," Lif said, and Orka nodded, not breaking her stride, just marching over the ridge and down the slope. It was about fifty paces through woodland and then another twenty across open ground to the steading's smashed gates.

Wolf, it is axe time, claw time, she said to the beast in her blood, and heard a deep-throated growl reverberate through her thought-cage, setting her limbs tingling. Everything sharpened, pine scent wafting up from needles underfoot, distinct screams and bellows from inside the longhouse, in the courtyard the fleshy folds of blue-grey skraeling hides becoming sharply clear, grime and sweat, patches of hair on their lopsided heads, rust on their blades. Orka's teeth drew back in a snarl as the ground levelled and she reached the treeline.

"Stay behind me," she growled at Lif, and then she was breaking into a loping run across the open ground, the soft beat of her feet on grass, breath rasping and eager, blood thrumming with the need to kill. At the gates and through them, a patter of dull thuds as she pounded across the smashed gate and into the courtyard.

The two skraeling skinning and dismembering a body were closest and, without breaking her stride, Orka swung her axe and hacked into the nearest one's back. A wet thump and crack, flesh and bone parting, a gurgled scream and Orka was turning, dragging the axe blade free as the skraeling fell, dead before it hit the ground, opened up from shoulder to hip. She raised her axe to swing at the other skraeling with the oversized cleaver but there was a flash of mail and a glimpse of red hair beneath an iron helm and then the skraeling was crashing to the ground, a red wound where its face had been, Halja standing over the dying vaesen, snarling and spitting curses.

Footsteps pounding behind, Lif catching up, the whirr of small wings. Ahead of her three skraeling looked up from a pile of guts and offal, two more that had been stripping a body already moving towards Orka and Halja. Orka did not wait for them to come to her. With a howl she leaped, gripping her long-axe two-handed across her body, ducked a looping blow from a jagged axe and swung up, her axe haft crunching into a skraeling's face, nose exploding, lips mushed, teeth spraying. With a howl the skraeling staggered a few steps, toppled backwards and Orka swung her axe overhead with a roar, buried it in the vaesen's chest. Blood and bone exploded. Put a foot on it to rip her blade free, wrenched, but the blade stuck in shattered ribs. A snarl and hint of fetid breath to her right and she let the axe go, dropped into a crouch, drawing hand-axe and seax, slashing and chopping simultaneously as another skraeling crashed into her. She snarled, spat and cursed, biting into thick-hided flesh, felt salty blood spurt into her mouth, kept stabbing and chopping and biting as she and the skraeling staggered and tottered around the yard, heard the skraeling's savage snarls become desperate squeals. A thud and the skraeling fell away, Gunnar Prow's face appearing, his eyes glinting green, mouth twisted, all rage, sharp teeth and snarling froth.

The wolf in Orka howled as she stood there, breathing hard, head snapping around the courtyard, searching for something living to kill.

All seven skraeling were down, Revna standing over two, Lif close by, his shield splintered, red claw marks down one side of his face. His spear blade dripped red. A skraeling lay at his feet, still twitching, red holes in its chest and belly and veins black and swollen. Spert hovered in the air above it, Vesli landing and hammering at the dying creature's teeth with the butt of her spear.

The Bloodsworn looked to Orka.

"Gunnar, Revna," she pointed at the longhouse roof. They nodded and moved, running fast and fluid around the side of the longhouse and leaping on to the turf roof, clambering up. A gout of black smoke rolled across the courtyard, stinging and choking. A sharp wind tore it away.

"With me," Orka told Halja and Lif, and then she was running again, axe and seax gripped in her bloodied fists. Pounding up timber steps and through the gaping black hole of the longhouse doors. She stumbled over corpses, human and skraeling locked together, jumped over them and skidded to a halt. A heartbeat for her eyes to adjust. Light streamed in a column through the hole in the roof. A hearth fire blazed, flames crackling, a body collapsed across it, clothes and hair burning, skin blackening, an overturned iron pot rolling.

There was a mass of skraeling at the far end of the hall, swarming around three or four people, maybe more. Orka glimpsing a white-haired old man, a younger woman and a youth, standing in a half-circle with shields raised and locked together, someone behind stabbing out with a long boar spear. More bodies littered the ground between Orka and them, none of them moving.

A presence at Orka's shoulder: Halja. Orka pointed to the right flank and Halja nodded, slapped Lif's arm to get his attention, pointed at the left flank of clustered skraeling, then she was moving again. Orka let out a snarling howl as she sped towards them, a handful of skraeling hearing her, turning, shouting out in their coarse, gravel-touched voices. Movement from above, Revna and Gunnar dropping down through the hole in the roof, and then Orka was leaping, crashing into them, axe and seax chopping and slicing, blood spraying as she smashed them apart like kindling. The wolf rose in her, howling, snarling, and Orka was lost in a sea of blood and teeth and sharp iron. Fractured moments filled with a skraeling's face, snarling then screaming, a blow to her back that sent her stumbling to one knee, flesh between her jaws, blood spurting into her throat, her axe chopping into a face, a clawed hand clamping around the mail of her helm, dragging her backwards. Lif's face appearing, stabbing his spear into the mouth of a skraeling, and then she was rolling on blood-slick ground, coming up in a crouched stance, axe raised high, seax low. Snarling.

Skraeling lay all around her in a heap, dead or dying. Wide-eyed faces stared out at her from behind shields. Halja standing close to Lif, skraeling dead on the ground before them. Lif swayed and dropped to one knee, Halja catching him. The thud of feet and she saw two or three skraeling running for the door. Without thought she was after them, crossing the longhouse in a handful of strides, then leaping, crashing into the back of one and sending it slamming into the others, all of them flying through the open door in a tangle of limbs. Orka's shoulder crunched into a step, then she was airborne again, spinning, smashed on to mud with a thud and expulsion of air, lost the grip of her hand-axe and clambered to one knee, seax still in her fist. She saw a skraeling rising, reaching for a thick-iron blade and she pushed off with one leg, threw herself into the creature and punched her seax into its belly, once, twice, three times before they both crashed back to the ground. Orka pushed herself free, rolled on to her back and saw another skraeling loom over her with an axe raised high. A moment as she sucked in a new breath, and then a shadow fell over her, the skraeling and the courtyard. Wind swept around her, the sound of beating wings and a raucous screech filled her ears, then talons were wrapping around the skraeling and it was being heaved up into the air with great, powerful beats of black feathered wings.

Orka gazed up, saw a huge raven with the skraeling in its claws, another raven swooping and raking another skraeling with razored talons. A ripping, cracking sound and then blood was raining down over Orka, lumps of flesh falling with wet thuds all around her as the skraeling in the raven's claws was ripped and torn apart.

Orka gripped the water barrel with both hands and submerged her head into the ice-cold water, held it there for a dozen heartbeats, then a dozen more, the world fading for a moment, just muffled echoes, and let the cold soak and seep into her skin. With a spray of pink water she pulled clear, washing and wiping the blood from her face. Coughed and spat more skraeling blood from her mouth. She walked around the courtyard, retrieving her weapons, wrenching her long-axe from the chest of a dead skraeling, and finding her hand-axe lying in a pool of blood.

Gunnar and Revna had gone to fetch Sæunn and the horses. Halja was standing over Lif, who sat on the timber steps to the longhouse with a deep gash across one cheek, blood sheeting down his face, ragged claw marks down the other. Vesli stood on his knee, spitting balls of stringy mucus into her hands and rubbing them together and Spert lay at Lif's feet like a hound, looking like he was fast asleep.

Other people were walking in and out of the longhouse, an old man with white hair pulled and tied neatly, and a tall, long-limbed youth with a wisp of blond beard. They were carrying bodies, skraeling being hurled on to a pile in the courtyard, and people laid neatly out in a line close to the longhouse. So far there were fourteen skraeling and seven people.

One of the giant ravens stood close over the dead skraeling, ripping into flesh with a huge black beak. The other raven was sitting at the top of the strange mound of timber in the centre of the courtyard, preening its feathers. Orka realised now that it was a giant nest. Ash lay thick on the ground, the barn had burned down to a black-husked skeleton.

The sound of hooves and Gunnar appeared, Revna and Sæunn with him, leading their horses. They tethered them to the post and rail fence of the pig pen. Revna walked across to where Vesli was tending to Lif, Halja sitting close by on the steps to the longhouse, cleaning her weapons.

"Still in one piece then, Lif," Revna said.

"Just about," Lif said as Vesli held the skin of his cheek together, waiting for her mucus to bind it.

"Come a long way from sleeping through a visit from a night-hag, haven't you?" She glanced at Halja. "He's turning into quite the warrior, don't you think, Flat-Nose?"

Halja looked up from scouring blood from her seax.

"He's still breathing," she said, nodding, "and his enemies lay cold in the mud."

Revna smiled and gave Lif a wink, then sauntered away, Lif's cheeks shifting to match the colour of the blood spattering his face. A smile twitched his lips, Vesli scolding him for moving.

The man with the white hair limped over to Orka. He was tall, lean and wire-muscled, a thick ridge of scar running through his chin. His eyes were red with grief, but he still dipped his head in thanks to Orka.

"Name's Gudleif Arnesson, and we are in your debt," he said to Orka.

"Huh, you can thank him for that," she grunted, nodding at Lif. "Helping you was his idea." Orka looked from the raven to the giant horn hanging from its timber scaffold, to the huge nest in the middle of the courtyard.

"What in the name of the dead gods is going on here?" she asked Gudleif.

"It's a trade," Gudleif said with a shrug. "Food, for news and protection."

"There wasn't much protection going on when we got here," Revna commented.

"They came," Gudleif shrugged.

True enough, Orka thought, looking about at the lumps of shredded skraeling that spattered the courtyard.

"And news?" Orka asked.

"Might like to live alone," Gudleif said, "but it's always good to know what's going on in the rest of the world, and those two ravens are the best source of news I've ever known. In return we feed them, give them a safe place to rest when they're around."

"Ha, am I still sleeping?" Gunnar laughed. "This is more moon-touched than some dreams I have."

"So, these ravens are your . . . friends?" Revna said.

The closest raven looked up from feasting on skraeling corpses and regarded Revna with a bright, intelligent eye.

"*Everyone needs a friend*," the raven squawked.

Gudleif nodded. Gunnar half choked and spat out a mouthful of water he'd been drinking.

"Strange friends you keep," Orka said, raising an eyebrow.

"Can't be too fussy with friends when you live north of the Bonebacks," Gudleif said.

Gunnar Prow snorted another laugh, shaking his head. "*Human* is usually one of the guiding principles for friendships."

"*Not always*," squeaked Vesli as she kneaded her mucus into Lif's cheek.

Orka took a few steps closer to the raven until she was close enough to reach out and touch its feathers.

"What are you exactly?" Revna asked.

"*Ravens*," the one in front of Orka squawked, feathers ruffling and peering at Revna as if she were half-witted.

"I mean, are you vaesen, or gods, or just . . . ravens?" Revna said.

"*NOT vaesen*," the raven sitting up in the nest screeched, sounding offended.

Spert lifted his head and looked at the two ravens as if *he* were offended.

"*Lik-Rifa made the vaesen*," the one with Orka rasped.

"*The crazy bitch*," muttered the raven in the nest.

"*But Snaka made us*," the one by Orka croaked, ignoring her mate in the nest. "*Like he did giants, and Froa, and you . . .*"

"Ahh," Revna nodded. "Thank you for clearing that up."

"*Welcome*," the raven in front of Orka rasped.

"Are you the same ravens that I met at the Grimholt?" Orka asked the one in front of her.

"*How many giant ravens do you think there are?*" it squawked. "*Name's Kló, and up there's Grok, my mate. He's the one you saved from the frost-spiders' web.*"

Grok hopped out of the giant nest, wings spreading wide, and he glided down to the courtyard.

"*Grok grateful for that*," the raven cawed.

Gunnar Prow leaned back on the fence and laughed some more, all in the courtyard looking at him.

"*There were more of us, once*," Grok squawked. "*We were Snaka's messengers, and his eyes and ears.*"

"His spies, then?" Revna said.

"*Yes*," Grok said, head bobbing.

"*Lik-Rifa didn't like that*," Kló added.

"Not sure what I find the strangest," Gunnar said when he'd caught his breath, "well-mannered, talking giant ravens, or Orka Skullsplitter wandering around Vigrið saving ravens from frost-spiders. That is not the reputation the Skullsplitter has."

Orka glowered at Gunnar.

"*It's a hard world, friends make it better*," Grok squawked. "*You helped me, we helped you.*" He ran a beak through black feathers on a wing, "*Favour for a favour. Everyone happy.*"

"Strange you should mention that," Orka said thoughtfully, "because I need a favour."

CHAPTER FIFTY-EIGHT

BIÓRR

Biórr cocked his head and listened. He was standing with his back to a wall of stone, his cloak pulled tight about him and his spear resting in the crook of his arm, working his shift on guard duty down by the subterranean docks where boats rose and fell on the sluggishly churning sea. There were many entrances to guard in the caverns of Nastrandir. Apparently the halls were a catacomb that spread beneath the Boneback Mountains, with entrances both north and south of where Snaka had fallen, so both humans and vaesen were used to guarding the halls. It was late now, darkness spread like an ink-stain through the sea-cavern, a brazier of oil burning on a wall, and it was quiet, just the gentle rock and creak of hulls shifting on the swell of the sea.

He let out a contented sigh.

I am happy, he realised. All his years he had lived in some state of fear, pain or anxiety, whether it was as a thrall, or trying to prove himself as a new member of Ilska's Raven-Feeders, or as a spy in the crew of Agnar's Battle-Grim. But now, he felt . . . home.

It had been a struggle, settling back into the company of Ilska's crew. His old friends had helped, no doubt, Fain and Storolf most of all, but there was something about those that had joined in his absence, mostly with Drekr's crew, that set the hairs on his neck prickling. Coupled with that was the unhelpful way that images of his time among the Battle-Grim would just resurface in his thought-cage, usually of Agnar's trusting expression just before Biórr stabbed him, and of Elvar's freckled face, of her smile and their snatched moments together. He missed talking to her, how she had been interested in *him*, asking him about his past, about his kin. No woman had ever bothered with those questions before. But Rotta's appearance had changed all that unease for him. Since the god's appearance Biórr had felt like he finally belonged somewhere, and that he mattered.

Something snagged his attention, a sound, faint as bats' wings in the night. He stopped nibbling his cheese and listened. Nothing for a moment, and then, there it was again, faint, on the very edge of sound. He closed his eyes and took a moment to let his beast trickle through his blood, the rat inquisitive and eager to help. His hearing sharpened, and his sense of smell. Now he could hear it clearly: gentle footfalls, the hiss of leather on stone. Something about it wasn't right. Like someone trying to go unheard.

He put the cheese down, held his spear tighter and shrunk back into the shadows, squeezing into the narrowest of gaps between a boulder and the cavern's wall. That was another benefit of having Rotta's blood in his veins: somehow his skeleton became more flexible when the rat was loose in his blood, allowing him to squash and squirm into the smallest of spaces, his skeleton compressing far more than usual.

A whispered voice cut off by a sharp hiss, and then two figures were slipping into the chamber. One tall, one short. Even before they stepped into the firelight Biórr knew them by their scent.

Kráka and Bjarn.

Have they come for a game of tafl?

He breathed out a sigh of relief, but something stopped him from stepping out from the shadows. A furtiveness in their movements, the sharp scent of fear-induced sweat that hovered around them like a miasma. Biórr pushed back into the shadows and watched them.

Kráka had a hemp sack slung over her back. She scanned the cavern and then hurried to one of the jetties carved from stone, where some of the boats were moored. Hurrying to the end she threw the sack into a small *snekke*, and then gestured for Bjarn to join her. He ran wide-eyed across the cavern, the slap of his feet echoing on stone.

Biórr stepped out of the shadows.

"Kráka, what are you doing?"

Bjarn skidded to a halt and Kráka froze, staring at Biórr. Her face twitched, a war of emotions.

"I am taking Bjarn back to his mother," Kráka said, a whispered hiss, her eyes flickering to the tunnel behind Bjarn.

"What?" Biórr blinked. "No, you cannot," he snapped. "Why would you betray us like this? You are free. I slew Agnar and set you free."

"I am *not* free," Kráka said bitterly, her face twisting in anger and despair. She pulled back the sleeve of her tunic and revealed an arm of knotted scars and red-raw wounds. Some scabbing over, some fresh, spotted with blood and weeping blisters.

And then Biórr remembered. Agnar Fire-Fist. Agnar telling them all of Oskutreð, and his pact with Uspa, the Seiðr-witch. A trade: Oskutreð for Bjarn, sealed by Seiðr-magic. Elvar had sworn that oath, too, but he had forgotten that Kráka had been in the backroom of the inn at Snakavik when that rune-magicked deal had been struck.

"The *blóð svarið*," he said.

Kráka nodded. "There is no fighting it," she said, a half-sob lurching from her mouth. "It knows my thoughts, knows my will, my intentions." She held her wounded arm up to him. "This is what happens when you think for an *instant* about breaking that vow."

"Why so long, then? Why did you not leave when we were near to Oskutreð, and you were still so close to Uspa?"

"Because Bjarn was under the Seiðr-spell, I couldn't break it, so it was impossible to move him anywhere. I told the *blóð svarið* this, and it . . . accepted it. But ever since Bjarn has awoken from his spell, I have had to plot for a way to escape with him. We were marching through icy, frozen wastes, so leaving then would have been our death. But now . . ." She looked at the rowing boat.

"I cannot let you leave," Biórr said.

"I cannot stay," Kráka said sadly, "it will be my death." She muttered unknown words under her breath and a red-glowing rune began to appear in the air before her.

Biórr summoned the rat in his blood and crouched, light on his feet, spear held high.

Bjarn stepped between them.

"Please, Biórr, let me go," the lad pleaded.

He looked down at him.

"This is the best place for you, Bjarn. You are safe here with us, among the Tainted. Among your own kind. Lik-Rifa will protect you. Out there, you are likely to end up with an iron collar around your neck, and worse than that."

Bjarn looked at his feet, then back up at Biórr.

"I want to be back with my mama," he said, a fat tear rolling down his cheek.

"She cannot protect you like we can."

"But, she's my *mama*."

All the logic and reason in Biórr's thought-cage could not fight the hope in Bjarn's eyes.

A long moment passed.

Biórr lowered his spear.

"Go, then," he said with a jerk of his head. Then, "Hold," he snapped. "They will hunt you, will know you took a boat. And I will be asked hard questions." He strode down the stone jetty to Kráka. "Here," he said, holding his spear out to her. "Put me on the ground, make it look realistic." He hesitated. "Not *too* realistic."

Kráka gave him a wan smile as she took the spear from him.

"You are a good man, Biórr," she said.

"Thank you," Bjarn said, hugging Biórr.

Biórr patted his head.

"Tell Storolf that . . ." Kráka began. "Tell him I am sorry for what might have been."

Then she hit him with the butt of his spear.

★

"Biórr, Biórr", a voice calling his name. Hands on him, lifting him.

"Guh," he moaned, his head feeling like it was cracked open and his thought-cage leaking out. Storolf's gap-toothed face was peering down at him, filling his vision.

"By the dead gods, you had me worried for a moment," Storolf breathed, a grin splitting his face.

Biórr tried to move, pain exploding in his head and his stomach lurched. Then he was vomiting on to stone.

"What . . . happened?" Biórr croaked when he felt there was nothing left in his belly to heave out. Alongside the pain in his head, his jaw was throbbing, lips swollen, words slurring. He wiped a long string of vomit and spittle from his lips, slimy in his beard.

"You've had a crack to the head," Storolf said. "Your face is none too pretty either, but I think that's because you fell on it."

A hand on Storolf's shoulder and the big man looked away, then moved quickly out of Biórr's blurred vision, replaced by another. Dark-haired, stern-featured.

Ilska squatted down to peer at him, taking long moments to look at his wounds. "Who did this?" she asked him again.

A memory of Bjarn, tears on his cheek, and Kráka, holding his spear.

"Gah," he mumbled, tried to shake his head and sent his world spinning. His stomach heaved again.

"They were here," a voice shouted, "took a boat."

Ilska looked away, gave Biórr one last look, then stood and disappeared from view.

"Take him to the hall", he heard Ilska's voice, but she sounded as if she were far, far away. Hands gripped and lifted him, and white spots burst before his eyes, his vision fading, darkness drawing in.

Biórr opened his eyes and peered up at darkness. Shapes moved in the shadows and he caught the reflection of firelight in clustered eyes. He tried to move, didn't like the idea of a frost-spider lurking directly over his head, but a wave of vertigo gripped, and then whatever was left in his stomach was coming up. Mostly hot bile that burned his throat.

"Here," Storolf said, grabbing Biórr under his arms and hoisting him so that he was propped against a cold stone column. He put a cup of water in Biórr's fist and stepped back. Slowly Biórr raised the cup to his lips and drank. It felt good on the raw pain in his throat.

"Was it Kráka?" Storolf asked him.

"Don't know," Biórr said. "One moment I was watching the boats, the next . . . I'm looking into your ugly face."

"Kráka's gone," Storolf said, not even a twitch of a smile at Biórr's words. "Bjarn, too."

Biórr put a hand up to his head and found that it had been wrapped in a linen bandage. He looked around, slowly. His spear lay on the ground beside him, blood caked on the butt-end. He was in the great hall, Lik-Rifa's serpent throne empty. The huge carcass of a whale lay spread across the hall, caught a few days ago by Lik-Rifa in her dragon form and brought back for her growing warband to feed upon. Pale ribs curled upwards, like a tunnel approaching Lik-Rifa's throne. A few faces were left in the hall, Breca and Harek sitting by a fire, heads together, whispering, and in a corner two troll-cubs each bigger than Storolf were playing or fighting. It was hard to tell the difference. A granite-faced bull troll towered over them, a club nestled in the crook of one arm. It looked like it was laughing. Here and there other people huddled around hearth fires.

"Where is everyone?" Biórr rasped.

"Most are trying to find Kráka," Storolf said with a shrug.

A burst of laughter and Biórr saw some silhouetted figures step away from a hearth fire where the dragon-worshippers had made their camp. Three people came striding towards Biórr and Storolf. As they drew closer Biórr saw that one was Rotta, each arm around a woman. He was talking and they were laughing.

"My poor Biórr," Rotta said, looking down on him. "You have a nasty injury there."

Biórr didn't know what to say, so he just nodded, immediately regretting that as it set off a burst of pain that spasmed into his belly.

"A blow to the head is a dangerous thing," Rotta murmured. "You must be careful." He took his arms from around the two women and crouched low, bent forward until his lips were almost touching Biórr's. "It can cloud the memory, and the judgement. Remember where your loyalties must lie," he whispered, too quiet even for Storolf to hear.

Biórr blinked at Rotta, feeling a ripple of fear.

He knows.

He opened his mouth to say something, but the words stuck in his throat.

"Shh, say nothing," Rotta said, "ignorance is bliss, and often much safer than knowledge. But I would hate for some misfortune to happen to you. There are too few of my kind left in this world as it is." He stood up and wrapped his arms around the two women, pulling them close. "Though I feel it is my sombre duty to change that sad state in the world. Less talking, more humping, that's what I say," and with that he was leading the giggling women away.

"Lucky shite," Storolf muttered, "what's he got that I haven't."

"All his teeth," Biórr said. "And he is a god."

"I meant apart from that," Storolf grunted.

Biórr tried not to laugh as it made his head spin, and took a sip of his water.

"How long have I been here?" he asked.

Storolf looked up at the cavernous roof, here and there a grey hint of light, where cracks in the granite walls let out into the day.

"Dawn's here, so, most of the night."

A murmur of sound echoed through the hall, coming from the eastern end, where the tunnel led to the underground docks. The tramp of feet, growing steadily louder, and then people were emerging into the great chamber. A whirr of wings and a cloud of tennúr burst from the tunnel, sweeping up high and disappearing into the murk, and then Ilska stepped into the light, Drekr towering at her shoulder, and a score more behind her.

They were dragging two figures.

Biórr reached out and gripped his spear, tried to use it to lever himself upright, got halfway and swayed. Storolf put a hand under his arm and heaved him the rest of the way as if he were made of straw. He tottered on his feet a moment, but took some deep breaths and slowly the world steadied around him. Storolf gave him a supporting arm and together they walked to the far side of the whale carcass, where Ilska stopped before Lik-Rifa's empty serpent throne. A crowd was gathering around Ilska and her crew, dragon-worshippers, more Raven-Feeders, skraeling, the bull troll who had been watching over his cubs. Biórr glimpsed the shifting of many limbs in the shadows above them.

"She is not here," Rotta said, hair dishevelled and looking perturbed as he appeared from behind a wide column, adjusting his breeches. "My sister is out hunting a fresh meal for us all." He smiled. "She is good to those who follow her, who are *loyal* to her." He looked pointedly at the two people Ilska and her crew had dragged into the hall and thrown to the ground in front of the empty throne.

Storolf shoved a path through the gathering crowd and Biórr followed in his wake, until they were standing close to Rotta and Ilska. And the two captives.

Kráka and Bjarn. Both of them were bound with seal-gut rope at wrist and ankle, and Kráka was gagged around her mouth. Her hair was matted with blood from a wound on her scalp. Bjarn looked at her with tear streaks through his grimy cheeks.

"Caught 'em," Brák Trolls-Bane said, grinning. He was standing behind Kráka, a cut that still leaked blood across one cheek and blood on his teeth. Ilmur stood beside him, stone-faced.

"Not easily, it appears," Rotta said, walking to Brák and looking at the cut on his face. He stood over Kráka and Bjarn.

"She's a Seiðr-witch," Brák said with a shrug, as if that explained everything. "You'd expect her to put up a bit of a struggle." His tongue moved around the inside of his mouth and he spat out a glob of blood.

"Ungag her," Rotta said.

"But—" Brák began, but Rotta's dark look stopped his words.

Ilska stepped forward and drew her seax.

"Anything foolish will end with more pain," she told Kráka, then cut the strip of fabric around her mouth and pulled it away. Kráka coughed and spat.

"Why would you want to leave the comfort of Nastrandir, and the company of my gentle sister?" Rotta asked her, voice calm, friendly.

Kráka pulled a face. "Didn't want to, had to," she wheezed. She tried to move her arms and Brák Trolls-Bane had his seax at Kráka's throat faster than Biórr could blink.

"Thank you for the concern," Rotta said to Brák, "but I can assure you, I am in no danger."

At a nod from Rotta, Brák sliced the sleeve of Kráka's tunic and pulled it up, Kráka holding her arm up to reveal the red lacerated wounds that coiled around her from wrist to elbow.

Rotta leaned close to the arm and sniffed deeply. Nodded respectfully. "A *blóð svarið*," he said, then wiped one finger across a weeping blister, put it in his mouth and sucked. Then spat. His eyes widened. "Who did this?" he asked her. "Not you; I can smell your power, and it is not enough for this."

"Another Seiðr-witch. Her name is Uspa," Kráka said. "She is Bjarn's mother."

"Uspa was thralled to another crew," Ilska explained. "She fought us at Oskutreð, when we set your sister free."

"Hmm, I think we should find this Uspa and offer her the pleasure of our company," Rotta said.

"She will not come," Ilska said. "I have already given her that offer. She made her answer very clear." Ilska turned her head and pulled at the tunic around her neck, revealing a white-ridged scar.

"Shame," Rotta muttered. He looked back to Kráka. "I am afraid there is no escaping the *blóð svarið*," he said. "The best I can offer you is a quick death."

Kráka nodded.

"No," Bjarn half sobbed.

"Ah, and then there is you, little bear," Rotta said.

"He is innocent," Kráka breathed. "I forced him to come with me."

"No, she didn't," Bjarn said. "I wanted to leave. I miss my mama."

Some of the children in the crowd sniggered at that.

"Your home is here, with us, now," Rotta said.

"We could make an example of the little brat," Brák said, stepping around Kráka and closer to Bjarn, his seax hovering. "A memorable death is better than a thousand words."

"Let him go," a voice said from the crowd, a small figure stepping forward.

Breca.

Brák stepped forward and pulled his arm back to slap Breca.

Breca looked up at him, his eyes shimmering green-brown in the firelight, and his lips pulled back in a snarl, revealing sharp-pointed teeth.

"Ha," Rotta laughed, clapping his hands.

Brák slapped Breca, fast as a snake, and Breca's head snapped back. He stumbled a step or two, then found his balance and crouched, snarling, and launched himself at Brák. There was a thud and they fell, Brák's seax spinning away.

Rotta stepped over them, laughing, leaned over and snatched Breca up with a fistful of his tunic. Breca turned on him, snapping and snarling in a frenzy.

"ENOUGH," roared Rotta, voice abruptly loud as a storm, filling the room. His face rippled, the hint of his nose elongating, incisors growing, and Breca fell limp in his grip. Brák scrambled back to his feet, wiping blood from his nose.

Rotta held Breca in his grip, glowering at him.

"You must learn to control the beast in your blood, not let it control you," he said, voice quiet where it had been thunderous, but no less terrifying. He waited for Breca to nod, then set him down and pushed him back into the crowd.

"Ilska, set the boy free," Rotta said, gesturing to Bjarn. "He cannot be held accountable for this. That must fall on her." He looked to Kráka as Ilska cut Bjarn's bonds and hoisted him to his feet, let him stumble towards Breca and Harek.

"As for you, Snaka's daughter, as I said, death is the only answer. My sister will not forgive you." He looked to the great doors of the chamber. "And it is best done quickly, before she returns, else you will end up in a dragon's belly, and the getting there won't be at all pleasant for you." He gave Ilska a sharp nod and she stepped towards Kráka with her seax drawn.

"The rat-boy should do it," Brák said, stepping forward and looking keenly at Biórr.

"What?" Rotta said.

"Something not right about how these two got away so easy. Biórr was on guard down there." He stepped closer to Biórr, eyes narrowed. "And they just walked up behind you and clumped you on the skull?"

"That's right," Biórr said.

Brák looked at the spear in Biórr's fist, at the dark stain of blood on the butt of the haft. "So, how'd they get hold of your spear to crack you with it?"

Biórr was blank for a moment. He felt a tremor of anger in his veins, wanting more than anything to bury his spear in Brák's gut. But he also felt fear. Fear of being discovered. Of ending up in Lik-Rifa's belly.

"Uh," Biórr mumbled. "Must have leaned it against the wall." He put a hand to the bandage around his head.

"So, you didn't help 'em, then?" Brák said.

"No," Biórr said, trying to keep the lie from his voice. He was keenly aware of every eye in the chamber staring at him, both human and vaesen.

"No soft feelings for 'em? You worked the same crew together, didn't you?"

"That means nothing," Storolf said, stepping forward.

"You stay out of this, big man," Brák said, looking up at Storolf. "You might be big, but that don't bother me none. They don't call me Troll-Slayer for nothing. Fought bigger than you and walked away from it."

Storolf's hand went to the axe at his belt.

"Stop," Ilska said, stepping forwards, Drekr at her shoulder.

Storolf sucked in a breath. Brák grinned and spat on the floor, not taking his eyes from Storolf. Then he looked back to Biórr.

"So, if you're telling the truth; that you had no part in it and she means nothing to you, then you do the deed. You put the blade in her."

"I'd rather put a blade in you," Biórr snarled.

"You're welcome to try, rat-boy," Brák said, spreading his arms wide and grinning.

"Enough of this," Ilska said. Brák dipped his head to her. She looked at Biórr. "Do what he says," she said to him.

"Huh? What?" Biórr asked.

"Kill Kráka. Now." She turned and strode back to Kráka, grabbing her by the hair and yanking her head high, exposing her throat.

Biórr stood there, frozen, looking into Kráka's eyes.

"She's one of us," he said.

"Takes more than a touch of god blood to be in this crew," Drekr said. "Takes loyalty. She swore her oath and broke it," he growled, then spat on Kráka. "That's the end of her."

Do it, a voice said in his thought-cage. *Kill her.* His eyes snapped to Rotta, who was staring intensely at him.

But she is my friend, Biórr told the voice.

She is already dead, but you might yet live. We are survivors, you and I. Do what you need to do to survive.

Biórr hovered one more moment, and then he stepped forwards and plunged his spear into Kráka's throat.

CHAPTER FIFTY-NINE

VARG

Varg stared out at a sight beyond his imagining.

Ulaz, gateway to Iskidan, stretched all around him, as far as his eyes could see. A never-ending landscape of white- and red-tiled buildings punctuated by towers and groves of green trees. They had first seen Ulaz soon after dawn, a white glow of rippling heat haze on the horizon as the *Sea-Wolf* passed out of the tangle of islands that clustered Iskidan's coast. As they had drawn closer, Varg had seen that it was a town built upon both banks of a river's estuary, harbours stretching on both sides, a horde of all manner of boats moored at countless piers, jetties and wharves.

But town wasn't the right word. The buildings spread far and as wide as a forest.

As they had rowed into the estuary, they had passed between two colossal statues that rose towering out of the water, a bull on one side with curling horns and a creature that reminded Varg of Spert, Orka's vaesen companion, only this was ten thousand times bigger. Bulbous, claw-like pincers and a segmented body, a needle-pointed sting set on the end of its tail, curled high over its back. He didn't much like the look of it. Tern and cormorants nested and screeched in their heights.

"It's a scorpion," Svik told him as Varg gawped open-mouthed. "They have strange gods in Iskidan."

The statues were stained and pitted by weather and bird shite, patches of green algae where the waves rolled and fell, barnacles clustered in dark, shining swathes, looking like scabbed wounds.

Now they were rowing slowly on a half-crew into the maw of the estuary, the port of Ulaz slipping by on both banks of the river. Glornir was standing at the steering oar and guiding the *Sea-Wolf* into the wide-banked river that curled away from the port into the heartlands of Iskidan. Ships of all manner and size ploughed the water, making it feel more like a crowded street in Darl than a river, and Varg could see no end of docks and wharves and a never-ending forest of masts. A constant hum of sound rippled out from the port, voices shouting, laughing, music playing, animals barking, braying, snarling, herring gulls swirling and screeching in the skies above the docks, thick as flies around a corpse. All of it merged into a constant, indistinct rising and falling rhythm, like the lapping of waves on a shore. Myriad scents rolled across the waters, the reek of rotting fish and vegetables, sweat, sharp-tanged ammonia, and unknown scents of something that Svik explained were spices, used to flavour food and drink.

"Stinks like shite, doesn't it," Røkia said as she came to stand beside them.

"It's . . . big," Varg muttered.

"Your powers of observation might not be your greatest strength," Svik said wryly.

"I mean, overwhelming," Varg said, feeling a smile twitch his mouth, the first since they had left the island of the tongue-eaters. He went to scratch his ear that wasn't there, and felt the scabbed, puckered skin instead. The mood of the crew had been sombre as they had rowed away from the island, and Einar's absence lay heaviest of all on them. Leaving Einar Half-Troll behind had felt wrong to Varg, and now that the big man was no longer on the ship he realised how much a huge part of the Bloodsworn he was. But part of Varg's thought-cage did understand the logic of it. They had camped the night there, tending to Einar, hoping that he would regain consciousness and recover enough to be able to travel, but when dawn came Einar was still unconscious, shivering and sweating in the grip of a fever. Taking him back on to the whale road, and then who knew where on a chase across Iskidan, did not seem like good sense for Einar's recovery.

So, Glornir had left him there, in the care of Æsa, who was a skilled healer and wounded herself. All the children had stayed, as well. Glornir had unloaded a third of their provisions, barrels of water and food.

"We will be back for you, hopefully before the barrels run low," he had said. *"If you do run out of water before we return, do not use that well. Find a stream, and boil everything that you pull from it before you put it into your mouth."*

Varg shivered at the thought of becoming infected by those tongue-eaters. Every day since they had left the island, he had scoured his mouth with sand, drunk water as hot as he could bear, and then painstakingly inspected his tongue by hand, using the polished boss of his shield to peer into his mouth. He ran a hand through his thick-growing hair, feeling anxious all over again at the thought of those nasty little parasites.

"Your hair," Svik said with a frown on his face.

"What about it?" Varg muttered.

"It's a mess." Svik shook his head.

"What's wrong with that?" Varg said. He thought very little about his hair or his appearance. All his life his hair had been shaved to stubble, as with all thralls, and since he had run from Kolskegg's farm his hair had grown steadily. Now he had a thick beard that made his chin itch, and hair that flopped and stuck out at all angles. The only thought he gave it was when it itched or irritated him.

"It's an embarrassment," Svik said. "You are one of the Bloodsworn now. You should make an effort to look your best."

Varg frowned, then looked to Røkia.

"Do you agree?" he asked her.

"You look like a wild bush," she said with a shrug.

"What can I do?" Varg said, putting his hands to his head, feeling clumps of matted, tangled hair.

"Just trust me," Svik smiled at him as he put a hand to his belt and drew a small, razor-sharp knife and a comb carved from bone.

Røkia snorted a laugh.

Svik set to work on Varg's beard, combing and trimming.

"It is not long enough to braid yet," Svik said after a while, his face serious as he concentrated, "but a beard ring will keep it neat, for now." He took a small silver ring from a pouch at his belt and threaded it on to Varg's beard, then tied it off. He stepped back to look at Varg, smiling.

"Better," he said. "Now, the hair. What shall I do with this over-grown forest?"

"Shave it," Varg said.

Svik scowled. "Then you will look like a thrall again."

"Not all of it," Varg explained. "Shave it like Helka's *Úlfhéðnar*, leave the top untouched, just shave the back and sides. When the top is long enough, I shall braid it." He looked from Svik to Røkia.

"I like it," Svik said, nodding, and set to work again.

"All those people in Ulaz," Varg said, eyeing the town as Svik cut his hair. "Where did they come from?"

Svik paused, frowning. "Please tell me you know how bairns are made."

"Of course I know that," Varg blurted, blushing at Røkia's raised eyebrow. "I mean, how are there so many people in one place? Is this all of Iskidan gathered into one town?"

Svik stopped cutting Varg's hair because he was laughing so hard.

"No, this is a port, like Liga. Iskidan is vast, as I have told you, and Gravka, the great city where the emperor Kirill dwells, is as Darl is to Liga, many, many times the size of Ulaz."

Varg puffed out his cheeks.

"How did so many come to be ruled by just one man?"

"You have not heard the tale of the three brothers and the Shadow-Walker?"

"No," Varg said. "In some ways I am coming to think that I have led a sheltered life."

Røkia snorted another laugh.

"Well, I shall educate you, then," Svik said, "although this really is a saga that should be told by the hearth fire, with some food on a plate and a skin of mead." He clicked his tongue as he went back to cutting Varg's hair. "I shall shorten the story for you."

"Thank the dead gods," Røkia muttered.

"Soon after the *Guðfalla*, where the gods fought and slew each other, and mankind was licking its wounds and fighting for a place in the new world, three brothers rose up among the survivors of Vigrið. Mag, Oleg and Aslog."

"Kirill the Magnificent is descended from their line," Røkia whispered.

"Tsk," Svik hissed with a scowl at Røkia, "you are spoiling the story."

"I am speeding the story up," Røkia answered.

Svik sighed and carried on. "The three brothers were strong and adventurous, and they had heard tales of warm, green lands to the south, beyond the sea, where land was for the taking and rivers of silver flowed in plenty. So, they gathered about them a warband of like-minded people and set about building a fleet of ships. They set sail with thirty sleek-prowed longships and rode the whale road, landing here, at Ulaz. Back then it was just a flea-bitten fishing village, but the brothers established their base here, building a stockaded hall. They found a land broken by the *Guðfalla*, just like Vigrið. The gods had made the world their Battle-Plain, you see, fighting and dying throughout all of Iskidan, just as they had done in the north. The people of Iskidan were divided, split into many petty realms and clans, all mistrusting each other and jostling for power."

"Much like Vigrið, then," Varg muttered.

"Exactly," Svik said. "Mag, Oleg and Aslog approached a neighbouring clan, and offered their help, in return for silver."

"Much like us Bloodsworn would do," Røkia said.

"Yes," Svik nodded. "And like this, the neighbouring clans were conquered, and the three brothers became silver-rich, and soon the north of Iskidan was ruled by one clan, with the brothers as their elite warriors."

"So, how did the three brothers come to rule Iskidan, and who is this shadow-walker?"

"I am getting to that," Svik huffed. "The three brothers and the clan they fought for became ever more powerful, increasing their dominion south, east and west. In time all the other clans joined against them, and the war was terrible. Mag, the eldest brother, proposed a truce, an end to the bloodletting, and all the clans agreed. A meeting was arranged, where all the leaders could gather and agree to the boundaries of their realms, and swear a blood oath to peace. The night of the meeting came, within a tent the size of a small town. It was filled with lords and ladies, the rulers of each clan come with a small retinue to swear their oaths to peace. The clans of Iskidan were like the stars in the sky, hundreds of them, so there must have been thousands gathered for the Great Meeting. But when the sun rose the next morning . . . they were all dead. Only Mag, Oleg and Aslog stepped out of that tent with breath in their bodies. They had slain everyone, even the clan they had fought for."

"But how could they kill so many?" Varg breathed.

"The Skuggar Ganga, the Shadow-Walker," Svik said, and Varg felt his skin gooseflesh, despite the sunshine.

"Who is the Shadow-Walker?" Varg whispered.

"No one knows," Svik smiled. "A Tainted thrall? A vaesen under some kind of Seiðr-spell. A Seiðr-witch or Galdurman?" He shrugged. "People in Iskidan still tell tales of the Shadow-Walker to their children, though, to keep them from straying in the dark."

"It is just another tale," Røkia said.

"Of course, but a good one, you must admit," Svik grinned, "and the fact remains, Iskidan has only one ruler, and that is a remarkable feat." He stepped back. "I am finished," he said, a pile of hair lying about Varg's feet.

"Like your beard, it is too short to braid, but you can tie it back, if you have a cord of leather. That would stop it falling in your eyes, which is not helpful in a scrap."

"I have some leather," Varg said and he felt the sea breeze on his skull. He rubbed a palm across the back of his head and felt smooth skin.

Varg looked up at Røkia. "What do you think?" he asked her.

She was silent a long moment, face unreadable.

"I like it," she said, then looked at Svik. "Do it to me," she said, sitting down on a barrel.

★

THE HUNGER OF THE GODS

"Like this," Røkia said, then raised her hand-axe and hooked the beard of its blade over Varg's shield rim and wrenched it down.

They were standing on the deck of the *Sea-Wolf* as they moved down the River Reka, the last buildings of Ulaz finally behind them. The sun was a molten glow on the horizon, reflecting from high clouds in a blaze of orange and pink as Røkia continued Varg's lessons in weapons craft. The fact that they were on the rolling deck of a ship had not dissuaded her.

"*What?*" she had said when Varg questioned the sense of training on a ship's deck, "*you will only fight when the ground beneath your feet is solid and unmoving? What kind and polite enemies you have, to allow you that choice.*" She had shaken her head in disappointment. "*No-Sense,*" she had muttered.

So here they were, training in Varg's break between oar-shifts as a half-crew rowed them into the land of Iskidan.

"You see?" Røkia continued. "Now if we are in the shield wall you are open to a spear-thrust from the second row, or a diagonal strike from seax or sword. It is called working together."

That is something I am not used to, Varg thought.

He nodded. Røkia had decided that he had learned enough with spear and shield to now start his education in axe work.

"So, how do I counter this?" Varg asked her.

Røkia raised an eyebrow. "A sensible question from No-Sense?" She stepped close and put the back of her hand upon his brow, her skin warm and rough. "Do you have a fever?"

A snort of laughter from Svik and others on their oar-benches. Varg just shrugged.

"To answer your question, there are four things you could do. First," she held up one finger. "Don't let them do it in the first place. Watch your enemy, read their eyes and movements, their weight and balance. Most will give away their attack that way. So you strike before them, move away, shift the angle of your shield."

"All right," Varg said.

"The second thing you can do," Røkia said, holding up two fingers. "You go with it, smash into the one with the axe; they will likely not be expecting that and so you might surprise them and end the fight quickly. Of course, you just end up leaping out of the shield wall among a host of your enemy, so, you also might die very quickly." She shrugged.

"Third?" Varg asked her.

"Drop your shield," she said. "Again, they will likely not be expecting that, so it will give you a moment in which to strike. Although, if you are in the shield wall, you will probably just get skewered by half a dozen spears from the second row."

"Sounds like a No-Sense thing to do, to me," Svik called out.

"And fourth?" Varg asked.

"Røkia scratched at her freshly shaved head, which made her look even more fierce than she had before, something that Varg had not thought possible.

"There is no fourth," she said.

"Ah, so, you've just told me three different ways of dying. Some quicker than others."

More laughter rippling along the deck.

"It depends how good you are, and how lucky," Røkia said. "Better to do it to them before they do it to you. Luck you cannot change, but your skill, now that is something you can bring to a scrap. I know your strategy is to leap in and chop, chop, chop," she said, "and people think because it is an axe and used for splitting wood that there is no weapons craft or skill to be had with it." She looked Varg in the eye. "They are wrong."

"So, all this you have been teaching me is in the shield wall," Varg said. "What if I'm not in the shield wall, though?"

Røkia took a step back and acted dizzy, as if she were fainting.

"Two sensible questions in one day. Who are you?" Svik called from his oar-bench.

Everyone within hearing was now laughing.

"I am glad you asked me that, No-Sense," Røkia said, when the laughter had subsided. "So, if you are fighting a *drengr* with a shield, no matter what their weapon is; spear, sword, axe, seax, you do the same. Get in close, using your shield to protect you, then you hook the top of the shield rim, as before." She hooked her bearded axe over the rim of Varg's shield. "Then, you do this." She tugged his shield rim down, dragging him forward a step, and then punched the top eye of the axe haft and iron poll into his face. Not hard enough to pulp lips and smash teeth, but enough for him to feel it. If the leather cover from her axe blade had not been in place then the top point of the axe blade would have ripped his face open from lip to brow. He stumbled back a step, putting a hand to his mouth.

"You see," she said, a vicious smile cracking her lean face. "Not a killing blow, true, but it will set one up nicely."

"You knocked my tooth loose," Varg said, frowning as he examined his mouth.

A voice rang out across the deck.

"There they are, chief," Ingmar Ice called out, standing in the prow of the *Sea-Wolf.* "East bank," he called out, pointing.

Glornir leaned on the tiller and the *Sea-Wolf* cut across the river, and was soon carving a path through dense reeds towards a muddy bank. Two figures stood waiting, and two hounds sat beside one of them, silhouetted by the sun.

Oars were raised and shipped as the *drakkar's* hull grated on silt, slowed and then stopped. Glornir tied off the tiller and strode to the prow.

It was Sulich, and Edel with her two hounds. They waded out among the reeds.

"Welcome back, brother and sister," Ingmar called down to them, grinning, and leaned over the top-rail to give Sulich his hand, pulling the shaven-haired man on board as if he weighed little more than a bundle of feathers. Edel leaped at the side and clambered agilely aboard, her hounds running and leaping on to the deck.

"What news?" Glornir asked them.

"Jaromir was in Ulaz two days ago," Sulich said. It looked like he had bought himself some new clothes from the markets of Ulaz, wearing a fine silk and wool kaftan in red and grey, baggy linen breeches and leather boots, his curved sword at his hip and a felt and fur cap on his head.

"Two days," Glornir muttered, his face clouding, a blend of anger and something else. Fear?

"But he only left at midday yesterday. He had to buy new horses and supplies for his crew. He rode out with over a hundred spears at his back." Sulich looked away, then back to Glornir. "I was told that two Seiðr-witches rode with him, one of them bound with chains. From her description it is definitely Vol." He spat over the side of the longship. "She has not been treated . . . kindly."

Glornir's cheek twitched, his knuckles whitening as he gripped the top-rail.

"What does that mean?" he growled, colours flickering and shifting in his eyes, his shoulders hunching, swelling.

"Beaten," Sulich said grimly. "And they have stitched her lips shut."

Glornir let out a deep, pain-filled roar and there was the sound of splintering wood, part of the top-rail cracking in his grip. He sucked in a deep, shuddering breath.

"Where are they going?" Glornir grated.

"His tower at Valdai," Edel said. "The *druzhina* on the island told the truth."

"How long?" Glornir asked Sulich.

"Valdai is a three-day ride from Ulaz. A twisting road through the mountains."

"Can we catch them?"

Sulich sucked his teeth. "Perhaps. If we row hard. There is a place to beach at the foot of the mountains. A narrow path through them that cuts across the road to Valdai. Horses couldn't travel it, but we could, on foot."

"Good," Glornir growled. "Anything else?"

Sulich and Edel looked at each other.

"Something strange is happening in Ulaz, chief," Edel said. "It is busier, with all manner of people; *druzhina*, craftsmen, merchants . . ."

"And the eastern harbour, it is patrolled, now, no one allowed in or out without birch-bark tablets."

"Why?" Glornir muttered. "What are they doing in this harbour?"

"Don't know," Edel said.

"We couldn't get close enough," Sulich added. He shrugged. "If we had more time, but we were moving fast."

"Hmm," Glornir rumbled, then he patted Sulich and Edel on their shoulders, making them both stagger. "You did the right thing. Vol is our only business," then turned to look at the rest of the Bloodsworn. "Everyone back to their oar-bench; we are rowing for Vol."

CHAPTER SIXTY

GUÐVARR

*A*mbition is overrated, thought Guðvarr as he swayed in his saddle and pulled his fur cloak tighter about him, a vain attempt to protect himself from cold-numbing snow and sleet that was falling thick and hard as hail. He twisted in his saddle to look at the man riding beside him, Frek the *Úlfhéðnar* wrapped in a wolfskin cloak, the head pulled up, and thought about complaining to him about how they had been riding for what felt like a hundred years without rest or food or drink, but then thought better of it.

He will just look at me with his curled lip and say nothing, so what is the point.

Guðvarr knew this because he had already shouted out to Frek at least a score of times since they had broken their camp and set out that morning.

Why am I here? What in the name of the dead gods possessed me to volunteer to do this? Go to Nastrandir, to the Corpse-Hall of Lik-Rifa, a dragon!

But he knew full well why he had volunteered.

Self-preservation. He knew that he had served his purpose for Skalk in helping to wheedle out the secret Hakon had been keeping. And what a secret. But he also knew that if he'd wanted to walk out of that Galdur tower still breathing he had to become useful again.

So here I am, at the arse-end of the world, freezing my stones off in the attempt to keep breathing a little longer. I wish this journey were over, wish that I could just arrive at my destination and get this job over and done with. Whatever solace that thought gave him did not last very long. One hand rose up to press against his chest. *But once I've done this task, there is still the problem of a monster living in my chest.*

If he had the strength in his body he would have wept. He did sniff, though, went to wipe his nose and felt ice snap.

Even my own snot is freezing in my nose in this frozen shite-hole. Where are we anyway? Somewhere north of the Bonebacks, that is all I know. Why, why, why did I not just stay in Fellur village? "Let's go to Darl," I said, "let's hunt Orka," I said, thinking to make my fair-fame name.

He shook his head morosely.

Ambition is overrated.

A flicker of movement beside him and he looked to see Frek reining in. Joy blossomed in his heart. *Stopping. Thank all the powers that be. Please let him strike a fire and cook a meal. Even if he doesn't, I don't care. My arse is frozen to my saddle and I just want to get off this horse and curl up behind a rock.*

Frek swung a leg over his saddle and slipped down to the ground, led his horse to a twisted, leafless tree and tethered his mount there.

Yes, yes, yes, Guðvarr thought, trying to prise his frozen fingers in his thick nålbinding mittens from his reins and rocking back and forth to unstick his arse from his saddle.

Frek trudged over to him through thick snow.

Ah, he's coming to help me. Perhaps he's not as bad as I thought after all. I take all the insults that I have hurled at him in my head back. The many, many insults. He smiled gratefully down at Frek.

"Help me down, my good man," he said through his chattering teeth and held a hand out.

"Not you," Frek said with a scowl.

"What do you mean?" Guðvarr said, his smile withering.

"Ride on," Frek said.

"What!" Guðvarr squeaked, "alone? In this? Don't be ridiculous."

"We are almost there. I cannot come any further, you know this," Frek said.

"But, but, but, what do you mean, almost there?"

Frek just scowled up at him.

Abruptly there was a knot of fear in his belly, swelling with every heartbeat, and he felt his bladder twitching.

Now that it was a reality, he didn't want to actually *arrive*. He would rather ride on forever through this eternal freezing blizzard than actually arrive at the hall of a dragon-god.

A dragon-god.

He gulped.

"I'll get lost," he whispered.

"You won't," Frek said. He pointed through the sheeting snow. "There is the peninsula. Follow this track until you meet the sea, then you are there. That is what Prince Hakon said."

But Prince Hakon is a niðing, arseling, troll-shiteing liar, he thought.

"Come a little further," Guðvarr said to him. "Please," he whined. *Begging a thrall. I have lost all my dignity, and yet, I do not care.*

"You value my company so much?" Frek said, teeth pulling back in a smile that revealed sharp-pointed teeth. He shook his head. "They may have guards about. They *should* have guards about. If they catch me, we are done, both of us a dragon's supper."

"But—" Guðvarr began but Frek lifted his head into the sheeting snow and sniffed. "There are strange scents in the air." He shook his head. "Go on, ride." And before Guðvarr could argue any more, Frek slapped the rear of Guðvarr's horse and sent the animal jumping forward. Guðvarr looked ahead and gulped. A sweeping curtain of white filled his world. A gust of wind blew, snatching snow and sleet and hurling it into his face. It felt like a bucket of ice had been flung at him and he swore ineffectually at the world around him, put his head down and let his horse guide him.

Through the blizzard he glimpsed a peninsula stabbing out into an icy sea that swelled and churned like thick gruel, and to his right cliffs reared far beyond his vision.

Have I really reached Nastrandir, Lik-Rifa's hall?

I hope not.

Offering to pose as a messenger for Prince Hakon had seemed

like a good idea back in the Galdur tower in Darl, enabling Guðvarr to walk away from Skalk and Queen Helka with his life intact and a long journey ahead, in which he would be able to work on his next plan, but he hadn't actually given much thought to the eventuality of meeting a dragon. Being lumbered with silent Frek had been something of a blow as well, but the man had said more to him just now than during the entire journey from Darl, up the River Drammur, through the abandoned Grimholt and then north and east along the northern rim of the Boneback Mountains, so he had not been too much of a burden and, as much as Guðvarr despised *Úlfhéðnar* and anyone who served Queen Helka or Skalk, he wished that Frek was riding at his side now.

He slipped a little in his saddle and realised he was riding down a slope. Ice-bright boulders reared out of the snow as he rode down a winding path, and then the ground began to level, the grinding of churning ice from the sea filling his ears.

Why choose here to make your hall? It might just possibly be the most inhospitable spot in the whole of Vigrið. Perhaps she doesn't like visitors.

A pressure across his chest, pushing him backwards as his horse walked on.

"What the—?" he grunted. He saw a length of rope stretched across the path, glistening with ice and almost invisible against the falling snow. Reaching up with one hand, he grabbed it, tried to tug it out of the way.

The rope was as strong as iron.

Who put this rope here?

A moment of worry as he looked wildly around, rapidly growing into panic as his horse bolted beneath him, neighing and leaping forward. He closed his eyes and braced himself for the bone-jarring crunch as he fell to the ground.

It didn't come.

Opening his eyes, he saw that he was hanging suspended in the air, somehow stuck to the rope, one hand still gripping it tight.

He frowned and made to draw his seax, but his hand was stuck to the rope.

It's . . . sticky?

Guðvarr pulled and tugged but his hand would not come free, so he twisted with his other hand to try and reach his seax.

A whirring sound and a figure appeared in the air before him, small and hairless with a head like a bald rat and a mouth too big for its face. Wings beat in a blur of speed as it hovered in front of him.

A tennúr.

"*Intruder,*" it hissed at him.

Guðvarr blew out a sigh of relief.

"Go away, before I chop you up and throw you into the sea," Guðvarr told the tennúr.

The tennúr just smiled at him, showing two rows of nasty looking teeth that Guðvarr found unsettling.

I need to get down.

Then he saw a flicker of movement, off in his peripheral vision.

A shape in the blizzard, indistinct, growing closer, sitting hunched upon a boulder to his right.

What is that?

Guðvarr had to stare a moment before its fragmented form coalesced through the ever-swirling snow. Many jointed legs. Small, clustered eyes. Blue-dripping fangs.

Oh no.

Fear, deep in his bones, deeper even than he had felt when Skalk's hyrndur had alighted upon his arm. Guðvarr's hand jerked for his weapons belt, grasping for a weapon, any weapon, and he bounced on the rope.

It moved in a startling burst of speed, scuttling down the rock and on to the rope, moving along it towards Guðvarr with frightening agility.

Not a rope, a web.

He opened his mouth and screamed, but the wind and snow snatched it away.

Guðvarr heard the murmur of voices and opened his eyes, then wished that he hadn't.

He was lying on a cold stone floor, shivering, unable to move, and looking up into the far-too-close clustered eyes of a frost-spider.

He whimpered.

"*Wake up*," a reed-thin voice squeaked and Guðvarr felt a blow on his shoulder. He twisted his head and saw the little tennúr standing there, kicking him.

When I have recovered my strength, I am going to put a sharp stick up your arse and roast you over a fire, you annoying little rat.

"Back," a deep voice growled, and the frost-spider scuttled out of Guðvarr's view, the tennúr disappearing in a whirr of wings, both of them replaced by a hulking man with apparently no neck, just slab upon slab of muscle. His black hair was braided and tied back, white-ridged scars running down one side of his face, as if he'd been clawed by a bear.

He is Drekr, Guðvarr thought, remembering Prince Hakon's description of the man. He tried to move, to show Drekr his proof, but found that he was held tight, tied up.

No, not tied, he realised as he looked down at his body and saw thick, pale-glistening strands of frost-spider web wrapped all around him.

He whimpered again.

"Who are you?" the hulking man said.

"I am G-G-G-Guðvarr, and I bring a message from P-P-Prince Hakon," Guðvarr said through stuttering teeth, tremors of cold wracking his body.

Drekr frowned.

"You are not the messenger I sent."

"K-K-K-Kalv is dead," Guðvarr shivered.

"What?" other voices snarled, an old, white-haired man and a younger red-haired warrior with a gap in his teeth appearing beside Drekr. The red-haired man leaned down and heaved Guðvarr up from the floor, slamming him to sit against a stone column. "Say that again," he said, spittle spraying through gaps in his teeth. The white-haired man loomed over his shoulder.

"Kalv was slain," Guðvarr said, "soon after he met with my prince. That is why Prince Hakon has sent me in his place."

The red-haired man stared at him, his face twitching, eyes shifting in colour from blue to flecked gold and hazel. His jaw seemed to grow in size and two teeth appeared from his lower lip, like tusks. He gnashed his teeth, spittle foaming upon his lips, and his eyes filled with tears. The white-haired man put a hand on his shoulder, tears welling in his eyes as well.

They must be kin to Kalv, Guðvarr realised, *red-hair is certainly ugly enough to be.*

"Fain, Storolf," Drekr said, looking from the white-haired man to red-hair, "is it true?"

"Ach," Fain, the white-haired man spat, bowing his head. "We knew something bad had happened, felt it in our blood."

Storolf glowered at Guðvarr. "How?" he growled.

"Skalk the Galdurman," Guðvarr said.

Fain made a deep, growling sound in the back of his throat. "Skalk is a dead man," he said.

"I will rip his head from his shoulders," Storolf promised.

I sincerely hope that you do.

Fain pulled Storolf into an embrace as he wept and shook, other warriors with black feathers tied in their hair gathering around them. One stepped up and put a hand on Fain's arm, a slim, dark-haired, handsome warrior of a similar age to Guðvarr.

Drekr squatted down, his face uncomfortably close.

"You're one of Hakon's, then, so you say?" the big man growled. Guðvarr felt Drekr's voice reverberate in his chest, like a bear growling.

"Yes," Guðvarr said, trying to deepen his own voice, and failing.

Drekr frowned. "Never seen you before."

"I am a *drengr* from the Fellur district," Guðvarr said. "My jarl's path is set in Queen Helka's shadow, but I want more."

Drekr said nothing, just stared into Guðvarr's eyes.

"Another youth in search of a fair-fame reputation, eh?" Drekr mused. "Hakon has a skill for rooting them out."

"Yes, I would be part of a saga-tale," Guðvarr said eagerly, "I would be part of the song that Skálds sing in the mead hall and around the hearth fire."

Not so long ago that was all perfectly true. But now all I wish for is a warm fire and a jug of mead in a place far from Galdurmen, Tainted and monsters.

"And what better way to do that than to follow the dragon," Guðvarr finished.

Drekr nodded. "You would not be the first," he said. Casually Drekr put his hand to an axe at his belt, then faster than thought he was raising it high and chopping down at Guðvarr's chest.

Guðvarr sucked in a breath to scream, then realised that he could move his arms. Drekr was hacking away the web that bound him. In a few short moments he was struggling to his feet.

A horn call echoed around the cavern and huge doors began to scrape open. Guðvarr took the opportunity to see where he had ended up.

A vast chamber lit by burning braziers, shadow and smoke clinging to the higher places. Thick granite columns carved with scaled, coiling serpents, and a dais close by with an empty serpent-carved throne. Pale bones lay scattered across the ground, bigger than the strakes of Helka's finest longships. But it was not the chamber that snatched the breath from Guðvarr, it was the cavern's inhabitants.

Warriors, of course, hard-looking men and women in mail and bristling with weapons, many of them with raven feathers tied in their hair. But there were also grey-skinned, wax-faced skraeling lounging around the dais, thick-knotted muscle clothed in rough hides with heavy weapons of iron hanging from their baldrics and belts. Frost-spiders scuttled across the stone floor and sat in vast webs spread between columns. Clouds of tennúr whirled. What looked like a whole village of trolls were going about their business, many gathered around a huge cauldron, others playing or fighting. Two trolls were humping on a sheepskin hide. In a dark corner Guðvarr saw dark, swirling shapes that hovered above the ground. They had pale, skeletal faces and long hair thick and were floating like mist.

Night-hags.

He shuddered.

This place is worse than Skalk's Galdur tower.

A figure was standing in the shadow of a column, a man, tall and striking, finely dressed in a wool-embroidered tunic and gold worked into his belt and weapons. He was looking at Guðvarr with an unnerving intensity. In fact, he was the only one in the hall looking at Guðvarr. All else in the cavern had stopped what they were doing and were stood staring at the opening doors, a gust of wind hurling snow in a swirling blizzard into the cavern.

And then a shape was bursting through the white haze, winged and fearsome, a dragon, impossibly huge, its body pale with scales that glistened and shimmered like a coat of mail. Great wings beat slowly, the turbulence of it buffeting Guðvarr, making him stagger.

Lik-Rifa, last of the gods.

Nothing in the world could ever have prepared him for the sight of her, vast and majestic and terrible, her jaws wide and rowed with teeth longer and sharper than spears, pale horns jagged and curling back upon her head like a crown, forge-fire eyes burning red and gold. In her talons she carried the colossal bulk of a whale, blue-skinned and slick with seawater and barnacles. There were huge rents in its flesh, blood falling like rain. Lik-Rifa opened her jaws and roared as she released the whale's carcass, the sound of her filling the cavern and making Guðvarr's bones shake. Deep in his chest he felt the hyrndur stir.

The whale hit the ground with a concussive slap, clouds of dust rising, and then Lik-Rifa was circling in the heights of the cavern, spiralling slowly down to land in the open space before the serpent throne.

Guðvarr's legs were trembling and he dropped to his knees and put his head to the ground in obeisance to this great and terrible vision before him. He was not even acting. He heard a series of cracks and snaps, like bones splintering, flesh tearing, and then there was a silence.

"Who have we here, then?" a voice said, deep and hypnotic, and a hand touched his shoulder. He looked up to see a woman standing over him, tall and regal, dark hair streaked with silver and tied in many braids. Her eyes burned red. Guðvarr did not know whether to weep or laugh, joy and fear storming through him like a gale.

"The messenger from Hakon, in Darl," Drekr said. "Or so he tells us." He nodded somewhere behind Guðvarr and then hands were gripping him and hauling him to his feet.

"M-m-my queen," Guðvarr said to Lik-Rifa.

She regarded him with feral intensity, which made him weak with fear, and then she smiled, which filled his heart with joy.

"What news from Darl?" Lik-Rifa asked him.

"Uh," Guðvarr mumbled.

Pull yourself together, you idiot. Do you want to end up in a dragon's belly? Think. Remember the plan. He had recited it in his thought-cage countless times during his journey here. Now, though, it felt faint and ephemeral, impossible to grasp. "P . . . Prince Hakon has sent me," he said, blurting it out, "told me to say that your messenger was caught by your enemies, but he took his own life rather than be put to the question. I have been sent in his stead. Prince Hakon says that he is overjoyed that you are free, and that he is making ready. He is desperate to know the time of your coming, as he longs to see the dragon banner fly over the fortress of Darl."

"Well, that all sounds wonderful," Lik-Rifa smiled. "And my messenger took his own life, rather than betray me. Admirable." Then she frowned, and a cloud formed over Guðvarr's heart. "Prince, did you say? But to be a prince, you must be the son of a queen." There was an edge to Lik-Rifa's voice now that turned Guðvarr's blood to ice. "Who is this *Prince* Hakon?" she said, her lips curling down, sharp teeth glinting. Her face flickered with scales.

"Hakon is Helka's son," Drekr said, stepping forward. "He has been useful and is in a valuable position for us." He shrugged. "He is a vain *niðing*."

I wholeheartedly agree.

"Hmm," Lik-Rifa nodded. She tapped a finger on her lip, regarding Guðvarr.

"And how do I know that you are telling me the truth?" she said. "How do I know that you are not a liar. I have been tricked before; I will not let that happen again."

It seemed that every eye in the cavern stared at him, silence settling about them, heavy as an ocean. Drekr loomed close, his axe still in his fist, and other warriors stepped in. The fear that flooded Guðvarr drained him of strength and made his bladder twitch.

"I bear your mark, O great queen," he said, and pulled up the sleeve of his tunic. A tattooed dragon coiled around his arm, jaws wide, tail curled as if it clung to him.

"A ruse, to gain our trust?" a woman behind Drekr said. Dark-haired with grey, slim and honed and sharp as new-forged steel. Guðvarr did not like the look of her, but he met her gaze.

"Yes, Ilska, you speak my thoughts," Lik-Rifa said.

Ilska. Ilska the Cruel?

Another ripple of fear shivered through him. *She has a fair-fame name, and not one I'd like to go against.* He took a deep breath. *Remember the plan, remember the plan.*

"I would have to be the world's greatest idiot to have the dragon tattooed on my arm and not be a follower," he said, though he could not help but see the irony of that statement. He licked his lips. "It is a death sentence to me across all Vigrið."

"That is a truth," Drekr said.

A long, fear-filled silence and Guðvarr turned his eyes back to Lik-Rifa, tried to meet her forge-fire gaze.

"It will soon be a death sentence if any do *not* bear my mark," Lik-Rifa said.

She believes me.

Inside his thought-cage Guðvarr smiled.

CHAPTER SIXTY-ONE

ELVAR

Elvar stood in the prow of the *Wave-Jarl* and stared up at the slopes of Snakavik.

The River Slågen was wide and slow now, close to the end of its course where it bled into the fjord at Snakavik, and Urt the Unwashed was beating a slow rhythm on a barrel with his axe haft for the half-crew at their oar-benches. On the western bank of the river dense swathes of pinewood and scree-covered slopes reared, and higher still Snaka's skull emerged from the detritus of his fall, towering high above them all, eyes and fanged jaws facing out into the fjord and western sea. At the skull's crown Elvar could just glimpse the walls of her father's fortress and the black smudge of his Galdur tower. Clouds bunched in the sky above the fortress and mountains, fat and glowing with the imminence of snow, and when Elvar breathed she could taste ice on the air.

Fear and excitement tremored through her, quickening the blood in her veins. It was one thing to make a plan, but another thing entirely to attempt it.

Can I do this? Should I do this?

A sound beside her, a low-grinding growl and she looked down. Ulfrir was sitting beside her, gazing up at Snaka's skull with his amber-glowing eyes, a twist of emotion on his wolf-sharp face. His lips were moving, but she could not hear his words.

We are both thinking on our fathers.

Skuld was standing close by, eyes fixed on the skull of Snaka.

What memories do they have? Each one a saga-song. But memories are no good to us, now. We must make a new saga-song, or die in the trying.

Elvar lifted her hand from the cover of her bearskin cloak and raised a scabbarded sword wrapped in a gold-fitted belt. The sword had gold wire wrapped around the three-lobbed pommel and wound tight around the hilt, in place of a leather grip. The scabbard was equally richly tooled.

Skuld saw the sword, her head twitching to stare at it, like a predatory bird.

"This is yours," Elvar said to her. "I took it from you when you were thrown from the depths of Oskutreð." She held it out to Skuld. "Here, take it."

Skuld frowned, then smiled, reached out hesitantly and paused. Looked to Elvar as if she did not quite believe her.

"Take it," Elvar said. "You will probably need it."

Skuld snatched the sword from Elvar's hand and unrolled the belt, wrapped it around her waist and cinched it tight over her fish-scale *brynja*. She wrapped her fist around the hilt.

"My . . . thanks," Skuld said.

"Only use it on my command, or to protect me or mine from harm," Elvar said.

Footsteps, and Grend prowled along the deck to stand silently at Elvar's shoulder.

They turned a bend in the river and saw the town of Snakavik appear, nestled within the huge jaws of great Snaka. Row upon row of docks and piers, the town rising in a tangled, tiered snarl of smoke and stench and gloom.

Elvar could feel Grend's eyes on her, so she tore her gaze away from her home and looked at him.

"We are here," he said.

"I have always valued your powers of observation," she snapped.

"As I have always valued your kind-hearted tongue," he replied. "Since the first day I met you."

Elvar sucked in a deep breath, regretting her words. Grend had been the only constant in her life and did not deserve to bear the brunt of her fears.

"Tell me of that day, again," she said.

A moment as Grend's eyes became distant.

"Your mother had sent for me, summoning me to her in Snakavik from her father's farm," he said. "She took me into the weapons court, and we found you hiding behind a barrel of spears, watching the warriors train and spar. You had four winters on your back. Your father wanted you to be seated at a stool and learn the distaff, but your mother said that weapons craft would weave the tapestry of your life, not a loom." A glimmer of a smile cracked Grend's crag of a face. "She asked me to teach you weapons craft, to teach you of war and battle, so, I put a wooden sword in your hand and told you to try and kill me. When told to do that most children will lunge at your chest or try to swipe at your head, if they can reach it. You chopped your wooden sword down on to my foot, broke three of my toes and put me on my arse." He laughed now, loud and genuine, many of the Battle-Grim at their oar-benches staring open-mouthed, for it was a rare thing, to hear Grend laugh. He lifted a hand and tapped Elvar's forehead. "I knew then that you were a deep-cunning thinker; that you would find the right path needed for each task, whatever it is." He looked up at the heights of Snakavik. "I have no doubt that you are doing the same, now."

Elvar smiled and put a hand to his cragged cheek, rested her forehead against his.

A snowflake landed on her cheek.

The screeching of gulls grew around them as the Hvítá spilled into the fjord, cliffs rearing high, snow falling gently, muting sound. Sighvat leaned on the steering oar and the *Wave-Jarl* cut a white-foamed arc through the green-black waters and then the world was darkening as they sailed beneath the fangs and jaws of Snaka and into the cavity of his mottled skull, sound changing, echoing within the dome of the serpent's great skull. The docks were a tangle of masts, *drakkars* pressed tight to merchant *knarrs*, *snekkes* and all manner of *byrdings*. Elvar was used to seeing the docks of Snakavik as a heaving mass of timber, but this exceeded anything she could remember. There were more longships here than she had ever seen gathered in one place, and she remembered the merchant woman on the *knarr* that she had questioned on her journey here.

"Jarl Störr has summoned his drengrs *and offered silver to any warband who would fight for him."*

She saw a space on the furthermost pier and shouted at Sighvat, pointing to it, and soon the *Wave-Jarl*'s hull was scraping on timber, mooring ropes tied off. Elvar did not wait for the boarding plank to be raised, just leaped from the top-rail to the pier and stood waiting for the harbour official.

A thud of wood and Grend was beside her, handing her a red-painted shield with black spear and axe crossed upon it. He was balancing a small chest upon one shoulder.

Elvar rolled her shoulders, settling her god-made *brynja* and bearskin cloak, tightened her weapons belt with her seax, and then slung the shield across her back. Out of habit her hand went to her sword hilt and checked it was loose in its scabbard, hung from a baldric, let it slip back into the wood and sheepskin lining.

The harbour official marched towards her, a fat man in fur-trimmed wool, two guards in leather and mail behind him. She rested one hand upon the hilt of her sword and waited.

"Are you here for the muster?" he asked brusquely as he reached Elvar, looking from her to her crew full of mail-clad warriors.

A pause as Elvar took that in.

"Well?"

"Yes," she answered, reaching into her pouch and jangling coins.

"No fees, then," the official said, waving a hand. "Any who fight for Jarl Störr are exempt from harbour duties. You may leave your longship docked here for the duration of your service to the jarl."

Elvar nodded. "Good to know."

He held out a birch-bark tablet, scratched something into it with a small sharp knife and handed it to Elvar.

"What's this?" Elvar frowned.

"Your pass to the fortress."

"For me?"

"For all of you. You will have to take your whole crew up on to Snaka's skull," he said. "Either that or sleep in your longship, for there is no room for another person in the whole of Snakavik, every inn is full to bursting. Besides, you will have to go to the fortress, first. Jarl Störr wishes to see all who will fight for him. Do you have tents?"

"A sail awning, and a spare," Elvar said.

"That will have to do you all," he said. He looked out over the fjord, at the snow falling. "It will be cold up there tonight." He looked back to Elvar. "Any questions?"

"No," Elvar shook her head, and then the official was turning on his heel and striding away.

Well, that was easier than I was expecting.

Elvar looked at Grend and smiled. "If the gods were not all dead, I would say they are smiling on me," she said, remembering Agnar's old saying.

Though three of them still live, and two of them are my companions. My thralls. She tugged on the troll tusk hanging about her neck. "Battle-Grim, you heard the man. It's a walk to the top of Snaka's skull for us all. You know what we are about, so make sure you're all dressed for the occasion."

She stood and waited while Sighvat raised the steering oar and secured it, all the Battle-Grim going about the business of slithering into *brynjas*, buckling on weapons belts and helms, reaching for shields.

In short time the Battle-Grim disembarked, all of them mail-clad and grim-faced. Sighvat carried a large chest balanced across one shoulder. He stopped beside Elvar and looked up at the murky heights of Snakavik, the town cast in a permanent dusk, a thousand torches flickering.

"Time to earn our pay then," he said good-naturedly.

Ulfrir and Skuld crossed on to the pier, Ulfrir with his cloak hood pulled high, Skuld with a cloak wrapped around her wings, making her look freakishly muscled, her sword hilt poking through the cloak.

Uspa was the only one left on the deck of the *Wave-Jarl*. She was standing by the heaped piles of Oskutreð's treasure, covered now in the spare sail.

"*Bráðið holdið frá hverjum þeim sem þorir að snerta þennan fjársjóð, þangað til ég kem aftur,*" she said, red-flickering tendrils weaving from her palm and spreading across the sail, like a protective web. As Elvar watched the red-fire veins faded.

"That should give anyone foolish enough to try thieving from the Battle-Grim an unpleasant surprise," Uspa said as she walked across the boarding plank to stand at Elvar's side.

Elvar nodded, then stared up at Snakavik, her eyes drawn to the spiral stair that curled around the back of Snaka's skull, the path to the bone tunnel that led to the summit. That led to her father.

"Ready?" Grend asked her.

Elvar did not answer him, but looked to Uspa instead.

The Seiðr-witch gave her a grim nod, a flicker of something in her eyes.

Hope.

"Time to get your husband back," Elvar said to Uspa, then she was walking down the pier, a Seiðr-witch, a wolf-god and a winged woman at her back. The Battle-Grim fell in behind them.

CHAPTER SIXTY-TWO

BIÓRR

Biórr checked over the kit he was packing, needing a moment of calm in the midst of what felt like a swirling storm, because all about him Lik-Rifa's warband were making ready to leave, to march on Svelgarth. Trolls were roaring, skraeling were shouting, tennúr were chittering and Drekr was bellowing commands. Lik-Rifa had already left, Ilska and most of the dragon-born galloping like a gale after her. Rotta was the only one who seemed to be unmoved by the excitement and fear that was surging through all in the cavern. He was lounging in Lik-Rifa's serpent throne, biting into an apple.

Biórr looked down at the kit spread across his straw mattress: his coat of mail rolled in sheepskin to keep it oiled and protected from the sea-rot. A spare wool tunic, breeches and *winnigas* leg-wraps. A copper box with dry tinder and kindling. Flint and striking iron, seal gut and fishhooks for the stitching of wounds. A roll of linen bandages and a heating iron for the cauterisation of wounds. His sword and seax were rolled in his weapons belt. An iron helm with a simple nasal guard.

He puffed out his cheeks and looked around the hall.

This is really happening, then. Excitement and fear shivered through him. *So many years I have lived in hope of this day. When we would march against the world and hold our heads high. Strike a blow for all those Tainted thralls who have bled and died for a slave-master.* Just at the thought of it he felt his anger building, a bubbling pot.

Storolf was standing close by, still and silent, gazing down at his hands. They bunched into fists, knuckles whitening.

He has taken his brother's death hard.

Storolf must have felt Biórr's eyes on him, because he looked over.

"Grief, it eats away at us, like rust on iron," Biórr said as he stepped closer to his friend. "But it can be a weapon, too. Avenge Kalv. Avenge all the Tainted put in the ground by *niðing* jarls and slave-owners."

Storolf just looked at him, eyes red-rimmed. His face hardened.

"Three hundred years of our kind wearing thrall-collars," Biórr said. "And we shall be the ones to end it."

"That is a lot of vengeance," Storolf breathed.

"Aye, but they have it coming," Biórr hissed, feeling a swell of anger. He turned and went back to his kit, set about shrugging into his coat of mail, shifting to settle it, then buckling his weapons belt about his waist, easing some of the weight of mail from his shoulders. The weight of sword and seax felt familiar and reassuring. He wrapped a sealskin cloak around his shoulders. Much of his small kit he put into a pouch at his belt, the rest going into a kitbag. Then he slung his shield across his back and carried his kitbag over towards the wagons. He passed a dark patch of ground, Kráka's blood still staining it. Not long ago he would have felt shame and anger intertwined, both at Kráka for involving him in her escape, and for Brák, who had backed him into a corner and made him become her executioner.

He should know, it is not wise to back a rat into a corner.

But he felt nothing. Just a cold, empty darkness.

A horn blast rang out, Biórr thinking it was time to move out. The plan was to travel south through the catacomb of caverns and tunnels that wound beneath the Boneback Mountains, leaving by one of Nastrandir's southern entrances and marching hard for Svelgarth, Jarl Orlyg's seat of power. Biórr had been assigned to the rearguard, following behind the wagon train and children. But instead of whips cracking and the wagons moving out, the northern gates began to open. A white crack that let in a blast of wind and snow and sea-spray. Through that crack a solitary rider came, surrounded by a handful of scuttling frost-spiders and a few tennúr.

Spiders and tooth-eaters: who would have thought they would make the finest of guards?

The rider was wrapped in a dark cloak, travel-stained, jet hair slick, and a bandage wrapped around their head, covering one eye.

"Someone call off these arseling pets, before I run out of patience and roast them," the rider called out, a flare of red in one eye.

And then Biórr recognised her.

Myrk.

Drekr barked an order as he strode to her, a crowd following him. The tennúr swirled up into the shadows and the frost-spiders scuttled to the nearest column and climbed up to their webs.

"I need a new sword, a score of Raven-Feeders, and maybe some of these fanged and clawed pets of yours, brother," Myrk snarled at Drekr. "I need to go and kill some people."

"What's happened?" Drekr scowled. "Where's father, and everyone else?"

Biórr shoved through the crowd gathering around Myrk, pushed through to the front and saw that she was pale and thin, her face hard lined and quivering with rage.

"All dead," Myrk said, a tremor in her voice.

A silent moment, the whole hall listening. Biórr saw Rotta step up silently behind Drekr, who was staring at Myrk with disbelief in his eyes, swiftly followed by tears.

"Tell me," Drekr snarled.

"It was the Bloodsworn," Myrk said. "Those *niðing*, steaming piles of goat-humping shite . . ." she trailed off into wordless sounds of rage, slowly reined her fury back in. "They were hired by Helka to investigate the mine." She sucked in a long, shuddering breath. "Someone named Varg slew father."

Drekr's jaw was working, but no words came out of his mouth, only guttural animal noises.

"I was ambushed moments after arriving," Myrk continued, "set upon by the Bloodsworn. And they had vaesen pets with them, just like I see here." She looked around. "Tennúr, and a spertus."

Rotta frowned at that.

"You escaped, though?" another voice said, Brák Trolls-Bane, who stood in Drekr's shadow.

Myrk looked at him with a twist of her lips.

"Eventually," she said, "by my own wits. But only after I had been their prisoner." She raised the bandage across one eye, revealing a scarred, puckered hole. "Their chief did this to me."

"That old grey-beard Glornir Shield-Breaker?" Brák asked.

"Not him. Another," Myrk said.

"Who?" Drekr growled.

"Someone you know, brother. She is hunting you. Kept me alive so that I would lead her to you. Her name is Orka, and she says you took her son."

"Orka," Drekr murmured as he raised a hand to his face, his fingertips brushing the scars on his face.

"Mother!" a voice gasped, and Biórr saw Breca standing in the crowd, hope blazing in his eyes. Harek and Bjarn stood behind him.

"She said she fought you in Darl, was the one who broke your thumb," Myrk said.

"Aye, that is her," Drekr said. "I knew she was going to be trouble, should have killed her when I had the chance." He shrugged. "If she is chasing you, then I will kill her when she finds us."

"She'll be the one killing you," Breca screamed at Drekr. His eyes were flickering amber and green and he sniffed the air. "I can smell your fear from here," he laughed.

With a growl Drekr stepped forward and backhanded Breca across the jaw, sent him crashing to the ground where he rolled, groaning.

"Your family are becoming more trouble than they are worth," Drekr snarled.

"Is that Breca, the brat Orka hunts?" Myrk said. "I will gut him now, make a belt from his entrails." She swung a leg over her saddle and slid to the ground, swayed and dropped to her knees.

Drekr stooped and lifted her up in his arms.

"Let me kill him," Myrk rasped.

"Where is this Orka now? Is she close?"

"No, brother, she thinks you and her maggot-child are in the Iskalt Islands." She looked at Breca again. "I want to kill him. I need to kill him."

Drekr walked to stand over Breca, who still lay on the ground.

"You should keep the lad alive," Rotta said, stepping forward.

"Who's this arseling?" Myrk snarled, frowning at Rotta.

"Ha, I think I like your sister," Rotta said to Drekr.

"He is Rotta, the rat god," Drekr told Myrk.

Myrk blinked up at Rotta, unbelieving.

"It is true, I am," Rotta said with a smile and a shrug. "You should let him live," he repeated.

"Why?" Myrk and Drekr said together.

"Because when trapping a hungry wolf, live bait always works best."

CHAPTER SIXTY-THREE

VARG

Varg ran, his lungs burning, legs aching, his coat of mail chaffing on his shoulders, the strap of his shield rubbing into his neck. He tried to shift it as he ran, then ignored it, setting his will to focus on the next step, and the next, and the next. Up ahead he saw the backs of Edel and Røkia pulling ahead of him, and the blur of movement that was Edel's hounds. He focused on the wolf in his soul, allowed it to seep through his blood. Almost immediately he felt its strength and energy pulse through him, and he increased his pace.

It had been two days since they had met Sulich and Edel at the riverbank. Two days of hard rowing down the River Reka, and then leaving the *Sea-Wolf* moored to a riverbank. At first they had drawn lots, as no one wanted to stay behind, but when protests had followed even that, Glornir had decided that they all would go, leaving the *Sea-Wolf* moored and hidden as well as they could.

We can buy a new drakkar, *if we have to*, Svik had said. So, all fifty-four members of the Bloodsworn were running now, had been running for over half a day through these mountains, setting out as soon as the sun had risen enough to chase darkness from the land. They were following Sulich as he led them along a narrow path that wound through steep-sided valleys, up treacherous slopes dotted with spruce and hawthorn and across meadows of sun-bleached, yellow grass, the occasional shadow of a buzzard skimming across the ground. Only goats stopped to watch them as they ran past, a ram placing himself protectively between his flock and Varg and stamping a hoof as they ran past.

Your flock are safe from the wolf today, old ram, Varg thought, *we are hunting bigger prey.*

Edel had picked Varg to run with her and Røkia as scouts, Sulich leading them because only he knew the way. Varg slowed a fraction to twist and look back over his shoulder. In the distance he saw the bulk of Glornir, bald head sweating and shining in the sun, long-axe in his fists, his shield on his back, and behind him the blurred smudge of the Bloodsworn stretching out into the distance.

His foot hit a loose patch of soil and he stumbled, slid, propping himself up with his spear and then he was running on again, Edel and Røkia only a score of paces ahead now. A last burst of speed and he was with them. Together they climbed a ridge, crested it and found Sulich a few paces down a slope leaning against a boulder, red-faced and sucking air.

"We . . . are . . . here," he gasped. He was dressed in his baggy breeches tied from ankle to knee with leg-wraps, and also the lamellar coat that Varg had given him. The quiver of arrows and bow case hung from his belt, along with his horsehair helm and curved sabre, and his shield was slung across his back. Varg knew that his own coat of mail was heavy, but the lamellar plate was heavier. He did not envy Sulich running for over half a day up and down mountains in that kit.

"You need to run more often," Røkia said to Sulich, "you are unfit."

"I have the . . . hawk in my . . . blood," he muttered, "not the . . . wolf or hound."

Røkia shrugged.

"When you have breath to speak, tell us where *here* is," Edel said, tugging on the ears of one of her hounds as it nudged her hip, tongue lolling.

"When Glornir arrives," Sulich said, "no point wasting breath and saying it twice."

Edel nodded and sat down with her back to the rock Sulich was leaning against.

"Varg, come down here," Røkia said, "get off the ridge."

"Why?" Varg asked as he hurried a few paces to stand beside Sulich.

"Because if there is anyone else in these mountains, then they will see your silhouette standing there, announcing to the world that we are here," she said, rolling her eyes.

"Oh," Varg said.

"No-Sense," Røkia breathed, shaking her head.

They drank from their water bottles as they waited for the rest of the Bloodsworn, Varg taking the time to practise using the wolf in his blood to look, smell and listen. The ridge they were standing upon sloped down to a vale, a dirt road running through it. To the south the road spilled on to a thin-grassed plain punctuated with dark boulders, a stream trickling through it and sparkling in the sun. The road led up to the dark smear of a timber fortress, thin lines of hearth smoke rising from it. He could taste the smoke in the air, and the smell of humanity, of stale sweat and shite, and faint as a sigh he could hear the murmur of life, blacksmiths' hammers pounding, horses whinnying, children shouting, dogs barking.

The sun was high in the sky and though Varg's blood was slowing, sweat was still dripping and stinging his eyes. He cuffed it away.

"Why is it so hot?" he muttered, "when the world is moving towards winter."

Røkia looked at him like he was moon-touched.

"Because we have travelled south," she said. "The further south you travel, the hotter it gets." She looked up at the sun, bright in a sheer blue sky. "This is nothing," she shrugged.

Back on Kolskegg's farm Varg had heard tales of vast oceans of sand, the land burned of all life by the furnace of the sun, but living his whole life on a farm where ice locked the land for more time than the sun warmed it, he had found it impossible to believe.

The growing sound of feet drumming and then Glornir was cresting the ridge, a wave of the Bloodsworn flowing down the slope behind him. They spread around Sulich and the boulder, some sitting, squatting, others spreading out to scan the land.

"Why have we stopped?" Glornir growled. He was sweat-soaked, his grey beard dark and matted, but he was not gasping for breath, as Varg had expected.

"What?" Glornir said, seeing Varg's puzzled expression.

"It's been a long run," Varg said with a shrug, "yet you are not even breathing hard."

"The bear is not a match for the wolf in a sprint, but he can run all day if need calls," Glornir said, then looked back to Sulich.

"We are here," Sulich said, pointing down the slope. "The road from Ulaz." Then he pointed south to the columns of smoke and the smudge of timber walls. "And that is Valdai, Jaromir's fortress."

Glornir looked both ways, eyes narrowed, face grim.

"You are sure we are here ahead of Jaromir?" he said.

"Yes," Sulich said. "That road curls east among the feet of mountains, like a lazy river. It is a long road to ride from Ulaz."

"Huh," Glornir grunted, taking in the terrain around them. The road ran between two steep-sided slopes, boulders and patches of hawthorn scattered across them. A little deeper into the vale there had been an old rockfall that narrowed the road.

"Will Jaromir have scouts riding ahead of him?"

"No," Sulich said. "This is his land, and he would not even countenance the thought of someone attacking him here, so close to his fortress."

"Are you sure?" Glornir pressed.

"I know him well, he is my half-brother," Sulich said with a shrug. "He is an arrogant arseling."

Glornir looked north and south.

"Edel, follow the road into the mountains, I want to know when they are close."

"Aye, chief," Edel said and loped off along the slope, her two hounds spreading around her.

"Røkia, go have a look at Valdai, see what you can see," he shrugged.

Røkia nodded and slid off down the slope towards the road. Varg felt the urge to go with her, like a rope tied around his waist.

"The rest of us, we'll get down there and make Jaromir a welcome he'll not be forgetting," Glornir growled.

CHAPTER SIXTY-FOUR

ORKA

Orka reined Trúr in, their breath misting as they stood at the crest of a slope leading down towards a peninsula of land that stretched out like a snow-crusted arm into the slow-churning sea. At the southern edge of the peninsula, granite cliffs towered as high as the sky, the easternmost end of the Boneback Mountains. The skies were clear and pale, the snow clouds of the last few days finally blown over with a westerly wind, leaving the land white and smooth and still.

Where are you, Myrk? Have you leaped into the sea? There is nowhere else for you to go.

The crunch of hooves on snow as the others rode up and reined in behind her.

About twenty paces ahead Sæunn crouched low to the ground, sniffing, studying.

Spert shifted where he was lying across Orka's saddle and looked up at her.

"*Stopping for food?*"

"No," Orka said, clicked her tongue and touched her heels to Trúr's sides, walking slowly towards Sæunn.

"She came this way," Sæunn said, scraping away the top layer of snow and pressing her nose low to the ground.

"And went where?" Orka said, looking around. *Scaled a mountain, or into the sea?*

Their progress had slowed with the snow. If not for Sæunn that would have been the end of tracking Myrk, but somehow the *Hundur*-thrall had managed to find traces of scent to lead them ever on.

Sæunn shrugged. "On," she said. She raised her head to the sky and breathed deep. "There are strange scents in the wind, but faint, so faint."

"Of what?"

Sæunn shrugged. "They are like the memory of a scent. The snow has scoured everything from the land." She rose to her feet and walked on down the winding track.

Orka and the others followed.

They passed between snow-covered boulders and wind-twisted, leafless trees and slowly the path levelled. Something glinted up ahead, catching Orka's eye, and Sæunn stopped, hand raised.

"Frost-spiders," the *Hundur*-thrall hissed.

Orka reached for her long-axe hanging on a saddle hook and rode slowly forward, past Sæunn.

"Stay behind me," she said to the *Hundur*-thrall.

A thick strand of web stretched across the path, roughly the height of Orka's chest. It was secured on either side to two boulders. Halja and Revna rode left and right of Orka, sword and spear levelled, ready for anything to appear, and Orka swung her axe, sliced through the thick strand of web. Each severed part snapped back to the boulder it was attached to, a puff of snow.

Nothing happened.

Sæunn took a few steps and broke into a bounding run, leaping up on to one of the boulders. She sat there, squatting, and stared across the peninsula.

"Nothing living here," she pronounced.

Orka frowned.

They moved on, Sæunn bounding ahead, then squatting, digging, sniffing, then loping on in a series of stuttering stops and starts, until eventually they stood between the sea and a cliff of granite. The sea crashed against boulders, salt spray soaking them, Orka sitting in her saddle and staring, willing Myrk to appear.

This cannot be the end. A seed of despair wormed in her belly, the wolf within her snarling at it, hackles raised. Giving up was not in her blood.

Sæunn was crawling across the base of the cliff on all fours, the ground smooth, the snow less deep here, as if it had been cleared recently, before the last snowfall. Orka looked up at the cliff face, wondering if Myrk had scaled it.

Impossible. Huge swathes of it were smooth as marble, not a seam or crack for purchase, although as Orka stared at it she saw there was something unusual about the cliff. Some distance up there were huge ridges curling across the granite, as if some giant, ancient worm had bored tunnels through the rock and left its ridged trail.

"Has old one-eye just learned how to walk through rock, then?" Revna Hare-Legs said, frowning at the cliff.

Sæunn scrambled back from the door, looking around wild-eyed.

Orka and the Bloodsworn reached for their weapons, spreading out.

"What is it?" Orka breathed.

"Something bad," Sæunn said, fear putting a tremor in her voice.

"Where?" Gunnar Prow muttered, eyeing the rock-strewn peninsula behind them.

"Everywhere," Sæunn said, twisting and spinning.

Spert shifted on Orka's saddle, his antennae twitching, caressing the air, and then he looked up at Orka with his grey-melted face.

"*Lik-Rifa,*" Spert said.

The dragon. Orka felt a shiver of fear at that, anger snapping at its heels. *The dragon that my son was stolen to free.*

Halja's horse whinnied, danced sideways, and Lif's head jerked as he tried to look everywhere at once.

"Where is she?" Orka said quietly to Spert.

"*In there,*" Spert said, pointing with one of his many legs at the cliff face.

"Inside a mountain?" Gunnar said.

"*Not a mountain. Nastrandir,*" Spert rasped.

"*That* is Lik-Rifa's hall?" Revna said, pointing at the cliff.

Spert muttered under his breath as his wings snapped out and he rose from Orka's lap to hover before the cliff face.

"*Opinn*," Spert rasped.

There was a long moment of silence, all of them staring, and then the cliff face began to move, loose snow falling from it as the rock heaved and writhed, huge serpents of granite emerging, twisting and coiling on sinuous necks to look down upon Spert.

A vertical crack appeared in the cliff face, the outline of doors, and then they began to open.

"Don't you think we are rushing things a bit?" Lif squeaked. "There might be a dragon in there."

Breca might be in there.

Orka slipped from Trúr's saddle and hit the ground running, her long-axe held two-handed across her body. She ran through the opening door just as it became wide enough for her to squeeze through. The sound of hooves and shouting behind her, but she was only thinking of what was ahead, of Breca, the wolf in her blood filling her senses. A huge chamber, braziers of flame flickering, great columns rising into deep shadows, Orka snarling, searching for her son, and for someone or something to kill.

She skidded to a halt, staring around the cavern as the doors opened fully, Lif and her companions surging in behind her.

The chamber was empty.

"Sæunn," Orka called.

The *Hundur*-thrall came loping tentatively in to stand beside Orka, her head raised, nose twitching and sniffing.

"Bad smells, lots of bad smells, but they are all old, mistress," she said.

"Search the place," Orka growled, feeling the need for violence still pulsing through her veins. She looked to the shadowed eaves and howled.

Sæunn sucked in a breath, clearly gathering her courage, then loped off, sniffing and searching. Revna and Gunnar dismounted and moved into the chamber. Footsteps, and Lif walked to stand with Orka, leading his horse and Trúr by the reins. Halja walked silently with him. Spert whirred into the room and landed beside Orka.

"How did you do that?" Orka asked him.

"*Don't know*," Spert said, a shrug rippling through his segmented body. "*Spert felt it, just knew what to do.*"

"It must be Lik-Rifa's Seiðr," Halja said. "The same way she called the vaesen to her."

"Aye," grunted Orka. She paced further into the chamber, between two rows of huge granite columns. All about were signs of life and recent habitation, not all of them human: straw mattresses, piles of ash in hearth fires, mounds of dung, discarded bones. Barrels with wooden weapons for training. Thick, blue-glinting webs hung between columns. Ahead of Orka was the huge carcass of a whale, mostly just white bones now that arched like a tunnel, and beyond them was a dais with a stone-carved chair upon it.

"So, this is Nastrandir, the corpse-hall of Lik-Rifa," Lif breathed as they walked through the chamber, even his soft words echoing. "It's more impressive than Rotta's chamber, it must be said." He sniffed. "Though, if anything, it smells worse than Rotta's chamber."

Halja stopped at a pile of dried dung as high as her knees, squatted and cracked some off in her hand, sniffed it. It was soft inside the outer crust, dripping through Halja's gloved fingers.

"Trolls," she said. "A day old, maybe less."

"*Lots of vaesen been here*," Spert muttered as he scuttled along beside them, his antennae twitching.

Orka saw a pile of carcasses, the remnants of elk and boar and reindeer. As she looked closer, she saw that not one of the skulls had a single tooth left in their jaws.

"*Filthy tooth-eating tennúr*," Spert rasped.

"Vesli's a tennúr," Lif said.

"*Vesli different*," Spert grunted. An indrawn breath. "*Spert miss Vesli.*"

"I do, too," Lif said.

Orka had asked the ravens, Kló and Grok, to carry Vesli to Darl in search of Glornir and the Bloodsworn, so that Orka could keep her bargain with Elvar. Vesli had agreed, though she had shed tears as she had climbed on to the back of one of the ravens.

They stopped at the steps to the dais, a huge stone-carved chair upon it, looking like it was crafted from intertwined serpents.

The clatter of hooves and echo of feet, Gunnar and Revna joining them there.

"Quite a gathering," Revna said. "Very cosy."

"A lot of vaesen," Gunnar agreed.

"And not just vaesen," Halja said, jutting her chin at the barrels of practice weapons and ash-filled hearth fires.

"And where have they gone?" Lif said as he strode up the dais towards the stone chair. Orka had noticed a difference in him since they had attacked the skraeling at Gudleif's steading. He had a new scar on his cheek that ran beneath his right eye, mending well thanks to Vesli's healing spit, but it was more than that. He walked taller, less hesitantly than he once had, a confidence in him that had not been there before.

Face death enough times, and you become used to the company of those raven-wings.

"To cause some mischief somewhere, that is for sure," Gunnar Prow said.

"Aye," Revna agreed, looking around the hall. "This is all going to end in blood."

The wolf in Orka growled, agreeing.

"Heya," muttered Halja Flat-Nose.

As Lif drew near to the chair it shifted, the rock rippling, dust falling away, and there was a series of cracks, the carved serpents moving, breaking away from the chair, coiling and baring their fangs at Lif in a silent hiss.

Lif stumbled away, spear raised, and fell on his backside.

Halja ran up the steps to stand beside Lif, her sword hissing into her fist, shield raised over him, but the serpents only writhed and watched them.

The slap of feet and Sæunn joined them, her eyes still wide with fear and awe.

"I have found Myrk's trail," she said.

CHAPTER SIXTY-FIVE

ELVAR

Two hundred and eleven, two hundred and twelve, Elvar counted the steps of the bone-tunnel, as she had always done since she was a child, the air thick with whale oil, oppressive and claustrophobic, and then stepped out of Snaka's skull and into a snowstorm.

Guards huddled around a blazing brazier, and one of them looked over at Elvar.

"Here for the muster," Elvar called out, raising the bark tablet in her hand, and the guard nodded, waving them on with his spear.

Elvar led the Battle-Grim along a road of timber planks that spanned the ground between the bone-tunnel and Jarl Störr's fortress, though the fortress was just a blur through the swirling blizzard. As they drew closer Elvar saw the glow of hearth fires either side of her, spread across the plateau of Snaka's skull, saw tents grouped in clusters, glimpsed warriors gathered around fires and cook-pots, heard the snatched sound of voices raised in song. Round shields were left leaning against tent-poles, all manner of symbols upon them, ravens, serpents, crossed axes, wolves in swirling knotwork. A host of *drengrs* gathered from every petty jarl's retinue in her father's realm, and other mercenary bands like the Battle-Grim.

The harbour official told no word of a lie; it looks like every man and woman in Vigrið has answered my father's call to battle.

She shared a look with Grend, who walked at her left shoulder, head down and one arm balancing the small chest on his shoulder.

"The lure of silver and battle-fame is a Seiðr-magic of its own," he said.

They walked on in silence and soon the walls and gate towers of the fortress loomed above them, the orange glow of torches flickering. Elvar pulled the hood of her bearskin cloak up, the snarling jaws putting her face in shadow, Grend pulling his own hood up. The gates were open, guards huddled close to braziers, just like at the bone-tunnel. One stepped forward, an old grey-beard, a scar running through his chin that cut a line through his beard.

"Here for the muster," Elvar said, holding up the bark tablet.

He looked from the tablet to Elvar, then at the warriors at her back.

"Who are you?" the grey-beard asked her.

"The Battle-Grim," Elvar said. Then, louder, "we are the slayers of vaesen, hunters of the Tainted, reapers of souls. And we are here to fight for Jarl Störr and help you win your battles." She flashed a grin, just the flicker of her teeth in the shadows and firelight.

"Heya," Sighvat said approvingly, and there were hooms and heyas rippling through the Battle-Grim behind her.

"Jarl Störr does not take everyone with a sword and a few spears at their back into his shield wall, just on the strength of their own fare-fame words," the grey-beard said. "He will meet with you first. Syr," he called, and a woman stepped away from the brazier. "More fair-fame gold-seekers," he said. "Take them to the jarl."

Syr nodded, gestured to Elvar and turned on her heel.

Elvar followed her, and the guard led her through the fortress, longhouses stretching either side of the timber road where Jarl Störr's oathsworn *drengrs* were barracked, then through a street of forges that belched acrid smoke and rang with hammers pounding iron. Elvar glimpsed buckets and barrels full of spearheads waiting to be riveted on to ash shafts, axe heads and arrowheads heaped and piled in long troughs. Men and women sitting with buckets of iron rings at their feet and hammering rivets together, crafting coats of mail.

My father is taking the business of war seriously. What has happened? Is it word of Lik-Rifa? They passed into another street, the echo of hammer on iron fading, and then finally into the courtyard before Jarl Störr's mead hall.

Syr the guard crossed the courtyard and climbed wide wooden steps, stopping at the oak-carved doors to speak to more guards.

Elvar climbed the steps behind her and leaned against a knot-carved column as if she were bored, though her blood was thrumming, nerves tight as a drawn bowstring, heart pounding an oar-beat in her chest.

"Come," Syr said to Elvar as the doors opened. "Not all of you," she added as all the Battle-Grim shifted to follow Elvar up the steps.

"Grend, Sighvat, Uspa, Ulfrir, with me," Elvar said, and then she was striding up the stairs and through the doors into her father's hall.

CHAPTER SIXTY-SIX

VARG

Varg wiped sweat from his face and pushed his unruly hair out of his eyes, felt the rasp of bristle on the back of his head. He drew his seax and started shaving the stubble away.

"Now this is what I like to see," Svik said, who was sitting alongside Sulich with their backs to a tree beneath a stand of spruce. Sulich was checking over each grey-feathered arrow in his bow case. "Varg No-Sense is taking pride in his appearance before a scrap."

"I don't like the stubble," Varg muttered. "Reminds me of being a thrall."

Svik nodded, serious for a moment. Then the smile was back. "Just be careful you don't go cutting your own head off. I'm sure one of Jaromir's *druzhina* would be happy to help you with that."

"Huh," grunted Varg as his blade slipped and he nicked his skin.

He was standing on the flat road of the vale, nestled between steep-sided slopes. The sun was beating down, not a cloud in the sky and, to Varg, it seemed that nothing was moving in the whole world. He heard the sounds of insects and the raucous croaking of an old crow, but other than that the world felt like it was holding its breath. Most of the Bloodsworn were gathered in clumps, resting in what little shade could be found, which was hardly any, especially as they had chopped most of the branches from the trees surrounding the vale. All the Bloodsworn were sweat-soaked, sitting quietly, tending to kit, tightening buckles and laces, dragging whetstones along the edges of blades. Varg found himself constantly looking over his shoulder, to where the road through the mountains spilled on to a grassy plain that led to the gates of Valdai.

Where is Røkia? She should be back by now.

The only one other than Varg who was not sitting in the shade was Glornir. He stood still as carved stone, staring down the vale, as if by will alone he could make Jaromir and his *druzhina* appear.

"Jaromir," Varg said to Sulich as he shaved his head and Sulich inspected arrows, "he is your brother, then?"

Sulich paused in his task.

"Half-brother," Sulich said. "We have the same father."

"Kirill the Magnificent, Khagan of Iskidan," Svik said casually.

"The Khagan? Ruler of all Iskidan?" Varg said. "So, you are a prince?"

Sulich shrugged. "My father has more children than Ingmar has lice in his beard," he said.

"My beard is clean," Ingmar called out, then plucked a louse from it and frowned, squashed the louse with a *pop* between nail and thumb.

"But technically, yes, I am a prince of Iskidan," Sulich finished.

"Is that why Jaromir hunts you, then?"

"Perhaps. He uses the fact that I am Tainted, with Hauker the hawk in my blood, to legitimise his hunt for me. Whether that is the truth or not, I do not know. He is ambitious, so perhaps he uses my Tainted blood to remove those he considers future rivals or competitors for the throne of Iskidan, once my father is gone. Jaromir has a twin brother, Rurik. When they were younger, they would often talk of how they would rule all Iskidan together. Many of my brothers and sisters have fallen to their ambition and malice already. Disappeared in the night . . ." He stood and stretched his neck. "Perhaps I will ask Jaromir, when we see him." He looked down the vale, eyes narrowed. Then reached for his shield that was leaning against a tree, slung it over his back and walked away.

"Have I offended him again?" Varg said as he wiped his seax across his breeches and sheathed the weapon.

"It is a painful subject for him," Svik said. "I have rarely heard him speak of it to anyone, but I do know that what he has just told you, that is just the tip of the blade. Jaromir is not . . . a kind man."

Varg nodded as he tied the long shock of hair that ran from forehead to crown with a thin strip of leather. Svik grunted approvingly, even as he was braiding his own beard. Varg turned on his heel and paced a dozen steps down the vale, peering across the plain with narrowed eyes.

"You should try and relax, little wolf," Ingmar Ice said. The big man was sitting beside a boulder, calmly checking over the straps and grip on his blood-spattered shield. "Worrying about a thing won't make it come any quicker."

"I can't," Varg said.

Then he saw a dark shape in the distance, running towards them. His wolf-eyes picked out the blonde braid of Røkia's hair, the sweat-glistening sides of her head that Svik had shaved for her, just like Varg's. A score of heartbeats and she was entering the vale, slopes rising steeply either side of her. Glornir broke his silent vigil and strode to meet her.

"Just a garrison, like a hundred others we've taken," Røkia said to Glornir as she skidded to a halt. "Timber walls high as two of you, the gates are closed and not well manned. Maybe fifty spears, from what I can see, but it would need twice that to guard it well. A stream runs beneath the wall, north to south. A tower and hall, stables, the usual."

Glornir nodded. "Good," he said.

"Welcome back," Varg said, handing Røkia a waterskin. She drank deep, then frowned as she looked at his fresh-shaven head.

"You're bleeding," she said. "Has the fighting started already?"

"Only between Varg's stubble and his seax," Svik called out.

Varg swiped blood from the shaving nick.

"Chief," Ingmar said, standing slowly and pointing down the vale with his spear.

Edel appeared around the distant bend in the road, her hounds loping at her side.

"They're coming," Varg heard her call out.

Glornir held up his long-axe, halting her, then gestured up the slope to her right. Edel loped up the steep slope and disappeared behind a boulder.

"Well, it's time," Glornir said. He looked at the Bloodsworn spread around him. "For Vol," he said.

Varg's heart pounded at that, a drumbeat of war.

For Vol. He remembered the last time he had seen her, showing him kindness in the damp of Rotta's chamber. Remembered Skalk clubbing her to the ground with his staff. Remembered Torvik stabbed in the throat by Yrsa.

The wolf in his blood snarled, wanting blood, wanting vengeance.

As do I, he told the wolf.

Instantly the Bloodsworn were moving, the calm of a moment before replaced with practised efficiency. Warriors were buckling on helms, shrugging shields from their backs. Varg strode back to where Svik was rising from his spot beneath the trees, to his shield and spear, both leaning against a trunk. He pulled his sweat-stained nålbinding cap on to his head, unbuckled his helm from his belt and slipped it over the wool cap, then fastened it tight beneath his chin, pulled his beard out free of the leather straps, adjusted the mail curtain across his neck and shoulders, checked his vision through the helm's eye sockets. A roll and shrug of his shoulders, shifting his coat of mail, and then he swept up his shield and spear, wrapping his fist around the wooden grip and tucking his knuckles in tight behind the iron boss.

The crunch of footsteps and Glornir strode down the dirt path a score of places, stopping where an old rockfall had choked and narrowed the road. On the other side a dense stand of hawthorn stood thick as a hedge. He planted his feet halfway between them, setting the prow of their shield wall and the warriors of the Bloodsworn settled around him, forming loosely into two rows behind him.

"Spears in the second row, No-Sense," Røkia told him, from her position at Glornir's right shoulder and Varg nodded, settling in behind her. A shadow to Varg's right and he saw Ingmar Ice come to stand beside him, his shield held loosely in one fist, a long spear, shaft thick as Varg's wrist in the other. A wickedly curved bearded axe was threaded through his belt. Ingmar looked up at the sky, then down the road.

"A good day for a scrap, eh," Ingmar said, smiling.

And then they waited.

A silence settled over them, the old crow in the tree squawking. Varg became aware of a sensation, a vibrating that he felt through his feet, and then he heard them. A rumbling, like distant thunder, growing with every heartbeat. Individual sounds became clear; the creak of leather harness, the jangle of tack and mail, the drum of hoofbeats.

Riders emerged around the bend in the road, sunlight gleaming on bright-polished helms, on lamellar coats, on a forest of spears.

Jaromir rode at their head, his hawk on his saddle pommel and a column of his *druzhina* behind him, four warriors wide and many deep, disappearing around the curl in the road like some elongated, segmented vaesen.

"Do not keep your beast on a leash," Glornir said, his voice low and deep as he pulled on his iron helm. "There is no need to hide what we are this day. This day we are the pack, and they are the prey." He let out a low, rumbling growl that vibrated in Varg's chest. "This will be their last day."

A ripple of fear and excitement shivered through Varg. This feeling of fear, it was an old friend to him, familiar from a hundred times that he had stepped into the pugil-ring at Kolskegg's farm. But this was different, though, fighting with sharp steel in your fist, there was more than a beating and a bucket of silver at stake. There was your life. And that made the fear and excitement thrum all the louder through his blood. He tried to swallow but his mouth was dry.

As Jaromir and his *druzhina* drew closer Varg saw that, close to the head of the column, a huge-muscled man walked, shaven-haired with skin rippling in hues of blacks and blues and purples, like one of the bruised men Varg had seen at the thrall-market in Darl. This man, too, wore an iron collar around his neck, though his neck was thick and muscled as a bull. Beside him rode a woman, her head shaved and covered with swirling tattoos. Her hands and arms were also tattooed, coiling up into the sleeves of her grey-woollen tunic. She, too, wore a thrall-collar.

The Seiðr-witch that Sulich spoke of.

A fresh seed of fear in Varg's gut, different from what had come before. Sharper, more intense. Fighting other warriors with sharp steel and tooth and claw was one thing, but fighting a Seiðr-witch, that was another thing entirely.

In his blood his wolf growled, its hackles rising, and it gave him courage.

Jaromir had seen them, but he rode on a while, until he was around a hundred paces away. Then he reined in, regarding Glornir with a downward curl of his lips.

"You *dare*," he snarled. Then, slowly, deliberately, he took the horsehair-plumed helm that was hanging from his saddle hook and buckled it on.

"You are food for crows, all of you, for this insult," Jaromir said. "I will show you no mercy, no matter how hard you beg. This night your bones will be picked clean by jackals." He raised a hand and the riders behind him moved, spreading wider across the path, eight, ten horses wide. That was all that could pass through the chokepoint on the road.

"Iva," Jaromir said with a contemptuous wave of his hand. "Clear this rabble from my way."

The tattooed Seiðr-witch rode forward a few paces, the hulking bruised man keeping pace with her and, as she moved, Varg saw another rider behind her. Shackled at her wrists with iron, swaying in her saddle, her head shaved to stubbled patches. A knotwork of tattoos coiled on her neck, though they were hard to see through the crusted blood and bruises. But it was to her face that Varg's eyes were drawn. A landscape of pain, her lips stitched together, swollen, scabbed, weeping pus. For a moment she stared dazedly out into nowhere, but then her eyes fell upon Glornir, standing solitary before the Bloodsworn. Her gaze sharpened and her body tensed.

"Vol," Varg heard Glornir breathe. His body shuddered, shoulders rippling, neck swelling, and he threw his head back and roared to the sky, making the ground shake.

"SHIELD WALL," Glornir bellowed as he stepped back into the first rank of the Bloodsworn.

CHAPTER SIXTY-SEVEN

ELVAR

Elvar strode along a corridor, her thought-cage full and churning with memories. Of her mother, lying on a straw mattress, coughing blood. Of her father, ordering Elvar to cease her wailing, to dry her tears, and forbidding her from visiting her mother's chamber. Of the horn that blew, announcing her mother's death. She had been with Grend in the weapons court, twelve winters on her shoulders, could still remember that sense of chill sweeping through her, turning her body weak, saw the wooden practice sword slipping through her fingers and tumbling to the hard-packed earth, could remember Grend staring up at the hall, his face draining of colour, corpse-pale, and how she had seen a tear run down his cheek. She glanced at Grend now, walking beside her, no clue on his face as to what was going on within his own thought-cage.

Syr, the guard Elvar was following, turned and looked back at her.

"Who are you?" she asked. "I will announce you to the jarl."

"We are the Battle-Grim," Elvar said as she followed Syr through open doors into Jarl Störr's mead hall.

"Wait here," Syr said and strode between two long tables and around a central hearth fire, climbing up on to the dais at the far end, where Jarl Störr was seated, talking with a handful of people.

Elvar walked on a few paces, giving her companions room to spread behind her. She felt a tremor of . . . something. *Fear?*

Excitement? It was the same feeling she had standing in the shield wall and seeing her enemy approaching. She sucked in a deep, shivering breath and held it, blew it out slowly and looked around the room.

A score of her father's *drengrs* lined each wall, standing still and looking bored. One of them stood straighter, though, looking past Elvar to stare at Grend. A woman, dark hair braided tight, a scar running through one cheek and down into her lip.

Gytha, Jarl Störr's champion.

Elvar turned away from her and looked down the hall. On the dais sat her father, the Galdurwoman Silrið at his shoulder, tall and fair, bones cast about her neck in a necklace that glinted in the flickering hearth fire. Her father looked older, his face thinner, nose sharper, more silver-grey in his dark hair. He wore a fine wool tunic, deep red with tablet weave at neck and hem, silver rings wrapped around his arms and a silver-tooled belt and seax scabbard at his waist. The serpent fang still hung on a silver chain about his neck. He was talking to a tall man dressed in mail, a tangle of black hair and a beard that covered most of his face. A shield was slung across his back, two ravens scrolled in knotwork upon it.

"Who is my father talking to?" Elvar whispered to Sighvat.

"That is Hjalmar Peacemaker," Sighvat said, stooping to Elvar's ear. "Chief of the Fell-Hearted. He is so named because he kills his enemies quickly, thus making peace. Or so he pays the skálds to sing."

Elvar nodded. She had heard his name in the skáld's saga-songs, and knew from Agnar that a few silver coins slipped into the right palms would spread a reputation quicker than the plague.

Her two brothers were seated in chairs close beside her father. Thorun, the eldest, broad-chested, dark-haired and heavy-browed, his nose would have been as thin and sharp as his father's if he had less meat on his bones.

You look like you have been spending more time feasting than sparring, big brother.

Beside him sat her younger brother, Broðir, similar in looks to Thorun, but leaner at the shoulder and slimmer at the waist.

Standing behind Jarl Störr and her brothers Elvar saw his *Berserkir*, lurking in the half-shadows. Tall, broad and hulking, wearing mail and fine silver, hair and beards braided and oiled, bound with gold and silver thread, axes protruding from belts. And thick collars of iron around their throats. One of them had stepped out of the shadows and was staring at Elvar's company, and she heard Uspa suck in a sharp breath behind her.

Berak still lives, then. He looked better than the last time Elvar had seen him, bloodied from his capture, hair and beard unkempt and matted, a stoop in his back and shoulders common to those recently come to thralldom.

And behind them all stood the broad outline of Hrung's giant head, seated upon his pedestal of stone. His eyes were closed, face slumped, mouth drooped in sleep, and Elvar heard a deep, rhythmic rumble filling the room.

Ancient Hrung is snoring. Her lips twitched in a smile.

Syr the guard was standing on the dais, waiting patiently and Jarl Störr's eyes flickered from Hjalmar to her. He held a hand up, silencing the mercenary warrior and gestured to Syr. She leaned close and spoke to him, and then Jarl Störr was looking down the hall at Elvar.

"Agnar Battle-Grim," Jarl Störr said. "Returned to us again. This time come to take my silver and fight in my shield wall, I hear. Is my ungrateful daughter still in your band of misfits, or has she moved on to leech from some new host?"

A silence filled the room, all looking at Elvar as she stepped forward a pace.

"Agnar is dead and the Battle-Grim have a new chief," Elvar said as she pushed the hood of her bearskin cloak back. "Hello, *Father.*"

CHAPTER SIXTY-EIGHT

VARG

The Bloodsworn's shields came together with a sharp crack, Varg raising his shield and shuffling close to Ingmar Ice, making sure that it was overlapping Ingmar's, and that the rim was tight to Ingmar's iron boss.

The Bloodsworn filled the road, almost forty of them, two rows deep.

"WEAPONS," Glornir roared and Varg raised his spear, holding it in an overhand grip for a longer reach, spear blade resting on his shield rim.

Iva the Seiðr-witch rode forward ten or twelve paces. She raised her hand, clenched it into a fist and Varg saw her lips moving. A ripple of fire snaked around her fist, crackling, expanding, breaking into tendrils that seethed towards the ground.

A snap and hissing sound, and then grey-fletched arrow feathers were sprouting from the Seiðr-witch's back. She spasmed, hands thrown up into the air, the tendrils of flame from her fist sputtering and evaporating. A wet thud and another arrow punched into her back, throwing her forward and she fell from her saddle. The bruised man caught her in tree-trunk arms, looked down at her in horror and confusion, slowly dropped to his knees. He lifted his head to the sky and bellowed.

More arrows hissed, a *druzhina* cried out, blood spurting from his throat. Spears flew from the slopes, punched warriors from horses. Screams and neighs, horses dancing, rearing. *Druzhina* all along the left flank of their column reached for bows from bow cases hanging at their hips, grabbed for arrows, and then a volley was curling up the slopes, falling with *thunks* into trees, skittering off boulders.

"Ilia," Jaromir shouted as he reached for the shield slung across his saddle horn and his hawk rose shrieking into the air, and another *druzhina* rode forward, a woman, her braided hair coiling like a serpent from beneath her plumed helm. She dragged her curved sabre free and raised it, snatched a shield into her left fist, and then roared a command.

The five or six lines of the *druzhina* rowed behind Jaromir rode forward, forming up behind Ilia, some gripping their long spears, others with their curved bows in their fists. Another shouted command and they were moving forward at a walk, then breaking into a canter.

"Here it comes," Røkia shouted. She glanced back at Varg and his spearhead.

"Watch where you go stabbing that thing."

He snorted and nodded.

The thunder of hooves drowned out any more conversation, the ground trembling, stones skittering down the vale's steep slopes as the *druzhina* hurtled towards the Bloodsworn. Arrows whipped and hissed through the air, *thunking* into shields, hissing overhead. Varg ducked behind his shield, heard a cry as an arrow found flesh.

"Never much liked standing against a charge of horse," Ingmar Ice shouted in Varg's ear. "All for show, though, no horse will ever charge into a shield wall. They'll break away before that, if they get close enough."

"Why are they doing it then?" Varg yelled back.

"To scare us into breaking. Even one crack in the shield wall and they'll be in it like maggots in a wound."

Varg snatched a glimpse over his shield rim, saw the *druzhina* were forty or fifty paces away, could see the individual expressions on warriors' faces, thick braids of hair trailing them like wind-whipped banners. Met a woman's eyes as she loosed her arrow and he ducked back down. A spray of splinters in his face and the tip of an arrowhead burst through his shield, a handspan from his eye.

The sound of timber cracking, horses falling, screams, and Varg looked up over his shield rim again, saw that the first line of *druzhina* was falling as the ground beneath them disappeared in an explosion of timber and loose soil.

Glornir had ordered a ditch dug across the road. It was less than knee-deep, but deep enough. It hadn't taken long, the Bloodsworn working furiously with their axes, and then they had set about chopping branches from trees, covering the ditch and scattering soil and stones to mask it. A lot of axes had needed the whetstone after that.

The first row of horses fell with terrified squeals, many crashing to the ground, throwing riders from saddles, only a handful remaining on their feet and carrying on. The row behind crashed into them, more horses falling, more riders hurled through the air, and the row behind dragged on their reins, skidding to a halt, milling, some guiding their horse up the slopes to edge around the ditch.

The few riders that managed to cross the ditch and remain in their saddles regrouped, the woman with her sabre among them. Twelve or fifteen riders spurred their horses forward, bows thrumming, the staccato slap of arrows hitting timber, spears levelled, and then they were on the Bloodsworn, riding and jostling along the line of shields, their long spears stabbing out, loosing arrows. The Bloodsworn held, sharp steel snaking out from behind the shields, stabbing into horses and riders. Ingmar thrust his huge spear over Røkia's right shoulder and buried his blade in the unprotected armpit of a rider. The *druzhina* screamed and toppled backwards, Ingmar wrenching the spear back, blood raining down.

One horse reared, guided by its rider, Ilia, the woman with the sabre, and lashed out with its hooves, smashing into a shield. Varg heard the splinter of wood and crack of breaking bones. A cry of pain as the shield was dropped, cut short as Ilia hacked down with her sabre.

Glornir was close and lashed out with his long-axe, holding it one-handed like it was a twig and chopped into Ilia's leg, between knee and hip. A spray of blood as Glornir ripped the axe free and Ilia was swaying, toppling from her saddle.

The first rush of riders was gone. Behind them *druzhina* warriors were clambering to their feet, reaching for spears and swords, riders behind them picking their way across the ditch.

Glornir did not wait for them.

"FORWARD," Glornir bellowed and the shield wall took a lumbering step forward, then another, and another, walking over the dead, stabbing down at the wounded, until they were almost upon the ditch. Some of the *druzhina* tried to leap back over the ditch, some stumbled and fell, others screamed wordless war cries and stood, shields raised, spears and curved swords levelled.

Behind them Varg glimpsed Jaromir yelling orders, his horse turning on the spot as a score of the Bloodsworn came pouring down the slopes from where they had been hidden behind boulders and trees, roaring as they came. Arrows were hissing through the sky like hornets, spears hurled, warriors screaming.

With a thunderous crunch *druzhina* and Bloodsworn came together, a deafening roar of screams and steel and wood as warriors stabbed and heaved and chopped. In front of Varg Røkia lashed out with her hand-axe, hooked a shield rim with its bearded blade and heaved, pulling the shield down and exposing the warrior behind it. Varg stabbed out with his spear, snaking across Røkia's left shoulder and punching into the *druzhina*'s throat. Heaved his spear back and the warrior staggered a step, tumbling into the ditch, replaced by another snarling face.

Horses milled the other side of the ditch, some warriors dismounting and leaping across to join the press against the Bloodsworn. Some were riding up the slopes at either end of the shield wall, trying to attack the Bloodsworn's flanks, and others stayed mounted, loosing arrows into the Bloodsworn's ranks. An arrow pinged from Varg's helm, another thumping into Ingmar's shield. In front of them Glornir roared and chopped, his axe head weaving trails of blood through the air, Røkia snarling and hacking with her hand-axe, Svik on Glornir's other side stabbing furiously above and below his shield with his seax.

Varg picked his moments, darting his spear out wherever he saw exposed flesh.

A deafening roar rang out, echoing over and above the din of battle and there was a moment's lull all along the shield-line, Bloodsworn and *druzhina* alike looking back down the vale.

The column of Jaromir's *druzhina* was seething chaos, the Bloodsworn among them. Varg glimpsed Sulich standing on a boulder loosing arrows at riders. But that was not what had made the deafening noise.

It was the bull man.

He had laid Iva the Seiðr-witch beneath a stand of trees and was now breaking into a run, straight down the vale towards where *druzhina* and Bloodsworn were crushed together around the ditch.

He roared as he ran, a feral, harrowing ululation of pain, filling the vale. He seemed to grow as he ran, swelling in size, his head dipping down like a charging bull. The ground shook. *Druzhina* spurred their mounts towards each slope in an effort to get out of his way, other warriors diving to left and right. Not all of them managed it.

Bodies flew spinning, bones cracking as the bull man surged into the mass of warriors, ploughing across the ditch full of bodies and into the Bloodsworn's shield wall. A concussive crash, the world seeming to explode and then Varg was spinning through the air. He hit the ground, losing all the air in his lungs, rolled, shield and spear spinning from his grip, and crunched into something solid, pain spiking through his shoulder and back.

He lay on the ground, for long moments an absence of sound or feeling, and then it came rushing back in a great wave. Men and women wailing, screaming, groaning, horses snorting, a throbbing pain in his back.

Varg pushed himself to one elbow, saw that the Bloodsworn's shield wall was broken, a hole four shields wide and two rows deep smashed through its centre. Figures littered the ground. He saw Ingmar Ice rise to one knee, hand reaching out to grasp his thick-shafted spear. Glornir rose growling, close to one of the slopes, where he had been hurled by the bull man. Varg searched for Røkia and Svik, saw Svik staggering to his feet, shaking his head, shield and seax still in his fists.

Druzhina were rising to their feet, others from further up the vale riding in the bull man's wake, and fresh battle erupted as they closed with the Bloodsworn.

"YOU HURT IVA," the bull man bellowed at the Bloodsworn, eyes bulging, snorting and frothing foam, nostrils flaring. He strode towards Ingmar, who was on one knee, grasping his spear two-handed, and the bull man raised his hands high, laced his fingers and smashed his hands down in a hammer blow.

Ingmar jerked his spear up in a reflex and there was a crack, the bull man's fists smashing through the thick spear haft like so much kindling and slamming down on to Ingmar's chest, hurling the big man back to the ground.

The wolf in Varg surged through his veins and he stumbled to his feet, snarling, running, fresh strength and energy flooding his muscles, powering him on. He fumbled for a weapon at his belt, found his seax and drew it. Saw Svik and Røkia moving on the bull man, who was standing over Ingmar, foot rising over his head. Leaped.

A crunch as Varg crashed into the bull man, stabbed wildly with his seax, his opponent stumbling and slamming his foot down next to Ingmar's head. Varg's momentum swung him around the bull man's torso as he clung to his linen tunic with one hand, losing the grip on his seax as it stuck in flesh. The Tainted thrall roared and lashed out at Varg, caught him a glancing blow across the shoulder and back that sent him spinning through the air, thudding to the ground and rolling again. Røkia leaped at the bull man and slipped beneath his hammer of a fist, jumping up his thick torso to chop at him with her axe. Blood spurted as she hacked into his shoulder. The thrall bellowed, grabbed a fistful of Røkia's mail shirt and flung her away. A blur of mail and red hair and Svik darted in, stabbing, ducking, and was backhanded with a meaty fist, sent spiralling through the air.

The Tainted thrall saw Varg lurch unsteadily to hands and knees, and strode after him, limping, Varg's seax deep in his thigh.

Varg stayed there, his head spinning, tried to stand, swayed and fell to one knee, just snarled at the looming bull man, reached fumbling fingers to his weapons belt.

Behind the bruised man a deep-rumbling growl.

Ingmar was on his feet, eyes yellow, teeth sharp, neck and shoulders hunched, the bear loose in his blood. In each fist he held a half of his splintered spear. He broke into a lumbering run, growling and roaring. The bull man scraped the ground with one foot, then charged at Ingmar.

Their collision shook the ground, a meaty slap that sounded like a whale breaching the sea. They stumbled around together, punching, headbutting, biting, gouging.

Varg rose unsteadily, drew his hand-axe and staggered towards them.

A thunder of hooves and riders were weaving through the chaos of combat, Varg leaping out of the way of a galloping horse. He glimpsed Jaromir in the saddle, a rope in one fist attached to a horse behind him, Vol sitting tied in the saddle. They thundered through the combat and burst through it, past it, galloped on down the vale towards the open plain. A dozen *druzhina* followed them.

A bellow of pain filled the vale, Varg spinning to see half of Ingmar's shattered spear jutting from the bull man's thick-muscled neck. His huge fists were wrapped around Ingmar's throat, squeezing, holding Ingmar off the ground. Ingmar's eyes were bulging, face purpling as he slammed the other half of his spear haft into the bull man's head, thick as a club. Blood spurted and the bull man staggered to the side but did not let go. Another crunching blow, then another, and another, and the bull man dropped to his knees, swayed and toppled to the ground. Ingmar rolled away, sucking in breaths.

Varg ran to Ingmar, knelt beside him.

"Are you all right?" he asked the big man.

"Do I look all right?" Ingmar wheezed, his throat mottled with bruises, his helm ripped from his head, one eye swollen shut, blood sluicing from a gash on his forehead.

Varg shrugged. "You're alive."

A roar rose up around them and Varg looked up to see the Bloodsworn all around him shouting and yelling a victory cry. All the *druzhina* were down.

Glornir appeared, blood-drenched, eyes yellow-brown, teeth sharp and bared in a snarl. He clutched his long-axe two-handed as he stared down the vale at the dust of Jaromir and his fleeing warriors.

"After them," Glornir growled and broke into a loping run.

CHAPTER SIXTY-NINE

ELVAR

Elvar enjoyed the shock in her father's eyes. It only flickered there for a moment, but Elvar saw it, and treasured it. Then his mask was back.

"So, Agnar is dead, and you are now chief of his band of mercenaries, then," Jarl Störr said with a sneer. "How high you have risen. How *proud* you must be."

Behind her Elvar heard Grend let out a low-rumbling growl.

She bit back the response forming on her lips.

"Why are you mustering for war, Father? Have you heard news of the dragon?"

"Dragon?" Jarl Störr said. "No. Helka has allied herself to Orlyg. They are meeting in Darl, uniting against me. Better to strike first, and strike hard, than wait for them." He paused. "What dragon?"

"Lik-Rifa is free," Elvar said. "She flies the skies of Vigrið."

Her father frowned. "My spies have brought me tales," he murmured, "but I thought them just that. No evidence . . ." He looked hard at Elvar. "How do you know?"

"I have seen her," Elvar said. "Was there when she burst her bonds at Oskutreð."

There were gasps around the hall, some laughter, too, but Elvar saw that Silrið was looking at her with a fierce intensity.

"Ignore her, Father," Thorun said, standing and taking a few steps forward. His face was shaking with rage. "She lives in a saga-song dream."

"It is good to see you, too, dear brother," Elvar said sarcastically, and saw his rage twitch and judder across his face. "Enough of this," Elvar said with a wave of her hand, "I didn't come here to debate with you on things I have seen with my own eyes."

"And why have you come here?" Jarl Störr said.

"To offer you a deal," she said. "You have something I want."

"Oh," Jarl Störr said, his composure back now as he regarded her with his calculating, heavy-lidded eyes, "and what is that."

"Him," Elvar said, pointing at Berak.

Her father looked back over his shoulder, saw Berak standing, staring at Uspa.

"Don't be ridiculous," he said. "I paid a chest of silver for him."

"And I will buy him from you for twice what you paid Agnar."

"You cannot afford it," her father laughed.

"Grend," Elvar said, and Grend walked forward, stopping a dozen paces before the dais. He put the chest he'd been carrying on the ground, kicked it so that the lid sprang open, then turned and walked back to Elvar. The glow of silver and gold radiated from the chest.

Jarl Störr rose from his seat and took a few steps closer, peering down into the chest.

"How did you come by such wealth?" he breathed.

"I told you," Elvar said. "I have seen Oskutreð."

There were murmurs and mutters now, Elvar noting the absence of laughter this time. Silrið strode down the dais steps and crouched over the chest. She cast a hand over the treasure within, murmuring, and her hand glowed a pale green, mist-like tendrils seeping down into the chest. She gasped and stood, took a step backwards.

"It is ancient," she hissed, "and . . ."

"What?" Jarl Störr said.

"Powerful," she said.

Her father regarded Elvar with a new expression entirely.

"And I have another offer for you, Father," Elvar said.

Jarl Störr smiled, even snorted half a laugh. "What a day this is turning out to be," he said. "Not what I expected at all. Go on, then, what is this other offer?"

"Sighvat," Elvar said, and Sighvat strode forward, deposited the chest he had been carrying next to Grend's. It was twice the size of Grend's. Sighvat gave it a kick and the lid creaked open, gasps and hisses echoing in the hall, everyone leaning to peer, wide-eyed. Elvar knew it was more treasure than anyone in the hall had ever seen in one place, including her father, and the thought that it came from fabled Oskutreð, well, Elvar could see the weave of that threading through hearts and heads like a Seiðr-spell.

"I would hire your *Berserkir*," Elvar said into the silence. "Pay you for their hire, as you are paying the likes of Hjalmar there for his warband and services." She gestured to the black-bearded warrior who stood on the dais, staring at the two chests of gold and silver with unconcealed lust. His eyes flickered to Elvar and he dipped his head to her.

"Hire them for what?" her father asked.

"Father, you cannot be seriously considering this mad bitch's—"

"Be quiet, Thorun," her father snapped. "For what?" he asked Elvar again.

"To rescue a child from Lik-Rifa. His child," she said, jutting her chin at Berak.

"My Bjarn?" Berak rumbled.

"Be silent," Jarl Störr said.

"The dragon has my son?" Berak said.

"*Verkir*," Jarl Störr murmured with a wave of his hand and red veins of fire crackled into life in the collar about Berak's throat. He grunted in pain, hissed, hands grasping at the collar, stumbled and dropped to one knee.

Uspa moved and Elvar held out a warning hand.

"*Nóg*," Jarl Störr said and the fire in the collar faded, returning to dull iron. Berak remained on his knees, gasping deep breaths. Jarl Störr stood on the dais, looking from the chests of gold and silver to Elvar, his heavy brows knotted, eyes in shadow.

"No," he said. "To do that I would have to give you power over their collars and that I will not do." A thin smile stretched his lips. "I do not trust that you would give them back, my dear daughter, and that I cannot risk as I have spent half my life collecting them."

Elvar nodded slowly and heaved a sigh.

"If you will not give them, then I must take them."

Her father laughed then, deep and loud. Elvar had never seen him laugh like that.

"I am liking this new Elvar," he said, wiping an eye. "I shall forgive your insolence, just this once. And I have an offer for you. Stay. Fight Helka and Orlyg with me."

"I cannot," Elvar said. "I have more . . . pressing things to do."

Her father looked at the chests of treasure. "You have clearly achieved something remarkable," he murmured. "Perhaps you are even telling the truth, have seen fabled Oskutreð. Whether you have or not, you have found this somewhere and, I imagine if you are willing to trade this, then you have much more hidden away." He was watching her carefully now, his eyes fixed on hers. "Most likely on your *drakkar*. I know what you mercenaries are like, that you think your longship is your fortress. But where is your *drakkar*? Moored in my harbour, I imagine. Is it guarded well? No matter how well it is guarded, a score of *Berserkir* will change any guard's mind."

Elvar frowned at that, thinking of the *Wave-Jarl* moored at Snakavik's docks.

Her father smiled. "So, you see, Elvar, you will not be taking anything from me. It is I who will be doing the taking."

He waved a hand and his *drengrs* that rowed the hall moved forward.

Grend and Sighvat stepped either side of Elvar, both of them drawing their hand-axes and shrugging shields into fists.

"Stand down, Grend," one of the *drengrs* said. Gytha, Jarl Störr's champion.

"I cannot," Grend said.

"And I cannot allow you to raise a weapon against the jarl or his oathsworn."

Grend shrugged. "We each do what we must," he said.

"Let me make this clear," Jarl Störr said, "you are mine, accept it and there will be no bloodshed. Chose to defy me, and . . . well." He glanced over his shoulder. "*Taktu hana,*" he said, and as one his

Berserkir moved out of the shadows, even Berak rising from his knees and lumbering across the dais.

"That is a bunch of nasty looking bastards," Sighvat muttered.

The *Berserkir* swept from the dais down on to the hall, a wall of mail and sharp iron. Their eyes glittered gold and green and brown. Gytha and her *drengrs* closed in from the sides.

"Ulfrir," Elvar said with a snarl, and the wolf-god stepped forward.

CHAPTER SEVENTY

VARG

Varg chased across the plain of sun-bleached grass, breath rasping in his throat, the sun high and hot overhead, his wolf growling in his blood.

Ahead of him Jaromir and the dozen or so *druzhina* who had followed him out of the vale were raising a cloud of dust, and in front of them were the timber walls of Valdai, growing ever larger. The thud of feet all about him as the Bloodsworn raced after Jaromir, fifty men and women, blood-spattered, weapons in their fists. Varg had swept up his spear and shield as Glornir had led them after Jaromir, his back, shoulder and arm now burning with the weight of his shield.

Some of them were gaining on Jaromir and his warriors, all of the Bloodsworn releasing the beast in their blood, all of them flooded with the animalistic gifts of their god-blood. Røkia was ahead of Varg, and Edel, too, her hounds loping, tongues lolling. A *druzhina* twisted in his saddle, looked back and saw the Bloodsworn gaining ground. A few moments later and arrows were streaking through the air. One buzzed over Varg's shoulder like an angry hornet and he raised his shield. A yelp and one of Edel's hounds collapsed, rolling. Edel skidded to a halt, bent over her hound, then let out a furious howl and sprinted on, rage giving her speed. Arrows hissed at her, but she swept them aside with her shield, gaining on the rearmost of the riders. Røkia reached him first, though, sweeping in from his flank and leaping, dragging herself up into the saddle behind the *druzhina*. A slice of her seax and a spurt of blood and she was shoving the dying warrior crashing to the ground. A few heartbeats later Edel was upon him, stabbing and stabbing and stabbing with her spear.

Røkia settled into the saddle, grabbed the reins and spurred her horse on, leaning low over the horse's neck.

Another *druzhina* saw her, his bow bending.

"No," Varg yelled, and then the rider stiffened in his saddle, his bow slipping from his fingers, an arrow sprouting from his throat. He swayed and fell. The drum of hooves behind Varg and a horse was galloping past him, Sulich on its back, already nocking his next arrow.

Shouts from the walls of Valdai, Jaromir approaching the gates and gesturing wildly. Answering calls and the gates were opening.

Arrows began to flit down from the walls.

In a thunder of hooves Jaromir galloped through the open gates, Vol on her horse behind him, then the rest of his surviving *druzhina*. All of them passed through the gates in a storm of hooves and dust, Røkia and Sulich among them, and then the gates began to close.

Varg dug deeper for more speed. He was sixty paces from the gates, fifty, forty, and then they were grating closed. A frantic burst of energy, trying to make the gate before the bar was slipped in place, but he heard it being dropped into the gate-hooks. Arrows *thunked* into the ground around him, slapped into his raised shield, pinged off his helm. He leaped, slammed into the gate, heard the timber creak but it held.

A flurry of hurled spears from the Bloodsworn, some sinking into the gates and wall, one taking a bowman high in the chest, throwing him back, out of sight in a spray of blood, and then other Bloodsworn were reaching the wall, Svik standing over Varg with his shield held high. Glornir loped out of the swirling dust, eyes blazing, lips pulled back in a rictus snarl, sharp teeth gnashing, and hurled himself at the barred gates. They shook, timber creaking, dust erupting from the timber joints. Glornir backed up a handful of paces, roared and threw himself at the gate again. Hefted his long-axe and hacked at the timber, splinters of wood spraying. Ingmar joined them and threw himself at the gate.

Screams, the clash of steel and battle-cries echoed out from behind the walls. A savage howling.

Røkia, Sulich. Varg looked around wildly, desperate for a way to get in to her, to them, looked up.

"Ingmar," he cried, grabbing the big man's arm. "On one knee."

Ingmar scowled at him, the bear blazing in his eyes.

"Trust me," Varg snarled, and Ingmar dropped to a knee.

Varg took a few paces back, then hurled his shield up at the heads leaning over the wall, smashed a space among them and then he was running, stepping up on to Ingmar's knee, then vaulting up his back and shoulder, legs bent, and he leaped, grabbed a spear protruding from the timber wall, swung around it and then he was flopping over the top of the wall and on to a wooden walkway.

A moment as he looked around, saw figures either side of him, men and women in lamellar and mail and leather, bows in their fists, staring at him.

Varg knew he was outnumbered, death hovering over his shoulder on raven's wings. He heard Røkia scream. Pain or rage, he did not know.

The wolf rose up in him, free of its leash, shuddering through his body and he snarled as he rolled, staggered to his feet, reaching for his weapons belt, drawing hand-axe and cleaver, swinging them as he rose. Chopped into a thigh with his axe, hacked through a bow and into a forearm with the cleaver, heard screams as he ripped the weapons free, spun, snarling, arms moving, weapons chopping, slicing, hacking, warriors falling away from him, one tumbling backwards, crashing to the courtyard with a thud. Glimpsed Sulich, still on the back of a horse, his sabre rising and falling, trading blows with Jaromir to one side and a *druzhina* on the other, a flash of Røkia below, blood-drenched, seax and axe in her fists, bodies at her feet. Warriors were pouring into the courtyard from all directions.

Movement to his left and a flash of steel. Varg swayed, a spear stabbing where his face had been. He thrust his seax along the spear shaft, met resistance, saw severed fingers spraying, blood spurting, dimly heard a scream, hacked his cleaver down into a mailed shoulder, carved through into flesh, felt the grate of bone, a savage wrench as he ripped the cleaver free in an explosion of blood and shattered mail, kicked the stumbling warrior away. Saw another figure appear close, raised his seax to stab and pulled back at the last moment, saw it was Svik on the walkway beside him, a fierce grin on his face, his eyes blazing yellow.

"You'll not be the only one in this saga-song," Svik snarled, half laughing as he shrugged his shield from his back and hacked his sword across the face of a bowman, sent the warrior reeling and crashing into the courtyard.

Then Edel was clambering over the wall and dropping on to the walkway, other Bloodsworn appearing behind her.

"Getting too crowded up here," Svik grinned and leaped from the walkway into the courtyard, slamming into a knot of warriors pressed against the shuddering gates. Without thought Varg followed him, fell snarling and chopping into the warriors, scattering them. He stood there a moment, crouched, cleaver held high, axe low, as Svik stabbed a warrior behind him and threw himself at the bar across the gates. Beyond Svik, Varg saw strips of the gate had been torn free, ragged holes in it, and through those holes he saw Glornir hacking, chopping, biting in a frenzy at the timber. *Druzhina* came at Varg in a flood and he ran at them, glimpsed Edel leaping down to his left, running alongside him, and then he was wading into bodies, fractured images of screaming faces, flesh parting, steel stabbing, blood trailing arcs. The sensation of flesh between his jaws, ripping, tearing, of blood spurting into his mouth. Screams, rising in pitch. Dimly he was aware of a roaring behind him, of more bodies around him, the gates open and the Bloodsworn sweeping into the courtyard, a wave of steel and iron and tooth and claw, the battle-din growing to shake the whole world, and inside him his wolf was slavering, urging him to bite and tear and rend.

A blow across his back and shoulders and he staggered and fell to one knee, twisted, lashing out, seax sparking on lamellar plates, a fraction of a moment later an impact on his jaw, rattling the teeth in his head and setting white lights exploding in front of his eyes. Then he was on his back, didn't know how he got there, how long he'd been there, just blinking up at a sheer blue sky between dark bodies that spun and fought and snarled curses all around him. A throbbing pain down one side of his face, a burning line of fire. He realised someone was standing over him, legs spread, crouching, blood-crusted weapons raised.

"Uh," he grunted, moved an arm. It was heavy, realised he was still gripping his cleaver in a blood-slick fist.

"Can you stand, No-Sense?" a voice filtered down to him, sounding as if he heard it through water.

Just want to lie here a while.

He heaved a sigh, rolled on to his side, pushed himself up with one arm.

"On your feet, then," the voice over him said, and he saw Røkia's face grow large as she bent and hooked her arm through his, heaved him up.

He stood on swaying legs and looked at Røkia. Her face was covered in blood, but Varg didn't think much of it was hers. She was standing protectively in front of him, her axe and seax raised.

"I'm supposed to be saving you," he mumbled, and saw her face part in a snarl or a smile, he could not tell. He put one hand to the burning line on his face, felt gaping flesh and his fingers came away red.

"No time to be worrying about your looks," Svik said, appearing on one side of him. Varg blinked, sound muted, shook his head, and then his hearing and vision snapped back into focus.

The courtyard was seething with combat. Glornir was bellowing and swinging his long-axe, horses rearing and falling away before him. Sulich, still mounted, slicing down at *druzhina* around him. Everywhere the Bloodsworn were killing. At the far end of the courtyard Jaromir was sitting on his horse on the steps to a wooden hall and tower, the rope to Vol's horse still gripped in his fist. Varg saw him tug on the rope, dragging Vol's horse closer and he leaned and grabbed her around the waist, heaved her across to sit in front of him.

"GLORNIR," Jaromir screamed, raising the blade of his curved sword to Vol's throat. "I'LL KILL HER."

Glornir dragged his axe from a corpse and stared, all around him warriors breaking off from their combat, Bloodsworn and *druzhina* stepping warily apart.

"Lay down your weapons," Jaromir said, "or I'll open her throat." He pressed his sword tighter, a trickle of blood running down Vol's neck.

"This is your last day, prince of Iskidan," Glornir said, his voice more growl than words. "Let her go and you will have a quick death. Harm her and your screams will fill the world."

Jaromir's lip curled. "You dare to speak to me this way, you goat-turd *niðing*," he snarled. Varg saw the muscles in his sword-arm tighten, his knuckles whiten around the grip of his hilt, a ripple across his shoulder and back.

Glornir roared, already moving, but too far away.

Vol smashed her head backwards, into Jaromir's nose. A crack of cartilage and spurt of blood, Jaromir swaying, but he still gripped Vol.

The drum of feet and Ingmar Ice appeared, running at Jaromir from his flank, crashing into Jaromir's horse and staggering it. Jaromir was thrown back in his saddle and Vol was hurled through the air. She fell into the courtyard amid *druzhina* and Bloodsworn. A *druzhina* moved to grab her and Edel punched her spear into his throat.

Battle erupted again, Glornir swinging his axe, a head sailing through the air, blood jetting. Røkia broke into a run at Jaromir, Varg following on unsteady legs. Jaromir righted himself in his saddle and chopped down at Ingmar with his sabre, the big man swiping the blade away, a red line opening along his forearm, a flap of flesh hanging. Ingmar reached for Jaromir, grabbed a fistful of his lamellar coat in his taloned hands, crushing iron plates as he tried to drag him from the saddle.

A keening screech and a bird came swooping down from above, Jaromir's hawk, talons raking Ingmar's head, claws ripping and tearing at his face, a hooked beak stabbing down. Ingmar bellowed and let go of Jaromir, swiping at the hawk, grabbing a wing in one huge hand and throwing it to the ground. He looked up, reaching again for Jaromir as the prince swung his sabre, chopping into Ingmar's neck. A grunt from Ingmar and Jaromir raised his arm high, blood arcing, Ingmar choking and gurgling, clasping a hand to his neck. The sabre chopped down again, and Ingmar dropped to his knees, toppled to the side. With a snarl Jaromir gripped his reins and kicked his mount on, trampling across Ingmar's body.

Varg screamed, heard others in the Bloodsworn cry out, saw Jaromir take in the faces running at him. He dragged on his reins and turned his mount, trampling over Ingmar again, then his horse was clattering up the remaining steps and through the open doors of his hall. A handful of *druzhina* flung the doors shut behind their prince.

Røkia and Svik reached Ingmar, both skidding to their knees, Varg a heartbeat behind them. At a glance Varg knew Ingmar was gone. His body seemed shrunken, empty now of the bear that had fought so ferociously, his eyes pale blue and staring, sightless. Varg stood there, all his rage and fury gone, swept away and replaced by a swelling wave of grief. Tears welled, blurring his vision, a sob building in his chest.

A howl behind him and he turned to see Glornir drop to his knees beside Vol. She lay on the courtyard, unmoving, hands bound with iron. Glornir's long-axe slid from his hands and he slipped his arms beneath her, raised her tenderly and held her to him, kissed her softly, her eyes, her cheeks, her scabbed lips, tears flowing down his face, tracing pale tracks through the blood and grime crusted upon him.

"Ach, my Vol, my Vol, my Vol," he repeated, over and over as he rocked her in his arms.

Vol groaned, moved. Slowly, gently, Glornir reached for a small seax at his belt and drew it, began carefully to slice through the twine that stitched Vol's lips together. He tugged on each strip, pulled it out, until Vol's lips were free.

"I . . . told him . . . you would come," Vol breathed.

"I would cross the oceans of the world for you," he said, stroking her cheek with a slabbed hand. "Only death would stop me."

"Help me . . . stand," Vol rasped through cracked, swollen lips.

Glornir stood, set Vol on her feet.

"*Logi, brennið þessi bönd til ösku*," Vol breathed. A shifting in the air around her fists, a flickering crackle of flame, and then the manacles and chains around her wrist were glowing, red, orange, then white-hot. There was a crack, and the manacles fell away, crumbling to ash before they hit the ground.

Vol lifted her hands, slowly moved them apart, as if it were a wondrous thing.

"Where is he?" she spat.

Glornir nodded to the hall. "In there."

Vol took a few unsteady steps, Glornir stooping to lift his long-axe and walking beside her. The Bloodsworn parted for Vol and she made her way to the hall, stopped as she reached Varg, Svik and Røkia, looked down at Ingmar's corpse. Her eyes softened, tears welling, and then her face hardened and she looked up at the closed doors of the hall.

Sulich clicked his tongue and rode his horse up the stairs, a clatter of hooves on timber, then stood before the doors. He leaned in his saddle and touched the reins and the horse reared, hooves lashing out and crashing into the doors. They burst inwards with a splinter of timber, and Vol strode up the stairs, muttering under her breath, hands glowing with crackling flame, the air rippling about her fists with heat haze.

The hiss of arrows and Vol swept a hand, the arrows bursting into flame, disintegrating and gone on the breeze. She strode into the hall, Glornir at her side. Sulich rode through the smashed doors, ducking beneath the crossbeam, Edel, Røkia, Varg, Svik and the rest of the Bloodsworn followed.

It was much like a mead hall inside, two rows of long tables and benches leading up to a dais with another table there. A huge tapestry covered the back wall, like a tablet-woven sail, filled with images of warriors on horseback. At another time, it would have been something that Varg would have marvelled at. Jaromir stood there, a handful of *druzhina* arrayed around him, shields raised, swords and spears levelled. A few more arrows hissed out at them and Vol gestured, incinerating them.

The few *druzhina* drew closer together, sheathing their bows in cases at their belts and drawing sabres. Jaromir dragged open a door in the back wall and fled through it.

Vol strode silently forwards, stopped before the dais. Swayed. Glornir gently steadied her.

"*Brenndu þá, brenndu þá alla,*" Vol snarled, and tendrils of flame crackled out from her fists, snaked to the ground and ran hissing across the timber floor and up the dais. The *druzhina* stumbled and backed away but the flames followed them, faster than they could move, and then fire was licking around their feet, climbing their legs, breeches bursting into flames, flaring in their tunics, and Varg smelled the stench of scorching flesh.

Vol stepped over the dying men, Glornir moving ahead of her and swinging his axe. The door Jaromir had fled through shattered to so much kindling, and then Glornir was striding through it, Vol behind him. They descended wide steps and then the ground levelled into a tunnel, still wide and high enough for Sulich to ride through. Vol led them on until she came to a thick, iron-banded oak door. She placed one hand upon it.

"*Eik og járn, beygja og brjóta,*" Vol snarled, and the door exploded inwards.

Jaromir cried out, fell stumbling backwards into a table that took up a smaller chamber, a tapestried wall at the back, images of mounted warriors fighting creatures Varg did not recognise.

Vol strode into the chamber, picking her way across the splintered oak door.

Jaromir tried to draw his sabre, but his sword arm hung limp, a splinter of wood buried in his shoulder.

"Rurik will kill you for this," Jaromir hissed.

"I am your death," Vol said to him.

"MY BROTHER WILL KILL YOU," he screamed.

"*Mölbrotna eik, verða að spjótum, verða að hnífum, gata óvin minn, gata kvalara mina,*" Vol cried out and the broken splinters of the door rose up, came together, quivering in the air, a sharp-pointed wall. With a flick of Vol's hand, they hurtled towards Jaromir, piercing him and throwing him tumbling across the table to lie at the foot of the huge tapestry, blood pooling from many wounds.

Vol stood there, snarling and breathing heavily, then swayed and staggered forward a few steps into the table. Glornir stepped forward and steadied her with one hand, then frowned at what he saw on the table.

"What is it?" Svik said, stepping closer, and Varg followed him, leaning to look at the table. A huge map was drawn upon a sheet of parchment and pinned to the table's corners, and all around were piles of birch-bark tablets, with runes carved into them. Rune-words were carved into the map as well, but Varg didn't understand them. He had never been taught his letters and could not read.

But he did not need to read to understand what he was looking at. He could see a mountain range curving sinuously across the northern part of the map, at one end the skeletal jaws of a serpent opening wide to spill into the sea.

"It is a map of Vigrið," he said.

"Aye," breathed Røkia beside him.

"Why is Vigrið of such interest to Jaromir?" Varg muttered, but no one answered as they all stared in silence.

A voice, faint and muted, calling for help.

The tapestry on the back wall moved.

The clack of hooves on stone as Sulich rode forward and slashed at the tapestry, chopping at the twine that tied it to a pole and it fell away. He grabbed a fistful and ripped it from the wall, throwing the tapestry into a pile atop Jaromir's corpse.

Sulich stared at what was behind the tapestry.

Thick iron bars, a room behind it. And people.

A figure walked out of the shadows to the bars, a thin man in a tattered tunic, fair-haired and pale as a corpse, a collar of iron about his neck. He gripped the bars and stared out at them all, blinking.

"Sulich?" he said.

Others stumbled forward, men and women, some pale-skinned

as milk, others varying hues of black and purple and blue, bruised men and women. They all stared at Sulich.

He stared back at them.

"Sulich," Glornir said. "Who are these people?"

"They are the Tainted children of the Great Khagan," Sulich said, with tears in his eyes. "They are my brothers and sisters."

CHAPTER SEVENTY-ONE

ELVAR

Elvar sucked in a long breath. A part of her had hoped things would not come to this. Another part of her had hoped that they would.

"Berak must live," she muttered to Ulfrir as he stepped forward.

"And who is this?" Jarl Störr asked, a smile twitching his lips. "Some relic from your travels who has listened to too many skáld-songs and thinks he can stand against over forty *Berserkirs*?"

"This is Ulfrir wolf-god, raised from the dead and thralled to *me*," Elvar cried out as Ulfrir pushed back the wolf-head hood of his cloak. Gytha and her *drengrs* paused a moment, and even the *Berserkir* slowed in their tracks.

"JUST KILL HER," Thorun yelled from the dais.

A loud yawning filled the chamber, Hrung's giant head shifting, mouth gaping. He slapped his fat lips.

"What does a severed head have to do to get some sleep around here?" he said, his rumbling voice echoing through the room. Then he blinked and sniffed, took another deep-snorting breath, seeming to suck all the air from the room. He frowned.

"Ulfrir? I must still be sleeping," Hrung muttered. Shook his head, sniffed again. "Ah, Ulfrir, my friend, if only this were no dream." A fat tear welled in his eye and rolled down one cheek.

"This is no dream, ancient Hrung," Ulfrir said, and the giant head stared at him with wide eyes. "Though reality is stranger, and far crueller, I fear." He put a hand to the thrall-collar about his neck.

Elvar saw her father look from Hrung to Ulfrir, a flicker of doubt in his eyes. "Enough of this," he snapped. "Kill him and take my daughter." The *Berserkir* still hesitated. "*Drepið hann og taktu dóttur mina,*" Jarl Störr snarled and red lines crackled in the *Berserkir's* collars. They growled and roared, began moving as one down the hall towards Ulfrir.

"Stop them, but try not to kill them, they are under his sway," Elvar said to Ulfrir.

The air around Ulfrir shimmered, rippling like a heat haze, and then he was changing, growing. Bones cracking, reshaping, face shifting, muzzle extending, teeth protruding, fur sprouting. People screamed as Ulfrir became the wolf, his bulk growing, filling the room. Timber rafters cracked in the eaves as his back and withers hunched into them, a splintering, tearing sound and parts of the roof fell crashing to the ground, snow and pale light cutting through in winter-bright beams. *Drengrs* stumbled away, only a handful standing their ground, Gytha among them.

The *Berserkir* came on reluctantly, a rolling wave now, bloodlust in their eyes, teeth and claws long and sharp, axes pulled from their belts.

More timber fell, parts of the hall falling away, collapsing, a blizzard of snow swirling in.

Ulfrir raised his head to the sky and howled, people cowering, putting hands to their ears.

There was a flash of red light from the dais and Uspa stepped in front of Elvar, her hands rising, glowing.

"*Eldhlíf, verndaðu okkur,*" Uspa said and the air rippled, a domed sheet of red-cast runes appearing before Elvar, spreading like a cobweb. There was an impact and a burst of sparks, Elvar seeing Silrið on the dais, her fists wreathed in flame, the Galdurwoman trying to melt the flesh from Elvar's bones.

Berserkirs and *drengrs* leaped at Ulfrir, axes chopping into his forelegs. Ulfrir snarled and shook, sent bodies flying, his head lunging down, teeth snapping and coming up with a body clamped in his jaws. A savage shake of his head and the *drengr* fell apart, legs and blood raining down, Ulfrir swallowing the upper body.

"Guard yourself," Grend shouted as he swung his shield, sweeping aside a spear-thrust from a *drengr* and stepping in, chopping down into the warrior's chest, his new axe slicing through mail and deep into flesh, cracking bone. He ripped the blade free and smashed the *drengr* to the ground with his shield.

Elvar drew her sword and pulled her shield from her back, saw her father's warriors slipping between Ulfrir's legs and moving around Uspa's Seiðr-cast barrier. A woman came at her, snarling, shield raised, axe held high. Elvar stepped away from the axe blow, punched her shield into the woman's side and sent her staggering. The woman found her balance, turned, and then Sighvat's axe crashed into her helm, splitting it and she dropped like a stone. He stood over her corpse and roared a challenge at a knot of *drengrs* moving on them.

"With me," Elvar said, marching forward. Uspa strode beside her, muttering her Seiðr-rune words, the shield of crackling flame held high before them, and Grend and Sighvat moved on her flanks, chopping and snarling at any who dared to approach Elvar.

Ulfrir howled and thrashed through the hall, more of it collapsing, tumbling away. The entirety of one side wall crashed outwards, revealing a snow-thick street, faces staring, mouths open. Snow whirled through the hall, hissing in the flames of the hearth fire. *Drengrs* flew through the air, hurled by Ulfrir's raking claws, eviscerated and thrown from his jaws, blood and body parts falling like rain. *Berserkir* were hacking at Ulfrir's legs, clawing their way up him. Elvar saw one clamber on to one of the mead hall's tables and leap, long-axe held high overhead. An arrow punched into his shoulder and he fell away, limbs flopping.

A figure dropped out of the sky, Orv the Sneak, landing and bending his legs.

"Chief," he said to Elvar with a flashed grin, at the same time drawing an arrow from his quiver, nocking and loosing, a *drengr* falling with a screech and a spurt of blood. More of the Battle-Grim materialised out of the snow, Sólín with shield and longseax in her fists, Urt the Unwashed punching his spear through a *drengr's* belly. Skuld swooped low overhead, russet wings spread wide as she glided through the ruin of the hall and dropped to the dais, Jarl Störr stumbling away from her. Thorun swung a sword at the red-haired goddess and she raised her own blade, a clash of steel and Thorun was spinning away and falling down the dais steps. Skuld strode forward, eyes blazing golden and grabbed a fist full of Jarl Störr's tunic, then her wings were beating, and she was lifting him up, Jarl Störr shouting, reaching for the seax at his belt. Skuld ripped the blade from his fingers and hurled it spinning away. A burst of red flame shot into the air from Silrið's fist, hissing past Skuld, singeing some of her feathers, and then Skuld was winging back through the hall, towards her father. She beat her wings, hovering before Ulfrir's jaws.

Ulfrir paused in his destruction, lips curling back in a snarl as he regarded Jarl Störr.

Skuld looked down at Elvar, waiting.

A memory, of her mother screaming, of her father's fist rising and falling. Elvar nodded.

"No," she saw her father's lips move.

Skuld threw Jarl Störr into the air, spinning, and Ulfrir's jaws lunged, snapped about him. There was a muffled scream, the crunch and crackle of bone and then blood was trickling over Ulfrir's matted lips.

A pause in the hall, like a breath held, as the *Berserkir* faltered in their frothing madness. Many of them stumbled and swayed, looking around, confused. Some raised their hands to their collars.

Elvar had often thought of her father's death, and of hers being the hand that killed him. Imagined it many times over. Imagined the things she would say to him, imagined his sharp, bitter words and then his pleading, imagined the sense of justice that she would feel at this moment. But she had never imagined it like this. She felt . . . nothing.

"F . . . F . . . FATHER," Thorun screamed, staring in wide-eyed horror. His gaze moved to Elvar, standing close to the dais. "You," he snarled. "*You* did this." He looked to his scattered *drengrs*. "KILL HER," he screeched.

A flare of red-veined flame crackled through the *Berserkir's* collars, roars of pain, snarls. And then their eyes were fixing on Elvar. Thorun looked confused, surprised, then gloating.

My father's control has passed to Thorun, then, as Uspa said it would. He is father's firstborn.

Elvar broke into a run for the dais and Thorun realised there were no guards between him and his sister. The only man was Hjalmar, leaning on a serpent-carved post. Elvar saw he had one of her chests of silver at his feet.

"Stop her," Thorun yelled at the chief of the Fell-Hearted.

"I would not interfere in what is obviously a family dispute," Hjalmar said, a wry smile twisting his lips.

"Silrið, melt her flesh," Thorun snarled as Elvar bounded up on to the dais, the drum of feet behind her, the sound of steel clashing, grunting, snarling and she knew that Grend and Sighvat were fighting *Berserkir*, knew that would not end well for her oar-mates.

"Uspa, help them," she barked as she ran at her brother, stabbing her sword at him, the strike hidden behind her shield until the last moment, but he was already stumbling back and so her blade sliced his cheek, blood sheeting.

Thorun shrieked, touched fingers to his face, looked at Elvar with her shield held high, grim-faced and draped in mail. He hefted his sword, and she could see the realisation dawning in his eyes, of how mismatched he was.

"Silrið, kill her," Thorun said to the Galdurwoman who was standing behind him, licking his lips, his voice edged with panic, "do this now and you will be first in my realm, above all others."

Silrið stepped forward, her hands raised, lips moving, flame crackling around her fists and forearms. Fire snaked out and wrapped around Thorun's wrists. He yelped and dropped his sword, tried to rip his hands away from the flame but it clung to him like a fiery leash.

"My gift to you, my jarl," Silrið said to Elvar, dipping her head but not taking her eyes from Elvar.

Elvar held the Galdurwoman's gaze, weighing up her options, then she stepped forward and stabbed Thorun in the throat, felt her blade grate on his spine, ripped it free in a torrent of blood.

Thorun opened his mouth but no words came out, only a gout of dark blood. He gurgled and choked, swayed, dropped to his knees, then fell on to his face.

Elvar stood over him, remembered how he had stopped her from helping their mother as Jarl Störr had beaten her, remembered how Thorun had laughed in Elvar's ear. She spat on her brother's corpse, then turned to look into the hall, saw *Berserkir* fighting with her Battle-Grim crew. Orv was running, small and light-footed, and swerved out of the grasping hands of a *Berserkir*, turned, dropped to his knees and skidded between the huge warrior's legs, stood and ran. Urt the Unwashed lay on the ground, a *Berserkir's* foot on his head, pinning him in place as he raised his axe. Uspa was casting her shield of runes, trying to hold the *Berserkir* back. There were a few knots of *drengrs* brave or foolish enough still to be attacking Ulfrir.

"Stop," Elvar said, and to her relief and pleasure saw the crackle of red flames in the iron collars about the *Berserkir's* throats.

In a heartbeat they were stepping away from their combat, disengaging and turning to look at her.

"Sister," a voice said, and she saw Broðir stepping hesitantly towards her, his eyes flickering from Elvar's face to her red-bladed sword.

"Broðir," she answered, tense and ready for his attack.

He knelt before her and took her hand, slick with blood, still gripping her sword, and he put his lips to it, kissed it.

"My jarl," Broðir said.

Elvar looked down on him, considered the thought of opening his throat. *He is the last of my bloodline, and the youngest, so would become master of these Berserkir if I were dead.*

But she had seen enough death for one day, and remembered Broðir fondly. She dropped her shield with a clatter and cupped his cheek.

"Brother," she whispered.

"JARL ELVAR," Sighvat bellowed, a grin splitting his beard.

Shouts rang through the hall, her Battle-Grim punching the air with their weapons. Gytha and her *drengrs* stood and stared in silent shock. The *Berserkir* remained silent but returned to stand around Elvar. She saw Uspa running through the hall and throwing herself into the arms of Berak. They held each other as if they were drowning.

Beyond the shattered hall Elvar saw figures appearing through the eddying snow. Warriors, hundreds of them, weapons drawn, shields raised with all manner of sigils upon them, shuffling into some semblance of a shield wall, filling the streets.

The host of *drengrs* and mercenaries she had seen camped beyond the walls of the fortress.

Ulfrir padded out from the wreckage of the mead hall, looked down upon them all and snarled, lips curling back from his bloodied teeth.

Many fled, and many more dropped to their knees in the snow before the great wolf.

"Jarl Elvar," a voice said, behind Elvar, deep and reverberating through the hall.

"Hrung," Elvar dipped her head.

"Well, I always said that you knew how to make an entrance," the giant said.

CHAPTER SEVENTY-TWO

ORKA

Orka reined in her horse and stared, Sæunn standing in front of her and the others moving to either side.

They were spread along a high mountain path, looking down on to a fortress that stretched along the banks of an ice-blue fjord. A tangle of boats bobbed at piers and jetties, mostly fisher boats and merchant *knarrs*, a few *snekkes* and *drakkars* scattered among them. A mead hall sat high on the bank and built against the side of a squat black tower nestled in the shadow of a looming cliff, and buildings spread down the slope from it like a spumed wake from a sharp prow. A single high wall sliced across the river valley that fed into the fjord, the town's protection from the land, and Orka could see the glint of mail from warriors stood upon it.

"Svelgarth," she muttered through a cloud of misted breath. Steep-sided slopes dotted with pine edged the fjord, frozen waterfalls like streaks of silver-bright tears carving down the dark granite cliffs. Horns were blowing from the wall of Svelgarth, the town seething like a kicked ant's nest, and Orka could see the reason why.

A warband was seeping towards Svelgarth's wall, filling the valley on the southern bank of the river like ink spreading through parchment. But this was no ordinary warband. Mounted warriors led the way, but they were followed by a tangled mass of creatures. Orka could see a dark cloud of tennúr swirling in the air, trolls striding along the river's bank, nailed clubs balanced on shoulders, many-legged frost-spiders creeping through the boughs of pine trees that edged the vale, a mass of skraeling, singing raucous songs as they marched. Dark patches of mist leaked from the treeline, moving against the wind that howled up the fjord.

Night-hags.

And behind it all rolled a line of wagons filled with barrels and people, more warriors around them with ravens scrawled on their shields.

Orka's eyes focused on the wagons and she allowed the wolf in her blood a little freedom, her sight sharpening.

Not people. Children.

She felt her heart begin to thump like a war-drum in her chest.

"Flat-Nose," she said and Halja rode close. "Down there, with the wagons. Tell me what your eagle eyes see?"

A moment as Halja stared, her head twitching like a predatory bird.

"Children," she murmured. "Lots of them. Many are huddled together in the wagons, but some walk alongside them."

He is down there. Breca. My son. He must *be.* The realisation hit her like a hammer blow, and she swayed in her saddle, clutched hard on her reins. All these many months of searching, desperate to find the faintest trace of him. And now he was there, within the range of her vision, close enough that he might hear her if she howled his name.

A hand touched her elbow and she blinked, looked to see Lif staring at her with worried eyes.

"Steady," he said to her.

"Huh," Orka grunted, sitting straighter in her saddle. She blew out a long breath, tore her eyes away from the wagons and children and saw that the warband was stuttering to a halt a few hundred paces from Svelgarth's wall, only a handful of the riders at the front riding closer. They stopped beneath the walls, looked like they were exchanging words. The rest of the warband were spreading out, seemed to be going about the business of making camp. She studied the terrain, eyes searching, then turned in her saddle to look at the others.

"We'll move closer, find somewhere to prepare before . . ." She left the rest unsaid, just touched her reins and kicked Trúr on down the mountain path.

Orka laid all her weapons out before her. Her long-axe, a hand-axe, a small seax that she had picked up in Starl that she had strapped to her arm beneath her two tunics and the mail sleeve of her *brynja*. Myrk's scabbarded sword wrapped in a belt. And the two seaxes with dragon-carved hilts that she had taken from Thorkel's corpse.

Drekr must be down there, too.

That sent a shiver through her blood.

The man who slew Thorkel, who stole my son from me.

She felt a muscle twitch in her jaw, and she rested the long-axe across her lap and drew her whetstone across its blade. Rasp, rasp, rasp.

They had made a small camp in a dell among the pines, a good distance from the warband, Lif setting about tending to their mounts first. Orka had set Sæunn on watch duty. Gunnar had cracked a hole through the crust of an iced-up stream, much to the joy of Spert, who had grumbled and moaned every waking moment that he needed water to sleep in. The vaesen had slipped through the cracked ice and into the stream with hardly a splash and Gunnar had refilled all their water bottles, the water so cold it was painful in the throat and felt like it would freeze your belly solid. Now all were sitting in silence, minding their own weapons and kit, chewing on cold, half-frozen strips of meat and hard flatbread.

"When are we moving, then?" Revna Hare-Legs asked Orka. She was leaning against a tree, rubbing sheepskin across her blades to grease them. One of her legs was resting casually over Gunnar's thighs, who was sitting beside her, using a seax to slice a worn fray of leather from his sword-hilt.

A deep breath from Orka and she looked around at them all.

"You do not have to do this," she said. The thought of them following her down there, into that nest of fang and claw and steel, was weighing heavily on her shoulders.

"We go where you go, chief," Gunnar Prow said.

"And the sooner the better," Revna said, "I need to do something to warm my blood. I hate being cold."

"You do not have to, is what I am saying," Orka grated. She opened her mouth, struggling to find the words.

"We know that," Halja Flat-Nose said as she scraped a whetstone along the edge of her sword. "We want to. We've come this far, and we will see it through. No more needs to be said."

A silence settled among them, Orka looking from one to another. Eventually she gave a curt nod.

"All right, then," she muttered.

"So, what's the plan?" Lif asked. "And please don't say *kill them all but one.*"

All of the Bloodsworn laughed at that, even Halja cracking her lips in a smile.

"That may be a little too much for even the Skullsplitter to achieve," Revna said, looking at Lif and giving him a wink. "It would be hard for even her to get through so many in just one night."

"No," Orka said, shaking her head. "That is not the plan. I have a new plan, just this once. I am going to go down to that camp, find my son and get him out of there. And I will only kill those who try to stop me."

CHAPTER SEVENTY-THREE

BIÓRR

Biórr grunted as Myrk rolled off him and tugged her breeches up. He lay on his back in the snow, breathing hard, his sweat already cooling, ice-fingers of cold beginning to seep into him. A cold wind was hissing through branches above him and he eyed them suspiciously. He had the distinct feeling something had been watching them.

Frost-spiders, night-hags, tennúr, spertus? The world has gone mad.

"Best pull your breeches up," Myrk said, "else your snake might freeze and snap off." She gave him a playful pinch, then frowned.

"You smile less than I remember," she said, "when you should be smiling more; especially as I've just given you a good humping." She grinned at him, a maniacal edge to it, reinforced by the dark hole of her missing eye.

I would, if Elvar would stop creeping into my head every time we hump. Why can I not get that woman out of my thought-cage? She is a trader in thralls, a slaver, a disease upon the land.

"You smile too much," Biórr said, though he took her advice about the cold, standing up and hopping on one foot as he tugged his wool breeches up, his coat of mail slithering back over his hips. He adjusted his belt and weapons.

"Better to smile than weep," Myrk muttered, her grin slipping for a moment.

Perhaps you're right. An image of Kráka's face as he stabbed her floated around his thought-cage, others that he had betrayed gathered behind the Seiðr-witch. Agnar of the Battle-Grim, reaching up to Biórr with his trusting gaze, and Elvar, her face shifting from confusion to understanding as she realised Biórr's betrayal.

Why? she had said to him.

Elvar, again.

With an act of will he pushed all the faces away and gave Myrk a soulless smile. It was the best he could do.

"Why haven't we attacked Svelgarth yet?" he asked her, wanting to change the subject.

"Some of our new crew-mates prefer to fight in the dark," Myrk said with a shrug. "I'd rather we just got on with it, but Lik-Rifa says we must be more understanding . . ."

Biórr nodded. It didn't make much difference to him, as the beast in his blood welcomed the night. He looked up at the sky, just streaks of grey through the branches.

"It's almost dark now."

"It is," Myrk said, following his gaze, "which means that I had better make my way to the wall. No doubt Svelgarth's Galdurmen will be on the walls, so there's rune-work to be done." She grabbed a fist full of his *brynja* and dragged him to her, kissed him hard. Something in her changed as she kissed him. Where she was tense and stiff, she softened, melting into him. The world seemed to slow. Eventually she pulled away, regarding him with her one eye, and then she stroked his cheek, tender as she had just been rough. "Don't go getting yourself killed," she said. "Through my long journey here you have been the thought that helped me rise each day, helped me take another step, and another."

Biórr just looked at her, had never heard Myrk talk like this before.

Life is changing us all in the heat of its forge-fire.

"I'll do my best," he said.

"I'll see you after," she said, flashing a smile at him as she stepped back and turned, walking away.

He stood there a moment, watching her fade through the trees, and then he set off back to his part of the camp, making his way to the wagons. He skirted a dense patch of mist, knew that night-hags were lurking within it. Even though they were all on the same side, he did not trust some of these vaesen and their appetites. Twilight lay heavy in the air, night's mantle settling about them. He saw skraeling gathered around a pot and playing knucklebone, laughing and singing as they drank ale from barrels, and then he was back at the wagons.

Storolf and Fain were standing before a fire, warming their hands, Tannbursta the tennúr hovering close to them. They looked like they were talking. Ilmur was with them, too. He had spent more time with them during the journey south. A score or so of warriors were scattered among and around the wagons at the rear of the camp, a mixture of Raven-Feeders and worshippers of the dragon. Most of them were huddled around a handful of hearth fires. A few skraeling were there, too, arguing over the slops of a cookpot. Some of the children were gathered around Storolf's fire, Breca and Harek among them. Biórr looked for Bjarn but could not see him.

"Good hump?" Fain asked as Biórr joined him at the fire.

"Aye, best thing for the cold," Biórr said.

"Heya," Fain agreed with a smile as he stamped his feet. He looked at Storolf, whose lips twitched in an attempt at a smile, though it did not reach his eyes. News of his brother's death still weighed on him.

"*Tooth?*" Tannbursta offered Storolf, hovering in the air and holding out his open palm, a bloodied tooth on it.

"No," Storolf grunted and Tannbursta shrugged, popping the tooth into his own mouth and crunching.

"*It's good,*" the tennúr said with a shrug.

"Aye, for you, maybe," Storolf said. He looked at Biórr. "Too cold to be standing around here," he muttered. "We should be in there, killing our enemies and sleeping warm in Orlyg's mead hall tonight." He jutted his red-bearded chin at the walls of Svelgarth, black against the grey of dusk, torches flickering to life upon them.

"Soon," Biórr said. "Myrk and the dragon-born are waiting for dark."

"It *is* dark," Fain said, looking up at the sky, the first stars flickering into life.

As if at Fain's words, horns rang out, echoing off the slopes and cliffs of the valley and fjord, and the camp shifted, the shadows growing and flowing.

Biórr allowed the rat in his blood to seep through him, his senses sharpening, the shadowed dark coming to life. Warriors moved, and so did vaesen. Trolls roared, moving in their clans, skraeling yelled war-songs and clashed weapons on shields. Frost-spiders scuttled through the canopy of trees, mist floated in dense clumps, night-hags gliding towards the wall. He heard a splash and ripple and saw the segmented bodies of spertus swimming in the river towards the fjord.

Some of the vaesen stayed, though. Ice-bright webs glistened around the camp's edge, many eyes glimpsed in furtive clusters, and here and there patches of deeper shadow revealed the lurking presence of night-hags.

Towards Svelgarth's wall a crackle of red light split the darkness, joined by another and another. Warriors roared battle-cries, and Biórr heard the hiss of loosed arrows.

"We should be up there with our brothers and sisters," Storolf said. He looked around, at the wagons piled with supplies, and children, most of them gathered in knots, here and there some in smaller groups, some standing alone. All of them were staring at the bursts of red incandescence that split and scarred the sky over Svelgarth.

"Heya," Biórr agreed.

"Ha, the wisdom of youth," Fain said, drinking from a cup of mead. "These old bones aren't so quick to rush at death."

"We should just go and join the fight," Storolf said, ignoring Fain.

"Brák is up there, somewhere," Ilmur muttered.

"So?" Storolf said.

"He is . . . cruel," Ilmur said.

"Has he hurt you?" Biórr snapped.

Ilmur looked at the fire. "No," he said. "But the air smells bad around him. Wrong. I would rather be around you three."

"Bad breath is no good cause to hate a man," Storolf grinned, slapping Ilmur's shoulder. "And Brák's bad breath or no, I'd still rather be doing something."

"We are doing something," Fain reminded him. "We are guarding, as Rotta told us."

"What is there to guard against back here, anyway?" Storolf said. "As if there's a warband creeping up on us from the frozen north." He snorted in disgust.

"Rotta's orders," Biórr said. "Who knows the mind of a god but I, for one, am not going to disobey him."

"I'll drink to that," Fain said with a grin, raising his drinking horn and Biórr filled his and raised it high.

"Huh," Storolf grunted, but he lifted his horn of ale and drank with them. "Looks like it's going to be a quiet night for us, then," he said, froth in his beard.

CHAPTER SEVENTY-FOUR

ORKA

Orka stood at the edge of the dell and looked out into the night. Trolls were roaring, a pack of them running at the wall of Svelgarth and pounding on the gates with their clubs. Even from here Orka could hear timber cracking and splintering. Arrows flitted down at them, but the trolls just roared and swung their great clubs. Flashes of red light ripped through the darkness and sparked against the wall's gate tower.

"What's happening?" Lif asked as he and Halja came to stand beside Orka.

"The dragon-born," Orka said.

As they watched, Orka saw tendrils of fire leap from the space before Svelgarth's great gate, wrapping like whips around the gate tower. Sparks flared and hissed, and warriors' yells drifted on the wind.

Orka stared with her wolf-eyes and saw a line of dark-mailed figures standing before the gate tower, ropes of red fire pulsing from their hands.

"Dragon-born," Orka growled. *Is Drekr among them? And where is Lik-Rifa?* She felt the hackles of her wolf rise.

As she watched, a dozen bull trolls approached the dragon-born, naked, huge and hulking, and then, somehow, the tendrils of fire were being passed to the trolls, wrapped around their waists like flaming belts. With a roar, the trolls were turning and lumbering away from the wall.

The ropes of flame pulled tight and taut, sparking and cracking, timber charring and creaking and catching alight, warriors on the gate tower shouting, throwing buckets of water at the burning timber.

With an ear-splitting crack and a ripping, tearing sound, the gate tower tore away from the wall and toppled slowly to the ground, crashing and exploding, splinters of timber hurled through the air.

A moment's silence as the dust settled, all staring at the gaping hole in the wall.

And then Lik-Rifa's host were roaring, screaming, running at the breach in the wall, a tide of mail and steel, of deep shadows and scuttling legs, of thick-trunked muscles.

"We move now," Orka said.

She turned and strode back into the dell, saw Spert come whirring out of the trees. He was muttering and grumbling under his breath.

"*Can't get any sleep around these filthy Maður,*" he rasped.

"What's wrong with you?" Lif asked him.

"*Those two,*" Spert spat, pointing with one of his antennae back into the trees, where Revna and Gunnar were appearing. "*Humping right next to Spert's stream. Gave Spert bad dreams and woke him up.*"

"Nothing wrong with a good hump," Gunnar said as they stepped into the dell.

"That's right," Revna said, smiling. "Especially before a scrap. Reminds you of what's worth fighting for." She looked at Lif and Halja. "You two should try it."

Lif's face turned the colour of blood and Gunnar laughed loudly.

Orka strode to Sæunn, who was adjusting girth straps on the horses and making sure their unneeded kit and provisions were all packed and secured well to the packhorses. Orka opened the pouch at her belt and took out a key, reached down to Sæunn and fitted the key into the thrall-collar at her neck. Turned it with a click and opened the collar, took it off of Sæunn and threw it into the dark. A thud and it was gone.

"You're free," Orka told Sæunn.

Sæunn just stared at Orka, then, slowly, hesitantly, she raised a hand to her neck, her fingertips brushing the ridged scars where her collar had chaffed her for years without end.

"W . . . what?" she whispered.

"You are free, and I thank you for your help," Orka said.

"You . . . don't want me to help get your son?"

Orka turned and looked through the trees, towards the clash of steel and screams of the dying. "No, that is no place for you."

Sæunn dropped her head, and when she looked up Orka saw tears glistening on her cheeks.

"I don't know what to do," she whispered.

"Whatever you wish," Orka told her.

"I could wait for you here, guard your horses," Sæunn said.

"Not here," Orka said. "This is too close. If we get out of there, it's likely we will have company." She looked to Spert. "Did you explore the stream as I asked?"

"*Of course, mistress,*" Spert rasped. "*It feeds into a river, which feeds into a lake, south, in the shadow of the mountains.*"

"How far?" Orka asked.

"*Far enough.*"

"Huh," Orka grunted. "Where the river meets the lake, that will be where we meet. All plans go wrong, so when this one goes wrong that is where we shall meet." She saw nods from her companions. "Sæunn, you could take our horses there. Wait for us if you wish, and you are welcome to travel with us. We will be heading south, hard, for Darl. But you are free to go, if you prefer. Take a horse, food, whatever you need." Orka shrugged.

"I will take your horses to this pool," Sæunn said.

"My thanks," Orka said. She turned to the others as Sæunn moved to the horses.

"This plan that will go wrong, then," Revna said. "What is it?"

Orka walked back to the edge of the dell and gazed down on the river valley and fjord. A tangle of combat raged on either side of the breach in Svelgarth's wall and was spreading along the dockside and into the town. Closer, at the rear of Lik-Rifa's camp, Orka could see pit fires burning around the wagons, dark shapes silhouetted against them, and other shadows shifting in the murk beyond.

"Still too many down there," she muttered. "Flat-Nose, Lif, I need a distraction to draw the camp guards. Make them think it is a counter-attack from Svelgarth, if you can."

"Chief," Halja nodded. Lif grunted.

"Spert, you go with them."

"*Yes, mistress*," Spert said.

"Gunnar, Revna, you come with me."

Gunnar nodded. Revna grinned.

"Lif, there are night-hags down there."

"Not much chance of me sleeping through this job," Lif said grimly.

Gunnar and Revna chuckled.

"If you meet one, you must speak rune-words as you strike it, or your blade will not bite. *Skuggar skilja*. Say it."

"*Skuggar skilja*," Lif said clumsily. "What are these words?"

"It is Snaka's god-tongue," Orka said. "Uspa the Seiðr-witch taught them to me, long ago."

Lif repeated them, more smoothly this time. "Got it," he said. Gave a wavering smile.

"Are you ready?" Orka asked them.

They buckled on helms, checked weapons, nodded.

Orka pulled on her nålbinding cap, that had once been Thorkel's. She could still smell him on it. Then her helm, buckled it tight, sound becoming muted. A deep breath and then she looked at them all, waiting, staring back at her. She turned and paced out of the dell and into the trees, moving careful and silent down the slope towards the river vale. She heard the soft tread of Gunnar and Revna behind her, moving wide on her flanks. Fifty paces, a hundred, choosing each step, and then she saw the treeline, beyond it flickering firelight, silhouettes around them all staring towards the battle din of Svelgarth.

Moonlight glinted on a movement above and in front, and Orka saw a fragment of web shudder, and not with the wind. The web was spread at shoulder height through the trees, and as Orka let her wolf fill her blood her eyesight sharpened, and she saw a deeper shadow nestled in the boughs of a pine tree. A hint of gleaming, clustered eyes. One hairy, thick-spined leg resting on the strand of web.

Like a tripwire.

Orka pointed with her long-axe, saw Gunnar and Revna were aware of the webbing. She shifted her long-axe to point at the shadows where the frost-spider lurked.

Now we wait.

Orka forced herself into stillness, breathing more slowly, waiting patiently as the wolf would for its prey. She studied the camp, eyes moving from fire to fire among the wagons. Saw a handful of skraeling dipping drinking horns in a barrel, maybe a score of men and women in mail scattered around the fires, some with raven-shields slung across their backs or leaning against wagons. And smaller figures. Children. Many children. Some clustered in the backs of wagons, just shadows, others huddled around fires, hands held out to ward against the cold.

My Breca is here.

Her breath caught in her throat at that thought, almost a physical pain in her chest, as if someone had clenched a fist around her heart.

A shout to her right, a scream. A spark of flame and a tent burst into flame, maybe two hundred paces away, quickly spreading to another tent, and then another. Figures running through them, shadows rippling, Orka seeing Halja and Lif speeding among the burning tents, hacking at warriors gathered around a fire, a few heartbeats filled with the sound of blades chopping into mail and meat, the ring of steel on steel, voices raised. A flitting shadow as Spert dropped out of the sky, more shouting, more screaming.

"'WARE," a voice rang out, echoing through the camp, "SVELGARTH ATTACKS," Orka thinking it was Halja's, and then the guards around the wagons were moving, lifting weapons, hurrying towards the chaos and flames among the tents.

Orka looked to Revna and nodded.

A hiss and *thunk*, the frost-spider falling from its shadowed lair. It hit the pine-needled ground with a thud, legs curled tight and twitching in death, Revna's spear protruding from it.

Orka took a step forward, glimpsed movement in her peripheral vision and swung her axe. Hacked into the hard shell of a frost-spider as it dropped on a strand of web, an explosion of slime and she was ripping her blade free, the spider dead before it hit the ground. She looked about, checking if any had seen or heard, saw the wagons emptying as more moved towards the tumult caused by Halja and Lif, and then she was moving, crouched low, running out from the treeline and into the camp. Gunnar and Revna moved silent as shadows either side of her.

A handful of skraeling, three or four of them, were still loitering around a fire, two of them arguing about a slab of spitted meat, the others laughing at them. Orka swung her axe and hacked halfway through a neck, the skraeling hurled into one of its companions. The two of them fell in a tangle of limbs, the dying one on top of the other, who scrambled and grunted and squealed as he tried to struggle free of the corpse's dead weight. Orka put a boot on the dead one's shoulder and ripped her axe free, heaved it up in a spray of blood and swung it down hard into the one struggling beneath. A wet slap and crack as she hacked into its skull. Either side of her Gunnar and Revna hit the other two skraelings and they were both down with hardly a sound, though one fell back on to the iron spit above the fire, blood jetting from its throat, black in the moonlight. Sparks erupted from the fire and iron grated, leather and flesh sizzling.

Orka looked up, saw that children were all about, pale faces staring at her, Revna and Gunnar snarling and looking for another foe to kill.

"Breca," she called, looking about wildly, saw wide-eyed, frightened faces looking back at her. Realised what these children were seeing. Three warriors, mailed, helmed, blood-drenched killers, hewers of men, rushing from the dark. She reached up to her helm, fumbled with the buckle, ripped it off with a snarl and cast it to the ground, turning, desperately searching the faces staring back at her.

"Mama?" a voice said.

A figure took a few hesitant steps towards her. A boy wrapped

in wool and fur, a shock of untidy black hair, taller than she remembered, thinner, too, gaunt hollows in his cheeks, and a silver-black
scar running beneath one eye. But she knew him in a heartbeat.

It was her Breca.

The world about her faded and Orka was running to him. Breca
was running, too. She dropped her long-axe, skidded to her knees
and then he was throwing himself into her arms, Orka stroking his
hair, vision blurred with her tears, smiling, laughing, weeping, kissing
his face, holding him tight to her in a crush of arms.

"Mama, I knew you'd come, I *knew* you'd come," he was saying,
over and over through his tears.

She tried to speak but her voice would not work.

He is here, in my arms.

The wolf in her blood growled, a reminder, and a hand touched
her shoulder.

"Chief," Revna said.

Orka pulled herself away and looked at her son.

"Papa?" Breca said. She could see a flicker of hope in his eyes.
She shook her head and fresh tears filled Breca's eyes.

"Come," she said to him, "I'm getting you out of here."

Breca nodded.

"Do you know Bjarn?" Orka asked him as she swept up her
long-axe.

"He is the son of our friend," Gunnar Prow added.

"Yes," Breca said, "but I don't know where he is. Bjarn," he called
out.

A figure stepped out of the shadows, another boy, dark-haired
like Breca, a heavy brow and a wide, big-boned face.

"You know my mother?" the boy said to Gunnar.

"Aye, lad," Gunnar Prow said. "She is sister to our chief's wife.
She is looking for you. We can take you to her."

Bjarn nodded, stood there hesitantly, then sucked in a deep breath
and strode to them.

Orka looked at the other children, knew that she could not take
them all, but felt a wave of sympathy for them. For their shattered
lives and murdered parents.

"You should run, *all* of you," Breca said. "Take what you can carry from those wagons and run. Go south, where it's warmer."

Many of them looked from Orka to the wagons, and some of them broke into sudden movement, running to the store-barrels. Some didn't bother to do that, just ran into the night.

Orka gripped Breca's hand and began to lead him away, Bjarn following them. Breca looked back over his shoulder.

"Harek," he called out. "Harek, come with us."

A thickset lad stepped out of the shadows, and Orka saw it was Harek, Asgrim's boy. He was changed, too, broader and longer-limbed. He was looking at them with a frown on his face.

"Come on, Harek," Breca called again.

"No," Harek said. "They're liars. All of them. That's what Lik-Rifa said."

"*She's* the liar," Breca snarled, more venom than Orka had ever seen in him.

Harek took a step back and opened his mouth.

"ENEMIES," he yelled, "ENEMIES IN THE CAMP."

CHAPTER SEVENTY-FIVE

BIÓRR

Biórr faltered as he ran towards the burning tents, Ilmur a little ahead and Storolf and Fain thundering along either side of him. Ahead of him fires were blazing, tents burning, shadows flickering, warriors shouting and milling about. But his rat ears heard something else behind him. Another voice, higher in pitch. A child's voice.

He slowed to a stop, turned and looked back.

Children were running in all directions. Some emptying barrels in the wagons, others disappearing into the gloom.

Harek was standing by the fire, shouting, looking towards Breca and . . .

Who is that? A woman dressed in mail, tall and broad, her fair hair pale and made shimmering silver and gold by the moonlight and flickering fire, a long-axe in one fist. She was holding Breca's hand. Two others stood in the shadows, a man and woman, mailed and helmeted, black shields and bearded axes in their fists. Bjarn was with them. They were walking quickly away from the fire, towards the treeline.

"Biórr, keep up," Fain called to him, but Biórr was staring at the shields on these warriors' arms. Black, with something spattered across them. A memory tugged at his thought-cage, and Myrk's words as she arrived at Nastrandir.

"Orka and the Bloodsworn," Biórr muttered.

Fain calling him, the big man's footsteps.

Let them go, a voice in his head said. *He is her son.* But he saw Bjarn leaving with them, too, and then Kráka's face was filling his thought-cage, her pleading eyes, blood jetting from her throat. He had paid a heavy price for helping them, almost died for her and Bjarn, and to allow Bjarn to escape again, when Biórr was one of those tasked with guarding the children.

Lik-Rifa will eat me.

"What is it?" Fain said at his shoulder.

Biórr pointed.

"Orka, who put out Myrk's eye, and the Bloodsworn," he said. "They've come for Breca." And then he was running, heard Fain calling to Storolf, heard footfalls behind him. He hefted his spear, abruptly aware that he carried no shield and wore no helm, though he wore his coat of mail. His pace faltered a moment, then footsteps drummed and Ilmur was speeding past him, the hound in his blood free, lips drawn back in a sharp-toothed snarl.

"I'll catch them for you, Biórr," he said as he swept past him, a spear in his fist and he was raising it as he ran, speeding at the back of one of the Bloodsworn as they passed the last fire before the trees. Dead skraeling were scattered across the ground.

Orka looked back first, must have heard Ilmur, shouted a warning and the Bloodsworn that Ilmur was charging at turned, the woman. She saw his spear raised for a thrust to her back. A shuffle of her feet, black shield swiping away Ilmur's spear lunge, a short, controlled chop of her axe and Ilmur was stumbling away, legs suddenly loose, spinning, blood spurting from his neck, collapsing in a heap of limbs.

Biórr hurled his spear and it flew hissing through the air, punched into the woman's chest, pierced her coat of mail and hurled her to the ground. A cry of pain. A roar from the other Bloodsworn warrior as he saw the woman fall, looked up to see Biórr running at him, drawing his sword and seax as he ran, Fain and Storolf a few paces behind him.

The warrior stood over the fallen woman and set his feet, raised his shield and hefted his axe. Biórr let the rat loose in his blood,

felt its speed and viciousness flood him. Twenty paces away, saw
that beneath his helm the warrior was a dark-haired man, tall and
long-limbed, a nose as big as his face, beard braided, standing over
a fair-haired woman who was flopping on the ground, plucking
feebly at Biórr's spear in her chest. Ten paces and he saw the animal
gleam in the man's eyes, saw lips peel back in a snarl to reveal sharp
teeth, knew he was Tainted.

That will not save you. He raised his sword high, kept his seax
low for the disembowelling stroke.

A shadow to his left and something slammed into his side, pain
blooming in his ribs, sent him careening through the air, weightless,
glimpsed a flash of fair hair and mail, Orka snarling at him, and
then he hit the ground with a crunch. A sharp pain in his shoulder
and he screamed, lost the grip on his sword and rolled into the
flames of a hearth fire, heat washing him, rolled to look in the face
of a dead skraeling, a hole in its skull and brains leaking like a
cracked egg. He shoved himself out of the fire, swatting at flames,
heard the clash of steel and pushed himself up on one knee, saw
Fain and Storolf trading blows with Orka while the other
Bloodsworn crouched over the fallen woman, trying to help her.

Storolf was swinging his long-axe, Fain chopping and slicing with
sword and hand-axe, and somehow Orka was meeting every blow,
her own long-axe gripped two-handed, just a flickering blur in the
firelight. The staccato beat of steel and wood. A flurry of blows given
and taken and Storolf grunted and fell staggering to one knee, blood
spurting from his mouth. Fain roared as his hand-axe went spinning
through the air and he stepped in close, headbutted Orka across the
nose, a gush of blood and she stumbled away. Fain raised his sword,
stepping after her, and then Orka was hooking her long-axe around
Fain's waist, snaring him with the head and heaving him into her,
arms wrapping around him, her jaws open in a gaping snarl, clamping
on to Fain's cheek and jaw and shaking him, ripping, tearing. Fain
screamed, beat at her with the pommel of his sword, his scream
fading to a gurgle and then a rasp, his sword dropping to the ground,
body slumping into her crushing grip.

Biórr staggered to his feet, saw his sword and swept it up, pain radiating from his shoulder, ignored it, eyes fixed on Fain as Orka spat him out and he crumpled to the ground, one side of his face a ragged wound, wheezing and frothing blood. Orka stood over him, mouth and chin slick with blood.

A bellow from Storolf and Biórr saw him charge into Orka, head down like a boar, and the two of them flew through the air together.

A cry of pain and fury from the man crouching over the woman. She was still, now, a pool of blood soaking the ground beneath her. The man rose, lips trembling, eyes flecked with green. He saw Biórr and hefted his shield and axe, ran at him.

Fight or flight? the rat in his blood whispered to him.

Fight, he snarled at the rat, felt a new rush of strength and speed, and he ran at the man.

They met with a crash of steel and wood, the man thrusting his shield and chopping with his axe, Biórr stepping around the shield blow, ducking the axe swing and slicing with sword and seax. His sword hissed through air as the warrior moved impossibly fast and his seax grated on mail, ripping links open but going no deeper, then their momentum was carrying them apart a few paces, both of them turning, twisting, snarling, weapons swinging.

Dimly Biórr heard other voices, shouts, the thud of feet, glimpsed warriors returning from the burning tents.

The Bloodsworn warrior came at him again, eyes blazing with grief and fury and power, axe chopping, shield boss crunching into him. Biórr stabbed with his sword but the Bloodsworn's axe parried the blow, the beard of the axe blade hooking around Biórr's sword and with a wrench the sword was ripped from his grip. He lunged in close, wrapped an arm around the Bloodsworn's neck and stabbed with his seax, sparks as it grated on more mail, then his leg was being kicked out behind him and he was falling, dragging the Bloodsworn with him. They rolled, the Bloodsworn's shield getting trapped beneath them, both of them snarling and frothing and growling at each other, teeth snapping.

Then hands were gripping him, heaving him up and away, a forest of spears pointing down at the Bloodsworn on the ground. The Bloodsworn tried to rise, and a spear blade touched his throat.

"Die now, or a little later," Rotta said, looking down on the Bloodsworn with a long spear in his fist.

The Bloodsworn froze.

"Wise choice," Rotta said. "Take his weapons, get him on his knees," he said to the score of warriors around him, a mixture of dragon-worshippers and skraeling, then he was striding towards Orka and Storolf.

CHAPTER SEVENTY-SIX

ORKA

Orka slammed a fist into the red-haired warrior's chin, his crushing grip on her slackening and she pulled her head back, jaws opening as she wrapped a fist in his hair, dragging his head back to reveal his throat.

"Enough of that, Ulfrir's child," a voice said, and the edge of a spear blade touched her neck. She looked, saw Breca held dangling in the grip of a man, tall and handsome, dark hair pulled back, a neat beard, wearing a fur-trimmed cloak and a tunic of wool. He reeked of wrongness, the wolf in Orka's blood snarling at him, her hackles rising.

That is no man, her wolf growled. Orka took in a deep breath, sifting through the scents of blood and death around her. There was something in the air that she had smelled once, not so long ago. Something that reminded her of Ulfrir.

"Not another *niðing* god," she spat.

"Very good," he said with a smile. "I am Rotta, cleverest and most handsome of the gods. Now, on your feet."

Orka held her hands up, rose slowly, the warrior beneath her groaning.

Breca was thrashing and snarling in Rotta's grip, trying to claw Rotta with his sharp-taloned hands, her son's eyes blazing with amber and green, his lips, teeth and chin all slick with blood. Orka recognised the wolf's fury in him, but there was something else as well.

"You have raised an ill-mannered little savage," Rotta said with a curl of his lip. "I like him."

"Let him go," Orka growled.

"First lesson: you do not command a god." He clubbed Breca with his spear haft, then threw him to the ground, gave him a kick in the stomach that took the wind and fury from him.

"I don't give a steaming troll-turd who or what you are. Harm my son and you're a dead man walking," she snarled as she moved, but Rotta swung his spear to hover over Breca.

Orka froze.

"A sensible wolf, then," Rotta smiled. "On your knees, beside your son."

She stretched her neck, bones clicking, holding back the straining wolf in her blood, dropped to the ground beside Breca.

"Mama," he wheezed.

She rested a hand on his shoulder as she looked around, saw that vaesen were all about her, frost-spiders, night-hags, tennúr flitting through the air, a few spertus scuttling across the ground. Skraeling and warriors marched Gunnar across to her, the warrior's eyes red-rimmed, muscles in his face twitching. A glance to Revna told Orka she was dead, felt a cold anger pulse through her at that.

The red-haired man she had been fighting pushed himself up from the ground. The blood of Svin the boar was in his veins, his jaw misshapen, tusks protruding from his lower jaw, and his skin had been thick, resistant to her blows.

Gunnar was pushed down to his knees beside Orka, and Breca struggled up to sit beside her. Vaesen ringed them, now, frost-spiders with their fangs dripping ice-blue venom, night-hags floating. A tennúr landed beside the red-haired man, who had staggered to the white-haired warrior that Orka had fought, who was wheezing ragged breaths through the holes in his face and neck. The red-haired man heaved him up on to his lap, weeping. "Keep breathing, Papa," he said as he stroked hair out of the wounded man's eyes. The tennúr rested a comforting hand on his arm.

"There are a lot of people who want to kill you," Rotta said, looking down at Orka. "Drekr, Myrk—"

"Let me kill her," the red-haired man snarled.

"See," Rotta said with a twitch of a smile. "Even Storolf wants to kill you, and he is usually a calm, measured man. You seem to bring out the worst in people. I must say, since I heard Myrk's tale about you I have been looking forward to meeting you." Rotta's nose twitched and he frowned, leaned forward until he was almost touching her skin, took in a long, deep breath. He jerked away, took a stumbling step back, face rippling and twitching, glimmers of fear and fury.

"You have seen my brother."

Orka said nothing. She could feel the weight of Drekr's two seaxes on her belt. Rolled her wrist and felt the small seax strapped to her arm beneath her sleeve.

"Where is he?" Rotta snarled

She shifted her weight.

"Ah, ah, ah," Rotta said as he took another step back, out of Orka's reach and wagged a finger at her, part smile, part snarl on his face. He raised his spear to Orka's throat. She felt a trickle of blood run down her neck and showed him her wolf-teeth. He moved the tip slowly to her chin, traced a line up it, over her mouth, her cheek, held it hovering over one eye. "Where is my brother?"

Orka let out a low-rumbling growl, her hairs standing like hackles.

Vaesen moved closer, a frost-spider's leg touching her foot. Spertus scuttled around her.

"I could hurt you. Introduce you to pain you have never imagined," Rotta said.

"Life is pain," Orka said, spitting a mouthful of blood at his feet.

A long moment, the spear-point hovering a hair's breadth from Orka's unblinking eye.

Rotta sighed and took a step back, regarding Orka thoughtfully. "Storolf, get that big axe of yours and come here," he said.

Footsteps, Storolf walking over to them, sweeping up his long-axe.

"Stand in front of her cub," Rotta said.

Storolf glowered at Orka as he placed himself in front of Breca.

"Now, raise your axe."

As Storolf moved Orka leaped, snarling, reaching for him. A blow to her back, slamming her down to the ground, a weight pressing her into the mud as she writhed and snarled.

"Your son lives or dies. Your choice," Rotta said calmly. Hands gripped her, heaved her back to her knees as something cold and sticky wrapped around her, a frost-spider winding her in a thick strand of web, pinning her arms. She saw warriors ringed around her, spears levelled. The one who had slain Revna with a spear-throw was among them, a sword in his fist, young, dark-haired, handsome if not for the cold, emotionless set of his features.

Other hands gripped Breca and Gunnar, holding them still beside her.

"Storolf, raise your axe," Rotta said again, and the blade glinted in moonlight high over Breca's head. A spertus opened its wings from its segmented carapace and rose into the air, hovering in front of Orka, the sting on its tail twitching, dripping a bead of black venom.

"*Move and you will feel my sting*," the spertus rasped. Then it smiled, wax-melted lips wriggling like maggots. "*I would like to kill you*," the spertus said.

Rotta stepped in front of Orka.

"So, now that I have your undivided attention, I shall ask you again. Where is my flea-bitten brother?"

"I do not know," Orka said.

Rotta back-handed Breca across the face, blood spurting from his lip.

"Where is my brother?" Rotta repeated.

"I'm going to rip your *niðing* throat out," Orka snarled at him, feeling the heat of her fury inside shifting to something colder and more deadly.

Rotta looked to Storolf and nodded.

The red-haired man raised the axe higher, muscles bunching.

"NO," Orka howled, straining at the thick web that bound her, veins bulging.

The spertus in front of Orka turned in the air and its sting darted out, adder-fast. Storolf grunted, swayed, black veins spreading beneath the flesh of his face. He tried to say something, but his tongue protruded from his mouth, black and swelling. Foam frothed over his lips and he toppled backwards. The spertus was already moving, opening its mouth and a black cloud hissed from its wide-gaping maw, like a plague of flies, straight into Rotta's face.

Rotta screamed and stumbled backwards.

A hiss, of iron slicing air, and a hurled spear punched into Rotta's chest, throwing him to the ground.

"*On your feet, mistress,*" Spert rasped as all stared down at the rat god. Rotta was screeching and writhing, limbs juddering in violent spasms. There was the sound of bones cracking, flesh tearing, and as Orka stumbled to her feet she saw that Rotta was growing, changing, his body swelling, fur sprouting, snout elongating, a hair-less tail whipping, cracking into a wagon, timber splintering. His bulk spread so quickly that those around the shapeshifting god were heaved into the air, Orka one of them. She was hurled towards the treeline, crunched to the ground and rolled, arms still pinned, and then hands were grabbing her, Lif's face looming close, pale in the moonlight, and he was chopping with a hand-axe at the web binding Orka. Halja stood with shield and sword, facing the camp. A whirr of wings and Spert appeared, hovering above Breca as he ran, guiding him into the woods.

Orka burst out of her bonds, threw them to the ground in a sticky heap.

"Here," she called, Breca running to her and throwing his arms around her waist, hugging her tight. She put a hand on his head, stroking his hair and looked back into the camp.

Rotta was still growing, shivering, twitching, screeching, and Orka could still see the spear in his chest, though it looked like a twig, now, as Rotta's bulk spread to fill the camp, big as a longship and growing larger. People and vaesen were running, fleeing lest they be flattened or smashed to pulp in the great rat's thrashing.

Orka took a step back towards the camp and Lif gripped her wrist.

"What are you doing?" he hissed at her.

"Gunnar Prow," Orka said. "We do not leave the living behind."

She took another step towards the camp, and then a shadowed figure was running towards them. Gunnar, carrying Revna's lifeless form in his arms. He was weeping, raging. "I will kill them all," he snarled as he reached them.

"Aye, brother," Orka said to him. "But not now."

"What then?" Lif said to her.

"Now, we run," and with that she was taking Breca's hand in her fist and loping into the trees.

CHAPTER SEVENTY-SEVEN

GUÐVARR

Guðvarr stamped his feet and blew into his cupped hands as he stood in the courtyard of Darl's fortress. He was dressed in his finest for this special day, but he was still cold. Felt as if he'd been cold since his return from Nastrandir, a chill seeping deep into his bones and not letting go. It was a little past dawn now, the air sharp and crisp, the sky pale, clouds high and gold-flecked with dawn's first touch, thin and frayed as stretched linen.

Today is the day, he thought as he looked up at the huge skeleton of Orna, the dead god. New scaffolding had been erected in the courtyard, so that Skalk could climb up to the eagle's skull and be within easy reach of her when he performed whatever Galdur-magic was needed to put flesh on this dead god's bones.

He was not the only one in the courtyard.

A few score *drengrs* sworn to Helka lined its edges, and a crowd was beginning to gather, filtering up from the town. The fortress gates were open, every resident of Darl having been summoned to witness this moment, to witness Queen Helka's ascendancy from one of a handful of rulers in Vigrið to the woman who raised the eagle-god and became ruler of all.

The skálds will be singing of this day for evermore.

The doors to the mead hall opened and Queen Helka emerged, surrounded by her *Úlfhéðnar* guard, more than a score of the shaven-headed, tattooed, braided warriors.

At Queen Helka's side strode Jarl Orlyg of Svelgarth. A barrel-chested, white-haired man, beard tied in a thick knot of braid, a wolfskin cloak about his shoulders and an axe thrust through his belt. A dark-haired Galdurman walked behind Orlyg, and a dozen warriors, all with collars around their necks.

Tainted warriors, Guðvarr realised and shivered.

Prince Hakon walked a step behind Orlyg and Helka, though Guðvarr was pleased to see he had lost much of his swagger. Guðvarr flashed the prince a grin as he looked over, but Hakon just looked at him as if Guðvarr were troll-shite on his shoe.

Arseling, Guðvarr thought, holding his smile.

Estrid walked at Helka's left, her dark hair tied back, a pale blue cloak edged in fox fur wrapped about her. The pommel and hilt of a sword poked from beneath her cloak.

Queen Helka and her retinue walked to a new-built platform that gave a fine view of dead Orna's skeleton, and also made her visible to all who would be cramming into the courtyard and streets of the fortress.

Footsteps behind Guðvarr and he turned to see his aunt entering the courtyard. She, too, was dressed in her finest gear, a gleaming *brynja*, sword and seax in fine-tooled scabbards at her belt, rings of gold and silver on her arm. The scar through her face was red from the cold. Forty *drengrs* marched at her back, all that were left of those who had escorted her from Fellur village.

"With me," Jarl Sigrún said as she reached him, not breaking her stride. "You have brought about this day, you should be close to the queen, to share in her glory."

This is one of the reasons I love you, Guðvarr thought. *You are one of the few people who already recognises my worth.* He thought about that a moment as he hurried to keep up with his aunt. *Perhaps the only person . . .*

They strode across the courtyard to the wooden platform, *Úlfhéðnar* stepping forward to block their passage to Helka.

"Sigrún and Guðvarr," the queen said and the *Úlfhéðnar* parted, allowing them to pass through and walk up the timber steps to stand beside the queen, her children and their guards. Sigrún's *drengrs* joined the warriors standing before the platform.

Looking out over the courtyard from the platform Guðvarr saw that the ground had been rune-carved, eight huge lines like the spokes of a wheel radiated out from the mead hall, Orna's skeleton at their centre, runes carved into the tip of each line.

"My prince," Guðvarr whispered, leaning close to Hakon. "I know we did not have the best of starts, but know this, I had no choice. Skalk held my life in his palm. I despise him."

Hakon gave him a surprised look, but before he could say anything voices were rising up from the courtyard. The petty jarls who had been summoned by Jarl Sigrún like Orlyg: Glunn Iron-Grip and Svard the Scratcher, all with their *drengrs* about them, and others that Guðvarr did not know. The jarls were permitted up on to the platform alongside Guðvarr, their *drengrs* settling around the court-yard, which was full to bursting, now, all manner of people from the town of Darl come for the great spectacle.

The mead hall doors creaked open again and Skalk stepped out into the pale day, holding his new staff in one fist, the many bones on his necklace shining white in the sun.

I hate that man.

His scars from Jaromir's hawk were mostly healed now, running through his face like thick, poorly stitched seams on a tunic, his empty eye socket a red-rimmed, puckered hole. Yrsa the *drengr* walked at his shoulder, stone-faced, one hand resting on the hilt of her sword, and behind them strode Sturla and a handful of Skalk's Galdur-apprentices. Sturla carried a small chest in her arms.

A hush settled over the courtyard, the crowd parting for Skalk. He strode out deep into the courtyard as his followers made for the new-built scaffold.

Skalk stopped before Helka's platform. He dipped his head to her, drew the seax at his belt and pricked a bead of blood from his thumb, smeared it over the head of his staff and touched the staff to the rune-carved ground.

"*Jörð og klettur lofi og himinn, kraftur blóðs og rúna, rís upp og fyllir bein Orna,*" he said.

There was a flare and crackle of flame and then fire was filling the rune carved into the ground and running down the spoke-like trench that led to the mead hall. People leaped out of the way of the flames as they spread hungrily and Guðvarr realised that a circle had been carved about the mead hall and Orna's skeleton, all of its sharp lines and runes now filling with flame.

Skalk walked to the scaffolding and climbed to the platform beneath Orna's head, joining Sturla and the other Galdur-apprentices. Sturla set the chest she carried down at his feet and Skalk reached in and took out a dull iron thrall-collar.

"*Opna og vaxa, kraga bundin við mig*," Skalk said as he raised the collar to Orna's skeletal neck and opened it. Guðvarr sucked in a hissed breath as red veins of heat threaded through the iron, the collar growing in size, stretching as if some invisible giant were moulding it, until it was wrapped around the highest point of the eagle's spine.

Skalk cried out more strange words in his Galdur-tongue, all in the courtyard silent, enraptured.

The collar closed with a snap, a final flicker of flame and then it was dull iron again.

Skalk held up his blood-smeared staff, tracing lines in the air, again chanting words in his unknown language.

Sharp-angled runes of flame and blood crackled into life in the air between Skalk and the skeleton, and Skalk turned to Sturla and the other Galdur-apprentices. They drew small seaxes and cut their hands, blood dripping, and then together they hurled their blood at the skeleton, bleached bones spattered red.

"*Hjarta sló aftur*," Skalk and the apprentices cried out together, and a hush fell over the world.

The glowing rune that hovered in the air grew and stretched like a giant net.

"*Kraftur orðs, kraftur blóðs, drekkur í dauða og lífgar*," Skalk and his apprentices chanted, and the flaming rune fell upon Orna's skeleton, from wingtips to tail to curved beak. The ancient bones flared, red and orange veins rippling through them, slowly faded.

Guðvarr felt a tremor ripple through the courtyard. The air about

Orna shimmered. A tremor passed through the bones of the dead
eagle, dust falling in a cloud over the courtyard, and then Guðvarr
saw strands of sinew and flesh appear from the fire-filled stave
marked on the ground, growing like vines. Veins and arteries wrapped
around bone, muscle appearing, a glimpse of lungs and heart beating
within the great ribcage. The skull moved as flesh appeared, a golden
glimmer in once-dark eye sockets, and then feathers were sprouting,
russet-red and gold and white.

Guðvarr stood and stared, frozen in awe, along with everyone else
around him. And then the eagle's wings were beating, slow and
ponderous, a great gale buffeting them, some in the courtyard falling.
Skalk and his companions scurried from the platform and scaffolding
like rats. There was a great creaking and ripping sound as Orna's
new body tore its way from the mead hall, timber splintering and
falling away and the eagle rose into the air and descended back on
to the shattered mead hall with a creak of timber, razored talons
flexing. She raised her head to the sky, opened her beak and screeched,
the sound sending Guðvarr tumbling to his knees, hands to his ears.

Orna stood on the ruined remains of the mead hall, larger than
Helka's hall had ever been, shook her body, feathers ruffling, and
folded her wings. Gazed down upon Helka and those on the platform with haughty, intelligent eyes.

"Where is Ulfrir?" she said, her voice rich, edged like a sharp
blade. "My daughters? And that bitch, Lik-Rifa?" She twisted her
head, trying to look at the thick iron collar about her neck. "What
is this?" she said.

"You have been long dead, mighty Orna," Queen Helka said,
"and the world has changed much in your absence. That collar
means you are mine."

"What?" Orna said, gold-flecked eyes blazing, her head rearing
back on her powerful neck, her taloned claws flexing, crushing
timber. Guðvarr fought the urge to run.

A sound, distant, filtering down from above and Orna's head
twitched, looking up into the pale sky.

People in the courtyard were pointing up. Someone screamed.

Guðvarr saw a dark speck high above, breaking through the thin clouds, growing larger with every heartbeat. Wide wings, a long tail and sinuous neck. A sound drifted down to them, rumbling like distant thunder.

"Lik-Rifa," Orna hissed, her voice filling the courtyard and she spread her wings wide, casting Guðvarr and the fortress of Darl in shadow, her great wings were beating, Orna rising into the air, higher and higher, Lik-Rifa growing huge as she hurtled down from above, roaring as she came.

The eagle flew at an angle, forcing Lik-Rifa to break and flatten her dive, and then they were slamming together in the skies above the fortress, a thunderclap of sound that exploded outwards, the turbulence of their clash battering people to the ground, rocking Guðvarr and all on the platform.

The eagle and the dragon whirled through the sky, roaring and screeching, spinning, wings buffeting, jaws biting, beak rending, taloned claws raking. Feathers and scales and blood rained down.

Hands gripped Guðvarr's cloak, Hakon dragging him close, Helka looming behind him, her face a thundercloud.

"You told us the dragon's attack was not planned for another nine-day," Hakon spat in Guðvarr's face, "told us we had time to prepare."

"I-I have been lied to, deceived," Guðvarr squeaked.

"SPEARS," Helka cried out, "ARCHERS." The initial shock was gone from Helka's face, Guðvarr impressed with how quickly she marshalled her fears.

Shouts and screams among the crowd, people throwing back cloaks to reveal rusted mail, striking about them with axes and spears. Guðvarr saw the flicker of flame, saw warriors in dark mail carving into the courtyard like a hurled spear, rune-cast fire flickering from their fists. A hulking man at their head hacked a *drengr* down with an axe in a spray of blood, a dark-haired woman at his side, sword stabbing, both of them the sharp tip of the spear, others in a wedge behind them.

Drekr and Ilska the Cruel.

"DRAGON-BORN," he yelled, pointing at them, drawing the sword at his side.

Jarl Sigrún heard him and grabbed Queen Helka's arm, pointing them out to her.

"PROTECT THE QUEEN," Jarl Sigrún cried out, and Helka shouted, her *Úlfhéðnar* moving to intercept the dragon-born, Frek and the others on the platform drawing blades and leaping to join their pack, screams and blood spraying as dragon-worshippers threw themselves at the *Úlfhéðnar*.

"TO ME," Jarl Orlyg bellowed and jumped from the platform, pulling an axe from his belt, his hard-looking *drengrs* rushing to him.

Hakon was standing open-mouthed, eyes moving from the dragon and eagle in the skies above to the blood and chaos in the court-yard.

Helka stood on the platform, proud and fierce, glaring at the dragon-born as her *Úlfhéðnar* surged towards them, and then Jarl Sigrún drew back her sword and stabbed Queen Helka through the back.

It was a powerful blow, slicing through wool and linen and deep into flesh, Helka crying out, her back arching as Sigrún thrust her blade on, the tip of her sword bursting out through Helka's stomach in an explosion of blood. Helka stood there a moment, eyes wide, mouth moving, and then Sigrún ripped her blade free and Helka toppled from the dais, falling and disappearing into the crowd below.

"No," Guðvarr heard Hakon say.

The *Úlfhéðnar* faltered in their charge at the dragon-born, stumbling to a halt and looking around in confusion, flickers of red fire rippling through their thrall-collars.

"MURDERER, TRAITOR," Hakon yelled, pointing at Jarl Sigrún, spittle spraying from his mouth. "Seize her, kill her," he screamed. The *Úlfhéðnar* turned and began forging a way back to the platform, their amber eyes fixed upon Jarl Sigrún.

It is true, then, that the thrall-power passes through the line of blood.

Guðvarr grabbed a fistful of Hakon's hair and pulled him back, dragged the edge of his sword across Hakon's throat. Blood spurted and Guðvarr pushed Hakon stumbling to the ground. He fell with a thud, rolled and flopped like a landed fish, hands grasping at his throat, slick with blood. Guðvarr stood over him and smiled as Hakon wheezed and rasped and became still. Then he looked around for Estrid.

Estrid was staring at Hakon, blood pooling about his corpse. She looked up at Guðvarr.

"TO ME," she yelled, "*Úlfhéðnar* to me."

She is no fool, has realised the power she now has, Guðvarr thought, glancing into the crowd and seeing a wave of *Úlfhéðnar* carving their way back to the platform. *She needs to die before they get back here.*

He stabbed his sword at her but Estrid was stepping away, grabbing Glunn Iron-Grip's sleeve and throwing him into Guðvarr, sending them both stumbling. A glimpse of flashing steel and then Guðvarr was parrying Estrid's sword, a strong overhead blow, another at his ribs, a stab at his throat, realising that she was far more skilled than he had expected, and that every moment she drew breath was another moment that the *Úlfhéðnar* were closer to ripping him apart. He swept her blade away, desperation and fear lending him strength and speed, stepped in and punched her on the jaw, sending her reeling, and raised his sword high.

The world exploded, Guðvarr flying through the air, spinning, people and splintered timber all around him. He crashed to the ground with a bone-jarring crunch, white lights exploding before his eyes. He pushed himself up on to one arm and knee, staggered to his feet. Saw that Lik-Rifa and Orna had crashed into the mead hall and courtyard, decimating it, and anyone who'd got in their way.

Orna rose out of the dust and ruin, screeching and stabbing with her beak, claws raking the body of Lik-Rifa, ripping out clumps of scaled flesh. Lik-Rifa roared and lashed her tail, crunching into Orna and sending her spinning away, Lik-Rifa beating her wings, rising and following the eagle.

Here and there pockets of people clambered back to their feet and fought on, Helka's *drengrs* fighting dragon-worshippers. Guðvarr saw a flicker of rune-cast fire and saw Skalk in the courtyard, Yrsa, Sturla and a knot of his apprentices about him, all of them striking down worshippers of the dragon and duelling with dragon-born. Yrsa was calling Helka's *drengrs* to her, more gathering around her with every moment, but even as Guðvarr watched he saw Ilska and Drekr plough into their flank, scattering them like chaff.

My sword, where is my sword. Guðvarr looked around wildly, saw it and swept it up, turned around, searching for Estrid, but he could not see her in the dust-choked, battle-filled din.

Skalk, then, time for him to die.

He stumbled through the tumult, slashing out at a *drengr* fighting three dragon-worshippers, stabbing at someone who stumbled across his path, and then he was close to where Skalk had been standing, the clash of steel louder here, dust swirling, red flames flickering. He glimpsed Yrsa trading blows with a Tainted, punching her shield boss into a face full of sharp-snarling teeth.

And then Skalk was staggering up from the ground, immediately in front of him. He had no weapon in his fist, his staff lying on the ground.

"You," Skalk snarled at him, "you betrayed us, you *fool.*"

"I did," Guðvarr said, smiling at this man that he hated.

"Your last, and most painful mistake," Skalk said. "Time for my hyrndur to return to me. *Hyrndur, vaknið af svefni, etið þig í gegnum hold, farðu aftur til húsbónda þíns,*" he said, hand closing into a fist, a savage grin on his face.

Guðvarr looked down at his chest and laughed. Slowly he pulled up the sleeve of his mail shirt, the wool and linen tunics, past his dragon-tattoo to reveal the scar on his arm where the hyrndur had entered him. It was fresh-scabbed again, still bleeding a little.

"It is gone," Guðvarr said.

"What?" Skalk frowned. "How?"

"She smelled it in me," Guðvarr said, eyes flickering up to Lik-Rifa in the skies above them. "What did you expect? She *created* the hyrndur, created all the vaesen. They are her children."

As if to prove Guðvarr's point, a new sound drifted into the courtyard, growing louder. Buzzing. A whirring of wings. Guðvarr and Skalk looked up to see dark clouds sweeping down on the courtyard, hyrndur diving to swarm around *drengrs*, screams ripping through the air, men and women staggering and stumbling, swelling from a multitude of stings and collapsing, twitching.

Other winged creatures swirled through the air, tennúr dropping on to warriors, biting with their too-big mouths and many rows of teeth, ripping and tearing teeth from the gums of their still-screaming victims. A deep-bellowed roaring and a bull troll appeared, iron-nailed club swinging, pulped figures flying through the air.

Guðvarr looked back at Skalk. "Once Lik-Rifa knew the hyrndur was living in my chest, she knew I was not Hakon's messenger. So, I told her *everything* and, in return, she called her hyrndur out of me, without killing me." He shuddered at the memory. "It hurt. Oh, how I screamed. But I survived. I am a survivor, that's what *you* told me, remember?" He lunged at Skalk with his sword, straight at his chest.

An impact on his back sent him sprawling, dust and dirt in his face, losing his grip on his sword. He turned and looked up, saw Yrsa standing over him, shield and sword in hand, a flap of her cheek hanging down, blood sheeting.

"I hoped I'd get to kill you, you pathetic pile of shite," she snarled, raising her sword.

A piercing shriek filled their ears, a shadow falling over them. Yrsa looked up, Guðvarr taking the opportunity to roll away, glimpsed the *drengr* leaping, Skalk running, and then there was a concussive crash, the ground heaving and bucking beneath him, hurling him into the air. He slammed into a broken post of the mead hall, screamed, fell to the ground with a thud and just lay there, staring.

Orna lay in the courtyard, one of her wings twisted beneath her. Her one good wing was flapping, half raising her from the ground. Blood was pouring from a hundred wounds where the dragon had raked her, but her beak was red with Lik-Rifa's blood, clumps of dragon flesh in her talons. And then Lik-Rifa was descending, and crashing into Orna, her dragon claws gouging, raking, her great jaws wide, clamping around Orna's neck and head.

The eagle screeched, fury and pain mingled, thrashed and writhed, but Lik-Rifa's grip was iron. Her neck reared high, dragging Orna from the ground, and then she shook the eagle like a dog shakes a rat. There was an ear-splitting crack, bones snapping, the sound of flesh tearing, fresh blood spurting in fountains, and Orna was sagging in the dragon's jaws, her wings loose, flopping.

Lik-Rifa spat the eagle out, beat her wings, rose into the air, then crashed down again, claws ripping, stamping, jaws tearing, feathers and flesh flying in all directions, Lik-Rifa's rage and fury a blood-soaked frenzy, Guðvarr clamping his hands over his ears.

Slowly, the sounds of butchery faded, the cloud of dust and blood and feathers settling. Skalk was gone. Yrsa was gone, and Lik-Rifa stood on the mangled remains of the eagle, just a torn, mutilated sack of skin and flesh and bone now, and the dragon lifted her head to the sky and roared.

CHAPTER SEVENTY-EIGHT

ORKA

"Spert, lead us to the stream," Orka said, "we'll follow it to the lake."

An ear-splitting screech echoed up from the vale.

"*FIND THEM*," a voice shrieked, loud enough to crack ice. Boughs shook and birds took to startled flight, pine needles falling like hail. The grey of dawn was leaking into the world, but it had not touched the valley and woodland yet.

They ran into the wooded darkness, Spert leading them, whirring ahead, and soon Orka saw a glint of light on ice, and they were at the stream, frost-crusted and frozen. They turned south, running as best they could along the streambank. Tree roots snared their feet, Lif tripping, falling, scrambling back up with Halja's help, and they ran on.

Soon Orka heard the sounds of pursuit behind them. A troll's roar, the splintering of timber, the drum of many feet, spreading across the wooded slopes behind them.

The whirr of wings and Orka looked up, saw the shape of a tennúr flitting through the canopy. Someone hurled a spear and it squawked, limbs folding, crashing to the ground. They ran on, Orka hearing Breca's breath start to rasp in his throat. The stream grew wider and then it was feeding into a river, flowing fast and fierce out of the mountains, white-flecked where it surged and frothed around sparkling, frost-slick boulders.

They ran on.

The sounds of pursuit were growing, echoing through the woodland around them.

"Chief," Halja said, veering to run closer to Orka, "we should split up, spread them out, might confuse them."

"Aye," Orka said, she had been thinking the same thing.

Halja barked it out to the others without breaking stride, and then Halja and Lif were veering away. Gunnar ran on with Orka and Breca a way, Revna lying across one shoulder.

"Will you help me kill them?" he breathed at Orka.

"I will," Orka growled back at him.

Gunnar gave her a nod. "See you at the lake, chief," he said to her, and then he was cutting away from the river into the darkness.

"Breca, are you well?" Orka asked him.

My son, my Breca, he is here, flesh and blood, running at my side. I have found him. It hit her like a hammer blow, the relief and joy of it flooding through her and she reached out a hand, stroking his sweat-soaked hair as they ran on.

He looked up at her, sweat-stained, breathless, but his mouth twitched in a smile at her and her heart lurched to see it. She felt her own smile crack her lips, a sensation she had almost forgotten.

"You have found the wolf in your blood. Let it fill you, it will help."

"And . . . the . . . bear . . . Mama," Breca breathed.

Ah, that is the other thing I sensed in you. Orka smiled, liking the thought that she and Thorkel were both present in his blood.

I swore to you, my Thorkel, that I would find our son.

They ran on.

Time passed, filled only by the thud of their feet, the rasp of breath, the drum of Orka's heartbeat, loud in her head. Other sounds filtered through to her. The snap of twigs behind them, movements at the edge of her vision, drawing her eye, flitting shapes in the canopy.

A flash of something ahead, a flicker of frost-touched web catching a gleam of moonlight.

"Breca, down," Orka cried out, pushing Breca and he fell tumbling beneath the hurried web that a frost-spider was weaving. Orka threw herself to the side, tripped and fell, crunched into a tree, saw a frost-spider descending on Breca from above on a thread of web. She thrust herself away from the tree, drawing her hand-axe from her belt, fell into the spider, chopping, its hard shell cracking, fluid exploding in great gouts as Orka fell with it. The spider shivered and shrieked, mandibled mouth clacking, fangs twitching, dripping fluid as it died.

Something slammed into Orka's back, a great weight bearing her down. She fell into pine needles, tried to turn, felt the cold-burn touch of frost web on her hand. A sharp pain in the back of her neck. The wolf surged through her blood, snapping and snarling, and she heaved herself from the floor, twisted over, the spider looming over her. Fangs darted forward and she thrust her head to the side, saw the fangs puncture the earth. She chopped with her axe, felt the blade bite into a furry leg, severing it, a spurt of fluid. Heard Breca shouting, incoherent screams and snarling, then a cracking, tearing sound, felt the spider shiver above her. Its strength faded, legs folding and it fell away, Breca on its back, his clawed hands thick with spider-slime, his teeth and jaws dripping.

Orka could see Thorkel in him, when the battle-rage fell on him, a cold fury in Breca's eyes, and she felt a flush of pride in her son, that he had killed the frost-spider.

We are pack.

She pushed herself to her feet, swayed, feeling slower, a chill spreading through her veins. She felt . . . wrong. The wolf in her blood whined. A pain throbbed in her neck and she put her hand to it, came away with blood on her fingers and something else, a thick ichor, tinged with blue. It was ice-cold to the touch, so cold it burned.

I've been bitten.

The creak of branches behind her, the scrape and scuttle of feet.

"Breca, we have to run," she managed to say, her mouth feeling thick and sluggish. She grabbed Breca's tunic and pulled him, broke into a loping run.

No, she snarled in her head, *I'll not lose him again.*

Breca followed her, still snarling and growling, the wolf-frenzy loose in his blood.

With every step Orka could feel the spider venom spreading through her limbs. It was pushing the wolf back in her blood, drowning it in a fight it did not understand. It whined and snapped at this new enemy inside her, but faded with every pulse of her heart. She ran fifty paces, stumbled over a root, her legs feeling heavy, feet beginning to grow numb. Ran on another dozen steps, then she was falling, scrabbling at the ground, trying to get back to her feet.

"Mama, what's wrong?" Breca cried as he ran back to her, tried to help her stand. His eyes widened as he looked at her, fear flickering in his gaze. "Your lips are blue."

"Spider v-venom," she mumbled through her chattering lips. She tried to walk, could not feel her feet. With a yell Breca took most of her weight, half carrying her, half dragging her.

"Where are we going, Mama?" he rasped as he laboured.

"A l-l-lake, end of r-r-river," Orka stuttered, "horses, f-f-friends." They got another dozen paces and Orka could no longer feel her legs. Breca tripped and fell and Orka dropped in a heap. She threw herself over, looked at the river, knew if she jumped in she would drown, her coat of mail weighing her down and her limbs frozen, unmoving.

"Mama, get up, get up," Breca cried, grabbing her arm and trying to drag her up.

Branches creaked above them and Orka looked up, saw many legs and clustered eyes. The scrape of clawed feet on the ground and frost-spiders came scuttling out of the trees. One began to drop down from above on a strand of web.

"Get up, Mama," Breca said, shaking her.

"Can't," Orka wheezed, her frost-misted breath clouding.

"Mama, what shall I do?" Breca cried, tears streaking his cheeks. He looked up at the descending spider, Orka seeing his eyes shimmer and shift in colour, lips peeling back in a sharp-toothed snarl.

"Live," Orka said, and with her fading strength she grabbed him and heaved him up, threw him through the air. He fell with a splash into the fast-flowing river. She saw him disappear under the water, then resurface, swept away by the current.

"MAMA," she heard him wail, and then he was gone.

She lifted her head and howled, a cry of grief and heartache, of rage and frustration.

She flopped against a tree, fumbled for a seax at her belt, drew it.

The spider dropped down in front of her, regarded her for a moment with its many eyes. More shapes moved behind it. With a terrifying silence it reared back, its forelegs high, fangs twitching and then it threw itself at her. Fangs stabbed at her chest but were turned on her mail, the spider's breath fetid, foul. Orka stabbed up with her seax, felt the blade puncture the hard outer shell and sink deep into fluid. The spider shrieked as it fell away from her, ripping the seax from her grip as it juddered and jerked in its death throes. Orka snarled a smile.

Another spider leaped at her, fangs flashing for her face and with her last strength she raised her arms and caught hold of it by its two thick fangs, held it above her, its great weight pressing down, legs thrashing, trying to wrench free.

Orka squeezed, snarled, with a last mammoth exertion of her fading strength she howled and ripped the fangs from the spider's body, splitting it open like an ale-skin, stinking fluid exploding over her. She cast the dead spider away, arms flopping at her side, felt a pain in her leg, saw more spiders swarming about her, darting forward and sinking their fangs into her legs. She felt her heartbeat slowing, everything touched with ice. Mist swirled out of the trees, a night-hag hovering over her, and then it was sinking on to her chest, a great weight crushing down upon her.

Live, my Breca, was her last thought before the blue, frost-tinged darkness took her.

The story continues in...

Book Three of The Bloodsworn Trilogy

ACKNOWLEDGEMENTS

As always, this book has taken a shield wall of warriors to bring it to the shelf, and I have many people to thank for their help.

First of all, my wife Caroline, who is the heart and soul of this family and keeps us all going. Without her I would not be writing books.

My three sons, James, Ed and Will, all of whom have literally stood at my side in the shield wall. Their passion and enthusiasm for my made-up worlds never fail to amaze and inspire me.

And my beautiful Harriett, of course, whose smiling eyes light up a room.

A big thank you to my wonderful agent, Julie Crisp, easily as loyal and fierce as any member of the Bloodsworn.

My fantastic editor James Long at Orbit UK, it has been a real pleasure working with you on this adventure.

The brilliant Priyanka Krishnan, my editor at Orbit US, for her unfailing hard work on my behalf.

And all of Team Orbit, both in the UK, US and beyond; you are all awesome and I am deeply grateful for all that you do to get the Bloodsworn Saga out into the big wide world.

I have to thank those who gave their time to read my first draft of this book.

My sons Ed and Will, who some of you may know as The Brothers Gwynne on YouTube, your passion for the world of the

Bloodsworn is a constant source of inspiration to me. Being able to chat about each book with you as I write it is so helpful, and also a lot of fun.

I must also thank Kareem Mahfouz, that indomitable force of nature, who has made time to read this during possibly the busiest time of his life. I'm writing this acknowledgement before he gets married to the lovely Avril, but by the time this book is published he will have been wed a significant amount of time. Congratulations to both of them.

Mark Roberson, thanks so much for giving the book your time, especially when I know you have cricket bats to restore. I'm looking forward to when we can chat books over a good breakfast.

Sadak – you really need to work on your time management and actually read these drafts before my deadlines . . . just saying.

I'd like to say a big thank you to all those that I have come into contact with through the internet, whether you be bloggers, reviewers, or readers, Twitterers, Instagramers or Facebookers. You know who you are. It's been a real pleasure to hear from you all, and I am deeply grateful for your support in spreading the word about the Bloodsworn and the Battle-Plain. The fantasy community is truly awesome.

And last but by no means least, I would like to thank you, the reader who is holding this book in your hands right now. Thank you for investing your time and your money into this book, these characters and this world. Without you I would not be writing, and I am both glad and grateful to see that you are ready to follow the Bloodsworn on another journey through the Battle-Plain. I am having so much fun writing this series, it's been a real pleasure playing in the sandbox of Norse mythology and Viking-era history and I am honoured that you are back for some more.

Keep your weapons sharp and your wits about you.

John

extras

orbit

meet the author

Photo Credit: Caroline Guynne

JOHN GWYNNE studied and lectured at Brighton University. He has played double bass in a rock 'n' roll band and traveled the United States and Canada. He is married with four children and lives in Eastbourne, where he is part of a Viking reenactment group. When not writing, he can often be found standing in a shield wall with his three sons about him. His dogs think he is their slave.

Find out more about John Gwynne and other Orbit authors by registering for the free monthly newsletter at orbitbooks.net.

if you enjoyed
THE HUNGER OF THE GODS

look out for

THE JUSTICE OF KINGS

Book One of
The Empire of the Wolf

by

Richard Swan

From a major new voice in epic fantasy, The Justice of Kings *introduces Sir Konrad Vonvalt, an Emperor's Justice, who is a detective, judge, and executioner all in one. But these are dangerous times to be a Justice....*

The Empire of the Wolf simmers with unrest, rife with rebels, heretics, and powerful patricians who would challenge the power of the Imperial throne.

Only the Order of Justices stands in the way of chaos. Sir Konrad Vonvalt is the most feared Justice of all, upholding the law by way of his sharp mind, arcane powers, and skill as a swordsman. In this he is aided by Helena Sedanka, his clerk and protégée, orphaned by the wars that forged the Empire.

When the pair investigates the murder of a provincial aristocrat, they unearth a conspiracy that stretches to the very top of Imperial society. As the stakes rise and become ever more personal, Vonvalt must make a choice: Will he abandon the laws he's sworn to uphold in order to protect the empire?

I

The Witch of Rill

"Beware the idiot, the zealot and the tyrant; each clothes himself in the armour of ignorance."

FROM CATERHAUSER'S THE SOVAN CRIMINAL
CODE: ADVICE TO PRACTITIONERS

It is a strange thing to think that the end of the Empire of the Wolf, and all the death and devastation that came with it, traced its long roots back to the tiny and insignificant village of Rill. That as we drew closer to it, we were not just plodding through a rainy, cold country twenty miles east of the Tolsburg Marches; we were approaching the precipice of the Great Decline, its steep and treacherous slope falling away from us like a cliff face of glassy obsidian.

Rill. How to describe it? The birthplace of our misfortune was so plain. For its isolation, it was typical for the Northmark of Tolsburg. It was formed of a large communal square of churned mud and straw, and a ring of twenty buildings with wattle-and-daub walls and thatched roofs. The manor was distinguishable only by its size, being perhaps twice as big as the biggest cottage, but there the differences ended. It was as tumbledown as the rest of them.

An inn lay off to one side, and livestock and peasants moved haphazardly through the public space. One benefit of the cold was that the smell wasn't so bad, but Vonvalt still held a kerchief filled with dried lavender to his nose. He could be fussy like that.

I should have been in a good mood. Rill was the first village we had come across since we had left the Imperial wayfort on the Jägeland border, and it marked the beginning of a crescent of settlements that ended in the Hauner fortress of Seaguard fifty miles to the north-east. Our arrival here meant we were probably only a few weeks away from turning south again to complete the eastern half of our circuit – and that meant better weather, larger towns and something approaching civilisation.

Instead, anxiety gnawed at me. My attention was fixed on the vast, ancient forest that bordered the village and stretched for a hundred miles north and west of us, all the way to the coast. It was home, according to the rumours we had been fed along the way, to an old Draedist witch.

"You think she is in there?" Patria Bartholomew Claver asked from next to me. Claver was one of four people who made up our caravan, a Neman priest who had imposed himself on us at the Jägeland border. Ostensibly it was for protection against bandits, though the Northmark was infamously desolate – and by his own account, he travelled almost everywhere alone.

"Who?" I asked.

Claver smiled without warmth. "The witch," he said.

"No," I said curtly. I found Claver very irritating – everyone did. Our itinerant lives were difficult enough, but Claver's incessant questioning over the last few weeks of every aspect of Vonvalt's practice and powers had worn us all down to the nub.

"I do."

I turned. Dubine Bressinger – Vonvalt's taskman – was approaching, cheerfully eating an onion. He winked at me as his horse trotted past. Behind him was our employer, Sir Konrad Vonvalt, and at the very back was our donkey, disrespectfully named the Duke of Brondsey, which pulled a cart loaded with all our accoutrements.

We had come to Rill for the same reason we went anywhere: to ensure that the Emperor's justice was done, even out here on the fringes of the Sovan Empire. For all their faults, the Sovans were great believers in justice for all, and they dispatched Imperial Magistrates like Vonvalt to tour the distant villages and towns of the Empire as itinerant courts.

"I'm looking for Sir Otmar Frost," I heard Vonvalt call out from the rear of our caravan. Bressinger had already dismounted and was summoning a local boy to make arrangements for our horses.

One of the peasants pointed wordlessly at the manor. Vonvalt grunted and dismounted. Patria Claver and I did the same. The mud was iron-hard beneath my feet.

"Helena," Vonvalt called to me. "The ledger."

I nodded and retrieved the ledger from the cart. It was a heavy tome, with a thick leather jacket clad in iron and with a lockable clasp. It would be used to record any legal issues which arose, and Vonvalt's considered judgments. Once it was full, it would be sent back to the Law Library in distant Sova, where clerks would review the judgments and make sure that the common law was being applied consistently.

I brought the ledger to Vonvalt, who bade me keep hold of it with an irritated wave, and all four of us made for the manor. I could see now that it had a heraldic device hanging over the door, a plain blue shield overlaid by a boar's head mounted on a broken lance. The manor was otherwise unremarkable, and a far cry from the sprawling town houses and country fortresses of the Imperial aristocracy in Sova.

Vonvalt hammered a gloved fist against the door. It opened quickly. A maid, perhaps a year or two younger than me, stood in the doorway. She looked frightened.

"I am Justice Sir Konrad Vonvalt of the Imperial Magistratum," Vonvalt said in what I knew to be an affected Sovan accent. His native Jägeland inflection marked him out as an upstart, notwithstanding his station, and embarrassed him.

The maid curtseyed clumsily. "I—"

"Who is it?" Sir Otmar Frost called from somewhere inside. It was dark beyond the threshold and smelled like woodsmoke and livestock. I could see Vonvalt's hand absently reach for his lavender kerchief.

"Justice Sir Konrad Vonvalt of the Imperial Magistratum," he announced again, impatiently.

"Bloody faith," Sir Otmar muttered, and appeared in the doorway a few moments later. He thrust the maid aside without ceremony. "My lord, come in, come in; come out of the damp and warm yourselves at the fire."

We entered. Inside it was dingy. At one end of the room was a bed covered in furs and woollen blankets, as well as personal effects which suggested an absent wife. In the centre was an open log fire, surrounded by charred and muddy rugs that were also mouldering thanks to the rain that dripped down from the open smoke hole. At the other end was a long trestle table with seating for ten, and a door that led to a separate kitchen. The walls were draped with mildewed tapestries that were faded and smoked near-black, and the floor was piled thick with rugs and skins. A pair of big, wolflike dogs warmed themselves next to the fire.

"I was told that a Justice was moving north through the Tolsburg Marches," Sir Otmar said as he fussed. As a Tollish knight and lord, he had been elevated to the Imperial aristocracy – "taking the Highmark", as it was known, for the payoffs they had all received in exchange for submitting to the Legions – but he was a far cry from the powdered and pampered lords of Sova. He was an old man, clad in a grubby tunic bearing his device and a pair of homespun trousers. His face was grimy and careworn and framed by white hair and a white beard. A large dent marred his forehead, probably earned as a younger man when the Reichskrieg had swept through and the Sovan armies had vassalised Tolsburg twenty-five years before. Both Vonvalt and Bressinger, too, bore the scars of the Imperial expansion.

"The last visit was from Justice August?" Vonvalt asked.

Sir Otmar nodded. "Aye. A long time ago. Used to be that we saw a Justice a few times a year. Please, all of you, sit. Food, ale? Wine? I was just about to eat."

"Yes, thank you," Vonvalt said, sitting at the table. We followed suit.

"My predecessor left a logbook?" Vonvalt asked.

"Yes, yes," Sir Otmar replied, and sent the maid scurrying off again. I heard the sounds of a strongbox being raided.

"Any trouble from the north?"

Sir Otmar shook his head. "No; we have a sliver of the Westmark of Haunersheim between us and the sea. Maybe ten or twenty miles' worth, enough to absorb a raiding party. Though I daresay the sea is too rough this time of year anyway to tempt the northerners down."

"Quite right," Vonvalt said. I could tell he was annoyed for having forgotten his geography. Still, one could be forgiven the occasional slip of the mind. The Empire, now over fifty years old, had absorbed so many nations so quickly the cartographers redrew the maps yearly. "And I suppose with Seaguard rebuilt," he added.

"Aye, that the Autun did. A new curtain wall, a new garrison and enough money and provender to allow for daily ranges during fighting season. Weekly, in winter, by order of the margrave."

The Autun. The Two-Headed Wolf. It was evens on whether the man had meant the term as a pejorative. It was one of those strange monikers for the Sovan Empire that the conquered used either in deference or as an insult. Either way, Vonvalt ignored it.

"The man has a reputation," Vonvalt remarked.

"Margrave Westenholtz?" the priest, Claver, chipped in. "A good man. A pious man. The northerners are a godless folk who cleave to the old Draedist ways." He shrugged. "You should not mourn them, Justice."

Vonvalt smiled thinly. "I do not mourn dead northern raiders, Patria," he said with more restraint than the man was due. Claver was a young man, too young to bear the authority of a priest. Over the course of our short time together we had all had grown to dislike him immensely. He was zealous and a bore, quick to anger and judge. He spoke at great length about his cause – that of recruiting Templars for the southern Frontier – and his lordly contacts.

Bressinger generally refused to talk to him, but Vonvalt, out of professional courtesy, had been engaging with the man for weeks.

Sir Otmar cleared his throat. He was about to make the error of engaging with Claver when the food arrived, and instead he ate. It was hearty, simple fare of meat, bread and thick gravy, but then in these circumstances we rarely went hungry. Vonvalt's power and authority tended to inspire generosity in his hosts.

"You said the last Justice passed through a while ago?" Vonvalt asked.

"Aye," Sir Otmar replied.

"You have been following the Imperial statutes in the interim?"

Sir Otmar nodded vigorously, but he was almost certainly lying. These far-flung villages and towns, months' worth of travel from distant Sova even by the fastest means, rarely practised Imperial law. It was a shame. The Reichskrieg had brought death and misery to thousands, but the system of common law was one of the few rubies to come out of an otherwise enormous shit.

"Good. Then I shouldn't imagine there will be much to do. Except investigate the woods," Vonvalt said. Sir Otmar looked confused by the addendum. Vonvalt drained the last of his ale. "On our way here," he explained, "we were told a number of times about a witch, living in the woods just to the north of Rill. I don't suppose you know anything about it?"

Sir Otmar delayed with a long draw of wine and then ostensibly to pick something out of his teeth. "Not that I have heard of, sire. No."

Vonvalt nodded thoughtfully. *"Who is she?"*

Bressinger swore in Grozodan. Sir Otmar and I leapt halfway out of our skin. The table and all the platters and cutlery on it were jolted as three pairs of thighs hit it. Goblets and tankards were spilled. Sir Otmar clutched his heart, his eyes wide, his mouth working to expel the words that Vonvalt had commanded him to.

The Emperor's Voice: the arcane power of a Justice to compel a person to speak the truth. It had its limitations – it did not work on other Justices, for example, and a strong-willed person could frustrate it if on their guard – but Sir Otmar was old and meek and not well-versed in the ways of the Order. The power hit him like a psychic thunderclap and turned his mind inside out.

"A priestess . . . a member of the Draeda," Sir Otmar gasped. He looked horrified as his mouth spoke against his mind's will.

"*Is she from Rill?*" Vonvalt pressed.

"Yes!"

"*Are there others who practise Draedism?*"

Sir Otmar writhed in his chair. He gripped the table to steady himself.

"Many . . . of the villagers!"

"Sir Konrad," Bressinger murmured. He was watching Sir Otmar with a slight wince. I saw that Claver was relishing the man's torment.

"All right, Sir Otmar," Vonvalt said. "All right. Calm yourself. Here, take some ale. I'll not press you any further."

We sat in silence as Sir Otmar summoned the terrified maid with a trembling hand and wheezed for some ale. She left and reappeared a moment later, handing him a tankard. Sir Otmar drained it greedily.

"The practice of Draedism is illegal," Vonvalt remarked.

Sir Otmar looked at his plate. His expression was somewhere between anger, horror and shame, and was a common look for those who had been hit by the Voice.

"The laws are new. The religion is old," he said hoarsely.

"The laws have been in place for two and a half decades."

"The religion has been in place for two and a half millennia," Sir Otmar snapped.

There was an uncomfortable pause. "Is there anyone in Rill that is not a practising member of Draedism?" Vonvalt asked.

Sir Otmar inspected his drink. "I couldn't say," he mumbled.

"Justice." There was genuine disgust in Claver's voice. "At the very least they will have to renounce it. The official religion of the Empire is the holy Nema Creed." He practically spat as he looked the old baron up and down. "If I had my way they'd all burn."

"These are good folk here," Sir Otmar said, alarmed. "Good, law-abiding folk. They work the land and they pay their tithes. We've never been a burden on the Autun."

Vonvalt shot Claver an irritated look. "With respect, Sir Otmar, if these people are practising Draedists, then they cannot, by definition, be law-abiding. I am sorry to say that Patria Claver is right – at least in part. They will have to renounce it. You have a list of those who practise?"

"I do not."

The logs smoked and crackled and spat. Ale and wine dripped and pattered through the cracks in the table planks.

"The charge is minor," Vonvalt said. "A small fine, a penny per head, if they recant. As their lord you may even shoulder it on their behalf. Do you have a shrine to any of the Imperial gods? Nema? Savare?"

"No." Sir Otmar all but spat out the word. It was becoming increasingly difficult to ignore the fact that Sir Otmar was a practising Draedist himself.

"The official religion of the Sovan Empire is the Nema Creed. Enshrined in scripture and in both the common and canon law. Come now, there are parallels. The Book of Lorn is essentially Draedism, no? It has the same parables, mandates the same holy days. You could adopt it without difficulty."

It was true, the Book of Lorn did bear remarkable parallels to Draedism. That was because the Book of Lorn *was* Draedism. The Sovan religion was remarkably flexible, and rather than replacing the many religious practices it encountered during the Reichskrieg, it simply subsumed them, like a wave engulfing an island. It was why the Nema Creed was simultaneously the most widely practised and least respected religion in the known world.

I looked over to Claver. The man's face was aghast at Vonvalt's easy equivocation. Of course, Vonvalt was no more a believer in the Nema Creed than Sir Otmar. Like the old baron, he had had the religion forced on him. But he went to temple, and he put himself through the motions like most of the Imperial aristocracy. Claver, on the other hand, was young enough to have known no other religion. A true believer. Such men had their uses, but more often than not their inflexibility made them dangerous.

"The Empire requires that you practise the teachings of the Nema Creed. The law allows for nothing else," Vonvalt said.

"If I refuse?"

Vonvalt drew himself up. "If you refuse you become a heretic. If you refuse to *me* you become an avowed heretic. But you won't do something as silly and wasteful as that."

"And what is the punishment for avowed heresy?" Sir Otmar asked, though he knew the answer.

"You will be burned." It was Claver who spoke. There was savage glee in his voice.

"No one will be burned," Vonvalt said irritably, "because no one is an avowed heretic. Yet."

I looked back and forth between Vonvalt and Sir Otmar. I had sympathy for Sir Otmar's position. He was right to say that Draedism was harmless, and right to disrespect the Nema Creed as worthless. Furthermore, he was an old man, being lectured and threatened with death. But the fact of the matter was, the Sovan Empire ruled the Tolsburg Marches. Their laws applied, and, actually, their laws were robust and fairly applied. Most everyone else got on with it, so why couldn't he?

Sir Otmar seemed to sag slightly.

"There is an old watchtower on Gabler's Mount, a few hours' ride north-east of here. The Draedists gather there to worship. You will find your witch there."

Vonvalt paused for a moment. He took a long draw of ale. Then he carefully set the tankard down.

"Thank you," he said, and stood. "We'll go there now, while there is an hour or two of daylight left."

orbit

Follow us:

f **/orbitbooksUS**

🐦 **/orbitbooks**

▶ **/orbitbooks**

Join our mailing list
to receive alerts on our
latest releases and deals.

orbitbooks.net

Enter our monthly
giveaway for the chance
to win some epic prizes.

orbitloot.com